Feb. 13 - 1956

THE THREE MUSKETEERS

Alexandre Dumas, the Elder, was born at Villers-Cotterets, France, on 24 July 1802, spent his early years in poverty, and in 1823 went to Paris, after which he commenced writing. He died at Puys on 5 December 1870.

He produced an astonishing number of novels and plays. His chief novels are The Three Musketeers (1844), The Count of Monte-Cristo (1844), Twenty Years After (1845), Marguerite de Valois (1847), The Queen's Necklace (1849–50), and The Black Tulip (1850).

THE
THREE MUSKETEERS

ALEXANDRE DUMAS

THOMAS NELSON AND SONS LTD
LONDON EDINBURGH PARIS MELBOURNE
TORONTO AND NEW YORK

THOMAS NELSON AND SONS LTD
Parkside Works Edinburgh 9
36 Park Street London W1
312 Flinders Street Melbourne C1
218 Grand Parade Centre   Cape Town

THOMAS NELSON AND SONS (CANADA) LTD
91–93 Wellington Street West   Toronto 1

THOMAS NELSON AND SONS
19 East 47th Street New York 17

SOCIÉTÉ FRANÇAISE D'EDITIONS NELSON
25 rue Henri Barbusse Paris V^e

CONTENTS

THE THREE MUSKETEERS

CHAPTER I.

THE THREE GIFTS OF M. D'ARTAGNAN THE ELDER.

ON the first Monday of the month of April 1625 the bourg of Meung, in which the author of the "Romance of the Rose" was born, appeared to be in as complete a state of revolution as if the Huguenots had come to make a second Rochelle of it. Many citizens, seeing the women flying towards the main street, hearing the children crying at the open doors, hastened to don the cuirass, and supporting their somewhat uncertain courage with a musket or a partisan, directed their steps towards the hostelry of the Jolly Miller, before which was gathered a compact and rapidly-increasing group, vociferous and full of curiosity.

In those times panics were common, and but few days passed without some city or other recording in its archives an event of this kind. There were nobles, who made war against one another; there was the king, who made war against the cardinal; there was the Spaniard, who made war against the king. Then in addition to these concealed or public, secret or open wars, there were robbers, mendicants, Huguenots, wolves, and lackeys, who made war upon everybody. The citizens were always in arms against thieves, wolves, or lackeys, often against nobles or Huguenots, sometimes against the king, but never against the cardinal or Spain. The result, therefore, of this habit was, that on the aforesaid first Monday of the month of April 1625 the citizens, hearing the clamour, and seeing neither the red and yellow standard nor the livery of the Duc de Richelieu, rushed toward the hostelry of the Jolly Miller.

On reaching there the cause of this hubbub was apparent to all.

A young man—let us outline his portrait with a stroke of the pen. Imagine Don Quixote at eighteen; Don Quixote without his corselet, without his coat of mail, without his cuisses; Don Quixote clothed in a woollen doublet, the blue colour of which had faded into a nameless shade between lees of wine and a heavenly azure; face long and brown; high cheek-bones, indicating craftiness; the maxillary muscles enormously developed, an infallible sign by which a Gascon may always be detected, even without his cap—and our young man wore a cap ornamented with a kind of feather; his eye open and intelligent; his nose hooked, but finely chiselled. Too big for a youth, too small for a grown man, an experienced eye might have taken him for a farmer's son upon a journey, had it not been for the long sword, which, dangling from a leathern baldric, hit against its owner's calves as he walked, and against his steed's rough side when he was on horseback.

For our young man had a steed, which was the observed of all observers. It was a Béarn pony, from twelve to fourteen years old, with yellow coat, not a hair in his tail, but not without wind-galls on his legs, which, though going with his head lower than his knees, rendering a martingale quite unnecessary, contrived, nevertheless, to perform his eight leagues a day. Unfortunately, the qualities of this horse were so well concealed under his strangely-coloured hide and his unaccountable gait, that at a time when everybody was a connoisseur in horseflesh the appearance of the said pony at Meung, which place he had entered about a quarter of an hour before by the gate of Beaugency, produced an unfavourable feeling that extended to his master.

And this feeling was the more painful to young D'Artagnan—for so was the Don Quixote of this second Rosinante named—because he was conscious himself of the ridiculous appearance he made on such a steed, good horseman as he was. He had sighed deeply, therefore, when accepting the gift of the pony from M. d'Artagnan the elder. He was not ignorant that such a beast was worth at least twenty pounds; and the words which accompanied the gift were above all price.

"My son," said the old Gascon nobleman, in that pure Béarn *patois* of which Henry IV. was never able to rid himself—"my son, this horse was born in your father's house about thirteen years ago, and has remained in it ever since, which ought to make you love it. Never sell it—allow it to die tranquilly and honourably of old age ; and if you make a campaign with it, take as much care of it as you would of an old servant. At court, provided you ever have the honour to go there," continued M. d'Artagnan the elder, " an honour to which, remember, your ancient nobility gives you the right, sustain worthily your name of *gentleman*, which has been worthily borne by your ancestors for more than five hundred years, both for your own sake and for those who belong to you. By the latter I mean your relatives and friends. Endure nothing from any one except the cardinal and the king. It is by his courage, you understand, by his courage alone, that a gentleman makes his way to-day. Whoever trembles for a second perhaps allows the bait to escape which during that exact second fortune held out to him. You are young : you ought to be brave for two reasons ; the first is that you are a Gascon, and the second is that you are my son. Never fear quarrels, but seek adventures. I have taught you how to handle a sword ; you have sinews of iron, a wrist of steel. Fight on all occasions ; fight the more because duels are forbidden, since, consequently, there is twice as much courage in fighting. I have nothing to give you, my son, but fifteen crowns, my horse, and the counsels you have just heard. Your mother will add to them a recipe for a certain balsam, which she got from a gypsy, and which has the miraculous virtue of curing all wounds that do not reach the heart. Take advantage of all, and live happily and long. I have but one more word to add, and that is to propose an example to you—not mine, for I myself have never appeared at court, and have only taken part in religious wars as a volunteer ; I speak of M. de Tréville, who was formerly my neighbour, and who had the honour to be, as a child, the playfellow of our king, Louis XIII., whom God preserve ! Sometimes their play degenerated into battles, and in these battles the king was not always the stronger. The blows which he received from him caused him to entertain great esteem and friendship for M. de Tréville. Afterwards, M. de Tréville fought with others : during his first journey to Paris, five times ; from the death of the late king to the majority of the young one, without reckoning wars and sieges, seven times ; and from that majority up to the present day, a hundred times perhaps ! So that in spite of edicts, ordinances, and decrees, behold him captain of the musketeers—that is to say, leader of a legion of Cæsars, whom the king holds in great esteem, and whom the cardinal dreads—he who dreads little, as every one knows. Moreover, M. de Tréville gains ten thousand crowns a year; he is, therefore, a very great noble. He began as you begin; go to him with this letter, and make him your model, in order that you may do as he has done."

Upon which M. d'Artagnan the elder girded his own sword round his son, kissed him tenderly on both cheeks, and gave him his blessing.

On leaving the paternal chamber the young man found his mother, who was waiting for him with the famous recipe, the use of which would be so frequently necessitated by the counsels we have just related. The farewells were, on this side, longer and more tender than they had been on the other; not that M. d'Artagnan did not love his son, who was his only offspring, but M. d'Artagnan was a man, and he would have considered it unworthy of a man to give way to his feelings; whereas Madame d'Artagnan was a woman, and, moreover, a mother. She wept profusely, and, let us tell it in praise of M. d'Artagnan the younger, notwithstanding the efforts he made to be as firm as a future musketeer ought to be, nature prevailed, and he shed many tears, half of which he had great difficulty in concealing.

The same day the young man set forward on his journey, provided with the three paternal gifts, which consisted, as we have said, of fifteen crowns, the horse, and the letter for M. de Tréville, the counsels, as may be supposed, being thrown into the bargain.

With such a *vade mecum* D'Artagnan was, morally and physically, an exact copy of the hero of Cervantes, to whom we so happily compared him when our duty as an historian placed us under the necessity of sketching his portrait. Don Quixote took windmills for giants and sheep for armies; D'Artagnan took every smile for an insult and every look as a provocation, the result of which was that from Tarbes to Meung his fist was constantly doubled, and his hand, on the average, ten times a day on the hilt of his sword; and yet the fist did not descend upon any jaw, nor did the sword issue from its scabbard. It was not that the sight of the wretched pony did not excite numerous smiles on the countenances of passers-by; but as against the side of this pony rattled a sword of respectable length, and as over this sword gleamed an eye rather ferocious than haughty, these said passers-by repressed their hilarity, or if hilarity prevailed over prudence, they endeavoured to laugh only on one side.

like the masks of the ancients. D'Artagnan, then, remained majestic and intact in his susceptibility till he came to this unlucky city of Meung.

But there, as he was alighting from his horse at the gate of the Jolly Miller, without any one—host, waiter, or hostler—coming to hold his stirrup or take his horse, D'Artagnan spied, through an open window on the ground floor, a man of fine figure and lofty bearing, but of rather grim countenance, talking with two persons who appeared to listen to him most respectfully. D'Artagnan fancied, as was natural for him to do, that he himself must be the object of their conversation, and listened. This time D'Artagnan was only in part mistaken: he himself was not the subject of remark, but his horse was. The gentleman appeared to be enumerating all his qualities to his auditors, and, as I have said, the auditors seeming to have great deference for the narrator, they every moment burst into fits of laughter. Now, as a half-smile was sufficient to awaken the irascibility of the young man, the effect produced upon him by this vociferous mirth may be easily imagined.

Nevertheless, D'Artagnan was desirous of examining the appearance of this impertinent personage who was laughing at him. He fixed his haughty eye upon the stranger, and perceived a man of from forty to forty-five years of age, with black and piercing eyes, a pale complexion, a strongly-marked nose, and a black and well-shaped moustache. He was dressed in a doublet and hose of violet colour, with aiguillettes of the same, without any other ornaments than the customary slashes through which the shirt appeared. This doublet and hose, though new, looked creased, as garments do which have been long packed in a travelling-bag. D'Artagnan noticed all this with the rapidity of a most minute observer, and doubtless from an instinctive feeling that this unknown was destined to have a great influence over his future life.

Now, as at the moment in which D'Artagnan fixed his eyes upon the man in the violet doublet the man made one of his most knowing and profound remarks respecting the Béarnese pony, his two auditors burst out laughing, and he himself, though contrary to his custom, suffered a pale smile (if I may be allowed to use such an expression) to stray over his countenance. This time there could be no doubt: D'Artagnan was really insulted. Full, then, of this conviction, he pulled his cap down over his eyes, and endeavouring to copy some of the court airs he had picked up in Gascony among young travelling nobles, he advanced, with one hand on the hilt of his sword and the other resting on his hip. Unfortunately, as he advanced his anger increased at every step, and instead of the proper and lofty speech he had prepared as a prelude to his challenge, he found nothing at the tip of his tongue but a gross personality, which he accompanied with a furious gesture.

"I say, sir—you, sir, who are hiding yourself behind that shutter—yes, you, sir, tell me what you are laughing at, and we will laugh together!"

The man withdrew his eyes slowly from the nag to his rider, as if he required some time to ascertain whether it could be to him that such strange reproaches were addressed; then, when he could no longer entertain any doubt of the matter, his eyebrows bent slightly, and after quite a long pause, with an accent of irony and insolence impossible to be described, he replied to D'Artagnan,—

"I was not speaking to you, sir!"

"But I am speaking to you!" replied the young man, exasperated by this mixture of insolence and good manners, of politeness and scorn.

The unknown looked at him for a moment longer with his faint smile, and retiring from the window, came out of the hostelry with a slow step, and placed himself before the horse within two paces of D'Artagnan. His quiet manner and the ironical expression of his countenance redoubled the mirth of those with whom he had been talking, and who still remained at the window.

D'Artagnan, seeing him approach, drew his sword a foot out of the scabbard.

"This horse is decidedly, or rather has been in his youth, a buttercup," resumed the unknown, continuing the remarks he had begun, and addressing himself to his auditors at the window, without seeming in any way to notice the exasperation of D'Artagnan, who, however, remained stiffly standing between them. "It is a colour very well known in botany, but till the present time very rare among horses."

"There are people who laugh at a horse that would not dare to laugh at the master of it," cried furiously the emulator of Tréville.

"I do not often laugh, sir," replied the unknown, "as you may perceive by the expression of my face; but nevertheless I insist upon retaining the privilege of laughing when I please."

"And I," cried D'Artagnan, "will allow no man to laugh when it displeases me!"

"Indeed, sir," continued the unknown, more quietly than ever. "Well, that is perfectly right!" and turning on his heel was about to re-enter the hostelry by the front gate, under which D'Artagnan as he came up had observed a saddled horse standing.

But D'Artagnan was not the person thus to allow a man to escape him who had once had the insolence to laugh at him. He drew his sword entirely from the scabbard, and followed him, crying,—

"Turn, turn, Master Joker, lest I strike you from behind!"

"Strike me!" said the other, turning sharply round and surveying the young man with as much astonishment as contempt. "Come, come, my good fellow, you must be mad!" Then in a suppressed tone, as if speaking to himself, "This is annoying," continued he. "What a godsend this would be for his Majesty, who is seeking everywhere for bravoes to recruit his musketeers!"

He had scarcely finished when D'Artagnan made such a furious lunge at him that if he had not sprung nimbly backward it is probable that he would have jested for the last time. The unknown then, perceiving that the matter was going beyond a joke, drew his sword, saluted his adversary, and gravely placed himself on guard. But at the same moment his two auditors, accompanied by the host, fell upon D'Artagnan with sticks, shovels, and tongs. This caused so rapid and complete a diversion to the attack that D'Artagnan's adversary, while the latter was turning round to face this shower of blows, sheathed his sword with the same precision as before, and from an actor, which he had nearly been, became a spectator of the fight, a *rôle* in which he acquitted himself with his usual impassibility, muttering, nevertheless,—

"A plague upon these Gascons! Put him on his yellow horse again and let him begone!"

"Not before I have killed you, poltroon!" cried D'Artagnan, showing the best front possible, and never falling back one step before his three assailants, who continued to shower their blows upon him.

"Another gasconade!" murmured the gentleman. "By my honour, these Gascons are incorrigible! Keep up the dance, then, since he will have it so. When he is tired, he will say that he has enough of it."

But the unknown did not yet know the headstrong personage he had to deal with; D'Artagnan was not the man ever to cry for quarter. The fight was therefore prolonged for some seconds; but at length D'Artagnan, worn out, let fall his sword, which was struck from his hand by the blow of a stick and broken in two pieces. Another blow full upon his forehead at the same moment brought him to the ground, covered with blood and almost fainting.

It was at this period that people came flocking to the scene of action from all sides. The host, fearful of consequences, with the help of his servants carried the wounded man into the kitchen, where some trifling attention was bestowed upon him.

As to the gentleman, he resumed his place at the window, and surveyed all that crowd with a certain air of impatience, evidently much annoyed by their persistence in remaining there.

"Well, how is it with this madman?" exclaimed he, turning round as the opening door announced the entrance of the host, who came to inquire whether he was hurt.

"Your Excellency is safe and sound?" asked the host.

"Oh yes! perfectly safe and sound, my good host; and I now wish to know what has become of our young man."

"He is better," said the host; "he fainted quite away."

"Indeed!" said the gentleman.

"But before he fainted he collected all his strength to challenge you, and to defy you while challenging you."

"Why, this fellow must be the devil in person!" cried the unknown.

"Oh no, your Excellency," replied the host, with a grin of contempt, "he is not the devil; for during his fainting we rummaged his valise, and found nothing but a clean shirt and twelve crowns, which, however, did not prevent his saying, as he was fainting, that if such a thing had happened in Paris you should have instantly repented of it, while here you will only repent of it later on."

"Then," said the unknown coldly, "he must be some prince of the blood in disguise."

"I have told you this, good sir," resumed the host, "in order that you may be on your guard."

"Did he name no one in his passion?"

"Yes. He struck his pocket and said, 'We shall see what M. de Tréville will think of this insult offered to his *protégé.*'"

"M. de Tréville?" said the unknown, becoming attentive. "He struck his pocket while pronouncing the name of M.

de Tréville ? Now, my dear host, while your young man was unconscious you did not fail, I am quite sure, to ascertain what that pocket contained. What was there in it ? "

" A letter addressed to M. de Tréville, captain of the musketeers."

" Indeed ! "

" Just as I have the honour to tell your Excellency."

The host, who was not endowed with great perspicacity, did not notice at all the expression which his words called up in the countenance of the unknown. The latter arose from the window, upon the sill of which he had been leaning his elbow, and knitted his brows like a man suddenly disturbed.

" The devil ! " muttered he between his teeth. " Can Tréville have set this Gascon upon me ? He is very young, but a sword-thrust is a sword-thrust, whatever be the age of him who gives it, and a youth is less to be suspected than an older man. A weak obstacle is sometimes sufficient to overthrow a great design."

And the unknown fell into a reverie which lasted some minutes.

" Host," said he, " could you not contrive to get rid of this frantic boy for me ? In conscience, I cannot kill him ; and yet," added he, with a coldly menacing expression—" and yet he annoys me. Where is he ? "

" In my wife's chamber, where they are dressing his wounds, on the first floor."

" His things and his bag are with him ? Has he taken off his doublet ? "

" On the contrary, everything is down in the kitchen. But if he annoys you, this crazy young fool——"

" To be sure he does. He causes a disturbance in your hostelry, which respectable people cannot put up with. Go, make out my bill, and call my servant."

" What, sir ! do you mean to leave us already ? "

" You knew I was going, as I ordered you to get my horse saddled. Have they not obeyed ? "

" Yes, sir ; and as your Excellency may have observed, your horse is in the great gateway, ready saddled for your departure."

" That is well. Do as I have directed you, then."

" What the devil ! " said the host to himself. " Can he be afraid of this boy ? " But an imperious glance from the unknown stopped him short ; he bowed humbly and retired.

"Milady * must see nothing of this fellow," continued the stranger. "She will soon pass by; she is already late. I had better get on horseback, and go and meet her. I should like, however, to know what this letter addressed to Tréville contains."

And the unknown, muttering to himself, directed his steps towards the kitchen.

In the meantime the host, who entertained no doubt that it was the presence of the young man which was driving the unknown from his hostelry, had gone up to his wife's chamber, and found D'Artagnan entirely returned to consciousness. Giving him to understand that the police could deal with him pretty severely for having sought a quarrel with a great lord (for in the opinion of the host the unknown could be nothing less than a great lord), he insisted that, notwithstanding his weakness, he should get up and depart as quickly as possible. D'Artagnan, half-stupefied, without his doublet, and with his head all swathed with bandages, arose then, and urged on by the host, began to descend the stairs ; but on arriving at the kitchen the first thing he saw was his antagonist, who stood quietly talking beside the step of a heavy carriage drawn by two large Norman horses.

His interlocutor, whose head appeared through the carriage window, was a woman of from twenty to two-and-twenty years of age. We have already observed with what rapidity D'Artagnan took in every feature of a face. He perceived then, at a glance, that this woman was young and beautiful ; and her style of beauty struck him the more forcibly on account of its being totally different from that of the southern countries in which D'Artagnan had hitherto resided. She was pale and fair, with long curls falling in profusion over her shoulders ; had large languishing blue eyes, rosy lips, and hands of alabaster. She was talking with great animation with the unknown.

"His Eminence, then, orders me——" said the lady.

"To return instantly to England, and to inform him immediately should the duke leave London."

"And my other instructions ? " asked the fair traveller.

"They are contained in this box, which you will not open until you are on the other side of the Channel."

"Very well : and you, what are you going to do ? "

"I—oh ! I shall return to Paris."

* We are well aware that this term *milady* is only properly used when followed by a family name. But we find it thus in the manuscript, and we do not choose to take upon ourselves to alter it.

"What! without chastising this insolent boy?" asked the lady.

The unknown was about to reply, but at the moment he opened his mouth D'Artagnan, who had heard all, rushed forward through the open door.

"This insolent boy chastises others," cried he; "and I sincerely hope that he whom he means to chastise will not escape him as he did before."

"Will not escape him?" replied the unknown, knitting his brow.

"No; before a woman you would not dare to fly, I presume?"

"Remember," cried milady, seeing the unknown lay his hand on his sword—"remember that the least delay may ruin everything."

"True," cried the gentleman. "Begone, then, your way, and I will go mine." And bowing to the lady, he sprang into his saddle, her coachman at the same time applying his whip vigorously to his horses. The two interlocutors thus separated, taking opposite directions, at full gallop.

"Your reckoning! your reckoning!" vociferated the host, whose respect for the traveller was changed into profound contempt on seeing him depart without settling his bill.

"Pay him, booby!" cried the unknown to his servant, without checking the speed of his horse; and the man, after throwing two or three pieces of silver at the foot of mine host, galloped after his master.

"Base coward! false nobleman!" cried D'Artagnan, springing forward, in his turn, after the servant. But his wound had rendered him too weak to support such an exertion. Scarcely had he gone ten steps when his ears began to tingle, a faintness seized him, a cloud of blood passed over his eyes, and he fell in the middle of the street, crying still,—

"Coward! coward! coward!"

"He is a coward indeed," grumbled the host, drawing near to D'Artagnan, and endeavouring by this little flattery to make up matters with the young man, as the heron of the fable did with the snail he had despised the evening before.

"Yes, a base coward," murmured D'Artagnan; "but she—she was very beautiful."

"What she?" demanded the host.

"Milady," faltered D'Artagnan, and fainted the second time.

"Ah! it's all one," said the host; "I have lost two

customers, but this one remains, of whom I am pretty certain for some days to come ; and that will be eleven crowns gained, at all events."

We must remember that eleven crowns was just the amount which remained in D'Artagnan's purse.

The host had reckoned upon eleven days of confinement at a crown a day, but he had reckoned without his guest. On the following morning, at five o'clock, D'Artagnan arose, and descending to the kitchen without help, asked, among other ingredients the list of which has not come down to us, for some oil, some wine, and some rosemary, and with his mother's recipe in his hand, composed a balsam with which he anointed his numerous wounds, replacing his bandages himself, and positively refusing the assistance of any doctor. Thanks, no doubt, to the efficacy of the gypsy's balsam, and perhaps, also, thanks to the absence of any doctor, D'Artagnan walked about that same evening, and was almost cured by the morrow.

But when the time of settlement came, the rosemary, the oil, and the wine were the only expenses the master had incurred on his own account, as he had preserved a strict abstinence ; while on the contrary, the yellow horse, by the account of the hostler, had eaten at least three times as much as a horse of his size could reasonably be supposed to have done. D'Artagnan found nothing in his pocket but his little worn velvet purse with the eleven crowns it contained ; as to the letter addressed to M. de Tréville, it had disappeared.

The young man commenced his search for the letter with the greatest patience, turning out his various pockets twenty times, rummaging and rummaging again in his valise, and opening and closing his purse ; but when he had reached the conclusion that the letter was not to be found, he flew, for the third time, into such a rage that it came near costing him a fresh consumption of wine, oil, and rosemary ; for upon seeing this hot-headed youth become exasperated and threaten to destroy everything in the establishment if his letter were not found, the host seized a spit, his wife a broom-handle, and the servants the same sticks they had used the evening before.

" My letter of recommendation ! " cried D'Artagnan ; " my letter of recommendation ! or, by God's blood, I will spit you all like so many ortolans ! "

Unfortunately there was one circumstance which created a powerful obstacle to the accomplishment of this threat, which was, as we have related, that his sword had been in the first conflict broken in two, a fact he had wholly forgotten. The consequence was that when D'Artagnan went to draw his sword in earnest, he found himself armed merely with a stump of a sword of about eight or ten inches in length, which the host had carefully placed in the scabbard. As to the rest of the blade, the master had slyly put that on one side to make for himself a larding-pin.

But this loss would probably not have stopped our fiery young man if the host had not reflected that the demand which his guest made was perfectly just.

"But after all," said he, lowering the point of his spit, "where is that letter?"

"Yes, where is that letter?" cried D'Artagnan. "In the first place, I warn you that the letter is for M. de Tréville, and it must be found. If it be not quickly found, he will know how to have it found, I'll answer for it!"

This threat completed the intimidation of the host. After the king and the cardinal, M. de Tréville was the man whose name was perhaps most frequently repeated by the military, and even by the citizens. There was, to be sure, Father Joseph, but his name was never pronounced except in a subdued voice, such was the terror inspired by his Gray Eminence, as the cardinal's confidant was called.

Throwing down his spit then, and ordering his wife to do the same with her broom-handle, and the servants with their sticks, he was the first to begin an earnest search for the lost letter.

"Does the letter contain anything valuable?" demanded the host, after a few minutes of useless investigation.

"Zounds! I think it does, indeed," cried the Gascon, who reckoned upon this letter for making his way at court; "it contained my fortune!"

"Bills upon Spain?" asked the disturbed host.

"Bills upon his Majesty's private treasury," answered D'Artagnan, who, reckoning upon entering into the king's service in consequence of this recommendation, thought he could make this somewhat hazardous reply without telling a falsehood.

"The devil!" cried the host, at his wit's end.

"But it's of no importance," continued D'Artagnan, with the assurance of his nation; "it's of no importance. The money is nothing; that letter was everything. I would rather have lost a thousand pistoles than have lost it." He would not have risked more if he had said twenty thousand, but a certain youthful modesty restrained him.

A ray of light all at once broke upon the mind of the host, who was uttering maledictions upon finding nothing.

"That letter is not lost!" cried he.

"What!" said D'Artagnan.

"No; it has been stolen from you."

"Stolen! by whom?"

"By the gentleman who was here yesterday. He came down into the kitchen, where your doublet was. He remained there some time alone. I would lay a wager he has stolen it."

"Do you think so?" answered D'Artagnan, but little convinced, as he knew better than any one else how entirely personal the value of this letter was, and saw nothing in it likely to tempt the cupidity of any one. The fact was that none of the servants, none of the travellers present, could have gained anything by becoming possessed of this paper.

"Do you say," resumed D'Artagnan, "that you suspect that impertinent gentleman?"

"I tell you I am sure of it," continued the host. "When I informed him that your lordship was the *protégé* of M. de Tréville, and that you even had a letter for that illustrious nobleman, he appeared to be very much disturbed, and asked me where that letter was, and immediately came down into the kitchen, where he knew your doublet was."

"Then he is the thief," replied D'Artagnan. "I will complain to M. de Tréville, and M. de Tréville will complain to the king." He then drew two crowns majestically from his purse, gave them to the host, who accompanied him, cap in hand, to the gate, remounted his yellow horse, which bore him without any further accident to the gate of St. Antoine at Paris, where his owner sold him for three crowns, which was a very good price, considering that D'Artagnan had ridden him hard on the last stretch. The dealer to whom D'Artagnan sold him for the said nine livres explained to the young man that he only gave that enormous sum for him on account of the originality of his colour.

So D'Artagnan entered Paris on foot, carrying his little packet under his arm, and wandered around till he found an apartment to be let on terms suited to the scantiness of his means. This chamber was a sort of garret, situated in the Rue des Fossoyeurs, near the Luxembourg.

As soon as the earnest-money was paid D'Artagnan took possession of his lodging, and passed the remainder of the day in sewing on to his doublet and hose some ornamental braiding which his mother had taken off from an almost new doublet of the elder M. d'Artagnan, and which she had given to him secretly. Then he went to the Quai de la Ferraille, to have a new blade put to his sword, and came back to the Louvre, and inquired of the first musketeer he met the situation of the hôtel of M. de Tréville, which proved to be in the Rue du Vieux-Colombier, in the immediate vicinity of the chamber hired by D'Artagnan, a circumstance which appeared to him to be a happy augury for the outcome of his journey.

After which, satisfied with the way in which he had conducted himself at Meung, without remorse for the past, confident in the present, and full of hope for the future, he retired to bed, and slept the sleep of the brave.

This sleep, rustic as it was, brought him to nine o'clock in the morning, at which hour he rose in order to repair to the residence of the famous M. de Tréville, the third personage in the kingdom, according to the estimation of his father.

CHAPTER II.

THE ANTECHAMBER OF M. DE TRÉVILLE.

M. DE TROISVILLE, as his family was still called in Gascony, or M. de Tréville, as he had ended by styling himself in Paris, had really commenced life as D'Artagnan now did— that is to say, without a sou in his pocket, but with a fund of courage, shrewdness, and intelligence which makes the poorest Gascon gentleman often derive more in his imagination from the paternal inheritance than the richest nobleman of Perigord or Berry receives in reality. His insolent bravery, his still more insolent success at a time when blows poured down like hail, had borne him to the top of that ladder called court favour, which he had climbed four rounds at a time.

He was the friend of the king, who honoured highly, as every one knows, the memory of his father, Henry IV. The father of M. de Tréville had served him so faithfully in his wars against the League that, for want of ready money—a thing to which the Béarnais was accustomed all his life, and who constantly paid his debts with the only thing which he never needed to borrow, namely, with wit—for want of money, we repeat, he authorized him, after the reduction of Paris, to assume for his arms a golden lion passant upon gules, with the motto *Fidelis et fortis*. This was a great matter in the way of honour, but very little in the way of wealth ; so that when the illustrious companion of the great Henry died, the only inheritance he was able to leave his son was his sword and his motto. Thanks to this double gift and the spotless name that accompanied it, M. de Tréville was admitted into the household of the young prince, where he made such good use of his sword, and was so faithful to his motto, that Louis XIII., one of the good swordsmen of his kingdom, was accustomed to say that, if he had a friend who was about to fight, he would advise him to choose as a second himself first and Tréville next, or even perhaps Tréville first.

Thus Louis XIII. had a real liking for Tréville, a royal liking, a selfish liking, it is true, but which was still a liking. At that unhappy period it was an important consideration to be surrounded by such men as De Tréville. Many might take for their motto the epithet of *strong*, which formed the second part of his device, but very few gentlemen could lay claim to the *faithful*, which constituted the first. Tréville was one of the latter ; his was one of those rare organizations endowed with an obedient intelligence like that of the dog, with a blind valour, a quick eye, and a prompt hand, to whom sight appeared only to be given to see if the king were dissatisfied with any one, and the hand to strike the one who displeased him, whether a Besme, a Maurevers, a Poltrot de Méré, or a Vitry. In short, up to this period, nothing had been wanting to De Tréville but opportunity ; but he was ever on the watch for it, and he promised himself that he would never fail to seize it by its three hairs whenever it came within reach of his hand. Louis XIII. then made De Tréville the captain of his musketeers, who were to Louis XIII., in devotedness, or rather in fanaticism, what his Ordinaries had been to Henry III., and his Scotch Guard to Louis XI.

On his part, and in this respect, the cardinal was not behindhand with the king. When he saw the formidable and chosen body by which Louis XIII. surrounded himself, this second, or rather this first, king of France became desirous that he too should have his guard. He had his musketeers, then, as Louis XIII. had his ; and these two powerful rivals vied with each other in procuring the most celebrated swordsmen, not only from all the provinces of France, but also from all foreign states. It was not uncommon for Richelieu and Louis XIII. to discuss, over their evening game of chess, the merits of their servants. Each boasted of the bearing and the courage of his own, and while exclaiming loudly against duels and broils, they excited them secretly to quarrel, leriving an immoderate satisfaction or a profound regret from the success or defeat of their own combatants. At least, so say the memoirs of a man who was concerned in some few of these defeats and in many of these victories.

Tréville had seized on the weak side of his master, and it was to this shrewdness that he owed the long and constant favour of a king who has not left behind him the reputation of having been very faithful in his friendships. He paraded his musketeers before the Cardinal Armand Duplessis with an insolent air, which made the gray moustache of his Eminence bristle with ire. Tréville was a master of the military science of that period, when he who did not live at the expense of the enemy lived at the expense of his compatriots ; his soldiers formed a legion of devil-may-care fellows, perfectly undisciplined as regarded every one but himself.

Loose, tipsy, gashed, the king's musketeers, or rather M. de Tréville's, spread themselves about in the saloons, in the public walks, and the public sports, shouting, twirling their moustaches, clanking their swords, and taking great pleasure in bustling against the guards of the cardinal whenever they could fall in with them ; then drawing their swords in the open streets, with a thousand jests ; sometimes killed, but sure in that case to be both wept and avenged ; often killing others, but then certain of not rotting in prison, M. de Tréville being there to claim them. And so M. de Tréville was praised in all keys by these men, who absolutely adored him, and who, ruffians as they were, trembled before him like scholars before their master, obedient to his least word, and ready to sacrifice themselves to wipe out the least insult.

M. de Tréville had employed this powerful machine for the king in the first place, and the friends of the king—and then for himself and his own friends. Besides, in none of the memoirs of this period, which has left so many memoirs, is this worthy gentleman accused even by his enemies—and he had many such among men of the pen, as well as among men of the sword ; in no instance, we say, was this worthy gentleman accused of being paid for the co-operation of his minions. Endowed with a rare genius for intrigue, which rendered him the equal of the ablest intriguers, he remained an honourable man. And further, in spite of sword-thrusts which weaken, and painful exercises which fatigue, he had become one of the most gallant frequenters of *salons*, one of the most exquisite dandies, one of the most refined purveyors of flattery of the times ; De Tréville's love affairs were talked about as those of M. de Bassompierre had been talked of twenty years before, and that was not saying a little. The captain of the musketeers, then, was admired, feared, and loved, and this constitutes the apogee of human fortunes.

Louis XIV. absorbed all the smaller stars of his court in his own vast radiance ; but his father, a sun *pluribus impar*, left his personal splendour for each of his favourites, his individual value for each of his courtiers. In addition to the levees of the king and the cardinal, there might be reckoned in Paris at that time more than two hundred smaller levees, more or less sought after. Among these two hundred levees, that of De Tréville was one of the most thronged.

The court of his hôtel, situated in the Rue du Vieux-Colombier, resembled a camp as early as six o'clock in the morning in summer and eight o'clock in winter. From fifty to sixty musketeers, who appeared to relieve each other there, in order always to present an imposing number, paraded constantly about, armed to the teeth and ready for anything. On one of those immense staircases, upon whose space modern civilization would build a whole house, ascended and descended the solicitors of Paris, who were in search of favours of any kind—gentlemen from the provinces anxious to be enrolled, and servants in all sorts of liveries, bringing messages from their masters to M. de Tréville. In the antechamber, upon long circular benches, reposed the elect—that is to say, those who were called. In this apartment a continued buzzing prevailed from morning till night, while M. de Tréville, in his office contiguous to this antechamber, received visits, listened to complaints, gave his orders, and, like the king in his balcony at the Louvre, had only to place himself at the window to review both men and arms.

The day on which D'Artagnan presented himself the assemblage was imposing, particularly for a provincial just arriving from his province. It is true that this provincial was a Gascon, and that, particularly at this period, the compatriots of D'Artagnan had the reputation of not being easily intimidated. When he had once passed the massive door, covered with long square-headed nails, he fell into the midst of a troop of military, who were passing each other in the court, calling out, quarrelling, and playing tricks one with another. To make way through these turbulent and conflicting waves it was necessary to be an officer, a great noble, or a pretty woman.

It was, then, in the midst of this tumult and disorder that our young man advanced with a beating heart. Holding his long rapier close to his lanky leg, and keeping one hand on the edge of his cap, he smiled with the embarrassment of a provincial who affects confidence. When he had passed one group he began to breathe more freely ; but he could not help observing that they turned round to look at him, and for the first time in his life D'Artagnan, who had till that day entertained a very good opinion of himself, felt that he was the object of ridicule.

When he arrived at the staircase it was still worse ; there were four musketeers on the bottom steps amusing themselves with the following exercise, while ten or twelve of their comrades on the landing-place awaited their turn in the game.

One of them, placed upon the top stair, naked sword in hand, prevented, or at least endeavoured to prevent, the three others from going up.

These three others fenced against him with their agile swords, which D'Artagnan at first took for foils, and believed to be buttoned ; but he soon perceived, by certain scratches, that every weapon was pointed and well sharpened, and that at each of these scratches not only the spectators, but even the actors themselves, laughed like so many madmen.

He who at that moment occupied the upper step kept his adversaries in check admirably. A circle was formed around them ; the conditions required that at every thrust the person hit should quit the game, losing his turn to the advantage of the person who had hit him. In five minutes three were slightly wounded, one on the wrist, another on the chin, and the third on the ear, by the defender of the stair, who himself remained intact—a piece of skill which was worth to him, according to the rules of the game, three additional turns.

However difficult it might be, or rather as he pretended it was, to astonish our young traveller, this pastime really astonished him. He had seen in his province—that land in which heads become so easily heated—a few of the preliminaries of duels, but the gasconades of these four fencers appeared to him the greatest he had ever heard, even in Gascony. He believed himself transported into that famous country of giants into which Gulliver has since gone and was so frightened ; and yet he had not gained the goal, for there were still the landing-place and the antechamber.

On the landing they were no longer fighting, but amused themselves with stories about women, and in the antechamber with stories about the court. On the landing D'Artagnan blushed ; in the antechamber he trembled. His warm and fickle imagination, which in Gascony had rendered him formidable to young chambermaids, and even sometimes to their mistresses, had never dreamed, even in moments of delirium, of half the amorous wonders, or a quarter of the feats of gallantry, which were here set forth, accompanied by names the best known and with details the least delicate. But if his morals were shocked on the landing, his respect for the cardinal was scandalized in the antechamber. There, to his great astonishment, D'Artagnan heard the policy which made all Europe tremble criticised aloud and openly, as well as the private life of the cardinal, for trying to pry into which so many great nobles had been punished. That great man, who was so revered by D'Artagnan the elder, served as an object of ridicule to M. de Tréville's musketeers, who cracked their jokes upon his bandy legs and his humpback; some sang ballads upon Madame d'Aiguillon, his mistress, and Madame de Combalet, his niece; while others formed parties and plans to annoy the pages and guards of the cardinal duke—all of which appeared to D'Artagnan monstrous impossibilities.

Nevertheless, when the name of the king was now and then uttered unexpectedly amidst all these cardinal jokes, a sort of gag seemed to close for a moment all these jeering mouths. They looked hesitatingly around them, and seemed to fear lest the walls of M. de Tréville's office should have ears; but a fresh allusion soon brought back the conversation to his Eminence, and then the laughter burst out anew, and all of his actions were dragged into full light.

"Certes, these fellows will all be either embastiled or hung," thought the terrified D'Artagnan, "and I, no doubt, with them; for from the moment I have either listened to or heard them, I shall be held to be an accomplice. What would my good father say, who so strongly pointed out to me the respect due to the cardinal, if he knew I was in the society of such pagans?"

We have no need, therefore, to say that D'Artagnan did not venture to join in the conversation; only he looked with all his eyes and listened with all his ears, stretching his five senses so as to lose nothing; and in spite of his confidence in the paternal monitions, he felt himself carried by his tastes and led by his instincts to praise rather than to blame the unheard-of things which were passing before him.

D'Artagnan being, however, a perfect stranger in the crowd of M. de Tréville's courtiers, and this his first appearance in that place, he was at length noticed, and a person came to him and asked him his business there. At this demand D'Artagnan gave his name very modestly, laid a stress upon the title of compatriot, and begged the servant who had put the question to him to request a moment's audience of M. de Tréville —a request which the other, with a patronizing air, promised to convey in time and season.

D'Artagnan, a little recovered from his first surprise, had now leisure to study costumes and countenances.

The centre of the most animated group was a musketeer of great height, of a haughty countenance, and dressed in a costume so peculiar as to attract general attention. He did not wear the uniform cloak—which, indeed, at that time of less liberty and greater independence was not obligatory—but a cerulean blue doublet, a little faded and worn, and over this a magnificent baldric worked in gold, which shone like water-ripples in the sun. A long cloak of crimson velvet fell in graceful folds from his shoulders, disclosing in front the splendid baldric, from which was suspended a gigantic rapier.

This musketeer had just come off guard, complained of having a cold, and coughed from time to time affectedly. It was for this reason, he said to those around him, he had put on his cloak ; and while he spoke with a lofty air and twirled his moustache, all admired his embroidered baldric, and D'Artagnan more than any one.

"What can you expect ? " said the musketeer. " The fashion is coming in. It is a folly, I admit, but still it is the fashion. Besides, one must lay out one's inheritance somehow."

" Ah, Porthos ! " cried one of his companions, " don't think to palm upon us that you obtained that baldric by paternal generosity : it must have been given to you by that veiled lady with whom I met you the other Sunday, near the gate Saint-Honoré."

" No, 'pon honour ; by the faith of a gentleman, I bought it with my own money," answered he whom they had just designated by the name of Porthos.

" Yes," said another musketeer, " you bought it as I did this new purse—with the money my mistress put into the old one."

" What I said is true, though," said Porthos ; " and the proof is that I paid twelve pistoles for it."

The wonder was increased, though the doubt continued to exist.

" Didn't I, Aramis ? " said Porthos, turning towards another musketeer.

This other musketeer formed a perfect contrast to his interrogator, who had just designated him by the name of Aramis.

He was a young man, of about two or three and twenty, with an open, ingenuous countenance, dark mild eyes, and cheeks rosy and downy as an autumn peach ; his delicate moustache marked a perfectly straight line upon his upper lip ; he appeared to dread to lower his hands lest their veins should swell, and he pinched the tips of his ears from time to time to preserve their delicate pink transparency. Habitually he spoke little and slowly, bowed frequently, laughed without noise, showing his teeth, which were fine, and of which, as of the rest of his person, he appeared to take the greatest care. He answered the appeal of his friend by an affirmative nod of the head.

This affirmation appeared to dispel all doubts with regard to the baldric. They continued to admire it, but said no more about it ; and by one of those rapid changes of thought, the conversation passed suddenly to another subject.

" What do you think of the story Chalais's esquire relates ? " asked another musketeer, without addressing any one in particular.

" And what does he say ? " asked Porthos, in a self-sufficient tone.

" He relates that he met at Brussels Rochefort, the cardinal's private tool, disguised as a capuchin ; and that this cursed Rochefort, thanks to his disguise, had tricked M. de Laigues, simpleton that he is."

" A simpleton, indeed ! " said Porthos. " But is the matter certain ? "

" I had it from Aramis," replied the musketeer.

" Indeed ! "

" Why, you know very well, Porthos," said Aramis ; " I told you of it yesterday. Say nothing more about it."

" Say nothing more about it—that's *your* opinion ! " replied Porthos. " Say nothing more about it ! Zounds ! you come to your conclusions quickly. What ! the cardinal sets a spy upon a nobleman, has his letters stolen from him by means of a traitor, a brigand, a rascal—has, with the help of this spy, and thanks to this correspondence, Chalais's throat cut, under the stupid pretext that he wanted to kill the king and marry Monsieur to the queen ! Nobody knew a word of this enigma. You unravelled it yesterday, to the great satisfaction of all ; and while we are still gaping with wonder at the news, you come and tell us to-day, ' Let us say no more about it.' "

" Well, then, let us speak about it, since you desire it," replied Aramis patiently.

"This Rochefort," cried Porthos, "if I were poor Chalais's esquire, should pass a minute or two very uncomfortably with me."

"And you—you would pass rather a sad half-hour with the Red Duke," replied Aramis.

"Oh! oh! the Red Duke! Bravo! bravo! the Red Duke!" cried Porthos, clapping his hands and nodding his head. "The Red Duke is capital. I'll circulate that saying, be assured, my dear fellow. Who says this Aramis is not a wit? What a misfortune it is you did not follow your first vocation; what a delightful abbé you would have made!"

"Oh, it's only a temporary postponement," replied Aramis. "I shall be one some day. You very well know, Porthos, that I continue to study theology for that purpose."

"He will be one, as he says," cried Porthos; "he will be one, sooner or later."

"Soon," said Aramis.

"He only waits for one thing to determine him to resume his cassock, which hangs behind his uniform," said another musketeer.

"What is he waiting for?" asked another.

"Only till the queen has given an heir to the crown of France."

"No jokes upon that subject, gentlemen," said Porthos. "Thank God, the queen is still of an age to give one."

"They say that the Duke of Buckingham is in France," replied Aramis, with a significant smile, which gave to this sentence, apparently so simple, a tolerably scandalous meaning.

"Aramis, my good friend, this time you are wrong," interrupted Porthos. "Your wit is always leading you astray. If M. de Tréville heard you, you would repent of speaking thus."

"Are you going to teach me better, Porthos?" cried Aramis, from whose usually mild eye a flash passed like lightning.

"My dear fellow, be a musketeer or an abbé. Be one or the other, but not both," replied Porthos "You know what Athos told you the other day: you eat at everybody's mess. Ah! don't be angry, I beg of you—that would be useless; you know what is agreed upon between you, Athos, and me. You go to Madame d'Aiguillon's, and you pay your court to her; you go to Madame de Bois-Tracy's, the cousin of Madame de Chevreuse, and you pass for being far advanced in the good graces of that lady. Oh, good Lord! don't trouble yourself to reveal your good fortunes ; no one asks for your secret—all the world knows your discretion. But since you possess that virtue, why the devil don't you make use of it with respect to her Majesty ? Let whoever likes talk of the king and the cardinal, and as he likes ; but the queen is sacred, and if any one speaks of her, let it be with respect."

"Porthos, you are as vain as Narcissus, I plainly tell you so," replied Aramis. "You know I hate moralizing, except when it is done by Athos. As to you, good sir, you wear too magnificent a baldric to be strong on that head. I will be an abbé if it suits me ; in the meanwhile I am a musketeer. In that quality I say what I please, and at this moment it pleases me to say that you annoy me."

"Aramis !"

"Porthos !"

"Gentlemen ! gentlemen !" cried the surrounding group.

"M. de Tréville awaits M. d'Artagnan," interrupted a servant, throwing open the door of the office.

At this announcement, during which the door remained open, every one became mute, and amidst the general silence the young man crossed the antechamber at one end, and entered the apartment of the captain of the musketeers, congratulating himself with all his heart at having so opportunely escaped the end of this strange quarrel.

CHAPTER III.

THE AUDIENCE.

M. DE TRÉVILLE was at this moment in a very ill-humour, nevertheless he politely saluted the young man, who bowed to the very ground, and he smiled on receiving his compliment, the Béarnese accent of which recalled to him at the same time his youth and his country, a double remembrance which makes a man smile at all ages. But stepping almost immediately towards the antechamber, and making a sign to D'Artagnan with his hand, as if to ask his permission to finish with others before he began with him, he called three times, with a louder voice at each time, so that he went through all the tones between the imperative accent and the angry accent.

"Athos ! Porthos ! Aramis !"

The two musketeers with whom we have already made

acquaintance, and who answered to the last two of these three names, immediately quitted the group of which they formed a part, and advanced towards the office, the door of which closed after them as soon as they had entered. Their bearing, though not entirely composed, was full of a dignified and submissive indifference, which excited the admiration of D'Artagnan, who beheld in these two men demigods, and in their leader an Olympian Jupiter, armed with all his thunders.

When the two musketeers had entered, when the door was closed behind them, when the buzzing murmur of the antechamber, to which the summons which had just been made had doubtless furnished fresh aliment, had recommenced, when M. de Tréville had three or four times paced in silence, and with a frowning brow, the whole length of his office, passing each time before Porthos and Aramis, who were as upright and silent as if on parade, he stopped all at once full in front of them, and looking at them angrily from head to foot,—

"Do you know what the king said to me," cried he, "and that no longer ago than yesterday evening—do you know, gentlemen?"

"No," replied the two musketeers, after a moment's silence; "no, sir, we do not."

"But I hope that you will do us the honour to tell us," added Aramis, in his politest tone and with the most graceful bow.

"He told me that he should henceforth recruit his musketeers from among the guards of the cardinal."

"The guards of the cardinal! And why so?" asked Porthos warmly.

"Because he plainly perceives that his piquette * stands in need of being enlivened by a mixture of good wine."

The two musketeers coloured up to the eyes. D'Artagnan did not know where he was, and would have liked to be a hundred feet underground.

"Yes, yes," continued M. de Tréville, growing warmer as he spoke, "and his Majesty was right, for, upon my honour, it is true that the musketeers make but a miserable figure at court. The cardinal related yesterday, while playing with the king, with an air of condolence not very pleasing to me, that the day before yesterday those damned musketeers, those dare-devils—he dwelt upon those words with an ironical tone still more displeasing to me—those cleavers, added

* A liquor squeezed out of grapes, when they have been pressed, and water poured upon them.

he, glancing at me with his tiger-cat's eye, had been out late in the Rue Férou, in a tavern, and that a patrol of his guards (I thought he was going to laugh in my face) had been forced to arrest the rioters. Zounds! you must know something about it! Arrest musketeers! You were among them—you were! Don't deny it; you were recognized, and the cardinal named you. But it's all my fault; yes, it's all my fault, because it is I myself who select my men. You, now, Aramis, why the devil did you ask me for a uniform when you were going to be so fine in a cassock? And you, Porthos, do you only wear such a fine golden baldric to suspend a sword of straw from it? And Athos—I don't see Athos! Where is he?"

"Sir," replied Aramis, in a sorrowful tone, "he is ill, very ill!"

"Ill—very ill, say you? And what is his malady?"

"It is feared that it is the smallpox, sir," replied Porthos, desirous of having a word in the conversation; "and what is sad is that it will certainly spoil his face."

"The smallpox! That's another fine story to tell me, Porthos! Sick of the smallpox at his age! No, no; but wounded, without doubt—perhaps killed. Ah, if I knew! S'blood! Sir musketeers, I will not have this haunting of bad places, this quarrelling in the streets, this sword-play at the cross-roads; and above all, I will not have any opportunity given to the cardinal's guards, who are brave, quiet, skilful men, who never put themselves in a position to be arrested, and who, besides, would never allow themselves to be arrested, to laugh at you! I am sure of it—they would prefer dying on the spot to being arrested or to retreating a step. To run, to clear out, to fly! a pretty thing to be said of the king's musketeers!"

Porthos and Aramis trembled with rage; they would willingly have strangled M. de Tréville if, at the bottom of all this, they had not felt it was the great love he bore them which made him speak thus. They stamped upon the carpet with their feet, they bit their lips till the blood came, and grasped the hilts of their swords with all their might. All in the next room had heard, as we have said, Athos, Porthos, and Aramis called, and had guessed from M. de Tréville's tone of voice that he was very angry about something. Ten curious heads were leaning against the tapestry and growing pale with rage. For their ears, glued to the door, did not lose a syllable of what was said, while their mouths repeated, as he went on, the insulting expressions of the captain to the whole population of the antechamber. In an instant, from the door of the office to the street gate, the whole house was in a state of commotion.

"Ah! the king's musketeers are arrested by the guards of the cardinal, are they?" continued M. de Tréville, as furious within as his soldiers, but emphasizing his words, and plunging them, one by one, like so many blows of a stiletto, into the bosoms of his auditors. "What! six of his Eminence's guards arrest six of his Majesty's musketeers! Zounds! my mind is made up. I will go straight to the Louvre. I will give in my resignation as captain of the king's musketeers, to take a lieutenancy in the cardinal's guards; and if he refuses me, 'sdeath! I will turn abbé."

At these words the murmur outside became an explosion; nothing was to be heard but oaths and blasphemies. Such expressions as zounds! 'sblood! the devil take us! clashed in the air. D'Artagnan looked round for some tapestry behind which he might hide himself, and felt an immense inclination to crawl under the table.

"Well, captain," said Porthos, quite beside himself, "the truth is that we were six against six. But we were not captured by fair means, and before we had time to draw our swords two of our party were dead; and Athos, grievously wounded, was very little better. For you know Athos. Well, captain, he endeavoured twice to get up, and fell again twice. And we did not surrender—no! they dragged us away by force. On the way we escaped. As for Athos, they believed him to be dead, and left him very quietly on the field of battle, not thinking it worth the while to carry him away. Now, that's the whole story. What the devil, captain, one cannot win all one's battles! The great Pompey lost that of Pharsalia; and Francis the First, who was, as I have heard say, as good as any one else, nevertheless lost the battle of Pavia."

"And I have the honour of assuring you that I killed one of them with his own sword," said Aramis, "for mine was broken at the first parry. Killed him, or poniarded him, sir, as is most agreeable to you."

"I did not know that," replied M. de Tréville in a somewhat softened tone. "The cardinal exaggerated, as I perceive."

"But pray, sir," continued Aramis, who, seeing his captain relenting, took courage to make a petition—"pray, sir, do not say that Athos is wounded. He would be in despair if that should come to the ears of the king; and as the wound is very serious, seeing that after crossing the shoulder it penetrates into the chest, it is to be feared——"

At this instant the tapestry was raised, and a noble and handsome face, but frightfully pale, appeared under the fringe.

"Athos!" cried the two musketeers.

"Athos!" repeated M. de Tréville to himself.

"You have sent for me, sir," said Athos to M. de Tréville in a feeble yet perfectly calm voice—"you have sent for me, as my comrades inform me, and I have hastened to receive your orders. I am here, sir; what do you want with me?"

And at these words the musketeer, in irreproachable costume, belted as usual, with a firm step entered the room. M. de Tréville, moved to the bottom of his heart by this proof of courage, sprang towards him.

"I was about to say to these gentlemen," added he, "that I forbid my musketeers to expose their lives needlessly; for brave men are very dear to the king, and the king knows that his musketeers are the bravest fellows on earth. Your hand, Athos!"

And without waiting until the newcomer should himself respond to this proof of affection, M. de Tréville seized his right hand, and pressed it with all his might, without perceiving that Athos, whatever might be his self-command, allowed a slight murmur of pain to escape him, and, if possible, grew paler than he was before.

The door had remained open, so strong was the excitement produced by the arrival of Athos, whose wound, though kept as secret as possible, was known to all. A loud murmur of satisfaction hailed the last words of the captain, and two or three persons, carried away by the enthusiasm of the moment, appeared through the openings of the tapestry. Doubtless M. de Tréville was about to reprehend severely this infringement on the rules of etiquette, when he suddenly felt the hand of Athos contract within his, and upon turning his eyes towards him, perceived he was about to faint. At the same instant Athos, who had rallied all his energies to contend against pain, at length overcome by it, fell upon the floor as if he was dead.

"A surgeon!" cried M. de Tréville; "mine! the king's! the best that can be found! A surgeon! or, 'sblood! my brave Athos will die!"

At the cries of M. de Tréville the whole assemblage rushed into the room without his thinking of shutting the door against any one, and all crowded round the wounded man.

But all this eager attention would have been useless if the doctor so loudly called for had not chanced to be in the hôtel itself. He pushed through the crowd, approached Athos, still insensible, and as all this noise and commotion inconvenienced him greatly, he required, as the first and most urgent thing, that the musketeer should be carried into another chamber. Immediately M. de Tréville opened the door and pointed the way to Porthos and Aramis, who carried off their comrade in their arms. Behind this group walked the surgeon, and as the surgeon passed through the door closed upon him.

The office of M. de Tréville, generally held so sacred, became for a moment the annex of the antechamber. Every one spoke, harangued, and vociferated, swearing, cursing, and consigning the cardinal and his guards to all the devils.

An instant after Porthos and Aramis returned, the surgeon and M. de Tréville alone remaining with the wounded man.

At length M. de Tréville himself came back. Athos had recovered his senses. The surgeon declared that the situation of the musketeer had nothing in it to render his friends uneasy, his weakness having been purely and simply caused by loss of blood.

Then M. de Tréville made a sign with his hand, and all retired except D'Artagnan, who did not forget that he had an audience, and with the tenacity of a Gascon remained in his place.

When all had gone out and the door was closed, M. de Tréville, on turning round, found himself alone with the young man. The stirring event which had just taken place had in some degree broken the thread of his ideas. He inquired what was the desire of his persevering visitor. D'Artagnan then repeated his name, and in an instant, recalling his memory of the past and the present, M. de Tréville was in possession of the situation.

"Pardon me," said he, smiling—"pardon me, my dear compatriot, but I had entirely forgotten you. But what help is there for it? A captain is nothing but a father of a family, charged with even a greater responsibility than the father of an ordinary family. Soldiers are big children; but as I maintain that the orders of the king, and more particularly the orders of the cardinal, should be executed——"

D'Artagnan could not restrain a smile. By this smile M. de Tréville judged that he had not to deal with a fool, and changing the subject, came straight to the point.

"I loved your father very much," said he. "What can

I do for the son? Tell me quickly—my time is not my own."

"Sir," said D'Artagnan, "on leaving Tarbes and coming hither, it was my intention to request of you, in remembrance of the friendship which you have not forgotten, the uniform of a musketeer. But after all that I have seen during the last two hours, I have become aware of the value of such a favour, and tremble lest I should not merit it."

"Well, young man," replied M. de Tréville, "it is, in fact, a favour, but it may not be so far beyond your hopes as you believe, or rather as you appear to believe. Yet his Majesty's decision is always necessary, and I inform you with regret that no one becomes a musketeer without the preliminary ordeal of several campaigns, certain brilliant actions, or a service of two years in some regiment less favoured than ours."

D'Artagnan bowed without replying, feeling his desire to don the musketeer's uniform vastly increased by the difficulties which he had learned must precede the attainment of it.

"But," continued M. de Tréville, fixing upon his compatriot a look so piercing that it might be said he wished to read the thoughts of his heart—"but on account of my old companion, your father, as I have said, I will do something for you, young man. Our cadets from Béarn are not generally very rich, and I have no reason to think matters have much changed in this respect since I left the province. I dare say you have not brought too large a stock of money with you?"

D'Artagnan drew himself up with an air that plainly said, "I ask charity of no man."

"Oh, that's all very well, young man," continued M. de Tréville, "that's all very well. I am well acquainted with all those lofty airs. I myself came to Paris with four crowns in my purse, and would have fought with any one who would have dared to tell me I was not in a condition to purchase the Louvre."

D'Artagnan drew himself up still more proudly. Thanks to the sale of his horse, he commenced his career with four crowns more than M. de Tréville had possessed at the commencement of his.

"You need, I say, then, to husband the means you have, however large the sum may be, but you ought also to endeavour to perfect yourself in the exercises becoming a gentleman. I will write a letter to-day to the director of the Royal Academy, and to-morrow he will admit you without any expense to yourself. Do not refuse this little service. Our best-born and richest gentlemen sometimes solicit it without being able to obtain it. You will learn riding, swordsmanship in all its branches, and dancing. You will make some desirable acquaintances, and from time to time you can call upon me, just to tell me how you are getting on, and to say whether I can be of any service to you."

D'Artagnan, stranger as he was to all the manners of a court, could not but perceive a little coldness in this reception.

"Alas, sir," said he, " I can but perceive how sadly I miss the letter of introduction which my father gave me to present to you."

" I certainly am surprised," replied M. de Tréville, " that you should undertake so long a journey without that necessary viaticum, the only resource of us poor Béarnese."

" I had one, sir, and, thank God, such as I could wish," cried D'Artagnan, " but it was perfidiously stolen from me."

He then related the adventure at Meung, described the unknown gentleman with the greatest minuteness, and all with a warmth and truthfulness that delighted M. de Tréville.

" This is all very strange," said the latter, after meditating a minute. " You mentioned my name, then, aloud ? "

" Yes, sir ; I certainly committed that imprudence. But why should I have done otherwise ? A name like yours was to serve me as a buckler on my way. You can fancy whether I often hid myself behind it or no ! "

Flattery was at that period very much in fashion, and M. de Tréville loved incense as well as a king, or even a cardinal. He could not then refrain from a smile of evident satisfaction ; but this smile soon disappeared, and returning to the adventure at Meung,—

" Tell me," continued he, " had not this gentleman a slight scar on his cheek ? "

" Yes, such a one as would be made by the grazing of a ball."

" Was he not a fine-looking man ? "

" Yes."

" Of lofty stature ? "

" Yes."

" Of pale complexion and brown hair ? "

" Yes, yes, that is he ! How is it, sir, that you are

acquainted with this man ? If ever I should meet him again, and I will find him, I swear, were it in hell——"

" He was waiting for a woman ? " continued Tréville.

" He at least departed immediately after having conversed for a minute with the one for whom he was waiting."

" You do not know what was the subject of their conversation ? "

" He gave her a box, told her that box contained her instructions, and desired her not to open it before she arrived in London."

" Was this an English woman ? "

" He called her Milady."

" It is he ! it must be he ! " murmured Tréville. " I thought he was still at Brussels ! "

" O sir, if you know who and what this man is," cried D'Artagnan, " tell me who he is and whence he is. I will then release you from all your promises—even that of procuring my admission into the musketeers. For, before everything, I wish to avenge myself."

" Beware, young man ! " cried De Tréville. " If you see him coming on one side of the street, pass by on the other. Do not cast yourself against such a rock ; he would break you like glass."

" That thought will not prevent me," replied D'Artagnan, " if ever I should happen to meet with him——"

" In the meantime, if you will take my advice, you will not seek him," said Tréville.

All at once the captain stopped, as if struck by a sudden suspicion. This great hatred which the young traveller manifested so loudly for this man, who (a rather improbable thing) had stolen his father's letter from him—was there not some perfidy concealed under this hatred ? Might not this young man be sent by his Eminence ? Might he not have come for the purpose of laying a snare for him ? This pretended D'Artagnan — was he not an emissary of the cardinal's whom he sought to introduce into his house, to place near him, and win his confidence, and afterwards to bring about his ruin, as had been practised in a thousand other instances ? He fixed his eyes upon D'Artagnan even more earnestly than before. He was moderately reassured, however, by the aspect of that countenance, full of shrewd intelligence and affected humility.

" I know indeed he is a Gascon," reflected he, " but he may be one for the cardinal as well as for me. Let us try him."

" My friend," said he slowly, " I wish, as the son of an old friend—for I consider this story of the lost letter perfectly true—I wish, I say, in order to repair the coldness you have noticed in my reception of you, to make you acquainted with the secrets of our policy. The king and the cardinal are the best of friends; their apparent bickerings are only feints to deceive fools. I am not willing that a compatriot, a handsome cavalier, a brave youth, quite fit to make his way, should become the dupe of all these artifices, and fall stupidly into the snare, after the example of so many others who have been ruined by it. Be assured that I am devoted to both these all-powerful masters, and that my earnest endeavour shall never have any other aim than the service of the king and that of the cardinal, one of the most illustrious geniuses that France has ever produced.

" Now, young man, regulate your conduct accordingly, and if you entertain, whether from your family, your associations, or even from your instincts, any of those enmities against the cardinal which we see constantly breaking out among the nobles, bid me adieu, and let us separate. I will aid you in many ways, but without attaching you to my person. I hope that my frankness, at all events, will make you my friend, for you are the only young man to whom I have hitherto spoken as I am now doing."

Tréville said to himself,—

" If the cardinal has set this young fox upon me, he will certainly not have failed—he who knows how bitterly I execrate him—to tell his spy that the best means of paying court to me is to rail at him. Therefore, in spite of my protestations, if it be as I suspect, my cunning gossip here will launch out in abuse of his Eminence."

It proved, however, entirely different from what Tréville expected. D'Artagnan answered, with the greatest simplicity,—

" I am come to Paris with exactly such intentions, sir. My father advised me to stoop to nobody but the king, the cardinal, and you—whom he considers the first three personages in France."

D'Artagnan added M. de Tréville to the two others, as may be perceived; but he thought this addition would do no harm.

" I therefore hold the cardinal in the greatest veneration," continued he, " and have the greatest respect for his actions. So much the better for me, sir, if you speak to me, as you say, with frankness, for then you will do me the honour to hold in esteem our similarity of taste; but if you have entertained any mistrust, as naturally you may, I feel that I am ruining myself by speaking the truth. But come what may, you will not fail to esteem me, and that is what I care for more than anything in the world."

M. de Tréville was surprised to the last degree. So much penetration, so much frankness, created admiration, but did not entirely remove his suspicions. The more this young man was superior to others the more he was to be dreaded, if he meant to deceive him. Nevertheless he pressed D'Artagnan's hand, and said to him,—

"You are an honest youth, but at the present moment I can only do for you that which I just now offered. My house will be always open to you. Hereafter, being able to ask for me at all hours, and consequently to take advantage of all opportunities, you will probably obtain what you desire."

"That is to say, sir," replied D'Artagnan, "that you will wait till I have made myself worthy of it. Well, be assured," added he, with the familiarity of a Gascon, " you will not wait long." And he bowed on retiring, as if he considered the future was his own concern.

"But wait a minute," said M. de Tréville, stopping him. "I promised you a letter to the director of the Academy. Are you too proud to accept it, young gentleman ?"

"No, sir," said D'Artagnan ; "and I will answer for it that this one shall not fare like the other. I will guard it so carefully that I swear it shall arrive at its address, and woe be to him who shall attempt to take it from me !"

M. de Tréville smiled at this bragging, and leaving his young compatriot in the embrasure of the window, where they had talked together, he seated himself at a table, in order to write the promised letter of recommendation. While he was doing this D'Artagnan, having no better employment, amused himself with beating a march upon the window, and with looking at the musketeers, who went away, one after another, following them with his eyes till they disappeared at the bend of the street.

M. de Tréville, after having written the letter, sealed it, and rising, approached the young man in order to give it to him. But at the very moment that D'Artagnan stretched out his hand to receive it, M. de Tréville was highly astonished to see his *protégé* make a sudden spring, become crimson with passion, and rush from the room, crying, " Ah, 'sblood ! he shall not escape me this time."

"Who ? who ?" asked M. de Tréville.

"He, my thief !" replied D'Artagnan. "Ah, the traitor !" and he disappeared.

"The devil take the madman!" murmured M. de Tréville, "unless," added he, "this is a cunning mode of escaping, seeing that he has failed in his purpose!"

CHAPTER IV.

D'ARTAGNAN, in a state of rage, crossed the antechamber in
three bounds, and was darting towards the stairs, which he
reckoned upon descending four steps at a time, when, in his
heedless course, he ran headforemost against a musketeer
who was coming out of one of M. de Tréville's private rooms,
and hitting his shoulder violently, made him utter a cry, or
rather a howl.

"Excuse me," said D'Artagnan, endeavouring to resume
his course—"excuse me, but I am in a hurry."

Scarcely had he descended the first stair when a hand of
iron seized him by the scarf and stopped him.

"You are in a hurry," said the musketeer, as pale as a
sheet. "Under that pretence you run against me. You
say 'Excuse me!' and you believe that that is sufficient?
Not at all, my young man. Do you fancy that because you
have heard M. de Tréville speak to us a little cavalierly
to-day that other people are to treat us as he speaks to
us? Undeceive yourself, companion; you are not M. de
Tréville."

"'Pon my word!" replied D'Artagnan, recognizing Athos,
who, after having his wounds dressed by the doctor, was going
to his own apartment—"on my word, I did not do it intentionally, and not having done it intentionally, I said,
'Excuse me!' It appears to me that that is quite enough.
I repeat to you, however—and this time it is too much, perhaps—on my word of honour I am in great haste, great
haste. Loose your hold, then, I beg of you, and let me go
where my business calls me."

"Sir," said Athos, letting him go, "you are not polite;
it is easy to perceive that you come from a distance."

D'Artagnan had already strode down three or four stairs
when Athos's last remark stopped him short.

"Zounds, sir!" said he, "however far I may have come,
it is not you who can give me a lesson in good manners, I
warn you."

"Perhaps!" said Athos.

"Ah! if I were not in such haste, and if I were not running after some one!" said D'Artagnan.

"Mr. Man-in-a-hurry, you can find me without running after me—me! Do you understand me?"

"And where, I pray you?"

"Near the Carmes-Deschaux."

"At what hour?"

"About noon."

"About noon. That will do; I will be there."

"Try not to make me wait, for at a quarter-past twelve I will cut off your ears as you run."

"Good!" cried D'Artagnan; "I will be there ten minutes before twelve."

And he set off, running as if the devil possessed him, hoping that he might yet find the unknown, whose slow pace could not have carried him far.

But at the street gate Porthos was talking with the soldier on guard. Between the two talkers there was just room for a man to pass. D'Artagnan thought it would suffice for him, and he sprang forward like a dart between them. But D'Artagnan had reckoned without the wind. As he was about to pass the wind blew out Porthos's long cloak, and D'Artagnan rushed straight into the middle of it. Without doubt Porthos had reasons for not abandoning this essential part of his vestments, for instead of letting go the flap, which he was holding, he pulled it towards him, so that D'Artagnan rolled himself up in the velvet by a movement of rotation explained by the resistance of the obstinate Porthos.

D'Artagnan, hearing the musketeer swear, wished to escape from under the cloak which blinded him, and endeavoured to make his way out of its folds. He was particularly anxious to avoid marring the freshness of the magnificent baldric we are acquainted with; but on timidly opening his eyes, he found himself with his nose fixed between the two shoulders of Porthos—that is to say, exactly upon the baldric.

Alas! like most of the things in this world which have nothing in their favour but appearance, the baldric was glittering with gold in the front, but was nothing but simple buff behind. Vainglorious as he was, Porthos could not afford to have an entirely gold-worked baldric, but had at least half a one. The pretext about the cold and the necessity for the cloak were thus exposed.

"Good Lord!" cried Porthos, making strong efforts to get rid of D'Artagnan, who was wriggling about his back, "the fellow must be mad to run against people in this manner."

"Excuse me," said D'Artagnan, reappearing under the shoulder of the giant, "but I am in such haste. I was running after some one, and——"

"And do you always forget your eyes when you happen to be in a hurry?" asked Porthos.

"No," replied D'Artagnan, piqued, "no; and, thanks to my eyes, I can see what other people cannot see."

Whether Porthos understood him or did not understand him, the fact is that giving way to his anger,—

"Sir," said he, "I warn you that you stand a chance of getting chastised if you run against musketeers in this fashion."

"Chastised, sir?" said D'Artagnan. "The expression is strong."

"It is one that becomes a man accustomed to look his enemies in the face."

"Ah, zounds! I know full well that you do not turn your back to yours."

And the young man, delighted with his joke, went away laughing with all his might.

Porthos foamed with rage, and started to rush after D'Artagnan.

"Wait awhile, wait awhile," cried the latter; "when you haven't your cloak on."

"At one o'clock, then, behind the Luxembourg."

"Very well; at one o'clock, then," replied D'Artagnan, turning the angle of the street.

But neither in the street through which he had passed, nor in the one which his glance now eagerly scanned, could he see any one. However slowly the unknown had walked, he had gained ground, or perhaps had entered some house. D'Artagnan inquired of every one he met, went down to the ferry, came up again by the Rue de Seine and the Croix Rouge, but he could see nothing of him, absolutely nothing! This race was, however, advantageous to him in one sense, for in proportion as the perspiration broke from his forehead his heart began to cool.

He began to reflect upon the events that had passed. They were numerous and inauspicious. It was scarcely eleven o'clock in the morning, and yet this morning had already brought him into disgrace with M. de Tréville, who could not fail to think the manner in which D'Artagnan had left him a little cavalier.

Besides this, he had drawn upon himself two good duels

with two men, each capable of killing three D'Artagnans—with two musketeers, in short, with two of those beings whom he esteemed so highly that he placed them in his mind and heart above all other men.

Conjectures were not encouraging. Sure of being killed by Athos, it may easily be understood that the young man was not very uneasy about Porthos. As hope, however, is the last thing extinguished in the heart of man, he ended by hoping that he might survive, although terribly wounded in both these duels; and in case of surviving he made the following reflections upon his own conduct:—

"What a harebrained, stupid fellow I am! That brave and unfortunate Athos was wounded exactly on that shoulder against which I must run headforemost, like a ram. The only thing that astonishes me is that he did not strike me dead at once; he had good cause to do so. The pain I gave him must have been horrible. As to Porthos—oh, as to Porthos, upon my word, that is stranger still!"

And in spite of himself the young man began to laugh aloud, looking round carefully, however, lest some one, hearing and not understanding his merriment, should be offended.

"As to Porthos, that is certainly strange, but I am not the less a giddy fool. Are people to be run against without warning? No! And have I any right to go and peep under their cloaks to see what is not there? He would have pardoned me—he would certainly have pardoned me—if I had not said anything to him about that cursed baldric, in ambiguous words, it is true, but rather neatly ambiguous! Ah, cursed Gascon that I am, I get from one hobble into another. Friend D'Artagnan," continued he, speaking to himself with all the amenity that he thought due to himself, "if you escape, of which there is not much chance, I would advise you to practise perfect politeness for the future. You must henceforth be admired and quoted as a model of it. To be obliging and polite does not necessarily make a man a coward. Look at Aramis now; Aramis is mildness and grace personified. Well, did ever anybody dream of saying that Aramis is a coward? No, certainly not; and from this moment I will endeavour to model myself after him. Ah, how strange, here he is!"

D'Artagnan, walking and soliloquizing, had arrived within a few steps of the Hôtel d'Aiguillon, and in front of that hôtel perceived Aramis chatting gaily with three gentlemen of the king's guards. Aramis also perceived D'Artagnan; but as he had not forgotten that it was in the presence of this young man that M. de Tréville had been so angry in the morning, and that a witness of the rebuke the musketeers had received was not likely to be at all agreeable, he pretended not to see him. D'Artagnan, on the contrary, quite full of his plans of conciliation and courtesy, approached the young men with a profound bow, accompanied by a most gracious smile. Aramis bowed his head slightly, but did not smile. All four of them immediately ceased talking.

D'Artagnan was not so dull as not to perceive that he was not wanted, but he was not sufficiently acquainted with the ways of the world to know how to withdraw with ease from the awkward position of having forced himself upon persons he scarcely knew, and having joined in a conversation which did not concern him. He was seeking in his mind, then, for the least disagreeable means of retreat, when he remarked that Aramis had let his handkerchief fall, and by mistake, no doubt, had placed his foot upon it, and it appeared a favourable opportunity to atone for his intrusion. He stooped, and with the most gracious air he could assume, drew the handkerchief from under the foot of the musketeer, in spite of the efforts the latter made to detain it, and holding it out to him, said,—

" I believe, sir, that this is a handkerchief you would be sorry to lose ? "

The handkerchief was, in fact, richly embroidered, and had a coronet and arms at one of its corners. Aramis blushed excessively, and snatched rather than took the handkerchief from D'Artagnan's hand.

" Ah, ah ! " cried one of the guards, " will you persist in saying, most discreet Aramis, that you are not on good terms with Madame de Bois-Tracy, when that gracious lady has the kindness to lend you her handkerchief ? "

Aramis darted at D'Artagnan one of those looks which inform a man that he has acquired a mortal enemy ; then resuming his mild air,—

" You are deceived, gentlemen," said he ; " this handkerchief is not mine, and I cannot fancy why the gentleman has taken it into his head to offer it to me rather than to one of you ; and as a proof of what I say, here is mine in my pocket."

So saying, he pulled out his own handkerchief, which was likewise a very elegant handkerchief, and of fine cambric, though cambric was then dear, but a handkerchief without embroidery and without arms, only ornamented with a single cipher, that of its owner.

This time D'Artagnan kept silence; he perceived his mistake. But the friends of Aramis were not at all convinced by his assertion; and one of them, addressing the young musketeer with affected seriousness,—

"If it were as you pretend it is," said he, "I should be forced, my dear Aramis, to reclaim it myself; for, as you very well know, Bois-Tracy is an intimate friend of mine, and I cannot allow the property of his wife to be sported as a trophy."

"You make the demand in bad form," replied Aramis; "and while I acknowledge the justice of your claim, I refuse it on account of the manner of its presentation."

"The fact is," hazarded D'Artagnan timidly, "I did not see the handkerchief fall from the pocket of M. Aramis. He had his foot upon it, that is all, and I thought from his having his foot upon it the handkerchief was his."

"And you were deceived, my dear sir," replied Aramis coldly, and little affected by the offer of atonement. Then turning towards that one of the guards who had declared himself the friend of Bois-Tracy, "Besides," continued he, "I have reflected, my dear intimate friend of Bois-Tracy, that I am not less tenderly his friend than you probably are, so that decidedly this handkerchief is as likely to have fallen from your pocket as mine."

"No, upon my honour!" cried his Majesty's guardsman.

"You are about to swear upon your honour and I upon my word, and then it will be pretty evident that one of us will have lied. Now here, Montaran, we will do better than that: let us each take a half."

"Of the handkerchief?"

"Yes."

"Perfectly just!" cried the two other guards; "the judgment of King Solomon! Aramis, you certainly are cram-full of wisdom."

The young men burst into a loud laugh, and as may be supposed, the affair had no other sequel. In a moment or two the conversation ceased, and the three guards and the musketeer, after having cordially shaken hands, separated, the guards going one way and Aramis another.

"Now is my time to make my peace with this gentleman," said D'Artagnan to himself, having kept at a little distance all the latter part of the conversation; and with this good feeling he drew near to Aramis, who was going away without paying any attention to him.

"Sir," said he, "you will excuse me, I hope."

"Ah!" interrupted Aramis, "allow me to call to your attention that you have not acted in this affair as a man of good breeding ought to have."

"What!" cried D'Artagnan; "you suppose——"

"I suppose, sir, that you are not a fool, and that you know very well, although coming from Gascony, that people do not tread upon pocket handkerchiefs without a reason. What the devil! Paris is not paved with cambric!"

"Sir, you do wrong in endeavouring to mortify me," said D'Artagnan, to whom his quarrelsome nature began to speak more loudly than his pacific resolutions. "I am from Gascony, it is true; and since you know it, there is no need of telling you that Gascons are not very patient, so that when they have asked pardon once, were it even for a folly, they are convinced that they have done already at least as much again as they ought to have done."

"Sir, what I say to you about the matter," said Aramis, "is not for the sake of seeking a quarrel. Thank God, I am not a bully; and being a musketeer only for a time, I only fight when I am forced to do so, and always with great repugnance. But this time the affair is serious, for here is a lady compromised by you."

"By us, you mean," cried D'Artagnan.

"Why did you so awkwardly give me the handkerchief?"

"Why did you so awkwardly let it fall?"

"I have said, sir, that the handkerchief did not fall from my pocket."

"Well, and by saying so you have lied twice, sir, for I saw it fall."

"Oh, oh! you take it up in that way, do you, Master Gascon? Well, I will teach you how to behave yourself."

"And I will send you back to your mass-book, Master Abbé. Draw, if you please, and right away."

"Not at all, if you please, my good friend—not here, at least. Do you not perceive that we are opposite the Hôtel d'Aiguillon, which is full of the cardinal's creatures? How do I know that it is not his Eminence who has honoured you with the commission to bring him my head? Now I really entertain a ridiculous partiality for my head, because it seems to suit my shoulders so admirably. I have no objection to killing you, depend upon that, but quietly, in a snug, remote place, where you will not be able to boast of your death to anybody."

"I agree, sir; but do not be too confident. Take away

your handkerchief. Whether it belongs to you or another, you may, perhaps, stand in need of it."

"The gentleman is a Gascon?" asked Aramis.

"Yes. The gentleman does not postpone a meeting through prudence."

"Prudence, sir, is a virtue quite useless to musketeers, I know, but indispensable to churchmen; and as I am only a musketeer provisionally, I deem it best to be prudent. At two o'clock I shall have the honour of expecting you at the hôtel of M. de Tréville. There I will point out to you the best place and time."

The two young men bowed and separated, Aramis ascending the street which led to the Luxembourg, while D'Artagnan, perceiving that the appointed hour was approaching, took the road to the Carmes-Deschaux, saying to himself, "Decidedly I can't draw back; but at least, if I am killed, I shall be killed by a musketeer!"

CHAPTER V.

THE KING'S MUSKETEERS AND THE CARDINAL'S GUARDS.

D'ARTAGNAN was not acquainted with anybody in Paris. He went, therefore, to his appointment with Athos without a second, determined to be satisfied with those his adversary should choose. Besides, his mind was fixed on making the brave musketeer all suitable apologies, but without meanness or weakness, fearing that the result of this duel would be the usual unfortunate result of an affair of this kind, when a young and vigorous man fights with an adversary who is wounded and enfeebled: if conquered, he doubles the triumph of his antagonist; if a conqueror, he is accused of foul play and cheap courage.

Now, we must have badly sketched the character of our adventurer, or our readers must have already perceived that D'Artagnan was not a common man. Therefore, while repeating to himself that his death was inevitable, he did not make up his mind to die as easily as another less courageous and less moderate than he might have done in his place. He reflected upon the different characters of the men he had to fight with, and began to see into his own situation more clearly. He hoped, by means of loyal excuses, to make a friend of Athos, whose lordly air and austere bearing were very pleasing to him. He flattered himself he should be able to frighten Porthos with the adventure of the baldric, which he could, if not killed upon the spot, relate to everybody—a story that, well managed, would cover Porthos with ridicule. As to the astute Aramis, he did not entertain much dread of him, and supposing that he should get so far, he determined to dispatch him in good style, or at least, by hitting him in the face, as Cæsar recommended his soldiers to do to those of Pompey, damage for ever that beauty of which he was so proud.

And, finally, D'Artagnan possessed that invincible stock of resolution which the counsels of his father had deposited in his heart, and which were summed up in " Endure nothing from any one but the king, the cardinal, and M. de Tréville." He flew, then, rather than walked, towards the monastery of the Carmes-Déchaussés, or rather Deschaux, as they said at that time, a sort of building without a window, surrounded by barren fields, an annex to the Pré-aux-Clercs, and which was generally employed as the place for the meetings of men who had no time to lose.

When D'Artagnan arrived in sight of the bare spot of ground which stretched out at the base of the monastery, Athos had been waiting about five minutes, and twelve o'clock was striking. He was, then, as punctual as the Samaritan woman, and the most rigorous casuist on duels could have nothing to say.

Athos, who still suffered grievously from his wound, though it had been freshly dressed by M. de Tréville's surgeon, was seated on a stone, awaiting his adversary with that placid countenance and that noble air which never forsook him. At sight of D'Artagnan he arose and politely came a few steps to meet him. The latter, on his part, saluted his adversary with hat in hand, and his feather even touching the ground.

" Sir," said Athos, " I have engaged two of my friends as seconds, but these two friends have not yet come. I am astonished at their delay, as it is not at all their custom to be behindhand."

" I have no seconds on my part, sir," said D'Artagnan ; " for, having reached Paris only yesterday, I as yet know no one but M. de Tréville, to whom I was recommended by my father, who has the honour to be, in some degree, one of his friends."

Athos reflected for an instant.

" You know no one but M. de Tréville ? " he asked.

" No, sir ; I know only him."

"Well, well," continued Athos, speaking partly to himself—"well, well, if I kill you, I shall have the air of a child-eater."

"Not too much so," replied D'Artagnan, with a bow that was not deficient in dignity—"not too much so, since you do me the honour to draw sword against me while suffering from a wound which must bother you very much."

"Very much, upon my word; and you hurt me devilishly, I can tell you. But I will use the left hand; I usually do so under such circumstances. Do not fancy, though, that I favour you: I use both hands equally. And it will be even a disadvantage to you: a left-handed man is very trouble-some to people who are not prepared for it. I regret I did not inform you sooner of this circumstance."

"You are truly, sir," said D'Artagnan, bowing again, "very courteous, for which, I assure you, I am extremely grateful."

"You confuse me," replied Athos, with his gentlemanly air. "I beg of you, let us talk of something else, unless it is displeasing to you. Ah, 'sblood! how you did hurt me! My shoulder really burns."

"If you would permit me——" said D'Artagnan timidly.

"What, sir?"

"I have a miraculous balsam for wounds—a balsam given to me by my mother, and of which I have made a trial upon myself."

"Well?"

"Well, I am sure that in less than three days this balsam would cure you; and at the end of three days, when you would be cured—well, sir, it would still do me a great honour to be your man."

D'Artagnan spoke these words with a simplicity that did honour to his courtesy, without casting the least doubt upon his courage.

"By God, sir!" said Athos, "that's a proposition which pleases me; not that I accept it, but it smacks of the gentle-man a league away. So spoke the gallant knights of the time of Charlemagne, in whom every knight ought to seek his model. Unfortunately, we do not live in the time of the great emperor. We live in the times of the cardinal; and three days hence, however well the secret might be guarded, it would be known, I say, that we were to fight, and our combat would be forestalled. Will these idlers never come?"

"If you are in a hurry, sir," said D'Artagnan, with the same simplicity with which a moment before he had proposed to put off the duel for three days—"if you are in a hurry, and if it be your will to dispatch me at once, do not inconvenience yourself, I beg of you."

"Well, that is again well said," cried Athos, nodding graciously to D'Artagnan ; "that did not come from a man without brains, and certainly not from a man without a heart. Sir, I love men of your kidney, and I foresee plainly that if we don't kill each other, I shall hereafter take real pleasure in your conversation. We will wait for these gentlemen, if you please ; I have plenty of time, and it will be more correct. Ah ! here is one of them, I think."

In fact, at the end of the Rue Vaugirard the gigantic form of Porthos began to loom.

"What ! " cried D'Artagnan, "is your first second M. Porthos ? "

"Yes. Does that displease you ? "

"Oh, not at all."

"And here comes the other."

D'Artagnan turned in the direction pointed to by Athos, and perceived Aramis.

"What ! " cried he, with an accent of greater astonishment than before, " is your second witness M. Aramis ? "

"Doubtless he is. Are you not aware that we are never seen one without the others, and that we are called in the musketeers and the guards, at court and in the city, Athos, Porthos, and Aramis, or the Three Inseparables ? And yet, as you come from Dax or Pau——"

"From Tarbes," said D'Artagnan.

"It is probable you are ignorant of this circumstance," said Athos.

"'Pon my word," replied D'Artagnan, "you are well named, gentlemen ; and my adventure, if it should make any noise, will prove at least that your union is not founded upon contrasts."

In the meantime Porthos had come up, waved his hand to Athos, and then turning towards D'Artagnan, stopped astonished.

Permit us to say in passing that he had changed his baldric and laid aside his cloak.

"Ah, ah ! " said he, " what does this mean ? "

"This is the gentleman I am going to fight with," said Athos, pointing to D'Artagnan with his hand, and saluting him with the same gesture.

"Why, it is with him I am also going to fight," said Porthos.

" But not before one o'clock," replied D'Artagnan.

" Well, and I also am going to fight with that gentleman," said Aramis, coming up in his turn.

" But not till two o'clock," said D'Artagnan, with the same calmness.

" But what are you going to fight about, Athos ? " asked Aramis.

" 'Pon my word, I don't very well know ; he hurt my shoulder.—And you, Porthos ? "

" 'Pon my word, I am going to fight because I am going to fight," answered Porthos, colouring deeply.

Athos, whose keen eye lost nothing, perceived a sly smile pass over the lips of the young Gascon as he replied,—

" We had a short discussion upon dress."

" And you, Aramis ? " asked Athos.

" Oh, ours is a theological quarrel," replied Aramis, making a sign to D'Artagnan to keep secret the cause of their dispute.

Athos saw a second smile on the lips of D'Artagnan.

" Indeed ? " said Athos.

" Yes ; a passage of St. Augustine, upon which we could not agree," said the Gascon.

" By Jove ! this is a clever fellow," murmured Athos.

" And now you are all assembled, gentlemen," said D'Artagnan, " permit me to offer you my excuses."

At this word *excuses* a cloud passed over the brow of Athos, a haughty smile curled the lip of Porthos, and a negative sign was the reply of Aramis.

" You do not understand me, gentlemen," said D'Artagnan, throwing up his head, on which was playing at that moment a ray of sunlight, gilding its clear and bold outlines. " I ask to be excused in case I should not be able to discharge my debt to all three ; for M. Athos has the right to kill me first, which must much diminish the face-value of your bill, M. Porthos, and render yours almost worthless, M. Aramis. And now, gentlemen, I repeat, excuse me, but on that account only, and—on guard ! "

At these words, with the most gallant air possible, D'Artagnan drew his sword.

The blood had mounted to the head of D'Artagnan, and at that moment he would have drawn his sword against all the musketeers in the kingdom as willingly as he now did against Athos, Porthos, and Aramis.

It was a quarter past twelve. The sun was in its zenith, and the spot chosen for the theatre of the duel was exposed to its full power.

"It is very hot," said Athos, drawing his sword in his turn, "and yet I cannot take off my doublet, for only just now I felt my wound begin to bleed again, and I should not like to annoy the gentleman with the sight of blood which he has not drawn from me himself."

"That is true, sir," replied D'Artagnan; "and whether drawn by myself or another, I assure you I shall always view with regret the blood of so brave a man. I will therefore fight in my doublet, as you do."

"Come, come, enough of such compliments," cried Porthos; "please remember we are waiting our turn."

"Speak for yourself when you are inclined to utter such incongruities," interrupted Aramis. "For my part, I think what they say is very well said, and quite worthy of two gentlemen."

"When you please, sir," said Athos, putting himself on guard.

"I was awaiting your order," said D'Artagnan, crossing swords.

But scarcely had the two rapiers clashed on meeting when a company of the guards of his Eminence, commanded by M. de Jussac, turned the angle of the convent.

"The cardinal's guards! the cardinal's guards!" cried Aramis and Porthos at the same time. "Sheathe swords, gentlemen! sheathe swords!"

But it was too late. The two combatants had been seen in a position which left no doubt of their intentions.

"Halloo!" cried Jussac, advancing towards them, and making a sign to his men to do the same—"halloo, musketeers! fighting here, then, are you? And the edicts—what has become of them?"

"You are very generous, gentlemen of the guards," said Athos with acrimony, for Jussac was one of the aggressors of the preceding day. "If we were to see you fighting, I can assure you that we would make no effort to prevent you. Leave us alone, then, and you will enjoy a little amusement without cost to yourselves."

"Gentlemen," said Jussac, "I greatly regret to declare the thing impossible. Duty before everything. Sheathe, then, if you please, and follow us."

"Sir," said Aramis, parodying Jussac, "it would afford us great pleasure to obey your polite invitation if it depended upon ourselves; but unfortunately the thing is impossible: M. de Tréville has forbidden it. Pass on your way, then; it is the best thing you can do."

This raillery exasperated Jussac.

"We will charge upon you, then," said he, "if you disobey."

"There are five of them," said Athos, half aloud, "and we are but three. We shall be beaten again, and must die on the spot; for, I swear it, I will never appear before the captain again as a conquered man."

Athos, Porthos, and Aramis instantly closed in, and Jussac drew up his soldiers.

This short interval was sufficient to determine D'Artagnan. It was one of those events which decide the life of a man. It was a choice between the king and the cardinal. The choice made, it must be persisted in. To fight was to disobey the law, to risk his head, to make at once an enemy of a minister more powerful than the king himself; all this the young man perceived, and yet, to his praise be it said, he did not hesitate a second. Turning towards Athos and his friends,—

"Gentlemen," said he, "allow me to correct your words, if you please. You said you were but three, but it appears to me we are four."

"But you are not one of us," said Porthos.

"That's true," replied D'Artagnan; "I do not wear the uniform, but I am with you in spirit. My heart is that of a musketeer. I feel it, sir, and that urges me on."

"Withdraw, young man," cried Jussac, who, doubtless by his gestures and the expression of his countenance, had guessed D'Artagnan's design. "You may retire; we allow you to do so. Save your skin; begone quickly."

D'Artagnan did not move.

"Well, you are a real good fellow," said Athos, pressing the young man's hand.

"Come, come, decide one way or the other," replied Jussac.

"Well," said Porthos to Aramis, "we must do something."

"You are very generous," said Athos.

But all three were thinking of the youthfulness of D'Artagnan, and dreaded his inexperience.

"We would be only three, one of whom is wounded, with the addition of a boy," resumed Athos, "and yet they will say none the less that we were four men."

"Yes, but to yield!" said Porthos.

"That's rather difficult," replied Athos.

D'Artagnan understood their hesitancy.

"Try me, gentlemen," said he, "and I swear to you by

my honour that I will not go hence if we are conquered."

"What is your name, my brave fellow?" said Athos.

"D'Artagnan, sir."

"Well, then, Athos, Porthos, Aramis, and D'Artagnan, forward!" cried Athos.

"Come, gentlemen, have you made your minds up?" cried Jussac for the third time.

"It is done, gentlemen," said Athos.

"And what do you mean to do?" asked Jussac.

"We are about to have the honour of charging you," replied Aramis, lifting his hat with one hand and drawing his sword with the other.

"Oh! you resist, do you?" cried Jussac.

"'Sblood! does that astonish you?"

And the nine combatants rushed at one another with a madness which, however, did not exclude a certain amount of method.

Athos fixed upon Cahusac, a favourite of the cardinal's, Porthos had Bicarat, and Aramis found himself opposed to two adversaries. As to D'Artagnan, he sprang towards Jussac himself.

The heart of the young Gascon beat as though it would burst its fetters—not from fear, God be thanked (he had not the shade of it), but with emulation. He fought like a mad tiger, turning ten times round his adversary, and changing his ground and his guard twenty times. Jussac was, as they said then, fond of the sword, and had had much practice; nevertheless it required all his skill to defend himself against an adversary who, active and energetic, departed every instant from received rules, attacking him on all sides at once, and yet parrying like a man who had the greatest respect for his own epidermis.

This contest at length exhausted Jussac's patience. Furious at being held in check by one whom he had considered a boy, he grew angry and began to make mistakes. D'Artagnan, who, though wanting in practice, had a profound theory, redoubled his agility. Jussac, anxious to put an end to this, springing forward, aimed a terrible thrust at his adversary, but the latter parried it; and while Jussac was recovering himself, glided like a serpent beneath his blade, and passed his sword through his body. Jussac fell in a heap.

D'Artagnan then cast an anxious and rapid glance over the field of battle.

Aramis had already killed one of his adversaries, but the other was pressing him warmly. Nevertheless Aramis was in a good situation and still able to defend himself.

Bicarat and Porthos had just made counter hits. Porthos had received a thrust through his arm, and Bicarat one through his thigh. But neither of the wounds was serious, and they only fought the more earnestly for them.

Athos, wounded again by Cahusac, was steadily growing paler, but did not give way a foot ; he had only changed his sword-hand, and was fighting with his left.

According to the laws of duelling at that period, D'Artagnan was at liberty to assist the one he pleased. While he was trying to find out which of his companions needed his aid, he caught a glance from Athos. This glance was of sublime eloquence. Athos would have died rather than appeal for help ; but he could look, and with that look ask assistance. D'Artagnan interpreted it. With a terrible bound he sprang to the side of Cahusac, crying,—

" To me, Sir Guard, or I will slay you ! "

Cahusac turned. It was time, for Athos, whose great courage alone supported him, sank upon his knee.

" 'Sblood ! " cried he to D'Artagnan, " do not kill him, young man, I beg of you. I have an old affair to settle with him when I am healed and sound again. Disarm him only ; make sure of his sword. That's it ! that's it ! well done ! very well done ! "

This exclamation was drawn from Athos by seeing the sword of Cahusac fly twenty paces from him. D'Artagnan and Cahusac sprang forward at the same instant, the one to recover, the other to obtain, the sword ; but D'Artagnan, being the more active, reached it first and placed his foot upon it.

Cahusac immediately ran to the guardsman whom Aramis had killed, seized his rapier, and returned towards D'Artagnan ; but on his way he met Athos, who, during the momentary relief which D'Artagnan had procured for him, had recovered his breath, and who, for fear that D'Artagnan should kill his own personal enemy, wished to resume the fight.

D'Artagnan perceived that it would be disobliging Athos not to leave him alone ; and in a few minutes Cahusac fell, with a sword-thrust through his throat.

At the same instant Aramis placed his sword-point on the breast of his fallen enemy, and compelled him to ask for mercy.

Only Porthos and Bicarat remained. Porthos was boasting merrily, asking Bicarat what o'clock it could be, and offering him his compliments upon his brother having just obtained a company in the regiment of Navarre ; but joke as he might, he gained no advantage. Bicarat was one of those iron men who never fall dead.

Nevertheless it was necessary to put an end to the affair. The watch might come up and take all the combatants, wounded or not, royalists or cardinalists. Athos, Aramis, and D'Artagnan surrounded Bicarat and summoned him to surrender. Though alone against all, and with a wound in his thigh, Bicarat wished to hold out ; but Jussac, who had risen upon his elbow, cried out to him to yield. Bicarat was a Gascon, as D'Artagnan was ; he turned a deaf ear, and contented himself with laughing ; and between two parries, finding time to point to a spot of earth with his sword,—

"Here," cried he, parodying a verse of the Bible—"here will Bicarat die, the only one of those who are with him ! "

"But there are four against you ; leave off, I command you ! "

"Ah, if you command me, that's another thing," said Bicarat ; "you being my sergeant, it is my duty to obey."

And springing backward, he broke his sword across his knee to avoid the necessity of surrendering it, threw the pieces over the convent wall, and crossed his arms, whistling a cardinalist air.

Bravery is always respected, even in an enemy. The musketeers saluted Bicarat with their swords, and returned them to their sheaths. D'Artagnan did the same ; then assisted by Bicarat, the only one left standing, he bore Jussac, Cahusac, and that one of Aramis's adversaries who was only wounded, under the porch of the convent. The fourth, as we have said, was dead. They then rang the bell, and carrying away four swords out of five, they took their road, intoxicated with joy, towards the hôtel of M. de Tréville.

They walked arm in arm, occupying the whole width of the street, and accosting every musketeer they met, so that in the end it became a triumphal march. The heart of D'Artagnan throbbed with wild delight ; he walked between Athos and Porthos, pressing them tenderly.

"If I am not yet a musketeer," said he to his new friends, as he passed through the gateway of M. de Tréville's hôtel, "at least I have entered upon my apprenticeship, haven't I?"

CHAPTER VI.

HIS MAJESTY KING LOUIS XIII.

THIS affair made a great noise. M. de Tréville scolded his musketeers in public and congratulated them in private; but as no time was to be lost in gaining the king, M. de Tréville made all haste to the Louvre. But he was too late; the king was closeted with the cardinal, and M. de Tréville was informed that the king was busy and could not receive him. In the evening M. de Tréville went to the king's card-table. The king was winning, and as his Majesty was very avaricious, he was in an excellent humour; therefore, perceiving M. de Tréville at a distance,—

"Come here, captain," said he—"come here, that I may scold you. Do you know that his Eminence has just made fresh complaints against your musketeers, and with so much emotion that his Eminence is indisposed this evening? Why, these musketeers of yours are very devils—fellows to be hanged!"

"No, sire," replied Tréville, who saw at the first glance which way things would turn—"no, sire; on the contrary, they are good creatures, as meek as lambs, and have but one desire, I'll be their warranty; and this is, that their swords may never leave their scabbards but in your Majesty's service. But what are they to do? The guards of the cardinal are for ever seeking quarrels with them, and for the honour of the corps even the poor young men are obliged to defend themselves."

"Listen to M. de Tréville," said the king, "listen to him! Would not one say he was speaking of a religious community? In truth, my dear captain, I have a great mind to take away your commission, and give it to Mademoiselle de Chemerault, to whom I promised an abbey. But don't fancy that I am going to take you on your bare word. I am called Louis the Just, Monsieur de Tréville, and by-and-by, by-and-by we will see."

"Ah! it is because I rely fully upon that justice that I shall wait patiently and quietly your Majesty's good pleasure."

"Wait, then, sir, wait," said the king; "I will not make you wait long."

In fact, fortune changed, and as the king began to lose what he had won, he was not sorry to find an excuse for playing Charlemagne, if we may be excused for using this gambling term, of the origin of which we confess we are ignorant. The king then arose a minute after, and putting the money which lay before him into his pocket, the major part of which arose from his winnings,—

"La Vieuville," said he, "take my place ; I must speak to M. de Tréville on an affair of importance. Ah, I had eighty louis before me ; put down the same sum, so that they who have lost may have nothing to complain of—justice before everything." Then turning towards M. de Tréville, and walking with him towards the embrasure of a window,—

"Well, monsieur," continued he, "you say it is his Eminence's guards who sought a quarrel with your musketeers ?"

"Yes, sire, as they always do."

"And how did the thing happen ? Let us see, for you know, my dear captain, a judge must hear both sides."

"Good Lord ! in the most simple and natural manner possible. Three of my best soldiers, whom your Majesty knows by name, and whose devotion you have more than once appreciated, and who have, I can assure the king, his service much at heart—three of my best soldiers, I say— Athos, Porthos, and Aramis—had made a party of pleasure with a young cadet from Gascony, whom I had introduced to them the same morning. The party was to take place at St. Germain, I believe, and they had appointed to meet at the Carmes-Deschaux, when they were disturbed by De Jussac, Cahusac, Bicarat, and two other guards, who certainly did not go there in a body without some ill intention against the edicts."

"Ah, ah ! you incline me to think so," said the king. "There is no doubt they went thither with the intention of fighting."

"I do not accuse them, sire ; but I leave your Majesty to judge what five armed men could possibly be going to do in such a retired spot as the environs of the Convent des Carmes."

"You are right, Tréville, you are right ! "

"Then, upon seeing my musketeers, they changed their minds, and forgot their private hatred for their corps feuds ; for your Majesty cannot be ignorant that the musketeers, who belong to the king, and to nobody but the king, are the natural enemies of the guards, who belong to the cardinal."

"Yes, Tréville, yes," said the king in a melancholy tone ; " and it is very sad, believe me, to see thus two parties in

France, two heads to royalty. But all this will come to an end, Tréville, will come to an end. You say, then, that the guards sought a quarrel with the musketeers ? "

" I say that it is probable that things did happen thus, but I will not swear to it, sire. You know how difficult it is to discover the truth ; and unless a man be endowed with that admirable instinct which causes Louis XIII. to be termed the Just——"

" You are right, Tréville. But they were not alone, your musketeers ; they had a youth with them ? "

" Yes, sire, and one wounded man ; so that three of the king's musketeers—one of whom was wounded—and a youth not only maintained their ground against five of the most terrible of his Eminence's guards, but absolutely brought four of them to the earth."

" Why, this is a victory ! " cried the king, glowing with delight, " a complete victory ! "

" Yes, sire ; as complete as that of the Bridge of Cé."

" Four men, one of them wounded, and a youth, say you ? "

" One scarcely a grown man, but who, however, behaved himself so admirably on this occasion that I will take the liberty of recommending him to your Majesty."

" What is his name ? "

" D'Artagnan, sire ; he is the son of one of my oldest friends—the son of a man who served under your father of glorious memory in the civil war."

" And you say that this young man behaved himself well ? Tell me how, De Tréville ; you know how I delight in accounts of war and fights."

And Louis XIII. twirled his moustache proudly and placed his hand upon his hip.

" Sire," resumed Tréville, " as I told you, M. d'Artagnan is little more than a boy, and as he has not the honour of being a musketeer, he was dressed as a private citizen. The guards of the cardinal, perceiving his youth, and still more that he did not belong to the corps, urged him to retire before they made the attack."

" So you may plainly see, Tréville," interrupted the king, " it was they who attacked ? "

" That is true, sire ; there can be no more doubt on that head. They called upon him, then, to retire, but he answered that he was a musketeer at heart, entirely devoted to your Majesty, and that he would therefore remain with the musketeers."

" Brave young man ! " murmured the king.

"Well, he did remain with them; and your Majesty has in fine so firm a champion that it was he who gave Jussac the terrible sword-thrust which has made the cardinal so angry."

"He who wounded Jussac!" cried the king—"he, a boy! Tréville, that's impossible!"

"It is as I have the honour to relate it to your Majesty."

"Jussac, one of the first swordsmen in the kingdom?"

"Well, sire, for once he found his master."

"I should like to see this young man, Tréville—I should like to see him; and if anything can be done—well, we will make it our business to do it."

"When will your Majesty deign to receive him?"

"To-morrow at midday, Tréville."

"Shall I bring him alone?"

"No, bring me all four together; I wish to thank them all at once. Devoted men are so rare, Tréville, we must recompense devotion."

"At twelve o'clock, sire, we will be at the Louvre."

"Ah! by the back staircase, Tréville, by the back staircase. It is useless to let the cardinal know."

"Yes, sire."

"You understand, Tréville; an edict is still an edict; it is forbidden to fight, after all."

"But this encounter, sire, is quite out of the ordinary conditions of a duel. It is a brawl; and the proof is that there were five of the cardinal's guards against my three musketeers and M. d'Artagnan."

"That is true," said the king; "but never mind, Tréville; come anyway by the back staircase."

Tréville smiled. But as it was already something to have prevailed upon this child to rebel against his master, he saluted the king respectfully, and with this agreement took leave of him.

That evening the three musketeers were informed of the honour which was bestowed upon them. As they had long been acquainted with the king, they were not much excited by the circumstance; but D'Artagnan, with his Gascon imagination, saw in it his future fortune, and passed the night in golden dreams. As early, then, as eight o'clock he was at the apartment of Athos.

D'Artagnan found the musketeer dressed and ready to go out. As the hour to wait upon the king was not till twelve, he had made a party with Porthos and Aramis to play a game at tennis in a tennis-court situated near the stables of the Luxembourg. Athos invited D'Artagnan to follow them; and although ignorant of the game, which he had never played, he accepted the invitation, not knowing what to do with his time till twelve o'clock, as it was then scarcely nine.

The two musketeers were already there and were playing together. Athos, who was very expert in all bodily exercises, went over with D'Artagnan to the opposite side and challenged them; but at the first effort he made, although he played with his left hand, he found that his wound was yet too recent to allow of such exertion. D'Artagnan remained, therefore, alone. As he declared he was too ignorant of the game to play it regularly, they only continued giving balls to each other without counting; but one of these balls, launched by Porthos's herculean hand, passed so close to D'Artagnan's face that he thought if instead of passing near it had hit him, his audience would have been probably lost, as it would have been impossible for him to have presented himself before the king. Now, as upon this audience, in his Gascon imagination, depended his future life, he saluted Aramis and Porthos politely, declaring that he would not resume the game until he should be prepared to play with them on more equal terms; and he went and took his place near the rope and in the gallery.

Unfortunately for D'Artagnan, among the spectators was one of his Eminence's guards, who, still irritated by the defeat of his companions, which had happened only the day before, had promised himself to seize the first opportunity of avenging it. He believed this opportunity was now come, and addressing his neighbour,—

"It is not astonishing," said he, "that that young man should be afraid of a ball; he is doubtless a musketeer apprentice."

D'Artagnan turned round as if a serpent had stung him, and fixed his eyes intently upon the guard who had just made this insolent speech.

"Zounds!" resumed the latter, twirling his moustache, "look at me as long as you like, my little gentleman; what I have said I have said."

"And as since that which you have said is too clear to require any explanation," replied D'Artagnan in a low voice, "I beg you will follow me."

"And when?" asked the guard, with the same jeering air.

"Immediately, if you please."

"And you know who I am, without doubt?"

" I ? No, I assure you I do not know you ; nor have I any desire to do so."

" You're in the wrong there ; for if you knew my name, perhaps you would not be in such a hurry."

" What is your name, then ? "

" Bernajoux, at your service."

" Well, then, Monsieur Bernajoux," said D'Artagnan quietly, " I will wait for you at the door."

" Go on, sir ; I will follow you."

" Do not appear to be in a hurry, sir, so as to cause it to be observed that we go out together. You must be aware that for that which we have in hand company would be inconvenient."

" That's true," said the guard, astonished that his name had not produced more effect upon the young man.

In fact, the name of Bernajoux was known to everybody, D'Artagnan alone excepted, perhaps ; for it was one of those which figured most frequently in the daily brawls which all the edicts of the king and cardinal had not been able to repress.

Porthos and Aramis were so engaged with their game, and Athos was watching them with so much attention, that they did not even see their young companion go out, who stopped outside the door, as he had told his Eminence's guard he would do. An instant after the guard descended. As D'Artagnan had no time to lose, on account of his audience with the king, which was fixed for midday, he cast his eyes around, and seeing that the street was empty,—

" Upon my word," said he to his adversary, " it is fortunate for you, although your name is Bernajoux, that you have only to deal with an apprentice musketeer. Never mind ; be content ; I will do my best. On guard ! "

" But," said he whom D'Artagnan thus provoked, " it appears to me that this place is very ill-chosen, and that behind the Abbey St. Germain or in the Pré-aux-Clercs would be better."

" What you say is very sensible," replied D'Artagnan ; " but unfortunately I have very little time to spare, having an appointment at twelve precisely. On guard, then, sir, on guard ! "

Bernajoux was not a man to have such a compliment paid to him twice. In an instant his sword glittered in his hand, and he sprang upon his adversary, whom, on account of his youth, he hoped to intimidate.

But D'Artagnan had on the preceding day gone through

his apprenticeship. Whetted by his victory, full of the hope
of future favour, he was resolved not to yield an inch. So the
two swords were crossed close to the hilts, and as D'Artagnan
stood firm, it was his adversary who made the retreating step ;
but D'Artagnan seized the moment at which, in this movement, the sword of Bernajoux deviated from the line. He
freed his weapon, made a lunge, and touched his adversary
on the shoulder. D'Artagnan immediately made a step
backwards and raised his sword ; but Bernajoux cried out that
it was nothing, and rushing blindly upon him, absolutely
spitted himself upon D'Artagnan's sword. As, however, he
did not fall, and as he did not declare himself conquered, but
only rushed away towards the hôtel of M. de la Trémouille,
in whose service he had a relative, D'Artagnan was ignorant
of the seriousness of the last wound his adversary had received, followed him closely, and without doubt would soon
have completed his work with a third blow, when the noise
which arose from the street being heard in the tennis-court,
two of the friends of the guard, who had seen him go out
after exchanging some words with D'Artagnan, rushed,
sword in hand, from the court, and fell upon the conqueror.
But Athos, Porthos, and Aramis quickly appeared in their
turn, and the moment the two guards attacked their young
companion, drove them back. Bernajoux now fell ; and as
the guards were only two against four, they began to cry,
" To the rescue ! the Hôtel de la Trémouille ! " At these
cries all who were in the hôtel rushed out, falling upon the
four companions, who on their part cried aloud, " To the
rescue, musketeers ! "

This cry was usually heeded ; for the musketeers were
known to be enemies to the cardinal, and were beloved on
account of the hatred they bore to his Eminence. Consequently the guards of other companies than those which belonged to the Red Duke, as Aramis had called him, generally
in these quarrels took part with the king's musketeers. Of
the three guardsmen of M. des Essarts's company who were
passing, two came to the assistance of the four companions,
while the other ran towards the hôtel of M. de Tréville,
crying, " To the rescue ! Musketeers, to the rescue ! "
As usual, this hôtel was full of soldiers of this corps, who
hastened to the assistance of their comrades. The *mêlée*
became general, but strength was on the side of the musketeers ; the cardinal's guards and M. de la Trémouille's
people retreated into the hôtel, the doors of which they
closed just in time to prevent their enemies from entering

with them. As to the wounded man, he had been taken in at once, and, as we have said, in a very bad condition.

Excitement was at its height among the musketeers and their allies, and they were already considering whether or not they should set fire to the hôtel to punish the insolence of M. de la Trémouille's domestics in daring to make a *sortie* upon the king's musketeers. The proposition had been made, and received with enthusiasm, when fortunately eleven o'clock struck. D'Artagnan and his companions remembered their audience, and as they would very much have regretted that such a feat should be performed without them, they succeeded in quieting their coadjutors. The latter contented themselves with hurling some paving-stones against the gates, but the gates were too strong. They then grew tired of the sport ; besides, those who must be considered as the leaders of the enterprise had quitted the group and were making their way towards the hôtel of M. de Tréville, who was waiting for them, having been already informed of this fresh disturbance.

"Quick, to the Louvre," said he—"to the Louvre without losing an instant, and let us endeavour to see the king before he is prejudiced by the cardinal. We will describe the thing to him as a consequence of the affair of yesterday, and the two will pass off together."

M. de Tréville, accompanied by his four young men, directed his course toward the Louvre ; but to the great astonishment of the captain of the musketeers, he was informed that the king was gone stag-hunting in the forest of St. Germain. M. de Tréville required this intelligence to be repeated to him twice, and each time his companions saw his brow become darker.

"Had his Majesty," asked he, "any intention of holding this hunting party yesterday ?"

"No, your Excellency," replied the valet ; "the master of the hounds came this morning to inform him that last night he had started a stag. He at first answered that he would not go, but could not resist his love of sport, and set out after dinner."

"Has the king seen the cardinal ?" asked M. de Tréville.

"Most probably he has," replied the valet, "for I saw the horses harnessed to his Eminence's carriage this morning, and when I asked where he was going, I was told to St. Germain."

"He has gotten ahead of us," said M. de Tréville. "Gentlemen, I will see the king this evening ; but as to you, I do not advise you to risk doing so."

This advice was too reasonable, and, moreover, came from a man who knew the king too well, that the four young men did not attempt to dispute it. M. de Tréville recommended them each to retire to his apartment and wait for news from him.

On entering his hôtel, M. de Tréville thought it best to be first in making the complaint. He sent one of his servants to M. de la Trémouille with a letter, in which he begged of him to eject the cardinal's guard from his house, and to reprimand his people for their audacity in making *sortie* against the king's musketeers. But M. de la Trémouille, already prejudiced by his esquire, whose relative we already know Bernajoux to be, replied that it was neither for M. de Tréville nor the musketeers to complain, but on the contrary for him, whose people the musketeers had assaulted, and whose hôtel they had endeavoured to burn. Now, as the debate between these two nobles might last a long time, each becoming, naturally, more firm in his own opinion, M. de Tréville thought of an expedient which might terminate it quietly, which was to go himself to M. de la Trémouille.

He repaired, then, immediately to his hôtel, and caused himself to be announced.

The two nobles saluted each other politely, for if no friendship existed between them, there was at least esteem. Both were men of courage and honour ; and as M. de la Trémouille, a Protestant, and seeing the king seldom, was of no party, he did not, in general, carry any partisan feeling into his social relations. This time, however, his greeting, though polite, was colder than usual.

"Sir," said M. de Tréville, "we fancy that we have each cause to complain of the other, and I am come to endeavour to clear up this affair."

"I have no objection," replied M. de la Trémouille ; "but I warn you that I have inquired well into it, and all the fault lies with your musketeers."

"You are too just and reasonable a man, sir," said De Tréville, "not to accept the proposition I am about to make to you."

"Make it, sir. I am attentive."

"How is M. Bernajoux, your esquire's relative ?"

"Why, sir, very ill indeed ! In addition to the sword-thrust in his arm, which is not dangerous, he has received

another right through his lungs, of which the doctor speaks
very unfavourably."

" But is the wounded man sensible ? "

" Perfectly."

" Can he speak ? "

" With difficulty, but he can speak."

" Well, sir, let us go to him ; let us adjure him, in the
name of the God before whom he is called upon, perhaps
quickly, to appear, to speak the truth. I will take him
for judge in his own cause, sir, and will believe what he
will say."

M. de la Trémouille reflected for an instant ; then, as it
was difficult to make a more reasonable proposition, agreed
to it.

Both descended to the chamber in which the wounded
man lay. The latter, on seeing these two noble lords enter
his room, endeavoured to raise himself up in his bed ; but
he was too weak, and exhausted by the effort, he fell back
again almost insensible.

M. de la Trémouille approached him, and made him
inhale some salts, which restored him to consciousness.
Then M. de Tréville, unwilling to be accused of having
influenced the wounded man, requested M. de la Trémouille
to question him himself.

What M. de Tréville had foreseen happened. Placed
between life and death, as Bernajoux was, he had no idea
for a moment of concealing the truth ; and he described
to the two nobles the affair exactly as it had taken place.

This was all that M. de Tréville wanted. He wished
Bernajoux a speedy recovery, took leave of M. de la Trémouille, returned to his hôtel, and immediately sent word
to the four friends that he awaited their company at dinner.

M. de Tréville received very good company, quite anti-
cardinalist, though. It may easily be understood, therefore, that the conversation during the whole of dinner
turned upon the two checks that his Eminence's guards
had just received. Now, as D'Artagnan had been the hero
of these two fights, all the felicitations fell to his share,
Athos, Porthos, and Aramis surrendering them all to him,
not only as good comrades, but as men who had so often
had their turn that they could very well afford to let him
have his.

Toward six o'clock M. de Tréville announced that it was
his hour to go to the Louvre ; but as the hour of audience
granted by his Majesty was past, instead of claiming the

entrée by the back stairs, he placed himself with the four young men in the antechamber. The king had not yet returned from hunting. Our young men had been waiting barely half an hour among the crowd of courtiers when all the doors were thrown open, and his Majesty was announced.

At this announcement D'Artagnan felt himself tremble to the very marrow of his bones. The instant which was about to follow would in all probability decide his future life. His eyes, therefore, were fixed in an agonized gaze upon the door through which the king would pass.

Louis XIII. appeared, walking in front. He was in hunting costume covered with dust, wearing large boots, and had a whip in his hand. At the first glance D'Artagnan perceived that the king was in a bad humour.

This disposition, visible as it was in his Majesty, did not prevent the courtiers from ranging themselves in view of him as he passed. In royal antechambers it is better to be looked upon with an angry eye than not to be looked upon at all. The three musketeers, therefore, did not hesitate to make a step forward. D'Artagnan, on the contrary, remained concealed behind them ; but although the king knew Athos, Porthos, and Aramis personally, he passed in front of them without speaking or looking—indeed, as if he had never seen them before. As for M. de Tréville, when the king's eyes fell for an instant upon him, he bore his glance with such equanimity that it was the king who looked away ; after which his Majesty, grumbling, entered his apartment.

" Matters go but badly," said Athos, smiling ; " and we shall not be made knights of the order this time."

" Wait here ten minutes," said M. de Tréville ; " and if at the expiration of ten minutes you do not see me come out, return to my hôtel, for it will be useless for you to wait for me longer."

The four young men waited ten minutes, a quarter of an hour, twenty minutes ; and seeing that M. de Tréville did not return, went away very uneasy as to what was going to happen.

M. de Tréville entered the king's closet boldly, and found his Majesty in a very ill humour, seated in an armchair, beating his boot with the handle of his whip. This, however, did not prevent his asking, with the greatest coolness, after his Majesty's health.

" Bad, sir, bad ! I am bored."

This was, in fact, the worst malady of Louis XIII., who would sometimes take one of his courtiers to a window, and say, "Mr. So-and-so, let us be bored together."

"What! your Majesty is bored? Have you not enjoyed the fine hunting to-day?"

"Fine hunting, indeed, sir! Upon my soul, everything degenerates; and I don't know whether it is the game leaves no scent, or the dogs that have no noses. We started a stag of ten branches. We chased him for six hours; and when he was near being taken—when St. Simon was already putting his horn to his mouth to sound the mort—crack, all the pack takes the wrong scent, and sets off after a yearling. I shall be obliged to give up hunting, as I have given up hawking. Ah, I am an unfortunate king, Monsieur de Tréville! I had but one gerfalcon, and he died the day before yesterday."

"Indeed, sire, I comprehend your vexation perfectly. It is a misfortune, but I think you have still a good number of falcons, sparrow-hawks, and tiercels."

"And not a man to instruct them. Falconers are dying out. I know no one but myself who is acquainted with the noble art of venery. After me it will be all over, and people will hunt with traps, snares, and deadfalls. If I had only the time to form pupils; but there is the cardinal always at hand, who does not leave me a moment's repose —who talks to me perpetually about Spain, about Austria, about England. Ah! *à propos* of the cardinal, Monsieur de Tréville, I am vexed with you."

This was what M. de Tréville was waiting for. He knew the king of old, and he knew that all these complaints were but a preface—a kind of excitation to encourage himself—and that he had now come to his point at last.

"And in what have I been so unfortunate as to displease your Majesty?" asked M. de Tréville, feigning the most profound astonishment.

"Is it thus you perform your office, sir?" continued the king, without directly replying to De Tréville's question. "Is it for this I named you captain of my musketeers, that they should assassinate a man, disturb a whole quarter, and endeavour to set fire to Paris, without your saying a word? But yet," continued the king, "without doubt I am too hasty in accusing you; without doubt the rioters are in prison, and you come to tell me justice is done."

"Sire," replied M. de Tréville calmly, "on the contrary, I come to demand it of you."

"And against whom, pray?" cried the king.

"Against calumniators," said M. de Tréville.

"Ah! this is something new," replied the king. "Will you tell me that your three damned musketeers—Athos, Porthos, and Aramis—and your cadet from Béarn, have not fallen, like so many furies, upon poor Bernajoux, and have not maltreated him in such a fashion that probably by this time he is at the point of death? Will you tell me that they did not lay siege to the hôtel of the Duc de la Trémouille, and that they did not endeavour to burn it?—which would not, perhaps, have been a great misfortune in time of war, seeing that it is nothing but a nest of Huguenots; but which is, in time of peace, a sorry example. Tell me, now, can you deny all this?"

"And who has told you this fine story, sire?" asked De Tréville quietly.

"Who has told me this fine story, sir? Who should it be but he who watches while I sleep, who labours while I amuse myself, who directs everything at home and abroad—in Europe as well as in France?"

"Your Majesty must be speaking of God, without doubt," said M. de Tréville; "for I know no one but God who can be so far above your Majesty."

"No, sir; I speak of the prop of the state, of my only servant, of my only friend—of the cardinal."

"His Eminence is not his Holiness, sire."

"What do you mean by that, sir?"

"That it is the Pope alone who is infallible, and that this infallibility does not extend to the cardinals."

"You mean that he deceives me—you mean that he betrays me? You accuse him, then? Come, speak; confess frankly that you accuse him."

"No, sire; but I say that he himself is deceived; I say that he is ill informed; I say that he has hastily accused your Majesty's musketeers, towards whom he is unjust, and that he has not obtained his information from good sources."

"The accusation comes from M. de la Trémouille—from the duke himself. What do you answer to that?"

"I might answer, sire, that he is too deeply interested in the question to be a very impartial witness; but far from that, sire, I know the duke to be a loyal gentleman, and I refer the matter to him—but upon one condition, sire."

"What is that?"

"It is that your Majesty will make him come here, will question him yourself, face to face, without witnesses, and that I shall see your Majesty as soon as you shall have seen the duke."

"What, then! and you will be bound," cried the king, "by what M. de la Trémouille shall say?"

"Yes, sire."

"You will abide by his judgment?"

"Doubtless; I will."

"And you will submit to the reparation he may require?"

"Certainly."

"La Chesnaye!" cried the king, "La Chesnaye!"

Louis XIII.'s confidential valet, who never left the door, entered in answer to the summons.

"La Chesnaye," said the king, "let some one go instantly and find M. de la Trémouille. I wish to speak with him this evening."

"Your Majesty gives me your word that you will not see any one after M. de la Trémouille until you see me?"

"Nobody, on the word of a gentleman."

"To-morrow then, sire?"

"To-morrow, sir."

"At what o'clock may it please your Majesty?"

"At whatsoever time you like."

"But I should be afraid of awakening your Majesty if I came too early."

"Awaken me! Do you think I ever sleep? I no longer sleep, sir. I sometimes dream, that's all. Come, then, as early as you like—at seven o'clock; but beware, if your musketeers are guilty."

"If my musketeers are guilty, sire, the guilty shall be placed in your Majesty's hands, and you can dispose of them at your good pleasure. Does your Majesty require anything further? Speak; I am ready to obey."

"No, sir, no. To-morrow, then, sir, to-morrow."

"Till then, God preserve your Majesty."

However poorly the king might sleep, M. de Tréville slept still worse. He had ordered his three musketeers and their companion to be with him at half-past six in the morning. He took them with him, without assuring them or promising them anything, and without concealing from them that their favour, and even his own, depended upon a single throw of the dice.

When they had reached the foot of the back stairs he desired them to wait. If the king was still irritated against

3 a

them, they should depart without being seen; if the king consented to see them, they would only have to be called.

On arriving at the king's private antechamber M. de Tréville found La Chesnaye, who informed him that they had not been able to find M. de la Trémouille on the preceding evening at his hôtel, that he had come in too late to present himself at the Louvre, that he had only just appeared, and that he was then with the king.

This circumstance pleased M. de Tréville much, as he thus became certain that no inimical suggestion could insinuate itself between M. de la Trémouille's deposition and himself.

In fact, ten minutes had scarcely passed away when the door of the king's closet opened, and M. de Tréville saw M. de la Trémouille come out. The duke came straight up to him and said,—

"M. de Tréville, his Majesty has just sent for me in order to inquire into the circumstances which took place yesterday at my hôtel. I have told him the truth—that is to say, that the fault lay with my people, and that I was ready to offer you my excuses for them. Since I have the good fortune to meet you, I beg you to receive them, and to consider me always as one of your friends."

"Duke," said M. de Tréville, "I was so confident of your loyalty that I did not wish any but you to defend me before his Majesty. I find that I have not been mistaken, and I am gratified to think that there is still one man in France of whom one may say, without being mistaken, what I have said of you."

"That's well said," said the king, who had heard all these compliments through the open door; "only tell him, Tréville, since he wishes to be considered as your friend, that I also wish to be one of his, but he neglects me; that it is nearly three years since I have seen him, and that I never do see him unless I send for him. Tell him all this for me, for these are things which a king cannot say himself."

"Thanks, sire, thanks," said M. de la Trémouille; "but your Majesty may be assured that it is not those—I do not speak of M. de Tréville—that it is not those whom your Majesty sees at all hours of the day who are the most devoted to you."

"Ah! you heard what I said? So much the better, duke, so much the better," said the king, advancing to the door.—"Ah! that's you, Tréville. Where are your musketeers ? I told you the day before yesterday to bring them with you. Why have you not done so ? "

" They are below, sire ; and with your permission La Chesnaye will tell them to come up."

" Yes, yes, let them come up immediately. It is nearly eight o'clock, and at nine I expect a visit.—Go, duke, and return, I beg of you.—Come in, Tréville."

The duke bowed and retired. At the moment he opened the door the three musketeers and D'Artagnan, led by La Chesnaye, appeared at the top of the staircase.

" Come in, my braves," said the king, " come in ; I have a scolding for you."

The musketeers advanced, bowing, D'Artagnan following closely behind them.

" How the devil ! " continued the king. " Seven of his Eminence's guards disabled by you four in two days ! That's too many, gentlemen, too many ! If you go on so, his Eminence will be obliged to renew his company in three weeks, and I to enforce the edicts to their fullest extent. One now and then I don't say much about ; but seven in two days—I repeat it is too many, it is far too many."

" Therefore, sire, your Majesty sees that they are come quite contrite and repentant to offer you their excuses."

" Quite contrite and repentant ! Hem ! " said the king, " I place no confidence in their hypocritical faces. In particular, there is one yonder with a Gascon face.—Come here, sir."

D'Artagnan, who understood that it was to him this compliment was addressed, approached, assuming a most despondent air.

" Why, you told me he was a young man ! This is a boy, Tréville, a mere boy ! Do you mean to say that it was he who bestowed that severe thrust upon Jussac ? "

" And those two equally fine thrusts upon Bernajoux."

" Truly ? "

" Without reckoning," said Athos, " that if he had not rescued me from the hands of Cahusac, I should not now have the honour of making my very humble reverence to your Majesty."

" Why, this Béarnais is a very devil ! *Ventre-saint-gris !* Monsieur de Tréville, as the king my father would have said. But at this sort of work many doublets must be slashed and many swords broken. But Gascons are always poor, are they not ? "

" Sire, I must say that they have not yet discovered

any gold mines in their mountains; though the Lord owes them this miracle in recompense for the manner in which they supported the claims of the king, your father."

"Which means that the Gascons made a king of me myself, seeing that I am my father's son, does it not, Tréville? Well, in good faith, I don't say nay to it.—La Chesnaye, go and see if, by rummaging all my pockets, you can find forty pistoles; and if you find them bring them to me.—And now let us see, young man, with your hand upon your conscience, how did all this come to pass?"

D'Artagnan related the adventure of the preceding day in all its details: how, not having been able to sleep for the joy he felt in the expectation of seeing his Majesty, he had gone to his three friends three hours before the hour of audience; how they had gone together to the tennis-court; and how, when he had manifested fear of receiving a ball in the face, he had been jeered at by Bernajoux, who had nearly paid for his jeer with his life, and M. de la Trémouille, who had nothing to do with the matter, with the loss of his hôtel.

"This is all very well," murmured the king; "yes, this is just the account the duke gave me of the affair. Poor cardinal! seven men in two days, and those of his very best. But that's quite enough, gentlemen; please to understand that's enough. You have taken your revenge for the Rue Férou, and even exceeded it; you ought to be satisfied."

"If your Majesty is," said Tréville, "we are."

"Oh yes, I am," added the king, taking a handful of gold from La Chesnaye and putting it into the hand of D'Artagnan. "Here," said he, "is a proof of my satisfaction."

At this period the ideas of pride which are in fashion in our days did not prevail. A gentleman received money directly from the king's hand, and was not in the least humiliated. D'Artagnan put his forty pistoles into his pocket without any scruple; on the contrary, he thanked his Majesty most heartily.

"There," said the king, looking at a clock—"there now, as it is half-past eight, you may retire; for, as I told you, I expect some one at nine. Thanks for your devotion, gentlemen. I may continue to rely upon it, may I not?"

"O sire!" cried the four companions with one voice, "we would allow ourselves to be cut to pieces in your Majesty's service!"

"Well, well, but keep whole ; that will be better, and you will be more useful to me. Tréville," added the king in a low voice, as the others were retiring, "as you have no room in your musketeers, and as we have besides decided that a novitiate is necessary before entering that corps, place this young man in the company of guards commanded by your brother-in-law, M. des Essarts. Ah, zounds ! I enjoy in advance the face the cardinal will make. He will be furious ; but I don't care. I am doing what is right."

And the king waved his hand to Tréville, who left him and rejoined the musketeers, whom he found sharing the forty pistoles with D'Artagnan.

And the cardinal, as his Majesty had said, was really furious, so furious that for a whole week he absented himself from the king's card-table, which did not prevent the king from being as complacent to him as possible, or, whenever he met him, from asking in the kindest tone,—

"Well, cardinal, how fares it with that poor Jussac, and that poor Bernajoux of yours ? "

CHAPTER VII.

THE MUSKETEERS' ESTABLISHMENTS.

WHEN D'Artagnan had left the Louvre, and consulted his friends upon the use he had best make of his share of the forty pistoles, he was advised by Athos to order a good repast at the Pomme-de-Pin, by Porthos to engage a lackey, and by Aramis to provide himself with a suitable mistress.

The repast was carried into effect that very day, and the lackey waited at table. The repast had been ordered by Athos, and the lackey furnished by Porthos. This fellow was a Picard, whom the vain musketeer had picked up that very day and for this occasion on the bridge De la Tournelle while he was spitting in the water to make rings.

Porthos pretended that this occupation was a proof of a reflective and contemplative organization, and he had brought him away without any other recommendation. The noble carriage of that gentleman, for whom he believed himself to be engaged, had seduced Planchet—that was the name of the Picard ; he felt a slight disappointment, however, when he saw that the place was already taken by a

compeer named Mousqueton, and when Porthos signified
to him that the state of his household, though great, would
not support two servants, and that he must enter into
the service of D'Artagnan. Nevertheless, when he waited
at the dinner given by his master, and saw him take out a
handful of gold to pay for it, he believed his fortune made,
and returned thanks to Heaven for having thrown him into
the service of such a Crœsus ; he preserved this opinion
even after the feast, with the remnants of which he made
up for his long abstinences. But when in the evening he
made his master's bed, Planchet's chimeras faded away.
The bed was the only one in the apartment, which consisted
of an antechamber and a bedroom. Planchet slept in the
antechamber upon a coverlet taken from D'Artagnan's
bed, and which D'Artagnan from that time made shift to
do without.

Athos, on his part, had a valet whom he had trained in
his service in a very peculiar fashion, and who was named
Grimaud. He was very taciturn, this worthy signor. Be
it understood we are speaking of Athos. During the five
or six years that he had lived in perfect intimacy with his
companions Porthos and Aramis, they could remember
having often seen him smile, but had never heard him laugh.
His words were brief and expressive, conveying all that was
meant, and no more—no embellishments, no embroidery,
no arabesques. His conversation was matter of fact, without any ornamentation.

Although Athos was scarcely thirty years old, and possessed of great physical and mental beauty, no one knew
that he had ever had a mistress. He never spoke of women.
He certainly did not prevent others from speaking of them
before him, although it was easy to perceive that this kind
of conversation, to which he contributed only bitter jests
and misanthropic opinions, was perfectly disagreeable to
him. His reserve, his roughness, and his silence made
almost an old man of him ; he had then, in order not to
interfere with his habits, accustomed Grimaud to obey him
upon a simple gesture, or at the mere movement of his lips.
He never spoke to him but upon the most extraordinary
occasions.

Sometimes Grimaud, who feared his master as he would
death, though entertaining for him a strong personal attachment, and a great veneration for his talents, believed he
understood perfectly what he wanted, flew to execute the
order received, and did precisely the contrary. Athos then

shrugged his shoulders, and without flying into a passion, gave Grimaud a good thrashing. On these days he did speak.

Porthos's character, as we have seen, was exactly opposite to that of Athos. He not only talked much, but he talked loudly, little caring, we must do him the justice to say, whether anybody listened to him or not. He talked for the pleasure of talking, and for the pleasure of hearing himself talk ; he discussed all subjects except the sciences, alleging as an excuse for this the inveterate hatred he had borne to the learned from his childhood. He had not so noble an air as Athos, and the consciousness of his inferiority in this respect had, at the commencement of their intimacy, often rendered him unjust towards that gentleman, whom he endeavoured to eclipse by his splendid dress. But with his simple musketeer's uniform, and nothing but the manner in which he threw back his head and advanced his foot, Athos instantly took the place which was his due, and consigned the ostentatious Porthos to the second rank. Porthos consoled himself by filling the antechamber of M. de Tréville and the guardroom of the Louvre with the accounts of his love affairs, while Athos never spoke of his ; and at the present moment, after having passed from the magistracy to the nobility, from the lawyer's dame to the baroness, there was question of nothing less for Porthos than a foreign princess, who was enormously fond of him.

An old proverb says, " Like master, like man." Let us pass then from the valet of Athos to the valet of Porthos, from Grimaud to Mousqueton.

Mousqueton was a Norman, whose pacific name of Boniface his master had changed into the infinitely more sonorous one of Mousqueton. He had entered Porthos's service upon condition that he should only be clothed and lodged, but in a handsome manner ; he claimed but two hours a day for himself to consecrate to an employment which would provide for his other wants. Porthos agreed to the bargain ; this arrangement suited him wonderfully well. He had doublets for Mousqueton cut out of his old clothes and cast-off cloaks, and thanks to a very intelligent tailor, who made his clothes look as good as new by turning them, and whose wife was suspected of wishing to make Porthos come down from his aristocratic habits, Mousqueton made a very good figure when attending on his master.

As for Aramis, whose character we believe we have sufficiently explained—a character, moreover, which, like that of his companions, we shall be able to follow in its development——his lackey was called Bazin. Thanks to the hopes which his master entertained of some day entering into orders, he was always clothed in black, as became the servant of a churchman. He was a Berrichon of from thirty-five to forty years of age, mild, peaceable, sleek, employing the leisure his master left him in the perusal of pious works, providing for the two, to be sure, a frugal but excellent dinner. In addition, he was dumb, blind, and deaf, and of unimpeachable fidelity.

And now that we are acquainted, superficially at least, with the masters and the valets, let us pass on to the dwellings occupied by each of them.

Athos dwelt in the Rue Férou, within two steps of the Luxembourg. His apartments consisted of two small chambers, very nicely fitted up, in a furnished house, the hostess of which, still young, and still really handsome, cast tender glances at him to no purpose. Some fragments of great splendour in the past appeared here and there upon the walls of this modest lodging—a sword, for example, richly damascened, which belonged by its make to the times of Francis I., the hilt of which alone, incrusted with precious stones, might be worth two hundred pistoles, and which, nevertheless, in his moments of greatest distress Athos had never pledged nor offered for sale. This sword had long been an object of ambition to Porthos. Porthos would have given ten years of his life to possess this sword.

One day, when he had an appointment with a duchess, he even endeavoured to borrow it of Athos. Athos, without saying anything, emptied his pockets, got together all his jewels, purses, shoulder-knots, and gold chains, and offered them all to Porthos ; but the sword, he said, was sealed to its place, and should never quit it until its master should himself quit his lodgings. In addition to the sword, there was a portrait representing a nobleman of the time of Henry III., dressed with the greatest elegance, and wearing the Order of the Holy Ghost; and this portrait had with Athos a certain family likeness, which indicated that this great noble, a knight of the king's orders, was his ancestor.

Besides these things, a casket of magnificent goldsmith's work, having the same arms as the sword and the portrait, formed a centre ornament to the mantelpiece, which assorted badly with the rest of the garnishings. Athos always carried the key of this coffer about him, but he one day opened it before Porthos, and Porthos was convinced that this coffer contained nothing but letters and papers—love letters and family papers, no doubt.

Porthos lived in apartments, large in size, and of a very sumptuous appearance, in the Rue du Vieux-Colombier. Every time he passed with a friend before his windows, at one of which Mousqueton was sure to be standing in full livery, Porthos raised his head and his hand, and said, "*That is my abode!*" But he was never to be found at home, he never invited anybody to go up with him, and no one could form an idea of what this sumptuous semblance contained in the shape of real riches.

As for Aramis, he dwelt in a little lodging composed of a boudoir, an eating-room, and a bedroom ; which room, situated, as the others were, on the ground floor, looked out upon a little, fresh, green garden, shady and impenetrable to the eyes of his neighbours.

With regard to D'Artagnan, we know how he was lodged, and we have already made acquaintance with his lackey, Master Planchet.

D'Artagnan, who was by nature very inquisitive, as people generally are who possess the genius of intrigue, did all he could to make out who Athos, Porthos, and Aramis really were ; for under these *noms de guerre* each of these young men concealed his family name—Athos in particular, who a league away looked like a noble. He addressed himself therefore to Porthos, to gain information respecting Athos and Aramis ; and to Aramis, in order to learn something of Porthos.

Unfortunately Porthos knew nothing of the life of his silent companion but what was known to every one. It was said he had had great misfortunes in his love affairs, and that a terrible deception had for ever poisoned the life of this gentleman. What could this deception be ? Nobody knew anything about it.

As to Porthos, except his real name, which no one but M. de Tréville knew, as he likewise knew those of his two comrades, his life was very easily fathomed. Vain and indiscreet, you could see through him like glass. The only thing which could have misled the investigator would have been for him to believe all the good he said of himself.

With respect to Aramis, though he had the air of having nothing secret about him, he was a young fellow made up of mysteries, making curt replies to questions put to him about others, and eluding those which concerned himself.

One day D'Artagnan, having for a long time asked him about Porthos, and having learned from him the report which prevailed concerning the intrigue of the musketeer with a princess, wished to gain a little insight into the amorous adventures of his interlocutor.

"And you, my dear companion," said he—" you who speak of the baronesses, countesses, and princesses of others?"

"Egad! I spoke because Porthos talks of them himself, because he cried out all these fine things before me. But be assured, my dear Monsieur d'Artagnan, that if I had obtained them from any other source, or if they had been confided to me, there would have been no confessor more discreet than I."

"Oh, I don't doubt that," replied D'Artagnan; "but it seems to me that you are tolerably familiar with coats of arms—a certain embroidered handkerchief, for instance, to which I owe the honour of your acquaintance."

This time Aramis did not get angry, but assumed the most modest air, and replied in a friendly tone,—

"My dear friend, do not forget that I wish to belong to the church, and that I avoid all mundane opportunities. The handkerchief you saw had not been given to me, but it had been forgotten, and left at my house by one of my friends. I was obliged to pick it up, in order not to compromise both him and the lady he loves. As for myself, I neither have nor do I desire to have a mistress, following in that respect the very judicious example of Athos, who has none, any more than I have."

"But what the devil! you are not an abbé; you are a musketeer!"

"A musketeer for a time, my friend, as the cardinal says, a musketeer against my will, but a churchman at heart, believe me. Athos and Porthos dragged me into this to give me occupation. I had, at the moment of being ordained, a little difficulty with—— But that would hardly interest you, and I am taking up your valuable time."

"Oh, not at all; it interests me very much," cried D'Artagnan; "and at this moment I have absolutely nothing to do."

"Yes, but I have my breviary to say," answered Aramis; "then some verses to compose, which Madame d'Aiguillon begged of me. Then I must go to Rue St. Honoré, in order to purchase some rouge for Madame de Chevreuse; so you see, my dear friend, that if you are not in a hurry, I am."

And Aramis held out his hand in a cordial manner to his young companion, and took leave of him.

Notwithstanding all the pains he took, D'Artagnan was unable to learn any more concerning his three new friends. He therefore made up his mind to believe in the present all that was said of their past, hoping for more certain and extended revelations in the future. In the meanwhile he looked upon Athos as an Achilles, Porthos as an Ajax, and Aramis as a Joseph.

Moreover, the life of the four young men was joyous enough. Athos played, and always with bad luck. Nevertheless, he never borrowed a sou of his companions, although his purse was ever at their service; and when he had played upon credit, he always awakened his creditor by six o'clock the next morning to pay the debt of the preceding evening.

Porthos had spells of gambling. On those days, if he won he was insolent and ostentatious; if he lost, he disappeared completely for several days, after which he reappeared with a pale face and long countenance, but with money in his purse.

Aramis never played. He was the worst musketeer and the most unconvivial companion imaginable. He had always something or other to do. Sometimes, in the midst of dinner, when every one, under the attraction of wine and in the warmth of conversation, believed they had two or three hours longer to enjoy themselves at table, Aramis looked at his watch, arose with a bland smile, and took leave of the company, to go, as he said, to consult a casuist, with whom he had an appointment. At other times he would return home to write a treatise, and requested his friends not to disturb him.

At this Athos would smile, with his charming, melancholy smile, so becoming to his noble countenance; and Porthos would drink, swearing that Aramis would never be anything but a village curate.

Planchet, D'Artagnan's valet, supported his good fortune nobly. He received thirty sous per day, and during one whole month he returned home gay as a lark, and affable towards his master. When the wind of adversity began to blow upon the household of Rue des Fossoyeurs—that is to say, when the forty pistoles of King Louis XIII. were consumed, or nearly so—he began a series of complaints, which Athos thought nauseous, Porthos unseemly, and Aramis ridiculous. Athos advised D'Artagnan to dismiss the fellow, Porthos was of the opinion that he should give him a good thrashing first, and Aramis contended that a master should never hear anything but the compliments paid him.

" This is all very easy for you to say," replied D'Artagnan ; " for you, Athos, who live like a dumb man with Grimaud, forbidding him to speak, and consequently never exchanging angry words with him ; for you, Porthos, who keep up such magnificent style, and are a god for your valet Mousqueton : and for you, Aramis, who, always abstracted by your theological studies, inspire your servant Bazin, a mild, religious man, with a profound respect ; but for me, who am without standing and without resources—for me, who am neither a musketeer nor even a guard, what am I to do to inspire either affection, terror, or respect in Planchet ? "

" The thing is serious," answered the three friends ; " it is a family affair. Valets are like wives : they must be placed at once upon the footing in which you wish them to remain. Reflect upon it."

D'Artagnan did reflect, and resolved to thrash Planchet provisionally, which was executed with the conscientiousness that D'Artagnan put in everything ; then, after having well beaten him, he forbade him to leave his service without his permission. " For," added he, " the future cannot fail to mend ; I inevitably look for better times. Your fortune is therefore made if you remain with me, and I am too good a master to allow you to miss such a chance by granting you the dismissal you require."

This manner of acting created much respect for D'Artagnan's policy among the musketeers. Planchet was equally seized with admiration, and said no more about going away.

The life of the four young men had become common to each and all. D'Artagnan, who had no settled habits of his own, since he had just dropped from his province into the midst of a world quite new to him, assumed immediately the habits of his friends.

They rose about eight o'clock in the winter, about six in summer, and went to get the countersign and see how things were at M. de Tréville's. D'Artagnan, although he was not a musketeer, performed the duty of one with touching punctuality. He was always mounting guard, because he always kept that one of his friends company who mounted his. He was well known at the hôtel of the musketeers, where every one considered him a good comrade. M. de Tréville, who had appreciated his worth at the first glance, and who bore him a real affection, never ceased recommending him to the king.

On their side, the three musketeers were much attached to their young comrade. The friendship which united these four men, and the need they felt for meeting three or four times a day, whether for duels, business, or pleasure, caused them to be continually running after one another like shadows; and you constantly met the inseparables looking one for the other, from the Luxembourg to the Place Saint-Sulpice, or from the Rue du Vieux-Colombier to the Luxembourg.

In the meanwhile the promises of M. de Tréville were accomplishing. One fine morning the king commanded the Chevalier des Essarts to admit D'Artagnan as a cadet in his company of guards. D'Artagnan, with a sigh, donned this uniform, which he would have exchanged for that of a musketeer at the price of ten years of his existence. But M. de Tréville promised this favour after a novitiate of two years—a novitiate which might, besides, be abridged if an opportunity should present itself for D'Artagnan to render the king any signal service, or to distinguish himself by some brilliant action. Upon this promise D'Artagnan withdrew, and the next day began service.

Then it became the turn of Athos, Porthos, and Aramis to mount guard with D'Artagnan when he was on duty. By admitting D'Artagnan, the company of the Chevalier des Essarts thus received four men instead of one.

CHAPTER VIII.

A COURT INTRIGUE.

MEANWHILE the forty pistoles of King Louis XIII., like all other things in this world, after having had a beginning, had had an end, and after this end our four companions began to be somewhat embarrassed. At first Athos supported the association for a time with his own means. Porthos succeeded him, and thanks to one of those disappearances to which people were accustomed, he was able to provide for the wants of all for a fortnight more. At last it became Aramis's turn, who performed it with a good grace, and who succeeded in procuring a few pistoles, as he said, by selling his theological books.

Then they, as usual, had recourse to M. de Tréville, who made some advances on their pay ; but these advances could not go far with three musketeers who were already much in arrears, and a guardsman who as yet had no pay at all.

At length, when they found they were likely to be quite in want, they got together, by a final effort, eight or ten pistoles, with which Porthos went to the gaming-table. Unfortunately luck ran against him. He lost all, together with twenty-five pistoles for which he pledged his word.

Then the embarrassment became distress. The hungry friends, followed by their lackeys, were seen haunting the quays and guardrooms, picking up among their friends abroad all the dinners they could meet with ; for, according to the advice of Aramis, it was prudent to sow repasts right and left in prosperity in order to reap a few in time of need.

Athos was invited four times, and each time took his friends and their lackeys with him ; Porthos had six chances, and made his friends enjoy them also ; Aramis had eight. He was a man, as must have been already perceived, who made little noise and did a great deal.

As to D'Artagnan, who as yet knew nobody in the capital, he only found one breakfast of chocolate at the house of a priest, his fellow-countryman, and one dinner with a cornet of the guards. He took his army to the priest's, where they devoured as much provision as would have lasted him for two months, and to the cornet's, who had a great spread ; but, as Planchet said, "People eat but one meal at a time, even though they eat a good deal."

D'Artagnan thus found himself rather humiliated in having had but one meal and a half to offer his companions —for the breakfast at the priest's could only be counted as half a repast—in return for the feasts which Athos, Porthos, and Aramis had procured for him. He fancied himself a burden to the society, forgetting in his perfectly youthful good faith that he had fed this society for a month, and he set his preoccupied mind actively to work. He reflected that this coalition of four young, brave, enterprising, and active men ought to have some other object than swaggering walks, fencing lessons, and practical jokes, more or less witty.

In fact, four men such as they were—four men devoted to one another, from their purses to their lives ; four men always supporting one another, never yielding, executing singly or together the resolutions formed in common; four arms threatening the four points of the compass, or turning towards a single point—must inevitably, either subterraneously or in open day, by mining or in the trench, by cunning or by force, open for themselves a way towards the object they wished to attain, however well it might be defended, or however distant it might seem. The only thing that astonished D'Artagnan was that his friends had never yet thought of this.

He was thinking of it seriously, and was racking his brain to find a direction for this single force increased fourfold, with which, as with Archimedes's lever, he had no doubt that they should succeed in moving the world, when some one tapped gently at his door. D'Artagnan awakened Planchet, and ordered him to go and see who was there.

From this phrase—"D'Artagnan awakened Planchet"—the reader must not suppose that it was night, or that the day had not yet come. No, it had just struck four. Planchet, two hours before, had asked his master for some dinner, and had been answered with the proverb, "He who sleeps dines." And Planchet dined by sleeping.

A man was introduced, of rather simple mien, who had the appearance of a tradesman.

Planchet, by way of dessert, would have liked to hear the conversation, but the bourgeois declared to D'Artagnan that what he had to say being important and confidential, he desired to be left alone with him.

D'Artagnan dismissed Planchet, and requested his visitor to be seated.

There was a moment of silence, during which the two men looked at each other, as if to make a preliminary acquaintance, after which D'Artagnan bowed as a sign that he was listening.

"I have heard M. d'Artagnan spoken of as a very brave young man," said the bourgeois; "and this reputation, which he justly enjoys, has determined me to confide a secret to him."

"Speak, sir, speak," said D'Artagnan, who instinctively scented something advantageous.

The bourgeois made a fresh pause, and continued,—

"I have a wife who is seamstress to the queen, sir, and who is not deficient in either good conduct or beauty. I was induced to marry her about three years ago, although she had but very little dowry, because M. de La Porte, the queen's cloak-bearer, is her godfather, and befriends her——"

" Well, sir ? " asked D'Artagnan.

" Well," resumed the bourgeois—" well, sir, my wife was carried off yesterday morning, as she was coming out of her workroom."

" And by whom was your wife carried off ? "

" I know nothing certain about the matter, sir, but I suspect some one."

" And who is the person you suspect ? "

" A man who has been pursuing her for a long time."

" The devil ! "

" But allow me to tell you, sir," continued the citizen, " that I am convinced that there is in all this less love than politics."

" Less love than politics," replied D'Artagnan, with a very meditative air.   " And what do you suspect ? "

" I do not know whether I ought to tell you what I suspect——"

" Sir, I beg you to observe that I ask you absolutely nothing. It is you who have come to me. It is you who have told me that you had a secret to confide to me. Act, then, as you think proper ; there is still time to retreat."

" No, sir, no ; you appear to be an honest young man, and I will place confidence in you. I believe, then, that it is not on account of any intrigues of her own that my wife has been carried off, but that it has been done on account of the amours of a much greater lady than she is."

" Ah, ah ! can it be on account of the amours of Madame de Bois-Tracy ? " said D'Artagnan, wishing to have the air, in the eyes of the bourgeois, of being up in court affairs.

" Higher, sir, higher."

" Of Madame d'Aiguillon ? "

" Higher still."

" Of Madame de Chevreuse ? "

" Higher, much higher."

" Of the——" D'Artagnan stopped.

" Yes, sir," replied the terrified bourgeois, in a tone so low that he was scarcely audible.

" And with whom ? "

" With whom can it be, if not with the Duke of—— "

" The Duke of —— "

" Yes, sir," replied the bourgeois, giving a still lower intonation to his voice.

" But how do you know all this ? "

" How do I know it ? "

"Yes, how do you know it? No half-confidence, or—you understand!"

"I know it from my wife, sir—from my wife herself."

"And she knows it, she herself, from whom?"

"From M. de la Porte. Did I not tell you that she was the goddaughter of M. de la Porte, the queen's confidential agent? Well, M. de la Porte placed her near her Majesty, in order that our poor queen might at least have some one in whom she could place confidence, abandoned as she is by the king, watched as she is by the cardinal, betrayed as she is by everybody."

"Ah, ah! it begins to grow clear," said D'Artagnan.

"Now my wife came home four days ago, sir. One of her conditions was that she should come and see me twice a week; for, as I had the honour to tell you, my wife loves me dearly. My wife, then, came and confided to me that the queen, at that very moment, entertained great fears."

"Indeed!"

"Yes. The cardinal, as it appears, pursues her and persecutes her more than ever. He cannot pardon her the story of the saraband. You know the story of the saraband?"

"Zounds! know it!" replied D'Artagnan, who knew nothing about it, but who wished to appear to know everything that was going on.

"So that it is now no longer hatred, but vengeance."

"Indeed!"

"And the queen believes——"

"Well, what does the queen believe?"

"She believes that some one has written to the Duke of Buckingham in her name."

"In the queen's name?"

"Yes, to make him come to Paris; and when once in Paris, to draw him into some snare."

"The devil! But your wife, sir, what has she to do with all this?"

"Her devotion to the queen is known, and they wish either to remove her from her mistress, or to intimidate her, in order to obtain her Majesty's secrets, or to seduce her and make use of her as a spy."

"That is all very probable," said D'Artagnan; "but the man who has carried her off—do you know him?"

"I have told you that I believe I know him."

"His name?"

"I do not know that. What I do know is that he is a creature of the cardinal's, his ready tool."

" But you have seen him ? "

" Yes, my wife pointed him out to me one day."

" Has he anything remarkable about him by which he may be recognized ? "

" Oh, certainly. He is a noble of lofty carriage, black hair, swarthy complexion, piercing eye, white teeth, and a scar on his temple."

" A scar on his temple ! " cried D'Artagnan ; " and also white teeth, a piercing eye, dark complexion, black hair, and haughty carriage. Why, that's my man of Meung."

" He is your man, do you say ? "

" Yes, yes ; but that has nothing to do with it. No, I am mistaken. It simplifies the matter greatly, on the contrary. If your man is mine, with one blow I shall obtain two revenges, that's all. But where is this man to be met with ? "

" I cannot inform you."

" Have you no information respecting his dwelling ? "

" None. One day, as I was conveying my wife back to the Louvre, he was coming out as she was going in, and she showed him to me."

" The devil, the devil ! " murmured D'Artagnan. " All this is vague enough. From whom did you learn the abduction of your wife ? "

" From M. de la Porte."

" Did he give you any of the particulars ? "

" He knew none himself."

" And you have learned none from any other quarter ? "

" Yes, I have received——"

" What ? "

" I fear I am committing a great imprudence."

" You still keep harping upon that ; but I beg leave to observe to you that this time it is too late to retreat."

" I do not retreat, 'sdeath ! " cried the bourgeois, swearing to keep his courage up. " Besides, by the word of Bonacieux——"

" Your name is Bonacieux ? " interrupted D'Artagnan.

" Yes, that is my name."

" You said, then, by the word of Bonacieux ! Pardon me for interrupting you, but it appears to me that that name is familiar to me."

" Very possibly, sir. I am your landlord."

" Ah, ah ! " said D'Artagnan, half rising and bowing ; " you are my landlord ? "

" Yes, sir, yes. And as it is three months since you came,

and, engaged as you must be in your important occupations, you have forgotten to pay me my rent—as, I say, I have not tormented you a single instant, I thought you would appreciate my delicacy."

"How can it be otherwise, my dear Bonacieux ?" replied D'Artagnan. "Believe me, I am wholly grateful for such conduct ; and if, as I have told you, I can be of any service to you——"

"I believe you, sir, I believe you ; and as I was about to say, by the word of Bonacieux, I have confidence in you."

"Finish, then, that which you were about to say."

The bourgeois took a paper from his pocket and presented it to D'Artagnan.

"A letter ?" said the young man.

"Which I received this morning."

D'Artagnan opened it, and as the daylight was fading, he drew near to the window to read it. The bourgeois followed him.

"'Do not seek for your wife,'" read D'Artagnan ; "'she will be restored to you when she is no longer needed. If you make a single step to find her, you are lost.' That's pretty positive," continued D'Artagnan ; "but, after all, it is only a threat."

"Yes ; but that threat terrifies me. I am not a swordsman at all, sir ; and I am afraid of the Bastille."

"Hum !" said D'Artagnan. "I have no greater regard for the Bastille than you. If it were nothing but a swordthrust——"

"I have counted upon you on this occasion, sir."

"You have ?"

"Seeing you constantly surrounded by musketeers of a very proud appearance, and knowing that these musketeers belonged to M. de Tréville, and were consequently enemies of the cardinal, I thought that you and your friends, while rendering justice to our poor queen, would not be displeased at having an opportunity of doing his Eminence an ill turn."

"Without doubt."

"And then I thought that owing me three months' rent, which I have said nothing about——"

"Yes, yes ; you have already given me that reason, and I find it excellent."

"And, besides, considering that as long as you do me the honour to remain in my house I shall never speak to you about your future rent——"

"Very good!"

"And adding to this, if necessary, that I mean to offer you fifty pistoles, if, against all probability, you should be short at the present moment."

"Admirable! But you are rich, then, my dear Monsieur Bonacieux?"

"I am comfortably off, sir, that's all. I have scraped together something like an income of two or three thousand crowns in the haberdashery business, and especially by investing some capital in the last voyage of the celebrated navigator Jean Mocquet; so that you understand, sir. But——" cried the bourgeois.

"What?" demanded D'Artagnan.

"Whom do I see yonder?"

"Where?"

"In the street, in front of your window, on the sill of that door—a man wrapped in a cloak."

"It is he!" cried D'Artagnan and the bourgeois, each at the same time having recognized his man.

"Ah, this time," cried D'Artagnan, leaping towards his sword—"this time he shall not escape me!"

Drawing his sword from the sheath, he rushed out of the apartment.

On the staircase he met Athos and Porthos, who were coming to see him. They separated, and D'Artagnan rushed between them like an arrow.

"Where the devil are you going?" cried the two musketeers in a breath.

"The man of Meung!" replied D'Artagnan, and disappeared.

D'Artagnan had more than once related to his friends his adventure with the unknown, as well as the apparition of the beautiful foreigner, to whom this man had confided some important letter.

The opinion of Athos was that D'Artagnan had lost his letter in the affray. A gentleman, in his opinion (and, according to D'Artagnan's portrait of him, the unknown must be a gentleman)—a gentleman would be incapable of the baseness of stealing a letter.

Porthos had seen nothing in all this but a tryst, given by a lady to a cavalier, or by a cavalier to a lady, which had been disturbed by the presence of D'Artagnan and his yellow horse.

Aramis said that as these sorts of affairs were mysterious, it was better not to attempt to unravel them.

They understood, then, from the few words which escaped from D'Artagnan, what affair was in hand ; and as they thought that after having overtaken his man or lost sight of him D'Artagnan would return to his rooms again, they kept on their way.

When they entered D'Artagnan's chamber it was empty. The landlord, dreading the consequences of the meeting which was doubtless about to take place between the young man and the unknown, had, consistently with the character he had given himself, judged it most prudent to decamp.

CHAPTER IX.

D'ARTAGNAN'S CHARACTER UNFOLDS.

As Athos and Porthos had foreseen, at the expiration of half an hour D'Artagnan returned. He had this time again missed his man, who had disappeared as if by enchantment. D'Artagnan had run, sword in hand, through all the neighbouring streets, but had found nobody resembling him whom he was looking for. Then at last he came back to the point where he should perhaps have started, which was to knock at the door against which the unknown was leaning ; but he had knocked uselessly ten or twelve times running, for no one answered, and some of the neighbours, who had put their noses out of their windows, or were brought to their doors by the noise, had assured him that the house, all the openings of which were in fact tightly closed, had been for six months completely uninhabited.

While D'Artagnan was running through the streets and knocking at doors, Aramis had joined his companions, so that on returning home D'Artagnan found the reunion complete.

" Well ? " cried the three musketeers all together, on seeing D'Artagnan enter with his brow covered with perspiration and his face clouded with anger.

" Well ! " cried he, throwing his sword upon the bed ; " this man must be the devil in person. He has disappeared like a phantom, like a shade, like a spectre."

" Do you believe in apparitions ? " asked Athos of Porthos.

" I never believe in anything I have not seen, and as I never have seen an apparition, I don't believe in them."

" The Bible," said Aramis, " makes our belief in them a law. The shade of Samuel appeared to Saul, and it is an article of faith that I should be very sorry to see any doubt thrown upon, Porthos."

"At all events, man or devil, body or shadow, illusion or reality, this man is born for my damnation, for his flight has caused us to miss a glorious affair, gentlemen—an affair by which there were a hundred pistoles, and perhaps more, to be gained."

"How is that ?" cried Porthos and Aramis in a breath.

As to Athos, faithful to his system of silence, he satisfied himself with interrogating D'Artagnan by a look.

"Planchet," said D'Artagnan to his domestic, who just then insinuated his head through the half-open door in order to catch some fragments of the conversation, "go down to my landlord, M. Bonacieux, and tell him to send me half a dozen bottles of Beaugency wine ; I prefer that."

"Ah, ah ! What ! you have full credit with your landlord, then ?" asked Porthos.

"Yes," replied D'Artagnan, "from this very day ; and mind, if his wine is bad, we will send to him for better."

"We must use and not abuse," said Aramis sententiously.

"I always said that D'Artagnan had the longest head of the four," said Athos, who, after having uttered this opinion, to which D'Artagnan replied with a bow, immediately resumed his habitual silence.

"But come, tell us what is this about ?" asked Porthos.

"Yes," said Aramis, "confide it to us, my dear friend, unless the honour of some lady be concerned in this confidence. In that case you would do better to keep it to yourself."

"Be calm," replied D'Artagnan ; "the honour of no one shall have to complain of what I have to tell you."

He then told his friends, word for word, all that had passed between him and his landlord, and how the man who had carried off the wife of his worthy landlord was the same with whom he had had a difference at the hostelry of the Jolly Miller.

"Your affair is not a bad one," said Athos, after having tasted the wine like a connoisseur, and indicated by a nod of his head that he thought it good, "and fifty or sixty pistoles may be got out of this good man. Now, the only thing left is to ascertain whether these fifty or sixty pistoles are worth the risk of four heads."

"But please to observe," cried D'Artagnan, "that there is a woman in the affair—a woman carried off, a woman who is doubtless threatened, tortured perhaps, and all because she is faithful to her mistress."

"Beware, D'Artagnan, beware," said Aramis; "you grow a little too warm, in my opinion, about the fate of Madame Bonacieux. Woman was created for our destruction, and from her came all our miseries."

At this saying of Aramis the brow of Athos became clouded, and he bit his lips.

"It is not Madame Bonacieux about whom I am anxious," cried D'Artagnan, "but the queen, whom the king abandons, whom the cardinal persecutes, and who sees the heads of all her friends fall one after the other."

"Why does she love what we hate most in the world— the Spaniards and the English?"

"Spain is her country," replied D'Artagnan; "and it is very natural that she should love the Spanish, who are children of the same soil as herself. As to the second reproach, I have heard it said that she does not love the English, but an Englishman."

"Well, by my faith," said Athos, "we must confess that this Englishman was worthy of being loved. I never saw a man with a nobler air than his."

"Without taking into consideration that he dresses as nobody else can," said Porthos. "I was at the Louvre the day he scattered his pearls; and, zounds! I picked up two that I sold for ten pistoles each.—Do you know him, Aramis?"

"As well as you do, gentlemen; for I was among those who seized him in the garden at Amiens, into which M. Putange, the queen's equerry, introduced me. I was at the seminary at the time, and the adventure appeared to me to be cruel for the king."

"Which would not prevent me," said D'Artagnan, "if I knew where the Duke of Buckingham was, to take him by the hand and lead him to the queen, were it only to make the cardinal angry; for our real, our only, our eternal enemy, gentlemen, is the cardinal, and if we could find means to play him a cruel trick, I confess that I would voluntarily risk my head in doing it."

"And did the mercer," rejoined Athos, "tell you, D'Artagnan, that the queen thought that Buckingham had been brought over by a forged letter?"

"She is afraid so."

"Wait a minute, then," said Aramis.

"What for?" demanded Porthos.

"Go on. I am trying to recall some circumstances."

"And now I am convinced," said D'Artagnan, "that this abduction of the queen's seamstress is connected with the events of which we are speaking, and perhaps with the presence of the Duke of Buckingham at Paris."

"The Gascon is full of ideas," said Porthos, with admiration.

"I like to hear him talk," said Athos; "his dialect amuses me."

"Gentlemen," cried Aramis, "listen to this."

"Listen to Aramis," said his three friends.

"Yesterday I was at the house of a learned doctor of theology whom I sometimes consult about my studies."

Athos smiled.

"He resides in a quiet quarter," continued Aramis; "his tastes and his profession require it. Now, at the moment that I left his house——"

Here Aramis stopped.

"Well," cried his auditors; "at the moment you left his house——"

Aramis appeared to make a strong inward effort, like a man who, in the midst of telling a lie, finds himself stopped by some unforeseen obstacle; but the eyes of his three companions were fixed upon him, their ears were wide open, and there was no means of retreat.

"This doctor has a niece," continued Aramis.

"A niece, has he?" interrupted Porthos.

"A very respectable lady," said Aramis.

The three friends began to laugh.

"Ah, if you laugh, or doubt what I say," replied Aramis, "you shall know nothing."

"We are as stanch believers as Mohammedans, and as mute as catafalques," said Athos.

"I will go on, then," resumed Aramis. "This niece comes sometimes to see her uncle, and by chance was there yesterday at the same time that I was, and I could do no less than offer to conduct her to her carriage."

"Oh, oh! Then this niece of the doctor's keeps a carriage, does she?" interrupted Porthos, one of whose faults was a great looseness of speech. "A very nice acquaintance, my friend!"

"Porthos," replied Aramis, "I have already had occasion to observe to you more than once that you are very indiscreet, and that this injures you with women."

"Gentlemen, gentlemen," cried D'Artagnan, who began

to get a glimpse of the result of the adventure, "the thing is serious. Endeavour, then, not to joke, if possible. Go on, Aramis, go on."

"All at once a tall, dark man, with the manner of a gentleman—— Come! the same style as yours, D'Artagnan."

"The same, perhaps," said he.

"Possibly," continued Aramis—"came towards me, accompanied by five or six men, who followed at about ten paces behind him; and in the politest tone, 'Duke,' said he to me, 'and you, madame,' continued he, addressing the lady, who had hold of my arm——"

"The doctor's niece?"

"Hold your tongue, Porthos," said Athos; "you are insupportable."

"'Be so kind as to get into this carriage, and that without offering the slightest resistance or making the least noise.'"

"He took you for Buckingham!" cried D'Artagnan.

"I believe so," replied Aramis.

"But the lady?" asked Porthos.

"He took her for the queen!" said D'Artagnan.

"Just so," replied Aramis.

"The Gascon is the devil!" cried Athos; "nothing escapes him."

"The fact is," said Porthos, "Aramis is of the same height and something of the form of the handsome duke; but it nevertheless appears to me that the uniform of a musketeer——"

"I wore a very large cloak," said Aramis.

"In the month of July, the devil!" said Porthos. "Is the doctor afraid you should be recognized?"

"I can understand that the spy may have been deceived by your figure; but your face——"

"I had a very large hat on," said Aramis.

"Oh, good Lord!" cried Porthos, "how many precautions in order to study theology!"

"Gentlemen, gentlemen," said D'Artagnan, "do not let us lose our time in jesting. Let us separate, and let us seek the mercer's wife; that is the key of the intrigue."

"A woman of such inferior condition! Do you believe it, D'Artagnan?" said Porthos, protruding his lip contemptuously.

"She is goddaughter to La Porte, the confidential valet of the queen. Have I not told you so, gentlemen? Besides, it has perhaps been a scheme of her Majesty's to have sought on this occasion for such lowly support. High heads can be seen from a distance; and the cardinal is far-sighted."

"Well," said Porthos, "in the first place, make a bargain with the mercer, and a good bargain, too."

"That's useless," said D'Artagnan; "for I believe if he does not pay us, we shall be well enough paid by another party."

At this moment a sudden noise of footsteps was heard upon the stairs, the door was thrown violently open, and the unfortunate mercer rushed into the chamber in which the council was being held.

"Save me, gentlemen, save me!" cried he. "There are four men come to arrest me! Save me! for the love of Heaven, save me!"

Porthos and Aramis arose.

"One moment," cried D'Artagnan, making them a sign to replace their half-drawn swords—"one moment. On this occasion we don't need courage; we need prudence."

"And yet," cried Porthos, "we will not leave——"

"You will let D'Artagnan act as he thinks proper," said Athos. "He has, I repeat, the longest head of us all, and for my part I declare I obey him.—Do as you think best, D'Artagnan."

At this moment the four guards appeared at the door of the antechamber; but seeing four musketeers standing with swords at their sides, they hesitated to advance farther.

"Come in, gentlemen, come in. You are here in my apartment, and we are all faithful servants of the king and the cardinal."

"Then, gentlemen, you will not oppose our executing the orders we have received?" asked the one who appeared to be the leader of the party.

"On the contrary, gentlemen, we would assist you if it were necessary."

"What is he saying?" grumbled Porthos

"That you are a simpleton," said Athos. "Hold your tongue."

"But you promised me——" said the poor mercer, in a very low voice.

"We can save you only by being free ourselves," replied D'Artagnan in a low and hurried tone; "and if we appear inclined to defend you, they will arrest us with you."

"It seems to me, nevertheless——"

"Come in, gentlemen, come in!" called out D'Artagnan;

"I have no motive for defending the gentleman. I saw him to-day for the first time, and he can tell you on what occasion. He came to demand the rent of my lodging.—Is not that true, M. Bonacieux ? Answer."

"That's the very truth," cried the mercer; "but the gentleman does not tell you——"

"Silence with respect to me ; silence with respect to my friends; silence about the queen, above all, or you will ruin everybody without saving yourself.—Now, gentlemen, come, take away this man ! "

And D'Artagnan pushed the half-stupefied mercer among the guards, saying to him,—

"You are a shabby old fellow, my dear. You come to demand money of me—of a musketeer !—To prison with him. Gentlemen, once more, take him to prison, and keep him under key as long as possible ; that will give me time to pay him."

The officers were full of thanks, and took away their prey.

At the moment they were going down D'Artagnan laid his hand on their leader's shoulder.

"Shall I not have the pleasure of drinking your health, and you mine ? " said D'Artagnan, filling two glasses with the Beaugency wine which he had obtained through the liberality of M. Bonacieux.

"That will do me great honour," said the chief of the officers, "and I accept with gratitude."

"Then to yours, sir—what is your name ? "

"Boisrenard."

"Monsieur Boisrenard ! "

"To yours, my good sir. In your turn, what is your name, if you please ? "

"D'Artagnan."

"To yours, Monsieur D'Artagnan."

"And above all others," cried D'Artagnan, as if carried away by his enthusiasm, "to that of the king and the cardinal."

The chief of the officers would perhaps have doubted the sincerity of D'Artagnan if the wine had been bad ; but the wine was good, and he was convinced.

"Why, what devilish villainy have you done there," said Porthos, when the head policeman had rejoined his companions, and the four friends were left alone. "Shame, shame, for four musketeers to allow an unfortunate devil who cried out for help to be arrested in their midst. And a gentleman to hobnob with a bailiff ! "

4

"Porthos," said Aramis, "Athos has already told you you are a simpleton, and I am quite of his opinion.—D'Artagnan, you are a great man, and when you occupy M. de Tréville's place, I will come and ask your influence to secure me an abbey."

"Well, I am quite lost!" said Porthos. "Do you approve of what D'Artagnan has just done?"

"Zounds! indeed I do!" said Athos. "I not only approve of what he has done, but I congratulate him upon it."

"And now, gentlemen," said D'Artagnan, without stopping to explain his conduct to Porthos, "all for one, one for all; that is our motto, is it not?"

"And yet——" said Porthos.

"Hold out your hand and swear!" cried Athos and Aramis at the same time.

Overcome by example, grumbling to himself, Porthos stretched out his hand, and the four friends repeated with one voice the formula dictated by D'Artagnan.

"All for one, one for all."

"That's well! Now let every one retire to his own house," said D'Artagnan, as if he had done nothing but command all his life; "and attention! for from this moment we are at war with the cardinal."

CHAPTER X.

A SEVENTEENTH-CENTURY MOUSE-TRAP.

THE invention of the mouse-trap does not date from our day: as soon as society, in developing, had invented any kind of police, that police in its turn invented mouse-traps.

As perhaps our readers are not familiar with the slang of the Rue de Jérusalem, and as, in all the fifteen years we have been writing, we now for the first time apply this word to the thing, let us explain to them what a mouse-trap is.

When in a house, of whatever kind it may be, an individual suspected of any crime is arrested, the arrest is kept secret. Four or five men are placed in ambuscade in the first apartment; the door is opened to all who knock; it is closed after them, and they are arrested; so that at the end of two or three days they have in their power almost all the frequenters of the establishment. And this is a mouse-trap.

The apartment of M. Bonacieux, then, became a mouse-trap, and whoever appeared there was taken and examined by the cardinal's people. It goes without saying that as a private passage led to the first floor, on which D'Artagnan lodged, those who called to see him were exempt from all search.

Besides, nobody came there but the three musketeers. They had all been engaged in earnest search and inquiries, but had discovered nothing. Athos had even gone so far as to question M. de Tréville—a thing which, considering the habitual reticence of the worthy musketeer, had very much astonished his captain. But M. de Tréville knew nothing, except that the last time he had seen the cardinal, the king, and the queen, the cardinal looked very thoughtful, the king uneasy, and the redness of the queen's eyes denoted that she had been deprived of sleep or had been weeping. But this last circumstance was not at all striking, as the queen since her marriage had slept badly and wept much.

M. de Tréville requested Athos, whatever might happen, to be observant of his duty to the king, but more particularly to the queen, begging him to convey the same request to his comrades.

As to D'Artagnan, he did not stir from his apartment. He had converted his chamber into an observatory. From his windows he saw all who came and were caught ; then, having removed some of the tiles of his floor and dug into the planking, and nothing remaining but a simple ceiling between him and the room beneath, in which the examinations were made, he heard all that passed between the inquisitors and the accused.

The examinations, preceded by a minute search of the persons arrested, were almost all conceived in this manner,—

" Has Madame Bonacieux given anything to you for her husband, or any other person ?

" Has Monsieur Bonacieux given anything to you for his wife, or for any other person ?

" Has either the one or the other confided anything to you by word of mouth ? "

" If they were acquainted with anything, they would not question people in this manner," said D'Artagnan to himself. " Now, what is it they want to know ? Why, whether the Duke of Buckingham is in Paris, and whether he has not had, or is not to have, some interview with the queen."

D'Artagnan was satisfied with this idea, which, according to all he had heard, was not wanting in probability.

In the meanwhile the mouse-trap continued in operation, as likewise did D'Artagnan's vigilance.

On the evening of the day after the arrest of poor Bonacieux, as Athos had just left D'Artagnan to go to M. de Tréville's, as nine o'clock had just struck, and as Planchet, who had not yet made the bed, was beginning his task, a knocking was heard at the street door. The door was instantly opened and shut: some one was caught in the mouse-trap.

D'Artagnan flew to his peek-hole, and laid himself down on the floor at full length to listen.

Cries were soon heard, and then moans, which some one was endeavouring to stifle. There were no questionings.

"The devil!" said D'Artagnan to himself; "it's a woman—they are searching her—she resists—they use force—the scoundrels!"

In spite of all his prudence, D'Artagnan had as much as he could do not to take part in the scene that was going on below.

"But I tell you that I am the mistress of the house, gentlemen! I tell you I am Madame Bonacieux! I tell you I belong to the queen!" cried the unfortunate woman.

"Madame Bonacieux!" murmured D'Artagnan. "Can I have been so lucky as to have found what everybody is looking for?"

"You are the very one we were waiting for," replied the examiners.

The voice became more and more indistinct; a tumultuous movement shook the wainscoting. The victim was resisting as much as one woman can resist four men.

"Pardon, gentlemen, par——" murmured the voice, which could now be heard only in inarticulate sounds.

"They are gagging her, they are going to drag her away," cried D'Artagnan to himself, springing from the floor. "My sword! Good! it is by my side. Planchet!"

"Sir."

"Run and get Athos, Porthos, and Aramis. One of the three will certainly be at home—perhaps all three are. Tell them to arm, to come here, and be quick about it! Ah, I remember; Athos is at M. de Tréville's."

"But where are you going, sir, where are you going?"

"I am going down by the window, in order to be there the sooner," cried D'Artagnan. "Do you put back the tiles, sweep the floor, go out at the door, and run where I bid you."

" O sir, sir, you will kill yourself ! " cried Planchet.

" Hold your tongue, you stupid fellow," said D'Artagnan ; and laying hold of the window-ledge, he let himself fall from the first story, which luckily was not far, without even scratching himself.

He then went straight to the door and knocked, murmuring,—

" I will go and be caught in the mouse-trap in my turn, but woe be to the cats that shall pounce upon such a mouse ! "

The knocker had scarcely sounded under the hand of the young man than the tumult ceased, steps approached, the door was opened, and D'Artagnan, sword in hand, rushed into M. Bonacieux's apartment, the door of which, doubtless moved by a spring, closed after him of itself.

Then those who were still living in Bonacieux's unfortunate house, together with the nearest neighbours, heard loud cries, stamping of feet, clashing of swords, and much breaking of furniture. Then a moment after those who, surprised by this tumult, had gone to their windows to learn the cause of it, could see the door open, and four men, clothed in black, not come out of it, but fly, like so many frightened crows, leaving on the ground, and on the corners of the furniture, feathers from their wings—that is to say, portions of their clothes and fragments of their cloaks.

D'Artagnan was conqueror, without much trouble, it must be confessed, for only one of the bailiffs was armed, and he defended himself only for form's sake. It is true that the three others had endeavoured to knock the young man down with chairs, stools, and crockery ; but two or three scratches made by the Gascon's blade terrified them. Ten minutes had sufficed for their defeat, and D'Artagnan remained master of the field of battle.

The neighbours who had opened their windows, with the indifference peculiar to the inhabitants of Paris in those times of perpetual riots and disturbances, closed them again as soon as they saw the four men in black fly away, their instinct telling them that for the moment all was over.

Besides, it began to grow late, and in those days, as at the present, people went to bed early in the Luxembourg quarter.

On being left alone with Madame Bonacieux, D'Artagnan turned towards her. The poor woman had fallen back upon an armchair in a half-fainting state. D'Artagnan examined her with a rapid glance.

She was a charming woman, of twenty-five or twenty-six years of age, with dark hair, blue eyes, a slightly turned-up nose, admirable teeth, and a pink and opal complexion. There, however, the signs stopped which might have confounded her with a lady of rank. Her hands were white, but pudgy; her feet did not bespeak the woman of quality. Fortunately, D'Artagnan had not yet reached the point of minding these details.

While D'Artagnan was examining Madame Bonacieux, and was, as we have said, close to her, he saw on the ground a fine cambric handkerchief, which he naturally picked up, and on the corner of which he recognized the same cipher that he had seen on the handkerchief which had nearly caused him and Aramis to cut each other's throats.

From that time D'Artagnan had been cautious with respect to handkerchiefs having arms on them, and he therefore, without a remark, placed the one he had just picked up in Madame Bonacieux's pocket.

At that moment Madame Bonacieux recovered her senses. She opened her eyes, looked around her with terror, saw that the apartment was empty, and that she was alone with her liberator. She immediately held out her hands to him with a smile. Madame Bonacieux had the sweetest smile in the world.

"Ah, sir!" said she, "you have saved me. Allow me to thank you."

"Madame," said D'Artagnan, "I have only done what every gentleman would have done in my place. You owe me, then, no thanks."

"Yes I do, sir, yes I do; and I hope to prove to you that you have not aided an ungrateful person. But what could these men, whom I at first took for robbers, want of me, and why is M. Bonacieux not here?"

"Madame, those men were much more dangerous than any robbers could have been, for they are the agents of the cardinal; and as to your husband, M. Bonacieux, he is not here, because he was yesterday evening taken away to the Bastille."

"My husband in the Bastille!" cried Madame Bonacieux. "Oh, my God, what can he have done? Poor, dear man—he is innocence itself!"

And something like a faint smile glided over the still terrified features of the young woman.

"What has he done, madame?" said D'Artagnan. "I believe that his only crime is to have at the same time the good fortune and the misfortune to be your husband."

"But, sir, you know then——"

"I know that you have been carried off, madame."

"And by whom? Do you know? Oh, if you know, tell me!"

"By a man of from forty to forty-five years of age, with black hair, a swarthy complexion, and a scar on his left temple."

"That is he, that is he; but his name?"

"Ah, his name? I do not know that."

"And did my husband know I had been carried off?"

"He was informed of it by a letter written to him by the abductor himself."

"And does he suspect," said Madame Bonacieux, with some embarrassment, "the cause of this event?"

"He attributed it, I believe, to a political cause."

"I suspected so myself at first, and now I think entirely as he does. So dear M. Bonacieux has not, then, for an instant suspected me?"

"Far from it, madame. He was too proud of your prudence, and particularly of your love."

A second smile stole almost imperceptibly over the rosy lips of the pretty young woman.

"But," continued D'Artagnan, "how did you escape?"

"I took advantage of a moment when they left me alone; and as I had known since morning what to think of my abduction, with the help of my sheets I let myself down from the window; then, as I thought my husband would be at home, I hastened here."

"To place yourself under his protection?"

"Oh no, poor, dear man! I knew very well that he was incapable of defending me; but as he could be otherwise useful to us, I wished to inform him."

"Of what?"

"Oh, that is not my secret; I therefore cannot tell you."

"Besides," said D'Artagnan—"pardon me, madame, if, guard as I am, I remind you of prudence—besides, I believe we are not here in a very proper place for imparting confidences. The men I have put to flight will return reinforced; if they find us here, we are lost. I have sent, to be sure, for three of my friends, but who knows whether they are at home?"

"Yes, yes; you are right," cried the terrified Madame Bonacieux; "let us fly, let us escape!"

At these words she passed her arm under that of D'Artagnan, and pulled him forward eagerly.

"But whither shall we fly—where escape to?"

"Let us in the first place get away from this house; when clear of it we shall see."

And the young woman and the young man, without taking the trouble to shut the door after them, descended the Rue des Fossoyeurs rapidly, turned into the Rue des Fossés-Monsieur-le-Prince, and did not stop till they came to the Place Saint-Sulpice.

"And now what are we to do, and where do you wish me to take you?" asked D'Artagnan.

"I am quite at a loss how to answer you, I confess," said Madame Bonacieux. "My intention was to inform M. de la Porte, by means of my husband, in order that M. de la Porte might tell us exactly what has taken place at the Louvre in the course of the last three days, and whether there were any danger in presenting myself there."

"But I," said D'Artagnan, "can go and inform M. de la Porte."

"No doubt you could; only there is one drawback in it, and this is that M. Bonacieux is known at the Louvre, and would be allowed to pass; whereas you are not known there, and the gate would be closed against you."

"Ah, bah!" said D'Artagnan; "there is no doubt you have at some wicket of the Louvre a porter who is devoted to you, and who, thanks to a password, would——"

Madame Bonacieux looked earnestly at the young man.

"And if I give you this password," said she, "would you forget it as soon as you had made use of it?"

"By my honour, by the faith of a gentleman!" said D'Artagnan, with an accent so truthful no one could mistake it.

"Then I believe you. You appear to be a brave young man; besides, your fortune, perhaps, will be the result of your devotion."

"I will do, without a promise, and conscientiously, all that I can do to serve the king and be agreeable to the queen. Use me, then, as a friend."

"But I—where shall I go in the meanwhile?"

"Do you know no one to whose house M. de la Porte can go to get you?"

"No, I will trust nobody."

"Stop," said D'Artagnan; "we are near Athos's door. Yes, here it is."

"Who is this Athos?"

"One of my friends."

"But if he should be at home and see me?"

"He is not at home; and I will carry away the key, after having placed you in his apartment."

"But if he should return?"

"Oh, he won't return; and if he should, he will be told that I have brought a lady with me, and that lady is in his apartment."

"But that will compromise me sadly, you know."

"Of what consequence can it be to you? Nobody knows you. Besides, we are in a situation in which we must not be too particular."

"Come, then, let us go to your friend's house. Where does he live?"

"Rue Férou, two steps from here."

"Come, then."

And both resumed their way. As D'Artagnan had foreseen, Athos was not at home. He took the key, which was usually given him as one of the family, ascended the stairs, and introduced Madame Bonacieux into the little apartment of which we have already given a description.

"Make yourself at home," said he. "Wait here, fasten the door inside, and open it to nobody unless you hear three taps like these." And he tapped thrice—two taps close together and pretty hard, the other after an interval, lighter.

"That is all right," said Madame Bonacieux. "Now it is my turn to give you my orders."

"I am all attention."

"Present yourself at the wicket of the Louvre, towards the Rue de l'Echelle, and ask for Germain."

"Well, and then?"

"He will ask you what you want, and you will answer by these two words—'Tours' and 'Brussels.' He will immediately put himself under your orders."

"And what shall I order him to do?"

"To go and fetch M. de la Porte, the queen's valet."

"And when he shall have found him, and M. de la Porte has come?"

"You will send him to me."

"Very well; but where and how shall I see you again?"

"Do you, then, wish very much to see me again?"

"Certainly I do."

"Well, let that care be mine, and do not worry."

"I depend upon your word."

"Certainly."

"Very well. Count on me for bringing this about, and have no fear."

"I may depend on your word ?"

"You may."

D'Artagnan bowed to Madame Bonacieux, darting at her the most loving glance that he could possibly concentrate upon her charming little person ; and while he descended the stairs he heard the door closed behind him and double-locked. In two bounds he was at the Louvre. As he entered the wicket of L'Echelle ten o'clock struck. All the events we have just described had taken place within half an hour.

Everything happened as Madame Bonacieux said it would. On hearing the password, Germain bowed ; ten minutes after La Porte was at the lodge ; with two words D'Artagnan told him what was going on, and informed him where Madame Bonacieux was. La Porte assured himself, by having it twice repeated, of the exact address, and set off at a run. He had, however, scarcely gone ten steps before he returned.

"Young man," said he to D'Artagnan, "I have a piece of advice to give you."

"What is it ?"

"You may get into trouble by what has taken place."

"Do you think so ?"

"Yes. Have you any friend whose clock is too slow ?"

"What then ?"

"Go and call upon him, in order that he may give evidence of your having been with him at half-past nine. In law that is called an alibi."

D'Artagnan found this advice prudent. He took to his heels, and was soon at M. de Tréville's ; but instead of going into the drawing-room with everybody, he asked to be introduced to M. de Tréville's office. As D'Artagnan was one of the frequenters of the hôtel, no difficulty was made in complying with his request, and a servant went to inform M. de Tréville that his young compatriot, having something important to communicate, solicited a private audience. Five minutes after, M. de Tréville was asking D'Artagnan what he could do for him, and to what he was indebted for his visit at so late an hour.

"Pardon me, sir," said D'Artagnan, who had profited by the moment he had been left alone to put back M. de Tréville's clock three-quarters of an hour; "I thought, as it was yet only twenty-five minutes past nine, it was not too late to wait upon you."

"Twenty-five minutes past nine!" cried M. de Tréville, looking at the clock; "why, that's impossible!"

"Look, rather, sir," said D'Artagnan; "the clock shows it."

"That's true," said M. de Tréville; "I should have thought it was later. But what can I do for you?"

Then D'Artagnan told M. de Tréville a long history about the queen. He expressed to him the fears he entertained with respect to her Majesty; he related to him what he had heard of the projects of the cardinal with regard to Buckingham; and all with a tranquillity and sereneness which deceived M. de Tréville the more because he had himself, as we have said, observed something new between the cardinal, the king, and the queen.

As ten o'clock was striking D'Artagnan left M. de Tréville, who thanked him for his information, recommended him to have the service of the king and queen always at heart, and returned to the drawing-room. But at the foot of the stairs D'Artagnan remembered he had forgotten his cane. He consequently rushed up again, re-entered the office, with a turn of his finger set the clock right again, that they might not perceive the next day it had been tampered with; and sure henceforth that he had a witness to prove his alibi, he ran downstairs and soon gained the street.

CHAPTER XI.

THE PLOT THICKENS.

His visit to M. de Tréville being paid, D'Artagnan, quite thoughtful, took the longest way homewards.

Of what was D'Artagnan thinking, that he strayed thus from his path, gazing at the stars in the heavens, and sometimes sighing, sometimes smiling?

He was thinking of Madame Bonacieux. For an apprentice musketeer the young woman was almost an ideal of love. Pretty, mysterious, initiated into almost all the secrets of the court, which reflected such a charming gravity over her pleasing features, he suspected her of not being insensible to wooing, which is an irresistible charm for novices in love. Besides, D'Artagnan had delivered her from the hands of the demons who wished to search and maltreat her; and this important service had established between them one of those sentiments of gratitude which so easily take on a more tender character.

So rapidly do our dreams move upon the wings of imagination that D'Artagnan already fancied himself accosted by a messenger from the young woman, who brought him some note appointing a meeting, or a gold chain, or a diamond. We have observed that young cavaliers received presents from their king without shame; let us add that, in those times of lax morality, they had no more delicacy with respect to their mistresses, and that the latter almost always left them valuable and durable remembrances, as if they endeavoured to conquer their fragile sentiments by solid gifts.

Men then made their way in the world by the means of women without blushing. Such as were only beautiful gave their beauty; whence, without doubt, comes the proverb that "The most beautiful girl in the world can give no more than she has." Such as were rich gave, in addition, a part of their money; and a vast number of heroes of that gallant period may be cited who would neither have won their spurs in the first place, nor their battles afterwards, without the purse, more or less garnished, which the mistress fastened to the saddle-bow.

D'Artagnan possessed nothing. Provincial diffidence—that slight varnish, that ephemeral flower, that down of the peach—had been blown away by the unorthodox counsels which the three musketeers gave their friend. D'Artagnan, following the strange custom of the times, considered himself at Paris as on a campaign, neither more nor less than if he had been in Flanders—Spain yonder, woman here. In each there was an enemy to contend with, and contributions to be levied.

But, we must say, at the present moment D'Artagnan was governed by a much more noble and disinterested feeling. The mercer had told him he was rich; the young man might easily guess that, with so weak a man as M. Bonacieux, it was most likely the young wife kept the purse. But all this had had no influence at all upon the feeling produced by the sight of Madame Bonacieux, and self-interest remained almost entirely foreign to that commencement of love which had been the consequence of it.

We say "almost entirely," for the idea that a young, handsome, kind, and witty woman is at the same time rich takes nothing from the charm of this beginning of love, but, on the contrary, strengthens it.

Affluence has a crowd of aristocratic cares and caprices which are highly becoming to beauty. A fine and white stocking, a silk dress, a lace kerchief, a pretty slipper on the foot, a new ribbon on the head, do not make an ugly woman pretty, but they make a pretty woman beautiful, without reckoning her hands, which gain by all this: the hands, among women particularly, must be idle to be beautiful.

Then D'Artagnan, as the reader, from whom we have not concealed the condition of his fortune, very well knows —D'Artagnan was not a millionaire. He hoped to become one some day, but the time which in his own mind he fixed upon for this happy change was still far distant. In the meanwhile, how disheartening to see the woman one loves long for those thousands of nothings which constitute a woman's happiness, and be unable to give her those thousand nothings! At least when the woman is rich and the lover is not, what he cannot offer her she offers to herself; and although it is generally with her husband's money that she procures herself this indulgence, the gratitude for it seldom reverts to him.

But D'Artagnan, disposed to become some day the most tender of lovers, was in the meantime a very devoted friend. In the midst of his amorous projects upon the mercer's wife he did not forget his friends. The pretty Madame Bonacieux was just the woman to walk with in the plain of St. Denis, or in the fair of Saint-Germain, in company with Athos, Porthos, and Aramis, to whom D'Artagnan would be so proud to display such a conquest. Then, when people walk for any length of time they become hungry, at least D'Artagnan had fancied so several times lately; and they could enjoy some of those little charming dinners in which we on one side touch the hand of a friend, and on the other the foot of a mistress. Besides, on pressing occasions, in extreme difficulties, D'Artagnan would become the preserver of his friends.

And Monsieur Bonacieux, whom D'Artagnan had pushed into the hands of the bailiffs, denying him aloud, although he had promised in a whisper to save him? We are compelled to admit to our readers that D'Artagnan thought nothing about him in any way; or that, if he did think of him, it was only to say to himself that he was very well where he was, wherever it might be. Love is the most selfish of all the passions.

Let our readers, however, be satisfied. If D'Artagnan forgets his host, or appears to forget him, under the pretence of not knowing where he has been taken to, we will not forget him, and we know where he is. But for the moment let us do as the amorous Gascon did. We will look after the worthy mercer presently.

D'Artagnan, reflecting on his future loves, addressing himself to the beautiful night and smiling at the stars, went up the Rue Cherche-Midi, or Chasse-Midi, as it was then called. As he found himself in the quarter in which Aramis lived, he took it into his head to pay his friend a visit, in order to explain to him why he had sent Planchet to him with a request that he would come instantly to the mouse-trap. Now, if Aramis was at home when Planchet came to his abode, he had doubtless hastened to the Rue des Fossoyeurs, and finding nobody but his two companions there, perhaps they would not be able to conceive, any of them, what all this meant. This result required an explanation ; at least, so D'Artagnan thought.

And he likewise whispered to himself that he thought this was an opportunity for talking about pretty little Madame Bonacieux, of whom his head, if not his heart, was already full. We must never look for discretion in first love. First love is accompanied by such excessive joy that unless this joy is allowed to overflow, it will stifle you.

Paris for two hours past had been dark, and began to be deserted. All the clocks of the Faubourg Saint-Germain were striking eleven. It was delightful weather. D'Artagnan was passing along a lane upon the spot where the Rue d'Assas is now situated, respiring the balmy emanations which were borne upon the wind from the Rue Vaugirard, and which arose from the gardens refreshed by the dews of evening and the breeze of night. From a distance resounded, deadened, however, by good shutters, the songs of the tipplers enjoying themselves in the scattered saloons of the plain. When he reached the end of the lane D'Artagnan turned to the left. The house in which Aramis dwelt was situated between the Rue Cassette and the Rue Servandoni.

D'Artagnan had just passed the Rue Cassette, and already caught sight of the door of his friend's house, shaded by a mass of sycamores and clematis, which formed a vast arch above it, when he perceived something like a shadow issuing from the Rue Servandoni. This something was enveloped in a cloak, and D'Artagnan at first believed it was a man ; but by the smallness of the form, the hesitation of the gait, and the indecision of the step, he soon discovered that it was a woman. Further, this woman, as if not certain of the house she was seeking, lifted up her eyes to look around her, stopped, went a little back, and then returned again. D'Artagnan was perplexed.

"Suppose I were to go and offer her my services," thought he. "By her step she must be young, perhaps pretty. Oh yes ! But a woman who wanders about the streets at this hour seldom does so but to meet her lover. Bah ! to go and disturb a rendezvous would not be the best means of commencing an acquaintance."

The young woman, however, continued advancing slowly, counting the houses and windows. This was neither a long nor a difficult affair. There were but three mansions in this part of the street, and two windows looking out upon that street, and one of them was the window of a pavilion parallel to that which Aramis occupied ; the other was Aramis's own window.

"Zounds !" said D'Artagnan to himself, whose mind reverted to the niece of the theologian—"zounds ! it would be droll if this belated flying dove should be in search of our friend's house. But, by my soul, that seems more than probable. Ah, my dear friend Aramis, this time I will find you out."

And D'Artagnan, making himself as small as he could, concealed himself on the darkest side of the street, near a stone bench placed at the back of a niche.

The young woman continued to advance, for, in addition to the lightness of her step, which had betrayed her, she had just given a slight cough which betrayed a clear, sweet voice. D'Artagnan believed this cough to be a signal.

Nevertheless, whether this cough had been answered by an equivalent signal which had driven away the hesitation of the nocturnal seeker, or whether she had recognized that she had arrived at the end of her journey, she boldly drew near to Aramis's shutter, and tapped at three equal intervals with her bent finger.

"She is certainly looking for Aramis," murmured D'Artagnan. "Ah, master hypocrite, this is the way you study theology, is it ?"

The three blows were scarcely struck when the inside casement was opened, and a light appeared through the panes of the shutter.

"Ah, ah!" said the listener, "not through doors, but through windows! Ah, ah! this was an expected visit. We shall see the windows open, and the lady enter by escalade! Very pretty!"

But to the great astonishment of D'Artagnan the shutter remained closed. Moreover, the light which had shone out for an instant disappeared, and all was dark again.

D'Artagnan thought this could not last long, and continued to look with all his eyes and listen with all his ears.

He was right. At the end of some seconds two sharp taps were heard on the inside. The young woman in the street replied by a single tap, and the shutter was opened a little way.

Judge whether D'Artagnan looked or listened eagerly. Unfortunately the light had been removed into another chamber. But the eyes of the young man were accustomed to the night. Besides, the eyes of Gascons, like those of cats, possess, it is said, the faculty of seeing in the dark.

D'Artagnan then saw that the young woman took from her pocket a white object which she unfolded quickly, and which took the form of a handkerchief. She made her interlocutor look at the corner of this unfolded object.

This immediately recalled to D'Artagnan's mind the handkerchief he had found at the feet of Madame Bonacieux, which had reminded him of the one he had dragged from under Aramis's foot.

"What the devil could that handkerchief mean?"

Placed where he was, D'Artagnan could not see the face of Aramis. We say the face of Aramis, because the young man entertained no doubt that it was his friend who held this dialogue inside with the lady outside. Curiosity prevailed over prudence, and taking advantage of the preoccupation in which the sight of the handkerchief appeared to have plunged the two personages now on the scene, he stole from his hiding-place, and quick as lightning, but stepping with the utmost caution, he went and placed himself close to the angle of the wall, from which his eye could plunge into the interior of the apartment.

Upon gaining this advantage D'Artagnan came near uttering a cry of surprise. It was not Aramis who was conversing with the nocturnal visitor; it was a woman! D'Artagnan, however, could only see enough to recognize the form of her vestments, not enough to distinguish her features.

At the same instant the woman of the apartment drew a second handkerchief from her pocket, and exchanged it for the one which had just been shown to her. Then some words were pronounced by the two women. At length the shutter was closed. The woman who was outside the window turned round, and passed within four steps of D'Artagnan, pulling down the hood of her cloak ; but the precaution was too late. D'Artagnan had already recognized Madame Bonacieux.

Madame Bonacieux ! The suspicion that it was she had crossed the mind of D'Artagnan when she drew the handkerchief from her pocket ; but what probability was there that Madame Bonacieux, who had sent for M. de la Porte in order to be led back to the Louvre, should be running about the streets of Paris at half-past eleven at night, at the risk of being carried off a second time ?

It must be, then, for some very important affair ; and what is the affair of the greatest importance to a pretty woman of twenty-five ? Love.

But was it on her own account or on account of another person that she exposed herself to such risks ? This was a question the young man asked himself, the demon of jealousy already gnawing at his heart, neither more nor less than at the heart of an accepted lover.

There was, besides, a very simple means of satisfying himself where Madame Bonacieux was going. This was to follow her. The means was so simple that D'Artagnan employed it quite naturally and instinctively.

But at the sight of the young man, who came out from the wall like a statue walking from its niche, and at the noise of the steps which she heard resound behind her, Madame Bonacieux uttered a little cry and fled.

D'Artagnan ran after her. It was not a very difficult thing for him to overtake a woman embarrassed with her cloak. He came up to her before she had traversed a third of the street. The unfortunate woman was exhausted, not by fatigue, but by terror ; and when D'Artagnan placed his hand upon her shoulder, she sank upon one knee, crying in a choking voice,—

" Kill me, if you will ; you shall know nothing ! "

D'Artagnan raised her by passing his arm round her waist ; but as he felt by her weight she was on the point of fainting, he made haste to reassure her by protestations of devotion. These protestations were nothing for Madame Bonacieux, for such protestations may be made with the worst intentions in the world ; but the voice was all. The young woman thought she recognized the sound of that voice. She opened her eyes, cast a quick glance upon the man who had terrified her so, and at once perceiving it was D'Artagnan, she uttered a cry of joy.

"Oh, it is you, it is you ! Thank God, thank God ! "

"Yes, it is I," said D'Artagnan—" it is I, whom God has sent to watch over you."

"Was it with that intention you followed me ? " asked the young woman, with a coquettish smile, whose somewhat bantering character resumed its influence, and whose fear had wholly disappeared from the moment when she recognized a friend in one whom she had taken for an enemy.

"No," said D'Artagnan—" no, I confess it ; it was chance that threw me in your way. I saw a female knocking at the window of one of my friends."

"Of one of your friends ? " interrupted Madame Bonacieux.

"Without doubt ; Aramis is one of my most intimate friends."

"Aramis ! Who is he ? "

"Come, come, you won't tell me you don't know Aramis ? "

"This is the first time I ever heard his name."

"This is the first time, then, that you ever went to that house ? "

"Certainly it is."

"And you did not know that it was inhabited by a young man ? "

"No."

"By a musketeer ? "

"Not at all."

"It was not he, then, you came to find ? "

"Not the least in the world. Besides, you must have seen that the person I spoke to was a woman."

"That is true ; but this woman may be one of the friends of Aramis——"

"I know nothing of that."

"Since she occupies his apartment."

"That does not concern me."

"But who is she ? "

"Oh, that is not my secret."

"My dear Madame Bonacieux, you are charming ; but at the same time you are the most mysterious of women."

"Do I lose much by that ? "

"No ; you are, on the contrary, adorable ! "

"Give me your arm, then."

"Most willingly. And now ? "

"Now take me with you."

"Where ? "

"Where I am going."

"But where are you going ? "

"You will see, because you will leave me at the door."

"Shall I wait for you ? "

"That will be useless."

"You will return alone, then ? "

"Perhaps I may, perhaps I may not."

"But will the person who will afterwards accompany you be a man or a woman ? "

"I don't know yet."

"But I will know it ! "

"How ? "

"I will wait for your coming out."

"In that case, adieu ! "

"Why so ? "

"I do not want you."

"But you had demanded——"

"The aid of a gentleman, not the watchfulness of a spy."

"That word is rather hard."

"How are they called who follow other people in spite of them ? "

"They are indiscreet."

"The word is too mild."

"Well, madame, I perceive I must act in accordance with your wishes."

"Why did you deprive yourself of the merit of doing so at once ? "

"Is there no merit in repentance ? "

"And you do really repent ? "

"I know nothing about that myself. But what I know is, that I promise to do all you wish if you will allow me to accompany you where you are going."

"And you will leave me afterwards ? "

"Yes."

"Without waiting for my coming out again ? "

"Yes."

"On your honour ? "

" By the faith of a gentleman. Take my arm, then, and let us go on."

D'Artagnan offered his arm to Madame Bonacieux, who took it, half laughing, half trembling, and both went up Rue la Harpe. When they reached there the young woman seemed to hesitate, as she had before done in the Rue Vaugirard. Nevertheless, by certain signs she appeared to recognize a door ; and approaching that door,—

" And now, sir," she said, " it is here I have business. A thousand thanks for your honourable company, which has saved me from all the dangers to which, alone, I might have been exposed. But the moment has come for you to keep your word ; I have reached the place of my destination."

" And you will have nothing more to fear on your return ? "

" I shall have nothing to fear but robbers."

" And is that nothing ? "

" What could they take from me ? I have not a farthing about me."

" You forget that beautiful embroidered handkerchief with the coat of arms."

" Which one ? "

" The one which I found at your feet, and put back into your pocket ! "

" Silence, silence, imprudent man ! " cried the young woman. " Do you wish to ruin me ? "

" You see very plainly that there is still danger for you, since a single word makes you tremble ; and you confess that if that word were heard you would be ruined. Come, come, madame ! " cried D'Artagnan, seizing her hand and surveying her with an ardent glance ; " come ! be more generous ; trust in me. Have you not read in my eyes that there is nothing but devotion and sympathy in my heart ? "

" Yes," replied Madame Bonacieux ; " therefore ask me my own secrets, and I will tell them to you ; but those of others—that is quite another thing."

" Very well," said D'Artagnan ; " I shall discover them. As these secrets may have an influence over your life, these secrets must become mine."

" Beware of what you do ! " cried the young woman, in a manner so serious that it made D'Artagnan start in spite of himself. " Oh, meddle in nothing which concerns me ; do not seek to assist me in what I am accomplishing. And this I ask of you in the name of the interest with which I inspire you, in the name of the service you have rendered me, and which I never shall forget while I have life. Rather place faith in what I tell you. No longer concern yourself about me. I exist no longer for you, any more than if you had never seen me."

"Must Aramis also do the same, madame?" said D'Artagnan, piqued.

"This is the second or third time, sir, that you have repeated that name, and yet I have told you that I do not know him."

"You do not know the man at whose shutter you went and knocked? Indeed, madame, you think me altogether too credulous!"

"Confess, now, that it is for the sake of making me talk that you invent this story and create this personage."

"I invent nothing, madame; I create nothing. I only speak the exact truth."

"And you say that one of your friends lives in that house?"

"I say so, and I repeat it for the third time: in that house lives one of my friends, and that friend is Aramis."

"All this will be cleared up at a later period," murmured the young woman; "now, sir, be silent."

"If you could see my heart," said D'Artagnan, "you would there read in it so much curiosity that you would pity me, and so much love that you would instantly satisfy my curiosity. We have nothing to fear from those who love us."

"You speak very soon of love, sir!" said the young woman, shaking her head.

"That is because love has come suddenly upon me, and for the first time, and because I am not twenty years old."

The young woman looked at him furtively.

"Listen! I am already upon the scent," resumed D'Artagnan. "About three months ago I was near fighting a duel with Aramis, concerning a handkerchief resembling the one you showed the woman in his house—concerning a handkerchief marked in the same manner, I am sure."

"Sir," said the young woman, "you tire me very much, I assure you, by your questions."

"But you, madame, prudent as you are, think, if you were to be arrested with that handkerchief on you, and that handkerchief were to be seized, would you not be compromised?"

"In what way? Are not the initials mine? C.B.— Constance Bonacieux."

"Or Camille de Bois-Tracy."

"Silence, sir! once again, silence! Ah, since the dangers I incur on my own account cannot stop you, think of those you may yourself run!"

"Danger for me?"

"Yes; there is risk of imprisonment, risk of life, in knowing me."

"Then I will leave you no more."

"Sir," said the young woman, supplicating him and clasping her hands together—"sir, in the name of Heaven, by a soldier's honour, by the courtesy of a gentleman, depart! There! hear midnight striking; that is the hour at which I am expected."

"Madame," said the young man, bowing, "I can refuse nothing asked of me thus. Be satisfied; I will go."

"But you will not follow me—you will not watch me?"

"I will return home instantly."

"Ah, I was quite sure you were an excellent young man," said Madame Bonacieux, holding out her hand to him, and placing the other upon the knocker of a little door almost hidden in the wall.

D'Artagnan seized the hand that was held out to him, and kissed it ardently.

"Ah, I wish I had never seen you!" cried D'Artagnan, with that ingenuous roughness which women often prefer to the affectations of politeness, because it reveals the entire thought, and proves that feeling prevails over reason.

"Well," resumed Madame Bonacieux, in a voice that was almost caressing, and pressing the hand of D'Artagnan, who had not let go of hers—"well, I will not say what you do. What is lost for to-day may not be lost for ever. Who knows, when I shall be some day at liberty, whether I may not satisfy your curiosity?"

"And will you make the same promise to my love?" cried D'Artagnan, beside himself with joy.

"Oh, as to that, I will not engage myself. That depends upon the sentiments you may inspire me with."

"So to-day, madame——"

"Oh, to-day I have got no further than gratitude."

"Ah, you are too charming," said D'Artagnan sorrowfully; "and you abuse my love."

"No, I make use of your generosity, that's all. But

be of good cheer. With certain people everything comes round all right."

"Oh, you make me the happiest of men! Do not forget this evening—do not forget your promise."

"Be satisfied. At the proper time and place I will remember everything. Well, now then, go; go, in the name of Heaven! I was expected exactly at midnight, and I am late."

"By five minutes."

"Yes; but in certain circumstances five minutes are five centuries."

"When one loves."

"Well, and who told you I had not to do with some one in love?"

"It is a man, then, that expects you!" cried D'Artagnan —"a man!"

"Come, come; the discussion is going to begin again!" said Madame Bonacieux, with a half-smile which was not free from a certain tinge of impatience.

"No, no; I am going, I am going! I believe in you, and I would have all the merit of my devotion, even though that devotion were a stupidity. Adieu, madame, adieu!"

And as if he felt that only a violent effort would give him the strength to detach himself from the hand he held, he sprang away, running; while Madame Bonacieux knocked, as she had done at the shutter, three slow regular taps. Then, when he had gained the corner of the street, he looked around. The door had been opened and shut again; the mercer's pretty wife had disappeared.

D'Artagnan pursued his way. He had given his word not to watch Madame Bonacieux, and if his life had depended upon the place to which she was going, or the person who should accompany her, D'Artagnan would still have returned home, since he had promised that he would do so. In five minutes he was in the Rue des Fosso-yeurs.

"Poor Athos!" said he; "he will never guess what all this means. He must have fallen asleep waiting for me, or else he must have returned home, where he will have learned that a woman had been there. A woman at Athos's house! After all," continued D'Artagnan, "there was certainly one in Aramis's house. All this is very strange; I should like to know how it will all end."

"Badly, sir, badly!" replied a voice, which the young man recognized as Planchet's; for, soliloquizing aloud, as very preoccupied people do, he had entered the alley, at the end of which were the stairs which led to his chamber.

"How badly? What do you mean by that, you stupid fellow?" asked D'Artagnan. "What has happened, then?"

"All sorts of misfortunes."

"What?"

"In the first place, M. Athos is arrested."

"Arrested! Athos arrested! What for?"

"He was found in your lodging; they took him for you."

"And who arrested him?"

"The guard brought by the men in black whom you put to flight."

"Why did he not tell them his name? Why did he not tell them he knew nothing about this affair?"

"He took care not to do so, sir. On the contrary, he came up to me, and said, 'It is your master who needs his liberty at this moment, and not I, since he knows everything and I know nothing. They will believe he is arrested, and that will give him time. In three days I will tell them who I am, and they cannot fail to set me at liberty again.'"

"Bravo, Athos! noble heart!" murmured D'Artagnan. "I know him well there. And what did the bailiffs do?"

"Four of them led him away, I don't know where—to the Bastille or Fort l'Evêque. Two remained with the men in black, who rummaged everywhere, and took all the papers. The last two mounted guard at the door during this examination; then, when all was over, they went away, leaving the house empty and the doors open."

"And Porthos and Aramis?"

"I could not find them; they did not come."

"But they may come at any moment, for you left word that I was expecting them?"

"Yes, sir."

"Well, don't stir from here, then. If they come, tell them what has happened. Let them wait for me at the Pomme de Pin. Here it would be dangerous; the house may be watched. I will run to M. de Tréville's to tell him all this, and will join them there."

"Very well, sir," said Planchet.

"But you will remain, will you not? You are not afraid?" said D'Artagnan, coming back to encourage his lackey.

"Be satisfied, sir," said Planchet; "you do not know me yet. I am brave when I am set about it—the difficulty lies wholly in starting; besides, I am a Picard."

" Then that's understood," said D'Artagnan. " You will be killed rather than desert your post ? "

" Yes, sir ; and there is nothing I would not do to prove my attachment to you."

" Good ! " said D'Artagnan to himself. " It appears that the method I have adopted with this fellow is decidedly a good one ; I shall employ it upon occasion."

And his legs, already a little fatigued with running about during the day, carried D'Artagnan as fast as they could towards the Rue du Colombier.

M. de. Tréville was not at his hôtel. His company was on guard at the Louvre ; he was at the Louvre with his company.

He must get at M. de Tréville ; it was important that he should be informed of what was going on. D'Artagnan resolved to endeavour to get into the Louvre. His costume of a guard in the company of M. des Essarts would, he thought, be a passport for him.

He therefore went down the Rue des Petits Augustins, and walked up the quay, in order to reach the Pont Neuf. He had had for a moment the idea of passing over by the ferryboat ; but on gaining the riverside, he had mechanically put his hand into his pocket, and perceived that he had not the wherewithal to pay the ferryman.

As he was arriving at the end of the Rue Guénégaud he saw, coming out of the Rue Dauphine, two persons whose appearance struck his attention. One was a man, and the other a woman.

The woman had Madame Bonacieux's figure, and the man resembled Aramis so much as to be mistaken for him.

Besides, the woman had on that black cloak, which D'Artagnan could still see outlined upon the shutter of the Rue de Vaugirard, and upon the door of the Rue de la Harpe.

And still further, the man wore the uniform of the musketeers.

The woman's hood was pulled down, and the man held his handkerchief up to his face. Both, as this double precaution indicated—both had an interest, then, in not being recognized.

They followed the bridge. That was D'Artagnan's road, since D'Artagnan was going to the Louvre. D'Artagnan followed them.

He had not gone twenty steps before he became con-

vinced that the woman was really Madame Bonacieux, and
the man Aramis.

He felt at that instant all the suspicions of jealousy
agitating his heart.

He was doubly betrayed—by his friend, and by her
whom he already loved as a mistress. Madame Bonacieux
had sworn by all that was holy that she did not know
Aramis, and a quarter of an hour after she had taken this
oath he found her hanging on Aramis's arm.

D'Artagnan did not reflect at all that he had known the
mercer's pretty wife for three hours only, that she owed
him nothing but a little gratitude for having delivered him
from the men in black who wished to carry her off, and
that she had promised him nothing. He considered himself to be an outraged, betrayed, and ridiculed lover. The
blood mounted angrily to his face. He resolved to unravel
the mystery.

The young man and woman had perceived they were
followed, and had redoubled their speed. D'Artagnan
hastened on, passed them, then turned on them at the
moment they were before the Samaritaine, which was
illuminated by a lamp that threw its light over all this part
of the bridge.

D'Artagnan stopped before them, and they stopped before
him.

"What do you want, sir?" demanded the musketeer,
drawing back a step, and with a foreign accent which
proved to D'Artagnan that he was deceived in one part of
his conjectures at least.

"It is not Aramis!" cried he.

"No, sir, it is not Aramis; and by your exclamation,
I perceive you have mistaken me for another, and pardon
you."

"You pardon me!" cried D'Artagnan.

"Yes," replied the unknown. "Allow me, then, to pass
on, since it is not with me you have anything to do."

"You are right, sir; it is not with you I have anything
to do. It is with madame here."

"With madame! You do not know her!" replied the
stranger.

"You are mistaken, sir; I know her very well."

"Ah," said Madame Bonacieux, in a tone of reproach
—"ah, sir, I had the promise of a soldier and the word
of a gentleman. I thought I might have depended upon
them!"

"And I, madame!" said D'Artagnan, embarrassed; "you promised me——"

"Take my arm, madame," said the stranger, "and let us proceed on our way."

D'Artagnan, however, stupefied, cast down, annihilated by all that had happened, stood, with his arms crossed, before the musketeer and Madame Bonacieux.

The musketeer advanced a step or two, and pushed D'Artagnan aside with his hand.

D'Artagnan made a spring backwards, and drew his sword.

At the same time, and with the rapidity of lightning, the unknown drew his.

"In the name of Heaven, milord!" cried Madame Bonacieux, throwing herself between the combatants, and seizing the swords with her hands.

"Milord!" cried D'Artagnan, enlightened by a sudden idea—"milord! Pardon me, sir, but are you not——"

"Milord, the Duke of Buckingham!" said Madame Bonacieux in an undertone; "and now you may ruin us all."

"Milord—madame—I ask a hundred pardons. But I love her, milord, and was jealous. You know what it is to love, milord. Pardon me, and then tell me how I can risk my life to serve your grace."

"You are a good young man!" said Buckingham, holding out his hand to D'Artagnan, who pressed it respectfully. "You offer me your services; I accept them. Follow us at a distance of twenty paces to the Louvre, and if any one watches us, slay him!"

D'Artagnan placed his naked sword under his arm, allowed the duke and Madame Bonacieux to proceed twenty steps, and then followed them, ready to carry out to the letter the instructions of the noble and elegant minister of Charles I.

But fortunately the young seid had no opportunity to give the duke this proof of his devotion, and the young woman and the handsome musketeer entered the Louvre by the wicket of L'Echelle without any interference.

As for D'Artagnan, he immediately repaired to the tavern of the Pomme de Pin, where he found Porthos and Aramis, who were waiting for him. But, without giving them any explanation of the inconvenience he had caused them, he told them that he had himself terminated the affair in which he had thought for a moment he should need their assistance.

And now, carried away as we are by our story, we must leave our three friends to return each to his own home, and follow the Duke of Buckingham and his guide through the windings of the Louvre.

CHAPTER XII.

GEORGE VILLIERS, DUKE OF BUCKINGHAM.

MADAME BONACIEUX and the duke entered the Louvre without difficulty. Madame Bonacieux was known to belong to the queen; the duke wore the uniform of the musketeers of M. de Tréville, who, as we have said, were that evening on guard. Besides, Germain was in the interests of the queen; and if anything should happen, Madame Bonacieux would only be accused of having introduced her lover into the Louvre. She took the risk upon herself. To be sure, her reputation was jeopardized, but of what value in society was the reputation of the mercer's pretty wife?

Once within the interior of the court, the duke and the young woman kept along the side of the wall for about twenty-five steps. This space passed, Madame Bonacieux pushed a little side door, open by day, but generally closed at night. The door yielded. Both entered, and found themselves in darkness. But Madame Bonacieux was acquainted with all the turnings and windings of this part of the Louvre, set apart for the royal attendants. She closed the door after him, took the duke by the hand, advanced a little, feeling her way, came to a balustrade, put her foot upon the bottom step, and began to ascend a flight of stairs. The duke counted two stories. She then turned to the right, followed a long corridor, descended a flight of steps, went a few steps farther, introduced a key into a lock, opened a door, and pushed the duke into an apartment lighted only by a night lamp, saying, " Remain here, my lord duke; some one will soon come." She then went out by the same door, which she locked, so that the duke found himself literally a prisoner.

Nevertheless, isolated as he was, we must say that the Duke of Buckingham did not experience a moment's fear. One of the salient points of his character was the search of adventures and a love of the romantic. Brave, bold, enterprising, this was not the first time he had risked his life in such attempts. He had learned that the pretended message from Anne of Austria, upon the faith of which he had come to Paris, was a snare; but instead of going back to England, he had, taking undue advantage of the position in which he had been placed, declared to the queen that he would not go back again without having seen her. The queen had at first positively refused, but at length became afraid that the duke, if exasperated, would commit some rash deed. She had already decided upon seeing him and urging his immediate departure, when, on the very evening of coming to this decision, Madame Bonacieux, who was charged with going to fetch the duke and conducting him to the Louvre, was carried off. During two days it was not known what had become of her, and everything remained in suspense. But when once free, and placed in communication with La Porte, matters resumed their course, and she accomplished the perilous enterprise which, but for her abduction, would have been executed three days earlier.

Buckingham, on being left alone, walked towards a mirror. His musketeer's uniform became him wonderfully well.

At thirty-five, which was then his age, he rightly passed for the handsomest gentleman and the most elegant cavalier in France or England.

The favourite of two kings, immensely rich, all-powerful in a kingdom which he threw into disorder at his fancy and calmed again at his caprice, George Villiers, Duke of Buckingham, had undertaken to live one of those fabled existences which survive in the course of centuries as an astonishment to posterity.

Therefore, sure of himself, convinced of his own power, certain that the laws which rule other men could not reach him, he went straight at the goal he had set for himself, even though this goal were so elevated and so dazzling that it would have been madness for any other even to have contemplated it. In this way he had succeeded in gaining access several times to the beautiful and haughty Anne of Austria, and in making himself loved by her by dazzling her.

George Villiers placed himself, then, before the mirror, as we have said, restored to his beautiful hair the curls which the weight of his hat had disordered, twisted his moustache, and, with a heart swelling with joy, happy and proud on approaching the moment he had so long sighed for, he smiled upon himself with pride and hope.

At this instant a door concealed in the tapestry was opened, and a woman appeared. Buckingham saw this apparition in the glass. He uttered a cry. It was the queen!

Anne of Austria was then twenty-six or twenty-seven years of age—that is to say, she was in the full splendour of her beauty.

Her carriage was that of a queen or a goddess. Her eyes, which reflected emerald hues, were perfectly beautiful, and yet were, at the same time, full of sweetness and majesty.

Her mouth was small and rosy, and although her under lip, like that of the princes of the house of Austria, protruded slightly beyond the other, it was eminently lovely in its smile, but also profoundly disdainful in its contempt.

Her skin was admired for its velvety softness, her hands and arms were of surpassing beauty. All the poets of the time sang of them as incomparable.

Lastly, her hair, which, from being light in her youth, had become chestnut, and which she wore in loose curls, and with much powder, admirably set off her face, in which the most rigid critic could only have desired a little less rouge, and the most fastidious sculptor a more delicate chiselled nose.

Buckingham remained for a moment dazzled. Never had Anne of Austria appeared to him so beautiful, amid balls, fêtes, or tournaments, as she appeared to him at this moment, dressed in a simple robe of white satin, and accompanied by Doña Estefana, the only one of her Spanish women that had not been driven from her by the jealousy of the king, or by the persecutions of Richelieu.

Anne of Austria advanced two steps. Buckingham threw himself at her feet, and before the queen could prevent him, kissed the hem of her robe.

"Duke, you already know that it is not I who caused you to be written to."

"Yes, yes, madame! yes, your Majesty!" cried the duke. "I know that I must have been mad, senseless, to believe that snow would become animated or marble warm. But what then? They who love easily believe in love; besides, this journey is not wholly lost, since I see you."

"Yes," replied Anne; "but you know why and how I see you, milord? Because, insensible to all my sufferings, you persist in remaining in a city where, by remaining, you run the risk of your own life, and make me run the risk of losing my honour. I see you to tell you that everything separates us—the depths of the sea, the enmity of kingdoms, the sanctity of vows. It is sacrilege to struggle against so many things, milord. In short, I see you to tell you that we must never see each other again."

"Speak on, madame, speak on, queen," said Buckingham; "the sweetness of your voice covers the harshness of your words. You talk of sacrilege; but the sacrilege lies in the separation of two hearts formed by God for each other."

"Milord," cried the queen, "you forget that I have never told you I loved you."

"But you have never told me that you did not love me; and, truly, to speak such words to me would be, on the part of your Majesty, too great an ingratitude. For, tell me, where can you find a love like mine—a love which neither time, nor absence, nor despair can extinguish—a love which contents itself with a lost ribbon, a stray look, or a chance word? It is now three years, madame, since I saw you for the first time, and during those three years I have loved you in this way. Shall I tell you how you were dressed the first time I saw you? Shall I describe to you every one of the ornaments you wore? Mark; I see you now! You were seated upon cushions, in the Spanish fashion. You wore a robe of green satin embroidered with gold and silver, with hanging sleeves fastened upon your beautiful arms, upon those lovely arms, with large diamonds. You wore a close ruff, a small cap upon your head, of the same colour as your dress, and in that cap a heron's feather. O madame, madame! I shut my eyes, and I can see you such as you then were. I open them again, and I see you such as you are now—a hundred times still more beautiful!"

"What folly," murmured Anne of Austria, who had not the courage to find fault with the duke for having so well preserved her portrait in his heart—"what folly to feed a useless passion with such memories!"

"And upon what, then, must I live? I have nothing but memories. They are my happiness, my treasures, my hopes. Every time that I see you is a fresh diamond, which I enclose in the casket of my heart. This is the fourth which you have let fall and I have picked up—for in three years, madame, I have only seen you four times—the first, which I have just described to you; the second, at the mansion of Madame de Chevreuse; the third, in the gardens at Amiens."

"Duke," said the queen, blushing, "never name that evening."

"Oh yes, let me speak of it; on the contrary, let me speak of it, madame. That was the happiest and most radiant evening of my life. Do you not remember what a beautiful night it was — how soft and perfumed the air, and how lovely the blue star-enamelled sky? Ah, that time, madame, I was able for one instant to be alone with you. That time you were about to tell me all—the isolation of your life, the griefs of your heart. You leaned upon my arm—upon this one, madame. I felt, in bending my head towards you, your beautiful hair touch my cheek; and every time that it did touch me, I trembled from head to foot. O queen, queen! you do not know what felicity from heaven, what joys from Paradise, are comprised in a moment like that. I would give all my wealth, all my fortune, all my glory, all the days I have to live, for such an instant, for a night like that! For that night, madame, that night you loved me, I will swear it."

"Milord, yes; it is possible that the influence of the place, the charm of the beautiful evening, the fascination of your look, the thousand circumstances, in short, which sometimes unite to ruin a woman, were grouped around me on that fatal evening. But, milord, you saw the queen come to the aid of the woman who was beginning to yield. At the first word you dared to utter, at the first freedom to which I had to reply, I summoned my attendants."

"Yes, yes, that is true; and any other love but mine would have sunk beneath this ordeal; but my love came out from it more ardent and more eternal. You believed you should fly from me by returning to Paris; you believed that I should not dare to quit the treasure over which my master had charged me to watch. What to me were all the treasures in the world, or all the kings of the earth? A week later I was back again, madame. That time you had nothing to say to me. I had risked my life and my favour to see you but for a second. I did not even touch your hand, and you pardoned me on seeing me so submissive and so repentant."

"Yes, but calumny seized upon all those follies in which I took no part, as you well know, milord. The king, excited by the cardinal, made a terrible scandal. Madame de Vernet was driven from me, Putange was exiled, Madame de Chevreuse fell into disgrace; and when you wished to come back as ambassador to France, the king himself, remember, milord, the king himself opposed it."

"Yes, and France is about to pay for her king's refusal

with a war. I am not allowed to see you, madame. Very well. I wish that each day you should hear me spoken of. What object, think you, have this expedition to Ré and this league with the Protestants of Rochelle which I am planning? The pleasure of seeing you. I have no hope of penetrating, sword in hand, to Paris; I know that well. But this war may bring about a peace; this peace will require a negotiator. I will be that negotiator. They will not dare to refuse me then; and I shall return to Paris, and I shall see you, and shall be happy for an instant. Thousands of men, it is true, will have to pay for my happiness with their lives; but what will that signify to me, provided I see you again! All this is perhaps madness, folly; but tell me what woman has a lover more truly in love? What queen has a more ardent servant?"

"Milord, milord! you invoke in your defence things which accuse you more strongly. Milord, all these proofs of love that you desire to give me are little better than crimes."

"Because you do not love me, madame. If you loved me you would see all this differently. If you loved me, oh! if you loved me, that would be too great happiness, and I should go mad. Ah, Madame de Chevreuse, of whom you spoke just now—Madame de Chevreuse was less cruel than you. Holland loved her, and she responded to his love."

"Madame de Chevreuse was not a queen," murmured Anne of Austria, overcome in spite of herself by the expression of so profound a passion.

"You would love me, then, if you were not a queen! Madame, you say that you would love me then! I am then to believe that it is the dignity of your rank alone that makes you cruel to me. I may then believe that if you had been Madame de Chevreuse, poor Buckingham might have hoped? Thanks for those sweet words, oh, my lovely queen! A hundred times, thanks!"

"O milord, you have misconceived, wrongly interpreted; I did not mean——"

"Silence, silence!" cried the duke. "If I am happy in an error, do not have the cruelty to deprive me of it. You have told me yourself, madame, that I have been drawn into a snare; and I, perhaps, shall leave my life in it—for, strangely enough, I have for some time had a presentiment that I shall shortly die." And the duke smiled, with a smile at once sad and charming.

"Oh, my God!" cried Anne of Austria, with an accent of terror which proved how much greater was the interest she took in the duke than she ventured to tell.

"I do not tell you this, madame, to terrify you; no, what I say to you is even ridiculous; and, believe me, I do not heed such dreams. But the words you have just spoken, the hope you have almost given me, will have richly paid for all, were it even my life."

"Oh, but I," said Anne—"I, duke, have had presentiments likewise; I have had dreams. I dreamed that I saw you lying bleeding, wounded."

"In the left side, was it not, and with a knife?" interrupted Buckingham.

"Yes, it was so, milord, it was so—in the left side, and with a knife. Who can possibly have told you I had had that dream? I have imparted it to no one but my God, and only then in my prayers."

"I ask for no more. You love me, madame. It is enough."

"I love you! I?"

"Yes, yes. Would God send the same dreams to you as to me if you did not love me? Should we have the same presentiments if our existences did not meet in our hearts? You love me, my queen, and you will weep for me?"

"Oh, my God, my God!" cried Anne of Austria, "this is more than I can bear. In the name of Heaven, duke, leave me—go! I do not know whether I love you or do not love you, but what I know is, that I will not be a perjured woman. Take pity on me, then, and go. Oh, if you are struck in France, if you die in France, if I could imagine that your love for me was the cause of your death, nothing could ever console me; I should go mad. Depart, then; go, I implore you!"

"Oh, how beautiful you are so! Oh, how I love you!" said Buckingham.

"Oh, but go—go back, I implore you, and return later on! Come as ambassador, come as minister, come surrounded with guards who will defend you, with servants who will watch over you, and then—then I shall no longer fear for your life, and I shall be happy in seeing you again."

"Oh, is this true, is what you say true?"

"Yes."

"Then, some pledge of your indulgence, some object which, coming from you, may assure me that I have not dreamed ; something you have worn, and that I may wear in my turn—a ring, a necklace, a chain !"

"Will you go then, will you go, if I give you what you ask for ? "

"Yes."

"This very instant ? "

"Yes."

"You will leave France, you will return to England ? "

"I will, I swear to you I will."

"Wait, then, wait."

And Anne of Austria went into her apartment, and came out again almost immediately, holding a casket in her hand made of rosewood, with her monogram incrusted in gold.

"Here, milord, here," said she ; "keep this in memory of me."

Buckingham took the casket, and fell a second time on his knees.

"You promised me you would go back," said the queen.

"And I keep my word. Your hand, madame, your hand, and I depart."

Anne of Austria stretched forth her hand, closing her eyes, and leaned the other upon Estefana, for she felt her strength was about to fail her.

Buckingham pressed his lips passionately to that beautiful hand, and then rising, said,—

"Within six months, if I am not dead, I shall have seen you again, madame, even if I have upset the whole world for it."

And, faithful to the promise he had made, he rushed out of the apartment.

In the corridor he met Madame Bonacieux, who was waiting for him, and who, with the same precautions and the same good fortune, led him out of the Louvre.

CHAPTER XIII.

MONSIEUR BONACIEUX.

THERE was in all this, as may have been noticed, one personage of whom, notwithstanding his precarious position, we have appeared to take but very little notice. This personage was M. Bonacieux, the respectable martyr of the political and amorous intrigues which were getting into such a tangle in this gallant and chivalric period.

Fortunately, as the reader may remember, or may not remember—fortunately we promised not to lose sight of him.

The officers who had arrested him conducted him straight to the Bastile, where, all of a tremble, he was made to pass before a platoon of soldiers who were loading their muskets.

Thence, introduced into a half-subterranean gallery, he became, on the part of those who had brought him, the object of the grossest insults and the harshest treatment. The bailiffs perceived that they had not to deal with a nobleman, and they treated him like a very beggar.

At the end of half an hour, or thereabouts, an officer came to put an end to his tortures, but not to his anxiety, by giving the order to lead M. Bonacieux to the examination chamber.

Ordinarily, prisoners were questioned in their own cells, but with M. Bonacieux they did not use so many formalities.

Two guards took hold of the mercer, made him cross a court, enter a corridor in which were three sentinels, then opened a door and pushed him unceremoniously into a low room, the whole furnishings of which consisted of one table, one chair, and a superintendent of police. The superintendent was seated in the chair, and was busily writing at the table.

The two guards led the prisoner towards the table, and upon a sign from the superintendent drew back so far as to be unable to hear anything.

The superintendent, who had till this time held his head down over his papers, looked up to see what sort of person he had to deal with. This superintendent was a man of repulsive mien, with a pointed nose, yellow and salient cheek-bones, small but keen, penetrating eyes, and an expression of countenance resembling at once the polecat and the fox. His head, supported by a long and flexible neck, issued from his large black robe, balancing itself, with a motion very much like that of the tortoise when drawing its head out of its shell.

He began by asking M. Bonacieux his full name, age, condition, and abode.

The accused replied that his name was Jacques Michel Bonacieux, that he was fifty-one years old, was a retired mercer, and lived at No. 11 Rue des Fossoyeurs.

The superintendent then, instead of continuing to question him, made him a long speech upon the danger there was for an obscure bourgeois to meddle with public matters.

He complicated this exordium by an exposition in which

he painted the power and the acts of the cardinal—that incomparable minister, that conqueror of past ministers, that example for ministers to come—acts and power which no one could thwart with impunity.

After this second part of his discourse, fixing his hawk's eye upon poor Bonacieux, he bade him reflect upon the seriousness of his situation.

The reflections of the mercer were already made. He consigned to the devil the moment when M. de la Porte had formed the idea of marrying him to his goddaughter, and particularly the moment when that goddaughter had been received mistress of the linen to her Majesty.

The character of M. Bonacieux was one of profound selfishness, mixed with sordid avarice, the whole seasoned with extreme cowardice. The love with which his young wife had inspired him was a secondary sentiment, and was not strong enough to contend with the primitive feelings we have just enumerated.

Bonacieux did reflect, in fact, upon what had just been said to him.

"But, superintendent," said he timidly, "I beg you to believe that I know and appreciate more than anybody the merit of the incomparable eminence by whom we have the honour to be governed."

"Really?" asked the superintendent, with an air of doubt—"really? If that is truly so, how came you in the Bastille?"

"How I came here, or rather why I came here," replied Bonacieux, "is entirely impossible for me to tell you, because I myself don't know; but to a certainty it is not for having—knowingly, at least—disobliged the cardinal."

"You must, nevertheless, have committed a crime, since you are here, and are accused of high treason."

"Of high treason!" cried the terrified Bonacieux—"high treason! How is it possible for a poor mercer, who detests all Huguenots, and who abhors all Spaniards, to be accused of high treason? Consider, sir, the thing is materially impossible."

"Monsieur Bonacieux," said the superintendent, looking at the accused as if his little eyes had the faculty of reading to the very depths of the heart—"Monsieur Bonacieux, you have a wife?"

"Yes, sir," replied the mercer, all of a tremble, feeling that this was the point at which affairs were likely to get mixed up—"that is to say, I had one."

"What! you had one ? What have you done with her, then, if you have her no longer ? "

" She has been carried off from me, sir."

" Been carried off from you ? " said the superintendent. " Ah ! "

Bonacieux felt, when he heard this " ah," that matters were becoming more and more entangled.

" She has been carried off," resumed the superintendent. " And do you know who the man is that has committed this outrage ? "

" I think I know him."

" Who is he ? "

" Remember that I affirm nothing, superintendent, and that I only suspect."

" Whom do you suspect ? Come, answer freely."

M. Bonacieux was in the greatest possible perplexity. Had he better deny everything or tell everything ? By denying all, it might be suspected that he knew too much to confess ; by confessing all, he would prove his goodwill. He decided, then, upon telling all.

" I suspect," said he, " a tall, dark man, of lofty carriage, who has the air of a great lord. He followed us several times, as I think, when I waited for my wife at the wicket of the Louvre to fetch her home."

The superintendent appeared to experience a little uneasiness.

" And his name ? " said he.

" Oh, as to his name, I know nothing about that ; but if I were ever to meet him, I should know him in an instant, I will answer for it, even if he were among a thousand persons."

The face of the superintendent grew still darker.

" You would recognize him among a thousand, say you ? " continued he.

" That is to say," cried Bonacieux, who saw he had gone wrong—"that is to say——"

" You answered that you would recognize him," said the superintendent. " That is very well, and enough for to-day. Before we proceed further, some one must be informed that you know the abductor of your wife."

" But I did not tell you that I know him ! " cried Bonacieux in despair. " I told you, on the contrary——"

" Take away the prisoner," said the superintendent to the two guards.

" Where shall we place him ? " demanded the officer.

" In a dungeon."

" Which one ? "

" Good Lord ! in the first you come to, provided it be a safe one," said the superintendent, with an indifference which filled poor Bonacieux with horror.

" Alas, alas ! " said he to himself, " misfortune hangs over me ; my wife must have committed some frightful crime. They believe that I am her accomplice, and will punish me with her ! She must have spoken, she must have confessed everything—a woman is so weak ! A dungeon, the first he comes to ! That's it ! One night is soon over ; and to-morrow to the wheel, to the gallows ! Oh, my God, my God, have pity on me ! "

Without listening the least in the world to the lamentations of M. Bonacieux — lamentations to which, indeed, they must have been pretty well accustomed—the two guards took the prisoner each by an arm, and led him away, while the superintendent wrote a letter in haste while his recorder was waiting.

Bonacieux could not close his eyes — not because his dungeon was so very disagreeable, but because his uneasiness was too great to allow him to sleep. He sat up all night upon his stool, starting at the least noise ; and when the first rays of the sun penetrated into his cell, the dawn itself appeared to him to have taken on a funereal tint.

All at once he heard his bolts drawn, and sprang up with a terrible bound, believing that they had come to lead him to the scaffold. Therefore when he saw purely and simply his superintendent and recorder of the preceding evening appear, instead of the executioner he was expecting, he was ready to embrace them both.

" Your affair has become more complicated since yesterday evening, my good man, and I advise you to tell the whole truth ; for your repentance alone can remove the cardinal's anger."

" Why, I am ready to tell everything," cried Bonacieux— " at least, all that I know. Question me, I entreat you ! "

" Where is your wife, in the first place ? "

" Why, did not I tell you she had been stolen away from me ? "

" Yes ; but yesterday, at five o'clock in the afternoon, thanks to you, she escaped."

" My wife escaped ! " cried Bonacieux. " Oh, unfortunate creature ! Sir, if she has escaped, it is no fault of mine, I will swear."

" What business had you, then, to go into the chamber of M. d'Artagnan, your lodger, with whom you had a long conference in the course of the day ? "

" Ah, yes, superintendent—yes, that is true, and I confess that I was in the wrong. I did go to M. d'Artagnan's apartment."

" What was the object of your visit ? "

" To beg him to assist me in finding my wife. I believed I had a right to endeavour to recover her. I was mistaken, as it appears, and I ask your pardon for so doing."

" And what did M. d'Artagnan reply ? "

" M. d'Artagnan promised me his assistance ; but I soon found out that he was betraying me."

" You are trifling with justice ! M. d'Artagnan made an agreement with you, and in virtue of that agreement put to flight the police officers who had arrested your wife, and placed her out of reach of all inquiries."

" M. d'Artagnan has carried off my wife ! What can that mean ? "

" Fortunately M. d'Artagnan is in our hands, and you shall be confronted with him."

" Ah, 'pon my word, I ask nothing better," cried Bonacieux ; " I shall not be sorry to see the face of an acquaintance."

" Bring in M. d'Artagnan," said the superintendent to the guards.

The two guards led in Athos.

" Monsieur d'Artagnan," said the superintendent, addressing Athos, " declare what passed between you and the gentleman here."

" But," cried Bonacieux, " that is not M. d'Artagnan whom you show me ! "

" What ! not M. d'Artagnan ! " exclaimed the superintendent.

" Not the least in the world like him," replied Bonacieux.

" What is this gentleman's name ? " asked the superintendent.

" I cannot tell you ; I don't know him."

" How ! you don't know him ? "

" No."

" Did you never see him ? "

" Yes, I have seen him, but I don't know what his name is."

" Your name ? " asked the superintendent.

" Athos," replied the musketeer.

" But that is not a man's name ; that is the name of a

mountain," cried the poor superintendent, who began to feel a little bewildered.

"That is my name," said Athos quietly.

"But you said that your name was D'Artagnan."

"Who ?—I ?"

"Yes, you."

"That is to say, some one asked me, 'You are Monsieur d'Artagnan?' I answered, 'You think so, do you?' My guards exclaimed that they were sure I was. I did not think it worth while to contradict them. Besides, I might myself be deceived."

"Sir, you insult the majesty of justice."

"Not at all," said Athos calmly.

"You are Monsieur d'Artagnan."

"You see, sir, that you persist in saying that I am."

"But I tell you, superintendent," cried Bonacieux in his turn, "there is not the least doubt about the matter. M. d'Artagnan is my tenant, and consequently, although he does not pay me my rent, and even the more on that account, I ought to know him. M. d'Artagnan is a young man, scarcely nineteen or twenty, and this gentleman must be thirty at least. M. d'Artagnan is in M. des Essarts's guards, and this gentleman is in the company of M. de Tréville's musketeers. Look at his uniform, superintendent, look at his uniform!"

"That's true," murmured the superintendent; "zounds! that's true."

At this moment the door was opened quickly, and a messenger, introduced by one of the gatekeepers of the Bastille, gave a letter to the superintendent.

"Oh, unhappy woman!" cried the superintendent.

"How? What do you say? Of whom do you speak? It is not of my wife, I hope!"

"On the contrary, it is of her. Your affair is becoming a pretty one."

"But," cried the exasperated mercer, "do me the pleasure, sir, to tell me how my own affair can become the worse by anything my wife does while I am in prison."

"Because what she does is part of a plan concerted between you—of an infernal plan!"

"I swear to you, superintendent, that you are profoundly mistaken; that I know nothing in the world about what my wife had to do; that I am an entire stranger to what she has done; and that if she has committed any follies, I renounce her, I abjure her, I curse her!"

"Bah!" said Athos to the superintendent; "if you have no further need of me, send me somewhere. Your Monsieur Bonacieux is very tiresome."

"Lead back the prisoners to their cells," said the superintendent, designating, by the same gesture, Athos and Bonacieux, "and let them be guarded more closely than ever."

"And yet," said Athos, with his habitual calmness, "if it be M. d'Artagnan who is concerned in this matter, I do not see very well how I can take his place."

"Do as I bade you," cried the superintendent, "and preserve the profoundest secrecy. You understand me?"

Athos shrugged his shoulders, and followed his guards, while M. Bonacieux uttered lamentations enough to break a tiger's heart.

They led back the mercer to the same dungeon in which he had passed the night, and left him to himself the whole day. Bonacieux wept the whole day like a true mercer, not being at all a military man, as he himself informed us.

In the evening, at the moment when he had made his mind up to lie down upon the bed, he heard steps in his corridor. These steps drew near to his cell, the door was thrown open, and the guards appeared.

"Follow me," said an officer, who came behind the guards.

"Follow you!" cried Bonacieux. "Follow you at this hour! Where, in God's name?"

"Where we have orders to lead you."

"But that is not an answer."

"It is, nevertheless, the only one we can give you."

"Ah, my God, my God!" murmured the poor mercer, "now, indeed, I am lost!"

And, mechanically and without resistance, he followed the guards who came for him.

He passed along the same corridor as before, crossed a first court, then a second part of the building. At length, at the gate of the outer court, he found a carriage surrounded by four guards on horseback. They made him get into this carriage, the officer placed himself by his side, the door was locked, and both were left in a rolling prison.

The carriage was put in motion as slowly as a funeral car. Through the padlocked gratings the prisoner could see the houses and the pavement, that was all; but, true Parisian as he was, Bonacieux could recognize every street by the mounting stones, the signs, and the lamps. At the moment of reaching Saint Paul, the spot where such as were condemned at the Bastille were executed, he came near fainting, and crossed himself twice. He thought the carriage was about to stop there. The carriage, however, passed on.

Farther on, a still greater terror seized him on passing by the cemetery of Saint Jean, where state criminals were buried. One thing, however, reassured him : he remembered that before they were buried their heads were generally cut off, and he felt that his head was still on his shoulders. But when he saw the carriage take the way to La Grève, when he perceived the pointed roofs of the city hall, when the carriage passed under the arcade, he then thought all was over with him, wished to confess to the officer, and upon his refusal, uttered such pitiable cries that the officer told him if he continued to deafen him in that manner he should put a gag in his mouth.

This menace somewhat reassured Bonacieux. If they meant to execute him at La Grève, it could scarcely be worth while to gag him, as they had nearly reached the place of execution. In fact, the carriage crossed the fatal square without stopping.

There remained, then, no other place to fear but the Croix-du-Trahoir. The carriage was taking the direct road to it.

This time there was no longer any doubt : it was at the Croix-du-Trahoir that obscure criminals were executed. Bonacieux had flattered himself by believing himself worthy of Saint Paul or of the Place de Grève. It was at the Croix-du-Trahoir that his journey and his destiny were to end. He could not yet see that dreadful cross, but he felt as if it were in some sort coming to meet him. When he was within twenty paces of it he heard a great stir, and the carriage stopped. This was more than poor Bonacieux could endure, depressed as he was by the successive emotions which he had experienced. He uttered a feeble groan, which might have been taken for the last sigh of a dying man, and fainted.

CHAPTER XIV.

THE MAN OF MEUNG.

THE crowd was occasioned not by the expectation of a man who was to be hanged, but by the contemplation of a man who was hanged.

The carriage, which had been stopped for a minute, resumed its way, passed through the crowd, threaded the Rue Saint Honoré, turned the Rue des Bons Enfants, and stopped before a low door.

The door opened, two guards received Bonacieux in their arms from the officer, who supported him. They carried him along an alley, up a flight of stairs, and deposited him in an antechamber.

All these movements had been effected mechanically, as far as he was concerned. He had moved along as if in a dream; he had had a glimpse of objects as though through a fog; his ears had perceived sounds without comprehending them; he might have been executed at that moment without his making a single gesture in his own defence, or his uttering a cry to implore mercy.

He therefore remained upon the bench, with his back leaning against the wall and his hands hanging down, exactly on the spot where the guards had placed him.

On looking round him, however, as he could see no threatening object, as nothing indicated that he ran any real danger, as the bench was comfortably covered with a well-stuffed cushion, as the wall was ornamented with beautiful Cordova leather, and as large red damask curtains, held back by gold fastenings, floated before the window, he perceived by degrees that his fear was exaggerated, and he began to turn his head to the right and the left, upwards and downwards.

At this movement, which nobody opposed, he gained a little courage, and ventured to draw up one leg and then the other. At length, with the help of both hands, he raised himself up upon the bench, and found himself upon his feet.

At that moment an officer of pleasant appearance opened a door, continued to exchange some words with a person in the next room, and then came up to the prisoner.

" Is your name Bonacieux ? " said he.

" Yes, officer," stammered the mercer, more dead than alive, " at your service."

" Come in," said the officer.

And he moved aside to let the mercer pass. The latter obeyed without reply, and entered the room, where it appeared he was expected.

It was a large, close, and stifling cabinet, the walls furnished with arms offensive and defensive, and where there was already a fire, although it was scarcely the end of September. A square table, covered with books and papers, upon which was unrolled an immense plan of the city of Rochelle, occupied the centre of the apartment.

Standing before the fireplace was a man of middle height, of a haughty, proud mien, with piercing eyes, a broad brow, and a thin face, which was made still longer by a royal (or imperial, as it is now called), surmounted by a pair of moustaches. Although this man was scarcely thirty-six or thirty-seven years of age, hair, moustaches, and royal all were growing gray. This man, though without a sword, had all the appearance of a soldier; and his buff leather boots, still slightly covered with dust, showed that he had been on horseback in the course of the day.

This man was Armand Jean Duplessis, Cardinal Richelieu, not such as he is generally represented—broken down like an old man, suffering like a martyr, his body bent, his voice almost inaudible, buried in a large armchair as in an anticipated tomb, no longer living save by the strength of his genius, and no longer maintaining the struggle with Europe but by the eternal application of his thoughts—but such as he really was at this period; that is to say, an active and gallant cavalier, already weak of body, but sustained by that moral force which made him one of the most extraordinary men that ever existed, preparing, after having supported the Duke of Nevers in his duchy of Mantua, after having taken Nîmes, Castres, and Uzes, to drive the English from the island of Ré, and lay siege to Rochelle.

At first sight nothing indicated the cardinal, and it was impossible for those who did not know his face to guess in whose presence they were.

The poor mercer remained standing at the door, while the eyes of the personage we have just described were fixed upon him, and appeared to wish to penetrate even into the depths of his past.

" Is this Bonacieux ? " asked he, after a moment of silence.

" Yes, monseigneur," replied the officer.

" Very well. Give me those papers, and leave us."

The officer took the papers pointed out from the table, gave them to him who asked for them, bowed to the ground, and retired.

Bonacieux recognized in these papers his examination at the Bastille. From time to time the man at the fireplace raised his eyes from the writings, and plunged them like daggers into the heart of the poor mercer.

At the end of ten minutes' reading, and ten seconds of examination, the cardinal had made up his mind.

"That head has never conspired," murmured he; "but no matter—let us investigate just the same."

"You are accused of high treason," said the cardinal slowly.

"So I have been told already, monseigneur," cried Bonacieux, giving his questioner the title he had heard the officer give him; "but I swear to you that I know nothing about it."

The cardinal repressed a smile.

"You have conspired with your wife, with Madame de Chevreuse, and with milord the Duke of Buckingham."

"In fact, monseigneur, I have heard her pronounce all those names."

"And on what occasion?"

"She said that Cardinal Richelieu had drawn the Duke of Buckingham to Paris to ruin him and to ruin the queen."

"She said that?" cried the cardinal angrily.

"Yes, monseigneur; but I told her she was wrong to talk about such things, and that his Eminence was incapable——"

"Hold your tongue! You are a fool," replied the cardinal.

"That's exactly what my wife said, monseigneur."

"Do you know who carried off your wife?"

"No, monseigneur."

"You have suspicions, nevertheless?"

"Yes, monseigneur; but these suspicions appeared to be disagreeable to the superintendent, and I no longer have them."

"Your wife has escaped. Did you know that?"

"No, monseigneur; I learned it since I have been in prison, and then from the conversation of the superintendent —a very pleasant man."

The cardinal repressed another smile.

"Then you are ignorant of what has become of your wife since her flight?"

"Absolutely, monseigneur; but she has most likely returned to the Louvre."

"At one o'clock this morning she had not returned."

"My God! what can have become of her, then?"

"We shall know, be assured. Nothing is concealed from the cardinal; the cardinal knows everything."

"In that case, monseigneur, do you believe the cardinal will be so kind as to tell me what has become of my wife?"

"Perhaps he may; but you must, in the first place, reveal

to the cardinal all you know of your wife's relations with Madame de Chevreuse."

" But, monseigneur, I know nothing about them. I have never seen her."

" When you went to fetch your wife from the Louvre, did you always return directly home ? "

" Scarcely ever. She had business to transact with linen-drapers, to whose shops I escorted her."

" And how many were there of these linen-drapers ? "

" Two, monseigneur."

" And where did they live ? "

" One Rue de Vaugirard, the other Rue de la Harpe."

" Did you go into these houses with her ? "

" Never, monseigneur ; I waited at the door."

" And what excuse did she make for thus going in alone ? "

" She gave me none. She told me to wait, and I waited."

" You are a very complacent husband, my dear Monsieur Bonacieux," said the cardinal.

" He calls me his dear monsieur," said the mercer to himself. " Bah ! matters are going all right."

" Should you know those doors again ? "

" Yes."

" Do you know the numbers ? "

" Yes."

" What are they ? "

" No. 25 in the Rue de Vaugirard ; 75 in the Rue de la Harpe."

" Very well," said the cardinal.

At these words he took up a silver bell and rang it. The officer entered.

" Go," said he in a subdued voice, " and find Rochefort. Tell him to come to me immediately, if he has returned."

" The count is here," said the officer, " and wishes to speak instantly with your Eminence."

" Let him come in, then—let him come in, then ! " said the cardinal eagerly.

The officer rushed out of the apartment with that alacrity which all the cardinal's servants displayed in obeying him.

" To your Eminence ! " murmured Bonacieux, rolling his eyes round in astonishment.

Five seconds had not elapsed after the disappearance of the officer when the door opened and a new personage entered.

" It is he ! " cried Bonacieux.

" He ! What he ? " asked the cardinal.

" The man who took away my wife ! "

The cardinal rang a second time.   The officer reappeared.

" Place this man in the care of his two guards, and let him wait till I send for him."

" No, monseigneur, no, it is not he ! " cried Bonacieux ; " no, I was mistaken.   This is quite a different man, and does not resemble him at all.   The gentleman is a very good sort of man ! "

" Take away this fool ! " said the cardinal.

The officer took Bonacieux by the arm, and led him into the antechamber, where he found his two guards.

The newly-introduced personage followed Bonacieux impatiently with his eyes till he was gone out, and the moment the door closed he advanced eagerly toward the cardinal and said,—

" They have seen each other."

" Who ? " asked his Eminence.

" He and she."

" The queen and the duke ? " cried Richelieu.

" Yes."

" Where ? "

" At the Louvre."

" Are you sure of it ? "

" Perfectly sure."

" Who told you of it ? "

" Madame de Lannoy, who is devoted to your Eminence, as you know."

" Why did she not let me know sooner ? "

" Whether by chance or mistrust, the queen made Madame de Surgis sleep in her chamber, and kept her all day."

" Well, we are beaten !   Now let us try to take our revenge."

" I will assist you with all my heart, monseigneur ; be assured of that."

" How did it take place ? "

" At half-past twelve the queen was with her women——"

" Where ? "

" In her bedchamber——"

" Go on."

" When some one came and brought her a handkerchief from her *dame de lingerie*."

" And then ? "

" The queen immediately exhibited strong emotion, and, in spite of the rouge which covered her face, grew pale."

" Go on, go on ! "

" She, however, rose, and with a trembling voice, ' Ladies,' said she, 'wait for me ten minutes; I shall soon return.' She then opened the door of her alcove and went out."

"Why did not Madame de Lannoy come and inform you instantly?"

"Nothing was certain as yet. Besides, her Majesty had said, 'Ladies, wait for me,' and she dared not disobey the queen."

"How long did the queen remain outside of the chamber?"

"Three-quarters of an hour."

"Did none of her women accompany her?"

"Only Doña Estefana."

"And she afterwards returned?"

"Yes; but only to take a little rosewood casket, with her monogram upon it, and to go out again immediately."

"And when she finally returned, did she bring that casket with her?"

"No."

"Does Madame de Lannoy know what was in that casket?"

"Yes; the diamond studs which his Majesty gave the queen."

"And she came back without this casket?"

"Yes."

"Madame de Lannoy, then, is of the opinion that she gave them to Buckingham?"

"She is sure of it."

"How can she be sure?"

"In the course of the day Madame de Lannoy, in her quality of tire-woman of the queen, looked for this casket, appeared uneasy at not finding it, and at length asked the queen if she knew anything about it."

"And the queen?"

"The queen became exceedingly red, and replied that having on the preceding evening broken one of those studs, she had sent it to her goldsmith to be repaired."

"He must be called upon, and so ascertain if the thing be true or not."

"I have just been at his shop."

"And the goldsmith says?"

"The goldsmith has heard of nothing of the kind."

"Good! good! Rochefort, all is not lost; and perhaps —perhaps everything is for the best."

"The fact is, that I do not doubt your Eminence's genius——"

"Will repair the blunders of his agent; is that it?"

"That is exactly what I was going to say, if your Eminence had permitted me to finish my sentence."

"Do you know where the Duchesse de Chevreuse and the Duke of Buckingham were concealed?"

"No, monseigneur. My people could tell me nothing positive in regard to that."

"But I know."

"You, monseigneur?"

"Yes, or at least I suspect. They were, one in the Rue de Vaugirard, No. 25, the other in the Rue de la Harpe, No. 75."

"Does your Eminence wish them both to be arrested?"

"It is too late; they will be gone."

"But still we can make sure of it."

"Take ten men of my guards, and search both houses thoroughly."

"Instantly, monseigneur."

The cardinal, upon being left alone, reflected for an instant, and then rang the bell a third time.

The same officer appeared.

"Bring the prisoner in again," said the cardinal.

M. Bonacieux was introduced anew, and upon a sign from the cardinal the officer retired.

"You have deceived me!" said the cardinal sternly.

"I," cried Bonacieux—"I deceive your Eminence!"

"Your wife, when going to Rue de Vaugirard and Rue de la Harpe, did not go to any linen-drapers."

"Then where, in God's name, did she go?"

"She went to the house of the Duchesse de Chevreuse, and she went to the Duke of Buckingham's."

"Yes," cried Bonacieux, recalling all the circumstances—"yes, that's it. Your Eminence is right. I told my wife several times that it was surprising that linen-drapers should live in such houses—in houses that had no signs—and every time she began to laugh. Ah, monseigneur!" continued Bonacieux, throwing himself at his Eminence's feet—"ah! how truly you are the cardinal, the great cardinal, the man of genius whom all the world reveres!"

However contemptible might be the triumph gained over so vulgar a being as Bonacieux, the cardinal did not the less enjoy it for an instant. Then, almost immediately, as if a new thought had entered his mind, a smile passed over his lips, and reaching out his hand to the mercer,—

"Rise, my friend," said he; "you are an honest man."

"The cardinal has touched me with his hand! I have

touched the hand of the great man!" cried Bonacieux. "The great man has called me his friend!"

"Yes, my friend, yes," said the cardinal, with that paternal tone which he sometimes knew how to assume, but which deceived only those who did not know him; "and as you have been unjustly suspected—well, you must be indemnified. Here! take this purse of a hundred pistoles, and pardon me."

"I pardon you, monseigneur!" said Bonacieux, hesitating to take the purse, fearing, doubtless, that this pretended gift was only a joke. "But you are free to have me arrested, you are free to have me tortured, you are free to have me hung. You are the master, and I should not have the least word to say about it. Pardon you, monseigneur! you cannot mean that."

"Ah, my dear Monsieur Bonacieux, you are generous in this matter, and I thank you for it. So you will take this purse, and you will go away without being too much dissatisfied with your treatment?"

"I shall go away enchanted."

"Farewell, then—that is to say, for the present, for I hope we shall meet again."

"Whenever monseigneur wishes. I am always at his Eminence's orders."

"And that will be frequently, I assure you, for I have found something extremely agreeable in your conversation."

"O monseigneur!"

"*Au revoir*, Monsieur Bonacieux, *au revoir!*"

And the cardinal made him a sign with his hand, to which Bonacieux replied by bowing to the ground. He then backed himself out, and when he was in the antechamber the cardinal heard him, in his enthusiasm, crying aloud, "Long life to monseigneur! Long life to his Eminence! Long life to the great cardinal!" The cardinal listened with a smile to this vociferous manifestation of M. Bonacieux's enthusiasm; and then, when Bonacieux's cries were no longer audible,—

"Good!" said he; "here's a man who, henceforward, would lay down his life for me."

And the cardinal began to examine with the greatest attention the map of Rochelle, which, as we have said, lay open upon the table, tracing with a pencil the line where the famous dike was to pass, which, eighteen months later, shut up the port of the besieged city.

As he was in the deepest part of his strategic meditations the door opened again, and Rochefort entered.

"Well?" said the cardinal eagerly, rising with a quickness which proved the degree of importance he attached to the commission with which he had charged the count.

"Well," said the latter, "a young woman of about twenty-six or twenty-eight years of age, and a man of from thirty-five to forty, have been lodging in fact at the two houses pointed out by your Eminence, the one four days and the other five; but the woman left last night, and the man this morning."

"They were the persons!" cried the cardinal, looking at the clock; "and now it is too late to have them pursued. The duchess is at Tours, and the duke at Boulogne. We can find them again only in London."

"What are your Eminence's orders?"

"Not a word of what has passed. Let the queen remain in perfect security; let her be ignorant that we know her secret; let her believe that we are in search of some conspiracy or other. Send me Séguier, the keeper of the seals."

"And that man—what has your Eminence done with him?"

"What man?" asked the cardinal.

"That Bonacieux."

"I have done with him all that could be done. I have made him a spy upon his wife."

The Comte de Rochefort bowed like a man who acknowledges the great superiority of his master, and retired.

Left alone, the cardinal sat down again, wrote a letter, which he sealed with his private seal, then rang the bell. The officer entered for the fourth time.

"Have Vitray sent to me," said he, "and tell him to be ready for a journey."

An instant after the man he required was before him, booted and spurred.

"Vitray," said he, "you will go with all speed to London. You must not stop an instant on the way. You will deliver this letter to milady. Here is an order for two hundred pistoles; call upon my treasurer and get the money. You shall have as much again if you are back within six days, and have executed your commission well."

The messenger, without replying a single word, bowed, took the letter, with the order for the two hundred pistoles, and went out.

These were the contents of the letter :—

"MILADY,—Be at the first ball at which the Duke of Buckingham shall be present. He will wear on his doublet twelve diamond studs. Get as near to him as you can, and cut off two of them.

"As soon as these studs are in your possession, inform me."

CHAPTER XV.

MAGISTRATES AND SOLDIERS.

ON the day after these events had taken place, Athos not having reappeared, M. de Tréville was informed by D'Artagnan and Porthos of his absence. As to Aramis, he had asked for a five days' furlough, and had gone, it was said, to Rouen on family business.

M. de Tréville was the father of his soldiers. The lowest or the most obscure among them, as soon as he assumed the uniform of the company, was as sure of his aid and support as his brother himself could have been.

He repaired, then, instantly to the residence of the chief of police. The officer who commanded the post of the Croix-Rouge was sent for, and by successive inquiries they found that Athos was then lodged in the Fort l'Évêque.

Athos had passed through all the examinations we have seen Bonacieux undergo.

We were present at the scene in which the two captives were confronted with each other. Athos, who had till that time said nothing, for fear that D'Artagnan, interrupted in his turn, should not have the time he needed—Athos from this moment declared that his name was Athos and not D'Artagnan. He added that he did not know either Monsieur or Madame Bonacieux ; that he had never spoken to either ; that he had come, at about ten o'clock in the evening, to pay a visit to his friend, M. d'Artagnan, but up to that hour he had been at M. de Tréville's, where he had dined. "Twenty witnesses," added he, "could attest the fact," and he named several distinguished gentlemen, and among them was the Duc de la Trémouille.

The second superintendent was as much bewildered as the first had been by the simple but firm declaration of the musketeer upon whom he was anxious to take revenge, which men of the robe like at all times to gain over men of the sword. But the name of M. de Tréville and that of M. de la Trémouille demanded consideration.

Athos was also sent to the cardinal, but unfortunately the cardinal was at the Louvre with the king.

It was precisely at this moment that M. de Tréville, coming from the residence of the chief of police and the office of the governor of the Fort l'Evêque, without having been able to find Athos, arrived at the palace.

As captain of the musketeers, M. de Tréville had at all times the right of entrance to the king.

It is well known how violent the king's prejudices were against the queen, and how skilfully these prejudices were kept up by the cardinal, who, in affairs of intrigue, mistrusted women much more than men. One of the principal causes of this prejudice was the friendship of Anne of Austria for Madame de Chevreuse. These two women gave him more uneasiness than the war with Spain, the quarrel with England, or the embarrassment of the finances. In his eyes and to his perfect conviction, Madame de Chevreuse not only served the queen in her political intrigues, but —and this troubled him still more—in her love affairs.

At the first word the cardinal uttered concerning Madame de Chevreuse—who, though exiled to Tours, and believed to be in that city, had come to Paris, remained there five days, and had outwitted the police—the king flew into a furious passion. Although capricious and unfaithful, the king wished to be called Louis the Just and Louis the Chaste. Posterity will have a difficulty in understanding this character, which history explains only by facts and never by reasonings.

But when the cardinal added that not only Madame de Chevreuse had been in Paris, but also that the queen had communicated with her by the means of one of those mysterious correspondences which at that time was called a cabal; when he affirmed that he, the cardinal, was about to unravel the most tightly twisted threads of this intrigue; when at the moment of arresting in the very act, with all the proofs on her, the queen's emissary to the exiled duchess, a musketeer had dared to interrupt violently the course of justice, by falling, sword in hand, upon the honest men of the law charged with investigating impartially the whole affair, in order to place it before the eyes of the king, Louis XIII. could contain himself no longer; he took a step toward the queen's apartment, showing that pale and mute

Indignation which, when it broke out, led this prince to the commission of the coldest cruelty.

And yet, in all this, the cardinal had not yet said a word about the Duke of Buckingham.

At this instant M. de Tréville entered, cold, polite, and in irreproachable costume.

Made aware of what had just gone on by the presence of the cardinal and the alteration in the king's countenance, M. de Tréville felt himself very much like Samson before the Philistines.

Louis XIII. had already placed his hand on the knob of the door. At the noise made by the entrance of M. de Tréville he turned round.

"You arrive in good time, sir," said the king, who, when his passions were raised to a certain point, could not dissemble. "I have learned some pretty things concerning your musketeers!"

"And I," said M. de Tréville coldly—"I have some pretty things to inform your Majesty concerning your magistrates."

"What?" said the king haughtily.

"I have the honour to inform your Majesty," continued M. de Tréville, in the same tone, "that a party of procurators, superintendents, and police officials, very estimable people, but, as it appears, very hostile to the uniform, have taken upon themselves to arrest in a house, to lead away through the open street, and throw into the Fort l'Evêque (all upon an order which they have refused to show me) one of my, or rather your, musketeers, sire—a man of irreproachable conduct, of an almost illustrious reputation, and whom your Majesty knows favourably—M. Athos."

"Athos!" said the king mechanically; "yes, indeed, I know that name."

"Let your Majesty remember," said M. de Tréville, "that M. Athos is the musketeer who, in the unfortunate duel which you are acquainted with, had the misfortune seriously to wound M. de Cahusac.—By the way, monseigneur," continued De Tréville, addressing the cardinal, "M. de Cahusac has entirely recovered, has he not?"

"Thank you!" said the cardinal, biting his lips with anger.

"M. Athos, then, had gone to pay a visit to one of his friends, absent at the time," continued M. de Tréville, "to a young Béarnais, a cadet in his Majesty's guards, the company of M. des Essarts; but scarcely had he arrived at his friend's and taken up a book, while waiting for his return, when a mixed crowd of bailiffs and soldiers came and laid siege to the house, broke open several doors——"

The cardinal made the king a sign, which signified, "That was on account of the affair about which I spoke to you."

"Oh, we all know that," interrupted the king ; "for all that was done for our service."

"Then," said Tréville, "it was also for your Majesty's service that one of my musketeers, who was innocent, was seized ; that he was placed between two guards, like a malefactor, and that this gallant man, who has ten times shed his blood in your Majesty's service, and is ready to shed it again, has been paraded through the midst of an insolent populace ! "

"Bah ! " said the king, who began to give way ; "was it managed in that way ? "

"M. de Tréville," said the cardinal, with the greatest coolness, "does not tell your Majesty that this innocent musketeer, this gallant man, had only an hour before attacked, sword in hand, four duly appointed examiners who were delegated by me to look into an affair of the highest importance."

"I defy your Eminence to prove it," cried M. de Tréville, with his Gascon freedom and military roughness ; "for, one hour before, M. Athos, who, I will confide it to your Majesty, is really a man of the highest quality, did me the honour, after having dined with me, to remain in the parlour of my hôtel, and converse there with the Duc de la Trémouille and the Comte de Châlus, who were present."

The king looked at the cardinal.

"A written examination attests it," said the cardinal, replying aloud to his Majesty's mute question ; "and the ill-treated people have drawn up the following, which I have the honour to present to your Majesty."

"And are the reports of magistrates to be compared with the word of soldiers ? " replied Tréville haughtily.

"Come, come, Tréville, hold your tongue," said the king.

"If his Eminence entertains any suspicion against one of my musketeers," said Tréville, "the cardinal's justice is sufficiently well known to induce me to demand an inquiry myself."

"In the house in which the judicial inquiry was made," continued the phlegmatic cardinal, "there lodges, I believe, a young Béarnais, a friend of the musketeer's."

"Your Eminence means M. d'Artagnan."

"I mean a young man who is under your protection, Monsieur de Tréville."

"Yes, your Eminence, it is the same."

"Do you not suspect this young man of having given bad advice——"

"To M. Athos, to a man double his age?" interrupted M. de Tréville. "No, monseigneur. Besides, M. d'Artagnan passed the evening at my hôtel."

"Well," said the cardinal, "everybody seems to have passed the evening at your hôtel!"

"Does your Eminence doubt my word?" said Tréville, his brow flushing with anger.

"No, God forbid!" said the cardinal; "but only let me inquire at what hour he was with you?"

"Oh, that I can affirm positively, your Eminence; for as he came in I remarked that it was but half-past nine by the clock, although I had believed it to be later."

"And at what hour did he leave your hôtel?"

"At half-past ten—an hour after the event."

"Well, but," replied the cardinal, who did not for an instant suspect De Tréville's loyalty, and who felt that the victory was escaping from his hands—"well, but Athos *was* taken in that house in the Rue des Fossoyeurs."

"Is one friend forbidden to visit another, or a musketeer of my company to fraternize with a guard of M. des Essarts's company?"

"Yes, when the house in which he fraternizes is under suspicion."

"That house is under suspicion, Tréville," said the king; "perhaps you were not aware of that?"

"Indeed, sire, I knew nothing of it. The house may be under suspicion, but I deny that it is so in that portion of it inhabited by M. d'Artagnan; for I can affirm, sire, if I can believe what he says, that there does not exist a more devoted servant of your Majesty, or a more profound admirer of the cardinal."

"Was it not this D'Artagnan who wounded Jussac, in that unfortunate encounter which took place near the monastery of the Carmes-Déchaussés?" asked the king, looking at the cardinal, who coloured with vexation.

"And the next day Bernajoux. Yes, sire, yes, it is the same. Your Majesty has an excellent memory."

"Come, what shall we decide?" said the king.

"That concerns your Majesty more than me," said the cardinal. "I should say that he was guilty."

"And I deny it," said De Tréville. "But his Majesty has judges, and these judges will decide."

"That is best," said the king. "Send the case before the judges; it is their business to judge, and they will judge."

"Only," replied Tréville, "it is a sad thing that in the unfortunate times in which we live, the purest life, the most incontestable virtue, cannot exempt a man from infamy and persecution. The army, I will answer for it, will be but little pleased at being exposed to rigorous treatment on account of police affairs."

The expression was imprudent; but M. de Tréville launched it with a full knowledge of his case. He was desirous of an explosion, because then the mine throws forth fire, and fire enlightens.

"Police affairs!" cried the king, taking up De Tréville's words—"police affairs! And what do you know about them, sir? Concern yourself with your musketeers, and do not annoy me in this way. It appears, according to your account, that if, unfortunately, a musketeer is arrested, France is in danger! Here's a piece of work about a musketeer! Why, I would arrest ten of them, 'sdeath! a hundred even, all the company; and I will not allow a whisper."

"From the moment they are suspected by your Majesty," said Tréville, "the musketeers are guilty; therefore you see me prepared to surrender my sword. For, after having accused my soldiers, there can be no doubt that the cardinal will end by accusing me. It is best to constitute myself at once a prisoner with M. Athos, who is already arrested, and with M. d'Artagnan, who most probably will be arrested."

"You Gascon head! will you have done?" said the king.

"Sire," replied Tréville, without lowering his voice in the least, "either order my musketeer to be restored to me, or let him be tried."

"He shall be tried," said the cardinal.

"Well, so much the better, for in that case I shall demand of his Majesty permission to plead for him."

The king began to fear an outbreak.

"If his Eminence," said he, "had not personal motives——"

The cardinal saw what the king was about to say, and anticipated him.

"Pardon me," said he; "but the instant your Majesty considers me a prejudiced judge, I withdraw."

"Come," said the king, "will you swear by my father that M. Athos was at your residence during the event, and that he took no part in it?"

"By your glorious father, and by yourself, who are those whom I love and venerate the most in the world, I swear it!"

"Be so kind as to reflect, sire," said the cardinal. "If we release the prisoner thus, we shall never be able to know the truth."

"M. Athos can always be found," replied Tréville, "always ready to answer, when it shall please the magistrates to question him. He will not desert, cardinal, be assured of that. I will answer for him."

"No, he will not desert," said the king; "he can always be found, as M. de Tréville says. Besides," added he, lowering his voice, and looking appealingly at the cardinal, "let us give them some security. There is policy in that."

This policy of Louis XIII.'s made Richelieu smile.

"Order it as you please, sire. You possess the right of pardoning."

"The right of pardoning applies only to the guilty," said Tréville, who was determined to have the last word, "and my musketeer is innocent. It is not mercy, then, that you are about to accord, sire. It is justice."

"And he is in the Fort l'Evêque?" said the king.

"Yes, sire, in solitary confinement, in a dungeon, like the lowest criminal."

"The devil, the devil!" murmured the king. "What must be done?"

"Sign the order for his release, and all will be done," replied the cardinal. "I believe, with your Majesty, that M. de Tréville's guarantee is more than sufficient."

Tréville bowed very respectfully, with a joy that was not unmixed with fear. He would have preferred an obstinate resistance on the part of the cardinal to this sudden yielding.

The king signed the order for release, and Tréville carried it away without delay.

At the moment he was going out, the cardinal gave him a friendly smile, and said to the king,—

"A perfect harmony seems to prevail in your musketeers, sire, between the leader and the soldiers, which must be good for the service, and very honourable to all."

"Now he will immediately play me some dog's trick or other," said Tréville; "there is no possibility of getting

the last word with such a man. But let us be quick; the
king may change his mind presently. And, at all events,
it is more difficult to put a man back into the Fort l'Evêque
or the Bastille when once he has got out than it is to keep
him a prisoner when he is there."

M. de Tréville made his entrance triumphantly into the
Fort l'Evêque, from which he delivered the musketeer,
whose calm indifference had not for a moment abandoned
him.

The first time he saw D'Artagnan, "You have come off
well," said he to him; "there is your Jussac thrust paid
for. There still remains Bernajoux, but you must not be
too confident."

Moreover, M. de Tréville had good reason to mistrust
the cardinal, and to think that all was not over, for scarcely
had the captain of the musketeers closed the door behind
him when his Eminence said to the king,—

"Now that we are at length by ourselves, we will, if your
Majesty pleases, converse seriously. Sire, Buckingham has
been in Paris five days, and left it only this morning."

CHAPTER XVI.

IN WHICH MONSIEUR SÉGUIER, THE KEEPER OF THE SEALS,
LOOKS MORE THAN ONCE FOR THE BELL, IN ORDER TO
RING IT, AS HE USED TO DO.

IT is impossible to form an idea of the impression these
few words made upon Louis XIII. He grew pale and red
alternately, and the cardinal saw at once that he had recovered, by a single blow, all the ground he had lost.

"Buckingham in Paris!" cried he; "and what does he
come to do there?"

"To conspire, no doubt, with your enemies, the Huguenots and the Spaniards."

"No, zounds, no! To conspire against my honour with
Madame de Chevreuse, Madame de Longueville, and the
Condés."

"O sire, what an idea! The queen is too prudent,
and, besides, loves your Majesty too well."

"Woman is weak, cardinal," said the king; "and as
to loving me much, I have my own opinion respecting that
love."

"I none the less maintain," said the cardinal, "that the

Duke of Buckingham came to Paris for a project purely political."

"And I am sure that he came for quite another purpose, cardinal. But if the queen be guilty, let her tremble!"

"Indeed," said the cardinal, "whatever repugnance I may have in fixing my mind on such a treason, your Majesty compels me to think of it. Madame de Lannoy, whom, according to your Majesty's command, I have frequently questioned, told me this morning that the night before last her Majesty sat up very late, that this morning she wept much, and that she was writing all day."

"That's it!" cried the king—"to him, no doubt. Cardinal, I must have the queen's papers."

"But how to get them, sire? It seems to me that neither your Majesty nor I can charge ourselves with such a mission."

"How did they act with regard to the Maréchale d'Ancre?" cried the king, in the highest state of irritation; "her closets were thoroughly searched, and then she herself was searched."

"The Maréchale d'Ancre was only the Maréchale d'Ancre, a Florentine adventuress, sire, and that was all; while the august spouse of your Majesty is Anne of Austria, queen of France—that is to say, one of the greatest princesses in the world."

"She is not the less guilty, duke! The more she has forgotten the high position in which she was placed, the more degrading is her fall. Long ago, in fact, I determined to put an end to all these petty intrigues of politics and love. She has also near her a certain La Porte."

"Who, I believe, is the mainspring of all this, I confess," said the cardinal.

"You think, then, as I do, that she deceives me?" said the king.

"I believe, and I repeat it to your Majesty, that the queen conspires against her king's power, but I have not said against his honour."

"And I—I tell you against both; I tell you the queen does not love me; I tell you she loves another; I tell you she loves that infamous Buckingham! Why did you not have him arrested while he was in Paris?"

"Arrest the duke! arrest the prime minister of King Charles I.! Can you think of it, sire? What a scandal! And suppose, then, the suspicions of your Majesty, which

I still continue to doubt, should prove to have any foundation, what a terrible disclosure, what a fearful scandal!"

"But since he played the part of a vagabond or a thief, he should have been——"

Louis XIII. stopped, terrified at what he was to say; while Richelieu, stretching out his neck, waited in vain for the word which had died on the lips of the king.

"He should have been——"

"Nothing," said the king, "nothing.   But all the time he was in Paris you, of course, did not lose sight of him ?"

"No, sire."

"Where did he lodge ?"

"Rue de la Harpe, No. 75."

"Where is that ?"

"Towards the Luxembourg."

"And you are certain that the queen and he did not see each other ?"

"I believe the queen to have too high a sense of her duty, sire."

"But they corresponded.   It is to him that the queen has been writing all the day.   Duke, I must have those letters!"

"Sire, notwithstanding——"

"Duke, at whatever price it may be, I will have them."

"I would, however, beg your Majesty to observe——"

"Do you, then, also join in betraying me, cardinal, by thus always opposing my will ?   Are you also in league with Spain and England, with Madame de Chevreuse and the queen ?"

"Sire," replied the cardinal, sighing, "I thought I was secure from such a suspicion."

"Cardinal, you have heard me.   I will have those letters."

"There is but one means."

"What is that ?"

"That would be to charge Séguier, the keeper of the seals, with this mission.   The matter belongs entirely to the duties of his office."

"Let him be sent for instantly."

"He is most likely at my hôtel.   I requested him to call ; and when I came to the Louvre, I left orders, if he came, to have him wait."

"Let him be sent for instantly."

"Your Majesty's orders shall be executed ; but——"

"But what ?"

"But the queen will perhaps refuse to obey."

"What! my orders ?"

"Yes, if she is ignorant that these orders come from the king."

"Well, that she may have no doubt on that head, I will go and inform her myself."

"Your Majesty will not forget that I have done everything in my power to prevent a rupture."

"Yes, duke, yes; I know you are very indulgent toward the queen—too indulgent, perhaps. We shall have occasion, I warn you, at some future period to speak of that."

"Whenever it shall please your Majesty. But I shall be always happy and proud, sire, to sacrifice myself to the good harmony which I desire to see reign between you and the queen of France."

"Very well, cardinal, very well; but, in the meantime, send for the keeper of the seals. I will go to the queen."

And Louis XIII., opening the communicating door, passed into the corridor which led to the apartments of Anne of Austria.

The queen was in the midst of her women, Madame de Guitaut, Madame de Sablé, Madame de Montbazon, and Madame de Guémenée. In a corner was the Spanish companion, Doña Estefana, who had followed her from Madrid. Madame de Guémenée was reading aloud, and everybody was listening to her with attention, with the exception of the queen, who had, on the contrary, desired this reading in order that she might be able, while feigning to listen, to pursue the thread of her own thoughts.

These thoughts, gilded as they were by a last reflection of love, were none the less sad. Anne of Austria, deprived of her husband's confidence, pursued by the hatred of the cardinal, who could not pardon her for having repulsed a more tender feeling, having before her eyes the example of the queen-mother, whom that hatred had tormented all her life—though Marie de Medici, if the memoirs of the time are to be believed, had begun by granting to the cardinal that love which Anne of Austria always refused to him—Anne of Austria had seen her most devoted servants fall around her, her most intimate confidants, her dearest favourites. Like those unfortunate persons endowed with a fatal gift, she brought misfortune upon everything she touched. Her friendship was a fateful portent of coming persecution. Madame de Chevreuse and Madame de Vernet were exiled, and even La Porte did not conceal from his mistress that he expected to be arrested at any moment.

At the very instant when she was plunged in the deepest

and darkest of these reflections the door of the chamber opened and the king entered.

The reader was instantly silent, all the ladies rose, and there was a profound silence. The king made no demonstration of politeness; only, stopping before the queen,—

"Madame," said he, in an unnatural voice, "you are about to receive a visit from the chancellor, who will communicate certain matters to you with which I have charged him."

The unhappy queen, who was constantly threatened with divorce, exile, and trial even, turned pale under her rouge, and could not refrain from saying,—

"But why this visit, sire? What can the chancellor have to say to me that your Majesty could not say yourself?"

The king turned upon his heel without reply, and almost at the same instant the captain of the guards, M. de Guitaut, announced the visit of the chancellor.

When the chancellor appeared, the king had already gone out by another door.

The chancellor entered, half smiling, half blushing. As we shall probably meet with him again in the course of this history, there is no harm in our readers making his acquaintance at once.

This chancellor was a pleasant man. Des Roches le Masle, canon of Notre Dame, who had formerly been the cardinal's valet, had introduced him to his Eminence as a perfectly reliable man. The cardinal trusted him, and profited by his confidence.

There were many stories related of him, and among them the following:—

After a wild youth, he had retired into a monastery, there to expiate, at least for some time, the follies of adolescence.

But, on entering this holy place, the poor penitent was unable to shut the door quick enough to prevent the passions he fled from entering with him. He was incessantly attacked by them, and the superior, to whom he confided this misfortune, wishing, as much as in him lay, to free him from them, had advised him, in order to conjure away the tempting demon, to have recourse to the bell-rope, and to ring with all his might. At the signal the monks would be made aware that temptation was besieging a brother, and all the community would offer prayers.

This advice seemed good to the future chancellor. Reinforced by the prayers offered up by the monks, he tried to exorcise the evil spirit ; but the devil does not suffer himself to be easily dispossessed of a place in which he has fixed his garrison. In proportion as they redoubled the exorcisms he redoubled the temptations, so that day and night the bell was ringing full swing, announcing the extreme desire for mortification which the penitent experienced.

The monks no longer had an instant of repose. By day they did nothing but ascend and descend the steps which led to the chapel. At night, in addition to compline and matins, they were further obliged to leap twenty times out of their beds and prostrate themselves on the flagging of their cells.

It is not known whether it was the devil who gave way or the monks who grew tired, but within three months the penitent reappeared in the world with the reputation of being the most terrible possessed one that ever existed.

On leaving the monastery he entered into the magistracy, became president of a court in the place of his uncle, embraced the cardinal's party, thereby showing no little sagacity, became chancellor, served his Eminence with zeal in his hatred against the queen-mother and in his vengeance on Anne of Austria, urged on the judges in the affair of Chalais, encouraged the endeavours of M. de Laffemas, chief gamekeeper of France ; then at length, clothed with the entire confidence of the cardinal, a confidence which he had so well earned, he received the singular commission for the execution of which he presented himself in the queen's apartments.

The queen was still standing when he entered, but scarcely had she perceived him when she reseated herself in her armchair, made a sign to her women to resume their cushions and stools, and, with an air of supreme hauteur, said,—

" What do you desire, sir, and with what object in view do you present yourself here ? "

" To make, madame, in the name of the king, and without prejudice to the respect which I have the honour to owe to your Majesty, a strict search into all your papers."

" How, sir ! a search into my papers—mine ! Truly, this is an unworthy proceeding ! "

" Be kind enough to pardon me, madame ; but on this occasion I am but the instrument which the king employs. Has not his Majesty just left you, and has he not himself desired you to prepare for this visit ? "

" Examine, then, sir. I am a criminal, as it appears.

6

—Estefana, give up the keys of my tables and my secretaries."

For form's sake the chancellor paid a visit to the pieces of furniture named, but he well knew that the queen would not place in a piece of furniture the important letter she had written in the course of the day.

When the chancellor had opened and shut twenty times the drawers of the secretaries, it became necessary, whatever hesitation he might experience—it became necessary, I say, to come to the conclusion of the affair ; that is, to search the queen herself. The chancellor advanced, therefore, toward Anne of Austria, and in a tone of great perplexity and with an embarrassed air,—

"And now," said he, "it remains for me to make the principal search."

"What is that ? " asked the queen, who did not understand, or rather did not wish to understand.

"His Majesty is certain that a letter has been written by you in the course of the day. He knows that it has not yet been sent to its address. This letter is not in your table-drawers nor in your secretary, and yet this letter must be somewhere."

"Would you dare to place your hand upon your queen ? " said Anne of Austria, drawing herself up to her full height, and fixing her eyes upon the chancellor with an expression which had become almost threatening.

"I am a humble subject of the king, madame, and all that his Majesty commands I shall do."

"Well, that is true," said Anne of Austria ; "and the cardinal's spies have served him faithfully. I have written a letter to-day ; that letter is not yet gone. That letter is here."

And the queen laid her beautiful hand on her bosom.

"Then give me that letter, madame," said the chancellor.

"I will give it to none but the king, sir," said Anne.

"If the king had desired that the letter should be given to him, madame, he would have demanded it of you himself ; and if you do not give it up——"

"Well ? "

"He has, then, charged me to take it from you."

"How ? What do you mean ? "

"That my orders go far, madame ; and that I am authorized to seek for the suspected paper, even on the person of your Majesty."

"What horror ! " cried the queen.

" Be kind enough, then, madame, to act more compliantly."

" This conduct is infamously violent! Do you know that, sir ? "

" The king commands it, madame. Excuse me."

" I will not suffer it ; no, no, I would rather die ! " cried the queen, in whom the imperious blood of Spain and Austria began to rise.

The chancellor made a profound reverence. Then, with the quite evident intention of not yielding an inch in the accomplishment of the commission with which he was charged, and as the attendant of an executioner might have done in the chamber of torture, he approached Anne of Austria, from whose eyes at the same instant sprang tears of rage.

The queen was, as we have said, of great beauty. The commission might, then, pass for a delicate one ; and the king, in his jealousy of Buckingham, had reached the point of being no longer jealous of any one.

Undoubtedly the chancellor Séguier looked about at that moment for the rope of the famous bell. But, not finding it, he summoned his resolution, and stretched out his hands toward the place where the queen had acknowledged the paper was to be found.

Anne of Austria took one step backward, grew so pale that it might be said she was dying, and leaning with her left hand, to keep herself from falling, upon a table behind her, she with her right hand drew the paper from her bosom, and held it out to the keeper of the seals.

" There, sir, there is that letter ! " cried the queen, in a broken and trembling voice ; " take it, and deliver me from your odious presence."

The chancellor, who on his part trembled with an emotion easily conceived, took the letter, bowed to the ground, and retired.

The door was scarcely closed upon him when the queen sank, half fainting, into the arms of her women.

The chancellor carried the letter to the king without having read a single word of it. The king took it with a trembling hand, looked for the address, which was wanting, became very pale, opened it slowly, then seeing by the first words that it was addressed to the king of Spain, he read it rapidly.

It was nothing but a plan of an attack against the cardinal. The queen urged her brother and the emperor of Austria, hurt as they really were by Richelieu's policy, the eternal object of which was the abasement of the house of Austria, to pretend to declare war against France, and as a condition of peace to insist upon the dismissal of the cardinal. But as to love, there was not a single word about it in all the letter.

The king, quite delighted, inquired whether the cardinal was still at the Louvre. He was told that his Eminence was waiting his Majesty's orders in his office.

The king went straight to him.

"There, duke," said he, "you were right, and I was wrong. The whole intrigue is political, and there is not the least question of love here in this letter. But, on the other hand, there is great question of you."

The cardinal took the letter and read it with the greatest attention. Then when he had reached the end of it he read it a second time.

"Well, your Majesty," said he, "you see how far my enemies go ; they threaten you with two wars if you do not dismiss me. In your place, in truth, sire, I should yield to such powerful demands ; and on my part, it would be a real happiness to withdraw from public affairs."

"What's that you are saying, duke ? "

"I say, sire, that my health is sinking under these burdensome struggles and these never-ending labours. I say that according to all probability I shall not be able to undergo the fatigues of the siege of Rochelle, and that it would be far better that you should appoint there either M. de Condé, M. de Bassompierre, or some valiant gentleman whose business is war, and not me, who am a churchman, and who am constantly turned aside from my real vocation to look after matters for which I have no aptitude. You would be the happier for it at home, sire, and I do not doubt you would be the greater for it abroad."

"Duke," said the king, "I understand you. Be assured, all who are named in that letter shall be punished as they deserve, and the queen herself."

"What do you say, sire ? God forbid that the queen should suffer the least uneasiness on my account ! She has always believed me to be her enemy, sire, although your Majesty can bear witness that I have always taken her part warmly, even against you. Oh, if she betrayed your Majesty on the side of your honour, it would be quite another thing, and I should be the first to say, ' No mercy, sire —no mercy for the guilty ! ' Fortunately, there is nothing of the kind, and your Majesty has just acquired a fresh proof of it."

"That is true, cardinal," said the king, "and you were right, as you always are; but the queen none the less deserves all my anger."

"Sire, you have now incurred hers. And even if she were to be seriously offended, I could well understand it. Your Majesty has treated her with severity——"

"So I shall always treat my enemies and yours, duke, however high they may be placed, and whatever peril I may incur in acting severely towards them."

"The queen is my enemy, but not yours, sire. On the contrary, she is a devoted, submissive, and irreproachable wife. Allow me then, sire, to intercede for her with your Majesty."

"Let her humble herself, then, and come to me first."

"On the contrary, sire, set the example. You have committed the first wrong, since it was you who suspected the queen."

"What! I make advances first?" said the king. "Never!"

"Sire, I entreat you to do so."

"Besides, how can I make advances first?"

"By doing a thing which you know will be agreeable to her."

"What is that?"

"Give a ball; you know how much the queen loves dancing. I will answer for it, her resentment will not hold out against such an attention."

"Cardinal, you know that I do not like mundane pleasures."

"The queen will only be the more grateful to you, as she knows your antipathy for that amusement. Besides, it will be an opportunity for her to wear those beautiful diamonds which you gave her recently, on her birthday, and with which she has since had no occasion to adorn herself."

"We shall see, cardinal, we shall see," said the king, who, in his joy at finding the queen guilty of a crime which he cared little about, and innocent of a fault of which he had great dread, was ready to make up all differences with her—"we shall see; but, upon my honour, you are too indulgent toward her."

"Sire," said the cardinal, "leave severity to your ministers. Clemency is a royal virtue; employ it, and you will find you will profit by it."

Upon which the cardinal, hearing the clock strike eleven, bowed low, demanding permission of the king to retire, and supplicating him to come to a good understanding with the queen.

Anne of Austria, who, in consequence of the seizure of her letter, expected reproaches, was much astonished the next day to see the king make some attempts at reconciliation with her. Her first movement was one of repulse; her womanly pride and her queenly dignity had both been so cruelly outraged that she could not come round at once. But, overcome by the advice of her women, she at last had the appearance of beginning to forget. The king took advantage of this favourable moment to tell her that he had the intention of shortly giving a fête.

A fête was so rare a thing for poor Anne of Austria that at this announcement, as the cardinal had predicted, the last trace of her resentment disappeared, if not from her heart, at least from her countenance. She asked upon what day this fête would take place, but the king replied that he must consult the cardinal upon that head.

In fact, every day the king asked the cardinal when this fête should take place, and every day the cardinal, under some pretence or other, deferred fixing it. Ten days passed away in this manner.

A week after the scene we have described the cardinal received a letter with the London stamp, which contained only these few lines:—

"I have them, but I am unable to leave London for want of money. Send me five hundred pistoles, and four or five days after I have received them I shall be in Paris."

On the same day that the cardinal received this letter the king put his customary question to him.

Richelieu counted on his fingers, and said to himself,—

"She will arrive, she says, four or five days after having received the money. It will require four or five days for the transmission of the money, four or five days for her to return; that makes ten days. Now, allowing for contrary winds, accidents, and woman's frailties, we cannot make it, altogether, less than twelve days."

"Well, duke," said the king, "have you made your calculations?"

"Yes, sire. To-day is the 20th of September. The provosts of the city give a fête on the 3rd of October. That will fall in wonderfully well. You will not appear to have gone out of your way to please the queen."

Then the cardinal added,—

"By the way, sire, do not forget to tell her Majesty, the evening before the ball, that you would like to see how her diamond studs become her."

CHAPTER XVII.

BONACIEUX'S HOUSEHOLD.

IT was the second time the cardinal had mentioned these diamond studs to the king. Louis XIII. was struck with his insistence, and began to fancy that this recommendation concealed some mystery.

More than once the king had been humiliated that the cardinal—whose police, without having yet attained the perfection of the modern police, was excellent—was better informed than himself even upon what was going on in his own household. He hoped, then, in a conversation with Anne of Austria, to obtain some additional information, and afterwards to come upon his Eminence with some secret which the cardinal either knew or did not know, but which, in either case, would raise him infinitely in his minister's eyes.

He went, then, to the queen, and, according to his custom, approached her with new threats against those who surrounded her. Anne of Austria hung down her head, allowed the torrent to flow on without replying, and hoped that it would finally cease of itself. But this was not what Louis XIII. wanted. Louis XIII. wanted a discussion, from which some light or other might break, convinced as he was that the cardinal was practising some dissimulation, and was preparing for him one of those terrible surprises which his Eminence was so skilful in getting up. He arrived at this end by his persistence in accusation.

"But," cried Anne of Austria, tired of these vague attacks—"but, sire, you do not tell me all that you have in your heart. What have I done, then ? Let me know what crime I have committed. It is impossible that your Majesty can make all this ado about a letter written to my brother !"

The king, attacked in so direct a manner, did not know what to answer. He thought that this was the moment to express the desire which he was to make only on the eve of the ball.

"Madame," said he, with dignity, "there will shortly be a ball at the City Hall. I wish that, in honour to our worthy provosts, you should appear at it in state dress, and particularly ornamented with the diamond studs which I gave you on your birthday. That is my answer."

It was a terrible answer. Anne of Austria believed that Louis XIII. knew all, and that the cardinal had persuaded him to employ this long dissimulation of seven or eight days, which, to be sure, was characteristic of the king also. She became excessively pale, leaned her beautiful hand upon a stand, a hand which then appeared like one of wax, and looking at the king, with terror in her eyes, she was unable to reply by a single syllable.

"You hear, madame," said the king, who enjoyed this embarrassment to its full extent, but without guessing the cause—"you hear, madame?"

"Yes, sire, I hear," stammered the queen.

"You will appear at this ball?"

"Yes."

"And with those studs?"

"Yes."

The queen's paleness increased, if possible. The king perceived it, and enjoyed it with that cold cruelty which was one of the worst sides of his character.

"Then that is agreed upon," said the king, "and that is all I had to say to you."

"But on what day will this ball take place?" asked Anne of Austria.

Louis XIII. felt instinctively that he ought not to reply to this question, the queen having put it in an almost inaudible voice.

"Oh, very shortly, madame," said he; "but I do not recollect the exact date of the day. I will ask the cardinal."

"It was the cardinal, then, who informed you of this ball?" cried the queen.

"Yes, madame," replied the astonished king. "But why do you ask that?"

"It was he who told you to ask me to appear there with those studs?"

"That is to say, madame——"

"It was he, sire, it was he!"

"Well, and what does it signify whether it was he or I? Is there any crime in this request?"

"No, sire."

"Then you will appear?"

" Yes, sire."

" Very well," said the king, retiring—" very well ; I count on it."

The queen made a curtsy, less from etiquette than because her knees were sinking under her.

" I am lost," murmured the queen, " lost ! for the cardinal knows all, and it is he who urges on the king, who as yet knows nothing, but will soon know everything. I am lost ! My God, my God ! "

She knelt upon a cushion and prayed, with her head buried between her palpitating arms.

In fact, her position was terrible. Buckingham had returned to London, Madame de Chevreuse was at Tours. More closely watched than ever, the queen felt certain that one of her women was playing her false, but she could not know to tell which. La Porte could not leave the Louvre. She had not a soul in the world in whom she could confide.

Thus, while contemplating the misfortune which threatened her and the abandonment in which she was left, she broke out into sobs and tears.

" Can I be of no service to your Majesty ? " said all at once a voice full of sweetness and pity.

The queen turned quickly round, for there could be no mistake in the tone of that voice. It was a friend who spoke thus.

In fact, at one of the doors which opened into the queen's apartment appeared the pretty Madame Bonacieux. She had been engaged in arranging the dresses and linen in a closet when the king entered. She could not get out, and had heard all.

The queen uttered a piercing cry at finding herself discovered, for in her trouble she did not at first recognize the young woman who had been given to her by La Porte.

" Oh, fear nothing, madame ! " said the young woman, clasping her hands, and weeping herself at the queen's sorrow ; " I am your Majesty's, body and soul, and however far I may be from you, however inferior may be my position, I believe I have discovered a means of extricating your Majesty from your trouble."

" You ! O heaven, you ! " cried the queen ; " but look me in the face. I am betrayed on all sides. Can I trust in you ? "

" O madame ! " cried the young woman, falling on her knees, " upon my soul, I am ready to die for your Majesty."

This expression came from the very bottom of the heart, and, like the first, there was no mistaking it.

"Yes," continued Madame Bonacieux—"yes, there are traitors here; but by the holy name of the Virgin, I swear that none is more devoted to your Majesty than I am. Those studs which the king speaks of, you gave them to the Duke of Buckingham, did you not? Those studs were in a little rosewood box, which he held under his arm? Am I mistaken? Is it not so, madame?"

"Yes."

"Well, those studs," continued Madame Bonacieux, "we must have them back again."

"Yes, without doubt, it is necessary," cried the queen. "But what can be done? How can it be effected?"

"Some one must be sent to the duke."

"But who, who? In whom can I trust?"

"Place confidence in me, madame. Do me that honour, my queen, and I will find a messenger."

"But I must write."

"Oh yes; that is indispensable. Two words from the hand of your Majesty and your own private seal."

"But these two words are my condemnation, divorce, exile!"

"Yes, if they fell into infamous hands. But I will answer for these two words being delivered to their address."

"Oh, my God! I must then place my life, my honour, my reputation, all in your hands?"

"Yes, yes, madame, you must, and I will save them all."

"But how—tell me at least how?"

"My husband was set at liberty two or three days ago. I have not yet had time to see him again. He is a worthy, honest man, who entertains neither love nor hatred for anybody. He will do anything I wish. He will set out, upon receiving an order from me, without knowing what he carries, and he will remit your Majesty's letter, without even knowing it is from your Majesty, to the address which it bears."

The queen took the young woman's two hands with a burst of emotion, gazed at her as if to read her very heart, and seeing nothing but sincerity in her beautiful eyes, kissed her tenderly.

"Do that," cried she, "and you will have saved my life, you will have saved my honour!"

"Oh, do not exaggerate the service I have the happiness

to render your Majesty. I have nothing to save for your Majesty. You are only the victim of perfidious plots.''

"That is true, that is true, my child," said the queen; "you are right."

"Give me, then, that letter, madame. Time presses."

The queen ran to a little table, upon which were pens, ink, and paper. She wrote two lines, sealed the letter with her private seal, and gave it to Madame Bonacieux.

"And now," said the queen, "we are forgetting one very necessary thing."

"What is that, madame?"

"Money."

Madame Bonacieux blushed.

"Yes, that is true," said she; "and I will confess to your Majesty that my husband——"

"Your husband has none. Is that what you mean?"

"Oh yes, he has some, but he is very close; that is his fault. Nevertheless, let not your Majesty be uneasy; we will find means——"

"And I have none either," said the queen. (Those who have read the Memoirs of Madame de Motteville will not be astonished at this reply.) "But wait a minute."

Anne of Austria ran to her jewel-case.

"Here," said she—"here is a ring of great value, as I have been told. It came from my brother, the king of Spain. It is mine, and I am at liberty to dispose of it. Take this ring, turn it into money, and let your husband set out."

"In an hour you shall be obeyed, madame."

"You see the address," said the queen, speaking so low that Madame Bonacieux could hardly hear what she said—"To my Lord Duke of Buckingham, London."

"The letter shall be given to him."

"Generous girl!" cried Anne of Austria.

Madame Bonacieux kissed the queen's hands, concealed the paper in the bosom of her dress, and disappeared with the lightness of a bird.

Ten minutes afterwards she was at home. As she told the queen, she had not seen her husband since his liberation; she was ignorant of the change that had taken place in him with respect to the cardinal—a change which had since been strengthened by two or three visits from the Comte de Rochefort, who had become Bonacieux's best friend, and who had persuaded him without great difficulty that noth-ing culpable had been intended by the carrying off of his wife, but that it was only a piece of political precaution.

She found Bonacieux alone. The poor man, with much trouble, was putting his house in order, the furniture of which he had found mostly broken, and his chests and drawers mostly empty, the administration of justice not being one of the three things which King Solomon named as leaving no traces of their passage. The maidservant had run away at the moment of her master's arrest. Terror had had such an effect upon the poor girl that after leaving Paris she had never stopped walking a minute till she reached Burgundy, her native place.

The worthy mercer had, immediately on entering his house, communicated to his wife the news of his happy return, and his wife had replied by congratulating him, and telling him that the first moment she could steal from her duties should be devoted to paying him a visit.

This first moment had been delayed five days, which, under any other circumstances, might have appeared rather long to M. Bonacieux. But he had, in the visit he had made to the cardinal, and in the visits Rochefort had made him, ample subjects for reflection; and, as everybody knows, nothing makes time pass more quickly than reflection.

This was the more so because Bonacieux's reflections were all rose-coloured. Rochefort called him his friend, his dear Bonacieux, and never ceased telling him that the cardinal thought a great deal of him. The mercer fancied himself already on the high road to honours and fortune.

Madame Bonacieux had also reflected, but, it must be admitted, upon something widely different from ambition. In spite of herself, her thoughts constantly reverted to that handsome young man who was so brave and appeared to be so much in love. Married at eighteen to M. Bonacieux, having always lived among her husband's friends, people thoroughly incapable of inspiring any sentiment whatever in a young woman whose heart was above her position, Madame Bonacieux had remained insensible to common seductions. But at this period the title of nobleman had a particularly great influence with the citizen class, and D'Artagnan was a nobleman. Besides, he wore the uniform of the guards, which, next to that of the musketeers, was most admired by the ladies. He was, we repeat, handsome, young, and bold; he spoke of love like a man who did love, and was anxious to be loved in return. There was certainly more than enough in all this to turn a head only twenty-three years old, and Madame Bonacieux had just attained that happy period of life.

The married couple, then, although they had not seen each other for more than a week, and although during that time serious events, in which both were concerned, had taken place, accosted each other with a certain amount of pre-occupation. Nevertheless, M. Bonacieux manifested real joy, and advanced towards his wife with open arms.

Madame Bonacieux offered him her forehead to kiss.

"Let us talk a little," said she.

"What!" said Bonacieux, astonished.

"Yes; I have something of great importance to tell you."

"True," said he; "and I also have some quite serious questions to put to you. Describe to me how you were carried off, I beg of you."

"Oh, that does not concern us now," said Madame Bonacieux.

"What? My captivity?"

"I heard of it the day it happened; but as you were not guilty of any crime, as you were not guilty of any intrigue, as you, in short, knew nothing that could compromise yourself or anybody else, I attached no more importance to that event than it deserved."

"You speak very lightly of it, madame," said Bonacieux, hurt at the little interest his wife seemed to take in him. "Do you know that I was buried during a whole day and a whole night in a dungeon of the Bastille?"

"Oh, a day and night soon pass away. Let us leave your imprisonment, then, and return to what brings me to you."

"What! to what brings you to me? Is it not the desire of seeing a husband again from whom you have been separated for a week?" asked the mercer, very much piqued.

"Yes, that first, and other things afterwards."

"Speak, then."

"It is a thing of the highest interest, and upon which our future fortune perhaps depends."

"The complexion of our fortune has changed very much since I saw you, Madame Bonacieux, and I should not be astonished if, in the course of a few months, it were to excite the envy of many folks."

"Yes, particularly if you will follow the instructions I am about to give you."

"Me?"

"Yes, you. There is a good and holy action to be performed, sir, and much money to be gained at the same time."

Madame Bonacieux knew that in speaking of money to her husband she attacked him on his weak side. But a man, even though he be a mercer, after he has talked ten minutes with the Cardinal Richelieu, is no longer the same man.

"Much money to be gained?" said Bonacieux, protruding his lip.

"Yes, much."

"About how much, pray?"

"A thousand pistoles, perhaps."

"Humph! What you have to ask of me, then, is very serious?"

"It is indeed."

"What is to be done?"

"You must set out immediately. I will give you a paper which you must not part with on any account, and which you will deliver into the proper hands."

"And where am I to go?"

"London."

"I go to London! You are joking. I have nothing to do in London."

"But others require that you should go there."

"But who are those others? I warn you that I will never again work in the dark, and that I will know not only to what I expose myself, but for whom I expose myself."

"An illustrious person sends you, an illustrious person awaits you. The recompense will exceed your expectations; that is all I promise you."

"More intrigues! nothing but intrigues! Thank you, madame; I am aware of them now. The cardinal has enlightened me on that head."

"The cardinal?" cried Madame Bonacieux. "Have you seen the cardinal?"

"He sent for me," answered the mercer proudly.

"And you went, you imprudent man!"

"Well, I can't say I had much choice in going or not going, for I was taken to him between two guards. I must also confess that as I did not then know his Eminence, if I had been able to decline the visit I should have been delighted to do so."

"He ill-treated you, then? He threatened you?"

"He gave me his hand, and he called me his friend—his

friend! Do you hear that, madame? I am a friend of the great cardinal!"

"Of the great cardinal!"

"Perhaps you would dispute his right to that title, madame?"

"Oh, I would dispute his right to nothing; but I tell you that a minister's favour is ephemeral, and that a man must be mad to attach himself to a minister. There are powers above his which do not depend upon the caprice of a man or the issue of an event; it is around these powers we must rally."

"I am sorry for it, madame, but I acknowledge no other power than that of the great man whom I have the honour to serve."

"You serve the cardinal?"

"Yes, madame; and as his servant I will not allow you to be concerned in plots against the safety of the state, or to assist in the intrigues of a woman who is not a French-woman, and who has a Spanish heart. Fortunately, we have the great cardinal; his vigilant eye watches over all and penetrates to the bottom of the heart."

Bonacieux was repeating, word for word, a sentence which he had heard the Comte de Rochefort use. But the poor woman, who had reckoned on her husband, and who, in that hope, had answered for him to the queen, trembled all the more, both at the danger into which she had nearly thrown herself, and at the helpless state to which she was reduced. Nevertheless, knowing her husband's weak-ness, and more particularly his cupidity, she did not de-spair of bringing him round to her purpose.

"Ah, you are a cardinalist, then, sir, are you?" cried she; "and you serve the party of those who ill-treat your wife and insult your queen?"

"Private interests are as nothing before the interests of all. I am for those who are saving the state," said Bona-cieux emphatically.

This was another of Comte de Rochefort's sentences which he had retained, and which he now found the opportunity to use.

"And do you know what that state is you talk about?" demanded Madame Bonacieux, shrugging her shoulders. "Be satisfied with being a plain, straightforward bourgeois, and turn your attention toward that side which holds out the greatest advantages."

"Eh, eh!" said Bonacieux, slapping a plump, round bag,

which gave back a silvery sound; "what do you think of this, my lady preacher?"

"Where does that money come from?"

"Can't you guess?"

"From the cardinal?"

"From him, and from my friend the Comte de Rochefort."

"The Comte de Rochefort! Why, it was he who carried me off!"

"Perhaps it was, madame."

"And you receive money from that man!"

"Did you not yourself tell me that the carrying off was entirely political?"

"Yes; but that abduction had for its object to make me betray my mistress, to draw from me, by tortures, confessions which might have compromised the honour and perhaps the life of my august mistress."

"Madame," replied Bonacieux, "your august mistress is a perfidious Spaniard, and what the cardinal does is well done."

"Sir," said the young woman, "I knew you to be cowardly, avaricious, and weak, but I never till now believed you to be infamous!"

"Madame," said Bonacieux, who had never seen his wife in a passion, and who retreated before this conjugal anger—"madame, what is that you say?"

"I say you are a miserable mean creature!" continued Madame Bonacieux, who saw she was regaining some little influence over her husband. "You meddle with politics, do you, and still more with cardinalist politics? Why, you are selling yourself, body and soul, to the devil for money!"

"No, but to the cardinal."

"It's the same thing!" cried the young woman. "Who names Richelieu names Satan."

"Hold your tongue! hold your tongue, madame! We may be overheard."

"Yes, you are right. I should be ashamed for any one to know your baseness."

"But what do you require of me, then? Come, let us see."

"I have told you. You must set out instantly, sir; you must accomplish loyally the commission with which I deign to charge you; and on that condition I pardon everything, I forget everything; and still further"—and she held out her hand to him—"I give you my love again."

Bonacieux was a coward, and he was avaricious, but he loved his wife ; he was softened. A man of fifty cannot long harbour malice against a pretty wife of twenty-three. Madame Bonacieux saw that he was hesitating.

"Come ! have you made up your mind ? " said she.

"But, my dear love, reflect a little upon what you require of me. London is far from Paris, very far, and perhaps the commission with which you charge me is not without dangers ? "

"Of what consequence is that, if you avoid them ? "

"Well, then, Madame Bonacieux," said the mercer— "well, then, I positively refuse. Intrigues terrify me. I have seen the Bastille. Brrrrou ! it's a frightful place that Bastille ! Only to think of it makes my flesh creep. They threatened me with torture. Do you know what the torture is ? Wooden points that they stick in between your legs till your bones break in pieces ! No, positively, I will not go. And, 'sdeath ! why do you not go yourself ? For, in truth, I think I have hitherto been deceived in you. I really believe you are a man, and a most violent one too."

"And you—you are a woman, a miserable woman, foolish and stupid. You are afraid, are you ? Well, if you do not go this very instant, I will have you arrested by the queen's orders, and I will have you placed in that Bastille which you dread so much."

Bonacieux fell into a profound reflection. He turned the two angers in his brain—the cardinal's and the queen's. The cardinal's predominated enormously.

"Have me arrested on behalf of the queen," said he, "and I—I will appeal to his Eminence."

At once Madame Bonacieux saw that she had gone too far, and she was terrified at having communicated so much. She for a moment contemplated with terror that stupid countenance, bearing the imprint of a resolution as invincible as the resolution of fools overcome by fear.

"Well, be it so ! " said she. "Perhaps, taking it all in all, you are right. In the long run, a man knows more about politics than a woman does—particularly you, Monsieur Bonacieux, who have conversed with the cardinal. And yet it is very hard," added she, "that a man upon whose affection I thought I might depend treats me thus unkindly, and will not comply with any of my fancies."

"That is because your fancies might lead too far," replied the triumphant Bonacieux, "and I mistrust them."

"Well, I will give it up, then," said the young woman, sighing. "It is well as it is; say no more about it."

"Supposing, at least, you should tell me what I should have to do in London," replied Bonacieux, who remembered a little too late that Rochefort had desired him to endeavour to obtain his wife's secrets.

"It is of no use for you to know anything about it," said the young woman, who drew back now by an instinctive mistrust. "It was about one of those follies of interest to women, a purchase by which much might have been gained."

But the more the young woman fought shy of committing herself, the more important Bonacieux conceived to be the secret which she declined to communicate to him. He resolved, then, that instant to hasten to the Comte de Rochefort, and tell him that the queen was looking for a messenger to send to London.

"Pardon me for leaving you, my dear Madame Bonacieux," said he; "but not knowing you would come to see me, I had made an engagement with a friend. I shall soon return; and if you will wait only a few minutes for me, as soon as I have concluded my business with that friend, I will come to get you; and as it is growing late, I will conduct you back to the Louvre."

"No, thank you, sir; you are not brave enough to be of any use to me whatever," replied Madame Bonacieux. "I shall return very safely to the Louvre by myself."

"As you please, Madame Bonacieux," said the ex-mercer. "Shall I have the pleasure of seeing you soon again?"

"Yes; next week I hope my duties will afford me a little liberty, and I will take advantage of it to come and set things to rights here, as they must be somewhat upset."

"Very well; I shall expect you. You are not angry with me?"

"Who?—I? Oh, not the least in the world."

"Farewell till then."

"Till then."

Bonacieux kissed his wife's hand and set off at a quick pace.

"Well," said Madame Bonacieux, when her husband had shut the street door and she found herself alone, "the only thing still lacking that fool was to become a cardinalist! And I, who have answered for him to the queen—I, who have promised my poor mistress—ah, my God! my God! she will take me for one of those wretches who swarm the palace, and are placed about her as spies! Ah, Monsieur

Bonacieux, I never did love you much, but now it is worse than ever. I hate you! and by my word you shall pay for this!"

At the moment she spoke these words a rap on the ceiling made her raise her head, and a voice which reached her through the ceiling cried,—

"Dear Madame Bonacieux, open the little side door for me, and I will come down to you."

CHAPTER XVIII.

THE LOVER AND THE HUSBAND.

"Ah, madame," said D'Artagnan, as he entered by the door which the young woman had opened for him, "allow me to tell you that you have a sorry husband there."

"Then you overheard our conversation?" asked Madame Bonacieux eagerly, and looking at D'Artagnan with much uneasiness.

"The whole of it."

"But, my God! how could you do that?"

"By a method known to myself, and by which I likewise overheard the more animated conversation which you had with the cardinal's bailiffs."

"And what did you understand by what we said?"

"A thousand things. In the first place, that, fortunately, your husband is a simpleton and a fool. In the next place, that you are in trouble, of which I am very glad, as it gives me an opportunity of placing myself at your service; and God knows I am ready to throw myself into the fire for you. And that the queen wants a brave, intelligent, devoted man to make a journey to London for her. I have, at least, two of the three qualities you stand in need of, and here I am."

Madame Bonacieux made no reply, but her heart beat with joy, and a secret hope shone in her eyes.

"And what pledge can you give me," asked she, "if I consent to confide this message to you?"

"My love for you. Speak! command! What must I do?"

"My God! my God!" murmured the young woman, "ought I to confide such a secret to you, sir? You are almost a boy!"

"I suppose, then, you require some one to answer for me?"

"I admit that that would reassure me greatly."

"Do you know Athos?"

"No."

"Porthos?"

"No."

"Aramis?"

"No; who are these gentlemen?"

"Three of the king's musketeers. Do you know M. de Tréville, their captain?"

"Oh yes, him; I know him—not personally, but from having heard the queen speak of him more than once as a brave and loyal gentleman."

"You are not afraid that he would betray you to the cardinal, are you?"

"Oh no, certainly not."

"Well, reveal your secret to him, and ask him whether, however important, however valuable, however terrible it may be, you may not safely confide it to me."

"But this secret is not mine, and I cannot reveal it in this manner."

"Why, you were going to confide it to M. Bonacieux," said D'Artagnan in vexation.

"As we confide a letter to the hollow of a tree, to the wing of a pigeon, or the collar of a dog."

"And yet—you see plainly that I love you."

"You say so."

"I am an honourable man."

"I believe so."

"I am brave."

"Oh, I am sure of that."

"Then put me to the proof."

Madame Bonacieux, restrained by a last hesitation, looked at the young man. But there was such ardour in his eyes, such persuasion in his voice, that she felt herself drawn on to place confidence in him. Besides, she was in one of those circumstances in which everything must be risked for the sake of everything. The queen might also be as much injured by too great discretion as by too great confidence, and—let us admit it—the involuntary sentiment which she felt for her young protector compelled her to speak.

"Listen," said she; "I yield to your protestations, I submit to your assurances. But I swear to you, before God who hears us, that if you betray me, and my enemies pardon me, I will kill myself while accusing you of my death."

"And I—I swear to you before God, madame," said

D'Artagnan, " that if I am taken while accomplishing the orders you give me, I will die sooner than do anything or say anything that may compromise any one."

Then the young woman confided to him the terrible secret, a part of which had already been revealed to him, by chance, in front of the Samaritaine.

This was their mutual declaration of love.

D'Artagnan was radiant with joy and pride. This secret which he possessed, this woman whom he loved—confidence and love made him a giant.

" I will go," said he ; " I will go at once."

" How ! you will go ! " said Madame Bonacieux ; " and your regiment, your captain ? "

" By my soul, you made me forget all that, dear Constance ! Yes, you are right ; I must obtain leave of absence."

" That is another obstacle," murmured Madame Bonacieux sorrowfully.

" Whatever it may be," cried D'Artagnan, after a moment of reflection, " I shall surmount it, be assured."

" How ? "

" I will go this very evening to M. de Tréville, whom I will request to ask this favour for me of his brother-in-law, M. des Essarts."

" But still there is another thing."

" What is that ? " asked D'Artagnan, seeing that Madame Bonacieux hesitated to proceed.

" You have, perhaps, no money ? "

" Perhaps is too much," said D'Artagnan, smiling.

" Then," replied Madame Bonacieux, opening a cupboard and taking from it the very bag which half an hour before her husband had caressed so affectionately, " take this bag."

" The cardinal's ? " cried D'Artagnan, breaking into a loud laugh, he having heard, as may be remembered, thanks to his broken floor, every syllable of the conversation between the mercer and his wife.

" The cardinal's," replied Madame Bonacieux. " You see it makes a very respectable appearance."

" Zounds ! " cried D'Artagnan, " it will be a doubly amusing affair to save the queen with his Eminence's money ! "

" You are an amiable and charming young man ! " said Madame Bonacieux. " Be assured you will not find her Majesty ungrateful."

"Oh, I am already more than recompensed!" cried D'Artagnan. "I love you; you permit me to tell you that I do; that is already more happiness than I dared to hope for."

"Silence!" said Madame Bonacieux, starting

"What!"

"Some one is talking in the street."

"It is the voice of——"

"Of my husband! Oh yes, I recognized it!"

D'Artagnan ran to the door and pushed the bolt.

"He shall not come in before I am gone," said he; "and when I am gone, you can open the door for him."

"But I ought to be gone too. And the disappearance of this money—how am I to justify it if I am here?"

"You are right. We must go out."

"Go out? How? He will see us if we go out."

"Then you must come up into my room."

"Ah," said Madame Bonacieux, "you say that in a tone which terrifies me!"

Madame Bonacieux pronounced these words with tears in her eyes. D'Artagnan saw these tears, and much disturbed, softened, he threw himself at her feet.

"In my apartment you will be as safe as in a temple. I give you my word as a gentleman."

"Let us go, then. I place full confidence in you, my friend."

D'Artagnan carefully drew back the bolt, and both, light as shadows, glided through the interior door into the passage, ascended the stairs as quietly as possible, and entered D'Artagnan's apartment.

Once in his apartment, for greater security the young man barricaded the door. They both went up to the window, and through a slit in the shutter they saw M. Bonacieux talking with a man in a cloak.

At the sight of this man D'Artagnan started, half drew his sword, and sprang towards the door.

It was the man of Meung.

"What are you going to do?" cried Madame Bonacieux. "You will ruin us all!"

"But I have sworn to kill that man!" said D'Artagnan.

"At this time your life is devoted, and does not belong to you! In the name of the queen I forbid you to throw yourself into any danger which is foreign to that of your journey!"

"And do you command nothing in your own name?"

"In my name," said Madame Bonacieux, with great emotion—"in my name I beg of you! But listen; they appear to be speaking of me."

D'Artagnan drew near the window and listened.

M. Bonacieux had opened his door, and seeing the apartment empty, had returned to the man in the cloak, whom he had left alone for an instant.

"She is gone," said he; "she must have gone back to the Louvre."

"You are sure," replied the stranger, "that she did not suspect the intention you had when you went out?"

"No," replied Bonacieux, with a self-sufficient air, "she is too superficial a woman."

"Is the young guardsman at home?"

"I do not think he is. As you see, his shutter is closed, and there is no light shining through the chinks of the shutters."

"That's true, but it's just as well to be certain."

"How can we be so?"

"By knocking at his door. Go."

"I will ask his servant."

Bonacieux went into the house again, passed through the same door that had afforded a passage for the two fugitives, went up to D'Artagnan's door, and knocked.

No one answered. Porthos, to make a greater display, had that evening borrowed Planchet. D'Artagnan himself took care not to give the least sign of existence.

At the moment that Bonacieux's fist sounded on the door the two young people felt their hearts bound within them.

"There is nobody in his room," said Bonacieux.

"All the same let us walk into your apartment. We shall be safer there than in the doorway."

"Oh, good God!" whispered Madame Bonacieux, "we shall hear no more."

"On the contrary," said D'Artagnan, "we shall hear all the better."

D'Artagnan raised the three or four tiles which made of his chamber another ear of Dionysius, spread a carpet, went down upon his knees, and made a sign to Madame Bonacieux to stoop down toward the opening, as he did.

"You are sure there is nobody there?" said the unknown.

"I will answer for it," said Bonacieux.

"And you think that your wife——"

"Has returned to the Louvre."

"Without speaking to any one but yourself?"

"I am sure of it."

"Please to understand that is an important point."

"So the news I brought you, then, has some value——"

"A very great value, my dear Bonacieux. I don't attempt to deny it."

"Then the cardinal will be pleased with me?"

"No doubt he will."

"The great cardinal!"

"Are you sure that in her conversation with you your wife mentioned no proper names?"

"I don't think she did."

"She did not name Madame de Chevreuse, the Duke of Buckingham, or Madame de Vernet?"

"No; she only told me she wished to send me to London to further the interests of an illustrious personage."

"Oh, the traitor!" murmured Madame Bonacieux.

"Silence!" whispered D'Artagnan, taking a hand which, without thinking of it, she suffered him to retain.

"Nevertheless," continued the man in the cloak, "it was very silly of you not to have feigned to accept the mission. You would now be in possession of the letter; the state, which is now threatened, would be safe; and you——"

"And I?"

"Well, you—the cardinal would have given you letters of nobility."

"Did he tell you so?"

"Yes, I know that he meant to afford you that agreeable surprise."

"Be calm," replied Bonacieux; "my wife adores me, and there is still plenty of time."

"The silly fool!" murmured Madame Bonacieux.

"Silence!" said D'Artagnan, pressing her hand more tightly.

"What do you mean by there being still time?" asked the man in the cloak.

"I will go to the Louvre; I will ask for Madame Bonacieux; I will tell her I have reflected upon the matter; I will resume the affair, obtain the letter, and then hasten directly to the cardinal's."

"Well, begone then! Make all possible haste. I will shortly come back to learn the result of your plan."

The unknown went out.

"The wretch!" said Madame Bonacieux, addressing this other affectionate epithet to her husband.

"Silence, once more!" said D'Artagnan, pressing her hand still more tightly.

A terrible howling interrupted these reflections of D'Artagnan and Madame Bonacieux. It was her husband, who had discovered the disappearance of his money-bag, and was screaming out, "Thieves! thieves!"

Bonacieux cried for a long time. But as such cries, on account of their frequency, did not attract much notice in the Rue des Fossoyeurs, and as, besides, the mercer's house had not been for some time in very good repute, finding that nobody came, he went out, continuing to cry aloud, and his voice died away in the direction of the Rue du Bac.

"Now he is gone, it is your turn to go," said Madame Bonacieux. "Have courage, but above all, prudence, and remember that it is your duty to the queen!"

"To her and to you!" cried D'Artagnan. "Be satisfied, lovely Constance. I shall become worthy of her gratitude, but shall I likewise return worthy of your love?"

The young woman replied only by the vivid blush which mounted to her cheeks. A few moments later D'Artagnan went out in his turn, enveloped in a large cloak, which the sheath of a long sword held back cavalierly.

Madame Bonacieux followed him with her eyes, with that long, fond look with which a woman accompanies the man whom she feels she loves. But when he had turned the angle of the street she fell on her knees, and clasping her hands,—

"Oh, my God!" cried she, "protect the queen, protect me!"

CHAPTER XIX.

PLAN OF CAMPAIGN.

D'ARTAGNAN went straight to M. de Tréville's hôtel. He had considered that in a few minutes the cardinal would be warned by this cursed unknown, who appeared to be his agent, and he rightly judged he had not a moment to lose.

The young man's heart overflowed with joy. An opportunity presented itself to him in which there would be both glory and money to be gained, and as a far higher encouragement still, had just brought him into close intimacy with the woman he adored. This chance was doing, then,

for him, almost at once, more than he would have dared
to ask of Providence.

M. de Tréville was in his drawing-room with his usual
court of gentlemen. D'Artagnan, who was known as a
familiar of the house, went straight to his office, and sent
word to him that he wished to see him upon an affair of
importance.

D'Artagnan had been there scarcely five minutes when
M. de Tréville entered. At the first glance, and by the joy
which was painted on his countenance, the worthy captain
plainly perceived that something fresh was on foot.

All the way along D'Artagnan had been deliberating
whether he should place confidence in M. de Tréville, or
whether he should only ask him to give him *carte blanche*
for a secret affair. But M. de Tréville had always been so
perfectly friendly, had always been so devoted to the king
and queen, and hated the cardinal so cordially, that the
young man resolved to tell him everything.

"You have something to say to me, my young friend?"
said M. de Tréville.

"Yes, sir," said D'Artagnan; "and you will pardon me,
I hope, for having disturbed you when you know the importance of my business."

"Speak, then; I am all attention."

"It concerns nothing less," said D'Artagnan, lowering
his voice, "than the honour, perhaps the life, of the
queen."

"What are you saying?" asked M. de Tréville, glancing
round to see if they were alone, and then fixing his scrutinizing look upon D'Artagnan.

"I say, sir, that chance has rendered me master of a
secret——"

"Which you will keep, I hope, young man, with your
life."

"But which I must impart to you, sir, for you alone can
assist me in the mission I have just received from her
Majesty."

"Is this secret your own?"

"No, sir; it is the queen's."

"Are you authorized by her Majesty to communicate it
to me?"

"No, sir; for, on the contrary, I am desired to preserve
the profoundest secrecy."

"Why, then, are you about to betray it to me?"

"Because, as I said, without you I can do nothing; and I

was afraid that you would refuse me the favour I have come to ask, if you did not know for what purpose I asked it."

"Keep your secret, young man, and tell me what you wish."

"I wish you to obtain for me, from M. des Essarts, leave of absence for a fortnight."

"When?"

"This very night."

"You are leaving Paris?"

"I am going on a mission."

"May you tell me where?"

"To London."

"Has any one an interest in preventing your reaching there?"

"The cardinal, I believe, would give anything in the world to hinder me from succeeding."

"And you are going alone?"

"I am going alone."

"In that case you will not get beyond Bondy. I tell you so, by the word of De Tréville."

"How so, sir?"

"You will be assassinated."

"And I shall die in the performance of my duty."

"But your mission will not be accomplished."

"That is true," replied D'Artagnan.

"Believe me," continued Tréville, "in enterprises of this kind, four must set out, for one to arrive."

"Ah, you are right, sir," said D'Artagnan; "but you know Athos, Porthos, and Aramis, and you know whether I can make use of them."

"Without confiding to them the secret which I did not wish to know?"

"We are sworn, once and for ever, to implicit confidence and devotion against all proof. Besides, you can tell them that you have full confidence in me, and they will not be more incredulous than you."

"I can send to each of them leave of absence for a fortnight, that is all—Athos, whose wound still gives him inconvenience, to go to the waters of Forges; Porthos and Aramis to accompany their friend, whom they are not willing to abandon in such a painful position. Sending their leave of absence will be proof enough that I authorize their journey."

"Thanks, sir. You are a hundred times too good!"

"Go, then, and find them instantly, and let all be done to-night. Ah! but first write your request to M. des Essarts.

You perhaps had a spy at your heels, and your visit—in that case already known to the cardinal—will be thus made regular."

D'Artagnan drew up his request, and M. de Tréville, on receiving it, assured him that before two o'clock in the morning the four furloughs should be at the respective domiciles of the travellers.

"Have the goodness to send mine to Athos's residence," said D'Artagnan. "I should fear some disagreeable encounter if I were to go home."

"I will. Farewell, and a prosperous journey! By the way," said M. de Tréville, calling him back.

D'Artagnan returned.

"Have you any money?"

D'Artagnan jingled the bag he had in his pocket.

"Enough?" asked M. de Tréville

"Three hundred pistoles."

"Excellent! That would carry you to the end of the world. Go, then!"

D'Artagnan bowed to M. de Tréville, who held out his hand to him. D'Artagnan pressed it with a respect mixed with gratitude. Since his first arrival at Paris he had had constant occasion to honour this excellent man, whom he had always found worthy, loyal, and great.

His first visit was to Aramis, at whose house he had not been since the famous evening when he had followed Madame Bonacieux. What was more, he had seldom seen the young musketeer; but every time he had seen him, he thought he noticed a deep sadness imprinted on his countenance.

That evening also Aramis was sitting up, melancholy and thoughtful. D'Artagnan asked a few questions about this deep melancholy. Aramis pleaded as his excuse a commentary upon the eighteenth chapter of St. Augustine that he was forced to write in Latin for the following week, and which preoccupied him a good deal.

After the two friends had been chatting a few moments, one of M. de Tréville's servants entered, bringing a sealed packet.

"What is that?" asked Aramis.

"The leave of absence you asked for," replied the lackey.

"For me! I have asked for no leave of absence."

"Hold your tongue and take it," said D'Artagnan.—"And you, my friend, there is a half-pistole for your trouble,

You will tell M. de Tréville that M. Aramis is very much obliged to him. Go!"

The lackey bowed to the ground and departed.

"What does all this mean?" asked Aramis.

"Pack up all you want for a fortnight's journey, and follow me."

"But I cannot leave Paris just now without knowing——" Aramis stopped.

"What has become of her, I suppose you mean," continued D'Artagnan.

"Become of whom?" replied Aramis.

"The woman who was here—the lady of the embroidered handkerchief."

"Who told you there was a woman here?" replied Aramis, becoming deathly pale.

"I saw her."

"And you know who she is?'

"Well, I think I can give a pretty good guess, at least."

"Listen," said Aramis. "Since you know so many things, can you tell me what has become of that lady?"

"I presume that she has gone back to Tours."

"To Tours? Yes, that may be. You know her. But why did she return to Tours without telling me anything about it?"

"Because she was in fear of being arrested."

"Why did she not write to me, then?"

"Because she was afraid of compromising you."

"D'Artagnan, you restore me to life," cried Aramis. "I fancied myself despised, betrayed. I was so delighted to see her again! I could not have believed she would risk her liberty for me, and yet for what other cause could she have returned to Paris?"

"For the cause which to-day carries us to England."

"And what is this cause?" demanded Aramis.

"Oh, you'll know it some day, Aramis; but at present I must imitate the discretion of *the doctor's niece*."

Aramis smiled as he remembered the tale he had related to his friends on a certain evening.

"Well, then, since she has left Paris, and you are sure of it, D'Artagnan, nothing prevents me, and I am ready to follow you. You say we are going——"

"To Athos's house now; and if you will come, I beg you to make haste, for we have already lost much time. By the way, inform Bazin."

"Will Bazin go with us?" asked Aramis.

"Perhaps so. At all events, it is best that he should follow us now to Athos's."

Aramis called Bazin, and after having ordered him to join them at Athos's residence, "Let us go, then," said he, taking his cloak, sword, and his three pistols, opening uselessly two or three drawers to see whether he could not find some stray coin or other.

When well assured this search was superfluous, he followed D'Artagnan, wondering how it happened that this young guardsman should know so well who the lady was to whom he had given hospitality, and that he should know better than he did what had become of her.

Only as they went out, Aramis placed his hand upon D'Artagnan's arm, and looking at him earnestly,—

"You have not spoken of this lady?" said he.

"To nobody in the world."

"Not even to Athos or Porthos?"

"I have not breathed a syllable to them."

"Good!"

And at ease on this important point, Aramis continued his way with D'Artagnan, and both soon arrived at Athos's dwelling.

They found him holding his leave of absence in one hand, and M. de Tréville's note in the other.

"Can you explain to me what this leave of absence and this letter I have just received mean?" said the astonished Athos.

"My DEAR ATHOS,—I wish, since your health absolutely requires it, that you should rest for a fortnight. Go, then, and take the waters of Forges, or any that may be more agreeable to you, and get well as quickly as possible.

"TRÉVILLE."

"Well, this leave of absence and this letter mean that you must follow me, Athos."

"To the waters of Forges?"

"There or elsewhere."

"In the king's service?"

"Either the king's or the queen's. Are we not their Majesties' servants?"

At that moment Porthos entered.

"Zounds!" said he, "here is a queer thing! Since when, I wonder, in the musketeers, did they grant men leave of absence without its being asked?"

"Since the time," said D'Artagnan, "they have had friends who ask it for them."

"Ah ha!" said Porthos; "it appears there's something fresh afoot?"

"Yes, we are going——" said Aramis.

"Going! To what country?" demanded Porthos.

"'Pon my word, I don't know much about it," said Athos. "Ask D'Artagnan here."

"To London, gentlemen," said D'Artagnan.

"To London!" cried Porthos. "And what the devil are we going to do in London?"

"That is what I am not at liberty to tell you, gentlemen. You must trust to me."

"But in order to go to London, a man should have some money; and I have none."

"Nor I," said Aramis.

"Nor I," said Athos.

"Well, I have," added D'Artagnan, pulling out his treasure from his pocket and placing it on the table. "There are in this bag three hundred pistoles. Let each take seventy-five, which will be quite enough to carry us to London and back. Besides, we may be sure that all of us will not reach London."

"Why so?"

"Because, according to all probability, some of us will be left on the road."

"What is this, then—a campaign upon which we are entering?"

"And a most dangerous one. I give you fair notice."

"Ah, ah! but since we run the risk of being killed," said Porthos, "at least I should like to know what for."

"Great good that will do you," said Athos.

"And yet," said Aramis, "I am somewhat of Porthos's opinion."

"Is the king accustomed to give you reasons? No. He says to you, very simply, 'Gentlemen, there is fighting going on in Gascony or in Flanders; go and fight.' And you go. Why? You don't even consider why."

"D'Artagnan is right," said Athos. "Here are our three leaves of absence, which came from M. de Tréville; and here are three hundred pistoles, which came from I don't know where. So let us go and get killed where we are told to go. Is life worth the trouble of so many questions? D'Artagnan, I am ready to follow you."

"And I," said Porthos.

"And I also," said Aramis. "And, indeed, I am not sorry to quit Paris. I need distractions."

"Well, you will have distractions enough, gentlemen, be assured," said D'Artagnan.

"And now, when are we to go?" asked Athos.

"Immediately," replied D'Artagnan; "we have not a minute to lose."

"Hello! Grimaud, Planchet, Mousqueton, Bazin!" cried the four young men, calling their lackeys; "clean my boots, and fetch the horses from the hôtel."

Each musketeer, in fact, was accustomed to leave at the central establishment, as at a barracks, his own horse and his lackey's.

Planchet, Grimaud, Mousqueton, and Bazin set off at full speed.

"Now let us draw up the plan of campaign," said Porthos. "Where do we go first?"

"To Calais," said D'Artagnan. "That is the straightest way to London."

"Well," said Porthos, "my advice is this——"

"Speak! What is it?"

"Four men travelling together would be suspicious. D'Artagnan will give each of us his instructions. I will set out first by the Boulogne road, to scout out the way. Athos will set out two hours later, by that of Amiens. Aramis will follow us by that of Noyon. As to D'Artagnan, he will go by what road he thinks best, in Planchet's clothes; while Planchet will follow us, dressed like D'Artagnan, in the uniform of the guards."

"Gentlemen," said Athos, "my opinion is that it is not proper to allow lackeys to have anything to do in such an affair. A secret may, by chance, be betrayed by gentlemen, but it is almost always sold by lackeys."

"Porthos's plan appears to me to be impracticable," said D'Artagnan, "inasmuch as I am myself ignorant of what instructions I can give you. I am the bearer of a letter, that is all. I have not, and I cannot make, three copies of that letter, because it is sealed. We must then, as it appears to me, travel in company. This letter is here, in this pocket." And he pointed to the pocket which contained the letter. "If I should be killed, one of you must take it and pursue the route. If he is killed, it will be another's turn; and so on. Provided a single one arrives, that is all that is necessary."

"Bravo, D'Artagnan! your opinion is mine," cried Athos. "Besides, we must be consistent. I am going to take the waters ; you will accompany me. Instead of taking the waters of Forges, I go and take sea-baths. I am free to do so. If any one wishes to stop us, I will show M. de Tréville's letter, and you will show your leaves of absence. If we are attacked, we will defend ourselves. If we are examined, we will stoutly maintain that we were only anxious to dip ourselves a certain number of times in the sea. They would have an easy time with four isolated men; whereas four men together make a troop. We will arm our four lackeys with pistols and carbines. If they send an army out against us, we will give battle; and the survivor, as D'Artagnan says, will carry the letter."

"Well said," cried Aramis. "You don't often speak, Athos, but when you do speak, it is like Saint John of the Golden Mouth. I agree to Athos's plan. And you, Porthos ? "

"I agree to it too," said Porthos, "if D'Artagnan approves of it. D'Artagnan, being bearer of the letter, is naturally the head of the enterprise. Let him decide, and we will execute."

"Well," said D'Artagnan, "I decide that we adopt Athos's plan, and that we set off in half an hour."

"Agreed ! " shouted the three musketeers in chorus.

And each one, putting his hand in the bag, took his seventy-five pistoles, and made his preparations to start at the time appointed.

CHAPTER XX.

THE JOURNEY.

At two o'clock in the morning our four adventurers left Paris by the gate St. Denis. As long as it was night they remained silent. In spite of themselves they felt the influence of the darkness, and saw ambushes everywhere.

With the first rays of the sun their tongues became loosened, with day their gaiety revived. It was like the eve of a battle : the heart beat, the eyes laughed, and they felt that the life they were perhaps going to lose was, after all, a pleasant thing.

The appearance of the caravan was indeed most formidable. The black horses of the musketeers, their martial carriage, the squadron-like step of these noble companions of the soldier, would have betrayed the strictest incognito.

The lackeys followed, armed to the teeth.

All went well as far as Chantilly, where they arrived about eight o'clock in the morning. They needed breakfast, and alighted at the door of an inn recommended by a sign representing St. Martin giving half his cloak to a poor man. They ordered the lackeys not to unsaddle the horses, and to hold themselves in readiness to set off again immediately.

They entered the public room, and seated themselves at table. A gentleman, who had just arrived by the route of Dammartin, was seated at the same table, and was taking his breakfast. He opened the conversation by talking of the rain and the fine weather; the travellers replied. He drank to their good health, and the travellers returned his politeness.

But at the moment Mousqueton came to announce that the horses were ready, and they were rising from the table, the stranger proposed to Porthos to drink the cardinal's health. Porthos replied that he asked no better, if the stranger in his turn would drink the king's health. The stranger cried that he acknowledged no other king but his Eminence. Porthos told him he was drunk, and the stranger drew his sword.

"You have committed a piece of folly," said Athos, "but it can't be helped; there is no drawing back. Kill your man, and rejoin us as soon as you can."

And all three mounted their horses and set out at a good pace, while Porthos was promising his adversary to perforate him with all the thrusts known in the fencing schools.

"There goes one!" cried Athos, at the end of five hundred paces.

"But why did that man attack Porthos, rather than any other of us?" asked Aramis.

"Because Porthos was talking louder than the rest, and he took him for the leader of the party," said D'Artagnan.

"I always said that this cadet from Gascony was a well of wisdom," murmured Athos.

And the travellers continued their route.

At Beauvais they stopped two hours, as much to breathe their horses a little as to wait for Porthos. At the end of the two hours, as Porthos did not come and they heard no news of him, they resumed their journey.

At a league from Beauvais, where the road was confined between two high banks, they fell in with eight or ten men who, taking advantage of the road being unpaved in this spot, appeared to be employed in digging holes and making muddy ruts.

Aramis, not liking to soil his boots with this artificial mortar, apostrophized them rather sharply. Athos wished to restrain him, but it was too late. The labourers began to jeer the travellers, and by their insolence disturbed the equanimity even of the cool Athos, who urged on his horse against one of them.

The men all immediately drew back to the ditch, from which each took a concealed musket. The result was that our seven travellers were outnumbered in weapons. Aramis received a ball which passed through his shoulder, and Mousqueton another ball which lodged in the fleshy parts at the lower portion of the back. Mousqueton alone fell from his horse, not because he was severely wounded, but from not being able to see the wound, he deemed it to be more serious than it really was.

"It is an ambuscade!" shouted D'Artagnan; "don't waste a shot! Forward!"

Aramis, wounded as he was, seized the mane of his horse, which carried him on with the others. Mousqueton's horse rejoined them, and galloped by the side of his companions.

"That horse will serve us for a relay," said Athos.

"I would rather have had a hat," said D'Artagnan; "mine was carried away by a ball. By my faith, it is very fortunate that the letter was not in it."

"Well, but they'll kill poor Porthos when he comes up," said Aramis.

"If Porthos were on his legs, he would have rejoined us by this time," said Athos. "My opinion is, that when they came to the point the drunken man proved to be sober enough."

They continued at their best speed for two hours, although the horses were so fatigued that it was to be feared they would soon refuse service.

The travellers had chosen cross-roads, in the hope that they might meet with less interruption. But at Crèvecœur Aramis declared he could proceed no farther. In fact, it required all the courage which he concealed beneath his elegant form and polished manners to bear him so far. He grew paler every minute, and they were obliged to support him on his horse. They lifted him off at the door of an inn, left Bazin with him—who, besides, in a skirmish was more embarrassing than useful—and set forward again in the hope of sleeping at Amiens.

"'Sdeath!" said Athos, as soon as they were again in motion—"reduced to two masters and Grimaud and Plan-

chet! 'Sdeath! I won't be their dupe, I will answer for it. I
will neither open my mouth nor draw my sword between here
and Calais. I swear by——"

"Let us waste no time in swearing," said D'Artagnan;
"let us gallop, if our horses are willing."

And the travellers buried their rowels in their horses'
flanks, who, thus vigorously stimulated, recovered their energies. They arrived at Amiens at midnight, and alighted
at the inn of the Golden Lily.

The host had the appearance of as honest a man as any
on earth. He received the travellers with his candlestick
in one hand and his cotton nightcap in the other. He proposed to lodge the two travellers each in a charming chamber, but, unfortunately, these charming chambers were at
the opposite extremities of the hotel, and D'Artagnan and
Athos declined them. The host replied that he had no
other worthy of their Excellencies, but the travellers declared they would sleep in the common chamber, each upon
a mattress, which could be thrown upon the floor. The host
insisted, but the travellers were firm, and he was obliged to
comply with their wishes.

They had just prepared their beds and barricaded their
door within when some one in the courtyard knocked at the
shutter. They demanded who was there, and upon recognizing the voices of their lackeys, opened the shutter.

In fact, it was Planchet and Grimaud.

"Grimaud can take care of the horses," said Planchet.
"If you are willing, gentlemen, I will sleep across your doorway, and you will then be certain that nobody can come to
you."

"And what will you sleep upon?" said D'Artagnan.

"Here is my bed," replied Planchet, producing a bundle
of straw.

"Come, then," said D'Artagnan, "you are right. Mine
host's face does not please me at all; it is too civil by half."

"Nor me either," said Athos.

Planchet got in through the window, and installed himself
across the doorway, while Grimaud went and shut himself
up in the stable, undertaking that, by five o'clock in the
morning, he and the four horses should be ready.

The night passed off quietly enough. About two o'clock
in the morning, to be sure, somebody endeavoured to open
the door; but as Planchet awoke in an instant and cried,
"Who is there?" this person replied he was mistaken, and
went away.

At four o'clock in the morning a terrible noise was heard in the stables. Grimaud had tried to waken the stable-boys, and the stable-boys were beating him. When the window was opened the poor lad was seen lying senseless, with his head split by a blow with a fork-handle.

Planchet went down into the yard, and proceeded to saddle the horses. But the horses were all used up. Mousqueton's horse, which had travelled for five or six hours without a rider the day before, alone might have been able to pursue the journey. But, by an inconceivable error, a veterinary surgeon, who had been sent for, as it appeared, to bleed one of the host's horses, had bled Mousqueton's.

This began to be annoying. All these successive accidents were, perhaps, the result of chance, but they might, quite as probably, be the fruits of a plot. Athos and D'Artagnan went out, while Planchet was sent to inquire if there were not three horses for sale in the neighbourhood. At the door stood two horses, fresh, strong, and fully equipped. These were just what they wanted. He asked where their owners were, and was informed that they had passed the night in the inn, and were then settling with the master.

Athos went down to pay the reckoning, while D'Artagnan and Planchet stood at the street door. The host was in a low room at the back, to which Athos was requested to go.

Athos entered without the least mistrust, and took out two pistoles to pay the bill. The host was alone, seated before his desk, one of the drawers of which was partly open. He took the money which Athos offered to him, and after turning and turning it over and over in his hands, suddenly cried out that it was bad, and that he would have him and his companions arrested as counterfeiters.

" You scoundrel ! " cried Athos, stepping towards him, " I'll cut your ears off ! "

But the host stooped, took two pistols from the half-open drawer, pointed them at Athos, and called out for help.

At the same instant four men, armed to the teeth, entered by side doors, and rushed upon Athos.

" I am taken ! " shouted Athos with all the power of his lungs. " Go on, D'Artagnan ! spur ! spur ! " And he fired two pistols.

D'Artagnan and Planchet did not require twice bidding. They unfastened the two horses that were waiting at the door, leaped upon them, buried their spurs in their sides, and set off at full gallop.

"Do you know what has become of Athos?" asked D'Artagnan of Planchet, as they galloped on.

"Ah, sir," said Planchet, "I saw one fall at each of his shots, and he appeared to me, through the glass door, to be fencing with the others."

"Brave Athos!" murmured D'Artagnan; "and to think that we must leave him, while the same fate awaits us, perhaps, two paces hence! Forward, Planchet, forward! You are a brave fellow!"

"Did not I tell you, sir," replied Planchet, "that we Picards are found out by being used? Besides, I am in my own country here, and that puts me on my mettle."

And both, with free use of the spur, arrived at St. Omer without drawing bridle. At St. Omer they breathed their horses with their bridles passed under their arms, for fear of accident, and ate a hasty morsel standing in the road, after which they departed again.

At a hundred paces from the gates of Calais D'Artagnan's horse sank under him, and could not by any means be made to get up again, the blood flowing from both his eyes and his nose. There still remained Planchet's horse, but he had stopped short, and could not be started again.

Fortunately, as we have said, they were within a hundred paces of the city. They left their two horses upon the highway, and ran toward the port. Planchet called his master's attention to a gentleman who had just arrived with his lackey, and who was about fifty paces ahead of them.

They made all haste to come up to this gentleman, who appeared to be in a great hurry. His boots were covered with dust, and he was asking whether he could not instantly cross over to England.

"Nothing would be more easy," said the captain of a vessel ready to set sail, "but this morning an order arrived that no one should be allowed to cross without express permission from the cardinal."

"I have that permission," said the gentleman, drawing a paper from his pocket; "here it is."

"Have it signed by the governor of the port," said the captain, "and give me the preference."

"Where shall I find the governor?"

"At his country house."

"Where is that situated?"

"A quarter of a league from the city. Look, you may see it from here, at the foot of that little hill, that slated roof."

"Very well," said the gentleman.

And with his lackey he started for the governor's country house.

D'Artagnan and Planchet followed the gentleman at a distance of five hundred paces.

Once outside the city, D'Artagnan quickly overtook the gentleman as he was entering a little wood.

"Sir," said D'Artagnan, "you appear to be in great haste?"

"No one can be more so, sir."

"I am sorry for that," said D'Artagnan, "for as I am in great haste likewise, I was going to beg you to do me a service."

"What service?"

"To let me go first."

"Impossible," said the gentleman. "I have travelled sixty leagues in forty-four hours, and by to-morrow at midday I must be in London."

"I have performed the same distance in forty hours, and by to-morrow at ten o'clock in the morning I must be in London."

"Very sorry, sir; but I was here first, and will not go second."

"I am sorry too, sir; but I arrived second, and will go first."

"The king's service!" said the gentleman.

"My own service!" said D'Artagnan.

"But this is a needless quarrel you are seeking with me, as I think."

"Zounds! what can you expect it to be?"

"What do you want?"

"Would you like to know?"

"Certainly."

"Well, then, I want that order of which you are the bearer, seeing that I have none and must have one."

"You are joking, I presume."

"I never joke."

"Let me pass!"

"You shall not pass."

"My brave young man, I will blow out your brains. Halloo, Lubin! my pistols!"

"Planchet," called out D'Artagnan, "take care of the lackey. I will manage the master."

Planchet, emboldened by his first exploit, sprang upon Lubin; and being strong and vigorous, he soon got him on his back, and placed his knee on his chest.

" Go on with your affair, sir," cried Planchet ; " I have finished mine."

Seeing this, the gentleman drew his sword, and sprang upon D'Artagnan ; but he had to deal with a tough customer.

In three seconds D'Artagnan had wounded him three times, exclaiming at each thrust,—

" One for Athos ! one for Porthos ! and one for Aramis ! "

At the third thrust the gentleman fell like a log.

D'Artagnan believed him to be dead, or at least insensible, and went toward him for the purpose of taking the order. But at the moment he stretched out his hand to search for it, the wounded man, who had not dropped his sword, pricked him in the breast, crying,—

" And one for you ! "

" And one for me—the best for the last ! " cried D'Artagnan in a rage, nailing him to the earth with a fourth thrust through his body.

This time the gentleman closed his eyes and fainted. D'Artagnan searched his pockets, and took from one of them the order for the passage. It was in the name of the Comte de Wardes.

Then casting a glance on the handsome young man, who was scarcely twenty-five years of age, and whom he was leaving lying there unconscious and perhaps dead, he uttered a sigh over that unaccountable destiny which leads men to destroy one another for the interests of people who are strangers to them, and who often do not even know of their existence.

But he was soon roused from these reflections by Lubin, who uttered loud cries, and screamed for help with all his might.

Planchet grasped him by the throat, and pressed as hard as he could.

" Sir," said he, " as long as I hold him in this manner he can't cry, I'll be bound ; but as soon as I let go, he will howl again as loud as ever. I have found out that he's a Norman, and Normans are obstinate."

In fact, tightly held as he was, Lubin endeavoured still to make a noise.

" Wait ! " said D'Artagnan ; and taking out his handkerchief, he gagged him.

" Now," said Planchet, " let us bind him to a tree."

This being properly done, they drew the Comte de Wardes close to his servant ; and as night was approaching, and as the wounded man and the bound man were both at some little distance within the wood, it was evident they would remain there till the next day.

"And now," said D'Artagnan, "to the governor's house."

"But you appear to me to be wounded," said Planchet.

"Oh, that's nothing! Let us dispatch what is most pressing first, and we will attend to my wound afterwards; besides, it does not seem a very dangerous one."

And they both set forward as fast as they could towards the worthy functionary's country seat.

The Comte de Wardes was announced.

D'Artagnan was introduced.

"You have an order signed by the cardinal?"

"Yes, sir," replied D'Artagnan; "here it is."

"Ah, ah! it is quite regular and explicit," said the governor.

"Most likely," said D'Artagnan; "I am one of his most faithful servants."

"It appears that his Eminence is anxious to prevent some one from reaching England?"

"Yes; a certain D'Artagnan, a Béarnese gentleman, who left Paris in company with three friends of his, with the intention of going to London."

"Do you know him personally?" asked the governor.

"Whom?"

"This D'Artagnan."

"Oh yes, perfectly well."

"Describe him to me, then."

"Nothing more easy."

And D'Artagnan gave, feature for feature, a description of the Comte de Wardes.

"Has he any one with him?"

"Yes; a lackey named Lubin."

"We will keep a sharp lookout for them. And if we lay hands upon them, his Eminence may be assured they shall be sent back to Paris under a good escort."

"And by doing so, governor," said D'Artagnan, "you will have merited well of the cardinal."

"Shall you see him on your return, count?"

"Doubtless I shall."

"Tell him, I beg you, that I am his humble servant."

"I will not fail."

And, delighted with this assurance, the governor signed the passport and delivered it to D'Artagnan, who lost no time in useless compliments, but thanked the governor, bowed, and departed.

Once out, he and Planchet set off as fast as they could, and by making a *détour*, avoided the wood, and re-entered the city by another gate.

The vessel was quite ready to sail, and the captain waiting on the wharf.

"Well?" said he, on perceiving D'Artagnan.

"Here is my pass, signed," said the latter.

"And that other gentleman?"

"He will not go to-day," said D'Artagnan; "but here, I'll pay you for us two."

"In that case we will be gone," said the captain.

"Yes; as soon as you please," replied D'Artagnan.

He leaped with Planchet into the boat. Five minutes after they were on board. And it was time; for they had sailed scarcely half a league when D'Artagnan saw a flash and heard a report. It was the cannon which announced the closing of the harbour.

It was time to look to his wound. Fortunately, as D'Artagnan had thought, it was not very dangerous. The point of the sword had met with a rib, and glanced along the bone. Besides, his shirt had stuck to the wound at once, and he had lost but very little blood.

D'Artagnan was worn out with fatigue. A mattress was laid upon the deck for him; he threw himself upon it, and fell fast asleep.

At break of day they were still three or four leagues from the coast of England. The breeze had been light during the night, and they had made but little progress.

At ten o'clock the vessel cast anchor in the harbour of Dover, and at half-past ten D'Artagnan placed his foot on English soil, crying,—

"Here I am at last!"

But that was not all: they had to get to London. In England the post was quite well served. D'Artagnan and Planchet took post-horses, a postilion rode before them, and in four hours they were at the gates of the capital.

D'Artagnan did not know London, he did not know one word of English, but he wrote the name of Buckingham on a piece of paper, and every one to whom he showed it pointed out to him the way to the duke's palace.

The duke was at Windsor hunting with the king.

D'Artagnan inquired for the duke's confidential valet, who, having accompanied him in all his travels, spoke

French perfectly well. He told him that he came from Paris on an affair of life and death, and that he must speak with his master instantly.

The confidence with which D'Artagnan spoke convinced Patrick, which was the name of the minister's minister. He ordered two horses to be saddled, and himself went as the young guardsman's guide. As for Planchet, he had been lifted from his horse as stiff as a stake. The poor lad's strength was exhausted. D'Artagnan seemed to be made of iron.

On their arrival at the castle they inquired for the duke, and learned that he was hawking with the king in the marshes, two or three leagues away.

In twenty minutes they were at the place designated. Patrick soon caught the sound of his master's voice recalling his falcon.

"Whom shall I announce to my Lord Duke?" asked Patrick.

"The young man who one evening sought a quarrel with him on the Pont Neuf, opposite the Samaritaine."

"Rather a singular introduction!"

"You will find that it is as good as any other."

Patrick galloped off, reached the duke, and announced to him in these very words that a messenger awaited him.

Buckingham at once remembered the circumstance, and suspecting that something was going on in France, concerning which news was now brought to him, he took only the time to inquire where the messenger was, and recognizing at a distance the uniform of the guards, he put his horse into a gallop, and rode straight up to D'Artagnan. Patrick discreetly kept in the background.

"Has any misfortune happened to the queen?" cried Buckingham, throwing all his fear and love into the question.

"I believe not. Nevertheless, I believe she is in some great peril from which your Grace alone can extricate her."

"I!" cried Buckingham. "What is it? I should be but too happy to render her any service. Speak! speak!"

"Take this letter," said D'Artagnan.

"This letter! From whom does this letter come?"

"From her Majesty, as I think."

"From her Majesty!" said Buckingham, becoming so pale that D'Artagnan feared he was going to be ill; and he broke the seal.

"What is this rent?" said he, showing D'Artagnan a place where it had been pierced through.

"Ah, ah!" said D'Artagnan, "I did not notice that; it must have been the Comte de Wardes's sword made that fine thrust, when he ran it into my breast."

"Are you wounded?" asked Buckingham, as he opened the letter.

"Oh, nothing," said D'Artagnan—"only a scratch."

"Just Heaven! what have I read?" cried the duke.— "Patrick, remain here, or rather join the king, wherever he may be, and tell his Majesty that I humbly beg him to excuse me, but an affair of the greatest importance calls me to London.—Come, sir, come!" And both set off toward the capital at full gallop.

CHAPTER XXI.

THE COMTESSE DE WINTER.

As they rode along the duke learned from D'Artagnan, not all that had passed, but all that D'Artagnan himself knew. By adding what he got from the young man to his own recollections, he was enabled to form a pretty exact idea of a condition of things the seriousness of which the queen's letter, short and vague as it was, conveyed to him quite clearly. But what astonished him most was that the cardinal, deeply interested as he was in preventing this young man from setting foot in England, had not succeeded in stopping him on the road. D'Artagnan then, on the expression of this astonishment, told him the precautions taken, and how, thanks to the devotion of his three friends, whom he had left dispersed and bleeding on the way, he had succeeded in getting off with the sword-thrust which had pierced the queen's letter, and for which he had repaid M. de Wardes in such terrible coin. While he was listening to this account, which was delivered with the greatest simplicity, the duke looked from time to time at the young man with astonishment, as if he could not comprehend how so much prudence, courage, and devotion could be displayed by a youth evidently not yet twenty years of age.

The horses went like the wind, and in a few moments they were at the gates of London. D'Artagnan imagined that on arriving in the city the duke would slacken his pace, but it was not so. He kept on at breakneck speed, heedless though he upset those who were in his way. In fact, in crossing the city two or three accidents of this kind happened. But Buckingham did not even turn his head to see what became of those he had knocked down. D'Artagnan followed him amidst cries which very much resembled curses.

On entering the court of his palace Buckingham sprang from his horse, and without caring what would become of him, threw the bridle on his neck and sprang toward the staircase. D'Artagnan did the same, with a little more concern, however, for the noble animals whose merits he could fully appreciate ; but he had the satisfaction of seeing three or four grooms run from the kitchens and stables and take charge of them at once.

The duke walked so fast that D'Artagnan had some trouble in keeping up with him. He passed through several apartments furnished with an elegance of which the greatest nobles of France had not even an idea, and arrived at length in a bedchamber which was at once a miracle of taste and of splendour. In the alcove of this chamber was a door, made in the tapestry, which the duke opened with a small gold key suspended from his neck by a chain of the same metal. D'Artagnan remained discreetly behind. But Buckingham, at the moment that he passed through the door, turned round, and seeing the young man's hesitation,—

"Come in ! come in !" cried he ; "and if you have the good fortune to be admitted to her Majesty's presence, tell her what you have seen."

Encouraged by this invitation, D'Artagnan followed the duke, who closed the door after him.

They then found themselves in a small chapel hung with a tapestry of Persian silk and embossed with gold, and brilliantly lit with a vast number of wax candles. Over a kind of altar, and beneath a canopy of blue velvet, surmounted by white and red plumes, was a life-size portrait of Anne of Austria, such a perfect likeness that D'Artagnan uttered a cry of surprise on beholding it. You might believe that the queen was about to speak.

On the altar, and beneath the portrait, was the casket containing the diamond studs.

The duke approached the altar, fell on his knees, as a priest might have done before a crucifix, then opened the casket.

"Here," said he, drawing from the casket a large bow of blue ribbon all sparkling with diamonds—"here," said he, "are the precious studs which I have taken an oath should be buried with me. The queen gave them to me; the queen takes them from me. Her will, like that of God, be done in all things."

Then he began to kiss, one after the other, those studs with which he was about to part. All at once he uttered a terrible cry.

"What is the matter?" exclaimed D'Artagnan anxiously; "what has happened to you, milord?"

"All is lost! all is lost!" cried Buckingham, turning as pale as death; "two of the studs are missing—there are but ten of them left!"

"Can you have lost them, milord, or do you think they have been stolen?"

"They have been stolen," replied the duke, "and it is the cardinal who has dealt me this blow. See! the ribbons which held them have been cut with scissors."

"If milord suspects they have been stolen, perhaps the person who stole them still has them."

"Let me reflect," said the duke. "The only time I wore these studs was at a ball given by the king a week ago at Windsor. The Comtesse de Winter, with whom I had had a quarrel, became reconciled to me at that ball. That reconciliation was a jealous woman's vengeance. I have never seen her since. The woman is an agent of the cardinal's."

"Why, then, he has agents throughout the whole world!" cried D'Artagnan.

"Yes, yes," said Buckingham, gnashing his teeth with rage; "he is a terrible antagonist! But when is the ball to take place?"

"Next Monday."

"Next Monday! Five days yet. That's more time than we need.—Patrick!" cried the duke, opening the door of the chapel—"Patrick!"

His confidential valet appeared.

"My jeweller and my secretary."

The valet went out with a mute promptness and silence that showed he was accustomed to obey blindly and without reply.

But although the jeweller had been summoned first, it was the secretary who first made his appearance. This was simple enough. He lived in the palace. He found Buckingham seated at a table in his bedchamber writing orders with his own hand.

"Master Jackson," said he, "go instantly to the lord

chancellor, and tell him that I desire him to execute these orders. I wish them to be promulgated immediately."

"But, your Grace, if the lord chancellor questions me about the motives which may have led your Grace to adopt such an extraordinary measure, what reply shall I make?"

"That such is my pleasure, and that I am responsible for my wishes to no man."

"Will that be the answer," replied the secretary, smiling, "which he must transmit to his Majesty, if, by chance, his Majesty should have the curiosity to know why no vessel is to leave any of the ports of Great Britain?"

"You are right, Master Jackson," replied Buckingham. "He will say, in that case, to the king that I am determined on war, and that this measure is my first act of hostility against France."

The secretary bowed and retired.

"We are safe on that side," said Buckingham, turning toward D'Artagnan. "If the studs are not yet gone to Paris, they will not arrive till after you."

"How so, milord?"

"I have just placed an embargo on all vessels at present in his Majesty's ports, and without special permission not one will dare raise an anchor."

D'Artagnan looked with stupefaction at a man who thus employed in the service of his amours the unlimited power with which he was clothed by a king's confidence. Buckingham saw by the expression of the young man's face what was passing in his mind, and he smiled.

"Yes," said he—"yes, Anne of Austria is my true queen. Upon a word from her I would betray my country, I would betray my king, I would betray my God. She asked me not to send the Protestants of Rochelle the assistance I promised them, and I did not do it. I broke my word, it is true; but never mind—I obeyed her wish. Have I not been richly paid for that obedience? It was to that obedience I owe her portrait!"

D'Artagnan was astonished to see by what fragile and unknown threads the destinies of a nation and the lives of men are sometimes suspended.

He was lost in these reflections when the goldsmith entered. He was an Irishman, one of the most skilful of his craft, and who himself confessed that he gained a hundred thousand pounds a year by the Duke of Buckingham.

"Master O'Reilly," said the duke to him, leading him into

the chapel, "look at these diamond studs, and tell me what they are worth apiece."

The goldsmith cast a glance at the elegant manner in which they were set, calculated, one with another, what the diamonds were worth, and without hesitation,—

"Fifteen hundred pistoles each, your Grace," replied he.

"How many days would it require to make two studs exactly like them? You see there are two wanting."

"A week, your Grace."

"I will give you three thousand pistoles each if I can have them by the day after to-morrow."

"Your Grace, you shall have them."

"You are a jewel of a man, Master O'Reilly. But that is not all. These studs cannot be trusted to anybody. They must be made in this palace."

"Impossible, your Grace; there is no one but myself who can make them so that the new may not be distinguished from the old."

"Therefore, my dear Master O'Reilly, you are my prisoner. And should you wish to leave my palace now, you cannot; so make the best of it. Name to me such of your workmen as you stand in need of, and point out the tools they must bring."

The goldsmith knew the duke. He knew all remarks would be useless, and instantly made up his mind.

"May I be permitted to inform my wife?" said he.

"Oh, you may even see her if you like, my dear Master O'Reilly. Your captivity shall be mild, be assured; and as every inconvenience deserves its indemnification, here is, in addition to the price of the studs, an order for a thousand pistoles, to make you forget the annoyance I cause you."

D'Artagnan could not get over the surprise created in him by this minister, who thus open-handed sported with men and millions.

As to the goldsmith, he wrote to his wife, sending her the order for the thousand pistoles, and charging her to send him in exchange his most skilful apprentice, an assortment of diamonds, of which he gave the names and the weight, and the necessary tools.

Buckingham led the goldsmith to the chamber destined for him, which, at the end of half an hour, was transformed into a workshop. Then he placed a sentinel at each door, with an order to admit nobody, upon any pretence, but his valet, Patrick. We need not add that the goldsmith, O'Reilly, and his assistant were prohibited from going out on any account.

This point settled, the duke turned to D'Artagnan.

"Now, my young friend," said he, "England is all our own. What do you wish for? What do you desire?"

"A bed," replied D'Artagnan. "I confess that is at present the thing I stand most in need of."

Buckingham assigned D'Artagnan a chamber adjoining his own. He wished to have the young man at hand, not at all that he mistrusted him, but for the sake of having some one to whom he could constantly talk about the queen.

An hour later the ordinance was published in London that no vessel bound for France should leave the ports—not even the packet-boat with letters. In the eyes of everybody this was a declaration of war between the two kingdoms.

On the day after the next, by eleven o'clock, the two diamond studs were finished; and they were such exact imitations, so perfectly like the others, that Buckingham could not tell the new ones from the old ones, and the most practised in such matters would have been deceived as he was.

He immediately called D'Artagnan.

"Here," said he to him, "are the diamond studs that you came to fetch; and be my witness that I have done all that human power could do."

"Rest assured, milord; I will tell what I have seen. But does your Grace mean to give me the studs without the casket?"

"The casket would only encumber you. Besides, the casket is the more precious from being all that is left to me. You will say that I keep it."

"I will perform your commission word for word, milord."

"And now," resumed Buckingham, looking earnestly at the young man, "how shall I ever acquit myself towards you?"

D'Artagnan coloured up to the eyes. He saw that the duke was searching for a means of making him accept something, and the idea that the blood of himself and his friends was about to be paid for with English gold was strangely repugnant to him.

"Let us understand each other, milord," replied D'Artagnan, "and let us weigh things well beforehand, in order that there may be no mistake. I am in the service of the king and queen of France, and form part of the company of M. des Essarts's guards, who, as well as his brother-in-law, M. de Tréville, is particularly attached to their Majesties. And, besides, it is very probable I should not have done anything of all this if it had not been to make myself agreeable to some one who is my lady, as the queen is yours."

"I understand," said the duke, smiling, "and I even believe that I know that other person. It is——"

"Milord, I have not named her!" interrupted the young man quickly.

"That is true," said the duke. "It is, then, to this person I am bound to discharge my debt of gratitude for your service."

"You have said it, milord; for truly at this moment, when there is question of war, I confess to you that I see in your Grace only an Englishman, and, consequently, an enemy, whom I should have much greater pleasure in meeting on the field of battle than in the park at Windsor or the corridors of the Louvre. All which, however, will not prevent me from executing my commission in every point, or from laying down my life, if there be need of it, to accomplish it, but—I repeat it to your Grace—without your having personally, on that account, more to thank me for in this second interview than for what I did for you in the first."

"We say, 'Proud as a Scotchman,'" murmured the Duke of Buckingham.

"And we say, 'Proud as a Gascon,'" replied D'Artagnan. "The Gascons are the Scots of France."

D'Artagnan bowed to the duke, and was retiring.

"Well, you are going away in that manner? But where, and how?"

"That's true!"

"Damn me! these Frenchmen have no forethought."

"I had forgotten that England is an island, and that you are the king of it."

"Go to the port, ask for the brig *Le Sund*, and give this letter to the captain. He will convey you to a little port where certainly no one is on the watch for you, and where only fishing-smacks ordinarily run in."

"What is the name of that port?"

"St. Valery; but listen. When you have arrived there, you will go to a mean inn, without a name and without a sign—a mere sailors' lodging-house. You cannot be mistaken; there is but one."

"And then?"

"You will ask for the host, and will repeat to him the word—*Forward !*"

"Which means ?"

"*En avant ;* that is the password. He will give you a horse all saddled, and will point out to you the road you are to take. You will find, in this manner, four relays on your route. If you wish, at each of these relays, to give your Paris address, the four horses will follow you there. You already know two of them, and you appeared to appreciate them like a lover of horseflesh. They were those we rode, and you may rely upon me for the others not being inferior to them. These horses are equipped for the field. However proud you may be, you will not refuse to accept one of them, and to request your three companions to accept the others. That is making war against us besides. The end excuses the means, as you Frenchmen say, does it not ?"

"Yes, milord, I accept them," said D'Artagnan ; "and if it please God, we will make good use of your gifts."

"Well now, your hand, young man. Perhaps we shall soon meet on the battlefield. But, in the meantime, we shall part good friends, I hope ?"

"Yes, milord ; but with the hope of soon becoming enemies ?"

"Be satisfied on that head ; I promise you."

"I depend upon your word, milord."

D'Artagnan bowed to the duke, and quickly made his way to the port opposite the Tower of London. He found the vessel that had been named to him, delivered his letter to the captain, who, after having it signed by the warden of the port, set sail at once.

Fifty vessels were waiting ready to sail.

As he was passing alongside of one of them D'Artagnan fancied he perceived on board the lady of Meung, the same whom the unknown gentleman had styled milady, and whom D'Artagnan had thought so handsome. But, thanks to the current of the river and a fair wind, his vessel passed so quickly that he lost sight of her in a moment.

The next day, about five o'clock in the morning, he landed at St. Valery.

D'Artagnan went instantly in search of the inn, and easily recognized it by the shouts proceeding from it. War between England and France was talked of as near and assured, and some jolly sailors were carousing over it.

D'Artagnan made his way through the crowd, advanced toward the host, and pronounced the word "*Forward !*"

The host instantly made him a sign to follow him, went out with him through a door which opened into the yard, led him to the stable, where a horse all saddled was waiting for him, and asked him if he needed anything else.

"I want to know the route I am to follow," said D'Artagnan.

"Go from here to Blangy, and from Blangy to Neufchâtel. At Neufchâtel go to the inn of the 'Golden Harrow,' give the password to the landlord, and you will find, as you found here, a horse ready saddled."

"Have I anything to pay?" demanded D'Artagnan.

"Everything is paid," replied the host, "and liberally. Go, then, and may God conduct you safely."

"Amen!" cried the young man, and set off at full gallop.

Four hours later he was in Neufchâtel. He strictly followed the instructions he had received. At Neufchâtel, as at St. Valery, he found a horse all saddled awaiting him. He was about to remove the pistols from the saddle he had vacated to the one he was about to occupy, but he found the holsters furnished with similar pistols.

"Your address at Paris?"

"Hôtel of the Guards, company of Des Essarts."

"Good," replied the landlord.

"Which route must I take?" demanded D'Artagnan in his turn.

"That of Rouen; but you will leave the city on your right. You must stop at the little village of Ecouis, in which there is but one inn, the Shield of France. Don't condemn it from appearances; you will find a horse in the stables quite as good as this."

"The same password?"

"Exactly."

"Farewell, master!"

"A good journey, gentleman! Do you want anything?"

D'Artagnan shook his head in reply, and set off at full speed. At Ecouis the same scene was repeated. He found as obliging a host and a fresh horse. He left his address as he had done before, and set off again, at the same pace, for Pontoise. At Pontoise he changed his horse for the last time, and at nine o'clock galloped into the court of M. de Tréville's hôtel. He had covered nearly sixty leagues in twelve hours.

M. de Tréville received him as if he had seen him that same morning; only, when pressing his hand a little more warmly than usual, he informed him that M. des Essarts's company was on duty at the Louvre, and that he might repair to his post.

CHAPTER XXII.

THE BALLET OF LA MERLAISON.

THE next day nothing was talked of in Paris but the ball which the provosts of the city were to give to the king and queen, and in which their Majesties were to dance the famous La Merlaison, the king's favourite ballet.

The whole of the last week had been occupied in preparations at the City Hall for this important evening. The city carpenter had erected a staging upon which the ladies invited were to sit. The city grocer had ornamented the chambers with two hundred white wax flambeaus, which was a piece of luxury unheard of at that period. Finally, twenty violins were ordered, and the price paid for them fixed at double the usual rate, upon condition, said the report, that they should play all night.

At ten o'clock in the morning the Sieur de la Coste, ensign in the king's guards, followed by two officers and several archers of that body, came to the city registrar, whose name was Clement, and demanded of him all the keys of the chambers and offices of the hall. These keys were given up to him instantly. Each of them had a ticket attached to it by which it might be known, and from that moment the Sieur de la Coste was charged with the guarding of all the doors and all the avenues of approach.

At eleven o'clock came in his turn Duhallier, captain of the guards, bringing with him fifty archers, who were distributed immediately through the hall, at the doors which had been assigned to them.

At three o'clock arrived two companies of the guards, one French, the other Swiss. The company of French guards was composed half of M. Duhallier's men, and half of M. des Essarts's men.

At six o'clock in the evening the invited guests began to enter. According to the order in which they entered they were shown places on the platform.

At nine o'clock Madame la Première Présidente arrived. As, next to the queen, she was the most important personage of the fête, she was received by the city officials, and seated in a box opposite to the one which the queen was to occupy.

At ten o'clock the king's collation of sweetmeats was prepared in a little chamber facing the church of St. John, in front of the silver buffet of the city, which was guarded by four archers.

At midnight great cries and loud acclamations were heard. It was the king passing through the streets which led from the Louvre to the City Hall, and which were all illuminated with coloured lanterns.

Immediately the provosts, clothed in their cloth robes, and preceded by six sergeants, each holding a torch in his hand, went out to wait upon the king, whom they met on the steps, where the provost of the merchants made him the welcoming speech, a courtesy to which his Majesty replied, apologizing for coming so late, but laying the blame on the cardinal, who had detained him till eleven o'clock, talking of affairs of state.

His Majesty, in full dress, was accompanied by his Royal Highness Monsieur, the Comte de Soissons, the Grand Prior, the Duc de Longueville, the Duc d'Elbœuf, the Comte d'Harcourt, the Comte de la Roche-Guyon, M. de Liancourt, M. de Baradas, the Comte de Cramail, and the Chevalier de Souveray.

Everybody observed that the king looked listless and preoccupied.

A closet had been prepared for the king, and another for Monsieur. In each of these closets were placed masquerade dresses. The same had been done with respect to the queen and Madame la Présidente. The nobles and ladies of their Majesties' suites were to dress, two by two, in rooms prepared for the purpose.

Before entering his closet the king desired to be informed the moment the cardinal arrived.

Half an hour after the king's entrance fresh acclamations were heard. These announced the queen's arrival. The provosts did as they had done before, and, preceded by their sergeants, went out to receive their illustrious guest.

The queen entered the great hall, and it was remarked that, like the king, she looked listless and especially fatigued.

At the moment she entered, the curtain of a small gallery, which up to that time had been closed, was drawn, and the cardinal, with a pale face and in the dress of a Spanish cavalier, appeared. His eyes were fixed on the queen's, and a smile of terrible joy passed over his lips. The queen did not have on the diamond studs.

The queen remained for a short time receiving the compliments of the city officials, and replying to the greetings of the ladies.

All at once the king appeared with the cardinal at one of the doors of the hall. The cardinal was speaking to him in a low voice, and the king was very pale.

The king, without his mask, and the ribbons of his doublet scarcely tied, made his way through the crowd, and going straight to the queen, in an altered voice asked,—

"Madame, why did you not wear your diamond studs, when you know it would have given me so much gratification?"

The queen cast a glance around her, and saw the cardinal behind, with a diabolical smile on his countenance.

"Sire," replied the queen, in a faltering voice, "because, in the midst of such a crowd as this, I feared some accident might happen to them."

"And you were wrong, madame! If I gave them to you, it was that you might adorn yourself with them. I tell you again you were wrong."

And the king's voice was tremulous with anger. The company looked and listened with astonishment, understanding nothing of what was going on.

"Sire," said the queen, "I can send for them to the Louvre, where they are, and thus your Majesty's wishes will be complied with."

"Do so, madame, do so; and as quick as possible, for within an hour the ballet will begin."

The queen bowed in token of submission, and followed the ladies who were to conduct her to her closet.

The king returned to his.

A moment of uncertainty and confusion ensued in the room. Every one had noticed that something had passed between the king and queen, but as both of them had spoken very low, and as all the company had, from respect, kept several feet away, no one had heard anything. The violins began to play with all their might, but no one listened to them.

The king was the first to come out from his closet. He was attired in a most elegant hunting costume, and Monsieur and the other nobles were dressed as he was. This was the costume that was most becoming to the king, and when thus clothed he really appeared the first gentleman of his kingdom.

The cardinal drew near to the king and placed a casket in his hand. The king opened it, and found in it two diamond studs.

"What does this mean ?" demanded he of the cardinal.

"Nothing," replied the latter; "only, if the queen has the studs—but I very much doubt if she has—count them, sire, and if you find only ten, ask her Majesty who can have stolen from her the two studs that are here."

The king looked at the cardinal as if to ask him what it meant. But he had no time to put any question to him. A cry of admiration burst from every mouth. If the king appeared to be the first gentleman of his kingdom, the queen was assuredly the most beautiful woman in France.

True, her huntress habit was admirably becoming; she wore a beaver hat with blue feathers, a surtout of pearl-gray velvet fastened with diamond clasps, and a petticoat of blue satin embroidered in silver. On her left shoulder sparkled the diamond studs, on a bow of the same colour as the plumes and the petticoat.

The king trembled with joy and the cardinal with vexation. However, at the distance they were from the queen, they could not count the studs. The queen had them; the only question was, had she ten or twelve ?

At that moment the violins sounded the signal for the ballet. The king advanced toward Madame la Présidente, with whom he was to dance, and his Highness Monsieur with the queen. They took their places, and the ballet began.

The king danced facing the queen, and every time that he passed by her he devoured with his eyes those studs, the number of which he could not make out. A cold sweat covered the cardinal's brow.

The ballet lasted an hour. It had sixteen figures.

The ballet ended amid the applause of the whole assemblage, and every one led his partner to her place. But the king took advantage of the privilege he had of leaving his lady to hasten to the queen.

"I thank you, madame," said he, "for the deference you have shown to my wishes; but I think two of your studs are missing, and I bring them back to you."

At these words he held out to the queen the two studs the cardinal had given him.

"How, sire ?" cried the young queen, affecting surprise; "you are giving me, then, two more. So now I shall have fourteen."

In fact, the king counted them, and the twelve studs were all on her Majesty's shoulder.

The king called the cardinal to him.

"What does this mean, cardinal?" asked the king in a severe tone.

"This means, sire," replied the cardinal, "that I was desirous of presenting her Majesty with these two studs, and that, not venturing to offer them myself, I adopted this means of inducing her to accept them."

"And I am the more grateful to your Eminence," replied Anne of Austria, with a smile that proved she was not the dupe of this ingenious piece of gallantry, "since I am certain these two studs have cost you as dearly as all the others cost his Majesty."

Then, after bowing to the king and the cardinal, the queen took her way to the chamber where she had dressed, and where she was to take off her ball costume.

The attention which we were obliged to give, at the beginning of this chapter, to the illustrious personages we have introduced in it diverted us for an instant from him to whom Anne of Austria owed the extraordinary triumph she had just obtained over the cardinal, and who, obscure, unknown, lost in the crowd gathered at one of the doors, was a witness of this scene, comprehensible only to four persons—the king, the queen, his Eminence, and himself.

The queen had just regained her chamber, and D'Artagnan was about to retire, when he felt a light touch on his shoulder. He turned round, and saw a young woman, who made him a sign to follow her. This young woman's face was covered with a black velvet mask, but notwithstanding this precaution, which was, in fact, taken rather against others than against him, he at once recognized his usual guide, the gay and witty Madame Bonacieux.

On the evening before, they had seen each other for a brief moment only at the porter Germain's apartment, where D'Artagnan had sent for her. The haste which the young woman was in to convey to her mistress the fine news of her messenger's happy return prevented the two lovers from exchanging more than a few words. D'Artagnan, therefore, followed Madame Bonacieux, moved by a double sentiment, love and curiosity. During the whole of the way, and in proportion as the corridors became more deserted, D'Artagnan wished to stop the young woman, seize her, and gaze upon her, were it only for a minute; but quick as a bird she slipped between his hands, and when he wished to speak to her, her finger placed on her mouth, with a little imperative gesture full of grace, reminded him that he was under the rule of a power which he had blindly to obey, and which forbade him even to make the slightest complaint. At length, after a minute or two of turns and counterturns, Madame Bonacieux opened the door of a closet, which was entirely dark, and led the young man into it. There she made a fresh sign of silence, and opening a second door, concealed by a tapestry which as it was drawn aside let in a sudden flood of brilliant light, she disappeared.

D'Artagnan remained for a moment motionless, asking himself where he could be; but soon a ray of light penetrating from the chamber, the warm and perfumed air reaching even to him, the conversation of two or three ladies in language at once respectful and elegant, and the word "Majesty" many times repeated, clearly indicated to him that he was in a closet adjoining the queen's chamber. The young man stood in the shadow and waited.

The queen appeared cheerful and happy, and this seemed to astonish very much the persons surrounding her, who were accustomed, on the contrary, to see her almost always sad and full of care. The queen attributed this joyous feeling to the beauty of the ball, to the pleasure she had experienced in the ballet; and as it is not permissible to contradict a queen, whether she smile or whether she weep, all rivalled one another in expatiating on the gallantry of the provosts of the city of Paris.

Although D'Artagnan did not know the queen, he soon distinguished her voice from the others, at first by a slightly foreign accent, and next by that tone of domination naturally impressed upon all royal words. He heard her approach and withdraw from the open door, and twice or three times he even saw the shadow of a body intercept the light.

At length a hand and an arm, surpassingly beautiful in form and whiteness, suddenly glided through the tapestry. D'Artagnan understood that this was his reward. He cast himself on his knees, seized the hand, and touched it respectfully with his lips; then the hand was withdrawn, leaving in his an object which he perceived to be a ring. The door immediately closed, and D'Artagnan found himself again in complete darkness.

D'Artagnan placed the ring on his finger, and again waited; it was evident that all was not yet over. After the reward of his devotion, the reward of his love was to come. Besides, although the ballet was danced, the evening's pleasures had scarcely begun. Supper was to be served at three, and the clock of St. John had struck three-quarters after two.

In fact, the sound of voices in the adjoining chamber diminished by degrees ; the company was then heard departing ; then the door of the closet in which D'Artagnan was was opened, and Madame Bonacieux entered quickly.

" You at last ? " cried D'Artagnan.

" Silence ! " said the young woman, placing her hand upon his lips—" silence ! and go the same way you came."

" But where and when shall I see you again ? " cried D'Artagnan.

" A note which you will find at home will tell you. Go ! go ! "

And at these words she opened the door of the corridor and pushed D'Artagnan out of the closet. D'Artagnan obeyed like a child, without the least resistance or objection, which proves that he was really in love.

CHAPTER XXIII.

THE RENDEZVOUS.

D'ARTAGNAN ran home immediately, and although it was after three o'clock in the morning, and he had the worst quarters of Paris to pass through, he met with no misadventure.

He found the door of his passage open, sprang up the stairs, and knocked softly, in a manner agreed upon between him and his lackey. Planchet, whom he had sent home two hours before from the City Hall, desiring him to sit up for him, came and opened the door.

" Has any one brought a letter for me ? " asked D'Artagnan eagerly.

" No one has *brought* a letter, sir," replied Planchet ; " but there is one come of itself."

" What do you mean by that, you stupid fellow ? "

" I mean that when I came in, although I had the key of your apartment in my pocket and that key had never been out of my possession, I found a letter on the green table-cover in your bedroom."

" And where is that letter ? "

" I left it where I found it, sir. It is not natural for letters to enter people's rooms in this manner. If the window had been open, or even ajar, I should think nothing of it. But no ; all was as close as possible. Beware, sir ; there is certainly some magic in it."

In the meantime the young man darted into his chamber and was opening the letter. It was from Madame Bonacieux, and was conceived in these terms:—

"Warm thanks are to be offered to you, and to be transmitted to you. Be at St. Cloud this evening about ten o'clock, in front of the pavilion at the corner of M. d'Estrées's hôtel.—C. B."

While reading this letter D'Artagnan felt his heart expand and close with that delicious spasm that tortures and caresses the hearts of lovers.

It was the first note he had received; it was the first rendezvous that had been granted him. His heart, swelled by the intoxication of joy, felt ready to faint at the very gate of that terrestrial paradise called Love!

"Well, sir," said Planchet, who had noticed his master grow red and pale successively, "did I not guess truly? Is it not some bad business or other?"

"You are mistaken, Planchet," replied D'Artagnan; "and, as a proof, there is a crown to drink my health."

"I am much obliged to you for the crown you have given me, and I promise you I will obey your instructions exactly. But it is not the less true that letters which come in this manner into shut-up houses——"

"Fall from heaven, my friend, fall from heaven."

"Then you are happy?" asked Planchet.

"My dear Planchet, I am the happiest of men!"

"And I may profit by your happiness, and go to bed?"

"Yes, go."

"May the blessings of heaven fall upon you. But it is not the less true that that letter——"

And Planchet retired, shaking his head with an air of doubt, which D'Artagnan's liberality did not entirely succeed in removing.

Left alone, D'Artagnan read and reread his note, then he kissed and kissed again twenty times the lines traced by the hand of his beautiful mistress. At length he went to bed, fell asleep, and had golden dreams.

At seven o'clock in the morning he arose and called Planchet, who, at the second summons, opened the door, his countenance not yet quite free from the anxiety of the preceding night.

"Planchet," said D'Artagnan, "I am going out for all day, perhaps. You are, therefore, your own master till seven o'clock in the evening; but at seven o'clock you must hold yourself in readiness with two horses."

"There!" said Planchet. "It appears we are going to have our skins pierced again in several places."

"You will take your carbine and your pistols."

"There now! did I not say so?" cried Planchet. "I was sure of it—cursed letter!"

"Come, don't be afraid, you silly fellow. There is nothing on hand but a pleasure party."

"Ah! like that charming journey the other day, when it rained bullets and grew a crop of snares."

"Well, if you are really afraid, Master Planchet," resumed D'Artagnan, "I will go without you. I prefer travelling alone to having a timid companion."

"You do me wrong," said Planchet; "I thought you had seen me at work."

"Yes; but I did not know whether you had not used up all your courage the first time."

"You shall see, on occasion, that I have some left; only I beg you not to be too prodigal of it, if you wish it to last long."

"Do you believe you still have a certain amount of it to expend this evening?"

"I hope I have, sir."

"Well, then, I depend upon you."

"At the appointed hour I shall be ready; only I believe you had but one horse in the guard stables."

"Perhaps there is but one at this moment, but by this evening there will be four."

"It appears that our journey is to be a journey for re-mounts, then?"

"Exactly so," said D'Artagnan; and nodding to Planchet, he went out.

M. Bonacieux was standing at his door. D'Artagnan's intention was to go out without speaking to the worthy mercer. But the latter made so polite and friendly a salutation that his tenant felt obliged not only to stop, but to enter into conversation with him.

Besides, how is it possible to avoid a little condescension toward a husband whose pretty wife has appointed a meeting with you that same evening at St. Cloud, opposite the pavilion of M. d'Estrées? D'Artagnan approached him with the most amiable air he could assume.

The conversation naturally fell upon the poor man's incarceration. M. Bonacieux, who was ignorant that D'Artagnan had overheard his conversation with the man of Meung, related to his young tenant the persecutions of that monster,

M. de Laffemas, whom he never ceased to qualify, during his account, with the title of the cardinal's executioner, and expatiated at great length upon the Bastille, the bolts, the wickets, the air-holes, the gratings, and the instruments of torture.

D'Artagnan listened to him with exemplary condescension, and when he had finished, said,—

"And Madame Bonacieux—do you know who carried her off? For I do not forget that I owe to that unpleasant circumstance the good fortune of having made your acquaintance."

"Ah," said Bonacieux, "they took good care not to tell me that; and my wife, on her part, has sworn to me, by all that's sacred, that she does not know. But you," continued M. Bonacieux, in a tone of perfect simplicity—"what have you been doing for several days past? I have not seen either you or any of your friends, and I don't think you could pick up from the pavement of Paris all that dust that I saw Planchet brush off your boots yesterday."

"You are right, my dear M. Bonacieux; my friends and I have been on a little journey."

"Far from Paris?"

"O Lord, no! About forty leagues only. We went to take M. Athos to the waters of Forges, where my friends have remained."

"And so you have returned, have you?" replied M. Bonacieux, giving his countenance his most jocular air. "A handsome young fellow like you does not obtain long leave of absence from his mistress; and we were impatiently waited for at Paris, were we not?"

"'Pon my word," said the young man, laughing, "I am fain to confess it; and so much the more readily, my dear M. Bonacieux, as I see there is no concealing anything from you. Yes, I was expected, and very impatiently, I assure you."

A slight shade passed over Bonacieux's brow, but so slight that D'Artagnan did not perceive it.

"And we are going to be rewarded for our diligence?" continued the mercer, with a trifling alteration in his voice— so trifling, indeed, that D'Artagnan did not perceive it any more than he had the shade which, an instant before, had darkened the worthy man's countenance.

"Ah, you are a deep one!" said D'Artagnan, laughing.

"No; what I say is only that I may know whether you will come in late."

" Why do you ask me that question, my dear landlord ? Do you intend to sit up for me ? "

" No ; only since my arrest and the robbery that was committed in my house I am alarmed every time I hear a door opened, particularly in the night. What the deuce can you expect ? I told you I was no swordsman."

" Well, don't be alarmed if I come home at one, two, or three o'clock in the morning ; indeed, do not be alarmed if I do not come at all."

This time Bonacieux became so pale that D'Artagnan could not do otherwise than perceive it, and asked him what was the matter.

" Nothing," replied Bonacieux, " nothing ; only since my misfortunes I have been subject to faintnesses, which seize me all at once, and I just felt a cold shiver. Pay no attention to it ; you have nothing to occupy yourself with but being happy."

" Then I have plenty of occupation, for I am happy."

" Not yet ; wait a little. This evening, you said."

" Well, this evening will come, thank God ! And perhaps you look for it with as much impatience as I do ; perhaps this evening Madame Bonacieux will visit the conjugal domicile."

" Madame Bonacieux is not at liberty this evening," replied the husband seriously ; " she is detained at the Louvre this evening by her duties."

" So much the worse for you, my dear host, so much the worse for you ! When I am happy, I wish everybody to be so ; but it appears that is not possible."

And the young man departed, laughing at the joke, which he thought he alone could comprehend.

" Ah, have your laugh out," replied Bonacieux, in a sepulchral tone.

But D'Artagnan was too far off to hear him, and if he had heard him, in the frame of mind he then was he certainly would not have remarked it.

He took his way toward M. de Tréville's hôtel. His visit the day before, we remember, had been very short, with little chances for confidential talk.

He found M. de Tréville in a most joyful mood. The king and queen had been charming to him at the ball. The cardinal, however, had been particularly ill-tempered ; he had retired at one o'clock under the pretence of being indisposed. Their Majesties did not return to the Louvre till six o'clock.

"Now," said M. de Tréville, lowering his voice and looking round at every corner of the apartment to see whether they were alone—"now let us talk about yourself, my young friend ; for it is evident that your fortunate return has something to do with the king's joy, the queen's triumph, and the cardinal's humiliation. You must look out for yourself."

"What have I to fear," replied D'Artagnan, "so long as I have the good fortune to enjoy their Majesties' favour ?"

"Everything, believe me. The cardinal is not the man to forget a mystification until he has settled his accounts with the mystifier. And the mystifier appears to me to have the air of being a certain young Gascon of my acquaintance."

"Do you believe the cardinal is as well informed as you are, and knows that I have been to London ?"

"The devil ! you have been to London ! Did you bring from London that beautiful diamond glittering on your finger ? Beware, my dear D'Artagnan ! A present from an enemy is not a good thing. Are there not some Latin verses upon that subject ? Stop a minute——"

"Yes, doubtless," replied D'Artagnan, who had never been able to cram even the first rudiments of that language into his head, and who, by his ignorance, had driven his master to despair—"yes, doubtless there is one."

"There certainly is one," said M. de Tréville, who had a smattering of letters, "and M. de Benserade was quoting it to me the other day. Stop a minute. Ah, it is this :

'*Timeo Danaos et dona ferentes,*'

which means, 'Beware of the emeny who makes you presents.'"

"This diamond does not come from an enemy, sir," replied D'Artagnan ; "it comes from the queen."

"From the queen ! oh, ho ! " said M. de Tréville. "Why, it is indeed a genuine royal jewel, worth a thousand pistoles if it is worth a farthing. By whom did the queen send you this jewel ? "

"She gave it to me herself."

"Where ? "

"In the closet adjoining the chamber in which she changed her dress."

"How ? "

"By giving me her hand to kiss."

"What ! you have kissed the queen's hand ? " said M. de Tréville, looking earnestly at D'Artagnan.

"Her Majesty did me the honour to grant me that favour."

"And that in the presence of witnesses! Imprudent woman! thrice imprudent!"

"No, sir; be assured no one saw her," replied D'Artagnan; and he told M. de Tréville how things had gone.

"O women, women!" cried the old soldier. "I know them by their romantic imaginations; everything that savours of mystery charms them. So you saw her arm, that was all. You would meet the queen and you would not know her; she might meet you and she would not know who you were?"

"No; but thanks to this diamond——" replied the young man.

"Listen to me," said M. de Tréville; "shall I give you a good piece of advice—a piece of friendly advice?"

"You will do me honour, sir," said D'Artagnan.

"Well, then, go to the nearest goldsmith's, and sell that diamond for the highest price you can get from him. However much of a Jew he may be, he will give you at least eight hundred pistoles. Pistoles have no name, young man, and that ring has a terrible one, which may betray him who wears it."

"Sell this ring—a ring which comes from my sovereign! Never!" said D'Artagnan.

"Then at least turn the stone inside, you silly fellow! For everybody must be aware that a cadet from Gascony does not find such gems in his mother's jewel-case."

"You think, then, I have something to fear?" said D'Artagnan.

"I mean, young man, that he who sleeps over a mine, the match of which is already lighted, may consider himself in safety in comparison with you."

"The devil!" said D'Artagnan, who, at M. de Tréville's positive tone, began to feel a little uneasy—"the devil! What must I do?"

"Be at all times on your guard. The cardinal has a tenacious memory and a long arm. You may depend upon it, he will repay you by some ill turn."

"But what sort of one?"

"Eh! how can I tell? Has he not all the devil's tricks at command? The least that might happen would be your arrest."

"What! would they dare to arrest a man in his Majesty's service?"

"Zounds! they did not scruple much in the case of Athos.

8

At all events, young man, believe one who has been thirty years at court. Do not lull yourself into security, or you will be lost; but, on the contrary—and I tell you so—see enemies in all directions. If any one seeks a quarrel with you, shun it, were it with a child of ten years old; if you are attacked by day or by night, draw back, without shame; if you cross a bridge, feel every plank of it with your foot, lest one should give way beneath you; if you pass before a house which is building, look up, for fear a stone should fall upon your head; if you stay out late, be always followed by your lackey, and let your lackey be armed—if, by-the-bye, you can be sure of your lackey. Mistrust everybody—your friend, your brother, your mistress—your mistress in particular."

D'Artagnan coloured.

"My mistress," repeated he mechanically; "and why mistrust her rather than any other?"

"Because a mistress is one of the cardinal's favourite means; he has not one that is more expeditious. A woman will sell you for ten pistoles—witness Delilah. You are acquainted with the Scriptures, eh?"

D'Artagnan thought of the appointment Madame Bonacieux had made with him for that very evening; but we are bound to say, to the credit of our hero, that the bad opinion entertained by M. de Tréville of women in general did not inspire him with the least suspicion of his pretty hostess.

"But, by the way," resumed M. de Tréville, "what has become of your three companions?"

"I was about to ask you if you had heard no news of them."

"None whatever, sir."

"Well, I left them on my road—Porthos at Chantilly, with a duel on his hands; Aramis at Crèvecœur, with a ball in his shoulder; and Athos at Amiens, detained by an accusation of counterfeiting."

"See there, now!" said M. de Tréville. "And how the devil did you escape?"

"By a miracle, sir, I must acknowledge, with a sword-thrust in my breast, and by nailing Comte de Wardes, on the road to Calais, like a butterfly on a tapestry."

"There again! De Wardes, one of the cardinal's men, a cousin of Rochefort's! But stop, my friend, I have an idea."

"Speak, sir."

" In your place, I would do one thing."

" What, sir ? "

" While his Eminence was seeking for me in Paris, I should take, without sound of drum or trumpet, the road to Picardy, and should go and make some inquiries concerning my three companions. What the devil ! they richly merit that piece of attention on your part."

" Your advice is good, sir, and to-morrow I will set out."

" To-morrow ! And why not this evening ? "

" This evening, sir, I am detained in Paris by urgent business."

" Ah, young man, young man ! Some love affair. Take care, I repeat to you, take care ! Woman was the ruin of us all, is the ruin of us all, and will be the ruin of us all, as long as the world stands. Take my advice and set out this evening."

" It is impossible, sir."

" You have given your word, then ? "

" Yes, sir."

" Ah, that's quite another thing. But promise me, if you should not happen to be killed to-night, that you will go to-morrow."

" I promise you, sir."

" Do you want money ? "

" I still have fifty pistoles. That, I think, is as much as I shall need."

" But your companions ? "

" I don't think they can be in need of any. We left Paris each with seventy-five pistoles in his pocket."

" Shall I see you again before your departure ? "

" I think not, sir, unless something new happens."

" Well, a pleasant journey to you, then."

" Thank you, sir."

And D'Artagnan left M. de Tréville, touched more than ever by his paternal solicitude for his musketeers.

He called successively at the abodes of Athos, Porthos, and Aramis. None of them had returned. Their lackeys likewise were absent, and nothing had been heard of either masters or servants.

He would have inquired after them of their mistresses, but he was not acquainted with Porthos's or Aramis's, and Athos had none.

As he passed the Hôtel des Gardes he took a glance into the stables. Three of the four horses had already arrived.

Planchet, much astonished, was busy grooming them, and had already finished with two.

"Ah, sir," said Planchet, on perceiving D'Artagnan, "how glad I am to see you!"

"Why so, Planchet?" asked the young man.

"Do you place confidence in our landlord, M. Bonacieux?"

"I? Not the least in the world."

"Oh, you do quite right, sir."

"But why do you ask?"

"Because, while you were talking with him, I watched you without listening to you; and, sir, his countenance changed colour two or three times."

"Bah!"

"Preoccupied as you were with the letter you had just received, you did not observe it; but, on the contrary, as I was put on my guard by the strange manner in which that letter had come into the house, I did not lose a movement of his face."

"And you found it——"

"Traitorous, sir."

"Indeed!"

"Besides, as soon as you had left, and disappeared round the corner of the street, M. Bonacieux took his hat, shut his door, and set off at a quick pace in an opposite direction."

"It seems you are right, Planchet. All this appears to be a little suspicious; and be assured that we will not pay him our rent until the matter shall be categorically explained to us."

"You joke, but you will see."

"What can you expect, Planchet? What must be shall be!"

"You have not, then, given up your excursion for this evening?"

"Quite the contrary, Planchet; the more ill-will I entertain toward M. Bonacieux, the more punctual I shall be in keeping the appointment made with me in that letter which gives you so much uneasiness."

"Then your determination is——"

"Is unalterable, my friend; so, then, be ready here, at nine o'clock, at the hôtel. I will come and get you."

Planchet, seeing there was no longer any hope of making his master abandon his project, heaved a deep sigh, and set to work to groom the third horse.

D'Artagnan, being at bottom a prudent youth, instead of returning home, went and dined with the Gascon priest, who, at the time of the four friends' poverty, had given them a breakfast of chocolate.

CHAPTER XXIV.

THE PAVILION.

At nine o'clock D'Artagnan was at the Hôtel des Gardes. He found Planchet under arms. The fourth horse had arrived.

Planchet was armed with his carbine and a pistol. D'Artagnan had his sword, and placed two pistols in his belt; then both mounted and departed quietly. It was quite dark, and no one saw them go out. Planchet followed his master, and kept at a distance of about ten paces from him.

D'Artagnan crossed the quays, went out by the gate of La Conférence, and went along the road, much more beautiful then than it is now, leading to St. Cloud.

As long as he was in the city Planchet kept at the respectful distance he had imposed upon himself. But as soon as the road began to be lonely and darker, he quietly drew nearer; so that when they entered the Bois de Boulogne, he found himself riding quite naturally side by side with his master. In fact, we must admit that the oscillation of the tall trees, and the moonlight flecking the dark underwood, gave him serious uneasiness. D'Artagnan perceived that something more than usual was passing in the mind of his lackey, and said,—

"Well, Master Planchet, what is the matter with us now?"

"Don't you think, sir, that woods are like churches?"

"How so, Planchet?"

"Because we dare not speak aloud in either."

"Why do you not dare to speak aloud, Planchet?—because you are afraid?"

"Afraid of being heard? Yes, sir."

"Afraid of being heard! Why, our conversation is quite proper, my dear Planchet, and no one could find fault with it."

"Ah, sir!" replied Planchet, recurring to his besetting idea, "that M. Bonacieux has something sly in his eyebrows, and something very unpleasant in the play of his lips."

"What the devil makes you think of Bonacieux now?"

"Sir, we think of what we can, and not of what we will."

"Because you are a coward, Planchet."

"Sir, we must not confound prudence with cowardice. Prudence is a virtue."

"And you are very virtuous, are you not, Planchet?"

"Is not that a musket barrel glittering yonder, sir? Had we not better duck our heads?"

"Truly," murmured D'Artagnan as M. de Tréville's advice recurred to him, "this animal will end by making me afraid."

And he put his horse into a trot. Planchet followed the movements of his master as if he had been his shadow, and was soon trotting by his side.

"Are we going to continue this pace all night?" asked Planchet.

"No, for you are at your journey's end."

"I, sir, at my journey's end? And you?"

"Why, I am going a few steps farther."

"And do you intend to leave me here alone?"

"You certainly are afraid, Planchet?"

"No; but I only beg leave to observe to you that the night will be very cold, that chills bring on rheumatism, and that a lackey who has the rheumatism makes but a poor servant, particularly to a master as active as you are."

"Well, if you are cold, Planchet, you can go into one of those saloons that you see yonder, and be waiting for me at the door by six o'clock in the morning."

"Sir, I have eaten and drunk in your honour the crown you gave me this morning, so that I have not a sou left, in case I should be cold."

"Here's a half-pistole. To-morrow morning, then."

D'Artagnan sprang from his horse, threw the bridle to Planchet, and departed at a quick pace, folding his cloak round him.

"Good Lord, how cold I am!" cried Planchet as soon as he had lost sight of his master; and in such haste was he to warm himself that he went straight to a house set out with all the attributes of a suburban inn, and knocked at the door.

In the meantime D'Artagnan, who had plunged into a bypath, continued his route, and reached St. Cloud; but instead of following the highway, he turned behind the château, reached a sort of retired lane, and found himself soon in front of the pavilion named. It was situated in a very private spot. A high wall, at the angle of which was the pavilion, ran along one side of this lane, and on the other a hedge protected from passers-by a little garden, at the rear of which stood a small cottage.

He was now on the place appointed, and as no signal had been given him by which to announce his presence, he waited.

Not the least noise was to be heard; one might have thought oneself a hundred miles from the capital. D'Artagnan leaned against the hedge, after having cast a glance behind him. Beyond that hedge, that garden, and that cottage a dark mist enveloped with its folds that immensity in which sleeps Paris, a vast void in which glittered a few luminous points, the funeral stars of that hell!

But for D'Artagnan all things visible wore a joyful dress, all ideas had a smile, all darknesses were diaphanous. The appointed hour was about to strike.

In fact, at the end of a few minutes the belfry of St. Cloud let fall slowly ten strokes from its huge, sonorous jaws.

There was something lugubrious in this brazen voice pouring out its lamentations in the midst of the night.

But every one of those strokes which made up the expected hour vibrated harmoniously in the young man's heart.

His eyes were fixed upon the little pavilion situated at the angle of the wall, all the windows of which were closed with shutters, except one on the first story.

Through this window shone a mild light, silvering the trembling foliage of two or three linden trees that formed a group outside the park. Evidently behind this little window, which threw forth such friendly beams, pretty Madame Bonacieux was awaiting him.

Wrapt in this sweet idea, D'Artagnan waited half an hour without the least impatience, his eyes fixed upon that charming little abode. He could perceive a part of the ceiling with its gilded mouldings, attesting the elegance of the rest of the apartment.

The clock on St. Cloud struck half-past ten.

This time, without at all knowing why, D'Artagnan felt a shiver run through his veins. Perhaps the cold was beginning to affect him, and he took a purely physical sensation for a mental impression.

Then the idea seized him that he had read incorrectly, and that the appointment was for eleven o'clock. He drew near to the window, so as to stand under a ray of light, and taking the letter out of his pocket, read it again. But he had not been mistaken; the appointment was for ten o'clock.

He went and resumed his post, beginning to be rather uneasy at this silence and this solitude.

It struck eleven!

D'Artagnan began now really to fear that something had happened to Madame Bonacieux.

He clapped his hands three times, the ordinary signal of lovers; but nobody replied to him—not even an echo.

He then thought, with a touch of vexation, that perhaps the young woman had fallen asleep while waiting for him.

He approached the wall and tried to climb it; but the wall had been recently pointed, and he could obtain no hold.

At that moment he noticed the trees, on the leaves of which the light still shone; and as one of them drooped over the road, he thought that from its branches he might succeed in looking into the pavilion.

The tree was easy to climb. Besides, D'Artagnan was scarcely twenty, and consequently had not yet forgotten his schoolboy habits. In an instant he was among the branches, and his eyes penetrated through the clear glass into the interior of the pavilion.

It was something strange, something that made D'Artagnan cold from the sole of his foot to the roots of his hair, to find that this soft light, this peaceful lamp, lighted up a scene of fearful disorder. One of the panes of glass was broken, the door of the room had been burst in, and hung, split in two, on its hinges; a table, which had been covered with an elegant supper, was overturned; the decanters, broken in pieces, and the crushed fruits, strewed the floor; everything in the apartment gave evidence of a violent and desperate struggle. D'Artagnan even fancied he could recognize, amid this strange disorder, fragments of garments, and some bloody spots staining the cloth and the curtains.

He hastened down into the street, with his heart throbbing frightfully. He wished to see if he could find any other traces of violence.

The little soft light continued to shine in the calm of the night. D'Artagnan then perceived a thing that he had not before remarked, for nothing had led him to this scrutiny— that the ground, trampled here and hoof-marked there, presented confused traces of men and horses. Besides, the wheels of a carriage, which appeared to have come from Paris, had made a deep impression in the soft earth, not extending beyond the pavilion, but turning again towards Paris.

At length D'Artagnan, in following up his researches, found near the wall a woman's torn glove. Yet this glove, wherever it had not touched the muddy ground, was of irreproachable freshness. It was one of those perfumed gloves that lovers like to snatch from a pretty hand.

As D'Artagnan pursued his investigations, at every fresh discovery a more abundant and more icy sweat stood in drops on his forehead; his heart was oppressed by a horrible anguish, his respiration was broken and short. And yet he said, to reassure himself, that this pavilion, perhaps, had nothing to do with Madame Bonacieux; that the young woman had made an appointment with him in front of the pavilion, and not in the pavilion; that she might have been detained in Paris by her duties, or perhaps by her husband's jealousy.

But all these reasons were combated, destroyed, overthrown by that sense of inward discomfort which occasionally takes possession of our being, and cries to us, in an unmistakable language, that some great misfortune is hanging over us.

Then D'Artagnan became almost wild. He ran along the highway, retraced his steps, and coming to the ferry, closely questioned the boatman.

About seven o'clock in the evening, the boatman said, he had taken over a young woman, enveloped in a black mantle, who appeared to be very anxious not to be recognized; but the boatman, simply on account of her precautions, had paid more special attention to her, and discovered that she was young and pretty.

There was then, as there is now, a crowd of pretty young women who came to St. Cloud, and who had good reasons for not being seen, and yet D'Artagnan did not for an instant doubt that it was Madame Bonacieux whom the boatman had noticed.

D'Artagnan took advantage of the lamp burning in the boatman's cabin to read Madame Bonacieux's note once again, and satisfy himself that he had not been mistaken, that the appointment was at St. Cloud and not elsewhere, before M. d'Estrées's pavilion and not in another street.

Everything conspired to prove to D'Artagnan that his presentiments had not deceived him, and that a great misfortune had happened.

He again ran back to the château. It appeared to him

that something might have happened at the pavilion in his absence, and that fresh information was awaiting him.

The lane was still empty, and the same calm, soft light shone from the window.

D'Artagnan then thought of that mute, blind cottage: it must have seen, and perhaps could speak !

The gate was locked, but he leaped over the hedge, and in spite of the barking of a chained dog, went up to the cabin.

There was no answer to his first knocking. A deathlike silence reigned in the cottage as in the pavilion ; but as the cottage was his last resource, he kept knocking.

It soon appeared to him that he heard a slight noise within, a timid noise, seeming itself to tremble.

Then D'Artagnan ceased to knock, and entreated with an accent so full of anxiety and promises, terror and persuasion, that his voice was of a nature to reassure the most timid. At length an old, worm-eaten shutter was opened, or rather pushed ajar, but closed again as soon as the light from a miserable lamp burning in the corner had shone upon D'Artagnan's baldric, sword-hilt, and pistol pommels. Nevertheless, rapid as the movement had been, D'Artagnan had had time to get a glimpse of an old man's head.

"In the name of Heaven," cried he, "listen to me ! I have been waiting for some one who has not come. I am dying with anxiety. Could any misfortune have happened in the neighbourhood ? Speak ! "

The window was again opened slowly, and the same face appeared again. Only it was paler than before.

D'Artagnan related his story simply, with the omission of names. He told how he had an appointment with a young woman before that pavilion, and how, seeing she did not come, he had climbed the linden tree, and by the lamplight had seen the disorder of the chamber.

The old man listened attentively, making a sign only that it all was so ; and then, when D'Artagnan had ended, he shook his head with an air that foreboded nothing good.

"What do you mean ? " cried D'Artagnan. " In the name of Heaven, tell me, explain yourself."

"Go, sir," said the old man—" ask me nothing ; for if I told you what I have seen, certainly no good would befall me."

"You have then seen something ? " replied D'Artagnan. "In that case, in the name of Heaven," continued he, throwing him a pistole, " tell me what you have seen, and I will pledge you the faith of a gentleman that not one of your words shall escape from my heart.''

The old man read so much truth and so much grief in the young man's face that he made him a sign to listen, and speaking in a low voice, said,—

" It was about nine o'clock when I heard a noise in the street, and was wondering what it could be, when, on coming to my gate, I found that somebody was endeavouring to open it. As I am poor, and am not afraid of being robbed, I went and opened the gate, and saw three men at a few paces from it. In the shade was a coach with horses, and some saddle-horses. These saddle-horses evidently belonged to the three men, who were dressed as cavaliers.

" ' Ah, my worthy gentlemen,' cried I, ' what do you want ?'

" ' Have you a ladder ? ' said the one who appeared to be the leader of the party.

" ' Yes, sir—the one with which I gather my fruit.'

" ' Lend it to us, and go into your house again. There is a crown for the trouble we cause you. Only remember this, if you speak a word of what you may see or hear (for you will look and listen, I am quite sure, however we may threaten you), you are lost.'

" At these words he threw me a crown, which I picked up, and he took my ladder.

" Well, then, after I had shut the gate behind them, I pretended to go into the house again ; but I immediately went out at a back door, and stealing along in the shade, I gained yonder clump of elder, from which I could see everything without being seen.

" The three men brought the carriage up quietly, and took out of it a little, short, stout, elderly man, poorly dressed in dark-coloured clothes. He climbed the ladder very carefully, looked slyly in at the window of the pavilion, came down as quietly as he had gone up, and whispered,—

" ' It is she ! '

" Immediately the one who had spoken to me approached the door of the pavilion, opened it with a key he had in his hand, closed the door, and disappeared, while at the same time the other two men mounted the ladder. The little old man remained at the coach door, the coachman took care of his horses, a lackey held the saddle-horses.

" All at once loud screams resounded in the pavilion, and a woman ran to the window and opened it, as if to throw herself out of it ; but as soon as she perceived the other two men, she sprang back, and they got into the chamber.

"Then I saw no more, but I heard the noise of breaking furniture. The woman screamed and cried for help, but her cries were soon stifled. Two of the men appeared, bearing the woman in their arms, and carried her to the carriage; the little old man entered it after her. The one who stayed in the pavilion closed the window, came out an instant after at the door, and satisfied himself that the woman was in the carriage. His two companions were already on horseback; he sprang into his saddle, the lackey took his place by the coachman, the carriage went off at a rapid pace, escorted by the three horsemen, and all was over. From that moment I have neither seen nor heard anything."

D'Artagnan, entirely overcome by such terrible news, remained motionless and mute, while all the demons of anger and jealousy were howling in his heart.

"But, my good gentleman," resumed the old man, upon whom this mute despair certainly produced a greater effect than cries and tears would have done, "do not take on so; they did not kill her—that's the main thing."

"Have you any idea," asked D'Artagnan, "who the man was who led this infernal expedition?"

"I did not know him at all."

"But, since he spoke to you, you must have seen him."

"Oh, you want a description of him, do you?"

"I do."

"A tall, swarthy man, with black moustaches, dark eyes, and the appearance of a gentleman."

"That's the man!" cried D'Artagnan; "again he, always he! He is my evil demon evidently. And the other?"

"Which?"

"The short one."

"Oh, he was not a gentleman, I'll answer for it. Besides, he did not wear a sword, and the others treated him with no consideration."

"Some lackey," murmured D'Artagnan.—"Poor woman! poor woman! What have they done with you?"

"You have promised me silence, sir," said the old man.

"And I repeat my promise. Have no anxiety; I am a gentleman. A gentleman has but his word, and I have given you mine."

With a broken heart D'Artagnan again bent his way toward the ferry. Sometimes he could not believe it was Madame Bonacieux, and hoped he should find her next day at the Louvre; sometimes he feared she had been having an intrigue with some one else, who, in a jealous fit; had surprised her and carried her off. His mind was torn by doubt, grief, and despair.

"Oh, if I had my three friends here," cried he, "I should have, at least, some hopes of finding her; but who knows what has become of them?"

It was almost midnight; the next thing was to find Planchet. D'Artagnan went successively into all the saloons where there was a light, but could not find Planchet in any of them.

At the sixth he began to reflect that the search was rather a matter of chance. Planchet's appointment was for six o'clock in the morning, and wherever he might be, he was acting according to directions.

It occurred to D'Artagnan that by remaining in the neighbourhood of the spot where this mysterious affair had taken place he should, perhaps, obtain some light on it. At the sixth saloon, then, as we said, D'Artagnan stopped, asked for a bottle of wine of the best quality, and taking his place in the darkest corner of the room, determined thus to wait till daylight. But this time again his hopes were disappointed, and although he listened with all his ears, he heard nothing amid the oaths, coarse jokes, and abuse passing between the workmen, servants, and carters who composed the honourable society of which he formed a part, that could put him at all on the track of the poor abducted woman. He was compelled, then, after having swallowed the contents of his bottle, in order to pass the time as well as to avoid suspicion, to find the easiest position possible in his corner, and to sleep as well as he could. D'Artagnan, be it remembered, was only twenty years old, and at that age sleep has imprescriptible rights, which it imperiously insists upon, even over the saddest hearts.

Towards six o'clock D'Artagnan awoke with that uncomfortable feeling which daylight generally brings after a bad night. He was not long in making his toilet. He examined himself to see if advantage had been taken to rob him while he was asleep, and having found his diamond ring on his finger, his purse in his pocket, and his pistols in his belt, he got up, paid for his wine, and went out to see whether he could have any better luck in his search for his lackey than he had had the night before. In reality the first thing he perceived through the damp, gray mist was honest Planchet, who, with the two horses in hand, was waiting for him at the door of an obscure little tavern, before which D'Artagnan had passed without even a suspicion of its existence.

CHAPTER XXV.

PORTHOS.

INSTEAD of returning directly home, D'Artagnan alighted at M. de Tréville's door and quickly ran upstairs. This time he was determined to relate all that had passed. As M. de Tréville saw the queen almost every day, he might be able to get from her Majesty some news of the poor young woman whom they were doubtless making pay very dearly for her devotion.

M. de Tréville listened to the young man's account with a seriousness which proved that he saw something else in all this adventure than a love affair; and when D'Artagnan had finished,—

"Hum!" said he; "all this smacks of his Eminence a league off."

"But what is to be done?" said D'Artagnan.

"Nothing, absolutely nothing, at present, but to leave Paris, as I told you, as soon as possible. I will see the queen; I will relate to her the details of this poor woman's disappearance, of which she is, no doubt, ignorant. These details will guide her on her part, and on your return I shall perhaps have some good news to tell you. Count on me."

D'Artagnan knew that, although a Gascon, M. de Tréville was not in the habit of making promises, and that when by chance he did promise, he generally more than kept his word. He bowed to him, then, full of gratitude for the past and for the future; and the worthy captain, who, on his side, felt a lively interest in this young man who was so brave and resolute, pressed his hand affectionately, while wishing him a pleasant journey.

Determined instantly to put M. de Tréville's advice into practice, D'Artagnan rode toward the Rue des Fossoyeurs, in order to superintend the packing of his portmanteau. On approaching the house he perceived M. Bonacieux, in morning costume, standing at his door. All that the prudent Planchet had said to him the preceding evening about his landlord's sinister character recurred to D'Artagnan's mind as he looked at him with more attention than he had done before. In fact, in addition to that yellow, sickly pallor which indicates infiltration of bile in the blood, and which might, however, be only accidental, D'Artagnan remarked something craftily perfidious in the play of the wrinkles of his face. A rogue does not laugh in the same way that an honest man does ; a hypocrite does not shed the same sort of tears that a man of good faith does. All falsehood is a mask, and however well made the mask may be, with a little attention we may always succeed in distinguishing it from the true face.

So it appeared to D'Artagnan that M. Bonacieux wore a mask, and likewise that this mask was most disagreeable to look upon.

Consequently, overcome by his repugnance for this man, he was about to pass him without speaking, when M. Bonacieux accosted him just as he had done the day before.

" Well, young man," said he, " we appear to pass rather gay nights ! Seven o'clock in the morning ! Hang it ! you seem to reverse ordinary customs, and come home at the hour when other people are going out."

" No one can reproach you for anything of the kind, M. Bonacieux," said the young man ; " you are a model for sober people. It is true that when a man has a young and pretty wife he has no need of seeking happiness elsewhere. Happiness comes to meet him, does it not, Monsieur Bonacieux ? "

Bonacieux grinned a ghastly smile.

" Ah, ha ! " said Bonacieux, " you are a jocular companion. But where the devil were you gadding last night, my young master ? It does not appear to be very clean in the crossroads."

D'Artagnan glanced down at his boots, all covered with mud, but that same glance fell upon the mercer's shoes and stockings. It might have been said they had been dipped in the same mudhole. Both were stained with splashes of the very same appearance.

Then a sudden thought crossed D'Artagnan's mind. That little, short, stout, elderly man, that sort of lackey, dressed in dark clothes, treated without consideration by the men wearing swords who composed the escort, was Bonacieux himself ! The husband had participated in the abduction of his wife !

A terrible inclination immediately took possession of D'Artagnan to seize the mercer by the throat and strangle him ; but, as we have said, he was a very prudent youth, and he restrained himself. The change, however, in his countenance was so manifest that Bonacieux was terrified at it, and endeavoured to draw back a step or two ; but he was exactly in front of the wing of the door which was shut, and the obstacle which he met compelled him to keep his place.

"Ah, ha! but you are joking, my worthy man," said D'Artagnan. "It appears to me that if my boots want sponging, your stockings and shoes stand in equal need of brushing. May you not have been philandering a little also, M. Bonacieux? Oh, the devil! that's unpardonable in a man of your age, and who, besides, has such a pretty young wife as yours is!"

"O Lord, no!" said Bonacieux; "but yesterday I went to St. Mandé, to make some inquiries after a servant, whom I cannot possibly do without, and as the roads were bad I brought back all this mud, which I have not yet had time to remove."

The place which Bonacieux named as the objective point of his journey was a fresh proof in support of the suspicions D'Artagnan had conceived. Bonacieux had named St. Mandé because Mandé was in an exactly opposite direction to St. Cloud. This probability afforded him his first consolation. If Bonacieux knew where his wife was, the mercer might at any time be forced, by the use of extreme means, to open his mouth and let his secret escape. The question, then, was only to change this probability into a certainty.

"I beg your pardon, my dear M. Bonacieux, if I don't stand on ceremony," said D'Artagnan, "but nothing makes one so thirsty as want of sleep. I am parched with thirst. Allow me to take a glass of water in your apartment; you know that is never refused among neighbours."

And without waiting for his host's permission, D'Artagnan went quickly into the house, and cast a rapid glance at the bed. The bed had not been slept in. Bonacieux had not been to bed. He had been back only an hour or two. He had accompanied his wife to the place where they took her, or else, at least, to the first relay.

"Many thanks to you, M. Bonacieux," said D'Artagnan, emptying his glass. "That is all I wanted of you. I will now go up into my room. I am going to have Planchet brush my boots; and when he has done, I will, if you like, send him to you to brush your shoes."

And he left the mercer quite astonished at his singular farewell, and asking himself if he had not been a little injudicious.

At the top of the stairs he found Planchet in a great fright.

"Ah, sir," cried Planchet, as soon as he perceived his master, "here is more trouble! I thought you would never come in!"

"What's the matter now, Planchet?"

"O sir, I give you a hundred, I give you a thousand guesses about the visit I received while you were out."

"When?"

"Half an hour ago, while you were at M. de Tréville's."

"Who has been here? Come, speak!"

"M. de Cavois."

"M. de Cavois?"

"In person."

"The captain of his Eminence's guards?"

"Himself."

"Did he come to arrest me?"

"I have no doubt he did, sir, for all his wheedling manner."

"Wheedling manner, did you say?"

"He was all honey, sir."

"Indeed!"

"He came, he said, on the part of his Eminence, who wished you well, to beg you to follow him to the Palais-Royal."

"What did you answer him?"

"That the thing was impossible, seeing that you were not at home, as he might perceive."

"Well, what did he say then?"

"That you must not fail to call upon him in the course of the day; and then he added in a low voice, 'Tell your master that his Eminence is very well disposed toward him, and that his fortune perhaps depends upon this interview.'"

"The snare is not very skilfully set, for the cardinal," replied the young man, smiling.

"I also saw the snare, and I answered you would be quite in despair on your return. 'Where has he gone?' asked M. de Cavois. 'To Troyes, in Champagne,' I answered. 'And when did he set out?' 'Yesterday evening.'"

"Planchet, my friend," interrupted D'Artagnan, "you are really a jewel of a man."

"You will understand, sir, I thought there would be still time, if you wish to see M. de Cavois, to give me the lie by saying you had not yet gone. The falsehood would then be mine, and as I am not a gentleman, I may be allowed to lie."

"Be of good heart, Planchet; you shall preserve your

reputation as a man of truth. In a quarter of an hour we start."

"That's just the advice I was going to give, sir. And where are we going, may I ask, without being too curious?"

"Zounds! in the opposite direction to that which you said I had gone. Besides, are you not as anxious to get news of Grimaud, Mousqueton, and Bazin as I am to know what has become of Athos, Porthos, and Aramis?"

"Oh yes, sir," said Planchet; "and I will go as soon as you please. Indeed, I think country air will suit us much better just now than the air of Paris. So then——"

"So then, pack up our necessaries, Planchet, and let us be off. On my part, I will go out ahead with my hands in my pockets, that nothing may be suspected. You can join me at the Hôtel des Gardes. By the way, Planchet, I think you are right with respect to our host; decidedly he is a frightfully low wretch."

"Ah, sir, you may take my word when I tell you anything. I am a physiognomist, I assure you!"

D'Artagnan went out first, as had been agreed upon. Then, that he might have nothing to reproach himself with, he went for the last time to the residences of his three friends. No news had been received of them; only a letter, all perfumed, and of an elegant and delicate handwriting, had come for Aramis. D'Artagnan took charge of it. Ten minutes afterwards Planchet joined him at the stables of the Hôtel des Gardes. D'Artagnan, in order that there might be no time lost, had saddled his horse himself.

"All right," said he to Planchet, when the latter added the portmanteau to the equipment. "Now saddle the other three horses."

"Do you think that we shall travel faster with two horses apiece?" said Planchet, with his cunning air.

"No, master joker," replied D'Artagnan; "but with our four horses we may bring back our three friends, if we find them living."

"Which would be great luck," replied Planchet. "But, indeed, we must not despair of God's mercy."

"Amen!" cried D'Artagnan, getting into his saddle.

As they left the Hôtel des Gardes they separated, going along the street in opposite directions, the one expecting to leave Paris by the gate of La Villette, and the other by the gate of Montmartre, with the understanding that they were to meet again beyond St. Denis. This, a strategic manœuvre, was executed with perfect punctuality, and was crowned with the most fortunate results. D'Artagnan and Planchet entered Pierrefitte together.

Planchet was more courageous, it must be admitted, by day than by night.

His natural prudence, however, never forsook him for a single instant. He had not forgotten one of the incidents of the first journey, and he looked upon everybody he met on the road as an enemy. It followed that his hat was for ever in his hand, which cost him some severe reprimands from D'Artagnan, who feared that his excess of politeness would lead people to think he was the lackey of a man of no consequence.

Nevertheless, whether the passers-by were really touched by Planchet's urbanity, or whether this time no one had been stationed in ambush on the young man's road, our two travellers arrived at Chantilly without any accident, and alighted at the hotel of the Great St. Martin, the same they had stopped at on their first trip.

The host, on seeing a young man followed by a lackey with two led horses, advanced respectfully to the door. Now, as they had already travelled eleven leagues, D'Artagnan thought it time to stop, whether Porthos were or were not in the hotel. And then, perhaps, it would not be prudent to ask at once what had become of the musketeer. The result of these reflections was that D'Artagnan, without asking for information of any kind, alighted, consigned the horses to the care of his lackey, entered a small room destined to receive those who wished to be alone, and asked the landlord to bring him a bottle of his best wine, and as good a breakfast as possible, a request which further corroborated the high opinion the innkeeper had formed of the traveller at first sight.

D'Artagnan was therefore served with miraculous celerity.

The regiment of the guards was recruited among the first gentlemen of the kingdom, and D'Artagnan, followed by a lackey with four magnificent horses, could not fail to make a sensation, in spite of the simplicity of his uniform. The host himself desired to wait upon him. D'Artagnan, perceiving this, ordered two glasses to be brought, and began the following conversation :—

" 'Pon my word, my good host," said D'Artagnan, filling the two glasses, " I asked for a bottle of your best wine, and if you have deceived me, your sin will bring its own punishment, for, seeing that I hate drinking by myself, you shall drink with me. Take your glass, then, and let us drink. But what shall we drink to, come, so as to avoid wounding any susceptibility? Let us drink to the prosperity of your establishment."

"Your Lordship does me much honour," said the host, "and I thank you sincerely for your kind wishes."

"But don't mistake," said D'Artagnan; "there is more selfishness in my toast than perhaps you may think, for it is only in prosperous establishments that one is well received. In hotels that are running down, everything is in confusion, and the traveller is a victim to his host's embarrassments. Now, I travel a great deal, particularly on this road, and I should like to see all landlords making a fortune."

"I was thinking," said the host, "that it was not the first time I had had the honour of seeing you."

"Bah! I have passed, perhaps, ten times through Chantilly, and out of the ten times I have stopped at least three or four times at your house. Why, I was here only ten or twelve days ago. I was conducting some friends, musketeers, one of whom, by-the-bye, had a dispute with a stranger, a man who, for some unknown reason, sought a quarrel with him."

"Ah, exactly so!" said the host; "I remember it perfectly. Is it not M. Porthos that your Lordship means?"

"Yes; that is my companion's name. Good Heavens! my dear host, has any misfortune happened to him?"

"Your Honour must have observed that he could not continue his journey."

"Why, but he promised to rejoin us, and we have seen nothing of him."

"He has done us the honour of remaining here."

"What! he has done you the honour of remaining here?"

"Yes, sir, in this hotel; and we are even very uneasy——"

"About what?"

"Certain debts he has incurred."

"Well, but whatever debts he may have incurred he will pay."

"Ah, sir, you pour balm into my heart! We have made considerable advances; and only this morning the surgeon declared that if M. Porthos did not pay him, he should look to me, as it was I who had sent for him."

"What! is Porthos wounded?"

"I cannot tell you, sir."

"What! you cannot tell me! Surely you ought to be able to tell me better than any other person."

"Yes; but in our situation we must not say all we know, particularly when we have been warned that our ears should answer for our tongues."

"Well, can I see Porthos?"

"Certainly, sir. Take the stairs on your right; go up the first flight, and knock at No. 1. Only warn him that it is you."

"Warn him! Why should I do that?"

"Because, sir, some mischief might happen to you."

"What mischief might happen to me, pray?"

"M. Porthos may suppose you are some one connected with the house, and in a fit of passion might run his sword through you, or blow out your brains."

"What have you been doing to him, then?"

"We asked him for money."

"The devil! Ah, I can understand that. Such a demand Porthos takes very ill when he is not in funds; but I know he ought to be."

"We thought so too, sir. As our house is very methodical, and as we make our bills every week, at the end of a week we presented our account; but it appeared we had chosen an unlucky moment, for at the first word on the subject he sent us to the very devil. It is true he had been playing the day before."

"Playing the day before! And with whom?"

"Lord, who can say, sir? With a gentleman, who was travelling this way, to whom he proposed a game of lansquenet."

"That's it, then; and the foolish fellow lost all he had."

"Even to his horse, sir; for when the gentleman was about to set out, we perceived that his lackey was saddling M. Porthos's horse. We called his attention to this, and he told us to mind our own business, as this horse belonged to him. We also informed M. Porthos of what was going on; but he told us we were scoundrels to doubt a gentleman's word, and that as the gentleman had said the horse was his, there could be no doubt that it was so."

"That's Porthos all over," murmured D'Artagnan.

"Then," continued the host, "I sent him word that from the moment we seemed unlikely to reach an understanding with respect to payment, I hoped he would have, at least, the kindness to grant the favour of his custom to my brother

host of the Golden Eagle ; but M. Porthos replied that, as
my hotel was the best, he preferred to remain here.

"This reply was too flattering to allow me to insist on his
departure. I confined myself, then, to begging him to give
up his room, which is the handsomest in the hotel, and to
be satisfied with a pretty little chamber on the third floor.
But to this M. Porthos replied that as he every moment
expected his mistress, who was one of the greatest ladies
of the court, I might easily comprehend that the room he did
me the honour to occupy in my house was itself very mean
for the visit of such a personage.

"Nevertheless, though acknowledging the truth of what
he said, I thought proper to insist ; but without even
giving himself the trouble to enter into any discussion with
me, he took one of his pistols, laid it on his nightstand, and
declared that, at the first word said to him about moving
either inside the house or out of it, he would blow out the
brains of the person imprudent enough to meddle with a
matter that concerned himself alone. So from that time,
sir, nobody enters his chamber except his servant."

"What ! Mousqueton is here, then ? "

"Yes, sir ; five days after his departure he came back
in a very bad humour. It appears that he had also met with
unpleasant experiences on his journey. Unfortunately he is
more nimble than his master, so that for his master's sake
he turns everything upside down; and as he thinks we might
refuse what he asks for, he takes all he wants without asking at all."

"Well, the fact is," said D'Artagnan, "I have always
observed a high degree of intelligence and devotion in
Mousqueton."

"Very possibly, sir. But suppose that I should happen
to be brought in contact, only four times a year, with such
intelligence and devotion—why, I should be a ruined man ! "

"No ; for Porthos will pay you."

"Hum ! " said the host, in a doubting tone.

"He is the favourite of a great lady, who will not allow
him to be inconvenienced for such a paltry sum as he owes
you."

"If I may venture to say what I think in regard to
that——"

"What you think ? "

"I ought rather to say, what I know."

"What you know ? "

"And even what I am sure of."

" Come ! what are you sure of ? "

" I would say that I know this great lady."

" You ? "

" Yes, I."

" And how did you become acquainted with her ? "

" O sir, if I could believe I might trust in your discretion——"

" Speak ! On the faith of a gentleman, you shall have no cause to repent of your confidence."

" Well, sir, you understand that uneasiness makes us do many things."

" What have you done ? "

" Oh, nothing that a creditor has not a right to do."

" Go on ! "

" M. Porthos gave us a note for this duchess, asking us to post it. This was before his servant had come. As he could not leave his room, we had to run on his errands."

" Well ! "

" Instead of putting the letter in the post, which is never safe, I took advantage of one of my lads going to Paris, and I ordered him to give the letter to this duchess himself. This was fulfilling the intentions of M. Porthos, who had desired us to be so careful of this letter, was it not ? "

" Nearly so."

" Well, sir, do you know who this great lady is ? "

" No. I have heard Porthos speak of her, that's all."

" Do you know who this pretended duchess is ? "

" I repeat I don't know her."

" Why, sir, she is the old wife of a solicitor of the Châtelet, named Madame Coquenard, who, although she is at least fifty, still gives herself jealous airs. It struck me as very odd that a princess should live in the Rue aux Ours."

" But how do you know all this ? "

" Because she flew into a great passion on receiving the letter, saying that M. Porthos was a fickle man, and that she was sure it was on account of some woman again that he had received this wound."

" What ! Has he been wounded ? "

" Oh, good Lord ! what have I said ? "

" You said that Porthos was wounded."

" Yes ; but he had so strictly forbidden me to say so ! "

" And why so ? "

" Zounds, sir ! only because he had boasted that he would perforate the stranger with whom you left him in dispute ; whereas the stranger, on the contrary, in spite of all his braggadocio, quickly brought him to the ground. Now, as M. Porthos is a very vainglorious man, he insists that nobody shall know he has received this wound, except the duchess, whom he endeavoured to interest by an account of his adventure."

"It is a wound, then, that confines him to his bed?"

"Ah! and a master thrust, too, I assure you. Your friend must have nine lives."

"Were you there, then?"

"Sir, I followed them from curiosity, so that I saw the combat without the combatants seeing me."

"And what took place?"

"Oh, the affair was not long, I assure you. They placed themselves on guard. The stranger made a feint and a lunge, and that so rapidly that when M. de Porthos came to parry he had already three inches of steel in his breast. He fell on his back. The stranger immediately placed the point of his sword on his throat; and M. Porthos, finding himself at the mercy of his adversary, confessed himself conquered. Whereupon the stranger asked his name, and learning that it was Porthos, and not D'Artagnan, assisted him to rise, brought him back to the hotel, mounted his horse, and disappeared."

"So this stranger meant to quarrel with M. d'Artagnan?"

"It appears so."

"And do you know what became of him?"

"No. I never saw him until that moment, and we have not seen him since."

"Very well. Now I know all that I wished to know. Porthos's room is, you say, on the first story, No. 1?"

"Yes, sir, the handsomest in the inn—a room that I could have let ten times over."

"Bah! don't be anxious," said D'Artagnan, laughing; "Porthos will pay you with the Duchess Coquenard's money."

"O sir, *procureuse* or duchess, if she will but loosen her purse-strings it will be all the same; but she positively answered that she was tired of M. Porthos's unreasonable demands and infidelities, and that she would not send him a farthing."

"And did you convey this answer to your guest?"

"We took good care not to do that. He would have found out how we had done his errand."

"So that he is still in expectation of his money?"

"Oh dear me, yes, sir! Yesterday he wrote again, but this time his servant posted his letter."

"Do you say the *procureuse* is old and ugly?"

"Fifty, at least, sir, and not at all handsome, according to Pathaud's account."

"In that case you may be quite at ease; she will soon be softened. Besides, Porthos cannot owe you much."

"What! not much? Twenty good pistoles already, without reckoning the doctor. Bless you, he denies himself nothing. You can see he has been accustomed to live well."

"Never mind! If his mistress abandons him, he will find friends, I will answer for it. So, my dear host, have no anxiety, and continue to take all the care of him that his situation requires."

"You have promised me not to open your mouth about the *procureuse*, and not to say a word about the wound?"

"That's a thing agreed upon. You have my promise."

"Oh, he would kill me, don't you see?"

"Don't be afraid. He is not so fierce as he seems."

Saying these words, D'Artagnan went upstairs, leaving his host a little better satisfied with respect to two things in which he appeared to be very much interested—his debt and his life.

At the top of the stairs, on the most conspicuous door of the corridor, was traced in black ink a gigantic "No. 1." D'Artagnan knocked, and upon being told from inside to enter, went into the chamber.

Porthos was in bed, and was playing a game of lansquenet with Mousqueton, to keep his hand in, while a spit loaded with partridges was turning before the fire, and at each side of a large chimney-piece, over two chafing-dishes, were boiling two stewpans, from which exhaled a double odour of rabbit and garlic stews, very grateful to the olfactory nerves. In addition to this, he perceived that the top of a wardrobe and the marble of a stand were covered with empty bottles.

At the sight of his friend Porthos uttered a loud cry of joy; and Mousqueton, rising respectfully, yielded his place to him, and went to give an eye to the two stewpans, over which he appeared to have especial care.

"Ah, zounds! is that you?" said Porthos to D'Artagnan. "Welcome! Excuse my not coming to meet you. But," added he, looking at D'Artagnan with a certain degree of uneasiness, "you know what has happened to me?"

"Not exactly."

"Has the landlord told you nothing, then?"

" I asked after you, and came straight up."

Porthos seemed to breathe more freely.

" And what, then, has happened to you, my dear Porthos ? " continued D'Artagnan.

" Why, on making a thrust at my adversary, whom I had already hit three times, and with whom I meant to finish by a fourth, my foot slipped on a stone, and I sprained my knee."

" Indeed ! "

" Honour bright ! Luckily for the rascal, for I should have left him dead on the spot, I assure you."

" And what became of him ? "

" Oh, I don't know. He had enough, and set off without wanting any more. But you, my dear D'Artagnan, what has happened to you ? "

" So that this sprain," continued D'Artagnan, " my dear Porthos, keeps you here in bed ? "

" Really that's all ! I shall be about again, however, in a few days."

" Why did you not have yourself carried to Paris ? You must be sadly bored here."

" That was my intention ; but, my dear friend, I have one thing to confess to you."

" What's that ? "

" It is that, as I was sadly bored, as you say, and as I had in my pocket the seventy-five pistoles which you had apportioned to me, in order to amuse myself I invited a gentleman who was travelling this way to walk up, and proposed a game of dice to him. He accepted my challenge, and, 'pon my word, my seventy-five pistoles quickly passed from my pocket to his, without reckoning my horse, which he won into the bargain. But you—I want to know about you, D'Artagnan."

" What can you expect, my dear Porthos ? A man is not privileged in all ways," said D'Artagnan. " You know the proverb, ' Unlucky at play, lucky in love.' You are too fortunate in love for play not to take its revenge. What consequence can the reverses of fortune be to you ? Have you not, lucky rogue that you are—have you not your duchess, who cannot fail to come to your assistance ? "

" Well, you see, my dear D'Artagnan, with what ill-luck I play," replied Porthos, with the most careless air in the world. " I wrote to her to send me fifty louis or so, of which I stood absolutely in need, on account of my accident——"

" Well ? "

" Well, she must be at her country seat, for she has not answered me."

" Indeed ! "

" No ; so yesterday I addressed another letter to her, still more urgent than the first. But you are here, my dear fellow ; let us speak of you. I confess I began to be rather uneasy on your account."

" But your host behaves very well towards you, as it appears, my dear Porthos," said D'Artagnan, directing the sick man's attention to the full stewpans and the empty bottles.

" So, so ! " replied Porthos. " Only three or four days ago the impertinent jackanapes gave me his bill, and I was forced to turn both him and his bill out of doors ; so that I am here something in the fashion of a conqueror, holding my position, as it were, by conquest. So, you see, being in constant fear of being forced in my position, I am armed to the teeth."

" And yet," said D'Artagnan, laughing, " it appears to me that from time to time you must make sorties."

And he again pointed to the bottles and the stewpans.

" No, not I, unfortunately," said Porthos. " This miserable sprain confines me to my bed, but Mosqueton forages and brings in provisions.—Friend Mousqueton, you see that we have a reinforcement, and we must have an increase of provisions."

" Mousqueton," said D'Artagnan, " you must do me a service."

" Of what kind, sir ? "

" You must give your recipe to Planchet. I may be besieged in my turn, and I should not be sorry for him to make me enjoy the same advantages with which you gratify your master."

" Lord, sir," said Mousqueton, with a modest air, " there is nothing easier. It only requires to have a little skill, that's all. I was brought up in the country, and my father, in his leisure moments, was something of a poacher."

" And the rest of the time what did he do ? "

" He carried on a trade, sir, which I have always found pretty lucrative."

" What was that ? "

" As it was in the time of the wars between the Catholics and the Huguenots, and as he saw the Catholics exterminating the Huguenots and the Huguenots exterminating the Catholics, and all in the name of religion, he adopted a mixed belief, which permitted him to be sometimes a Catholic, sometimes a Huguenot. Now, he was accustomed to walk, with his fowling-piece on his shoulder, behind the hedges which border the roads; and when he saw a Catholic coming alone, the Protestant religion immediately prevailed in his mind. He levelled his gun in the direction of the traveller; then, when he was within ten paces of him, he began a conversation which almost always ended by the traveller abandoning his purse to save his life. Of course, when he saw a Huguenot coming, he felt himself seized with such an ardent Catholic zeal that he could not understand how, a quarter of an hour before, he had been able to have any doubts upon the superiority of our holy religion. For, sir, I am a Catholic. My father was faithful to his principles, and made my elder brother a Huguenot."

"And what was the end of this worthy man?" asked D'Artagnan.

"Oh, of the most unfortunate kind, sir. One day he was caught in a sunken road between a Huguenot and a Catholic, with both of whom he had already had to do, and who both recognized him; so they united against him, and hung him on a tree. Then they came and boasted of their fine exploit in the tavern at the next village, where my brother and I were drinking."

"And what did you do?" said D'Artagnan.

"We let them tell their story out," replied Mousqueton. "Then, as in leaving the tavern they took different directions, my brother went and hid himself on the Catholic's road, and I on the Protestant's. Two hours after, all was over; we had done the business of both of them, admiring the foresight of our poor father, who had taken the precaution to bring each of us up in a different religion."

"Well, as you say, your father must have been a very intelligent fellow. And you say, then, that in his leisure moments the worthy man was a poacher?"

"Yes, sir; and he taught me to lay a snare and ground a line. The result is, that when I saw our rascal of a host wanted to feed us upon lumps of fat meat fit for workmen, which did not at all suit such delicate stomachs as ours, I had recourse to a little of my old trade. While walking in the prince's wood, I laid a few snares in the runs; and while reclining on the banks of his Highness's pools, I slipped a few lines into his ponds. So that now, thanks be to God! as you yourself can testify, we do not lack for partridges, rabbits, carp, or eels—all light, wholesome food, suitable for sick persons."

"But the wine?" said D'Artagnan. "Who furnishes the wine? That, at least, must be your landlord?"

"That is to say, yes and no."

"How yes and no?"

"He furnishes it, it is true, but he does not know that he has that honour."

"Explain yourself, Mousqueton; your conversation is full of instructive things."

"This is the way of it, sir. Chance brought it about that I met with a Spaniard in my peregrinations who had seen many countries, and among them the New World. This Spaniard had in his service a lackey who had accompanied him in his voyage to Mexico. This lackey was a compatriot of mine, and we became intimate the more quickly from there being many resemblances of character between us. We loved hunting of all kinds better than anything, so that he related to me how, in the plains of the pampas, the natives hunt the tiger and the wild bull with simple running-nooses, which they throw round the necks of those terrible animals. At first I would not believe that they could attain such skill as to throw the end of a cord with such precision to a distance of twenty or thirty paces; but in face of the proof I was obliged to acknowledge the truth of the account. My friend placed a bottle at the distance of thirty paces, and at each cast he caught the neck of the bottle in his running-noose. I practised this exercise, and since nature has endowed me with some faculties, to-day I can throw the lasso with any man in the world. Well, do you understand? Our host has a well-furnished cellar, the key of which is never out of his possession; but his cellar has a loophole. Now, through this loophole I throw my lasso, and as I now know which part of the cellar the best wine is in, I draw from there. Now, will you taste our wine, and, without prejudice, tell us what you think of it?"

"No, thank you, my friend—no, thank you; unfortunately I have just breakfasted."

"Well," said Porthos, "set the table, Mousqueton, and while we breakfast D'Artagnan will tell us what has happened to him during the ten days since he left us."

"Willingly," said D'Artagnan.

While Porthos and Mousqueton were breakfasting with the appetites of convalescents, and with that brotherly cordiality which unites men in misfortune, D'Artagnan related how Aramis had been wounded, and was obliged to stop at Crèvecœur; how he had left Athos fighting at Amiens with four

men, who accused him of being a counterfeiter ; and how he,
D'Artagnan, had been forced to pass over the Comte de
Wardes's body in order to reach England.

But there D'Artagnan's disclosure ended. He only added
that on his return from Great Britain he had brought back
four magnificent horses—one for himself, and one for each
of his companions ; finally, he informed Porthos that the
one intended for him was already installed in the stable of
the hotel.

At that moment Planchet entered. He informed his
master that the horses were sufficiently refreshed, and that
it would be possible to sleep at Clermont.

As D'Artagnan was tolerably reassured with regard to
Porthos, and as he was anxious to obtain news of his two
other friends, he held out his hand to the sick man, and
told him he was going to resume his route in order to prose-
cute his researches. However, as he reckoned upon returning by the same road, if, in seven or eight days, Porthos
were still at the hotel of the Great St. Martin, he would call
for him on his way.

Porthos replied that, according to all probability, his
sprain would not permit him to depart during that time.
Moreover, it was necessary for him to stay at Chantilly to
wait for an answer from his duchess.

D'Artagnan wished that her answer might be prompt and
favourable ; and after having again recommended Porthos
to the care of Mousqueton, and paid his reckoning to the
landlord, he resumed his route with Planchet, who was now
relieved of one of his led horses.

CHAPTER XXVI.

ARAMIS'S THESIS.

D'ARTAGNAN had said nothing to Porthos of his wound or
of his *procureuse*. He had appeared to believe all that
the vainglorious musketeer had told him, convinced that
no friendship will hold out against a secret obtained by
accident, particularly when pride is deeply interested in
that secret. Besides, we always enjoy a certain mental superiority over those whose lives we know about without their
suspecting it. Now, in his projects of intrigue for the
future, and determined as he was to make his three friends
the instruments of his fortune, D'Artagnan was not sorry

at uniting in his grasp beforehand the invisible strings by which he counted upon moving them.

And yet, as he journeyed along, a profound sadness weighed upon his heart. He thought of the young and pretty Madame Bonacieux, who was to have paid him so richly for all his devotion. But let us hasten to say this sadness came upon the young man less from the regret for the happiness he had missed than from the fear he entertained that some misfortune had befallen the poor woman. In his mind there was no doubt that she was a victim of the cardinal's vengeance, and, as we well know, his Eminence's vengeance was terrible. He did not know in the least how he could have found grace in the minister's eyes, but doubtless M. de Cavois would have revealed it to him if the captain of the guards had found him at home.

Nothing makes time pass more quickly or shortens a journey more than a thought which absorbs in itself all the faculties of the being of him who thinks. External existence then resembles a sleep of which this thought is the dream. Through its influence time no longer has measure, space no longer has distance. We depart from one place and arrive at another; that is all. Of the interval covered, nothing remains in the memory but a vague mist in which a thousand confused images of trees, mountains, and landscapes are dimly seen. Under the spell of this hallucination D'Artagnan, letting his horse take his own gait, traversed the six or eight leagues between Chantilly and Crèvecœur. He was unable to remember, when he had reached that village, any of the things he had met with on the road.

There only memory returned to him. He shook his head, perceived the tavern where he had left Aramis, and putting his horse to the trot, pulled up at the door.

This time not a host but a hostess received him. D'Artagnan was a physiognomist. His eye took in at a glance the plump, cheerful countenance of the mistress of the place, and he at once perceived there was no occasion for dissembling with her, or of fearing anything from such a jolly woman.

"My good dame," asked D'Artagnan, "could you tell me what has become of a friend of mine whom we were obliged to leave here about ten days ago?"

"A handsome young man, of twenty-three or twenty-four, mild, amiable, and well made?"

"That's it."

"Wounded, moreover, in the shoulder?"

"Just so."

"Well, sir, he is still here."

"Ah, zounds! my dear dame," said D'Artagnan, springing from his horse and throwing the bridle to Planchet, "you restore me to life. Where is my dear Aramis? Let me embrace him! for, I confess it, I am quite anxious to see him again."

"I beg your pardon, sir, but I doubt whether he can see you at this moment."

"Why so? Is he with a lady?"

"Dear me! what do you mean by that? Poor lad! No, sir, he is not with any woman."

"With whom is he, then?"

"With the Vicar of Montdidier and the superior of the Jesuits of Amiens."

"Good Heavens!" cried D'Artagnan; "is the poor fellow worse, then?"

"Oh no, sir—quite the contrary; but after his illness grace touched him, and he determined to take orders."

"Oh, that's it!" said D'Artagnan. "I had forgotten that he was only a musketeer temporarily."

"Are you still anxious to see him?"

"More so than ever."

"Well, you have only to take the right-hand staircase in the yard, and knock at No. 5 on the second floor."

D'Artagnan hastened in the direction pointed out, and found one of those outside staircases such as are still to be seen in the yards of old-fashioned inns. But there was no getting in this way at the future abbé's room. The defiles of Aramis's chamber were neither more nor less guarded than the gardens of Armida. Bazin was stationed in the corridor, and barred his passage with the greater intrepidity because, after many years of trial, he found himself on the point of attaining the result which had ever been his ambition.

In fact, poor Bazin's dream had always been to serve a churchman, and he was waiting impatiently the moment, anticipated so long, when Aramis should at last throw aside the uniform and assume the cassock. The promise renewed every day by the young man, that the moment would not long be delayed, had alone kept him in the service of a musketeer—a service in which, he said, his soul was in constant jeopardy.

Bazin was, then, at the summit of delight. According to

all probability, this time his master would not retract. The union of physical pain with moral pain had produced the effect so long desired. Aramis, suffering at once in body and mind, had at length fixed his eyes and his thoughts upon religion, and he had considered as a warning from Heaven the double accident which had happened to him—that is to say, his mistress's sudden disappearance and the wound in his shoulder.

We can understand that, in his present frame of mind, nothing could be more disagreeable to Bazin than D'Artagnan's arrival, which might cast his master back again into the vortex of mundane affairs that had so long carried him away. He resolved, then, to defend the door bravely ; and as, betrayed by the mistress of the inn, he could not say that Aramis was absent, he endeavoured to prove to the newcomer that it would be the height of indiscretion to disturb his master in the pious conference which had begun early that morning, and could not be, as Bazin said, terminated before night.

But D'Artagnan took very little heed of Master Bazin's eloquent discourse, and as he had no desire to support a polemic discussion with his friend's valet, he simply pushed him aside with one hand, and with the other turned the handle of the door No. 5.

The door opened, and D'Artagnan went into the chamber.

Aramis, in a black gown, his head covered with a sort of round, flat headdress, much like a calotte, was seated before an oblong table, covered with rolls of paper and enormous folio volumes ; at his right hand was seated the superior of the Jesuits, and on his left the Vicar of Montdidier. The curtains were half drawn, and admitted only a mysterious light calculated for beatific reveries. All the mundane objects that generally strike the eye on entering a young man's room, particularly when that young man is a musketeer, had disappeared as by enchantment ; and for fear, no doubt, that the sight of them might bring his master back to the ideas of this world, Bazin had laid violent hand on sword, pistols, plumed hat, embroideries and laces of all kinds and descriptions.

But in their stead and place D'Artagnan thought he perceived, in an obscure corner, something like a scourge hanging from a nail in the wall.

At the noise made by D'Artagnan in entering, Aramis raised his head and recognized his friend. But to the young man's great astonishment the sight of him did not

9

produce much effect upon the musketeer, so completely was his mind detached from the things of this world.

"Good-afternoon to you, dear D'Artagnan," said Aramis. "Believe me, I am very glad to see you."

"So am I delighted to see you," said D'Artagnan, "although I am not yet very sure that it is Aramis I am speaking to."

"Yes, it is I, my friend, it is I! But what makes you doubt?"

"I was afraid I had made a mistake in the chamber, and that I had found my way into the apartment of some churchman. Then I made another error on finding you in company with these gentlemen: I was afraid you were dangerously ill."

The two men in black, guessing D'Artagnan's meaning, darted at him a glance that was almost threatening; but D'Artagnan took no heed of it.

"I disturb you, perhaps, my dear Aramis," continued D'Artagnan, "for by what I see I am led to believe you are confessing to these gentlemen."

Aramis coloured imperceptibly.

"You disturb me? Oh, quite the contrary, dear friend, I swear; and as a proof of what I say, allow me to rejoice at seeing you safe and sound."

"Ah, he'll come round after a while," thought D'Artagnan; "that's not bad."

"For this gentleman, who is my friend, has just escaped from a serious danger," continued Aramis with unction, pointing to D'Artagnan, and addressing the two ecclesiastics.

"Give God praise, sir," replied they, bowing in unison.

"I have not failed to do so, your Reverences," replied the young man, returning their salutation.

"You arrive very opportunely, D'Artagnan," said Aramis, "and, by taking part in our discussion, may assist us with your learning. The Principal of Amiens, the Vicar of Montdidier, and I are arguing certain theological questions in which we have been interested for some time. I should be delighted to have your opinion."

"A soldier's opinion can have very little weight," replied D'Artagnan, who began to get uneasy at the turn things were taking, "and you had better be satisfied, believe me, with the knowledge of these gentlemen."

The two men in black bowed in their turn.

"On the contrary," replied Aramis, "your opinion will be

very valuable. The question is this : The principal thinks that my thesis ought to be especially dogmatic and didactic.''

" Your thesis ! Are you, then, preparing a thesis ? "

" Certainly," replied the Jesuit ; " in the examination which precedes ordination a thesis is always requisite."

" Ordination ! " cried D'Artagnan, who could not believe what the hostess and Bazin had successively told him—" ordination ! "

And he gazed with astonished eyes on the three persons before him.

" Now," continued Aramis, taking the same graceful position in his easy-chair that he would have assumed at a morning reception, and complacently examining his hand, which was as white and plump as a woman's, and which he held up to cause the blood to descend—" now, as you have heard, D'Artagnan, the principal is desirous that my thesis should be dogmatic, while I, for my part, would rather it should be ideal. This is the reason why the principal has proposed to me the following subject, which has not yet been treated, and in which I perceive there is material for magnificent developments : ' *Utraque manus in benedicendo clericis inferioribus necessaria est.*' "

D'Artagnan, whose erudition we are well acquainted with, evinced no more interest in this quotation than in the one made by M. de Tréville regarding the gifts which he supposed the Duke of Buckingham had bestowed on the young man.

" That means," resumed Aramis, that he might make the matter perfectly plain, "' Both hands are indispensable for priests of the inferior orders when they give the benediction.' "

" An admirable subject ! " cried the Jesuit.

" Admirable and dogmatic ! " repeated the vicar, who, being about as strong in his Latin as D'Artagnan, carefully watched the Jesuit, in order to keep step with him, and repeat his words like an echo.

As to D'Artagnan, he remained perfectly indifferent to the enthusiasm of the two men in black.

" Yes, admirable ! *prorsus admirabile !* " continued Aramis ; " but it requires a profound study of both the Scriptures and the Fathers. Now, I have confessed to these learned ecclesiastics, and that in all humility, that the duties of mounting guard and the service of the king have caused me to neglect my studies a little. I should find myself, therefore, more at my ease, *facilius natans,* in a subject

of my own choice, which would be to these hard theological
questions what morals are to metaphysics in philosophy."

D'Artagnan began to be bored, and so did the vicar.

"See what an exordium!" cried the Jesuit.

"Exordium," repeated the vicar, for the sake of saying
something.

"*Quemadmodum inter cœlorum immensitatem.*"

Aramis glanced at D'Artagnan, and found his friend yawn-
ing enough to dislocate his jaw.

"Let us speak French, worthy Father," said he to the
Jesuit; "M. d'Artagnan will enjoy our conversation more."

"Yes," replied D'Artagnan; "I am fatigued with riding,
and I fail to grasp all this Latin."

"Agreed," replied the Jesuit, a little put out, while the
vicar, greatly delighted, threw on D'Artagnan a look full of
gratitude. "Well, let us see what is to be derived from
this gloss.

"Moses, the servant of God—he was but a servant, please
to understand!—Moses blessed with his hands; he held out
both his arms while the Hebrews were beating their enemies.
Therefore he blessed them with his two hands. Besides,
what does the gospel say? '*Imponite manus,*' and not
'*manum*'—lay on the hands, and not the hand."

"Lay on the hands," repeated the vicar, making a gesture.

"For St. Peter, on the contrary, whose successors the
popes are," continued the Jesuit: "'*Porrige digitos*'—present
the fingers. Do you see that now?"

"Certainly," replied Aramis, in a pleased tone; "but the
thing is subtle."

"The fingers!" resumed the Jesuit; "St. Peter blessed
with the fingers. The pope, therefore, blesses also with the
fingers. And with how many fingers does he bless? With
three fingers: one for the Father, one for the Son, and one
for the Holy Ghost."

All crossed themselves. D'Artagnan thought it was proper
to follow their example.

"The pope is St. Peter's successor, and represents the
three divine powers. The rest, *ordines inferiores,* of the
ecclesiastical hierarchy, bless in the name of the holy arch-
angels and angels. The most humble clerks, such as our
deacons and sacristans, bless with aspergills or holy-water
sprinklers, which are like an indefinite number of blessing
fingers. Here's the subject simplified. *Argumentum omni
denudatum ornamento.* I could make of that subject,"
continued the Jesuit, "two volumes of the size of this."

· And in his enthusiasm he pounded on a folio volume of St. Chrysostom, which was making the table bend beneath its weight.

D'Artagnan trembled.

"Certainly," said Aramis, "I do justice to the beauties of this thesis, but at the same time I perceive it would be overwhelming for me. I had chosen this text—tell me, dear D'Artagnan, if it is not to your taste : ' *Non inutile est desiderium in oblatione ;*' or, still better, ' A little regret is not unsuitable in an offering to the Lord.' "

"Stop there ! " cried the Jesuit, " for that thesis smacks of heresy. There is a proposition almost like it in the ' Augustinus ' of the heresiarch Jansenius, whose book will, sooner or later, be burnt by the hangman. Take care, my young friend ; you will be lost ! "

"You will be lost," said the vicar, shaking his head sorrowfully.

"You are nearing that famous point of freewill which is a fatal reef. You are sailing dangerously close to the insinuations of the Pelagians and the semi-Pelagians."

"But, my reverend——" replied Aramis, somewhat dumbfounded by the hail of arguments that poured on his head.

"How will you prove," continued the Jesuit, without allowing him time to speak, "that we ought to regret the world when we offer ourselves to God ? Listen to this dilemma : God is God, and the world is the devil. To regret the world is to regret the devil. That is my conclusion."

"And mine also," said the vicar.

"But for Heaven's sake——" resumed Aramis.

"*Desideras diabolum,* unhappy man," cried the Jesuit.

"He regrets the devil ! Ah, my young friend," added the vicar, groaning, " do not regret the devil, I implore you ! "

D'Artagnan felt himself growing idiotic ; it seemed to him he was in a madhouse, and that he was becoming as mad as those he saw. He was, however, forced to hold his tongue, as he did not comprehend the language they employed.

"But listen to me, now," resumed Aramis, with a politeness under which began to show a little impatience. " I do not say I regret. No, I will never pronounce that sentence, as it would not be orthodox."

The Jesuit raised his hands toward heaven, and the vicar did the same.

"No ; but grant at least that it is bad grace to offer to the

Lord only that with which we are perfectly disgusted. Don't you think so, D'Artagnan ? "

" Zounds ! I think so, indeed," cried he.

The Jesuit and the vicar started from their chairs.

" This is my point of departure ; it is a syllogism. The world is not wanting in attractions. I quit the world ; therefore I make a sacrifice. Now, the Scripture says positively, ' Make a sacrifice unto the Lord.' "

" That is true," said his antagonists.

" And then," said Aramis, pinching his ear to make it red, as he smoothed his hands to make them white—" and then I made a little rondeau on it last year, which I showed to M. Voiture, and that young man paid me a thousand compliments."

" A rondeau ! " said the Jesuit disdainfully.

" A rondeau ! " said the vicar mechanically.

" Repeat it ! repeat it ! " cried D'Artagnan ; " it will give some variety."

" Not so, for it is religious," replied Aramis ; " it is theology in verse."

" The devil ! " said D'Artagnan.

" Here it is," said Aramis, with a somewhat modest air, which was not exempt from a certain shade of hypocrisy :—

> " *Vous qui pleurez un passé plein de charmes,*
>   *Et qui traînez des jours infortunés,*
>   *Tous vos malheurs se verront terminés,*
> *Quand à Dieu seul vous offrirez vos larmes,*
>   *Vous qui pleurez !* "

> (Oh, you who weep for joys that long have flown,
>   Whose mournful days in vain regrets now creep,
>   Your woes will all in deep oblivion sleep,
> If you will offer up your tears to God alone—
>   Oh, you who weep !)

D'Artagnan and the vicar appeared pleased. The Jesuit persisted in his opinion.

" Beware of a profane taste in your theological style. What, indeed, says St. Augustine ? ' *Severus sit clericorum sermo.*' "

" Yes, let the sermon be clear," said the vicar.

" But," hastily interrupted the Jesuit, on seeing that his acolyte was going astray—" but your thesis would please the ladies ; it would have the same kind of success as one of M. Patru's pleadings."

" I hope to God it may ! " cried Aramis, transported.

"There it is," cried the Jesuit; "the world still speaks within you in a loud voice, *altissimâ voce*. You follow the world, my young friend, and I tremble lest grace prove ineffectual."

"Rest assured, my reverend father, I can answer for myself."

"Mundane presumption!"

"I know myself, father; my resolution is irrevocable."

"Then you persist in continuing this thesis?"

"I feel myself called upon to treat this, and no other. I shall then continue it, and to-morrow I hope you will be satisfied with the corrections I shall have made in consequence of your advice."

"Work slowly," said the vicar. "We leave you in an excellent frame of mind."

"Yes, the ground is all sown," said the Jesuit, "and we have not to fear that one portion of the seed may have fallen upon stony ground, another by the wayside, or that the birds of heaven have eaten the rest, *aves cœli comederunt illam*."

"Plague take you and your Latin!" said D'Artagnan, who felt all his patience exhausted.

"Farewell, my son," said the vicar, "till to-morrow."

"Till to-morrow, my rash young friend," said the Jesuit. "You promise to become one of the lights of the Church. Heaven grant that this light prove not a devouring fire!"

D'Artagnan, who for an hour past had been gnawing his nails with impatience, was now beginning to attack the flesh.

The two men in black rose, bowed to Aramis and D'Artagnan, and advanced toward the door. Bazin, who had been standing listening to all this controversy with a pious jubilation, sprang toward them, took the vicar's breviary and the Jesuit's missal, and walked respectfully before them to clear their way.

Aramis conducted them to the foot of the stairs, and then immediately came back again to D'Artagnan, who was still dreaming.

When left alone, the two friends at first kept silence from embarrassment. It, however, was necessary for one of them to break it first, and as D'Artagnan appeared determined to leave that honour to his friend,—

"You see," said Aramis, "that I have returned to my original ideas."

"Yes; saving grace has touched you, as that gentleman said just now."

"Oh, these plans of retreat have been formed for a long time. You have often heard me speak of them, have you not, my friend?"

"Yes; but I must confess that I always thought you were joking."

"About such things! O D'Artagnan!"

"Yes, indeed! People can joke about death."

"And people are wrong, D'Artagnan; for death is the door which leads to perdition or to salvation."

"Granted. But, if you please, let us not theologize, Aramis; you must have had enough for to-day. As for me, I have almost forgotten the little Latin I ever knew. Then I confess to you that I have eaten nothing since ten o'clock this morning, and I am devilish hungry."

"We will dine directly, my friend; only you must please to remember that this is Friday. Now, on such a day I cannot eat meat or see it eaten. If you can be satisfied with my dinner, it consists of cooked tetragones and fruits."

"What do you mean by tetragones?" asked D'Artagnan anxiously.

"I mean spinach," replied Aramis; "but on your account I will add some eggs. Even that is a serious infraction of the rule, for eggs are meat, since they engender chickens."

"This feast is not very nutritious; but never mind—I will put up with it for the sake of remaining with you."

"I am grateful to you for the sacrifice," said Aramis. "But if your body be not greatly benefited by it, be assured your soul will."

"And so, Aramis, you are decidedly going into the Church? What will our friends say? What will M. de Tréville say? They will treat you as a deserter, I warn you."

"I do not enter the Church—I re-enter it. I deserted the Church for the world, for you know that I did violence to myself when I became a musketeer."

"I know nothing about it."

"You don't know how I quitted the seminary?"

"Not at all."

"Here's my story. Besides, the Scriptures say, 'Confess yourselves one to another,' and I confess to you, D'Artagnan."

"And I give you absolution beforehand. You see I am good-natured."

"Do not jest with sacred things, my friend."

"Go on, then; I am listening."

"I had been at the seminary ever since I was nine years old; I lacked only three days of being twenty. I was expecting to be an abbé, and all was settled. One evening, when I had gone, according to my custom, to a house which I enjoyed frequenting (when you are young, what can you expect? You are weak), an officer who saw me, with a jealous eye, reading the 'Lives of the Saints' to the mistress of the house, entered suddenly, without being announced. That evening, as it happened, I had translated an episode of Judith, and had just communicated my verses to the lady, who was making me all sorts of compliments, and, leaning on my shoulder, was reading them a second time with me. Her attitude, which, I must admit, was rather free, wounded this gentleman's feelings. He said nothing, but when I went out he followed, and coming up to me,—

"'Abbé,' said he, 'do you like canings?'

"'I cannot say, sir,' answered I, 'no one having ever dared to give me any.'

"'Well, listen to me, then, abbé: if you venture again into the house where I met you this evening, I will dare.'

"I really think I must have been frightened. I became very pale; I felt my legs fail me. I sought a reply, but could find none. I was silent.

"The officer waited for my reply, and seeing it so long coming, he burst into a laugh, turned on his heel, and re-entered the house. I returned to my seminary.

"I am a gentleman born, and my blood is hot, as you may have remarked, my dear D'Artagnan. The insult was terrible, and although it remained unknown to the rest of the world, I felt it live and fester at the bottom of my heart. I informed my superiors that I did not feel myself sufficiently prepared for ordination, and at my request the ceremony was postponed for a year.

"I sought out the best fencing-master in Paris. I made an agreement with him to take a lesson every day, and every day during a year I took that lesson. Then, on the anniversary of the day on which I had been insulted, I hung my cassock on a peg, assumed the costume of a cavalier, and went to a ball given by a lady friend of mine, and where I knew my man would be. It was in the Rue des Francs-Bourgeois, close to La Force.

"As I expected, my officer was there. I went up to him as he was singing a love ditty and looking tenderly at a lady, and interrupted him exactly in the middle of the second couplet.

" ' Sir,' said I, ' does it still displease you that I should return to a certain house in Rue Payenne ? And would you still give me a caning if I took it into my head to disobey you ? '

" The officer looked at me with astonishment, and then said,—

" ' What is your business with me, sir ? I do not know you.'

" ' I am,' said I, ' the little abbé who used to read the " Lives of the Saints," and translate Judith into verse.'

" ' Ah, ha ! I recollect now.' said the officer in a jeering tone. ' Well, what do you want with me ? '

" ' I should like you to spare the time to take a walk with me.'

" ' To-morrow morning, if you like, and with the greatest pleasure.'

" ' No, not to-morrow morning, but immediately, if you please.'

" ' If you absolutely insist upon it——'

" ' I do ; I insist upon it.'

" ' Come, then.—Ladies,' said the officer, ' do not disturb yourselves. Allow me time simply to kill this gentleman, and I will return and finish the last couplet.'

" We went out. I took him to the Rue Payenne, to exactly the same spot where, a year before, at the very same hour, he had paid me the compliment I have related to you. It was a superb moonlight night. We drew, and at the first pass I laid him stark dead."

" The devil ! " cried D'Artagnan.

" Now," continued Aramis, " as the ladies did not see their singer come back, and as he was found in the Rue Payenne with a great sword-thrust through his body, it was supposed that I was the one who had accommodated him thus, and the matter created some scandal. So I was obliged to renounce the cassock for a time. Athos, whose acquaintance I made about that period, and Porthos, who had, in addition to my lessons, taught me some fine passes, prevailed upon me to solicit the uniform of a musketeer. The king entertained great regard for my father, who was killed at the siege of Arras, and the uniform was granted. You understand, then, that the moment has now come for me to re-enter the bosom of the Church."

" And why now, rather than yesterday or to-morrow ? What, then, has happened to you to-day which gives you such sorry ideas ? "

"My wound, my dear D'Artagnan, has been a warning to me from Heaven."

"Your wound? Bah! it is nearly healed, and I am sure it is not that which at the present moment gives you the most pain."

"What wound?" asked Aramis, colouring.

"You have one in your heart, Aramis, deeper and more painful—a wound made by a woman."

The eye of Aramis kindled in spite of himself.

"Ah," said he, dissembling his emotion under a feigned carelessness, "do not talk of such things. What! I think of such things? I have love-pangs? *Vanitas vanitatum!* According to your idea, then, my brain is turned! And for whom? For some grisette, some chambermaid, whom I have courted in some garrison! Fie!"

"I crave your pardon, my dear Aramis, but I thought you aimed higher."

"Higher? And who am I, to nourish such ambition? A poor musketeer, a beggar and unknown, who hates slavery, and finds himself out of place in the world."

"Aramis, Aramis!" cried D'Artagnan, looking at his friend with an air of doubt.

"Dust I am, and to dust I return. Life is full of humiliations and sorrows," continued he, becoming still more melancholy; "all the ties which attach it to happiness break one after another in the hand of man, particularly the golden ties. Oh, my dear D'Artagnan," resumed Aramis, giving to his voice a slight tone of bitterness, "believe me; conceal your wounds when you have any. Silence is the last joy of the unhappy. Beware of giving any one the clue to your griefs. The curious suck our tears as flies suck the blood of a wounded hart."

"Alas! my dear Aramis," said D'Artagnan, in his turn heaving a profound sigh, "that is my own history you are relating!"

"How?"

"Yes; a woman whom I love, whom I adore, has just been torn from me by force. I do not know where she is, or where she has been taken. Perhaps she is a prisoner, perhaps she is dead!"

"Yes, but you have at least this consolation, that you can say to yourself she has not quitted you voluntarily, that if you have no news of her, it is because all communication with you is forbidden; while——"

"While what?"

" Nothing," replied Aramis, " nothing."

" So you renounce the world, then, for ever. That is a settled thing, a resolution fixed upon ? "

" For ever ! You are my friend to-day ; to-morrow you will no longer exist for me. As for the world, it is a sepulchre, and nothing else."

" The devil ! What you say is very sad."

" What can you expect ? My vocation attracts me, it carries me away."

D'Artagnan smiled, but made no answer. Aramis continued,—

" And yet, while I still belong to the earth, I should have liked to speak of you and of our friends."

" And on my part," said D'Artagnan, " I should have liked to speak of you, but I find you so completely detached from everything ! Love you cry fie upon ! friends are shadows ! the world is a sepulchre ! "

" Alas ! you will find it so yourself," said Aramis, with a sigh.

" Well, then, let us say no more about it," said D'Artagnan ; " and let us burn this letter, which, no doubt, announces to you some fresh infidelity of your grisette or your chambermaid."

" What letter ? " cried Aramis eagerly.

" A letter which was sent to your rooms in your absence, and which was given to me for you."

" But whom is that letter from ? "

" Oh, from some tearful waiting-maid, some despairing grisette ; from Madame de Chevreuse's chambermaid, perhaps, who must have been obliged to return to Tours with her mistress, and who, in order to make herself attractive, stole some perfumed paper, and sealed her letter with a duchess's coronet."

" What are you saying ? "

" There ! I really think I must have lost it," said the young man mischievously, while pretending to search for it. " But fortunately the world is a sepulchre ; men, and consequently women also, are only shadows, and love is a sentiment upon which you cry, ' Fie, fie ! ' "

" D'Artagnan ! D'Artagnan ! " cried Aramis, " you are killing me ! "

" At last, here it is ! " said D'Artagnan. He drew the letter from his pocket.

Aramis sprang towards him, seized the letter, read it, or rather devoured it, his countenance absolutely beaming with delight.

"**Your** waiting-maid seems to have an agreeable style," said the carrier carelessly.

"Thanks, D'Artagnan, thanks!" cried Aramis, almost in a state of delirium. "She was forced to return to Tours; she is not faithless; she still loves me! Come, dear friend, come, let me embrace you; happiness stifles me!"

And the two friends began to dance round the venerable St. Chrysostom, kicking about famously the sheets of the thesis, which had fallen on the floor.

At that moment Bazin entered with the spinach and the omelet.

"Be off, you scoundrel!" cried Aramis, throwing his calotte into his face; "return to where you came from. Take back those horrible vegetables and that frightful side-dish! Order a larded hare, a fat capon, a leg of mutton with garlic, and four bottles of old Burgundy!"

Bazin, who looked at his master without comprehending the cause of this change, gloomily let the omelet slip into the spinach, and the spinach on to the floor.

"Now is the moment to consecrate your existence to the King of kings," said D'Artagnan, "if you persist in offering Him a civility. *Non inutile desiderium in oblatione.*"

"Go to the devil with your Latin. Let us drink, my dear D'Artagnan. 'Sdeath! let us drink while the wine is fresh. Let us drink heartily, and tell me something about what is going on in the world yonder."

CHAPTER XXVII.

THE WIFE OF ATHOS.

"Now we still have to get news of Athos," said D'Artagnan to the vivacious Aramis, when he had informed him of all that had passed since their departure from the capital, and when a good dinner had made one of them forget his thesis and the other his fatigue.

"Do you think any harm can have happened to him?" asked Aramis. "Athos is so cool, so brave, and handles his sword so skilfully."

"There is no doubt of that. Nobody has a higher opinion of the courage and skill of Athos than I have; but I like better to hear my sword clang against lances than against staves. I fear lest Athos has been carried down by a mob of menials. Those fellows strike hard, and don't leave off in a hurry. This is my reason for wishing to set out again as soon as I possibly can."

" I will try to accompany you," said Aramis, " though I scarcely feel in a condition to mount on horseback. Yesterday I undertook to employ that scourge you see hanging on the wall, but pain prevented my continuing the pious exercise."

" This is the first time I ever heard of anybody trying to cure gunshot wounds with a cat-o'-nine-tails ; but you were ill, and illness makes the head weak, therefore you may be excused."

" When do you set out ? "

" To-morrow at daybreak. Sleep as soundly as you can to-night, and to-morrow, if you are well enough, we will start together."

" Till to-morrow, then," said Aramis ; " for though you are made of iron you must need repose."

The next morning, when D'Artagnan entered Aramis's chamber, he found him standing at the window.

" What are you looking at there ? " asked D'Artagnan.

" 'Pon my word, I am admiring those three magnificent horses which the stable-lads are leading about. It would be a pleasure worthy of a prince to travel on such horses."

" Well, my dear Aramis, you may enjoy that pleasure, for one of those horses is yours."

" Ah, bah ! which of them ? "

" Whichever of the three you like. I have no preference."

" And the rich caparison is mine too ? "

" Certainly."

" You are laughing, D'Artagnan."

" No ; I have left off laughing, now that you speak French again."

" What ! those gilded holsters, that velvet housing, that silver-mounted saddle are all mine ? "

" Yours ; and the horse that is pawing the ground is mine, and the other horse which is caracoling belongs to Athos."

" By Jove ! they are three superb animals ! "

" I am glad they please you."

" Was it the king who made you such a present ? "

" Certainly it was not the cardinal. But don't trouble yourself about where they come from ; be satisfied that one of them is your property."

" I choose the one which the red-headed boy is holding."

" Have it, then."

" Good heavens ! That is enough to drive away all my

remaining pains. I could ride on him with thirty balls in my body. On my soul, what handsome stirrups!——Helloo, Bazin! come here this minute."

Bazin made his appearance at the door, dull and spiritless.

"Polish my sword, press my hat, brush my cloak, and load my pistols!" said Aramis.

"That last order is useless," interrupted D'Artagnan; "there are loaded pistols in your holsters."

Bazin sighed.

"Come, Master Bazin, make yourself easy; people gain the kingdom of heaven in all conditions of life."

"You were already such a good theologian," said Bazin, almost weeping; "you might have become a bishop, perhaps a cardinal."

"Well, but, my poor Bazin, reflect a little. Of what use is it to be a churchman, pray? You do not avoid going to war by that means: you see the cardinal is about to make the next campaign, helm on head and partisan in hand. And what do you say of M. de Nogaret de la Valette? He is a cardinal likewise. Ask his lackey how often he has had to prepare lint for him."

"Alas!" sighed Bazin, "I very well know, sir; everything is turned topsy-turvy in the world nowadays."

During this dialogue the two young men and the poor lackey had gone down into the yard.

"Hold my stirrup, Bazin," cried Aramis.

And Aramis sprang into his saddle with his usual grace and lightness; but after a few vaults and curvets of the noble animal, his rider felt his pains come on so insupportably that he turned pale and became unsteady in his seat. D'Artagnan, who, foreseeing such an event, had kept his eye on him, sprang toward him, caught him in his arms, and assisted him to his chamber.

"All right, my dear Aramis; take care of yourself," said he; "I will go alone in search of Athos."

"You are a man of bronze," replied Aramis.

"No, I have good luck, that is all. But how do you mean to pass your time till I come back? No more glosses on the fingers or upon benedictions, hey?"

Aramis smiled. "I will make verses," said he.

"Yes; verses perfumed with the odour of the note from Madame de Chevreuse's serving-maid. Teach Bazin prosody, then; that will console him. As to the horse, ride him a little every day, and that will accustom you to his movements."

"Oh, make yourself easy on that head," replied Aramis; "you will find me ready to follow you."

They took leave of each other, and ten minutes later, after commending his friend to the care of Bazin and the hostess, D'Artagnan was trotting along in the direction of Amiens.

How was he going to find Athos, and should he even find him at all? The position in which he had left him was critical. He might, very probably, have succumbed. This idea, while darkening his brow, drew several sighs from him, and caused him to formulate to himself a few vows of vengeance.

Of all his friends, Athos was the eldest, and consequently the least like him, apparently, in his tastes and sympathies.

Yet he entertained a marked preference for this gentleman. Athos's noble and distinguished air, the flashes of greatness which from time to time broke out from the shade in which he voluntarily kept himself, his unalterable equality of temper, which made him the pleasantest companion in the world, his forced and bitter gaiety, his bravery which might have been termed blind if it had not been the result of the rarest coolness—all these qualities attracted more than D'Artagnan's esteem, more than his friendship: they attracted his admiration.

Indeed, when placed beside M. de Tréville, the elegant and noble courtier, Athos in his days of good spirits might advantageously sustain a comparison. He was of middle height, but his person was so admirably shaped and so well proportioned that more than once, in his struggles with Porthos, he had overcome the giant, whose physical strength was proverbial among the musketeers. His head, with piercing eyes, a straight nose, a chin cut like that of Brutus, had altogether an indefinable character of grandeur and grace. His hands, of which he took no care at all, were the despair of Aramis, who cultivated his with a great deal of almond paste and perfumed oil. The sound of his voice was at once penetrating and melodious; and then what was indefinable in Athos, who was always modest and retiring, was his knowledge of the world, and of the usages of the most brilliant society, his high-bred manners, which appeared, as if unconsciously to himself, in his least actions.

If a repast were on foot, Athos presided over it better than any other man in society, placing every guest exactly in the rank which his ancestors had earned for him, or which he had made for himself. If a question in heraldry were started,

Athos knew all the noble families of the kingdom, their genealogy, their alliances, their arms, and the origin of their arms. Etiquette had no details unknown to him. He knew what were the rights of the great landowners ; he was profoundly versed in venery and falconry, and had one day, when conversing on this great art, astonished even Louis XIII. himself, who, nevertheless, had taken his master's degree in it.

Like all the great nobles of that period, he rode and fenced to perfection. But still further, his education had been so little neglected, even with respect to scholastic studies, so rare at this time among gentlemen, that he smiled at the scraps of Latin which Aramis sported, and which Porthos pretended to understand. Twice or thrice even, to the great astonishment of his friends, he had, when Aramis allowed some rudimentary error to escape him, replaced a verb in its right tense and a noun in its right case. Besides, his probity was irreproachable, in that age when soldiers so easily compromised with their religion and their consciences, lovers with the rigorous delicacy of our days, and the poor with God's seventh commandment. Athos, then, was a very extraordinary man.

And yet this nature so well bred, this creature so beautiful, this essence so fine, was seen to turn insensibly toward material life, as old men turn toward physical and moral imbecility. In his hours of privation—and such hours were frequent—the whole of the luminous portion of Athos was extinguished, and his brilliant side disappeared as if in profound eclipse.

Then, the demigod having vanished, he remained almost less than a man. With head hanging down, dull eye, speech slow and painful, Athos would look for hours together at his bottle, his glass, or at Grimaud, who, accustomed to obey him by signs, read in his master's faint glance his least desire, and immediately satisfied it. If the four friends were together during one of these moods, a word, uttered occasionally with a violent effort, was the one share Athos furnished to the conversation. To make up for his silence, Athos alone drank enough for four, nor did he appear to be otherwise affected by wine than by a more marked contraction of the brow and by a deeper sadness.

D'Artagnan, with whose inquisitive and penetrating disposition we are acquainted, whatever interest he might have in satisfying his curiosity on this subject, had not been able to assign any cause for these fits, or to note periods of their recurrence.   Athos never received any letters ; Athos never had concerns which were not known to all his friends.

It could not be said that wine produced this sadness, for, in truth, he only drank to combat this sadness, and the wine, as we have said, only rendered it still more gloomy.   This excess of bilious humour could not be attributed to play, for, unlike Porthos, who accompanied the variations of chance with songs or oaths, Athos, when he had won, remained as impassive as when he had lost.   He had been known, in the musketeers' club, to win one night a thousand pistoles, lose them, even with his gold-embroidered gala-day belt to boot, gain it all back, with the addition of a hundred louis, without his beautiful black eyebrows rising or falling half a line, without his hands losing their pearly hue, without his conversation, which was cheerful that evening, ceasing for a moment to be calm and agreeable.

Nor was it, as with our neighbours the English, an atmospheric influence that darkened his countenance, for his sadness generally became more intense toward the fine season of the year.   June and July were Athos's terrible months.

For the present he had no care.   He shrugged his shoulders when people spoke of the future.   His secret, then, was in the past, as D'Artagnan had vaguely been told.

This mysterious shadow, spread over his whole person, rendered still more interesting the man whose eyes or mouth had never, even in the moments of the most complete intoxication, revealed anything, however skilfully questions had been put to him.

"Well," remarked D'Artagnan, "poor Athos is perhaps at this moment dead, and dead through my fault ; for I dragged him into this affair, the origin of which he did not know, the result of which he will not know, and from which he could derive no advantage."

"Without reckoning, sir," added Planchet, "that we probably owe our lives to him. Do you remember how he cried, ' On, D'Artagnan ! I am taken ! ' And when he had discharged his two pistols, what a terrible noise he made with his sword ! One might have said that twenty men or rather twenty mad devils were fighting."

And these words redoubled D'Artagnan's eagerness, and he spurred on his horse, which stood in no need of any stimulus, but carried his master along at a gallop.

About eleven o'clock in the morning they perceived Amiens.   At half-past eleven they were at the door of the cursed inn.

D'Artagnan had often meditated against the perfidious landlord one of those hearty revenges which are consoling even in the thought of them. He entered the hostelry with his hat pulled over his eyes, his left hand on the pommel of the sword, and cracking his whip with his right hand.

"Do you remember me?" said he to the landlord, who advanced, bowing, toward him.

"I have not that honour, monseigneur," replied the latter, his eyes still dazzled by the brilliant turnout with which D'Artagnan appeared.

"What! you don't know me?"

"No, monseigneur."

"Well, two words will refresh your memory. What have you done with that gentleman whom you had the audacity, about two weeks ago, to accuse of passing bad money?"

The host grew pale, for D'Artagnan had assumed the most threatening attitude, and Planchet had followed his master's example.

"Ah, monseigneur, do not mention it!" cried the landlord, in the most piteous voice imaginable; "ah, seigneur, how dearly have I paid for my mistake, unhappy wretch that I am!"

"I say, what has become of that gentleman?"

"Deign to listen to me, monseigneur, and be merciful! Sit down, I beg!"

D'Artagnan, mute with anger and uneasiness, sat down as threatening as a judge. Planchet stood fiercely at the back of his armchair.

"Here is the story, monseigneur," resumed the trembling landlord, "for I now recollect you. It was you who rode off at the moment I had that unfortunate difference with the gentleman you speak of."

"Yes, it was I; so you may plainly perceive that you have no mercy to expect if you do not tell me the whole truth."

"Then please listen to me, and you shall know it all."

"I am listening."

"I had been warned by the authorities that a celebrated counterfeiter would arrive at my inn with several of his companions, all disguised as guards or musketeers. I was furnished with a description of your horses, your lackeys, your countenances; nothing was omitted."

"Go on! go on!" said D'Artagnan, who quickly recognized the source of such an exact description.

"In conformity with the orders of the authorities, who

sent me a reinforcement of six men, I took, then, such measures as I thought necessary to get possession of the persons of the pretended counterfeiters."

"What, again!" exclaimed D'Artagnan, whose ears were terribly wounded by the repetition of this word counterfeiters.

"Pardon me, monseigneur, for saying such things, but they are really my excuse. The authorities had terrified me, and you know that a tavern-keeper must keep on good terms with the authorities."

"But, once again, where is the gentleman? What has become of him? Is he dead? Is he living?"

"Patience, monseigneur, we are coming to it. What you know about then happened, the outcome of which your precipitate departure," added the landlord, with a shrewdness that did not escape D'Artagnan, "appeared to authorize. The gentleman, your friend, defended himself desperately. His lackey, who, by an unforeseen piece of ill-luck, had got up a quarrel with the police, disguised as stable-lads——"

"Miserable scoundrel!" cried D'Artagnan; "you were all in the plot then! And I really don't know what prevents me from exterminating you all."

"Alas, monseigneur, we were not all in the plot, and you will soon see we were not. Your friend (I ask pardon for not calling him by the honourable name which no doubt he bears, but we do not know his name)—your friend, having disabled two men with his pistols, retreated fighting with his sword, with which he mutilated another one of my men, and stunned me with a blow of the flat side."

"Hangman! when will you come to the end?" cried D'Artagnan. "Athos—what has become of Athos?"

"While fighting and retreating, as I have told monseigneur, he found behind him the cellar stairs, and as the door was open, he took possession of the key, and barricaded himself inside. As we were sure of finding him there, we let him alone."

"Yes," said D'Artagnan; "there wasn't any particular reason for killing him; it was enough to keep him a prisoner."

"Good God! a prisoner, monseigneur? Why, he imprisoned himself—upon my oath he did. Besides, he had made rough work of it. One man was killed on the spot, and two others were severely wounded. The dead man and the two who were wounded were carried off by their companions, and I have heard nothing of any of them since.

As for myself, as soon as I recovered my senses I went to the governor, to whom I related all that had passed, and whom I asked what I should do with my prisoner. But the governor was thunderstruck. He told me he did not know at all what I meant, that the orders I had received did not come from him, and that if I had the misfortune to tell any one whatsoever that he was at all concerned in all this disturbance, he would have me hanged. It appears that I had made a mistake, sir, that I had arrested the wrong person, and that he whom I ought to have arrested had escaped.''

"But Athos!" cried D'Artagnan, whose impatience was increased by the abandoned state in which the authorities left the matter—"Athos! where is he?''

"As I was anxious to repair the wrongs I had done the prisoner," resumed the innkeeper, "I took my way straight to the cellar, in order to set him at liberty. Ah, sir, he was no longer a man; he was a devil! To my offer of liberty he replied that it was nothing but a snare set for him, and that before he came out he intended to impose his own conditions. I told him very humbly—for I could not conceal from myself the scrape I had got into by laying hands on one of his Majesty's musketeers—I told him I was ready to submit to his conditions.

"'In the first place,' said he, 'I insist upon having my lackey handed over to me, fully armed.' We hastened to obey this order, for you will please to understand, sir, we were disposed to do everything your friend could desire. M. Grimaud (he told us his name, he did, although he does not talk much)—M. Grimaud, then, was sent down to the cellar, wounded as he was; then his master, having received him, barricaded the door anew, and ordered us to remain in our shop."

"Well, but where is he now?" cried D'Artagnan. "Where is Athos?"

"In the cellar, sir."

"What! you wretch! What! you have kept him in the cellar all this time?"

"Merciful Heaven! No, sir! We keep him in the cellar! You do not know what he is up to in the cellar! Ah, if you could but persuade him to come out, sir, I should be grateful to you all my life; I should adore you as my patron saint!''

"Then he is there? I shall find him there?"

"Certainly you will, sir; he persists in remaining there. Every day we pass through the airhole some bread at the end of a fork, and some meat when he asks for it; but, alas! it is not of bread and meat that he consumes the greatest quantity. I once endeavoured to go down with two of my servants, but he flew into a terrible rage. I heard the noise he made in loading his pistols, and his servant in loading his musketoon. Then, when we asked them what were their intentions, the master replied that he had forty shots to fire, and that he and his lackey would fire them to the last one before he would allow a single soul of us to set foot in the cellar. Upon this I went and complained to the governor, who replied that I only had what I deserved, and that it would teach me to insult honourable gentlemen who took up their abode in my house."

"So that from that time——" replied D'Artagnan, totally unable to refrain from laughing at the landlord's pitiable face.

"So that from that time, sir," continued the latter, "we have led the most miserable life imaginable. For you must know, sir, that all our provisions are in the cellar: there is our wine in bottles, and our wine in the butt; beer, oil, groceries, bacon, and large sausages; and as we are prevented from going down there, we are forced to refuse food and drink to the travellers who come to the house, so that our hostelry is daily going to rack and ruin. If your friend remains another week in my cellar we shall be ruined."

"And that will be justice, you rascal! Could you not perceive by our appearance that we were people of quality, and not counterfeiters—say?"

"Yes, sir, yes, you are right," said the landlord. "But, hark, hark! there he is in a passion again!"

"Somebody has disturbed him, no doubt," said D'Artagnan.

"But he must be disturbed," cried the landlord. "Here are two English gentlemen just arrived."

"Well?"

"Well, the English like good wine, as you know, sir; these have asked for my best. My wife, then, must have asked M. Athos to let her go into the cellar to satisfy these gentlemen, and he, as usual, must have refused. Ah, good heavens! there is the hullabaloo louder than ever!"

D'Artagnan, in fact, heard a great noise in the direction of the cellar. He rose, and preceded by the landlord, who was wringing his hands, and followed by Planchet with his musketoon all loaded, he approached the scene of action.

The two gentlemen were exasperated. They had had a long ride, and were desperately hungry and thirsty.

"But this is a tyranny," cried they, in very good French, though with a foreign accent, "that this madman will not allow these good people access to their own wine! Come! we will break open the door, and if he is too far gone in his madness—well, we will kill him!"

"Softly, gentlemen!" said D'Artagnan, drawing his pistols from his belt; "you will kill no one, if you please!"

"Good, good!" said Athos calmly, from the other side of the door. "Just let them come in, these devourers of little children, and we shall see!"

Brave as they appeared to be, the two English gentlemen looked at each other hesitatingly. One would have said that there was in that cellar one of those hungry ogres, the gigantic heroes of popular legends, into whose cavern nobody can force a way with impunity.

There was a moment of silence; but at length the two Englishmen felt ashamed to draw back, and the more quarrelsome one descended the five or six steps which led to the cellar, and gave the door a kick hard enough to split a wall.

"Planchet," said D'Artagnan, cocking his pistols, "I will take charge of the one at the top; you look to the one below. —Now, gentlemen, if it's battle you want, you shall have it."

"My God!" cried the hollow voice of Athos, "I can hear D'Artagnan, I think."

"Yes," cried D'Artagnan, raising his voice in his turn; "I am here, my friend."

"Ah, ah, then," replied Athos, "we will give it to these breakers-in of doors!"

The gentlemen had drawn their swords, but they found themselves caught between two fires. They still hesitated an instant; but, as before, pride prevailed, and a second kick split the door from bottom to top.

"Stand on one side, D'Artagnan, stand on one side!" cried Athos; "I am going to fire!"

"Gentlemen," exclaimed D'Artagnan, whose presence of mind never abandoned him—"gentlemen, think of what you are about!—Patience, Athos!—You are running your heads into a very silly affair; you will be riddled. My lackey and I will have three shots at you, and you will get as many from the cellar. We will then have our swords, with which, I can assure you, my friend and I play tolerably well. Let me manage your business and my own. You shall soon have something to drink; I give you my word."

"If there is any left!" grumbled Athos's jeering voice.

The landlord felt a cold sweat creep down his back.

"How! if there is any left!" murmured he.

"What the devil! there must be plenty left," replied D'Artagnan; "be satisfied of that. These two can never have drunk up the whole cellar.—Gentlemen, return your swords to their scabbards."

"We will, provided you replace your pistols in your belt."

"Willingly."

And D'Artagnan set the example. Then turning towards Planchet, he made him a sign to uncock his musketoon.

The Englishmen, convinced, sheathed their swords grumblingly. The history of Athos's imprisonment was then related to them; and as they were really gentlemen, they pronounced the host in the wrong.

"Now, gentlemen," said D'Artagnan, "go up to your room again; and in ten minutes, I will answer for it, you shall have all you desire."

The Englishmen bowed and went upstairs.

"Now I am alone, my dear Athos," said D'Artagnan; "open the door, I beg of you."

"Instantly," said Athos.

Then a great noise of the knocking down of fagots was heard, and of the groaning of beams; these were Athos's counterscarps and bastions which the besieged himself was demolishing.

An instant later the door moved, and the pale face of Athos appeared, who with a rapid glance took a survey of the situation.

D'Artagnan fell on his neck and embraced him tenderly. He then endeavoured to draw him from that moist abode, but, to his surprise, perceived that Athos staggered.

"Why, you are wounded?" said he.

"I! Not at all. I am dead drunk, that's all, and never did a man do it better. Gracious heavens! my good host, I must at least have drunk for my part a hundred and fifty bottles."

"Mercy on us!" cried the landlord. "If the lackey has drunk only half as much as the master, I am a ruined man."

"Grimaud is a well-bred lackey. He would never think of faring in the same way as his master. He only drank from the butt. Hark! I believe he forgot to turn the faucet in again. Do you hear it? It is running now."

D'Artagnan burst into a loud laugh, which changed the landlord's trembling into a burning fever.

In the meantime, Grimaud appeared in his turn, behind

his master, with his musketoon on his shoulder, and his head shaking like one of those drunken satyrs in Rubens's pictures. He was bedewed before and behind with a thick liquid which the host recognized as his best olive oil.

The party crossed the public room, and proceeded to take possession of the best apartment in the house, which D'Artagnan seized arbitrarily.

In the meantime the landlord and his wife hurried down with lamps into the cellar, which had so long been forbidden them, and where a frightful spectacle awaited them.

Beyond the fortifications, through which Athos had made a breach in order to get out, and which were composed of fagots, planks, and empty casks, heaped up according to all the rules of the strategic art, they found, swimming in puddles of oil and wine, the bones and fragments of all the hams they had eaten ; while a heap of broken bottles filled the whole left-hand corner of the cellar, and a keg, the cock of which was left running, was losing through the opening the last drops of its blood. " The image of devastation and death," as the ancient poet says, " reigned as over a field of battle."

Of fifty large sausages, that had been suspended from the joists, scarcely ten remained.

Then the lamentations of the landlord and landlady pierced the vault of the cellar. D'Artagnan himself was moved by them. Athos did not even turn his head.

But rage succeeded grief. The landlord armed himself with a spit, and in his despair rushed into the chamber occupied by the two friends.

" Wine ! " said Athos on perceiving the host.

" Wine ! " cried the stupefied landlord, " wine ! Why, you have drunk more than a hundred pistoles' worth ! I am a ruined man—lost ! destroyed ! "

" Bah ! " said Athos. " Why, we always stopped thirsty."

" If you had been contented with drinking, why, well and good ; but you have broken all the bottles."

" You pushed me upon a heap which rolled down. That was your fault."

" All my oil is lost ! "

" Oil is a sovereign balm for wounds, and my poor Grimaud here was obliged to dress those you had inflicted on him."

" All my sausages gnawed ! "

" There is an enormous number of rats in that cellar."

" You shall pay me for all this," cried the exasperated host.

" You triple ass ! " said Athos, rising ; but he sank down again immediately. He had tried his strength to the utmost. D'Artagnan came to his relief, with his whip raised in the air.

The landlord drew back and burst into tears.

" This will teach you," said D'Artagnan, " to treat more courteously the guests God sends you."

" God ! Say rather the devil ! "

" My dear friend," said D'Artagnan, " if you keep stunning us in this manner, we will all four go and shut ourselves up in your cellar, and see if the mischief be as great as you say."

" O gentlemen, gentlemen," said the landlord, " I have been wrong, I confess it ; but there is pardon for every sin ! You are noblemen, and I am a poor innkeeper ; you will have pity on me."

" Ah, if you speak in that way," said Athos, " you will break my heart, and the tears will flow from my eyes as the wine flowed from your casks. We are not such devils as we appear to be. Come here, and let us talk the matter over."

The landlord approached hesitatingly.

" Come here, I say, and don't be afraid," continued Athos. " At the moment when I was about to pay you, I had laid my purse on your table."

" Yes, monseigneur."

" That purse contained sixty pistoles. Where is it ? "

" Deposited in the justice's office. They said it was counterfeit money."

" Very well ; get me my purse back, and keep the sixty pistoles."

" But monseigneur knows very well that justice never lets go what it once lays hold of. If it were counterfeit money, there might be some hopes ; but unfortunately they are good pieces."

" Manage the matter as well as you can, my good man. It does not concern me, the more so as I have not a livre left."

" Come," said D'Artagnan, " where is Athos's former horse ? "

" In the stable."

" How much is it worth ? "

" Fifty pistoles at most."

" It's worth eighty. Take it, and let that end the matter."

" What ! " cried Athos, " are you selling my horse—

selling my Bajazet ? And pray, on what shall I make my campaign ? On Grimaud ? "

" I have brought you another," said D'Artagnan.

" Another ? "

" And a magnificent one too ! " cried the landlord.

" Well, since there is another finer and younger, why, you may take the old one, and let us have some wine."

" What kind ? " asked the landlord, quite cheerful again.

" Some of that at the bottom, near the laths. There are twenty-five bottles of it left ; all the rest were broken by my fall. Bring up six of them."

" Why, this man is a tun ! " said the host aside. " If he will only remain here a fortnight, and pay for what he drinks, my affairs will soon be right again."

" And don't forget," said D'Artagnan, " to bring up four bottles of the same sort for the two English gentlemen."

" And now, D'Artagnan," said Athos, " while they are bringing up the wine, tell me what has become of the others —come ! "

D'Artagnan related how he had found Porthos in bed with a sprained knee, and Aramis at a table between two theologians. As he finished, the landlord entered with the wine and a ham, which, fortunately for him, had been left out of the cellar.

" Good ! " said Athos, filling his glass and D'Artagnan's. " Here's to Porthos and Aramis ! But, my friend, what is the matter with you, and what has happened to you personally ? You don't look happy."

" Alas ! " said D'Artagnan, " it is because I am the most unfortunate of all."

" You unfortunate ! " said Athos. " Come ! how the devil can you be unfortunate ? Tell me that."

" Presently," said D'Artagnan.

" Presently ! And why presently ? Because you think I am drunk, D'Artagnan ? Keep this in mind : my ideas are never so clear as when I have had plenty of wine. Speak, then ; I am all ears."

D'Artagnan related his adventure with Madame Bonacieux. Athos listened to him without moving a muscle, and when he had finished,—

" Trifles all that," said Athos — " nothing but trifles ! " That was Athos's favourite expression.

" You always say trifles, my dear Athos," said D'Artagnan, " and that comes very ill from you, who have never been in love."

Athos's dull eye flashed suddenly, but it was only a flash; it became dull and vacant as before.

"True," said he quietly, "I have never been in love."

"Acknowledge, then, you stony-hearted man," said D'Artagnan, "that you have no right to be so hard on us whose hearts are tender."

"Tender hearts! wounded hearts!" said Athos.

"What do you say?"

"I say that love is a lottery, in which he who wins wins death! You are very fortunate to have lost, believe me, my dear D'Artagnan. And if I may be allowed to advise you, always lose."

"Oh, but she seemed to love me so!"

"She seemed, did she?"

"Oh, she did love me."

"You boy! Why, not a man lives who has not believed as you do that his mistress loved him, and no man lives who has not been deceived by his mistress."

"Except you, Athos, who never had one."

"True," said Athos, after a moment's silence—"true, I never had one! Let us drink!"

"But then, philosopher that you are," said D'Artagnan, "instruct me, support me. I need to know and to be consoled."

"Consoled! for what?"

"For my misfortune."

"Your misfortune is laughable," said Athos, shrugging his shoulders. "I should like to know what you would say if I were to relate to you a real tale of love."

"Which concerns you?"

"Or one of my friends. What difference does it make?"

"Tell it, Athos, tell it."

"Let us drink! That will be better."

"Drink while you tell it!"

"Not a bad idea!" said Athos, emptying and filling his glass; "the two things go marvellously well together."

"I am all attention," said D'Artagnan.

Athos collected himself, and in proportion as he did so, D'Artagnan saw that he became paler. He was at that period of intoxication in which vulgar drinkers fall on the floor and go to sleep. But he dreamed aloud, without sleeping. This somnambulism of drunkenness had something frightful about it.

"You absolutely wish it?" asked he.

"I beg you to do it," said D'Artagnan.

" Be it, then, as you desire.   A friend of mine—please to observe, a friend of mine, not myself," said Athos, interrupting himself with a gloomy smile—" one of the counts of my province (that is to say, of Berry), noble as a Dandolo or a Montmorency, when he was twenty-five years old fell in love with a girl of sixteen, beautiful as an angel.   Through the ingenuousness of her age beamed an ardent mind—not a woman's mind, but a poet's.   She did not please; she intoxicated.   She lived in a small town with her brother, who was a vicar.   Both had recently come into the country. Nobody knew where they came from ; but on seeing her so lovely and her brother so pious, nobody thought of asking where they came from.   They were said, however, to be of good extraction.   My friend, who was lord of the country, might have seduced her; or he might have seized her forcibly, at his will, for he was master.   Who would have come to the assistance of two strangers, two unknown persons ? Unfortunately, he was an honourable man ; he married her. The fool ! the ass ! the idiot ! "

" How so, if he loved her ? " asked D'Artagnan.

" Wait ! " said Athos.   " He took her to his château, and made her the first lady in the province ; and, in justice, it must be allowed she supported her rank becomingly."

" Well ? " asked D'Artagnan.

" Well, one day when she was hunting with her husband," continued Athos, in a low voice, and speaking very quickly, " she fell from her horse and fainted.   The count flew to her help ; and as she appeared to be oppressed by her clothes, he ripped them open with his poniard, and in so doing laid bare her shoulder.   Guess, D'Artagnan," said Athos, with a loud burst of laughter—" guess what she had on her shoulder."

" How can I tell ? " said D'Artagnan.

" A fleur-de-lis ! " said Athos.   " She was branded ! "

And Athos emptied at a single draught the glass he held in his hand.

" Horrors," cried D'Artagnan.   " What are you telling me ? "

" The truth.   My friend, the angel was a demon.   The poor young girl had been a thief."

" And what did the count do ? "

" The count was a great noble.   He had on his estates the right of life and death.   He tore the countess's dress to pieces, tied her hands behind her, and hanged her on a tree ! "

" Heavens ! Athos, a murder ! " cried D'Artagnan.

"Yes, a murder—nothing else," said Athos, pale as death. "But methinks I am left without wine!" And he seized by the neck the last bottle that remained, put it to his mouth, and emptied it at a single draught, as he would have emptied an ordinary glass.

Then he let his head fall on his two hands, while D'Artagnan sat facing him, overwhelmed with dismay.

"That has cured me of beautiful, poetical, and loving women," said Athos, getting to his feet, and neglecting to pursue the apologue of the count. "God grant you as much! Let us drink!"

"Then she is dead ?" stammered D'Artagnan.

"Zounds !" said Athos. "But hold out your glass. Some ham, my man !" cried Athos ; "we can drink no longer !"

"And her brother ?" asked D'Artagnan timidly.

"Her brother ?" replied Athos.

"Yes, the priest."

"Oh, I inquired after him for the purpose of hanging him likewise ; but he was beforehand with me—he had quitted the curacy instantly."

"Was it ever known who this miserable fellow was ?"

"He was doubtless the fair lady's first lover and accomplice—a worthy man, who had pretended to be a curate for the purpose of getting his mistress married and securing her a position. He has been quartered before this time, I hope."

"My God ! my God !" cried D'Artagnan, quite stunned by the relation of this horrible adventure.

"Pray eat some of this ham, D'Artagnan ; it is exquisite," said Athos, cutting a slice, which he placed on the young man's plate. "What a pity it is there are only four like this in the cellar ! I could have drunk fifty bottles more."

D'Artagnan could no longer endure this conversation, which would have driven him crazy. He let his head fall on his hands and pretended to go to sleep.

"Young men no longer know how to drink," said Athos, looking at him pityingly, "and yet this is one of the best of them, too ! "

CHAPTER XXVIII.

THE RETURN.

D'ARTAGNAN was astounded by the terrible story Athos had confided to him, and yet many things still appeared obscure to him in this partial revelation. In the first place, it had been made by a man decidedly drunk to one who was half drunk ; and yet, in spite of the uncertainty which the fumes of three or four bottles of Burgundy carry with them to the brain, D'Artagnan, on awaking the following morning, found every word of Athos as vividly written on his brain as if, when they had fallen from his mouth, they had, in fact, been imprinted on his mind. All this doubt only gave rise to a more lively desire of arriving at a certainty, and he went into his friend's chamber with a fixed determination of renewing the conversation of the preceding evening ; but he found Athos quite himself again—that is to say, the most shrewd and impenetrable of men. Besides, the musketeer, after having exchanged a hearty shake of the hand with him, broached the matter first.

"I was pretty drunk yesterday, my dear D'Artagnan," said he. "I can tell that by my tongue, which was still very thick this morning, and by my pulse, which was still very tremulous. I would lay a wager I uttered a thousand absurdities."

And while saying this he looked at his friend with an earnestness that embarrassed him.

"No," replied D'Artagnan ; "if I recollect well what you said, it was nothing out of the common."

"Indeed, you surprise me. I thought I had related a most lamentable story to you."

And he looked at the young man as if he would like to read to the very depths of his heart.

"'Pon my word," said D'Artagnan, "it appears that I was drunker than you, since I remember nothing of the kind."

But this did not satisfy Athos, who went on,—

"You cannot have failed to remark, my dear friend, that every one has his own kind of drunkenness, sad or gay. My drunkenness is always sad, and when I am thoroughly intoxicated my mania is to relate all the dismal stories with which my foolish nurse filled my brain. That is my failing —a great failing, I admit ; but, with that exception, I am a sound drinker."

Athos said this so naturally that D'Artagnan was shaken in his conviction.

"Oh, that was it, then," replied the young man, trying to get at the truth—"that was it, then. I remember, as we remember a dream ; we were speaking of hanging people."

"Ah ! you see how it is," said Athos, turning pale, but

yet attempting to laugh. "I was sure it was so. The hanging of people is my nightmare."

"Yes, yes," replied D'Artagnan; "I remember now. Yes, it was about—stop a minute—yes, it was about a woman."

"That's it," replied Athos, becoming almost livid; "that is my great story of the fair lady. And when I relate that, I must be drunk indeed."

"Yes, that was it," said D'Artagnan—"the story of a lady, tall, fair, and beautiful, with blue eyes."

"Yes, who was hanged."

"By her husband, who was a nobleman of your acquaintance," continued D'Artagnan, looking intently at Athos.

"Well, you see how a man may compromise himself when he does not know what he says," replied Athos, shrugging his shoulders as if he thought himself an object of pity. "I certainly never will get drunk again, D'Artagnan; it is too bad a habit."

D'Artagnan remained silent.

Then Athos, changing the conversation all at once,—

"By-the-bye, I thank you for the horse you have brought me," said he.

"Does it suit you?" asked D'Artagnan.

"Yes; but it is not a horse for hard work."

"You are mistaken. I have ridden him ten leagues in less than an hour and a half, and he appeared no more distressed than if he had only made the tour of the Place St. Sulpice."

"Ah, ha! you begin to awaken my regret."

"Regret?"

"Yes; I have parted with him."

"How?"

"Why, here is a simple fact. This morning I awoke at six o'clock. You were still fast asleep, and I did not know what to do with myself. I was still stupid from our yesterday's revel. As I came into the public room I saw one of our Englishmen bargaining with a dealer for a horse, his own having died yesterday from blind staggers. I drew near, and found he was bidding a hundred pistoles for a chestnut nag.

"'Zounds!' said I, 'my good gentleman, I have a horse to sell too.'

"'Ay, and a very fine one! I saw him yesterday; your friend's lackey was leading him.'

"'Do you think he is worth a hundred pistoles?'

"'Yes. Will you sell him to me for that sum?'

" ' No ; but I will gamble with you for him.'

" ' You will gamble with me for him ? '

" ' Yes.'

" ' What with ? '

" ' Dice.'

" No sooner said than done, and I lost the horse. Ah, ah ! but please to observe I won back the trappings," cried Athos.

D'Artagnan looked much disconcerted.

" This vexes you ? " said Athos.

" Well, I must confess it does," replied D'Artagnan. " That horse was to have assisted in making us known in the day of battle. It was a pledge—a remembrance. Athos, you have done wrong."

" But, my dear friend, put yourself in my place," replied the musketeer. " I was bored to death ; and then, upon my honour, I don't like English horses. If it is only a question of being recognized by some one, why, the saddle will suffice for that ; it is quite remarkable enough. As to the horse, we can easily find some excuse for its disappearance. What the devil ! a horse is mortal. Let us play mine had the glanders or the farcy."

D'Artagnan remained gloomy.

" It vexes me greatly," continued Athos, " that you attach so much importance to these animals, for I am not yet at the end of my story."

" What else have you done ? "

" After losing my own horse, nine against ten—see how near !—the notion occurred to me of staking yours."

" Yes ; but you stopped at the notion, I hope ? "

" No ; for I put it in execution that very minute."

" That's too much ! " said D'Artagnan, in great anxiety.

" I threw, and I lost."

" What ! my horse ? "

" Your horse—seven against eight. One point short—you know the proverb."

" Athos, you are not in your right senses—I swear you are not."

" My dear lad, you ought to have told me that yesterday, when I was telling you silly stories, and not this morning. I lost him, then, with all his appointments and harnesses."

" Really this is frightful ! "

" Stop a minute ; you don't know all yet. I should make an excellent gambler if I were not too obstinate. But I get obstinate, just as when I drink. Well, I got obstinate, then——"

"Well, but what else could you play for? You had nothing left?"

"Oh, yes, yes, my friend; there was still that diamond left which sparkles on your finger, and which I had observed yesterday."

"This diamond!" said D'Artagnan, placing his hand eagerly on his ring.

"And as I am a connoisseur in such things, having had a few of my own once, I estimated it at a thousand pistoles."

"I hope," said D'Artagnan seriously, half dead with fright, "you made no mention of my diamond."

"On the contrary, my dear friend, your diamond became our only resource. With it I might regain our horses and their outfit, and, still further, money to pay our expenses on the road."

"Athos, you make me tremble!" cried D'Artagnan.

"I mentioned your diamond, then, to my adversary, who had likewise noticed it. What the devil! do you think you can wear a star from heaven on your finger and nobody observe it? Impossible!"

"Oh, go on, go on!" said D'Artagnan, "for, on my honour, you will kill me with your coolness!"

"So we divided your diamond into ten parts, of a hundred pistoles each."

"You are laughing at me, and want to try me!" said D'Artagnan, whom anger began to take by the hair, as Minerva takes Achilles in the "Iliad."

"No, I am not joking. 'Sdeath! I should like to have seen you in my place! I had been a fortnight without seeing a human face, and had been left to grow besotted in the company of bottles."

"That was no reason for staking my diamond!" replied D'Artagnan, doubling his fist with a nervous spasm.

"But hear the end. Ten throws of a hundred pistoles each—ten throws, without revenge; in thirteen throws I lost all—in thirteen throws. The number thirteen was always fatal to me. It was on the 13th of July that——"

"Great heavens!" cried D'Artagnan, rising from the table, that day's story making him forget that of the preceding one.

"Patience!" said Athos; "I had a plan. The Englishman was an original character. I had seen him conversing that morning with Grimaud, and Grimaud had told me that he made him proposals to enter his service. I staked Grimaud—the silent Grimaud—divided into ten portions."

"Well, what next?" said D'Artagnan, laughing in spite of himself.

"Grimaud himself, understand; and with the ten parts of Grimaud, who is not worth a ducatoon, I won back the diamond. Tell me, now, whether you don't think persistence is a virtue."

"'Pon my word, but this is a droll story!" cried D'Artagnan, a little consoled, and holding his sides with laughter.

"You may easily guess that, finding the luck turned, I again staked the diamond at once."

"The devil!" said D'Artagnan, growing sober again.

"I won back your trappings, then your horse, then my trappings, then my horse, and then I lost again. In short, I regained your trappings and then mine. That's where we left off. That was a superb throw, so I left off there."

D'Artagnan breathed as if the whole hostelry had been removed from his breast.

"Then I understand," said he timidly, "the diamond is safe?"

"Intact, my dear friend—plus the trappings of your Bucephalus and mine."

"But what shall we do without horses?"

"I have an idea concerning them."

"Athos, you keep me in a fever."

"Listen to me. You have not played for a long time, D'Artagnan."

"Neither have I any inclination to play."

"Swear to nothing. You have not played for a long time, I said. You ought, then, to have good luck."

"Well, what then?"

"Well, the Englishman and his companion are still here. I remarked that he regretted the trappings very much. You appear to think much of your horse. In your place, now, I would stake the harness against the horse."

"But he will not be satisfied with one equipment."

"Stake both, by Jove! I am not selfish if you are."

"You would do so?" said D'Artagnan, undecided, so strongly did the confidence of Athos begin to overcome him unconsciously.

"On my honour, in one single throw."

"But having lost the horses, I am particularly anxious to preserve the trappings."

"Stake your diamond, then!"

"No, thank you. That's quite another thing. Never! never!"

"The devil!" said Athos. "I would propose to you to stake Planchet; but as that has already been done, the Englishman would not, perhaps, be willing."

"Decidedly, my dear Athos, I prefer not to risk anything."

"That's a pity," said Athos coolly. "The Englishman is overflowing with pistoles. Good Lord! try one throw. One throw is soon thrown!"

"And if I lose?"

"You will win."

"But if I lose?"

"Well, you will surrender the trappings."

"Well, one throw it is," said D'Artagnan.

Athos went in search of the Englishman, and found him in the stable, examining the trappings with a greedy eye. The opportunity was good. He proposed the conditions—the two trappings against one horse or a hundred pistoles, to choose. The Englishman quickly calculated. The two trappings were worth three hundred pistoles by themselves. He consented.

D'Artagnan threw the dice with a trembling hand, and turned up the number three. His paleness terrified Athos, who, however, contented himself with saying,—

"That's a sorry throw, comrade. You will have the horses fully equipped, sir."

The Englishman, quite triumphant, did not even give himself the trouble to shake the dice; he threw them on the table without looking at them, so sure was he of victory. D'Artagnan had turned away to conceal his vexation.

"There! there! there!" said Athos, in his tranquil voice; "that throw of the dice is extraordinary. I have seen it only four times in my life. Two aces, gentlemen!"

The Englishman looked, and was filled with astonishment. D'Artagnan looked, and was filled with pleasure.

"Yes," continued Athos, "four times only: once at M. Créquy's; another time at my own house in the country, in my chateau at ——, when I had a château; a third time at M. de Tréville's, where it surprised us all; and the fourth time at a tavern, where it fell to my lot, and where I lost a hundred louis and a supper on it."

"Then the gentleman takes his horse back again," said the Englishman.

"Certainly," said D'Artagnan.

"Then there is no revenge?"

"Our conditions said no revenge, you will please to recollect."

"That is true. The horse shall be restored to your lackey, sir."

"A moment!" said Athos. "With your permission, sir, I wish to speak a word with my friend."

"If you please."

Athos drew D'Artagnan on one side.

"Well, tempter, what more do you want of me?" said D'Artagnan. "You want me to throw again, do you not?"

"No; I wish you to reflect."

"On what?"

"You mean to take your horse, do you not?"

"Without doubt, I do."

"You are wrong, then. I would take the hundred pistoles. You know you have staked the trappings against the horse or a hundred pistoles, at your choice."

"Yes."

"I would take the hundred pistoles."

"And I take the horse."

"In which, I repeat, you are wrong. What is the use of one horse for us two? I could not get up behind. We should look like the two sons of Aymon, who lost their brothers. You would not want to humiliate me by riding by my side, prancing along upon that magnificent charger. For my part, I should not hesitate a moment, but take the hundred pistoles. We want money to carry us back to Paris."

"I am much attached to that horse, Athos."

"And there again you are wrong. A horse gets a sprain; a horse stumbles and breaks his knees; a horse eats out of a manger in which a glandered horse has eaten. There is a horse or rather a hundred pistoles lost. A master must feed his horse; while, on the contrary, the hundred pistoles feed their master."

"But how shall we get back to Paris?"

"Upon our lackeys' horses, by Jove! Everybody will see by our looks that we are people of condition."

"Very pretty figures we shall cut upon ponies, while Aramis and Porthos will be caracoling upon their war steeds!"

"Aramis and Porthos!" cried Athos, and he began to laugh.

"What is it?" asked D'Artagnan, who did not at all comprehend his friend's hilarity.

"It's all right. Come on!" said Athos.

"Your advice, then, is——"

"To take the hundred pistoles, D'Artagnan. With the

hundred pistoles we can live well to the end of the month. We have undergone a great deal of fatigue, remember, and a little rest will do us no harm."

"I rest? Oh no, Athos. The moment I am in Paris I shall set about looking for that poor woman."

"Well, you may be assured that your horse will not be half so serviceable to you for that purpose as good louis d'or. Take the hundred pistoles, my friend, take the hundred pistoles!"

D'Artagnan only required one reason to be satisfied. This last reason appeared convincing. Besides, he feared that by resisting longer he should appear selfish in the eyes of Athos. He acquiesced, then, and chose the hundred pistoles, which the Englishman immediately paid down.

Their only anxiety now was to depart. Peace signed with the landlord cost six pistoles in addition to Athos's old horse. D'Artagnan and Athos took the nags of Planchet and Grimaud, and the two lackeys started on foot, carrying the saddles on their heads.

Badly as our two friends were mounted, they soon got far in advance of their servants, and arrived at Crévecœur. From a distance they perceived Aramis, seated in a melancholy manner at his window, looking out, like Sister Anne, at the dust in the horizon.

"Hello, ha, Aramis! what the devil are you doing there?" cried the two friends.

"Ah, it is you, D'Artagnan, and you, Athos," said the young man. "I was reflecting upon the rapidity with which the blessings of this world leave us; and my English horse, which has just disappeared amid a cloud of dust, has furnished me with a living image of the fragility of the things of the earth. Life itself may be resolved into three words: *Erit, est, fuit.*"

"Which means——" said D'Artagnan, who began to suspect the truth.

"Which means that I have just been duped. Sixty louis for a horse which, by his gait, can trot at least five leagues an hour."

D'Artagnan and Athos burst into a loud laugh.

"My dear D'Artagnan," said Aramis, "don't be too angry with me, I beg of you; necessity has no law. Besides, I am the person punished, as that rascally horse-dealer has robbed me of fifty pistoles at least. Ah, you fellows are good managers! You ride on your lackeys' horses, and have your own gallant steeds led along carefully by hand, in short stages."

At the same instant a market cart, which some minutes before had appeared upon the Amiens road, pulled up at the inn, and Planchet and Grimaud got out of it with the saddles on their heads. The cart was returning to Paris empty, and the two lackeys had agreed as the condition of their transportation to keep the driver in liquor the whole way.

"What's this?" said Aramis, on seeing what was going on. "Nothing but the saddles?"

"Now, do you understand?" said Athos.

"My friends, that is exactly my case. I retained my trappings instinctively.—Hello, Bazin! Bring my new harness, and carry it with those of these gentlemen."

"And what have you done with your curates?" asked D'Artagnan.

"Why, I invited them to a dinner the next day," replied Aramis. "They have some capital wine here, by the way. I made them drunk; then the vicar forbade me to quit my uniform, and the Jesuit entreated me to get him made a musketeer."

"Without a thesis!" cried D'Artagnan, "without a thesis! For my part, I request the thesis may be suppressed."

"From that time," continued Aramis, "I have lived very agreeably. I have begun a poem in verses of one syllable. That is rather difficult, but merit in all things consists in the difficulty. The matter is high-flown. I will read the first canto to you. It has four hundred verses, and lasts a minute."

"'Pon my word, my dear Aramis," said D'Artagnan, who detested verses almost as much as he did Latin, "add to the merit of difficulty that of brevity, and you are sure your poem will at least have two merits."

"Then," continued Aramis, "it breathes irreproachable passion, as you will see. And so, my friends, we are returning, then, to Paris? Bravo! I am ready. We are going, then, to rejoin our good Porthos! So much the better. You don't believe that he will fail me, the great simpleton! He would not sell his horse—not for a kingdom! I think I can see him now, mounted upon his animal and seated in his saddle. He will look like the Great Mogul!"

They made a halt for an hour to refresh their horses. Aramis discharged his bill, placed Bazin in the cart with his comrades, and then set forward to join Porthos.

They found him up, not so pale as when D'Artagnan left him, and seated at a table, on which, though he was alone, was spread dinner enough for four persons. This dinner consisted of meats nicely dressed, choice wines, and superb fruit.

"Ah, by Jove!" said he, rising, "you came in the nick of time. Gentlemen, I was just at the soup, and you will dine with me."

"Oh, ho!" said D'Artagnan, "these bottles are not the fruits of Mousqueton's lasso! Besides, here is a larded veal and a fillet of beef."

"I am getting back my strength," said Porthos; "I am recruiting myself. Nothing weakens a man more than these cursed sprains. Did you ever suffer from a sprain, Athos?"

"Never! Only I remember that in our affair of the Rue Férou I received a sword-wound, which at the end of fifteen or eighteen days produced exactly the same effect."

"But this dinner was not intended for you alone, my dear Porthos?" said Aramis.

"No," said Porthos; "I expected some gentlemen of the neighbourhood, who have just sent me word they could not come. You will take their places, and I shall not lose by the exchange.—Hello, Mousqueton! Chairs, and order the number of bottles to be doubled."

"Do you know what we are eating here?" said Athos at the expiration of about ten minutes.

"Zounds!" replied D'Artagnan, "for my part, I am eating larded veal with cardoons and marrow."

"And I some lamb fillets," said Porthos.

"And I a breast of fowl," said Aramis.

"You are all mistaken, gentlemen," answered Athos, with a serious countenance; "you are all eating horse."

"Eating what?" said D'Artagnan.

"Horse!" said Aramis, with a look of disgust.

Porthos alone made no reply.

"Yes, real horse.—Are we not, Porthos, eating horse, and perhaps his trappings?"

"No, no, gentlemen; I have kept the trappings," said Porthos.

"'Pon my word!" said Aramis, "we are all alike. One would think we tipped one another the wink."

"What could I do?" said Porthos. "This horse made my visitors ashamed of theirs, and I didn't like to humiliate them."

"So your duchess is still taking the waters, is she?" asked D'Artagnan.

"Yes, still," replied Porthos. "And the governor of the province, one of the gentlemen I expected to-day, seemed to have such a desire for it that I gave it to him."

"Gave it?" cried D'Artagnan.

"Lord! yes, gave it to him. You can't call it anything but a gift," said Porthos, "for the animal was worth at least a hundred and fifty louis, and the stingy fellow would only give me eighty!"

"Without the saddle?" said Aramis.

"Yes, without the saddle."

"You will please to observe, gentlemen," said Athos, "that Porthos has made the best bargain of any of us."

And then there was a roar of laughter, much to poor Porthos's astonishment. But when he was informed of the cause of their hilarity, he took part in it, as usual, boisterously.

"At any rate, we are all in cash, aren't we?" said D'Artagnan.

"Well, for my part," said Athos, "I found Aramis's Spanish wine so good that I sent on a hamper of sixty bottles of it with the lackeys. That has weakened my purse not a little."

"And I," said Aramis—"you can imagine that I had given almost my last sou to the church of Montdidier and the Jesuits of Amiens; that I, moreover, had formed engagements which I had to keep. I ordered masses for myself, and for you, gentlemen, which will be said, gentlemen, and for which I have not the least doubt we will be very much the better."

"And I," said Porthos—"do you think my sprain cost me nothing, without reckoning Mousqueton's wound, on account of which the surgeon was obliged to come twice a day, and who charged me double on the pretext that this stupid Mousqueton had allowed himself to be wounded in a part which people generally show only to apothecaries. So I advised him to try never to get wounded there any more."

"Ay, ay!" said Athos, exchanging a smile with D'Artagnan and Aramis, "it is very clear you acted nobly with regard to the poor lad; that is like a good master."

"In short," said Porthos, "when all my expenses are paid, I shall have, at most, thirty crowns left."

"And I about ten pistoles," said Aramis.

"Well, then, D'Artagnan, it appears that you and I are the Crœsuses of the society. How much have you left of your hundred pistoles?"

"Of my hundred pistoles? Why, in the first place, I gave you fifty."

"You did?"

"Zounds! yes."

"Ah yes, so you did; I recollect now."

"Then I paid the landlord six."

"What a beast that landlord was! Why did you give him six pistoles?"

"Why, you told me to give them to him yourself!"

"Ah, so I did; but I am too good-natured. In short, how much have you left?"

"Twenty-five pistoles," said D'Artagnan.

"And I," said Athos, taking some small change from his pocket, "I——"

"You? Why, nothing!"

"'Pon my word! so little that it is not worth reckoning in with the general stock. Now, then, let us calculate how much we possess in all. Porthos?"

"Thirty crowns."

"Aramis?"

"Ten pistoles."

"And you, D'Artagnan?"

"Twenty-five."

"That makes in all——" said Athos.

"Four hundred and seventy-five livres!" said D'Artagnan, who reckoned like Archimedes.

"Then on our arrival in Paris we shall still have four hundred, besides the trappings," said Porthos.

"But our troop horses?" said Aramis.

"Well, we will take two of the four lackeys' horses for the masters, and we will draw lots for them. The four hundred livres will be sufficient to furnish half a mount for the third of us, and then we will give all our loose change to D'Artagnan of the steady hand, who will go and play in the first gaming-house we come to. There, that's arranged."

"Let us finish the dinner, then," said Porthos; "it is getting cold."

The four friends, having set their minds at ease with regard to the future, did honour to the repast, the remains of which were abandoned to MM. Mousqueton, Bazin, Planchet, and Grimaud.

On arriving in Paris, D'Artagnan found a letter from M. de Tréville, informing him that, at his request, the king had just promised him his immediate admission into the musketeers.

As this was the height of D'Artagnan's worldly ambition —apart, of course, from his desire of finding Madame Bonacieux—he ran, full of joy, to seek his comrades, whom he had left only half an hour before. He found them very sad and deeply preoccupied. They were assembled in council at the residence of Athos, which always indicated an event of some seriousness.

M. de Tréville had just informed them that since it was his Majesty's fixed intention to open the campaign on the first of May, they must immediately get ready all their equipments.

The four philosophers looked at one another in a state of bewilderment. M. de Tréville never joked in matters relating to discipline.

"And what do you reckon your equipments will cost?" said D'Artagnan.

"Oh, we can scarcely venture to say. We have just made our calculations with Spartan niggardliness, and we each require fifteen hundred livres."

"Four times fifteen make sixty—ah! six thousand livres," said Athos.

"For my part, I think," said D'Artagnan, "with a thousand livres each—it is true I do not speak as a Spartan, but as a *procureur*——"

The word *procureur* roused Porthos.

"Stop!" said he; "I have an idea."

"Well, that's something. For my part, I have not the shadow of one," said Athos coolly. "But as to D'Artagnan, the hope of soon being one of us, gentlemen, has made him crazy. A thousand livres! I declare I want two thousand myself."

"Four times two make eight, then," said Aramis. "It is eight thousand that we want to complete our outfit, of which, it is true, we have already the saddles."

"One thing more!" said Athos, waiting till D'Artagnan, who was going to thank M. de Tréville, had shut the door, "one thing more—that beautiful diamond which glitters on our friend's finger. What the devil! D'Artagnan is too good a comrade to leave his brothers in embarrassment while he wears a king's ransom on his middle finger."

CHAPTER XXIX.

THE HUNT FOR EQUIPMENTS.

THE most preoccupied of the four friends was certainly D'Artagnan, although D'Artagnan, as a guardsman, would be much more easily equipped than the musketeers, who were all grandees. But our Gascon cadet was, as may have been observed, of a provident and almost avaricious character, and at the same time—explain the paradox—so vainglorious as almost to rival Porthos.

To this preoccupation of his vanity D'Artagnan at this moment joined an uneasiness much less selfish. Notwithstanding all his inquiries respecting Madame Bonacieux, he could obtain no news concerning her. M. de Tréville had spoken of her to the queen; the queen did not know where the mercer's young wife was, but had promised to have a search made for her. But this promise was very vague, and did not at all reassure D'Artagnan.

Athos did not leave his chamber; he made up his mind not to risk a single step to provide for his equipment.

"We have still a fortnight before us," said he to his friends. "Well, if at the end of a fortnight I have found nothing, or, rather, if nothing has come to find me, as I am too good a Catholic to kill myself with a pistol bullet, I will seek a good cause of quarrel with four of his Eminence's guards, or with eight Englishmen. I will fight until one of them has killed me, which, considering the number, cannot fail to happen. It will then be said of me that I died for the king, so that I shall have performed my duty without having needed an outfit."

Porthos continued to walk about, with his hands behind him, shaking his head, and repeating,—

"I shall follow up my idea."

Aramis, anxious, and negligently dressed, said nothing.

It may be seen by these disastrous details that desolation reigned in the community.

The lackeys, on their part, like the coursers of Hippolytus, shared their masters' sadness. Mousqueton collected a store of crusts; Bazin, who had always been inclined to devotion, never quitted the churches; Planchet watched the flies flying; and Grimaud, whom the general distress could not induce to break the silence imposed by his master, heaved sighs enough to melt a stone.

The three friends—for, as we have said, Athos had sworn

not to stir a foot to equip himself—the three friends went out, then, early in the morning and returned late at night. They wandered about the streets, looking at every cobblestone to see whether some passer-by had not dropped a purse. One might have thought that they were following a trail, so attentive were they wherever they went. When they met they looked desolately at each other, as much as to say, " Have you found anything ? "

However, as Porthos had first found his idea, and had thought of it earnestly afterwards, he was the first to act. This worthy Porthos was a man of execution. D'Artagnan perceived him one day walking toward the church of St. Leu, and followed him instinctively. He entered the holy place, after having twirled his moustache and pulled his royal, which always announced, on his part, the most triumphant resolutions. As D'Artagnan took some precautions to conceal himself, Porthos believed he had not been seen. D'Artagnan entered behind him. Porthos went and leaned against one side of a pillar. D'Artagnan, still unperceived, leaned against the other side of it.

There happened to be a sermon, and this made the church very full of people. Porthos took advantage of this circumstance to ogle the women. Thanks to Mousqueton's care, the exterior was far from announcing his inward distress. His hat was, to be sure, a little worn on the nap, his feather was a little faded, his gold lace was a little tarnished, his laces were decidedly frayed ; but in the obscurity of the church all these trifles were not seen, and Porthos was still the handsome Porthos.

D'Artagnan observed, on the bench nearest to the pillar against which he and Porthos were leaning, a sort of ripe beauty, rather yellow and rather dry, but erect and haughty under her black hood. Porthos's eyes were furtively cast upon this lady, and then roved about at large over the nave.

On her side, the lady, who from time to time blushed, darted with the rapidity of lightning a glance toward the inconstant Porthos, and then immediately Porthos's eyes went wandering over the church anxiously. It was plain that this was a mode of proceeding that deeply piqued the lady in the black hood, for she bit her lips till they bled, scratched the end of her nose, and sat very uneasily in her seat.

Porthos, seeing this, again twirled his moustache, pulled his royal a second time, and began to make signals to a beautiful lady who was near the choir, and who was not only a beautiful lady, but also, no doubt, a great lady, for she had behind her a negro boy, who had brought the cushion on which she knelt, and a female servant, who held the emblazoned bag in which was placed the book from which she followed the service.

The lady in the black hood followed through all their wanderings the looks of Porthos, and perceived that they rested on the lady with the velvet cushion, the little negro, and the maidservant.

Meantime he, Porthos, was playing his game prudently. He employed winks, fingers placed on lips, little assassinating smiles, which really assassinated the disdained beauty.

Therefore, as a *mea culpa*, and in striking her breast, she uttered an " Ahem ! " so vigorously that everybody, even the lady with the red cushion, turned round toward her. Porthos paid no attention. Nevertheless, he understood it all, but pretended to be deaf.

The lady of the red cushion produced a great effect—for she was very handsome—on the lady in the black hood, who saw in her a rival to be really dreaded ; a great effect on Porthos, who thought her much prettier than the lady in the black hood ; a great effect upon D'Artagnan, who recognized in her the lady of Meung, of Calais, and of Dover, whom his persecutor, the man with the scar, had saluted by the name of milady.

D'Artagnan, without losing sight of the lady of the red cushion, continued to watch Porthos's proceedings, which amused him greatly. He guessed that the lady of the black hood was the solicitor's wife of the Rue aux Ours, and this was the more likely because the church of St. Leu was not far from that street.

He guessed, then, by induction, that Porthos was trying to take his revenge for his defeat at Chantilly, when the *procureuse* had proved so refractory with respect to her purse.

But amid all this, D'Artagnan remarked also that not one countenance responded to Porthos's gallantries. There was nothing but chimeras and illusions. But for a real love, for a true jealousy, is there any other reality than illusions and chimeras ?

The sermon over, the solicitor's wife advanced toward the font of holy water. Porthos went before her, and instead of a finger, dipped his whole hand in. The *procureuse* smiled, thinking that it was for her that Porthos was exerting himself. But she was cruelly and promptly undeceived.

When she was only about three steps from him, he turned his head round, fixing his eyes steadily on the lady of the red cushion, who had risen, and was approaching, followed by her black boy and her maid.

When the lady of the red cushion came close to Porthos, Porthos drew his dripping hand from the font. The fair worshipper touched Porthos's great hand with her delicate fingers, smiled as she made the sign of the cross, and left the church.

This was too much for the solicitor's wife. She entertained no doubt that this lady and Porthos were engaged in an intrigue. If she had been a great lady she would have fainted; but as she was only a *procureuse*, she contented herself with saying to the musketeer, with concentrated fury,—

"Eh, Monsieur Porthos, you don't offer me any holy water?"

Porthos, at the sound of her voice, started like a man awakened from a sleep of a hundred years.

"Ma—madame!" cried he, "is that you? How is your husband, our dear Monsieur Coquenard? Is he still as stingy as ever? Where can my eyes have been not to have even perceived you during the two hours the sermon has lasted?"

"I was within two paces of you, sir," replied the solicitor's wife; "but you did not perceive me, because you had eyes only for the pretty lady to whom you just now gave the holy water."

Porthos pretended to be confused.

"Ah," said he, "you have noticed——"

"I must have been blind if I had not."

"Yes," said Porthos carelessly, "that is a duchess of my acquaintance, whom I have great trouble to meet on account of her husband's jealousy, and who sent me word that she would come to-day, solely for the purpose of seeing me in this poor church, in this vile quarter."

"Monsieur Porthos," said the *procureuse*, "will you have the kindness to offer me your arm for five minutes? I have something to say to you."

"Certainly, madame," said Porthos, winking to himself, as a gambler does who laughs at the dupe he is about to pluck.

At that moment D'Artagnan was passing in pursuit of milady. He cast a glance at Porthos, and beheld his triumphant look.

"Ah, ha!" said he to himself, reasoning in accordance with the strangely easy morality of that gallant period, "here is one of us, at least, on the road to be equipped in time."

Porthos, yielding to the pressure of the *procureuse's* arm as a boat yields to the rudder, arrived at the cloister St. Magloire, a somewhat unfrequented passage, shut in by a turnstile at each end. In the daytime nobody was seen there but beggars devouring their crusts, and children.

"Ah, Monsieur Porthos," cried the *procureuse*, when she was assured that no one a stranger to the population of the locality could either see or hear her—" ah, Monsieur Porthos, you are a great conqueror, it appears!"

"Who? I, madame?" said Porthos, drawing himself up proudly. "How so?"

"And the signals just now, and the holy water? But that lady with her negro boy and her maid must be a princess, at least."

"Zounds! madame, you are mistaken. No, no, she is simply a duchess."

"And that running footman who was waiting at the door, and that carriage with a coachman in full livery, who sat waiting on his seat?"

Porthos had seen neither the footman nor the carriage, but Madame Coquenard, with a jealous woman's eye, had seen everything.

Porthos regretted that he had not at once made the lady of the red cushion a princess.

"Ah, you are quite the pet of the ladies, Monsieur Porthos!" resumed the *procureuse*, with a sigh.

"Why, you may well imagine that. With the person with which nature has endowed me, I am not wanting for ladies' favours."

"Good Lord! how quickly men forget!" cried the *procureuse*, raising her eyes to heaven.

"Less quickly than the women, in my opinion," replied Porthos. "As a proof, I, madame, I may say I was your victim, when wounded, dying, I was abandoned by the surgeons. I, the offspring of a noble family, placed reliance upon your friendship; but I nearly died of my wounds at first, and of hunger afterwards, in a beggarly inn at Chantilly, and not once did you even deign to reply to the burning letters I addressed to you."

"But, Monsieur Porthos——" murmured the solicitor's wife, who began to feel that, judged by the conduct of the greatest ladies of the time, she was wrong.

"I, who had sacrificed for you the Baroness of——"

"Well, I know you did."

"The Countess of——"

"Monsieur Porthos, do not overwhelm me quite!"

"The Duchess of——"

"Monsieur Porthos, be generous!"

"You are right, madame, and I will not finish."

"But my husband would not hear of lending——"

"Madame Coquenard," said Porthos, "remember the first letter you wrote me, and which I preserve engraven in my memory."

The *procureuse* uttered a groan.

"Besides," said she, "the sum you required me to borrow was rather large."

"Madame Coquenard, I gave you the preference. I had but to write to the Duchess of—— I won't repeat her name, for I am incapable of compromising a woman. But this I know, that I had but to write to her, and she would have sent me fifteen hundred."

The *procureuse* let fall a tear.

"Monsieur Porthos," said she, "I can assure you you have severely punished me; and if in the time to come you should find yourself in a similar situation, you have only to apply to me."

"Fie, madame, fie!" said Porthos, as if disgusted; "let us not talk about money, if you please. It is humiliating."

"Then you no longer love me!" said the solicitor's wife, slowly and sadly.

Porthos maintained a majestic silence.

"And is this your reply? Alas! I understand."

"Think of the offence you have committed toward me, madame! It remains here!" said Porthos, placing his hand on his heart, and pressing it strongly.

"I will repair it—indeed I will, my dear Porthos."

"Besides, what did I ask of you?" resumed Porthos, with a good-natured shrug of the shoulders. "A loan—nothing more! After all, I am not an unreasonable man. I know you are not rich, Madame Coquenard, and that your husband is obliged to bleed his poor clients to squeeze a few paltry crowns from them. Oh, if you were a duchess, a marchioness, or a countess, it would be quite a different thing; it would be unpardonable."

The solicitor's wife was piqued.

"Please know, Monsieur Porthos," said she, "that my strong-box, though it may be only the strong-box of a solicitor's wife, is better filled than those of all your ruined minxes."

"That, then, doubles the offence," said Porthos, disengaging his arm from the *procureuse's* : "for if you are rich, Madame Coquenard, then there is no excuse for your refusal."

"When I said rich," replied the solicitor's wife, who saw that she had gone too far, "you must not take the word literally. I am not exactly rich ; I am only pretty well off."

"Come, madame," said Porthos ; "let us say no more upon the subject, I beg of you. You misunderstand me : all sympathy is extinct between us."

"Ungrateful man that you are !"

"Ah ! I advise you to complain !" said Porthos.

"Begone, then, to your beautiful duchess. I will detain you no longer."

"And she is not so shabby, in my opinion."

"Now, Monsieur Porthos, once more, and this is the last ! Do you love me still ?"

"Alas, madame," said Porthos, in the most melancholy tone he could assume, "when we are about to enter upon a campaign—a campaign in which my presentiments tell me I shall be killed——"

"Oh, don't talk of such things !" cried the solicitor's wife, bursting into tears.

"Something tells me so," continued Porthos, becoming more and more melancholy.

"Rather say that you have a new love affair."

"No, not so. I speak frankly to you. No new object affects me ; and I even feel here, at the bottom of my heart, something which speaks for you. But in a fortnight's time, as you know, or perhaps you do not know, this fatal campaign is to open. I shall be frightfully busy providing for my equipment. Then I am obliged to make a journey to my family, in the very depths of Brittany, to obtain the sum necessary for my departure."

Porthos observed a last struggle between love and avarice.

"And as," continued he, "the duchess you saw at the church has estates near to those of my family, we mean to make the journey together. Journeys, you know, appear much shorter when you travel two in company."

"Have you no friends in Paris, then, Monsieur Porthos ?" said the solicitor's wife.

"I thought I had," said Porthos, resuming his melancholy air, "but I have clearly seen that I was mistaken."

"You have some, Monsieur Porthos, you have some!" cried the solicitor's wife, in a transport that surprised even herself. "Come to our house to-morrow. You are my aunt's son, consequently my cousin. You come from Noyon, in Picardy; you have several lawsuits at Paris and no attorney. Can you recollect all that?"

"Perfectly, madame."

"Come at dinner-time."

"Very well."

"And be on your guard before my husband, who is rather shrewd, notwithstanding his seventy-six years."

"Seventy-six years! Plague on it! that's a fine age!" replied Porthos.

"An advanced age, you mean, Monsieur Porthos. Yes, the poor man may leave me a widow at any moment," continued she, throwing a significant glance at Porthos. "Fortunately, by our marriage contract, the survivor comes into the possession of everything."

"Everything?"

"Yes, everything."

"You are a woman of precaution, I see, my dear Madame Coquenard," said Porthos, squeezing the *procureuse's* hand tenderly.

"We are, then, reconciled, dear Monsieur Porthos?" said she, simpering.

"For life," said Porthos, in the same manner.

"Till we meet again, then, dear traitor!"

"Till we meet again, my forgetful charmer!"

"To-morrow, my angel!"

"To-morrow, flame of my life!"

CHAPTER XXX.

MILADY.

D'ARTAGNAN had followed milady, without being perceived by her. He saw her get into her carriage, and heard her order the coachman to drive to St. Germain.

It was useless to endeavour to keep pace on foot with a carriage drawn by two powerful horses, so D'Artagnan returned to the Rue Férou.

In the Rue de Seine he met Planchet, who had stopped before a bake-shop, and was contemplating with ecstasy a cake of the most appetizing appearance.

He ordered him to go and saddle two horses in M. de Tréville's stables, one for himself (D'Artagnan), and one for Planchet, and to come and meet him at Athos's—M. de Tréville having once for all given D'Artagnan the freedom of his stables.

Planchet proceeded toward the Rue du Colombier, and D'Artagnan toward the Rue Férou. Athos was at home, emptying in solitary sadness a bottle of the famous Spanish wine he had brought back with him from his journey into Picardy. He made a sign to Grimaud to bring a glass for D'Artagnan, and Grimaud obeyed, silent as usual.

D'Artagnan related to Athos all that had passed at the church between Porthos and the *procureuse*, and how their comrade was probably by that time in a fair way to be equipped.

"As for me," said Athos, in comment on this recital, "I am quite at my ease. Women are not going to defray the expense of my equipment."

"And yet, handsome, well-bred, great noble as you are, my dear Athos, neither princesses nor queens would be safe from your amorous darts."

"How young this D'Artagnan is!" said Athos, shrugging his shoulders, and making a sign to Grimaud to bring another bottle.

At that moment Planchet put his head modestly in at the half-open door, and told his master that the horses were ready.

"What horses?" asked Athos.

"Two horses that M. de Tréville lends me for a ride, and with which I am now going to make an excursion to St. Germain."

"Well, and what are you going to do at St. Germain?" asked Athos.

Then D'Artagnan described the meeting which he had had at the church, and how he had once more found the lady who, like the noble with the black cloak and a scar near his temple, was ever on his mind.

"That is to say, you are in love with this lady as you were with Madame Bonacieux," said Athos, shrugging his shoulders contemptuously, as if he pitied human weakness.

"I? Not at all!" said D'Artagnan. "I am only curious to unravel the mystery in which she is involved. I do not know why, but I have a strong feeling that this woman, though she is perfectly unknown to me, and though I am unknown to her, has an influence over my life."

"Well, you are right," said Athos. "I do not know a woman worth the trouble of being sought for when once she is lost. Madame Bonacieux is lost—so much the worse for her ; let her find herself."

"No, Athos, no ; you are mistaken," said D'Artagnan. "I love my poor Constance more than ever, and if I knew the place where she is, were it at the end of the world, I would go and free her from the hands of her enemies. But I cannot find out where she is ; all my researches have proved in vain. What can you expect ? I must divert my attention by something."

"Amuse yourself, then, with milady, my dear D'Artagnan, I wish you may, with all my heart, if that can amuse you."

"Hear me, Athos," said D'Artagnan. "Instead of shutting yourself up here as if you were under arrest, get on horseback, and come and take a ride with me to St. Germain."

"My dear fellow," said Athos, "I ride a horse when I have one, otherwise I go on foot."

"Well, for my part," said D'Artagnan, smiling at Athos's misanthropy, which from any other person would certainly have offended him, "I am not so proud as you are, my dear Athos. I ride what I can get. So good-bye."

"Good-bye," said the musketeer, making a sign to Grimaud to uncork the bottle he had just brought.

D'Artagnan and Planchet got into the saddle, and took the road to St. Germain.

As he rode along, what Athos had said respecting Madame Bonacieux recurred to the young man's mind. Although D'Artagnan was not of a very sentimental turn, the mercer's pretty wife had made a real impression on his heart. As he said, he was ready to go to the end of the world to seek her. But as the world is round, it has many ends, so that he did not know in which direction to turn.

In the meantime he was going to try to find out who milady was. Milady had spoken to the man in the black cloak, therefore she knew him. Now, in D'Artagnan's opinion it was certainly the man in the black cloak who had carried off Madame Bonacieux the second time, as he had carried her off the first. D'Artagnan, then, only told half a lie, which is lying but little, when he said that by going in search of milady he was at the same time going in search of Constance.

Thinking of all this, and from time to time giving his horse a touch of the spur, D'Artagnan completed his journey, and

arrived at St. Germain. He had just passed by the pavilion
in which ten years later Louis XIV. was to be born. He was
riding along a very quiet street, gazing right and left to see
whether he could find any trace of his beautiful Englishwoman, when from the ground floor of a pretty house, which,
according to the fashion of the time, had no window on the
street, he saw a form appear that looked familiar. This
person in question was walking along a kind of terrace,
ornamented with flowers. Planchet recognized who it was
first.

"Eh, sir!" said he, addressing D'Artagnan, "don't you
remember that face gaping yonder?"

"No," said D'Artagnan; "and yet I am certain I have
seen it before."

"By Jove, I believe you have!" said Planchet. "Why, it
is poor Lubin, the lackey of the Comte de Wardes, whom
you so well accommodated a month ago at Calais, on the
road to the governor's country house."

"So it is," said D'Artagnan; "I know him now. Do
you think he would recollect you?"

"'Pon my word, sir, he was so greatly disturbed that I
don't think he can have retained a very clear recollection
of me."

"Well, go and get into conversation with him, and find
out, if you can, whether his master is dead or not."

Planchet dismounted and went straight up to Lubin, who
did not recognize him, and the two lackeys began to chat
with the best understanding possible, while D'Artagnan
turned the two horses into a lane, and went round the
house so as to be present at the conference, coming back
to take his place behind a hedge of hazels.

After a moment's watching from behind the hedge he heard
the noise of a carriage, and saw milady's coach stop in front
of him. He could not be mistaken; milady was in it.
D'Artagnan bent over on his horse's neck in order to see
everything without being seen.

Milady put her charming fair head out at the window,
and gave some orders to her maid.

The latter, a pretty girl of about twenty years of age,
active and lively, the typical soubrette for a great lady,
jumped down from the step on which, according to the
custom of the time, she was seated, and went toward the
terrace where D'Artagnan had perceived Lubin.

D'Artagnan followed the maid with his eyes, and saw her
going toward the terrace. But it happened that some one

in the house had called Lubin, so that Planchet remained alone, looking in all directions for D'Artagnan.

The maid approached Planchet, whom she took for Lubin, and holding out a little note to him,—

"For your master," said she.

"For my master?" replied Planchet in astonishment.

"Yes, and very urgent. Take it quick."

Thereupon she ran toward the carriage, which had turned round in the direction it had come; she jumped on the step, and the carriage drove off.

Planchet turned the note over and over; then, accustomed to passive obedience, he jumped down from the terrace, ran through the lane, and at the end of twenty paces met D'Artagnan, who, having seen all, was coming to him.

"For you, sir," said Planchet, presenting the note to the young man.

"For me!" said D'Artagnan. "Are you sure of that?"

"Zounds! sir, I can't be more sure. The maid said for your master. I have no other master but you; so—— A pretty little lass, 'pon my word, that maid!"

D'Artagnan opened the letter and read these words:—

"A person who takes more interest in you than she is willing to confess wishes to know on what day you will be in condition to walk in the forest. To-morrow, at the Hôtel Field of the Cloth of Gold, a lackey in black and red will wait for your reply."

"Oh, ho!" said D'Artagnan, "this is rather lively. It appears that milady and I are anxious about the health of the same person.—Well, Planchet, how is our good M. de Wardes? He is not dead, then?"

"Oh no, monsieur; he is as well as a man can be with four sword-wounds in his body—for you, without question, inflicted four upon the dear gentleman, and he is still very weak, having lost almost all his blood. As I told you, Lubin did not know me, and he related to me our adventure from one end to the other."

"Well done, Planchet! you are the king of lackeys. Now jump up on your horse, and let us overtake the carriage."

This they soon did. At the end of five minutes they perceived the carriage drawn up by the roadside. A cavalier richly dressed was close to the coach door.

The conversation between milady and the cavalier was so animated that D'Artagnan stopped on the other side of the carriage without any one but the pretty maid being aware of his presence.

The conversation took place in English—a language which D'Artagnan could not understand ; but by the accent the young man plainly saw that the beautiful Englishwoman was in a great rage. She terminated it by a gesture which left no doubt as to the nature of this conversation : this was a blow with her fan, applied with such force that the little feminine weapon flew into a thousand pieces.

The cavalier broke into a loud laugh, which appeared to exasperate milady.

D'Artagnan thought this was the moment to interfere. He approached the other door, and taking off his hat respectfully,—

"Madame," said he, " will you permit me to offer you my services ? This cavalier seems to have made you very angry. Speak one word, madame, and I will take it on myself to punish him for his lack of courtesy."

At the first word milady turned round, looking at the young man in astonishment ; and when he had finished,—

"Sir," said she, in very good French, "I should with great confidence place myself under your protection, if the person who is picking a quarrel with me were not my brother."

"Ah, excuse me, then," said D'Artagnan ; "you must be aware that I was ignorant of that, madame."

"What is that presumptuous fellow troubling himself about ? " cried the cavalier whom milady had designated as her brother, stooping down to the height of the coach window, " and why does he not go on ? "

"Presumptuous fellow yourself ! " said D'Artagnan, also bending down on his horse's neck and answering through the carriage window. " I do not go on because it pleases me to stop here."

The cavalier addressed some words in English to his sister.

"I speak to you in French," said D'Artagnan ; " be kind enough, then, to reply to me in the same language. You are madame's brother : be it so ; but, fortunately, you are not mine."

You might think that milady, timid as women are in general, would have interposed at this beginning of mutual provocations in order to prevent the quarrel from going too far ; but, on the contrary, she threw herself back in her carriage, and called out coolly to the coachman, " **Drive home !** "

The pretty maid cast an anxious glance at D'Artagnan, whose good looks seemed to have produced an impression on her.

The carriage went on, and left the two men face to face, no material obstacle separating them any longer.

The cavalier made a movement as if to follow the carriage; but D'Artagnan, whose anger, already excited, was much increased by recognizing in him the Englishman of Amiens who had won his horse and had come very near winning his diamond from Athos, caught at his bridle and stopped him.

"Well, sir," said he, "you appear to be more presumptuous than I am, for you forget there is a little quarrel to arrange between us."

"Ah, ha!" said the Englishman; "is it you, my master? Must you, then, always be playing some game or other?"

"Yes; and that reminds me that I have a revenge to take. We will see, my dear sir, if you can handle a sword as skilfully as you can a dice-box."

"You see well enough that I have no sword," said the Englishman. "Do you wish to play the braggart with an unarmed man?"

"I hope you have a sword at home," replied D'Artagnan. "But, at all events, I have two, and if you like I will throw with you for one of them."

"Quite unnecessary," said the Englishman; "I am well furnished with such sorts of playthings."

"Very well, my worthy gentleman," replied D'Artagnan; "pick out the longest, and come and show it to me this evening."

"Where?"

"Behind the Luxembourg. That's a charming place for such strolls as the one I propose to you."

"Very well; I will be there."

"Your hour?"

"Six o'clock."

"By the way, you probably have one or two friends?"

"Yes, I have three who would be greatly honoured by joining in the game with me."

"Three? That's fortunate! That fits exactly," cried D'Artagnan. "It is just my number!"

"Now, then, who are you?" asked the Englishman.

"I am M. d'Artagnan, a Gascon gentleman, serving in the guards, in the company of M. des Essarts. And you?"

"I am Lord Winter, Baron of Sheffield."

"Well, then, I am your servant, baron," said D'Artagnan, "though your names are rather difficult to remember."

And touching his horse with his spur, he galloped back to Paris.

As he was accustomed to do on such occasions, D'Artagnan went straight to the residence of Athos.

He found Athos reclining upon a large sofa, waiting, as he said, for his equipment to come and find him.

He related to Athos all that had just passed, except the letter to M. de Wardes.

Athos was delighted to hear that he was going to fight an Englishman. We have said that was his dream.

They immediately sent their lackeys for Porthos and Aramis, and made them acquainted with the affair in hand.

Porthos drew his sword from the scabbard, and began to make passes at the wall, springing back from time to time, and making bends like a dancer.

Aramis, who was constantly at work on his poem, shut himself up in Athos's closet, and begged not to be disturbed until the moment of drawing swords.

Athos, by signs, desired Grimaud to bring another bottle of wine.

And D'Artagnan employed himself in arranging a little plan, the carrying out of which we shall see later on, and which promised him an agreeable adventure, as might be seen by the smiles which from time to time passed over his countenance, lighting up his thoughtful expression.

CHAPTER XXXI.

ENGLISH AND FRENCH.

THE hour having come, they repaired, with their four lackeys, to a yard behind the Luxembourg where goats were kept. Athos threw a piece of money to the goat-keeper to withdraw. The lackeys were charged to act as sentinels.

A silent party soon drew near to the same enclosure, came into it, and joined the musketeers. Then, according to English custom, the presentations took place.

The Englishmen were all men of the highest rank; consequently their adversaries' extraordinary names were, for them, not only a matter of surprise, but of uneasiness.

"But after all," said Lord Winter, when the three friends

had been named, " we do not know who you are, and we are not going to fight against such names. Why, they are shepherds' names."

" Therefore, as you may suppose, milord, they are only assumed names," said Athos.

" That only gives us the greater desire to know your real ones," replied the Englishman.

" You gambled very willingly with us without knowing our names," said Athos, " as is plain by your having won our two horses."

" That is true. But we then only risked our pistoles ; this time we risk our lives. Men play with anybody, but fight only with equals."

" You are right," said Athos, and he took aside the one of the four Englishmen with whom he was to fight, and whispered his name.

Porthos and Aramis did the same.

" Does that satisfy you ? " said Athos to his adversary. " Do you think me sufficiently noble to do me the honour of crossing swords with me ? "

" Yes, sir," said the Englishman, bowing.

" Well, now, shall I tell you another thing ? " asked Athos coolly.

" What is that ? " demanded the Englishman.

" That you would have done as well not to require me to make myself known."

" Why so ? "

" Because I am believed to be dead, and I have reasons for wishing nobody should know that I am alive ; so that I shall be obliged to kill you to prevent my secret getting out."

The Englishman looked at Athos, believing that he was joking, but Athos was not joking the least in the world.

" Gentlemen," said Athos, addressing at the same time his companions and their adversaries, " are we ready ? "

" Yes ! " answered the Englishmen and the Frenchmen, as with one voice.

" On guard, then ! " cried Athos.

And immediately eight swords glittered in the rays of the setting sun, and the combat began with an animosity very natural to men who were twofold enemies.

Athos fought with as much calmness and method as if he had been fencing in a school.

Porthos, cured, no doubt, of his too great confidence by his adventure at Chantilly, parried with skill and prudence.

Aramis, who had the third canto of his poem to finish, made quick work, like a man pressed for time.

Athos killed his adversary first. He gave him but one blow, but, as he had foretold him, that blow was mortal; the sword passed through his heart.

Porthos next stretched his opponent on the grass, with a wound through his thigh. Then, as the Englishman, without making any further resistance, surrendered his sword, Porthos took him up in his arms and carried him to his carriage.

Aramis pushed his so vigorously that, after retreating fifty paces, he at last ran away as fast as he could go, and disappeared amid the hooting of the lackeys.

As to D'Artagnan, he fought purely and simply on the defensive. Then when he saw his adversary pretty well fatigued, with a vigorous side-thrust he knocked his sword from his grasp. The baron, finding himself disarmed, retreated two or three paces; but at this moment his foot slipped, and he fell backward.

D'Artagnan was on him at a bound, and placing his sword on his throat,—

"I could kill you, sir," said he to the Englishman; "you are quite at my mercy, but I spare your life for your sister's sake."

D'Artagnan was overjoyed. He had just realized the plan which he had conceived, the development of which had occasioned the smiles we mentioned.

The Englishman, delighted at having to do with such a generous gentleman, pressed D'Artagnan in his arms, and paid a thousand compliments to the three musketeers; and as Porthos's adversary was already installed in the carriage, and as Aramis's had run away, they had nothing to think about but the dead man.

As Porthos and Aramis were undressing him, in the hope of finding his wound not mortal, a large purse dropped from his belt. D'Artagnan picked it up and held it out to Lord Winter.

"What the devil shall I do with that?" asked the Englishman.

"You can restore it to his family," said D'Artagnan.

"His family will care vastly about such a trifle as that! They will inherit fifteen thousand louis a year from him. Keep the purse for your lackeys."

D'Artagnan put the purse into his pocket.

"And now, my young friend—for you will permit me, I

hope, to call you by that name," said Lord Winter—" on this very evening, if agreeable to you, I will present you to my sister, Lady Clarick. For I am desirous that she in her turn should take you into her good graces ; and as she is in favour at court, perhaps, in the future, a word spoken by her might prove useful to you."

D'Artagnan reddened with pleasure and bowed his assent. Meanwhile Athos had come up to D'Artagnan.

" What are you going to do with that purse ? " whispered he.

" Why, I meant to pass it over to you, my dear Athos."

" To me ! Why to me ? "

" Why, you killed him, didn't you ? They are the spoils of victory."

" I inherit from an enemy ! " said Athos. " What do you take me for ? "

" It is the custom in war," said D'Artagnan. " Why should it not be the custom in a duel ? "

" Even on the field of battle I have never done that."

Porthos shrugged his shoulders. Aramis, by a movement of his lips, applauded Athos's opinion.

" Then," said D'Artagnan, " let us give the money to the lackeys, as Lord Winter desired us to do."

" Yes," said Athos, " let us give the money to the lackeys, but not to our lackeys—to the Englishmen's lackeys."

Athos took the purse and threw it into the coachman's hand.

" For you and your comrades," said he.

This lordly way of doing things in a man who was entirely destitute struck even Porthos, and this story of French generosity, repeated by Lord Winter and his friend, was highly applauded by every one except MM. Grimaud, Bazin, Mousqueton, and Planchet.

Lord Winter, on quitting D'Artagnan, gave him his sister's address. She lived at No. 6 Place Royale, then the fashionable quarter. Moreover, he promised to call and get him in order to present him. D'Artagnan appointed eight o'clock at Athos's residence.

This introduction to milady fully occupied our Gascon's thoughts. He remembered in what a strange manner this woman had hitherto been mixed up in his destiny. According to his conviction, she was one of the cardinal's creatures, and yet he felt himself irresistibly drawn toward her by one of those sentiments for which we cannot account. His only fear was that milady would recognize in him the man of

Meung and of Dover. Then she knew that he was one of
M. de Tréville's friends, and consequently that he belonged
body and soul to the king, which would instantly make him
lose a part of his advantage, because as soon as he became
known to milady as he knew her, he played only an equal
game with her. Our presumptuous hero gave but little
heed to the intrigue already begun between her and M. de
Wardes, although the marquis was young, handsome, rich,
and high in the cardinal's favour. Not for nothing are we
twenty years old, particularly if we are born at Tarbes.

D'Artagnan went straight home and made a brilliant toilet.
Then he returned to Athos's, and, as his custom was, told
him everything. Athos listened attentively to his projects,
then shook his head, and with a shade of bitterness recommended prudence to him.

"What!" said he, "you have just lost one woman, who,
you say, was good, charming, perfect, and here you are
already running after another!"

D'Artagnan felt the truth of this reproach.

"I loved Madame Bonacieux with my heart, while I only
love milady with my head," said he. "By getting introduced to her, my principal object is to ascertain what part
she plays at court."

"The part she plays at court, by Jove, is not difficult to
divine after all you have told me. She is some emissary of
the cardinal's, a woman who will draw you into a snare in
which you will leave your head for good and all."

"The devil! my dear Athos, you view things on the
dark side, it seems to me."

"D'Artagnan, I mistrust women (can it be otherwise?
I bought my experience dearly), particularly fair women.
Milady is fair, you say?"

"She has the most beautiful light hair imaginable!"

"Ah, my poor D'Artagnan!" exclaimed Athos.

"Listen. I want to be enlightened on a certain subject.
Then, when I shall have learned what I desire to know, I
will withdraw."

"Be enlightened!" said Athos phlegmatically.

Lord Winter arrived at the appointed time; but Athos,
being warned of his coming, went into the other chamber.
The Englishman accordingly found D'Artagnan alone, and
as it was nearly eight o'clock, he took the young man with
him.

An elegant coach below, drawn by two excellent horses,
was waiting. They were soon at the Place Royale.

Milady Clarick received D'Artagnan seriously. Her hôtel was remarkably sumptuous; and while most of the English, on account of the war, had left or were about to leave France, milady had just been laying out much money upon her residence. This proved that the general measures which sent the English home did not affect her.

"You see," said Lord Winter, presenting D'Artagnan to his sister, "a young gentleman who has held my life in his hands, and who has not abused his advantage, although we were doubly enemies, since it was I who insulted him, and since I am an Englishman. Thank him, then, madame, if you have any affection for me."

Milady frowned slightly; a scarcely visible cloud passed over her brow, and such a peculiar smile appeared on her lips that the young man, observing this triple shade, almost shuddered at it.

The brother saw nothing. He had turned round to play with milady's favourite monkey, which had pulled him by the doublet.

"You are welcome, sir," said milady, in a voice the singular sweetness of which contrasted with the symptoms of ill-humour which D'Artagnan had just remarked; "you have to-day acquired eternal rights to my gratitude."

The Englishman then turned round and described the combat, without omitting a single detail. Milady listened with the greatest attention, and yet it was easy to see that, in spite of her efforts to conceal her impressions, this recital was not agreeable to her. The blood mounted to her face, and her foot moved impatiently beneath her dress.

Lord Winter perceived nothing of this. When he had finished, he went to a table on which was a salver with Spanish wine and glasses. He filled two, and by a sign invited D'Artagnan to drink.

D'Artagnan knew that an Englishman regards as an insult the refusal to drink his health. He therefore went to the table and took the second glass. He did not, however, lose sight of milady, and in a mirror perceived the change that had just taken place in her face. Now that she believed herself to be no longer observed, a sentiment like ferocity animated her countenance. She bit her handkerchief with all her might.

The pretty little maid whom D'Artagnan had already observed then came in. She spoke some words in English to Lord Winter, who immediately requested D'Artagnan's permission to retire, excusing himself on account of the urgency of the business that called him away, and charging his sister to obtain his pardon.

D'Artagnan shook hands with Lord Winter, and then returned to milady. Her countenance, with surprising mobility, had recovered its gracious expression.

The conversation took a cheerful turn. She told D'Artagnan that Lord Winter was only her brother-in-law, and not her brother. She had married a younger brother of the family, who had left her a widow with one child. This child was Lord Winter's sole heir, if Lord Winter did not marry. All this showed D'Artagnan that there was a veil hiding something, but he could not yet see under this veil.

Moreover, after half an hour's conversation D'Artagnan was convinced that milady was his compatriot. She spoke French with a purity and an elegance that left no doubt on that head.

He was profuse in gallant speeches and protestations of devotion. To all the nonsense which escaped our Gascon, milady replied with a smile of kindness. The hour for retiring arrived. D'Artagnan took leave of milady, and left the parlour the happiest of men.

On the stairs he met the pretty maid, who brushed gently against him as she passed, and then, blushing to the eyes, asked his pardon for having touched him in so sweet a voice that the pardon was granted instantly.

D'Artagnan came again on the morrow, and was even better received than on the day before. Lord Winter was not at home, and milady this time did all the honours of the evening. She appeared to take a great interest in him, and asked him where he was from, who were his friends, and whether he had not at some times thought of attaching himself to the cardinal.

D'Artagnan, who, as we have said, was exceedingly prudent for a young man of twenty, then remembered his suspicions regarding milady. He launched into a eulogy of his Eminence, and said that he should not have failed to enlist in the cardinal's guards instead of the king's if he had only known M. de Cavois instead of M. de Tréville.

Milady changed the conversation without any appearance of affectation, and asked D'Artagnan, in the most careless manner possible, if he had never been in England.

D'Artagnan replied that he had been sent there by M. de Tréville to bargain for some new horses, and that he had even brought back four as specimens.

At the same hour as on the preceding evening D'Artagnan

retired. In the corridor he again met the pretty Kitty; that was the maid's name. She looked at him with an expression of good-will which it was impossible to mistake. But D'Artagnan was so preoccupied by her mistress that he noticed absolutely nothing which did not come from her.

D'Artagnan came again on the morrow and the day after that, and each day milady gave him a more gracious welcome.

Every evening, either in the antechamber, the corridor, or on the stairs, he met the pretty maid. But, as we have said, D'Artagnan paid no attention to poor Kitty's persistence.

CHAPTER XXXII.

A SOLICITOR'S DINNER.

MEANTIME the duel in which Porthos had played such a brilliant part had not made him forget the dinner of his *procureuse*.

On the morrow, about one o'clock, he received the last brushing from Mousqueton, and walked toward the Rue aux Ours with the step of a man who was doubly in favour with fortune.

His heart beat, but not, like D'Artagnan's, with a young and impatient love. No; a more material interest stirred his blood. He was about at last to pass that mysterious threshold, to climb those unknown stairs by which, one by one, the old crowns of Master Coquenard had mounted.

He was about to see, in reality, a certain coffer, the image of which he had twenty times beheld in his dreams—a coffer long and deep, padlocked, barred, bolted to the floor; a coffer of which he had so often heard, and which the *procureuse's* hands, a little wrinkled, it is true, but still quite elegant, were about to open to his admiring looks.

And then he—a wanderer on the earth, a man without a fortune, a man without family, a soldier accustomed to inns, saloons, taverns, and hostelries, a high liver forced to depend generally on chance invitations—was about to have an experience of family meals, to enjoy a comfortable establishment, and to accept those little attentions which, the tougher one is the more they please, as veterans say.

To come as a cousin and take his place every day at a good table; to smooth out the wrinkles on the old solicitor's creased and yellow brow; to pluck the young clerks a little

by teaching them " basset," " passe-dix," and " lansquenet,"
in their finest points, and by winning from them, by way of
fee for the lesson he would give them in an hour, their savings
of a month—all this was an enormously delightful outlook
for Porthos.

The musketeer now and then remembered the ugly stories
then afloat, and indeed prevalent even at the present day,
regarding solicitors—their meanness, stinginess, days of
fasts ; but as, after all, except for some few fits of economy,
which Porthos had always considered very untimely, the
procureuse had been tolerably liberal—that is, of course, for
a *procureuse*—he hoped to find a house kept up in comfortable style.

However, at the very door the musketeer felt some
doubts. The approach was not prepossessing,—an ill-smell-
ing, dark passage ; a staircase ill-lighted by bars through
which stole a glimmer from a neighbouring court ; on the
first floor a low door studded with enormous nails, like the
principal door of the Grand Châtelet.

Porthos knocked with his knuckle. A tall, pale clerk,
with a face shaded by a virgin forest of hair, opened the
door, and bowed with the air of a man forced to respect in
another the combination of lofty stature, indicating strength ;
the military dress, indicating rank ; and a ruddy countenance, indicating the habit of living well. Another shorter
clerk came behind the first, another taller clerk behind the
second, an errand boy of twelve behind the third. In all,
three clerks and a half. This, for the time, argued a very
extensive clientage.

Though the musketeer was not expected before one o'clock,
the *procureuse* had been on the watch ever since twelve,
reckoning that her lover's heart, and perhaps also his
stomach, would bring him ahead of time.

Madame Coquenard therefore entered the office from the
house almost at the instant that her guest entered from the
stairs, and the worthy lady's appearance relieved him from
great embarrassment. The clerks looked at him inquisi-
tively ; and he, not knowing exactly what to say to this
ascending and descending scale, remained mute.

" It is my cousin ! " cried the solicitor's wife.—" Come in,
come in, Monsieur Porthos ! "

The name of Porthos produced its effect upon the clerks,
who began to laugh ; but Porthos turned round, and every
countenance quickly recovered its gravity.

They went into the solicitor's library, after passing through the antechamber in which the clerks were, and the office in which they ought to have been. This last apartment was a kind of dark room, stocked with old papers. As they passed from the office they left the kitchen on the right, and entered the drawing-room.

All these intercommunicating rooms did not inspire Porthos with pleasant ideas. Conversation would be likely to be heard at a distance through all these open doors. Then, as he passed by, he cast a rapid, investigating glance into the kitchen, and was obliged to acknowledge, to the shame of the *procureuse* and his own deep regret, that he did not see that fire, that animation, that bustle, which, just before a good dinner, generally prevail in that sanctuary of gluttony.

The solicitor had unquestionably been warned of his visit, for he betrayed no surprise at the sight of Porthos, who advanced toward him with a free and easy air, and saluted him courteously.

"We are cousins, it appears, Monsieur Porthos?" said the solicitor, rising in his cane chair by means of his arms.

The old man, enveloped in a large black doublet, which concealed the whole of his slender body, was well preserved and dry; his little gray eyes shone like carbuncles, and appeared, with his grimacing mouth, to be the only part of his face in which life survived. Unfortunately, his legs had begun to refuse their service to all this bony machine. During the five or six months that this weakness had been growing on him the worthy solicitor had become almost the slave of his wife.

The cousin was accepted submissively, that was all. Master Coquenard on his legs would have declined all relationship with M. Porthos.

"Yes, monsieur, we are cousins," said Porthos, without being disconcerted; he had never reckoned on being received enthusiastically by the husband.

"On the female side, I believe?" said the solicitor maliciously.

Porthos did not feel the satire of this, and took it for a piece of naïveté, at which he laughed in his big moustache. Madame Coquenard, who knew that a naïve solicitor was a very rare variety in the species, smiled a little, and turned very red in the face.

Master Coquenard, ever since Porthos's arrival, had anxiously kept his eyes on a large chest placed in front of his oak desk. Porthos realized that this chest, though it did not correspond in shape with the one he had seen in his dreams, must be the blessed coffer, and congratulated himself that the reality was six feet higher than this dream.

Master Coquenard did not carry his genealogical investigations any further ; but, withdrawing his anxious eyes from the chest, and fixing them on Porthos, he contented himself with saying,—

" Our cousin will do us the favour of dining with us once before his departure for the campaign, will he not, Madame Coquenard ? "

This time Porthos received the blow full in his stomach, and felt it. It appeared, likewise, that Madame Coquenard was not insensible to it, for she added,—

" My cousin will not return if he finds that we ill-treat him ; but, on the other hand, he has too little time to pass in Paris, and consequently to see us, for us not to entreat him for every moment he can spare us before he goes."

" Oh, my legs ! my poor legs ! where are you ? " murmured Coquenard.

And he endeavoured to smile.

This aid, received by Porthos at the moment when he was attacked in his gastronomic hopes, inspired in him great gratitude toward his *procureuse*.

The hour of dinner soon arrived. They passed into the dining-room, a large dark apartment facing the kitchen.

The clerks, who apparently had smelt unusual perfumes in the house, displayed military punctuality, and stood with their stools in their hands, quite ready to sit down. Their jaws could be seen moving, in anticipation, with fearful threatenings.

" Ye gods ! " thought Porthos, casting a glance at the three hungry clerks, for the errand boy, as you may easily imagine, was not admitted to the honours of the master's table—" ye gods ! In my cousin's place, I would not keep such gluttons ! They look like shipwrecked sailors who have had nothing to eat for six weeks."

Master Coquenard entered, pushed along in his roller chair by Madame Coquenard. Porthos helped her in getting her husband up to the table.

He had scarcely got into the room when he began to move his nose and his jaws after the example of his clerks.

" Oh, ho ! " said he ; " here is a soup that is rather inviting ! "

" What the devil can they smell so extraordinary in this soup ? " said Porthos at the sight of a pale, abundant, but perfectly clear bouillon, on the surface of which swam a few crusts, as widely scattered as the islands of an archipelago.

Madame Coquenard smiled, and on a sign from her every one eagerly sat down.

Master Coquenard was first served, then Porthos. Afterwards Madame Coquenard filled her own plate, and distributed the crusts without bouillon to the impatient clerks.

At this moment the dining-room door opened of itself with a creak, and through the crack Porthos perceived the little clerk, who, not being allowed to partake of the feast, was eating his bread in the double odour of the kitchen and the dining-room.

After the soup the maid brought in a boiled fowl, a piece of magnificence which caused the eyes of all to open so wide that they seemed ready to burst.

"It is evident you love your family, Madame Coquenard," said the solicitor, with a smile that was almost tragic; "you are certainly treating your cousin very handsomely!"

The poor fowl was thin, and covered with one of those thick, bristly skins which the bones cannot make their way through, in spite of all their efforts. They must have sought for the fowl a long time before finding it on the perch, to which it had retired to die of old age.

"The devil!" thought Porthos; "this is very painful. I respect old age, but I don't think much of it boiled or roasted."

And he looked round to see whether anybody shared his opinion; but, on the contrary, he saw nothing but eager eyes devouring, in anticipation, that sublime fowl, the object of his contempt.

Madame Coquenard drew the dish toward her, skilfully detached the two great black feet, which she placed on her husband's plate; cut off the neck, which, with the head, she put aside for herself; took off the wing for Porthos, and then returned the bird otherwise intact to the servant who had just brought it in; and thus it disappeared before the musketeer had time to examine the variations which disappointment produces on faces, according to the characters and temperaments of those who experience it.

In place of the fowl appeared a dish of beans, an enormous dish, where some mutton bones, which at first sight might be supposed to be accompanied by meat, pretended to show themselves.

But the clerks were not the dupes of this deceit, and their lugubrious looks spoke of settled resignation.

Madame Coquenard distributed this dish to the young men with a good housewife's moderation.

The time for the wine came. Master Coquenard poured, from a very small stone bottle, the third of a glass to each of the young men, served himself in about the same proportion, and passed the bottle to Porthos and Madame Coquenard.

The young men filled up their third of a glass with water; then, when they had drunk half the glass, they filled it up again, and thus they kept doing. By the end of the repast, they were swallowing a drink which from the colour of a ruby had passed to that of a pale topaz.

Porthos ate his wing of the fowl very timidly, and shuddered when he felt under the table the *procureuse's* knee coming in search of his. He also drank half a glass of this sparingly served wine, and found it to be nothing but that horrible raw vintage of Montreuil, the terror of all practised palates.

Master Coquenard saw him swallowing this wine undiluted, and sighed deeply.

"Will you eat any of these beans, Cousin Porthos?" asked Madame Coquenard, in that tone which says, "Take my advice; don't touch them."

"Devil take me if I taste one of them!" murmured Porthos. Then aloud,—

"No, thank you, my dear cousin; I am no longer hungry."

A general silence prevailed. Porthos knew not what to make of it. The solicitor repeated several times,—

"Ah, Madame Coquenard! I give you my compliments. Your dinner has been a real feast. Lord, how well I have eaten!"

Master Coquenard had eaten his soup, the black feet of the fowl, and the only mutton bone on which there was the least appearance of meat.

Porthos fancied that he was being hoaxed, and began to twirl his moustache and scowl; but Madame Coquenard's knee came, and gently advised him to be patient.

The silence and the interruption in serving, though unintelligible to Porthos, had a terrible meaning for the clerks. On a look from the solicitor, accompanied by a smile from Madame Coquenard, they slowly arose from table, folded their napkins more slowly still, bowed, and retired.

"Go, young men; go and promote digestion by working," said the solicitor gravely.

After the clerks had gone Madame Coquenard rose and took from a sideboard a piece of cheese, some preserved quinces, and a cake which she herself had made of almonds and honey.

Master Coquenard frowned because there were too many good things. Porthos looked to see if the dish of beans was still on the table ; the dish of beans had disappeared.

"A positive feast !" cried Master Coquenard, squirming in his chair—"a real feast, *epulæ epularum*. Lucullus dining at Lucullus's."

Porthos looked at the bottle, which was near him, and hoped that with wine, bread, and cheese he might make a dinner ; but the wine was out, the bottle was empty. Master and Madame Coquenard did not seem to notice it.

"This is fine !" said Porthos to himself ; "I am neatly caught !"

He passed his tongue over a small spoonful of preserves, and stuck his teeth into Madame Coquenard's sticky pastry.

"Now," said he, "the sacrifice is consummated ! Ah ! if I had not the hope of having a peep with Madame Coquenard into her husband's strong-box !"

Master Coquenard, after the luxuries of such a repast, which he called an excess, felt the need of a siesta. Porthos began to hope that he would take it sitting where he was. But the solicitor would listen to nothing ; he insisted on being taken to his chamber, and was not satisfied till he was close to his chest, on the edge of which, for still greater precaution, he placed his feet.

The *procureuse* took Porthos into an adjoining chamber, and they began to lay the foundations of their reconciliation.

"You may come and dine three times a week," said Madame Coquenard.

"No, thank you, madame !" said Porthos ; "I don't like to take advantage. Besides, I must think of my equipment."

"True," said the solicitor's wife, groaning—"that unfortunate equipment !"

"Alas, yes," said Porthos, "that's the trouble !"

"But what, pray, does the equipment of your corps consist of, Monsieur Porthos ?"

"Oh, many things !" said Porthos. "The musketeers, as you know, are picked soldiers, and they require a quantity of things that are useless to the guards or the Swiss."

"But mention them to me, one by one."

"Why, they may amount to——" said Porthos. who preferred discussing the total to taking them in detail.

The *procureuse* waited tremblingly.

" How much ? " said she. " I hope it does not exceed——"

She stopped ; speech failed her.

" Oh no," said Porthos, " it does not exceed twenty-five hundred livres. I think that, with economy, I could manage it even with two thousand livres."

" Heavens ! two thousand livres ! " cried she. " Why, that is a fortune ! "

Porthos made a most significant grimace ; Madame Coquenard understood it.

" I wished to know the details," said she, " because, as I have many relatives and much experience in business, I should be almost sure of getting things at a hundred per cent. less than you could get them yourself."

" Ah, ha ! " said Porthos, " is that what you meant ? "

" Yes, my dear Monsieur Porthos. Thus, for instance, in the first place, don't you want a horse ? "

" Yes, I want a horse."

" Well, then, I can just suit you."

" Ah ! " said Porthos, brightening, " that's well as regards my horse ; but I must have the trappings complete, and these are composed of things that only a musketeer can purchase. They wouldn't amount to more than three hundred livres, however."

" Three hundred livres ! Then put down three hundred livres," said the *procureuse,* with a sigh.

Porthos smiled. It may be remembered that he still had the saddle that came from Buckingham. These three hundred livres, then, he reckoned upon putting slyly into his pocket.

" Then," continued he, " there is my lackey's horse and my valise. I need not trouble you about my arms ; I have them."

" A horse for your lackey ? " resumed the solicitor's wife hesitatingly ; " you do things in a very noble style, my dear."

" Well, madame," said Porthos haughtily, " do you take me for a peasant ? "

" No, no ; I only thought that a pretty mule made sometimes as good an appearance as a horse, and it seemed to me that by getting you a pretty mule for Mousqueton——"

" Well, agreed for a pretty mule," said Porthos. " You are right ; I have seen very great Spanish nobles, whose whole suite were mounted on mules. But then you understand, Madame Coquenard, a mule with tassels and bells."

"Very well," said the solicitor's wife.

"Then there remains my valise."

"Oh, don't let that disturb you," cried Madame Coquenard. "My husband has five or six valises ; you shall choose the best. There is one in particular which he himself selects whenever he travels. It's large enough to hold everything."

"The valise is empty, I suppose ? " asked Porthos naïvely.

"Certainly it is empty," naïvely replied the *procureuse*.

"Ah ! but the valise I want," cried Porthos, "is one well filled, my dear."

Madame Coquenard sighed again. Molière had not as yet written that famous scene in "L'Avare." Madame Coquenard therefore really anticipated Harpagon.

In short, the rest of the outfit was likewise debated in detail ; and the result of the session was that Madame Coquenard agreed to give eight hundred livres in money, and to furnish the horse and mule that were to have the honour of carrying Porthos and Mousqueton to glory.

These conditions being settled, Porthos took leave of Madame Coquenard. The latter tried to detain him by casting tender glances at him, but Porthos urged the demands of duty, and the *procureuse* was obliged to give way to the king.

The musketeer returned home atrociously hungry and in very ill-humour.

CHAPTER XXXIII.

MAID AND MISTRESS.

MEANTIME, in spite of the warnings of his conscience and the wise counsels of Athos, D'Artagnan hour by hour grew more and more deeply in love with milady. So the venturesome Gascon paid court to her every day, and he was convinced that sooner or later she could not fail to respond. One day when he arrived with his head in the air and as light at heart as a man who is expecting a shower of gold, he found the maid at the gateway of the hôtel. But this time the pretty Kitty was not satisfied with merely touching him as he passed ; she took him gently by the hand.

"Good !" thought D'Artagnan ; "she is charged with some message to me from her mistress. She is about to appoint a meeting which she probably has not the courage

to speak of." And he looked down at the pretty girl with
the most triumphant air imaginable.

"I should like to speak a few words with you, Chevalier,"
stammered the maid.

"Speak, my dear, speak," said D'Artagnan; "I am
all attention."

"Here? That's impossible. What I have to say is too
long, and, still more, too secret."

"Well, what is to be done?"

"If you will follow me?" said Kitty timidly.

"Wherever you please."

"Come, then."

And Kitty, who had not let go D'Artagnan's hand, led
him up a little dark, winding staircase, and, after ascending
about fifteen steps, opened a door.

"Come in here, Chevalier," said she; "here we shall be
alone, and can talk."

"And whose chamber is this, my pretty friend?"

"It is mine, Chevalier. It communicates with my mistress's by that door. But you need not fear; she will not
hear what we say; she never goes to bed before midnight."

D'Artagnan glanced around him. The little apartment
was charmingly tasteful and neat. But in spite of himself
his eyes were directed to the door which Kitty said led to
milady's chamber.

Kitty guessed what was passing in the young man's mind,
and sighed.

"You love my mistress, then, very dearly, Chevalier?"
said she.

"Oh, more than I can say, Kitty! I am madly in love
with her!"

Kitty sighed again.

"Alas, sir," said she, "that is a great pity."

"What the devil do you see so pitiable in it?" said
D'Artagnan.

"Because, sir," replied Kitty, "my mistress does not
love you at all."

"Hah!" said D'Artagnan; "can she have charged you
to tell me so?"

"Oh no, sir. Out of the regard I have for you I have
taken on myself to tell you so."

"I am much obliged, my dear Kitty, but for the intention
only—for the information, you must agree, is not very
pleasant."

" That is to say, you don't believe what I have told you, do you ? "

" We always have some difficulty in believing such things, if only from self-love."

" Then you don't believe me ? "

" Why, I confess that unless you give me some proof of what you advance——"

" What do you say to this ? "

And Kitty drew a little note from her bosom.

" For me ? " said D'Artagnan, snatching the letter from her.

" No ; for another."

" For another ? "

" Yes."

" His name ! his name ! " cried D'Artagnan.

" Read the address."

" The Comte de Wardes."

The remembrance of the scene at St. Germain presented itself to the mind of the presumptuous Gascon. As quick as thought he tore open the letter, in spite of the cry which Kitty uttered on seeing what he was going to do, or rather what he was doing.

" Oh, good Lord ! Chevalier," said she, " what are you doing ? "

" I ? " said D'Artagnan ; " nothing." And he read,—

" You have not answered my first note. Are you indisposed, or have you forgot the glances you gave me at Madame de Guise's ball ? You have an opportunity now, Count ; do not allow it to escape."

D'Artagnan became very pale.

" Poor dear Monsieur d'Artagnan ! " said Kitty, in a voice full of compassion, and pressing the young man's hand again.

" You pity me, my kind little creature ? " said D'Artagnan.

" That I do, and with all my heart, for I know what it is to be in love."

" You know what it is to be in love ? " said D'Artagnan, looking at her for the first time with some attention.

" Alas, yes."

" Well, then, instead of pitying me you would do much better to assist me in wreaking my revenge on your mistress."

" And what sort of revenge would you take ? "

" I would triumph over her, and supplant my rival."

" I will never help you in that, Chevalier," said Kitty warmly.

" Why not ? "

" For two reasons."

" What are they ? "

" The first is, that my mistress will never love you."

" How do you know that ? "

" You have offended her to the very heart."

" I ?   In what can I have offended her — I who, ever since I have known her, have lived at her feet like a slave ? Speak, I beg of you ! "

" I would never confess that except to the man who should read to the bottom of my soul ! "

D'Artagnan looked at Kitty for the second time.   The young girl possessed a freshness and beauty which many duchesses would have purchased with their coronets.

" Kitty," said he, " I will read to the bottom of your soul whenever you like.   Don't let that disturb you."

And he gave her a kiss, at which the poor girl became as red as a cherry.

" Oh no," cried Kitty, " you love me not ; you love my mistress ; you told me so only just now."

" And does that hinder you from telling me the second reason ? "

" The second reason, Chevalier," replied Kitty, emboldened by the kiss in the first place, and still further by the expression in the young man's eyes, " is, that in love, every one for herself ! "

Then only D'Artagnan remembered Kitty's languishing glances and stifled sigh ; how she constantly met him in the antechamber, in the corridor, or on the stairs ; how she touched him with her hand every time she met him.   But absorbed by his desire to please the great lady, he had disdained the maid.   He who hunts the eagle heeds not the sparrow.

But this time our Gascon saw at a glance all the advantage that he might derive from the love which Kitty had just confessed so naïvely, or so boldly—the interception of letters addressed to the Comte de Wardes, bits of secret information, entrance at all hours into Kitty's chamber, which was near her mistress's.   The perfidious fellow, as may be seen, was already sacrificing in idea the poor girl to obtain milady willingly or by force.

" Well, my dear Kitty," said he to the young girl, " do

you want me to give you a proof of that love of which you doubt ? "

" What love ? " asked the girl.

" Of that which I am ready to feel for you."

" And what proof is that ? "

" Do you want me to spend with you this evening the time I generally spend with your mistress ? "

" Oh yes ! " said Kitty, clapping her hands, " indeed I do."

" Well, then, my dear girl," said D'Artagnan, establishing himself in an armchair, " come here and let me tell you that you are the prettiest maid I ever saw."

And he told her so much, and so well, that the poor girl, who asked nothing better than to believe him, believed him. Nevertheless, to D'Artagnan's great astonishment, the pretty Kitty defended herself with considerable resolution.

Time passes very rapidly in attacks and repulses.

Twelve o'clock struck, and almost at the same time the bell was rung in milady's chamber.

" Great Heavens ! " cried Kitty, " there is my mistress calling me ! Go, go quick ! "

D'Artagnan rose, took his hat as if it had been his intention to obey ; then quickly opening the door of a large wardrobe, instead of the door of the staircase, he crouched down in the midst of milady's robes and dressing-gowns.

" What are you doing ? " cried Kitty.

D'Artagnan, who had secured the key, locked himself into the wardrobe without replying.

" Well," cried milady, in a sharp voice, " are you asleep, that you don't answer when I ring ? "

And D'Artagnan heard the communicating door opened violently.

" Here I am, milady, here I am ! " cried Kitty, springing forward to meet her mistress.

Both went into the bedroom, and as the door remained open, D'Artagnan could hear milady for some time scolding her maid. Then at last she grew cooler, and the conversation turned upon him while Kitty was assisting her mistress to undress.

" Well," said milady, " I have not seen our Gascon this evening."

" What, milady ! has he not been here ? " said Kitty. " Could he be inconstant before having been made happy ? "

" Oh no ; he must have been prevented by M. de Tréville or M. des Essarts. I understand my game, Kitty. I have him safe."

"What are you going to do with him, madame?"

"Do with him? O Kitty, there is something between that man and me that he is quite ignorant of. He very nearly made me lose my credit with his Eminence. Oh, I will be revenged for that!"

"I thought you loved him."

"Love him? I detest him — a fool, who held Lord Winter's life in his hands and did not kill him, so that I missed three hundred thousand livres a year!"

"That's true," said Kitty; "your son was his uncle's only heir, and until his coming of age you would have had the enjoyment of his fortune."

D'Artagnan shuddered to his very marrow at hearing this gentle creature reproach him in that sharp voice, which she took such pains to conceal in conversation, for not having killed a man whom he had seen load her with kindnesses.

"Therefore," continued milady, "I should long ago have had my revenge on him, if the cardinal—I don't know why—had not requested me to treat him kindly."

"Oh yes; but you have not treated very kindly the little woman he was so fond of."

"What! the mercer's wife of the Rue des Fossoyeurs? Has he not already forgotten she ever existed? Fine vengeance that, 'pon my word!"

A cold sweat broke from D'Artagnan's brow. This woman was a monster!

He resumed his listening, but unfortunately the toilet was completed.

"That will do," said milady. "Go into your own room, and to-morrow try again to get for me an answer to the letter I gave you."

"For M. de Wardes?" said Kitty.

"To be sure; for M. de Wardes."

"He is a man," said Kitty, "who appears to be quite different from that poor M. d'Artagnan."

"Go to bed, miss," said milady; "I don't like comments."

D'Artagnan heard the door close, then the noise of two bolts by which milady fastened herself in. Kitty on her side, as softly as possible, turned the key of the lock, and then D'Artagnan opened the closet door.

"O Heavens!" said Kitty, in a low voice, "what is the matter with you? How pale you are!"

" The abominable creature ! " murmured D'Artagnan.

" Silence, silence ! do go ! " said Kitty. " There is nothing but a thin partition between my chamber and milady's ; every word spoken in one can be heard in the other."

" That's just the reason I won't go," said D'Artagnan.

" What ! " said Kitty, blushing.

" Or, at least, I will go—later."

And he drew Kitty to him. There was no way to resist— resistance makes so much noise. Therefore Kitty yielded. This was an impulse of vengeance on milady. D'Artagnan realized the truth of the saying that vengeance is the delight of the gods. Therefore, with a little natural affection, he might have been satisfied with this new conquest ; but D'Artagnan knew only ambition and pride.

However, it must be said to his praise that the first use he made of his influence over Kitty was to try to learn from her what had become of Madame Bonacieux ; but the poor girl swore on the crucifix to D'Artagnan that she was entirely ignorant in regard to that, her mistress never letting her know half her secrets. Only she believed she could say she was not dead.

Kitty knew no more about the cause which had almost made milady lose the cardinal's confidence ; but this time D'Artagnan was better informed than she was. As he had seen milady on board an embargoed vessel at the moment he was leaving England, he had no doubt that it was on account of the studs.

But what was clearest in all this was, that milady's true hatred, her deep hatred, her inveterate hatred, arose from his not having killed her brother-in-law.

D'Artagnan came the next day to milady's. As she was in a very ill humour, he suspected that the lack of an answer from M. de Wardes provoked her to be so. Kitty came in, but milady was very cross with her. She glanced at D'Artagnan, as much as to say, " See how I suffer on your account ! "

Toward the end of the evening, however, the beautiful lioness became milder. She smilingly listened to D'Artagnan's soft speeches ; she even gave him her hand to kiss.

When D'Artagnan took his departure he scarcely knew what to think ; but as he was a youth not easily carried away by his emotions, even while he was continuing to pay court to milady he framed a little plan.

He found Kitty at the gate, and, as on the evening before,

went up to her chamber. Kitty had been severely scolded; she was charged with negligence. Milady could not at all understand the Comte de Wardes's silence, and she ordered Kitty to come at nine o'clock in the morning to take a third letter to him.

D'Artagnan made Kitty promise to bring him that letter on the following morning. The poor girl promised all her lover desired; she was madly in love.

Everything occurred as it had the night before. D'Artagnan concealed himself in his wardrobe, milady called, undressed, sent Kitty away, and shut the door. As before, D'Artagnan returned home at five o'clock in the morning.

At eleven o'clock he saw Kitty coming; she held in her hand a fresh note from milady. This time the poor girl did not even hesitate at giving up the note to D'Artagnan. She let him do as he pleased. She belonged, body and soul, to her handsome soldier.

D'Artagnan opened the letter, and read as follows:—

"This is the third time I have written to you to tell you that I love you. Beware lest I write to you a fourth time to tell you that I detest you.

"If you repent of the manner in which you have treated me, the young girl who brings you this note will tell you how a gentleman may obtain his pardon."

D'Artagnan coloured and grew pale several times as he read this note.

"Oh, you love her still," said Kitty, who had not for an instant taken her eyes off the young man's face.

"No, Kitty, you are mistaken; I do not love her, but I wish to revenge myself for her contempt of me."

"Oh yes, I know your vengeance! You told me!"

"What difference does it make to you, Kitty? You know I love only you."

"How can I be sure of that?"

"By the contempt I will cast on her."

D'Artagnan took a pen and wrote,—

"MADAME,—Until the present moment I could not believe that your two first letters were addressed to me, so unworthy did I feel myself of such an honour; besides, I was so seriously indisposed that I should, in any case, have hesitated to reply to them.

"But now I must believe in the excess of your kindness,

since not only your letter but your servant assures me that I have the good fortune to be loved by you.

"She has no occasion to teach me the way in which a gentleman may obtain his pardon. I will come and ask mine at eleven o'clock this evening.

"To delay it a single day would be, in my eyes, now to commit a fresh offence.

"He whom you have rendered the happiest of men,
"COMTE DE WARDES."

This note was in the first place a forgery; it was likewise an indelicate thing to do. It was even, according to our present morals, something like an infamous action; but at that period people were not so scrupulous. Besides, D'Artagnan, from her own admission, knew milady to be treacherous in matters of more importance, and he felt no great respect for her.

D'Artagnan's plan was very simple. By Kitty's chamber he could gain her mistress's. He would take advantage of the first moment of surprise, shame, and terror to triumph over her. He might fail, but something must be left to chance.

The campaign was to open in a week, and he would be compelled to leave Paris. D'Artagnan had no time for a prolonged love-making.

"There!" said the young man, handing Kitty the letter sealed and addressed; "give this note to milady. It is the Comte de Wardes's reply."

Poor Kitty turned deathly pale: she suspected what the letter contained.

"Listen, my dear girl!" said D'Artagnan; "you understand that all this must end in one way or another. Milady may discover that you gave the first note to my lackey instead of the count's; that I opened the others which should have been opened by M. de Wardes. Milady will then turn you off, and you know she is not a woman to let her vengeance stop there."

"Alas!" cried Kitty, "for whom have I exposed myself to all this?"

"For me, as I well know, my sweet girl," said D'Artagnan. "But I swear to you I am very grateful."

"But what does your note say?"

"Milady will tell you."

"Ah, you do not love me," cried Kitty, "and I am very wretched."

To such a reproach there is one answer that always deceives women. D'Artagnan replied in a way that left Kitty entirely convinced. Yet she wept a great deal before she could make up her mind to give the letter to milady. But at last she decided to do so, and that was all that D'Artagnan wanted.

Besides, he promised her that he would leave her mistress early that evening, and on coming out of the parlour would go up to Kitty's room. This promise completely consoled poor Kitty.

CHAPTER XXXIV.

WHICH TREATS OF THE OUTFIT OF ARAMIS AND PORTHOS.

SINCE the four friends had each been outfit-hunting they had had no regular meeting. They dined separately wherever they happened to be, or rather wherever they might find a dinner. Military duty likewise claimed its share of the precious time that was gliding away so swiftly.

They had agreed, however, to meet once a week about one o'clock at Athos's, since he, in conformity with his vow, no longer crossed his threshold.

The day that Kitty went to see D'Artagnan was the day for their reunion.

Kitty had barely left him before D'Artagnan directed his steps toward the Rue Férou.

He found Athos and Aramis philosophizing. Aramis was manifesting a decided inclination to resume the cassock. Athos, according to his principles, neither encouraged nor dissuaded him. Athos was for leaving every man to his own free will. He never proffered advice, and those who asked him had to ask him twice.

" People, as a rule," he said, " ask advice only in order to disregard it; and if they follow it, it is only for the sake of having some one to blame for having given it."

Porthos arrived a minute after D'Artagnan. Thus the four friends were all assembled.

Their four faces expressed four different feelings—Porthos's, tranquillity; D'Artagnan's, hope; Aramis's, anxiety; and Athos's, carelessness.

After a moment's conversation, in which Porthos hinted that a lady of high rank had condescended to relieve him from his embarrassment, Mousqueton entered.

He came to request his master to come home instantly,

where, he said, with a very pitiful air, his presence was urgently required.

"Is it my equipment?"

"Yes and no," replied Mousqueton.

"Well, but can't you say?"

"Come, monsieur!"

Porthos rose, saluted his friends, and followed Mousqueton.

An instant after, Bazin made his appearance at the door.

"What do you want of me, my friend?" said Aramis, with that mildness of language which was observable in him every time that his ideas led toward the church.

"A man is waiting for you at home," replied Bazin.

"A man! What man?"

"A mendicant."

"Give him alms, Bazin, and bid him pray for a poor sinner."

"But this mendicant insists on speaking to you, and pretends that you will be very glad to see him."

"Has he sent no special message for me?"

"Yes. 'If M. Aramis hesitates to come,' he said, 'tell him I am from Tours.'"

"From Tours!" cried Aramis. "A thousand pardons, gentlemen, but no doubt this man brings me the news I expected."

And instantly arising, he went off at a quick pace.

Athos and D'Artagnan only remained.

"I believe those fellows have got what they were after. What do you think, D'Artagnan?" said Athos.

"I know that Porthos was in a fair way," replied D'Artagnan; "and as for Aramis, to tell the truth, I have never been seriously uneasy on his account. But you, my dear Athos—you who so generously distributed the Englishman's pistoles, which were yours legitimately—what are you going to do?"

"I am satisfied with having killed that knave, seeing that it is holy bread to kill an Englishman. But if I had pocketed his pistoles, they would have weighed me down like remorse."

"Come, my dear Athos; you have truly extraordinary ideas!"

"Well, let that pass, let that pass! What did M. de Tréville mean, when he did me the honour to call upon me yesterday, by saying that you associate with those suspicious English whom the cardinal protects?"

" That is to say, I visit an Englishwoman — the one I
have told you about."

" Oh yes! the fair woman in regard to whom I gave you
advice, which, naturally, you took care not to adopt."

" I gave you my reasons."

" Yes; you see your equipment in it, I think you said."

" Not at all! I am certain that that woman was concerned in Madame Bonacieux's abduction."

" Yes, and I understand; to find one woman you make
love to another. It is the longest road, but certainly the
most amusing."

D'Artagnan was on the point of telling Athos all, but one
consideration restrained him. Athos was a gentleman punc-
tilious in all points of honour, and there were in all the little
plans which our lover had devised with regard to milady
certain things that he was sure would not obtain his approbation. He therefore preferred to keep silent; and as
Athos was the least inquisitive man on earth, D'Artagnan's
confidences stopped there.

We will therefore leave the two friends, who had nothing
very important to say to each other, and follow Aramis.

On the news that the person who wanted to speak to him
came from Tours, we saw with what rapidity the young man
followed or rather hastened ahead of Bazin : he ran without
stopping from the Rue Férou to the Rue de Vaugirard.

On entering, he found a man of short stature and intelligent eyes, but covered with rags.

" Did you ask for me ? " said the musketeer.

" I wish to speak with Monsieur Aramis. Is that your
name, sir ? "

" Yes. You have brought me something ? "

" Yes, if you can show me a certain embroidered handkerchief."

" Here it is," said Aramis, taking a key from his breast,
and opening a little ebony box inlaid with mother-of-pearl—
" here it is—look ! "

" That is right," replied the mendicant; " dismiss your
lackey."

In fact, Bazin, curious to know what the mendicant could
want with his master, had kept pace with him, and arrived
almost at the same time as he did. But his quickness was
not of much use to him; at the mendicant's hint, his master
made him a sign to retire, and he had to obey.

Bazin being gone, the mendicant cast a rapid glance
around him, in order to be sure that nobody could either

see or hear him, and opening his ragged jacket, badly held together by a leather strap, he began to rip the upper part of his doublet, and drew a letter from it.

Aramis uttered a cry of joy at the sight of the seal, kissed the superscription, and with almost religious respect opened the letter, which contained the following :—

"LOVE,—Fate wills that we should be still for some time separated ; but the delightful days of youth are not lost beyond return. Perform your duty in camp ; I will do mine elsewhere. Accept what the bearer brings you ; take part in the campaign like a true gentleman, and think of me, who tenderly kiss your black eyes !

"Adieu ! or, rather, *au revoir !* "

The mendicant kept ripping. He drew one by one from out his rags a hundred and fifty Spanish double pistoles, and laid them down on the table. Then he opened the door, bowed, and went out before the young man, stupefied, had a chance to address a word to him.

Aramis then re-read the letter, and perceived there was a postscript.

"P.S.—You may welcome the bearer, who is a count and a grandee of Spain."

"Golden dreams !" cried Aramis. "Oh, beautiful life ! Yes, we are young ; yes, we shall yet have happy days ! Oh, my love, my blood, my life ! All, all, my adored mistress ! "

And he passionately kissed the letter, without even looking at the gold sparkling on the table.

Bazin scratched at the door, and as Aramis had no longer any reason to exclude him, he bade him come in.

Bazin was dazed at the sight of the gold, and forgot that he was coming to announce D'Artagnan, who, curious to know who the mendicant was, came to Aramis's residence on leaving Athos's.

Now, as D'Artagnan used no ceremony with Aramis, when he saw that Bazin forgot to announce him, he announced himself.

"The devil ! my dear Aramis," said D'Artagnan, "if these are the prunes that are sent to you from Tours, you will make my compliments to the gardener who gathers them."

"You are mistaken, my dear," said Aramis, who was always discreet; "my bookseller has just sent me the price of that poem in one-syllable verse which I began yonder."

"Ah, indeed!" said D'Artagnan. "Well, my dear Aramis, your bookseller is generous, that's all I can say."

"How, sir?" cried Bazin—"a poem sell so dear as that! It is incredible! O sir, you do everything you want; you may become equal to M. de Voiture and M. de Benserade. I like that. A poet is almost as good as an abbé. Ah, Monsieur Aramis, become a poet, I beg of you."

"Bazin, my friend," said Aramis, "I believe you are interfering with my conversation."

Bazin perceived he was wrong; he bowed and went out.

"Ah!" said D'Artagnan, with a smile, "you sell your productions at their weight in gold; you are very fortunate, my friend. But take care, or else you will lose that letter which is peeping out from your doublet, and which comes, no doubt, from your bookseller likewise."

Aramis pushed the letter in, and buttoned up his doublet.

"My dear D'Artagnan," said he, "if you please, we will rejoin our friends; and since I am rich, we will to-day begin to dine together again, until you are rich in your turn."

"'Pon my word," said D'Artagnan, with great pleasure, "it is long since we have had a good dinner together; and as I have a somewhat hazardous expedition for this evening, I shall not be sorry, I confess, to fortify myself with a few glasses of good old Burgundy."

"Agreed, as to the old Burgundy; I have no objection to that," said Aramis, from whom the sight of the gold had removed, as by magic, his ideas of a pious retreat.

And having put two or three double pistoles into his pocket to answer the needs of the moment, he locked the others in the ebony box inlaid with mother-of-pearl, where he kept the famous handkerchief which served him as a talisman.

They first went to find Athos, and he, faithful to his vow of not going out, took it on him to have the dinner served in his room. As he was perfectly acquainted with the details of gastronomy, D'Artagnan and Aramis had no objection to abandoning this important care to him.

They were on their way to Porthos's, when, at the corner of the Rue Bac, they met Mousqueton, who, with a pitiable air, was driving forward a mule and a horse.

D'Artagnan uttered a cry of surprise, which was not free from a mixture of joy.

"Ah, my yellow horse!" cried he. "Aramis, look at that horse!"

"Oh, the frightful brute!" said Aramis.

"Well, my dear," replied D'Artagnan, "that is the very horse on which I came to Paris."

"What! do you know this horse?" asked Mousqueton.

"It is of an original colour," said Aramis; "I never saw one with such a hide in my life."

"I believe you," replied D'Artagnan; "and that was how I got three crowns for him. It must have been for his hide, for surely the carcass is not worth eighteen livres. But how did this horse come into your hands, Mousqueton?"

"Oh," said the lackey, "don't speak of it, sir. It is a frightful trick played us by the husband of our duchess!"

"How is that, Mousqueton?"

"Why, we are looked upon with a very favourable eye by a lady of quality, the Duchess of —— But, excuse me; my master has commanded me to be discreet. She had forced us to accept, as a little keepsake, a magnificent Spanish jennet and an Andalusian mule, which were beautiful to look on. The husband heard of the affair; on their way he confiscated the two magnificent beasts which she was sending us, and substituted these horrible animals in their places."

"Which you are taking back to him, I suppose?" said D'Artagnan.

"Exactly so!" replied Mousqueton. "You may well believe that we cannot accept such steeds as these in exchange for those which had been promised to us."

"No, by Jove! though I should have liked to see Porthos on my yellow horse. That would give me an idea of how I looked when I reached Paris. But don't let us hinder you, Mousqueton; go and perform your master's orders. Is he at home?"

"Yes, sir," said Mousqueton, "but very ugly! Go on!"

And he continued his way toward the Quai des Grands Augustins, while the two friends went to ring the bell of the unfortunate Porthos. He had seen them crossing the yard, and he refrained from answering. So they rang in vain.

In the meanwhile Mousqueton kept on his way, and crossing the Pont Neuf, still driving the two sorry animals before him, he reached the Rue aux Ours. Having arrived there, he fastened, according to his master's orders, both the horse and the mule to the knocker of the solicitor's door; then, without bothering about their future fate, he returned to Porthos, and told him that his errand was done.

In a short time the two wretched beasts, not having eaten anything since morning, made such a noise, by lifting the knocker and letting it fall again, that the solicitor ordered his errand-boy to go and inquire in the neighbourhood to whom this horse and mule belonged.

Madame Coquenard recognized her present, and could not at first comprehend why it was returned ; but a visit from Porthos soon enlightened her. The anger which fired the eyes of the musketeer, in spite of his efforts to suppress it, terrified his sensitive mistress. In fact, Mousqueton had not concealed from his master that he had met D'Artagnan and Aramis, and that D'Artagnan had recognized in the yellow horse the Béarnais pony on which he had come to Paris, and which he had sold for three crowns.

Porthos went away after having appointed a meeting with the *procureuse* in the cloister of St. Magloire. The solicitor, seeing he was going, invited him to dinner, an invitation which the musketeer refused with a majestic air.

Madame Coquenard repaired trembling to the cloister of St. Magloire, for she anticipated the reproaches that awaited her there ; but she was fascinated by Porthos's lofty airs.

All that a man wounded in his self-love can let fall in the shape of imprecations and reproaches on a woman's head, Porthos let fall on the bowed head of his *procureuse*.

"Alas ! " said she, " I did all for the best. One of our clients is a horse-dealer ; he owes money to the office, and was backward in payment. I took the mule and the horse for what he owed us ; he promised me two noble steeds."

"Well, madame," said Porthos, "if he owed you more than five crowns, your horse-dealer is a thief."

"There is no harm in trying to buy things cheap, Monsieur Porthos," said the solicitor's wife, seeking to excuse herself.

"No, madame ; but they who so earnestly try to buy things cheap ought to allow others to seek more generous friends."

And Porthos, turning on his heel, took a step as though to retire.

"Monsieur Porthos ! Monsieur Porthos ! " cried the solicitor's wife, " I have done wrong ; I confess it. I ought not to have driven a bargain when the point was to equip a cavalier like you."

Porthos, without reply, retreated another step.

The *procureuse* fancied she saw him in a brilliant cloud, all surrounded by duchesses and marchionesses, casting bags of money at his feet.

"Stop, in the name of Heaven, Monsieur Porthos!" cried she; "stop, and let us talk."

"Talking with you brings me misfortune," said Porthos.

"But, tell me, what do you ask?"

"Nothing, for that amounts to the same thing as if I asked you for something."

The solicitor's wife clung to Porthos's arm, and in the violence of her grief cried out,—

"Monsieur Porthos, I am ignorant of all such matters. How should I know what a horse is? How should I know what trappings are?"

"You should have left it to me, then, madame, for I do know what they are; but you were anxious to drive a sharp bargain, and consequently lend at usury."

"I have done wrong, Monsieur Porthos, but I will make reparation; on my word of honour, I will."

"And how?" asked the musketeer.

"Listen! This evening Master Coquenard is going to the Duc de Chaulnes's, who has sent for him. It is upon a consultation which will last two hours at least. Come, we shall be alone, and can make up our accounts."

"Well and good! That's the talk, my dear!"

"You will pardon me, then?"

"We will see," said Porthos majestically.

And they separated, both saying, "Till this evening."

"The devil!" thought Porthos, as he walked away; "it seems to me that I am at last getting nearer to Master Coquenard's strong-box."

CHAPTER XXXV.

AT NIGHT ALL CATS ARE GRAY.

THE evening so impatiently awaited by Porthos and D'Artagnan at length arrived.

D'Artagnan, as usual, presented himself about nine o'clock at milady's house. He found her in a charming humour. Never had she received him so kindly. Our Gascon saw at the first glance that his note had been delivered and was doing its work.

Kitty entered, bringing some sherbet. Her mistress was

very pleasant to her, and greeted her with her most gracious smile. But, alas! the poor girl was so sad that she did not even notice milady's kindness.

D'Artagnan looked at these two women, first at one, then at the other, and was forced to avow to himself that Nature had made a mistake in their composition. To the great lady she had given a vile and venal soul; to the maid she had given the heart of a duchess.

At ten o'clock milady began to appear uneasy. D'Artagnan understood what it meant. She looked at the clock, got up, sat down again, and smiled at D'Artagnan as much as to say, "You are doubtless very likable, but you would be charming if you would go away."

D'Artagnan rose and took his hat; milady gave him her hand to kiss. The young man felt that she pressed his hand, and he understood that she did so, not out of coquetry, but from a feeling of gratitude at his departure.

"She loves him devilishly," murmured he. Then he went out.

This time Kitty was not waiting for him, either in the anteroom, or in the corridor, or under the gateway. D'Artagnan was obliged alone to find the staircase and the little chamber. Kitty was sitting down, her head hidden in her hands, and was weeping.

She heard D'Artagnan enter, but did not raise her head at all. The young man went up to her, took her hands; then she burst out into sobs.

As D'Artagnan had supposed, milady, on receiving the letter, had, in the delirium of her joy, told her maid everything. Then, as a reward for the manner in which she had this time done her errand, she had given Kitty a purse.

On returning to her room Kitty had flung the purse into a corner, where it was lying wide open, disgorging three or four gold coins on the carpet.

The poor girl lifted her head at D'Artagnan's caresses. He was terrified at the change in her countenance. She clasped her hands supplicatingly, but without venturing to speak a word.

Though D'Artagnan's heart was not at all sensitive, he was softened by such mute grief. But he held too tenaciously to his plans, and especially to this particular one, to change in any way the line of action he had marked out. He therefore allowed Kitty no hope that he would yield, but he represented to her his conduct as actuated by vengeance pure and simple.

This vengeance, moreover, became all the easier because milady, doubtless to hide her blushes from her lover, had ordered all the lights put out even in her own room, and M. de Wardes was to depart before daybreak, in the darkness.

Almost immediately they heard milady enter her chamber. D'Artagnan instantly glided into the wardrobe. Scarcely was he hidden there when the mistress's bell rang. Kitty replied to the summons, taking care to shut the door after her. But the partition was so thin that almost all that was said by the two women could be heard.

Milady appeared intoxicated with joy. She made Kitty repeat the minutest details of her pretended interview with De Wardes—how he had received the letter, how he had answered, what was the expression of his face, whether he appeared much in love—to all of which poor Kitty, obliged to keep up a brave countenance, answered in a stifled voice, the sad accents of which her mistress did not even notice, so selfish is happiness.

At last, as the time for the interview with the count drew near, milady had all the lights in her chamber extinguished, and dismissed Kitty with an injunction to introduce De Wardes the moment he arrived.

Kitty was not kept waiting long. Scarcely had D'Artagnan seen, by the keyhole of the wardrobe, that the whole apartment was in darkness, when he sprang from his hiding-place just as Kitty was closing the door.

"What is that noise?" asked milady.

"My God! my God!" murmured Kitty. "He could not wait even for the hour he had himself appointed."

"It is I, the Comte de Wardes," replied D'Artagnan in a whisper.

"Well," said milady in a trembling voice, "why do you not come in? Count, count!" added she, "you well know I am waiting for you."

At this appeal D'Artagnan pushed Kitty gently aside and darted into the chamber.

If a soul is ever tortured by rage and grief, it is when a lover receives, under a name not his own, the protestations of love intended for his fortunate rival.

D'Artagnan was in a painful situation which he had not foreseen. Jealousy gnawed at his heart, and he suffered almost as much as poor Kitty, who at that very moment was weeping in the next room.

"Yes, count," said milady, in her sweetest voice, and pressing his hand tenderly in hers—"yes, I am happy in the love which your looks and words have expressed to me each time we have met. I love you also. To-morrow, to-morrow, I wish some pledge from you to prove to me that you think of me. And lest you forget me, take this ! "

She took a ring from her finger and put it on D'Artagnan's.

D'Artagnan remembered seeing that ring on milady's hand. It was a magnificent sapphire encircled by brilliants.

His first impulse was to give it back to her, but milady added,—

"No, no ; keep this ring for love of me. Besides, you do me a service in accepting it," she added, with a voice full of emotion, " a far greater service than you could imagine."

"This woman is full of mysteries," murmured D'Artagnan to himself.

At that moment he felt ready to reveal everything. He opened his mouth to tell milady who he was, and with what revengeful purpose he had come, when she added,—

" Poor dear angel, whom that monster of a Gascon came so near killing ! "

The monster was himself !

" Do you suffer still from your wounds ? " continued she.

" Yes, a great deal," said D'Artagnan, hardly knowing what to answer.

" Be assured," murmured she, " I will avenge you, and cruelly."

" Damn it ! " thought D'Artagnan, " the time for a revelation has not yet come."

D'Artagnan needed some time to recover from this short dialogue. But all the ideas of vengeance he had brought had vanished completely. This woman exercised over him an unaccountable fascination : he hated her and adored her at the same moment. He had never believed that two sentiments so opposite could ever dwell in the same heart, and by their union form a passion so strange and almost devilish.

But one o'clock had just struck, and they had to separate. D'Artagnan at the moment of leaving milady felt only a keen regret at departing, and in the passionate farewell they mutually bade each other a new interview was agreed upon for the following week. Poor Kitty hoped she might say some words to D'Artagnan when he came into her room ; but milady herself guided him through the darkness, and left him only on the staircase.

The next morning D'Artagnan hastened to Athos's room.

He had started on such a strange adventure that he wished to ask his advice. He told him everything. Athos frowned more than once. "Your milady," said he, "appears to me an infamous creature, but none the less you did wrong in deceiving her. Now you have, in one way or another, a terrible enemy on your hands."

While talking to him Athos was gazing earnestly at the sapphire surrounded with diamonds which had replaced on D'Artagnan's finger the queen's ring, now carefully kept in a jewel-case.

"You are looking at my ring?" said the Gascon, proud of showing off such a rich gift before his friend.

"Yes," said Athos; "it reminds me of a family jewel."

"It is beautiful, isn't it?" said D'Artagnan.

"Magnificent!" replied Athos. "I did not think there existed two sapphires of such fine water. Did you exchange it for your diamond?"

"No," said D'Artagnan; "it is a gift from my beautiful Englishwoman, or rather from my beautiful Frenchwoman, for though I never have asked her, I am convinced she was born in France."

"This ring comes from milady!" cried Athos in a tone which revealed great emotion.

"From herself. She gave it to me last night."

"Show me your ring, I beg of you," said Athos.

"Here it is," replied D'Artagnan, drawing it from his finger.

Athos examined it and grew very pale. Then he tried it on the ring-finger of his left hand. It fitted his finger as if it had been made for it. A shadow of anger and vengeance passed over the nobleman's brow, usually so calm.

"It is impossible it can be she," said he. "How could that ring be in Milady Clarick's possession? And yet it is very difficult to find such an exact resemblance between two jewels."

"Do you know that ring?" asked D'Artagnan.

"I thought I did," said Athos; "but no doubt I was mistaken."

And he gave it back to D'Artagnan, without ceasing, however, to eye it.

"Come, D'Artagnan," said he after a moment, "take that ring off your finger, or turn the stone inside. It brings up to me such cruel memories that I could not keep cool enough to talk with you. Didn't you come to ask advice of me? Didn't you tell me you were in doubt what to do?

But stop! let me take that sapphire again. The one I mentioned had one of its faces scratched in consequence of an accident."

D'Artagnan took the ring again from his finger and gave it to Athos.

Athos shuddered. "Ha!" said he; "look, isn't it strange?" And he showed D'Artagnan the scratches he remembered should be there.

"But from whom did you get this sapphire, Athos?"

"From my mother. As I tell you, it is an old family jewel, which never was to leave the family."

"And you—sold it?" asked D'Artagnan hesitatingly.

"No," replied Athos, with a singular smile; "I gave it away in a night of love, as it was given to you."

D'Artagnan became thoughtful in his turn. He seemed to see in milady's soul abysses the depths of which were full of darkness and mystery. He took back the ring, but put it in his pocket and not on his finger.

"D'Artagnan," said Athos, taking his hand, "you know I love you. If I had a son I could not love him more. Take my advice; renounce this woman. I do not know her, but a kind of intuition tells me she is wicked, and that there is something fatal about her."

"You are right," said D'Artagnan. "Therefore I have done with her. I confess this woman terrifies me."

"Will you have the courage?" said Athos.

"I shall," replied D'Artagnan, "and instantly."

"Truly, my young friend, you will act rightly," said the nobleman, pressing the Gascon's hand with an almost paternal affection; "and God grant that this woman, who has scarcely entered into your life, may not leave a terrible trace in it."

And Athos bowed to D'Artagnan like a man who wishes it understood that he would not be sorry to be left alone with his thoughts.

On reaching home D'Artagnan found Kitty waiting for him. A month of fever would not have changed the poor girl more than that night of sleeplessness and grief.

She was sent by her mistress to the false De Wardes. Her mistress was mad with love, intoxicated with joy. She wished to know when her lover would meet her again. And poor Kitty, pale and trembling, awaited D'Artagnan's reply.

Athos had a great influence over the young man. His friend's counsels, joined to the cries of his own heart, made him determine, now that his pride was saved and his vengeance satisfied, not to see milady again. As his reply he took a pen and wrote the following letter:—

"Do not depend upon me, madame, for the next meeting. Since my convalescence I have so many affairs of this kind on my hands that I am compelled to take them in a certain order. When your turn comes, I shall have the honour to inform you of it. I kiss your hands.

"COMTE DE WARDES."

Not a word about the sapphire. The Gascon wished to reserve one weapon against milady; moreover, after what Athos had said, should it not go to him rather than to her?

D'Artagnan handed the open letter to Kitty, who at first was unable to comprehend it, but who became almost wild with joy on reading it a second time. She could scarcely believe her happiness. D'Artagnan was obliged to repeat to her orally the assurances which the letter gave her in writing; and whatever the danger might be which the poor girl incurred in giving this note to her mistress, considering milady's violent character, she nevertheless ran back to the Place Royale as fast as her feet could carry her.

The heart of the best of women is pitiless for the griefs of a rival.

Milady opened the letter with eagerness equal to Kitty's in bringing it. But at the first words she read she became livid. She crushed the paper in her hand, and turning with flashing eyes on Kitty,—

"What is this letter?" cried she.

"The answer to yours, madame," replied Kitty, all in a tremble.

"Impossible!" cried milady. "It is impossible that a gentleman could have written such a letter to a woman."

Then all at once starting up,—

"My God!" cried she, "could he have——"

And she stopped.

She ground her teeth; she became ashen pale. She tried to take a step toward the window for air, but she could only stretch out her arms; her legs failed her, and she sank into an armchair.

Kitty thought she was ill, and hastened to open her dress; but milady started up quickly,

"What do you want?" said she; "and why do you put your hand on me?"

"I thought you were faint, milady," answered the maid, terrified by the frightful expression that had come on her mistress's face.

"I faint?—I? I? Do you take me for a weak, silly woman, then? When I am insulted I do not faint; I avenge myself! Do you understand?"

And she made a sign for Kitty to leave the room.

CHAPTER XXXVI.

DREAM OF VENGEANCE.

THAT evening milady gave orders that when M. d'Artagnan came as usual, he should be immediately admitted. But he did not come.

The next day Kitty went to see the young man again, and related to him all that had passed the evening before. D'Artagnan smiled. Milady's jealous anger was his revenge.

That evening milady was still more impatient than on the preceding one. She renewed the order relative to the Gascon; but, as before, she expected him in vain.

The next morning, when Kitty presented herself at D'Artagnan's, she was no longer joyous and alert, as she had been on the two preceding days, but, on the contrary, melancholy as death.

D'Artagnan asked the poor girl what was the matter; but her only reply was to draw a letter from her pocket and give it to him.

This letter was in milady's handwriting, only this time it was addressed to D'Artagnan, and not to M. de Wardes.

He opened it and read as follows:—

"DEAR MONSIEUR D'ARTAGNAN,—It is wrong thus to neglect your friends, particularly when you are about to leave them for such a long time. My brother-in-law and myself expected you yesterday and the day before, but in vain. Will it be the same this evening?

"Your very grateful
"LADY CLARICK."

"It's very simple," said D'Artagnan; "I was expecting this letter. My credit rises by the Comte de Wardes's fall."

"And will you go?" asked Kitty.

"Listen to me, my dear girl," said the Gascon, who sought for an excuse in his own eyes for breaking the promise he had made Athos; "you must understand it would be impolitic not to accept such a positive invitation. Milady, seeing that I ceased coming, would not be able to understand the interruption of my visits, and might suspect something. Who could say how far such a woman's vengeance would go?"

"O Heavens!" said Kitty, "you know how to represent things in such a way that you are always right. You are going now to pay your court to her again, and if this time you should succeed in pleasing her in your own name and with your own face, it would be much worse than before."

Instinct caused poor Kitty to guess a part of what was going to happen. D'Artagnan reassured her as well as he could, and promised to remain insensible to milady's seductions. He desired Kitty to tell her mistress that he was most grateful for her kindnesses, and that he would be obedient to her orders. But he dare not write, for fear of not being able sufficiently to disguise his writing to deceive such experienced eyes as milady's.

As nine o'clock was striking, D'Artagnan was at the Place Royale. It was evident that the servants waiting in the antechamber had been instructed, for as soon as D'Artagnan appeared, even before he had asked if milady was at home, one of them ran to announce him.

"Show him in," said milady curtly, but so piercingly that D'Artagnan heard her from the antechamber.

He was introduced.

"I am at home to nobody," said milady—"mind, to nobody."

The lackey went out.

D'Artagnan looked curiously at milady. She was pale, and her eyes looked red, either from tears or lack of sleep. The number of lights had been intentionally diminished, but the young woman could not conceal the traces of the fever which had been consuming her during the last two days.

D'Artagnan approached her with his usual gallantry. She then made an extraordinary effort to receive him, but never did a face more distressed belie a more amiable smile.

To the questions which D'Artagnan put concerning her health,—

"Bad!" replied she—"very bad!"

"Then," replied he, "my visit is ill-timed; no doubt you need to rest, and I will retire."

"No, no," said milady; "on the contrary, stay, Monsieur d'Artagnan; your agreeable company will divert me."

"Oh, ho!" thought D'Artagnan. "She has never been so kind before. I must be on my guard."

Milady assumed the most friendly air possible, and conversed with more than her usual brilliancy. At the same time the fever, which for an instant had left her, returned to give lustre to her eyes, colour to her cheeks, and vermilion to her lips. D'Artagnan was again in the presence of the Circe who had before surrounded him with her enchantment. His love, which he believed to be extinct, but which was only asleep, awoke again in his heart. Milady smiled, and D'Artagnan felt that he could go to perdition for that smile.

There was a moment when he felt something like remorse.

By degrees milady became more communicative. She asked D'Artagnan if he had a mistress.

"Alas!" said D'Artagnan, with the most sentimental air he could assume, "can you be cruel enough to put such a question to me—to me who, from the moment I saw you, have only breathed and sighed by reason of you and for you!"

Milady smiled with a strange smile.

"Then you do love me?" said she.

"Have I any need to tell you so? Have you not perceived it?"

"Yes; but you know the prouder hearts are, the more difficult they are to be won."

"Oh, difficulties do not frighten me," said D'Artagnan. "I shrink before nothing but impossibilities."

"Nothing is impossible," replied milady, "to true love."

"Nothing, madame?"

"Nothing," repeated milady.

"The devil!" thought D'Artagnan. "Her note is changed. Can this fair inconstant, perchance, be going to fall in love with me, and be disposed to give me another sapphire like the one she gave me when she took me for De Wardes?"

D'Artagnan impetuously drew his seat nearer to milady's.

"Well, now," she said, "let us see what you would do to prove this love of which you speak."

"All that could be required of me. Order; I am ready."

" For everything ? "

" For everything," cried D'Artagnan, who knew beforehand that he had not much risk in engaging himself thus.

" Well, now, let us talk a little seriously," said milady, drawing her armchair nearer to D'Artagnan's chair.

" I am all attention, madame," said he.

Milady remained thoughtful and apparently undecided for a moment ; then, as if appearing to have formed a resolution,—

" I have an enemy," said she.

" You, madame ! " said D'Artagnan, affecting surprise ; " is it possible ? Heavens ! good and beautiful as you are ! "

" A mortal enemy."

" Really ? "

" An enemy who has insulted me so cruelly that between him and me it is war to the death. May I count on you as my ally ? "

D'Artagnan at once perceived what the vindictive creature was aiming at.

" You may, madame," said he, with emphasis. " My arm and my life are yours, as my love is."

" Then," said milady, " since you are as generous as you are loving——"

She paused.

" Well ? " demanded D'Artagnan.

" Well," replied milady, after a moment's silence, " from now on cease to talk of impossibilities."

" Do not overwhelm me with happiness ! " cried D'Artagnan, throwing himself on his knees, and covering with kisses the hands which she let him keep.

" Avenge me of that infamous De Wardes," said milady to herself, " and I shall soon know how to get rid of you, double fool, animated sword-blade ! "

" Fall voluntarily into my arms, after having made sport of me with such effrontery, hypocritical, dangerous woman," said D'Artagnan, likewise to himself, " and afterwards I will laugh at you with the man whom you wish me to kill."

D'Artagnan lifted up his head.

" I am ready," said he.

" You have understood me, then, dear Monsieur D'Artagnan," said milady.

" I could read one of your looks."

" Then you would use for me that arm of yours which has already acquired so much renown ? "

" This instant ! "

" But," said milady, " how shall I repay such a service ?
I know what lovers are : they are men who will not do
anything for nothing."

" You know the only reply that I desire," said D'Artagnan—" the only one worthy of you and of me ! "

And he drew her gently to him.

She scarcely resisted.

" Selfish man ! " cried she, smiling.

" Ah ! " cried D'Artagnan, really carried away by the
passion this woman had the power to kindle in his heart—
" ah ! because my happiness appears so incredible to me,
and because I am always afraid of seeing it fly away from
me like a dream, I am anxious to make a reality of it."

" Well, deserve this pretended happiness, then ! "

" I am at your disposal," said D'Artagnan.

" Quite certain ? " said milady, with a last doubt.

" Only name to me the scoundrel who has brought tears
into your beautiful eyes ! "

" Who told you that I had been weeping ? "

" It seemed to me——"

" Such women as I am don't weep," said milady.

" So much the better. Come, tell me what his name is."

" Remember that his name is my whole secret."

" Yet I must know his name."

" Yes, you must. See what confidence I have in you ! "

" You overwhelm me with joy. What is his name ? "

" You know him."

" Indeed."

" Yes."

" It is surely not a friend of mine ? " replied D'Artagnan,
feigning hesitation, in order to make her believe in his
ignorance.

" If he were a friend of yours, you would hesitate, then ? "
cried milady ; and a threatening glance darted from her eyes.

" Not if it were my own brother ! " cried D'Artagnan, as
if carried away by his enthusiasm.

Our Gascon ran no risk in this, for he knew what he was
doing.

" I love your devotion," said milady.

" Alas ! is that all you love in me ? " asked D'Artagnan.

" I love you also—you ! " said she, taking his hand.

And the warm pressure made D'Artagnan tremble, as if
the fever consuming milady communicated itself to him
by the touch.

" You love me—you ! " cried he. " Oh, if that were so, I should lose my reason ! "

And he folded her in his arms. She made no effort to avoid the kiss which he pressed upon her lips, only she did not return it.

Her lips were cold ; it appeared to D'Artagnan that he had kissed a statue.

He was not the less intoxicated with joy, electrified by love. He almost believed in milady's tenderness ; he almost believed in De Wardes's crime. If De Wardes had at that moment been at hand, he would have killed him.

Milady seized her opportunity.

" His name is——" said she, in her turn.

" De Wardes ; I know," cried D'Artagnan.

" And how do you know ? " asked milady, seizing both his hands, and trying to read with her eyes to the bottom of his heart.

D'Artagnan felt that he had gone too far, and that he had made a mistake.

" Tell me ! tell me ! tell me, I say ! " repeated milady ; " how do you know ? "

" How do I know ? " said D'Artagnan.

" Yes."

" I know, because yesterday M. de Wardes, in a parlour where I was, displayed a ring which he said you gave him."

" Scoundrel ! " cried milady.

The epithet, as may be easily understood, resounded to the very bottom of D'Artagnan's heart.

" Well ? " continued she.

" Well, I will avenge you of this ' scoundrel,' " replied D'Artagnan, giving himself the airs of Don Japhet of Armenia.

" Thanks, my brave friend ! " cried milady. " And when shall I be avenged ? "

" To-morrow—immediately—when you please ! "

Milady was about to cry out " immediately," but she reflected that such precipitation would not be very gracious toward D'Artagnan.

Besides, she had a thousand precautions to take, a thousand counsels to give to her defender, in order that he might avoid explanations with the count before witnesses. All this was answered by an expression of D'Artagnan's.

" To-morrow," said he, " you will be avenged, or I shall be dead."

"No," said she, "you will avenge me, but you will not be
dead.   He is a coward."

"Toward women he may be, but not toward men.   I know
something of him."

"But it seems you had no reason to complain of your
fortune in your encounter with him."

"Fortune is a courtesan.   Though favourable yesterday,
she may turn her back to-morrow."

"Which means that now you hesitate ? "

"No, I do not hesitate.   God forbid !   But would it be
just to allow me to go to a possible death without having
given me at least something more than hope ? "

Milady answered by a glance which said, "Is that all ?
Speak, then."   And then, accompanying the glance with
explanatory words,—

"That is only too just," said she tenderly.

"Oh, you are an angel ! " exclaimed the young man.

"Then all is agreed ? " said she.

"Except what I ask of you, dear love ! "

"But when I tell you that you may rely on my tenderness ? "

"I have no to-morrow to wait for."

"Silence !   I hear my brother.   It will be better that he
should not find you here."

She rang the bell.   Kitty appeared.

"Go out this way," said she, opening a small private door,
"and come back at eleven o'clock ; we will then finish our
conversation.   Kitty will conduct you to my chamber."

The poor girl thought she should faint at hearing these
words.

"Well, miss, what are you doing, standing there like a
statue ?   Come, show the chevalier the way ; and this evening at eleven o'clock—you understand ! "

"It seems her appointments are all made for eleven
o'clock," thought D'Artagnan.   "That's a fixed habit."

Milady held out her hand to him, and he kissed it tenderly.

"There, now," said he, as he withdrew, scarcely heeding
Kitty's reproaches—" there, I must not play the fool.   This
woman is certainly very bad.   I must be on my guard."

CHAPTER XXXVII.

MILADY'S SECRET.

D'ARTAGNAN left the hôtel instead of going up at once to Kitty's chamber, as she tried to persuade him to do, and for this he had two reasons : the first, because in this way he avoided reproaches, recriminations, and entreaties ; the second, because he was not sorry to have an opportunity to read his own thoughts, and, if possible, to fathom this woman's.

The most palpable thing was that D'Artagnan loved milady like a madman, and that she did not love him the least in the world. For an instant D'Artagnan realized that the best thing for him to do would be to go home and write milady a long letter, in which he would confess to her that he and De Wardes were, up to the present moment, the same, and that consequently he could not undertake to kill De Wardes without committing suicide. But he also was spurred on by a ferocious desire of revenge. He wished to master this woman in his own name ; and as such a revenge seemed to him to have a certain sweetness in it, he could not make up his mind to renounce it.

He walked six or seven times round the Place Royale, turning every ten steps to look at the light in milady's apartment, which was to be seen through the blinds. It was evident that this time the young woman was not in such haste to retire to her bedroom as she had been the first.

At length the light disappeared.

With this light was extinguished the last irresolution in D'Artagnan's heart. He recalled to his mind the details of the first night, and with beating heart and brain on fire he re-entered the hôtel and rushed up to Kitty's chamber.

The young girl, pale as death, and trembling in all her limbs, wished to delay her lover ; but milady, listening intently, had heard the noise made by D'Artagnan, and opening the door,—

" Come," said she.

All this showed such incredible lack of discretion, such monstrous audacity, that D'Artagnan could scarcely believe his eyes or his ears. He imagined himself drawn into one of those fantastic intrigues which we meet with in our dreams.

He, however, darted none the less quickly toward milady, yielding to that magnetic attraction which the lodestone exercises over iron.

The door closed after them.

Kitty rushed toward it.

Jealousy, fury, offended pride, all the passions, in short, that wrangle for the heart of a woman in love, impelled her to make a revelation ; but she was lost if she confessed having aided in such a plot, and above all, D'Artagnan would also be lost to her for ever. This thought of love counselled her to make this last sacrifice.

D'Artagnan, on his part, had gained the height of all his desires : a rival was no longer beloved in him ; it was himself who was apparently beloved. To be sure, a secret voice at the bottom of his heart whispered to him that he was only an instrument of her revenge, that she would caress him only until he should inflict death. But pride, but self-love, but madness silenced this voice, stifled its whisper. And then our Gascon, with the amount of conceit we know he possessed, compared himself with De Wardes, and asked why, after all, he also should not be loved for his own qualities.

He there gave himself up to the sensations of the moment. Milady was no longer, for him, a woman of fatal designs who had for a moment terrified him. She was an ardent, passionate mistress, abandoning herself entirely to a love she really seemed to feel.

Some two hours thus glided away. But the transports of the two lovers moderated. Milady, not having the same motives that D'Artagnan had for forgetfulness, was the first to return to reality. She asked the young man if the measures destined to bring about a meeting between him and De Wardes the next day were already clear in his mind.

But D'Artagnan, whose ideas had taken quite another direction, forgot himself like a fool, and gallantly replied that it was rather late to think of duels and sword-thrusts.

This coldness toward the only thing that really occupied her thoughts alarmed milady, and her questions became more pressing.

Then D'Artagnan, who had never had any serious thought of such an impossible duel, tried to turn the conversation, but could not. Milady, with her irresistible spirit and iron will, kept him within the limits which she had predetermined.

D'Artagnan fancied that he was very clever in advising milady to pardon De Wardes, and thus renounce the furious projects she had formed.

But at the first word he spoke the young woman started,

drew away, and in a sharp, bantering tone that sounded strangely in the darkness, exclaimed,—

" Are you afraid, dear D'Artagnan ? "

" You cannot think me so, dear love ! " replied D'Artagnan. " But now, suppose poor Comte de Wardes should prove to be less guilty than you imagine him to be."

" At all events," said milady seriously, " he has deceived me, and from the moment he deceived me he deserved death."

" He shall die, then, since you condemn him," said D'Artagnan, in such a firm tone that it seemed to milady the expression of a devotion superior to every trial.

She immediately came close to him again.

We cannot say how long the night seemed to milady, but D'Artagnan imagined he had been with her scarcely two hours when day began to appear at the window-blinds, and soon invaded the chamber with its pallid light.

Then milady, seeing that D'Artagnan was about to quit her, recalled to his mind for the last time the promise he had made to avenge her on the Comte de Wardes.

" I am quite ready," said D'Artagnan ; " but in the first place, I should like to be certain of one thing."

" What ? "

" Whether you love me."

" I have proved to you that I do."

" Yes, and so I am yours body and soul. But if you love me as you say," continued he, " do you not feel a little fear on my account ? "

" What have I to fear ? "

" Why, that I may be dangerously wounded—even killed."

" Impossible ! " cried milady ; " you are such a valiant man, and such an expert swordsman."

" You would not, then, prefer a means," resumed D'Artagnan, " which would avenge you all the same, while rendering the combat useless ? "

Milady looked at her lover in silence. The wan light of the first rays of day gave to her clear eyes a strangely baneful expression.

" Really," said she, " I believe you are now beginning to hesitate."

" No, I do not hesitate ; but I really pity poor Comte de Wardes, since you have ceased to love him. And it seems to me that a man must be so severely punished merely by the loss of your love that he needs no other chastisement."

"Who told you that I ever loved him?" asked milady sharply.

"At least, I am now at liberty to believe, without too much self-conceit, that you love some one else," said the young man in a caressing tone, "and I repeat that I am really interested for the count."

"You are?" asked milady.

"Yes, I am."

"And why?"

"Because I alone know——"

"What?"

"That he is far from being, or rather from having been, so guilty toward you as he seems."

"Indeed!" said milady, with a look of some anxiety. "Explain yourself, for I really cannot tell what you mean."

And she looked at D'Artagnan, who held her in his arms, while his eyes seemed gradually to turn into flames.

"Yes; I am a man of honour," said D'Artagnan determined to end the matter, "and since your love is mine, and I am sure I possess it—for I do possess it, do I not?"

"Absolutely and entirely. Go on."

"Well, I feel as if transformed—a confession weighs on my mind."

"A confession!"

"If I had any doubt of your love I would not make it; but you love me, my beautiful mistress, do you not? You love me?"

"Certainly."

"Then if, through excess of love, I have rendered myself culpable toward you, you will pardon me?"

"Perhaps."

D'Artagnan tried, with the most winning smile he could put on, to touch milady's lips, but she avoided his kiss. It had no effect; he had alarmed milady, and she involuntarily turned from him.

"Your confession," said she, growing paler—"what is this confession of yours?"

"You invited De Wardes on Thursday last to meet you here, in this very room, did you not?"

"I? No, certainly not!" said milady, in a tone so firm and with a face so unconcerned that if D'Artagnan had not been so absolutely certain he would have doubted.

"Do not tell a lie, my angel!" exclaimed D'Artagnan, smiling; "it would do no good."

"What do you mean? Speak! You frighten me to death!"

"Oh, reassure yourself; you are not guilty toward me, and I have already pardoned you."

"What more? what more?"

"De Wardes cannot boast of anything."

"How so? You yourself told me that my ring——"

"My love, I have your ring. The Duc de Wardes of last Thursday and the D'Artagnan of to-night are one and the same person."

The imprudent young man expected to see surprise mixed with shame—a slight storm resolving itself into tears. But he was strangely mistaken, and his error was of brief duration.

Pale and terrible, milady started up, repulsed D'Artagnan with a violent blow on the chest, and leaped from the bed. It was then almost broad daylight.

D'Artagnan held her back by her nightdress, of fine India muslin, in order to implore her pardon, but by a powerful and determined effort she struggled to escape. Then the cambric gave way, leaving her neck bare, and on one of her beautiful, white, round shoulders D'Artagnan, with an indescribable shock, recognized the fleur-de-lis, that indelible stamp imprinted by the executioner's debasing hand.

"Great God!" cried D'Artagnan, loosing his hold of her nightrobe; and he remained on the bed, mute, motionless, and frozen.

But milady felt herself denounced by his very terror. Doubtless he had seen all. The young man now knew her secret, her terrible secret, of which every one, except him, was ignorant.

She turned on him, no longer like a furious woman, but like a wounded panther.

"Ah, wretch," she cried, "you have basely betrayed me! And what is worse, you know my secret. You shall die!"

And she flew to a little marquetry casket standing on the toilet-table, opened it with a feverish, trembling hand, took out of it a small gold-handled poniard with a sharp, slender blade, and then half-naked flung herself on D'Artagnan with one bound.

Though the young man was brave, as we have seen, he was terrified at her wild face, her horribly staring eyes, her pale cheeks, her bleeding lips. He crept over to the farther side of the bed as he would have done if a viper had been crawling toward him, and as his hand, covered with sweat, touched his sword, he drew it from the scabbard.

But without heeding the sword, milady tried to climb on the bed again so that she might stab him, nor did she desist till she felt the keen point at her throat.

She then tried to seize the blade with her hands; but D'Artagnan kept it free from her grasp, and while presenting the point, sometimes at her eyes, sometimes at her breast, he slid off the bed, designing to make his escape by the door leading to Kitty's apartment.

Milady meantime kept rushing at him with horrible fury, screaming in a blood-curdling manner.

As all this, however, was like a duel, D'Artagnan soon began to recover himself.

"Very well, pretty lady, very well," said he; "but, by the gods, if you don't calm yourself, I will mark you with a second fleur-de-lis on one of those pretty cheeks!"

"Scoundrel! scoundrel!" howled milady.

But D'Artagnan, while approaching the door, kept all the time on the defensive.

At the noise they made, she in overturning the furniture in her efforts to get at him, he in screening himself behind the furniture to keep out of her reach, Kitty opened the door. D'Artagnan, who had constantly manœuvred to gain this door, was not more than three paces from it. With one spring he flew from milady's chamber into the maid's, and, quick as lightning, shut the door, against which he leaned with all his weight, while Kitty bolted it.

Then milady, with a strength far above a woman's, attempted to tear down the doorposts which kept her in her room. Then, when she found she could not accomplish it, she kept stabbing at the door with her poniard, and more than once drove it through the thickness of the wood. Every blow was accompanied by a terrible imprecation.

"Quick, quick, Kitty!" said D'Artagnan, in a low voice, as soon as the bolts were fast, "let me get out of the hôtel; for if we leave her time to turn round, she will have me killed by the servants!"

"But you can't go out so," said Kitty; "you have hardly any clothes on."

"That's true," said D'Artagnan, then, for the first time, taking note of the costume in which he appeared—"that's true. But dress me as well as you are able, only make haste. Think, my dear girl, it's life and death!"

Kitty was but too well aware of that. In a moment she

muffled him up in a flowered dress, a capacious hood, and a cloak. She gave him some slippers, which he put on his naked feet, then she conducted him downstairs. It was time. Milady had already rung her bell, and roused the whole hôtel. The porter had just opened the street door as milady, only half-dressed, was shouting down from her window,—

"Don't open the door!"

CHAPTER XXXVIII.

HOW, WITHOUT INCOMMODING HIMSELF, ATHOS GOT HIS OUTFIT.

THE young man made his escape while she was still threatening him with an impotent gesture. At the moment she lost sight of him milady sank back fainting into her bedroom.

D'Artagnan was so completely upset that, without considering what would become of Kitty, he ran at full speed across half Paris, and did not stop till he reached Athos's door. The confusion of his mind, the terror which spurred him on, the cries of some of the patrol who started in pursuit of him, and the jeers of the passers-by, who, notwithstanding the early hour, were going to their work, only made him run the faster.

He crossed the court, ran up the two flights to Athos's apartment, and knocked at the door hard enough to break it down.

Grimaud, his eyes swollen with sleep, came to open for him. D'Artagnan darted so violently into the room that he nearly knocked him over.

In spite of his habitual silence, the poor fellow this time found his tongue.

"Helloa, there!" cried he; "what do you want, you strumpet? What's your business here, you hussy?"

D'Artagnan threw off his hood, and freed his hands from the folds of the cloak. At sight of his moustaches and naked sword. the poor devil perceived he had to deal with a man.

He then concluded it must be an assassin.

"Help! murder! help!" cried he.

"Hold your tongue, you villain!" said the young man; "I am D'Artagnan. Don't you know me? Where is your master?"

"You, Monsieur d'Artagnan!" cried Grimaud. "Impossible!"

"Grimaud," said Athos, coming out of his apartment in a dressing-gown——"Grimaud, I believe you are permitting yourself to speak?"

"Ah, monsieur, but——"

"Silence!"

Grimaud contented himself with pointing at D'Artagnan.

Athos recognized his comrade, and phlegmatic as he was, he burst into a laugh made quite excusable by the strange masquerade before his eyes—hood askew, petticoats falling over shoes, sleeves tucked up, and moustaches stiff with agitation.

"Don't laugh, my friend!" cried D'Artagnan; "for Heaven's sake, don't laugh, for, on my soul, I tell you it's no laughing matter!"

And he pronounced these words with such a solemn air and with such genuine terror that Athos instantly seized his hand, crying,—

"Are you wounded, my friend? How pale you are!"

"No; but I have just met with a terrible adventure! Are you alone, Athos?"

"Zounds! whom do you expect to find with me at this hour?"

"Well, well!"

And D'Artagnan rushed into Athos's chamber.

"Come, speak!" said the latter, closing the door and bolting it, that they might not be disturbed. "Is the king dead? Have you killed the cardinal? You are quite upset. Come, come, tell me; I am dying with anxiety!"

"Athos," said D'Artagnan, getting rid of his female garments and appearing in his shirt, "prepare to hear an incredible, an unheard-of history."

"Well, but take this dressing-gown first," said the musketeer to his friend.

D'Artagnan put on the dressing-gown, taking one sleeve for the other, so greatly was he still agitated.

"Well?" said Athos.

"Well," replied D'Artagnan, bending down to Athos's ear, and lowering his voice, "milady is marked with a fleur-de-lis on her shoulder!"

"Ah!" cried the musketeer, as if he had received a ball in his heart.

"Come, now," said D'Artagnan, "are you sure that the *other* is dead?"

" *The other?* " said Athos, in such a stifled voice that D'Artagnan scarcely heard him.

" Yes ; she of whom you told me one day at Amiens."

Athos uttered a groan and let his head sink into his hands.

" This one is a woman of from twenty-six to twenty-eight years of age."

" Fair," said Athos, " is she not ? "

" Very."

" Clear, blue eyes, of a strange brilliancy, with black eyelashes and eyebrows ? "

" Yes."

" Tall, well-made ? She has lost a tooth, next to the eyetooth on the left ? "

" Yes."

" The fleur-de-lis is small, rose-coloured, and somewhat faint from the coat of paste applied to it ? "

" Yes."

" But you say she is an Englishwoman ? "

" She is called milady, but she may be French. Lord Winter is only her brother-in-law."

" I will see her, D'Artagnan ! "

" Beware, Athos, beware. You tried to kill her ; she is a woman to return you the same, and not to fail."

" She will not dare to say anything, for it would be denouncing herself."

" She is capable of everything. Did you ever see her furious ? "

" No," said Athos.

" A tigress ! a panther ! Ah, my dear Athos, I am greatly afraid I have drawn a terrible vengeance on both of us ! "

D'Artagnan then told the whole story—milady's insane anger and her menaces of death.

" You are right ; and 'pon my soul I would give my life for a hair," said Athos. " Fortunately, the day after tomorrow we leave Paris. We are going, according to all probability, to Rochelle ; and once gone——"

" She will follow you to the end of the world, Athos, if she recognizes you ; so let her hate be wreaked on me alone."

" My dear friend, of what consequence is it if she kills me ? " said Athos. " Do you think, perchance, I set any great store by life ? "

" There is something horribly mysterious under all this, Athos. This woman is one of the cardinal's spies, I am certain."

" In that case, take care of yourself. If the cardinal does

not hold you in high admiration for the London affair, he entertains a great hatred for you ; but as, considering everything, he cannot accuse you openly, and as hatred must be satisfied, particularly when it's a cardinal's hatred, take care of yourself.   If you go out, do not go out alone.   When you eat, use every precaution.   In short, mistrust everything, even your own shadow.''

"Fortunately," said D'Artagnan, " all this will be necessary only until after to-morrow evening, for when once with the army, I hope we shall have only men to dread.''

"In the meantime," said Athos, "I renounce my plan of seclusion, and I will go wherever you go.   You must return to the Rue des Fossoyeurs.   I will accompany you.''

"Yes ; but near as it is, I cannot go there in this rig.''

"That's true," said Athos ; and he rang the bell.

Grimaud entered.

Athos made him a sign to go to D'Artagnan's residence and bring back some clothes.

Grimaud replied by another sign that he understood perfectly, and set off.

"Come, now, my dear friend, but this does not help toward your equipment," said Athos, " for if I am not mistaken, you have left all your clothes at milady's, and she certainly will not have the politeness to return them to you. Fortunately, you have the sapphire.''

"The sapphire is yours, my dear Athos ! Did you not tell me it was a family ring ? ''

"Yes ; my father gave two thousand crowns for it, as he once told me.   It formed part of the wedding present he made my mother, and it is magnificent.   My mother gave it to me ; and I, madman that I was, instead of keeping the ring as a holy relic, gave it to that wretched woman.''

"Then, my dear, take back your ring, to which, it is plain, you attach much value.''

"I take back the ring after it has passed through that infamous creature's hands ! Never ! D'Artagnan, this ring is defiled.''

"Sell it, then.''

"Sell a jewel that came from my mother ! I confess I should regard it as a sacrilege.''

"Pawn it, then.   You can raise at least a thousand crowns on it.   With such a sum you will be master of the situation. Then, when you get more money, you can redeem it, and have it back cleansed from its stains, for it will have passed through the usurer's hands.''

Athos smiled.

"You are a capital comrade, my dear D'Artagnan," said he. "Your never-failing cheerfulness lifts up poor souls in affliction. Well, let us pawn the ring, but on one condition."

"What?"

"That five hundred crowns of it shall be yours and five hundred mine."

"Don't think of such a thing, Athos. I don't need the quarter of such a sum. I am in the guards; and if I sell my saddle, I shall get it. What do I lack? A horse for Planchet, that's all. Besides, you forget that I too have a ring."

"Yes; and you seem to attach more value to it than I do to mine—at least, so it has seemed to me."

"Of course, for in any extremity it may help us out of some great difficulty or even danger. It is not only a precious diamond, but it is also an enchanted talisman."

"I don't know what you mean, but I have faith in what you say. Now as to my ring, or rather yours: you are to have half the sum advanced on it, or I will throw it into the Seine; and I doubt whether any fish, as in the case of Polycrates, would be polite enough to bring it back."

"Well, then, I will take it," said D'Artagnan.

At this moment Grimaud came in accompanied by Planchet, who was anxious about his master and curious to know what had happened to him, and so had taken advantage of the opportunity and brought the clothes himself. D'Artagnan dressed; Athos did the same. Then when both were ready to go out, Athos imitated the action of a person taking aim, and Grimaud immediately took down his musketoon and got ready to follow his master.

They arrived without mishap at the Rue des Fossoyeurs. Bonacieux was at the door; he looked banteringly at D'Artagnan.

"Ah, my dear tenant!" said he. "Hurry up; you have a very pretty girl waiting at your room, and you know women don't like to be kept waiting."

"It's Kitty," said D'Artagnan to himself, and darted into the passage.

In fact, there on the landing that led to his chamber he found the poor girl all of a tremble and crouching against the door.

As soon as she saw him,—

"You promised me your protection; you promised to

save me from her anger," said she.   " Remember, you are the one who ruined me ! "

" Yes, certainly I did," said D'Artagnan.   " Be at ease, Kitty.   But what happened after I left ? "

" How can I tell ? " said Kitty.   " The lackeys came when they heard her cries.   She was mad with anger.   Every imaginable curse she poured forth against you.   Then I thought she would remember that you went through my chamber into hers, and that then she would suppose I was your accomplice.   So I took what little money I had, and the best of my things, and I ran away."

" Poor girl !   But what can I do with you ?   I am going away the day after to-morrow."

" Do what you please, chevalier.   Help me out of Paris ; help me out of France ! "

" I cannot take you, however, to the siege of Rochelle," said D'Artagnan.

" No ; but you can get me a place in the provinces with some lady of your acquaintance—in your own country, for instance."

" Ah, my dear love, in my country the ladies do without chambermaids.   But stop !   I can manage it for you.— Planchet, go and find M. Aramis.   Have him come here immediately.   We have something very important to say to him."

" I understand," said Athos ;   " but why not Porthos ?   I should have thought that his marchioness——"

" Oh, Porthos's marchioness is dressed by her husband's clerks," said D'Artagnan, laughing.   " Besides, Kitty would not like to live in the Rue aux Ours. — Would you, Kitty ? "

" I am willing to live anywhere you please," said Kitty, " provided I am well concealed, and it is not known where I am."

" And now, Kitty, that we are about to separate, and, consequently, you are no longer jealous of me——"

" Chevalier, far off or near," said Kitty, " I shall always love you."

" Where the devil will constancy next take up its abode ? " whispered Athos.

" And I also," said D'Artagnan—" I also shall always love you ; be sure of that.   But now, answer me.   I attach great importance to the question I am going to ask you.   Did you never hear a young woman spoken of who was carried off one night ? "

" There now ! O Heavens, chevalier, do you love that woman still ? "

" No ; it is a friend of mine who loves her—here, M. Athos ; this gentleman here."

" I ? " cried Athos, with an accent like that of a man who perceives he is about to tread on an adder.

" Certainly, you ! " said D'Artagnan, pressing Athos's hand. " You know the interest we both take in this poor little Madame Bonacieux. Besides, Kitty will tell nothing— will you, Kitty ? You understand, my dear girl," continued D'Artagnan, " she is the wife of that frightful booby you saw at the door as you came in."

" Oh, good Heavens ! you remind me of my fright. If he should have recognized me ! "

" What ! recognize you ? Did you ever see that man before ? "

" He came twice to milady's."

" That's it. About what time ? "

" Why, about a fortnight or eighteen days ago."

" Exactly so."

" And yesterday evening he was there again."

" Yesterday evening ? "

" Yes, just before you came."

" My dear Athos, we are enveloped in a network of spies. —And do you believe he recognized you, Kitty ? "

" I pulled down my hood as soon as I saw him, but perhaps it was too late."

" Go down, Athos—he mistrusts you less than me—and see whether he is still at his door."

Athos went down, and returned immediately.

" He has gone," said he, " and the house door is shut."

" He has gone to make his report, and to say that all the pigeons are at this moment in the dovecot."

" Well, then, let us all fly away," said Athos, " and leave nobody here but Planchet to bring us news."

" Hold on a minute. How about Aramis, whom we have sent for ? "

" That's true," said Athos ; " we must wait for Aramis."

At that moment Aramis arrived.

The matter was explained to him, and he was told that he must find a place for Kitty with some of his high connections.

Aramis reflected for a minute, and then said, colouring,—

" Will it be really rendering you a service, D'Artagnan ? "

" I shall be grateful to you all my life."

"Very well. Madame de Bois-Tracy asked me, in behalf of a friend of hers who resides in the provinces, I believe, for a trustworthy chambermaid; and, my dear D'Artagnan, if you can answer for this young girl——"

"O sir, be assured that I shall be entirely devoted to the person who will afford me the means of leaving Paris."

"Then," said Aramis, "this turns out all for the best."

He sat down at the table and wrote a little note, which he sealed with a ring and gave to Kitty.

"And now, my dear girl," said D'Artagnan, "you know that it is not well for any of us to be here. Therefore let us separate. We shall meet again in better days."

"And whenever and wherever we meet again," said Kitty, "you will find that I love you as devotedly as I love you to-day."

"A gambler's vow!" said Athos, while D'Artagnan went to conduct Kitty downstairs.

An instant afterwards the three young men separated, agreeing to meet again at four o'clock at Athos's residence, and leaving Planchet to guard the house.

Aramis returned home, and Athos and D'Artagnan went to see about pawning the sapphire.

As our Gascon had foreseen, they found no difficulty in obtaining three hundred pistoles on the ring. Still further, the Jew told them that he would give five hundred pistoles for it if they would sell it to him, as it would make a magnificent pendant for an earring.

Athos and D'Artagnan, with the activity of two soldiers, and the knowledge of two connoisseurs, spent scarcely three hours in purchasing the musketeer's entire outfit. Besides, Athos was very easy to please, and a great noble to his fingers' ends. Whenever anything suited him, he paid the price asked, without any thought of dickering. D'Artagnan would have remonstrated at this, but Athos put his hand on his shoulder with a smile, and D'Artagnan understood that it was all very well for such a little Gascon gentleman as himself to drive a bargain, but not for a man who had the bearing of a prince.

The musketeer found a superb Andalusian horse, black as jet, nostrils of fire, legs clean and elegant, rising six years. He examined him, and found him sound and without blemish. A thousand livres was asked for him.

He might, perhaps, have been bought for less; but while D'Artagnan was discussing the price with the dealer, Athos was counting the hundred pistoles on the table.

Grimaud had a stout, short Picard cob, which cost three hundred livres.

But when the saddle and arms for Grimaud were purchased, Athos had not a sou left of his hundred and fifty pistoles. D'Artagnan offered his friend a part of his share, which he should return when convenient.

But Athos only replied to this proposal by shrugging his shoulders.

"How much did the Jew say he would give for the sapphire if he purchased it?" said Athos.

"Five hundred pistoles."

"That is to say, two hundred more—a hundred pistoles for you, and a hundred pistoles for me. Well, now, that would be a real fortune to us, my friend; let us go back to the Jew's again."

"What! will you——"

"This ring would certainly only recall very bitter remembrances. Then we shall never be masters of three hundred pistoles to redeem it, so that we really should lose two hundred pistoles by the bargain. Go, tell him the ring is his, D'Artagnan, and come back with the two hundred pistoles."

"Reflect, Athos!"

"We need ready money just now, and we must learn how to make sacrifices. Go, D'Artagnan, go; Grimaud will accompany you with his musketoon."

Half an hour afterwards D'Artagnan returned with the two thousand livres, and without having met with any accident.

Thus it was that Athos found at home resources which he did not expect.

CHAPTER XXXIX.

A VISION.

At four o'clock the four friends were all assembled in Athos's apartments. Their anxiety about their outfits had all disappeared, and each face preserved now only the expression of its own secret anxieties, for behind all present happiness is concealed a fear for the future.

Suddenly Planchet entered, bringing two letters for D'Artagnan.

The one was a little note neatly folded, with a pretty seal

in green wax, on which was impressed a dove bearing a green branch.

The other was a large square epistle, resplendent with the terrible arms of his Eminence the cardinal-duke.

At the sight of the little letter D'Artagnan's heart bounded, for he thought he recognized the writing ; and though he had seen it but once, the memory of it remained at the bottom of his heart.

He therefore seized the little letter and opened it eagerly.

"On Thursday next, at seven o'clock in the evening," said the letter, "be on the road to Chaillot. Look carefully into the carriages that pass ; but if you value your own life, or the life of those who love you, do not speak a word, do not make a motion which may lead any one to believe that you recognize her who exposes herself to everything for the sake of seeing you for an instant only."

No signature.

"That's a snare," said Athos ; "don't go, D'Artagnan."

"And yet," replied D'Artagnan, "I think I recognize the writing."

"That may be forged," said Athos. "Between six and seven o'clock the road to Chaillot is quite deserted ; you might as well go and ride in the forest of Bondy."

"But suppose we all go," said D'Artagnan. "What the devil ! they won't devour us all four, besides four lackeys, besides horses, besides arms."

"And besides, it will be a good chance to show off our new equipments," said Porthos.

"But if it is a woman who writes," said Aramis, "and she desires not to be seen, remember you compromise her, D'Artagnan. That is not behaving like a gentleman."

"We will remain in the background, and he will advance alone."

"Yes ; but a pistol shot is easily fired from a carriage, however fast it may be going."

"Bah !" said D'Artagnan, "they will miss me ; if they fire, we will ride after the carriage, and exterminate those who may be in it. That will make so many enemies the less."

"He is right," said Porthos ; "war ! Besides, we need to try our new arms."

"Bah ! let us enjoy that pleasure," said Aramis, in his mild and careless manner.

"As you please," said Athos.

"Gentlemen," said D'Artagnan, "it is half-past four,

and we have no more than time to be on the road to Chaillot by six."

"Besides, if we go out too late, nobody will see us," said Porthos, "and that would be a pity. Come, gentlemen, let us get ready."

"But your second letter," said Athos—"you forget that. It appears to me, however, the seal shows it well deserves to be opened. For my part, I declare, D'Artagnan, I think it of much more consequence than the little piece of waste paper you have so slyly slipped into your bosom."

D'Artagnan grew red.

"Well," said the young man, "let us see, gentlemen, what his Eminence wants of me." And D'Artagnan unsealed the letter and read,—

"M. d'Artagnan, of the king's guards, company Des Essarts, is expected at the Palais-Cardinal this evening at eight o'clock.

"LA HOUDENIÈRE, Captain of the Guards."

"The devil!" said Athos; "here's a rendezvous much more serious than the other."

"I will go to the second after attending the first," said D'Artagnan. "One is for seven o'clock, and the other for eight; there will be time for both."

"Hum! Now, I would not go at all," said Aramis. "A gallant knight cannot decline an appointment made by a lady; but a prudent gentleman may excuse himself from not waiting on his Eminence, particularly when he has reason to believe he is not invited in order to receive compliments."

"I am of Aramis's opinion," said Porthos.

"Gentlemen," replied D'Artagnan, "I have already received through M. de Cavois a similar invitation from his Eminence. I neglected it, and on the morrow a serious misfortune happened to me. Constance disappeared. Whatever may ensue, I shall go."

"If you are determined," said Athos, "do so."

"Yes; but the Bastille?" said Aramis.

"Bah! you will get me out," said D'Artagnan.

"To be sure we will," replied Aramis and Porthos, with admirable coolness, as if it were the simplest thing in the world—"to be sure we will get you out, if there; but in the meantime, as we are to set off the day after to-morrow, you would do much better not to risk the Bastille."

" Let us do better than that," said Athos ; " do not let us leave him during the whole evening. Let each of us wait at a gate of the palace with three musketeers behind him ; if we see any carriage come out with closed windows, and of suspicious appearance, let us fall on it. It is a long time since we have had a skirmish with the cardinal's guards. M. de Tréville must think we are dead."

" To a certainty, Athos," said Aramis, " you were meant to be a general. What do you think of the plan, gentlemen ? "

" Admirable ! " replied the young men in chorus.

" Well," said Porthos, " I will run to the hôtel, and engage our comrades to hold themselves in readiness by eight o'clock ; the rendezvous will be the Place du Palais-Cardinal. In the meantime, you have the lackeys saddle the horses."

" I have no horse," said D'Artagnan ; " but I will take one of M. de Tréville's."

" That is not worth while," said Aramis ; " you shall have one of mine."

" One of yours ! How many have you, pray ? " asked D'Artagnan.

" Three," replied Aramis, smiling.

" My dear ! " cried Athos, " you are the best-mounted poet of France or Navarre."

" Listen, my dear Aramis : you don't want three horses, do you ? I cannot comprehend why you bought three."

" No ; the third was brought to me this very morning by a groom without livery, who would not tell me in whose service he was, and who affirmed he had received orders from his master——"

" Or his mistress," interrupted D'Artagnan.

" It makes no difference," said Aramis — " and who affirmed, as I said, that he had received orders from his mistress to place the horse in my stable, without informing me where it came from."

" Well, this being so, we can manage famously," said D'Artagnan. " Which of the two horses will you ride— the one you bought, or the one that was given to you ? "

" The one that was given to me, of course. You cannot for a moment imagine, D'Artagnan, that I should commit such an offence toward——"

" The unknown giver," interrupted D'Artagnan.

" Or the mysterious benefactress," said Athos.

" So the one you bought will be useless to you ? "

" Nearly so."

" And you selected it yourself ? "

" With the greatest care. The safety of the horseman, you know, almost always depends on his horse."

" Well, let me have it at the price it cost you."

" I was going to make you the offer, my dear D'Artagnan, giving you all the time necessary for repaying me such a trifle."

" How much did it cost you ? "

" Eight hundred livres."

" Here are forty double pistoles, my dear friend," said D'Artagnan, taking the sum from his pocket ; " I know this is the coin in which you are paid for your poems."

" You are abounding in money, are you ? " said Aramis.

" Money ! Rolling in it, my dear fellow ! "

And D'Artagnan ostentatiously jingled the rest of his pistoles in his pocket.

" Send your saddle, then, to the hôtel of the musketeers, and your horse will be brought back with ours."

" Very well ; but it is almost five o'clock, so make haste."

A quarter of an hour afterwards Porthos appeared at the end of the Rue Férou, mounted on a very handsome jennet ; Mousqueton followed him upon an Auvergne horse, small, but very good-looking. Porthos was resplendent with joy and pride.

At the same time Aramis made his appearance at the other end of the street on a superb English charger ; Bazin followed him on a roan, leading a vigorous Mecklenburg horse. This last was D'Artagnan's.

The two musketeers met at the gate. Athos and D'Artagnan were watching their approach from the window.

" The devil ! " cried Aramis ; " you have a magnificent horse there, my dear Porthos."

" Yes," replied Porthos, " it is the one that ought to have been sent to me at first. A bad joke of the husband's substituted the other ; but the husband has been punished since, and I have obtained full satisfaction."

Planchet and Grimaud then appeared leading their masters' horses. D'Artagnan and Athos came down, joined their comrades, and all four set forward — Athos on a horse he owed to his wife, Aramis on a horse he owed to his mistress, Porthos on a horse he owed to his *procureuse*, and D'Artagnan on a horse he owed to his good fortune, the best mistress possible.

The lackeys followed.

As Porthos had foreseen, the cavalcade produced a good effect ; and if Madame Coquenard had met Porthos, and seen what a superb appearance he made on his handsome Spanish jennet, she would not have regretted the bleeding she had inflicted on her husband's strong-box.

Near the Louvre the four friends chanced to meet M. de Tréville, who was returning from St. Germain. He stopped them to offer his compliments on their superb outfit, and this in an instant drew round them some hundreds of gapers.

D'Artagnan took advantage of the opportunity to speak to M. de Tréville of the letter with the great red seal and the ducal arms.

M. de Tréville approved the resolution he had adopted, and assured him that if on the next day he did not appear, he himself would be able to find him, wherever he was.

At this moment the clock of La Samaritaine struck six ; the four friends pleaded an engagement, and took leave of M. de Tréville.

A short gallop brought them to the Chaillot road. The day was beginning to decline, carriages were passing and repassing. D'Artagnan, watched at some distance by his friends, darted a scrutinizing glance into every carriage that appeared, but saw no face with which he was acquainted.

At length, after waiting a quarter of an hour, and just as it was quite twilight, a carriage appeared, coming at full speed, on the road to Sèvres. A presentiment instantly told D'Artagnan that this carriage contained the person who had appointed the rendezvous. The young man was himself astonished to feel his heart beating so violently. Almost instantly a woman put her head out at the window, with two fingers placed on her mouth, either to enjoin silence or to send him a kiss. D'Artagnan uttered a slight cry of joy. This woman, or rather this apparition—for the carriage passed with the rapidity of a vision—was Madame Bonacieux.

By an involuntary movement, and in spite of the injunction given, D'Artagnan started his horse to a gallop, and in a few strides overtook the carriage. But the window was hermetically shut ; the vision had disappeared.

D'Artagnan then remembered the injunction contained in the anonymous note : " If you value your own life, or the life of those who love you, do not speak a word, do not make a motion which may lead any one to believe that you recognize her who exposes herself to everything for the sake of seeing you for an instant only."

He stopped, therefore, trembling, not for himself, but for the poor woman who had evidently exposed herself to great danger by appointing this rendezvous.

The carriage pursued its way, still going at a full pace, till it dashed into Paris and disappeared.

D'Artagnan remained fixed to the spot, astounded, and not knowing what to think. If it was Madame Bonacieux, and if she was returning to Paris, why this fugitive interview? why this simple exchange of a glance? why this last kiss? If, on the other side, it was not she, which was still quite possible—for the little light that remained rendered a mistake easy—if it was not she, might it not be the beginning of some machination against him with the bait of this woman with whom it was known he was in love?

His three companions joined him. All had plainly seen a woman's head appear at the window, but none of them, except Athos, knew Madame Bonacieux. Athos's opinion was that it was she; but, less preoccupied by her pretty face than D'Artagnan, he had fancied he saw another head, a man's head, in the carriage.

"If that be the case," said D'Artagnan, "they are doubtless transferring her from one prison to another. But what can they intend to do with the poor creature, and how shall I ever meet her again?"

"Friend," said Athos gravely, "remember that the dead are the only beings whom we are not likely to meet again on this earth. You know something of that, as well as I, do you not? Now, if your mistress is not dead, if we have just seen her, you will certainly find her again some day. And perhaps, my God!" added he, with that misanthropic tone which was characteristic of him—"perhaps sooner than you wish."

Half-past seven struck. The carriage was twenty minutes behind the time appointed. D'Artagnan's friends reminded him that he had a visit to pay, but at the same time observing that there was still time to recede.

But D'Artagnan was both impetuous and inquisitive. He had made up his mind that he would go to the Palais-Cardinal, and that he would learn what his Eminence had to say to him. Nothing could turn him from his purpose.

They reached the Rue St. Honoré, and in the Place du Palais-Cardinal they found the twelve musketeers who had been summoned, walking about in expectation of their comrades. Then only they were informed of the matter in question.

D'Artagnan was well known in the honourable corps of the king's musketeers, where it was understood that he would one day take his place ; he was regarded, therefore, as already their comrade. The result was that each cordially accepted the duty for which he had been summoned. Besides, in all probability, they were going to have a chance to play the cardinal and his people an ill turn, and for such expeditions these worthy gentlemen were always ready.

Athos divided them into three groups, assumed the command of one, gave the second to Aramis, and the third to Porthos ; and then each group went and took up its position opposite one of the entrances.

D'Artagnan, on his part, entered boldly at the front gate.

Though he felt himself ably supported, the young man was not without some anxiety as he ascended the great staircase of the palace step by step. His treatment of milady bore a strong resemblance to treachery, and he suspected the political relations which existed between that woman and the cardinal ; still further, De Wardes, whom he had treated so ill in their encounter at the gates of Calais, was one of his Eminence's faithful followers, and D'Artagnan knew that while his Eminence was terrible to his enemies, he was strongly attached to his friends.

" If De Wardes has related all our affair to the cardinal, which is not to be doubted, and if he recognized me, which is probable, I may consider myself almost as a condemned man," said D'Artagnan, shaking his head. " But why has he waited till now ? It's all plain enough : milady must have entered her complaint against me with that hypocritical grief which renders her so interesting, and this last offence must have made the cup overflow.

" Fortunately," he added, " my good friends are down yonder, and they will not allow me to be carried away without taking my part. Still, M. de Tréville's company of musketeers alone cannot maintain a war against the cardinal, who disposes of the forces of all France, and before whom, alas ! the queen is without power and the king without will. D'Artagnan, my dear, you are brave, you are prudent, you have excellent qualities, but the women will be the ruin of you."

He came to this melancholy conclusion as he entered the antechamber. He placed his letter in the hands of the usher on duty, who showed him into the waiting-room and passed on into the interior of the palace.

In this waiting-room were five or six of the cardinal's

guards, who recognized D'Artagnan, and knowing that it was he who had wounded Jussac, looked upon him with a smile of singular significance.

This smile seemed ominous to D'Artagnan ; but as our Gascon was not easily intimidated, or rather, by reason of the great pride natural to the men of his country, he did not readily reveal what was passing in his mind when what was passing resembled fear, he stood haughtily in front of the guards, and waited with his hand on his hip, in an attitude by no means deficient in majesty.

The usher returned and made a sign to D'Artagnan to follow him. It appeared to the young man that the guards, on seeing him depart, were whispering among themselves.

He passed along a corridor, crossed a large drawing-room, entered a library, and found himself in the presence of a man seated at a desk and writing.

The usher introduced him and retired without speaking a word. D'Artagnan remained standing and examined this man.

D'Artagnan at first believed that he had to do with some judge examining his papers, but he perceived that the man at the desk was writing, or rather correcting, lines of unequal length by scanning the words on his fingers. He saw that he was in presence of a poet. In an instance the poet closed his manuscript, on the cover of which was written *Mirame, a Tragedy in Five Acts*, and raised his head.

D'Artagnan recognized the cardinal.

CHAPTER XL.

A TERRIBLE VISION.

THE cardinal leaned his elbow on his manuscript, his cheek on his hand, and looked at the young man for a moment. No one had a more searching eye than Cardinal Richelieu, and D'Artagnan felt this look run through his veins like a fever.

He, however, kept up a brave face, holding his hat in his hand, and awaiting his Eminence's good pleasure, without too much assurance, but without too much humility.

" Sir," said the cardinal, " are you a D'Artagnan from Béarn ? "

" Yes, monseigneur," replied the young man.

" If I am not mistaken, there are several branches of the

D'Artagnans at Tarbes and its vicinity," said the cardinal. "To which do you belong ? "

" I am the son of the one who served in the religious wars under the great King Henry, his gracious Majesty's father."

" That is it.   Seven or eight months ago you started from your country to seek your fortune in the capital ? "

" Yes, monseigneur."

" You came through Meung, where something befell you —I don't very well remember what, but still something."

" Monseigneur," said D'Artagnan, "this is what happened to me——"

" No matter, no matter ! " resumed the cardinal, with a smile which proved that he knew the story as well as he who wished to relate it.   " You had a letter of introduction to M. de Tréville, had you not ? "

" Yes, monseigneur ; but in that unfortunate affair at Meung——"

" The letter was lost," replied his Eminence ; " yes, I know that.   But M. de Tréville is a skilful physiognomist, who knows men at first sight ; and he placed you in the company of his brother-in-law, M. des Essarts, leaving you to hope that some day you should enter the musketeers."

" Monseigneur is quite correctly informed," said D'Artagnan.

" Since that time many things have happened to you. You were walking one day behind the Chartreux, when it would have been better for you if you had been elsewhere. Then you took with your friends a journey to the waters of Forges ; they stopped on the way, but you went on.   That is all very simple : you had business in England."

" Monseigneur," said D Artagnan, quite confused, " I went——"

" Hunting at Windsor or elsewhere ; that concerns nobody.   I am acquainted with the circumstances, because it is my business to know everything.   On your return you were received by an august personage, and I perceive with pleasure that you preserve the souvenir she gave you."

D'Artagnan placed his hand on the diamond which the queen had given him.

" The day after that you received a visit from Cavois," resumed the cardinal ; " he went to desire you to call at the palace.   You did not make that visit, and you were wrong."

" Monseigneur, I feared I had incurred your Eminence's disfavour."

" How could that be, sir ? By following the orders of your

superiors with more intelligence and courage than another would have done, would you incur disfavour when you deserve praise ? I punish people who do not obey, and not those who, like you, obey but too well. As a proof, remember the date of the day when I had you summoned to me, and search in your memory for what happened that very night."

It was the very evening when Madame Bonacieux's abduction took place. D'Artagnan trembled. And he likewise recollected that half an hour before the poor woman had passed close to him, without doubt carried away once more by the same power that had caused her disappearance.

" In short," continued the cardinal, " as I have heard nothing of you for some time, I wished to know what you were doing. Besides, you owe me some thanks : you must yourself have remarked how considerately you have been treated in all these circumstances."

D'Artagnan bowed respectfully.

" That," continued the cardinal, " arose not only from a feeling of natural justice, but also from a plan I had marked out with respect to you."

D'Artagnan became more and more astonished.

" I wished to explain this plan to you on the day you received my first invitation ; but you did not come. Fortunately nothing is lost by this delay, and now you are about to hear it. Sit down there before me, Monsieur d'Artagnan ; you are enough of a nobleman not to listen standing."

And the cardinal pointed with his finger to a chair for the young man, who was so amazed at what was going on that he waited for a second sign from the cardinal before he obeyed.

" You are brave, Monsieur d'Artagnan," continued his Eminence ; " you are prudent, which is still better. I like men of head and heart. Don't be afraid," said he, smiling ; " by men of heart I mean men of courage. But though you are young and have hardly entered on life, you have powerful enemies ; if you do not take heed, they will destroy you ! "

" Alas, monseigneur ! " replied the young man, " very easily, no doubt ; for they are strong and well supported, while I am alone."

" Yes, that's true. But alone as you are, you have already done much, and will do still more, I doubt not. And yet you need, I believe, to be guided in the adventurous career you have chosen, for, if I mistake not, you came to Paris with the ambitious idea of making your fortune."

"I am at the age of extravagant hopes, monseigneur," said D'Artagnan.

"There are no extravagant hopes save for fools, sir, and you are a man of brains. Now, what would you say to an ensign's commission in my guards, and a company after the campaign ?"

"Ah, monseigneur !"

"You accept, do you not ?"

"Monseigneur," replied D'Artagnan, with an embarrassed air.

"What ! do you decline ?" cried the cardinal, in astonishment.

"I am in his Majesty's guards, monseigneur, and I have no reason to be dissatisfied."

"But it seems to me that my guards are also his Majesty's guards, and whoever serves in a French corps serves the king."

"Monseigneur, your Eminence has misunderstood my words."

"You want a pretext, do you not ? I understand. Well, a pretext you have : advancement, the opening campaign, the opportunity which I offer you—so much for the world. As regards yourself, the need of certain protection ; for it is well for you to know, Monsieur d'Artagnan, that I have received serious complaints against you. You do not consecrate your days and nights to the king's service alone."

D'Artagnan coloured.

"In fact," said the cardinal, laying his hand on a pile of papers, "I have here a whole bundle concerning you ; but before reading them I wanted to talk with you. I know you are a man of resolution, and your services, well directed, instead of leading you to misfortune, might bring you great advantage. Come, reflect and decide."

"Your goodness confounds me, monseigneur," replied D'Artagnan, "and I recognize in your Eminence a generosity that makes me mean as an earthworm ; but since monseigneur permits me to speak freely——"

D'Artagnan paused.

"Yes ; speak."

"Then I will tell your Eminence that all my friends are in the king's musketeers and guards, and, by an inconceivable fatality, all my enemies are in your Eminence's service. I should, therefore, be ill received here and ill regarded there if I accepted what monseigneur offers me."

"Do you possibly conceive the proud idea that I do not offer you a place equal to your merit, sir?" asked the cardinal, with a disdainful smile.

"Monseigneur, your Eminence is a hundred times too good to me; on the contrary, I think I have not yet proved myself worthy of your goodness. The siege of Rochelle is about to begin, monseigneur. I shall serve under your Eminence's eye, and if I have the good fortune to conduct myself at this siege in such a manner as to attract your attention, well and good. Then I shall at least have behind me some brilliant action to justify the protection with which you deign to honour me. Everything must have its own time, monseigneur. Hereafter, perhaps, I shall have the right of giving myself; at present, I should appear to be selling myself."

"That is to say, you refuse to serve me, sir," said the cardinal in a tone of vexation, through which, however, a sort of esteem manifested itself. "Remain free, then, and preserve your hatreds and your sympathies."

"Monseigneur——"

"Well, well!" said the cardinal, "I am not angry with you, but you are aware it is enough to defend and reward our friends; we owe nothing to our enemies. And yet I will give you a piece of advice: take good care of yourself, Monsieur d'Artagnan, for from the moment I withdraw my hand from you I would not give an obole for your life."

"I will try to do so, monseigneur," replied the Gascon, with a noble confidence.

"Remember by-and-by, at some moment when mischance may happen to you," said Richelieu pointedly, "that I came to seek you, and that I did all in my power to prevent this misfortune befalling you."

"Whatever may happen," said D'Artagnan, placing his hand on his heart and bowing, "I shall entertain an eternal gratitude toward your Eminence for what you are now doing for me."

"Well, let it be, then, as you have said, Monsieur d'Artagnan; we shall meet again after the campaign. I will have my eye on you, for I shall be there," replied the cardinal, pointing with his finger to a magnificent suit of armour he was to wear; "and on our return—well, we will settle our account!"

"Ah, monseigneur!" cried D'Artagnan, "spare me the

weight of your disfavour; remain neutral, monseigneur, if you find that I act as a gentleman ought to act."

"Young man," said Richelieu, "if I am able once again to say to you what I have said to you to-day, I promise you to do so."

This last expression of Richelieu's conveyed a terrible doubt; it alarmed D'Artagnan more than a threat would have done, for it was a warning. The cardinal, then, was trying to preserve him from some threatened misfortune. He opened his mouth to reply, but with a gesture the cardinal dismissed him.

D'Artagnan went out, but at the door his heart almost failed him, and he was on the point of going back. But Athos's noble, stern face recurred to him; if he made with the cardinal the proposed compact, Athos would no longer give him his hand—Athos would renounce him.

This was the fear that restrained him. Thus powerful is the influence of a truly great character on all its surroundings.

D'Artagnan descended by the same staircase at which he had entered, and found Athos and the four musketeers waiting for him at the gate, and beginning to grow uneasy. With a word D'Artagnan reassured them, and Planchet ran to inform the other sentinels that it was needless to keep guard longer, as his master had come out safe and sound from the Palais-Cardinal.

When they reached Athos's residence, Aramis and Porthos inquired as to the cause of this strange interview; but D'Artagnan confined himself to telling them that Richelieu had sent for him to propose to him to enter his guards with the rank of ensign, and that he had refused.

"And you were right," cried Aramis and Porthos, with one voice.

Athos fell into a deep reverie and made no remark. But when they were alone,—

"You have done your duty, D'Artagnan," said Athos; "but yet perhaps you have done wrong."

D'Artagnan sighed deeply, for this voice responded to a secret voice of his soul, which told him that great misfortunes were awaiting him.

The whole of the next day was spent in preparations for departure. D'Artagnan went to take leave of M. de Tréville. At that time it was still believed that the separation of the musketeers and the guards would be only temporary, as the king was holding his parliament that very day, and proposed to set out the day after. M. de Tréville contented himself with asking D'Artagnan if he could do anything for him, but D'Artagnan answered that he was supplied with all he wanted.

That night all the comrades of the company of M. des Essarts's guards and of the company of M. de Tréville's musketeers who had struck up a mutual friendship came together. They were parting to meet again when it should please God, and if it should please God. The night, therefore, was a somewhat riotous one, as may be imagined, for in such cases extreme preoccupation can be combated only by extreme carelessness.

At the first sound of the morning trumpet the friends separated, the musketeers hastening to M. de Tréville's hôtel, the guards to M. des Essarts's. Each of the captains then led his company to the Louvre, where the king reviewed them.

The king was dull and appeared ill, which detracted somewhat from his lofty bearing. In fact, the evening before, a fever had seized him in the midst of parliament, while he was holding his Bed of Justice. He had nevertheless decided on setting out that same evening; and in spite of all remonstrances he persisted in holding the review, hoping, by a vigorous effort at first, to conquer the disease which was beginning to lay hold of him.

The review over, the guards set forward alone on their march, the musketeers waiting for the king. This allowed Porthos time to go and take a turn in his superb equipment in the Rue aux Ours.

The solicitor's wife saw him pass in his new uniform and on his fine horse. She loved Porthos too dearly to allow him to depart thus: she made him a sign to dismount and come to her. Porthos was magnificent: his spurs jingled, his cuirass glittered, his sword knocked proudly against his leg. This time the clerks had no desire to laugh, such an ear-clipper did Porthos appear.

The musketeer was brought into the presence of Master Coquenard, whose little gray eye sparkled with anger at seeing his cousin all blazing new. Nevertheless, one thing afforded him inward consolation: it was expected by every one that the campaign would be severe; he hoped quietly in the bottom of his heart that Porthos might be killed in the course of it.

Porthos paid his compliments to Master Coquenard, and bade him farewell. Master Coquenard wished him all sorts of prosperities. Madame Coquenard could not restrain her tears, but no evil conclusions were deducible from her grief; she was known to be much attached to her relatives, about whom she was constantly having bitter quarrels with her husband.

But the real adieus were made in Madame Coquenard's chamber; they were heartrending.

As long as the *procureuse* could follow her lover with her eyes, she waved her handkerchief, leaning so far out of the window as to lead people to believe she was about to throw herself out. Porthos received all these marks of friendship like a man accustomed to such demonstrations. Only as he turned the corner of the street he lifted his hat and waved it to her as a sign of adieu.

On his part, Aramis wrote a long letter. To whom? No one knew. Kitty, who was to set out that evening for Tours, was waiting in the next chamber, where she had found refuge.

Athos sipped the last bottle of his Spanish wine.

Meantime, D'Artagnan was marching off with his company. On arriving at the Faubourg St. Antoine, he turned round to look gaily at the Bastille; but as he looked at the Bastille alone he did not observe milady, who, mounted upon a light bay horse, was pointing him out to two ill-looking men who immediately came close up to the ranks to take notice of him. To a questioning look milady signified that it was he. Then, certain that there could no longer be any mistake in the execution of her orders, she gave spurs to her horse and disappeared.

The two men then followed the company, and on leaving the Faubourg St. Antoine mounted two horses properly equipped, which a servant out of livery was holding in expectation of their coming.

CHAPTER XLI.

THE SIEGE OF ROCHELLE.

THE siege of Rochelle was one of the great political events of Louis XIII.'s reign, and one of the cardinal's great military enterprises. It is therefore interesting and even necessary that we should say a few words about it; moreover, many details of this siege are connected in too important a manner with the story we have undertaken to relate to allow us to pass it over in silence.

The cardinal's political views when he undertook this siege were considerable. Let us unfold them first, and then we will pass on to his private views, which, perhaps, had not less influence on his Eminence than the former.

Of the important cities given up by Henry IV. to the Huguenots as places of safety there remained only Rochelle. It became necessary, therefore, to destroy this last bulwark of Calvinism—a dangerous leaven, with which the ferments of civil revolt and foreign war were constantly mingling.

Spaniards, English and Italian malcontents, adventurers of all nations, soldiers of fortune of every sect, flocked at the first summons to the standard of the Protestants, and organized themselves, as it were, into a vast association, the various branches of which spread at leisure over all parts of Europe.

Rochelle, which had derived a new importance from the ruin of the other Calvinist cities, was then the focus of dissensions and ambitions. Moreover, its port was the last gateway in the kingdom of France open to the English, and by closing it against England, our eternal enemy, the cardinal completed the work of Joan of Arc and the Duc de Guise.

Thus Bassompierre, who was at once a Protestant and a Catholic—a Protestant by conviction and a Catholic as commander of the order of the Holy Ghost ; Bassompierre, who was a German by birth and a Frenchman at heart ; in short, Bassompierre, who had an especial command at the siege of Rochelle—said, as he charged at the head of several other Protestant nobles like himself,—

" You will see, gentlemen, that we shall be fools enough to take Rochelle.''

And Bassompierre was right : the cannonade of the Isle of Ré presaged to him the dragonnades of the Cévennes ; the taking of Rochelle was the preface to the revocation of the Edict of Nantes.

But as we have hinted, by the side of these views of the minister, which belong to history, the chronicler is forced to recognize the petty aims of the lover and the jealous rival.

Richelieu, as every one knows, had been in love with the queen. Was this love a purely political affair, or was it naturally one of those deep passions which Anne of Austria inspired in those who approached her ? We cannot tell. But at all events we have seen, by the preceding developments of this story, that Buckingham had got the advantage over him, and in two or three circumstances, particularly in the affair of the diamond studs, had, thanks to the three musketeers' devotion and D'Artagnan's courage, cruelly cheated him.

Richelieu's object was therefore not only to rid France of an enemy, but to avenge himself on a rival. Moreover, this vengeance was to be great and brilliant, and worthy in every way of a man who holds in his hand the forces of a whole kingdom.

Richelieu knew that in fighting England he was fighting Buckingham; that in triumphing over England he would triumph over Buckingham; in short, that in humiliating England in the eyes of Europe he humiliated Buckingham in the eyes of the queen.

On his side, Buckingham, while pretending to maintain the honour of England, was moved by interests exactly similar to the cardinal's. Buckingham, also, was pursuing a private vengeance. Under no pretext had Buckingham been able to enter France as an ambassador: he wished to enter it as a conqueror.

The result was that the real stake of this game, which two most powerful kingdoms were playing for the good pleasure of two men in love, was simply a look from Anne of Austria.

The first advantage had been gained by the Duke of Buckingham. Arriving unexpectedly in sight of the Isle of Ré, with ninety vessels and nearly twenty thousand men, he had surprised the Comte de Toirac, who commanded for the king in the island. He had, after a sanguinary conflict, effected his landing.

Let us observe, by the way, that in this fight perished the Baron de Chantal. The Baron de Chantal left a little orphan daughter of eighteen months. This little girl was afterwards Madame de Sévigné.

The Comte de Toirac withdrew into the citadel of St. Martin with his garrison, and threw a hundred men into a little fort called the fort of La Prée.

This event had hastened the cardinal's resolutions, and until the king and he could come to take the command of the siege of Rochelle, which was determined on, he had sent Monsieur to direct the first operations, and had ordered all the troops he could dispose of to march toward the scene of war. Our friend D'Artagnan belonged to this detachment, sent as a vanguard.

The king, as we have said, was to follow as soon as his Bed

of Justice was held. But on rising from his Bed of Justice on the 28th of June, he felt himself attacked by fever. He was, notwithstanding, anxious to set out; but his illness becoming more serious, he was obliged to stop at Villeroi.

Now, whenever the king stopped the musketeers stopped. The consequence was that D'Artagnan, who was still in the guards, found himself, for the time at least, separated from his good friends Athos, Aramis, and Porthos. This separation, which was only an unpleasant circumstance for him, would surely have become a cause of serious anxiety if he could have guessed by what unknown dangers he was surrounded.

He arrived, however, without accident in the camp established before Rochelle toward the 10th of September, 1627.

Everything was unchanged. The Duke of Buckingham and his English, masters of the Isle of Ré, were still besieging, but unsuccessfully, the citadel of St. Martin and the fort of La Prée; and hostilities with Rochelle had begun, two or three days before, about a fort which the Duc d'Angoulême had just built near the city.

The guards, under M. des Essarts's command, took up their quarters at the Minimes.

But, as we know, D'Artagnan, preoccupied by the ambition of passing into the musketeers, had formed but few friendships among his comrades. He found himself isolated, and given over to his own reflections. His reflections were not cheerful. During the time he had been in Paris, by mixing in public affairs, he, a puny creature, had made a great enemy of the cardinal, before whom the most powerful grandees of the kingdom, even the king himself, trembled. That man had the power to crush him, and yet he had not done it. For a mind so quick as D'Artagnan's, this indulgence was a light by which he caught a glimpse of a better future.

And then he had made another enemy—not so much to be feared, he thought, but nevertheless he instinctively felt not to be despised: the enemy was milady.

True, he had acquired the queen's protection and good-will; but the queen's good-will was, just then, an additional cause of persecution, and her protection, we know, was a very poor one, as instanced in Chalais and Madame Bonacieux.

The most certain thing he had clearly gained in all this was the diamond, worth five or six thousand livres, which he wore on his finger; and even this diamond—supposing that D'Artagnan, in his ambitious projects, wished to keep it, to make it some day a reminder of the queen's gratitude—had not, in the meanwhile, since he could not part with it, more value than the pebbles he trod under his feet. We say than the pebbles he trod under his feet, for D'Artagnan made these reflections while walking alone along a pretty little road leading from the camp to the village of Angoutin. Now, these reflections had led him farther than he intended, and the day was beginning to decline, when, in the last ray of the setting sun, he thought he saw a musket-barrel glittering behind a hedge.

D'Artagnan had a quick eye and ready wit. He realized that the musket had not come there of itself, and that he who carried it had not concealed himself behind a hedge with any friendly intentions. He determined, therefore, to direct his course as far away from it as he could, when, behind a rock on the opposite side of the road, he perceived the muzzle of another musket-barrel.

It was evidently an ambuscade.

The young man cast a glance at the first musket, and with a certain degree of anxiety saw that it was levelled in his direction; but as soon as he perceived that the mouth of the barrel was motionless, he threw himself flat on the ground. At the same instant the gun was fired, and he heard a ball whistle over his head.

No time was to be lost. D'Artagnan sprang up with a bound, and at the same instant the ball from the other musket tore up the stones on the very place on the road where he had thrown himself face to the ground.

D'Artagnan was not one of those uselessly brave men who seek a ridiculous death, in order that it may be said of them that they did not give way a single step; besides, courage was out of the question now: he had fallen into a trap.

"Should there be a third shot," said he to himself, "I am a lost man."

And immediately taking to his heels, he ran toward the camp, with the swiftness of the young men of his country, so renowned for their agility; but great as was his speed, the one who had first fired, having had time to reload, fired a second shot, so well aimed this time that the bullet struck his hat and carried it ten paces from him.

However, as D'Artagnan had no other hat, he picked up this as he ran, and arrived at his quarters, very pale and quite out of breath. He sat down without saying a word to anybody, and began to reflect.

This event might have three causes.

The first and the most natural—it might be an ambuscade of the Rochellais, who would not be sorry to kill one of his Majesty's guards, first because there would be one enemy less, and then because this enemy might have a well-furnished purse in his pocket.

D'Artagnan took his hat, examined the hole made by the bullet, and shook his head. The ball was not a musket-ball; it was an arquebuse-ball. The accuracy of the aim had first given him the idea that a particular kind of weapon had been employed. It could not, then, be a military ambuscade, as the ball was not of the regulation calibre.

It might be a kind remembrance of the cardinal's. We remember that at the very moment when, owing to the blessed ray of the sun, he perceived the gun-barrel, he was thinking with astonishment on his Eminence's forbearance toward him.

But D'Artagnan shook his head. For people against whom he had only to stretch out his hand, his Eminence had rarely recourse to such means.

It might be a vengeance of milady's.

That was the most probable.

He vainly tried to remember the faces or dress of the assassins; he had run away so swiftly that he had not had leisure to notice anything.

"Ah, my poor friends!" murmured D'Artagnan, "where are you? How sadly I need you!"

D'Artagnan passed a very bad night. Three or four times he started up, imagining that a man was approaching his bed to stab him. Nevertheless, day dawned without the darkness bringing any event.

But D'Artagnan realized that what was deferred was not lost. He remained all day in his quarters, assigning as a reason to himself that the weather was bad.

At nine o'clock the next morning the drums beat the salute. The Duc d'Orléans was inspecting the posts. The guards ran to their arms, and D'Artagnan took his place in the midst of his comrades.

Monsieur passed along the front of the line. Then all the superior officers approached him to pay him their compliments, M. des Essarts, captain of the guards, among the rest.

At the end of a moment D'Artagnan imagined that M. des

Essarts made him a sign to come to him. He waited for a fresh gesture on the part of his superior, for fear he might be mistaken; but when this gesture was repeated, he left the ranks, and advanced to receive his orders.

"Monsieur is about to ask for some gallant men for a dangerous mission, but one that will do honour to those who shall accomplish it, and I made you a sign in order that you might hold yourself in readiness."

"Thank you, captain," replied D'Artagnan, who desired nothing more than to distinguish himself in the lieutenant-general's eyes.

It seems the Rochellais had made a sortie during the night, and had retaken a bastion which the royal army had gained possession of two days before; the point was to ascertain, by reconnoitring, how the enemy guarded this bastion.

In fact, at the end of a few minutes, Monsieur raised his voice and said,—

"I want for this mission three or four volunteers, led by a trusty man."

"As to the trusty man, I have him at hand, monseigneur," said M. des Essarts, pointing to D'Artagnan; "and as to the four or five volunteers, monseigneur has but to make his intentions known, and the men will not be wanting."

"Four gallant men who will risk being killed with me!" said D'Artagnan, raising his sword.

Two of his comrades of the guards immediately sprang forward, and two soldiers having joined them, the number was deemed sufficient; so D'Artagnan declined all others, as he was unwilling to injure the chances of those who came forward first.

It was not known whether, after taking the bastion, the Rochellais had evacuated it or left a garrison in it; so the object was to examine the place near enough to ascertain.

D'Artagnan set out with his four companions, and followed the trench. The two guardsmen marched abreast with him, and the two soldiers followed behind.

Screened by the revetment, they came within a hundred paces of the bastion. There, on turning round, D'Artagnan perceived that the two soldiers had disappeared.

He thought that they had stayed behind from fear, and so he continued to advance.

At the turning of the counterscarp they found themselves within about sixty paces of the bastion.

No one was to be seen, and the bastion seemed abandoned. The three men of the forlorn hope were deliberating whether to proceed any farther, when suddenly a circle of smoke enveloped the stone giant, and a dozen balls came whistling round D'Artagnan and his two companions.

They knew what they wanted to know : the bastion was guarded. A longer stay in this dangerous spot would therefore have been uselessly imprudent. D'Artagnan and his two companions turned their backs, and beat a retreat like a flight.

On arriving at the angle of the trench which was to serve them as a rampart, one of the guardsmen fell ; a ball had passed through his breast. The other, who was safe and sound, kept on his way to camp.

D'Artagnan was not willing to abandon his companion thus, and stooped down to raise him and assist him in regaining the lines. But at this moment two shots were fired. One ball hit the head of the already wounded guardsman, and the other flattened itself against a rock, after passing within two inches of D'Artagnan.

The young man turned quickly round, for this attack could not come from the bastion, which was masked by the angle of the trench. The idea of the two soldiers who had abandoned him occurred to his mind, and reminded him of the assassins of two evenings before. So he resolved this time to satisfy himself on this point, and fell on his comrade's body as though he were dead.

He instantly saw two heads appearing above an abandoned work, within thirty paces of him ; they were the heads of his two soldiers. D'Artagnan had not been mistaken : these two men had followed him only for the purpose of assassinating him, expecting that the young man's death would be placed to the enemy's account.

But as he might be merely wounded and might accuse them of their crime, they came up to him with the purpose of making sure of him. Fortunately, deceived by D'Artagnan's trick, they neglected to reload their guns.

When they were within ten paces of him, D'Artagnan, who in falling had taken great care not to let go his sword, suddenly got up, and with one leap came upon them.

The assassins realized that if they fled toward the camp without killing their man they should be accused by him ; therefore their first idea was to desert to the enemy. One of them took his gun by the barrel, and used it as he would a club. He aimed a terrible blow at D'Artagnan, who dodged it by springing on one side ; but by this movement he left free passage to the bandit, who at once darted off toward the bastion. As the Rochellais who guarded the bastion were ignorant of the intentions of the man they saw coming toward them, they fired at him, and he fell, struck by a ball which broke his shoulder.

Meantime D'Artagnan had thrown himself on the other soldier, attacking him with his sword. The struggle was not long. The wretch had nothing to defend himself with but his discharged arquebuse. The guardsman's sword slipped down the barrel of the now useless weapon, and pierced the thigh of the assassin, who fell.

D'Artagnan immediately placed the point of the weapon at his throat.

" Oh, do not kill me ! " cried the bandit. " Pardon, pardon, officer, and I will tell you all ! "

" Is your secret important enough for me to spare your life, I wonder ? " asked the young man, withholding his arm.

" Yes ; if you think existence worth anything to a man of twenty-two, as you are, and who have everything to hope for, being handsome and brave, as you are."

" Wretch," cried D'Artagnan, " see here, speak quickly ! Who employed you to assassinate me ? "

" A woman whom I don't know, but who is called milady."

" But if you don't know this woman, how do you know her name ? "

" My comrade knew her and called her so. She made the bargain with him, and not with me ; he has even now in his pocket a letter from that person, which must be of great importance to you, judging by what I have heard."

" But how are you concerned in this ambuscade ? "

" He proposed to me to undertake it with him, and I agreed."

" And how much did she give you for this fine enterprise ? "

" A hundred louis."

" Well, good enough ! " said the young man, laughing ; " she thinks I am worth something. A hundred louis ! Well, that was a temptation for two miserable creatures like you. So I understand you accepted, and I grant you my pardon, but on one condition."

" What is that ? " said the soldier, uneasy at perceiving that all was not over.

" That you go and fetch me the letter your comrade has in his pocket."

" Why," cried the bandit, " that is only another way of killing me. How can you wish me to go and fetch that letter under the fire from the bastion ? "

"Nevertheless you must make up your mind to go and fetch it, or I swear you shall die by my hand."

"Pardon, sir; have pity on me! In the name of the young lady you love, and who you perhaps think is dead, but is not!" cried the bandit, throwing himself on his knees and leaning on his hand, for he began to lose his strength with his blood.

"And how do you know there is a young woman whom I love, or that I thought that woman dead?" asked D'Artagnan.

"By the letter which my comrade has in his pocket."

"You see, then," said D'Artagnan, "that I must have that letter. So no more delay, no more hesitation, or else, whatever may be my repugnance to soiling my sword a second time with the blood of a wretch like you, I swear on the faith of an honourable man——"

And at these words D'Artagnan made such a threatening gesture that the wounded man sprang up.

"Stop, stop!" cried he, regaining courage from his very terror; "I will go—I will go!"

D'Artagnan took the soldier's arquebuse, made him go on before him, and drove him toward his companion by pricking him behind with his sword.

It was a frightful thing to see this unfortunate being, leaving a long track of blood on the ground he passed over, pale with approaching death, trying to drag himself along, without being seen, to his accomplice's body, which lay at twenty paces from him.

Terror was so strongly painted on his face, covered with a cold sweat, that D'Artagnan took pity on him, and casting on him a look of contempt,—

"Well," said he, "I will show you the difference between a man of true courage and a coward, as you are. Stay, I will go."

And with a light step, an eye on the watch, observing the movements of the enemy and taking advantage of all the aid afforded by the nature of the ground, D'Artagnan succeeded in reaching the second soldier.

There were two means of attaining his object—to search him on the spot, or to carry him away, making a buckler of his body, and then search him in the trench.

D'Artagnan preferred the second means, and lifted the assassin on his shoulders at the very moment the enemy fired.

A slight shock, the dull thud of three balls penetrating the flesh, a last cry, a convulsion of agony, proved to D'Artagnan that the man who had just tried to assassinate him had saved his life.

D'Artagnan regained the trench, and threw the body down by the wounded man, who was as pale as death.

He instantly began the search. A leather pocket-book, a purse in which was evidently a part of the sum which the bandit had received, a dice-box and dice, formed the dead man's heritage.

He left the box and dice where they fell, flung the purse to the wounded man, and eagerly opened the pocket-book.

Among some unimportant papers he found the following letter, the one which he had gone to get at the risk of his life :—

" Since you have lost track of that woman, and she is now in safety in the convent, which you should never have allowed her to reach, try, at least, not to miss the man. If you do, you know that my hand reaches far, and that you shall repay me very dearly the hundred louis you have had of me."

No signature. Nevertheless it was plain the letter came from milady. He consequently kept it as a piece of evidence, and as he was in safety behind the angle of the trench, he began to question the wounded man. He confessed that he had undertaken, with his comrade, the man just killed, to abduct a young woman about to leave Paris by the gate of La Villette ; but having stopped to drink at a saloon, they had missed the carriage by ten minutes.

" But what were you to have done with the woman ? " asked D'Artagnan, in great agitation.

" We were to have conveyed her to a hôtel in the Place Royale," said the wounded man.

" Yes, yes," murmured D'Artagnan ; " that's the place—milady's own residence."

Then the young man, shuddering, felt what a terrible thirst of vengeance impelled this woman to destroy him, as well as those who loved him, and how well acquainted she must be with affairs of the court, since she had discovered everything. Doubtless she owed this information to the cardinal.

But he also perceived, with a feeling of genuine joy, that the queen must have at last discovered the prison in which poor Madame Bonacieux was expiating her devotion, and that she had freed her from that prison. And the letter he had received from the young woman, and her passing along the Chaillot road like an apparition, were now explained.

Hereafter, as Athos had predicted, it was possible that he should find Madame Bonacieux, and a convent was not impregnable.

This idea completely restored clemency to his heart. He turned to the wounded man, who had watched with intense anxiety all the varying expressions of his countenance, and holding out his arm to him,—

"Come," said he ; "I will not abandon you thus. Lean upon me, and let us return to camp."

"Yes," said the man, who could scarcely believe in such magnanimity ; "but is it not to have me hanged ?"

"You have my word," said he. "For the second time I give you your life."

The wounded man sank upon his knees, and again kissed his preserver's feet ; but D'Artagnan, who no longer had a motive for staying so near the enemy, cut short the evidences of his gratitude.

The guardsman who had returned at the first discharge had announced the death of his four companions. There was therefore much astonishment and delight in the regiment when the young man was seen to come back safe and sound.

D'Artagnan explained the sword-wound of his companion by a sortie which he improvised. He told of the other soldier's death and the perils they had encountered. This recital was for him the occasion of a veritable triumph. The whole army talked of this expedition for a day, and Monsieur sent him his compliments on it.

Moreover, as every great action brings its own recompense, D'Artagnan's resulted in the restoration of the tranquillity he had lost. In fact, D'Artagnan believed that he might indulge in a little tranquillity since one of his two enemies was killed, and the other devoted to his interests.

This tranquillity proved one thing, which was, that D'Artagnan did not yet know milady.

CHAPTER XLII.

THE ANJOU WINE.

AFTER almost hopeless news of the king's health, the report of his convalescence began to prevail in the camp ; and as he was very anxious to be at the siege in person, it was said that as soon as he could mount on horseback he would set forward.

Meantime Monsieur, who knew that from one day to another he might be superseded in his command by the Duc d'Angoulême, or Bassompierre, or Schomberg, who were all eager for the post, did but little, wasted his time in idle experiments, and dared not risk any great enterprise to drive the English from the Isle of Ré, where they still besieged the citadel of St. Martin and the fort of La Prée, while on their side the French were besieging Rochelle.

D'Artagnan, as we have said, had become more tranquil. He felt only one uneasiness, and that was at not hearing from his three friends.

But one morning early in November everything was explained to him by this letter, dated from Villeroi :—

"MONSIEUR D'ARTAGNAN,—MM. Athos, Porthos, and Aramis, after giving an entertainment at my house, and having a very gay time, created such a disturbance that the provost of the castle, a very rigid man, has had them confined for some days ; but I fulfil the order they have given me by forwarding to you a dozen bottles of my Anjou wine, with which they are much taken. They are desirous that you should drink to their health in their favourite wine. I have done so, and am, sir, with great respect, your very humble and obedient servant,

"GODEAU, Steward of the Musketeers."

"That's good !" cried D'Artagnan ; "they think of me in their pleasures, as I thought of them in my troubles. Well, I will certainly drink to their health with all my heart, but I will not drink alone."

And D'Artagnan went after two guardsmen with whom he had formed greater intimacy than with the others, to invite them to drink with him this delicious Anjou wine which had just been sent him from Villeroi.

One of the two guardsmen was engaged that evening, and the other for the next. So the meeting was fixed for the day after that.

D'Artagnan, on his return, sent the twelve bottles of wine to the messroom of the guards, enjoining that great care be taken of it. Then at nine in the morning of the day appointed, as the dinner was fixed for twelve o'clock, D'Artagnan sent Planchet to assist in making the preparations.

Planchet, very proud of being raised to the dignity of

butler, thought he would get everything ready, like an intelligent man; and with this object in mind called in the assistance of the lackey of one of his master's guests, named Fourreau, and the sham soldier who had tried to kill D'Artagnan, and who, belonging to no corps, had been in D'Artagnan's service, or rather Planchet's, ever since D'Artagnan had saved his life.

The hour of the banquet having come, the two guests arrived, took their places, and the dishes were served on the table. Planchet waited, towel on arm; Fourreau uncorked the bottles; and Brisemont, as the convalescent was named, carefully poured into glass decanters the wine, which seemed to be rather muddy after the joltings of the journey. As the first bottle of this wine was a little thick at the bottom, Brisemont poured the dregs into a glass, and D'Artagnan allowed him to drink it, for the poor devil had not as yet much strength.

The guests, after having eaten their soup, were on the point of touching the first glass of wine to their lips, when suddenly the cannon roared from Fort Louis and Fort Neuf. Instantly the guardsmen, imagining this to be caused by some unexpected attack, either of the besieged or the English, sprang to their swords. D'Artagnan, not less eager than they, did the same, and all three ran out, in order to repair to their posts.

But scarcely were they out of the messroom when they learned the cause of the noise. Cries of "Hurrah for the king! hurrah for the cardinal!" were resounding on every side, and drums were beating in all directions.

In fact, the king, impatient, as we have said he was, had made forced marches, and had just arrived with all his household and a reinforcement of ten thousand troops. His musketeers rode in front of him and behind him. D'Artagnan, standing with his company drawn up in line, saluted with an expressive gesture his friends, whom he followed with his eyes, and M. de Tréville, who instantly recognized him.

The ceremony of reception over, the four friends were soon in one another's arms.

"By Jove!" cried D'Artagnan, "you could not have arrived more opportunely; the dinner cannot have had time to cool.—Can it, gentlemen?" added the young man, turning to the two guardsmen, whom he introduced to his friends.

"Ah, ha!" said Porthos, "so it seems we were feasting!"

"I hope," said Aramis, "there are no women at your dinner-party."

"Is there any drinkable wine in your shanty?" asked Athos.

"Well, by Jove! there is your own, my dear friend," replied D'Artagnan.

"Our wine!" exclaimed Athos in astonishment.

"Yes, the wine you sent me."

"We sent you wine?"

"Yes; you know what I mean—the wine from the slopes of Anjou."

"Yes, I know very well the wine you mean."

"The wine you prefer."

"Doubtless, when I can get neither champagne nor chambertin."

"Well, in the absence of champagne and chambertin, you must be satisfied with this."

"And so, connoisseurs as we are, we have had some Anjou wine sent us, have we?" exclaimed Porthos.

"No; it is the wine that was sent me with your compliments."

"With our compliments?" exclaimed the three musketeers.

"Did you send this wine, Aramis?" said Athos.

"No; and you, Porthos?"

"No; and you, Athos?"

"No!"

"Well, but if it was not you, it was your steward," said D'Artagnan.

"Our steward!"

"Yes, your steward—Godeau, the steward of the musketeers."

"'Pon my word! never mind where it comes from," said Porthos; "let us taste it, and if it is good, let us drink it."

"No," said Athos; "don't drink wine which comes from an unknown source."

"You are right, Athos," said D'Artagnan. "Did none of you order Godeau to send me wine?"

"No; and yet you say he has sent you some with our compliments?"

"Here is his letter," said D'Artagnan, and he exhibited the note to his comrades.

"That is not his writing!" said Athos; "I know it. Before we left Villeroi I settled the accounts of our crowd."

"It is a forged letter," said Porthos. "We have not been under arrest."

"D'Artagnan," said Aramis in a reproachful tone, "how could you believe that we had made a disturbance?"

D'Artagnan grew pale, and a convulsive trembling shook all his limbs.

"Thou alarmest me!" said Athos, who never used *thee* and *thou* but upon very particular occasions. "What has happened?"

"Hasten! hasten, friends!" cried D'Artagnan; "a horrible suspicion crosses my mind! Can this be another vengeance on that woman's part?"

Athos now turned pale.

D'Artagnan rushed towards the messroom, the three musketeers and the two guards following him.

The first object that met D'Artagnan's eyes on entering the dining-room was Brisemont stretched on the ground and rolling in horrible convulsions.

Planchet and Fourreau, pale as death, were trying to aid him; but it was plain that all assistance was useless—all the features of the dying man were distorted with the death struggle.

"Ah!" cried he, perceiving D'Artagnan—"ah! it is frightful! You pretend to pardon me, and you poison me!"

"I," cried D'Artagnan—"I, wretched man! What do you mean?"

"I say that you gave me the wine; I say that you told me to drink it; I say you wished to avenge yourself on me, and I say that it is horrible!"

"Do not think so, Brisemont," said D'Artagnan, "do not think so. I swear to you—I protest——"

"Oh, but God is above! God will punish you!—My God, grant that he may one day suffer what I suffer!"

"I swear to you on the Gospel," said D'Artagnan, throwing himself down by the dying man, "that I didn't know the wine was poisoned, and I was going to drink of it as you did."

"I do not believe you," cried the soldier.

And he expired under redoubled torments.

"Frightful! frightful!" murmured Athos, while Porthos broke the bottles and Aramis gave orders, a little too late, to send for a confessor.

"Oh, my friends," said D'Artagnan, "you come once more to save my life—not only mine, but the lives of these gentlemen.—Gentlemen," continued he, addressing the guardsmen, "I request you say nothing about this adventure. Great personages may have had a hand in what you have seen, and if talked about, the evil would only recoil on us."

"Ah, sir," stammered Planchet, more dead than alive—"ah, sir, what a narrow escape I have had!"

"How, sirrah! so you were going to drink my wine, were you?"

"To the king's health, sir; I was going to drink a small glass of it, if Fourreau had not told me some one was calling me."

"Alas!" said Fourreau, whose teeth chattered with terror, "I wanted to get him out of the way that I might have a drink by myself."

"Gentlemen," said D'Artagnan, addressing the guardsmen, "you will easily see that such a feast can only be very melancholy after what has just taken place; so I beg you to accept my excuses, and put off the party till another day."

The two guardsmen courteously accepted D'Artagnan's excuses, and perceiving that the four friends desired to be alone, they retired.

When the young guardsman and the three musketeers were without witnesses, they looked at each other with an air which plainly expressed that each of them realized the seriousness of the situation.

"In the first place," said Athos, "let us leave this room; a dead man, especially the victim of a violent death, is not agreeable company."

"Planchet," said D'Artagnan, "I commit this poor devil's body to your care. Let him be interred in holy ground. He committed a crime, it is true, but he repented of it."

And the four friends left the room. Planchet and Fourreau undertook the duty of paying the mortuary honours to Brisemont.

The manager gave them another room, and served them with boiled eggs, while Athos went himself to draw water at the spring. In a few words Porthos and Aramis were informed of all that had occurred.

"Well," said D'Artagnan to Athos, "you see, dear friend, that it is war to the death!"

Athos shook his head.

"The fact is, we cannot remain in this way, with a sword hanging eternally over our heads," said Athos; "we must get out of this position."

" But how ? "

" Listen ! Try to have an interview with her, and make an agreement with her. Say to her : ' Peace or war, my word of honour as a gentleman never to say anything of you, never to do anything against you ; on your part, a solemn oath to remain neutral with respect to me. If not, I will apply to the chancellor, I will apply to the king, I will apply to the hangman, I will move the courts against you, I will denounce you as branded, I will bring you to trial, and if you are acquitted—well, on the word of a gentleman, I will kill you, at the corner of some wall, as I would a mad dog.' "

" I like the scheme well enough," said D'Artagnan, " but how meet her ? "

" Time, dear friend, time brings opportunity ; opportunity is man's martingale. The more we venture, the more we gain, when we know how to wait."

" Yes, but to wait surrounded by assassins and poisoners."

" Bah ! " said Athos ; " God has preserved us hitherto ; God will preserve us still."

" Yes, He has. Besides, we are men ; and all things considered, it is our lot to risk our lives. But she——" added he in an undertone.

" She ? Who ? " asked Athos.

" Constance."

" Madame Bonacieux ! Ah, that's true ! " said Athos. " My poor friend, I had forgotten."

" Well," said Aramis, " but have you not learned by the letter you found on the dead assassin that she is in a convent ? One may be very comfortable in a convent ; and as soon as the siege of Rochelle is over, I promise you, as far as I am concerned——"

" It seems some time since he heard from his mistress," said Athos, in a low voice. " But take no notice of it ; we know what that means."

" Well," said Porthos, " it appears to me that there is a very simple way."

" What ? " asked D'Artagnan.

" You say she is in a convent ? " replied Porthos.

" Yes."

" Well, as soon as the siege is over, we'll carry her off from that convent."

" But we must find out what convent she is in."

" You are right," said Porthos.

" But I think I have it," said Athos. " Do you not

believe, D'Artagnan, that it is the queen who has selected the convent for her ? "

" At least I imagine so."

" In that case, Porthos will assist us."

" And how, please ? "

" Why, by your marchioness, your duchess, your princess ; she must have a long arm."

" Hush ! " said Porthos, placing his finger on his lips. " I believe she is of the cardinal's party. She must know nothing of the matter."

" Then," said Aramis, " I take upon myself to get news of her."

" You, Aramis ! " cried the three friends. " How ? "

" By the queen's almoner, with whom I am very intimately acquainted."

And with this assurance the four friends, having finished their modest repast, separated, promising to meet again that evening. D'Artagnan returned to the Minimes, and the three musketeers repaired to the king's quarters, where they had to prepare their lodging.

CHAPTER XLIII.

THE TAVERN OF THE RED DOVECOT.

MEANWHILE the king, who, though he had so recently arrived, was in such haste to face the enemy, and, with more reason than the cardinal, shared his hatred for Buckingham, desired every disposition to be made, first to drive the English from the Isle of Ré, and afterwards to press the siege of Rochelle. But in spite of himself, he was delayed by the dissensions which broke out between Bassompierre and Schomberg against the Duc d'Angoulême.

Bassompierre and Schomberg were marshals of France, and claimed their right to command the army under the king's orders ; but the cardinal, fearing that Bassompierre, who was Huguenot at heart, might but feebly press the English and Rochellais, his co-religionists, supported the Duc d'Angoulême, whom the king, at his instigation, had named lieutenant-general. The result was that, to avoid seeing Bassompierre and Schomberg desert the army, they had to give a separate command to each. Bassompierre took up his quarters to the north of the city between

La Leu and Dompierre ; the Duc d'Angoulême to the east,
between Dompierre and Perigny ; and M. de Schomberg
to the south, between Perigny and Angoutin.

Monsieur's headquarters were at Dompierre.

The king's headquarters were sometimes at Étré, sometimes at La Jarrie.

The cardinal's quarters were upon the downs, at the bridge
of La Pierre, in a simple house without any entrenchment.

Thus Monsieur watched Bassompierre ; the king, the Duc
d'Angoulême ; and the cardinal, M. de Schomberg.

As soon as this organization was effected, they set about
driving the English from the island.

The opportunity was favourable. The English, who
require, above everything, good living in order to be good
soldiers, having only salt meat and bad biscuit to eat, had
many sick men in their camp. Furthermore, the sea was
very rough at this period of the year on all the coasts of
the ocean, and every day wrecked some vessel or other,
and the shore from the point of L'Aiguillon to the trench
was, at every tide, literally covered with flotsam and
jetsam from pinnaces, row-barges, and feluccas. The
consequence was, that even if the king's troops should
remain quietly in camp, evidently some day or other
Buckingham, who only remained on the Isle of Ré out of
obstinacy, would be obliged to raise the siege.

But as M. de Toirac reported that everything in the
enemy's camp was getting ready for a fresh assault, the
king judged that it would be best to put an end to the
affair, and gave the necessary orders for a decisive action.

As it is not our intention to write a journal of the siege,
but, on the contrary, only to introduce such events of it
as are connected with the story we are telling, we will content ourselves with saying in a word or two that the expedition succeeded, to the king's great astonishment and the
cardinal's great glory. The English, driven back foot by
foot, beaten in every skirmish, and overwhelmed in the
passage of the Isle of Loix, were obliged to re-embark,
leaving on the battlefield two thousand men, among
whom were five colonels, three lieutenant-colonels, two
hundred and fifty captains, and twenty gentlemen of
rank, four pieces of cannon, and sixty colours, which were
taken to Paris by Claude de St. Simon, and suspended with
great pomp in the arches of Notre Dame.

Te Deums were sung in the camp, and afterwards
throughout France.

The cardinal was left free to carry on the siege without having, at least for the moment, anything to fear from the English.

An envoy of the Duke of Buckingham, named Montague, was taken, and proof was obtained of a league between the Empire, Spain, England, and Lorraine. This league was directed against France. Furthermore, in Buckingham's headquarters, which he had been forced to abandon more precipitately than he expected, papers were found confirming this league, and, as the cardinal asserts in his Memoirs, strongly compromising Madame de Chevreuse, and consequently the queen.

All the responsibility rested on the cardinal, for one cannot be a despotic minister without responsibility; therefore all the resources of his mighty genius were expended night and day engaged in listening to the slightest rumour heard in any of the great kingdoms of Europe.

The cardinal was acquainted with Buckingham's activity, and more particularly his hatred. If the league threatening France should triumph, all his influence would be lost. Spanish policy and Austrian policy would have their representatives in the cabinet of the Louvre, where they had only partisans as yet; he, Richelieu, the French minister, the really national minister, would be ruined. The king, who, while obeying him like a child, hated him as a child hates his master, would abandon him to the personal vengeance of Monsieur and the queen; so his ruin was perhaps the ruin of France. All this had to be guarded against.

So couriers, constantly growing more numerous, were seen succeeding one another, day and night, in the little house of the bridge of La Pierre, where the cardinal had established his residence.

These were monks wearing the frock with such an ill grace that it was easy to see they belonged especially to the church militant; women, rather awkward in their costume of pages, while their large breeches could not entirely conceal their rounded forms; and peasants with blackened hands but fine limbs, who smacked of the man of quality a league off. In addition to these there were less agreeable visitors, for two or three times it was bruited that the cardinal had narrowly escaped assassination.

True, the cardinal's enemies declared that it was he himself who set these bungling assassins to work, in order, if need were, to have the right of retaliation ; but what ministers say, or what their enemies say, is not to be believed.

The cardinal, to whom his most inveterate detractors have never denied personal bravery, was not prevented, however, from making excursions by night, sometimes to communicate to the Duc d'Angoulême important orders ; sometimes to go and confer with the king ; sometimes to have an interview with a messenger whom he did not wish to receive at his headquarters.

On their part, the musketeers, who had not much to do with the siege, were not under very strict orders, and led a jolly life. This was all the easier for them, and for our three companions in particular, because, as they were M. de Tréville's friends, they readily obtained from him special permission to remain outside after the closing of camp.

Now, one evening, when D'Artagnan, who was in the trenches, was not able to accompany them, Athos, Porthos, and Aramis, mounted on their war-horses, enveloped in their military cloaks, with their hands on their pistol-butts, were returning from an ale-house called the Red Dovecot, which Athos had discovered two days before on the road to La Jarrie. They were riding along on the road leading to the camp, and quite on their guard, as we have stated, for fear of an ambuscade, when, about a quarter of a league from the village of Boinar, they fancied they heard the trampling of horses approaching them. All three instantly halted, closed in, and waited, occupying the middle of the road. In an instant, just as the moon broke out from behind a cloud, they saw appear at a turn of the road two horsemen, who, on perceiving them, stopped in their turn, seemingly to deliberate whether they should continue their route or go back. Their hesitation aroused some suspicion in the three friends, and Athos, riding a few paces in advance of the others, cried in a firm voice,—

" Who goes there ? "

" Who goes there, yourselves ? " replied one of the two horsemen.

" That is not an answer," replied Athos. " Who goes there ? Answer, or else we charge."

" Beware of what you are doing, gentlemen ! " said a ringing voice, which appeared accustomed to command.

" It is some superior officer making his night rounds," said Athos. " What do you mean to do, gentlemen ? "

"Who are you?" said the same voice in the same commanding tone. "Answer in your turn, or you may repent of your disobedience."

"The king's musketeers," said Athos, more than ever convinced that he who questioned them had the right to do so.

"What company?"

"Tréville's."

"Advance, and account for what you are doing here at this time."

The three companions advanced rather humbly, for all three were now convinced that they had to do with some one more powerful than themselves, and leaving to Athos the post of spokesman.

One of the two horsemen, the one who had spoken second, was ten paces in advance of his companion. Athos signed to Porthos and Aramis to remain behind, and went forward alone.

"Your pardon, officer," said Athos; "but we were ignorant of whom we were speaking to, and you see we were keeping good guard."

"Your name?" demanded the officer, whose face was partly covered by his cloak.

"But yourself, sir," said Athos, who began to be annoyed by this inquisition—"I beg you to prove to me that you have the right to question me."

"Your name?" insisted the horseman, letting his cloak fall, and leaving his face uncovered.

"The cardinal!" cried the astonished musketeer.

"Your name?" cried his Eminence for the third time.

"Athos," said the musketeer.

The cardinal made a sign to his attendant, who drew near to him.

"These three musketeers shall follow us," said he in an undertone. "I do not wish it known I left the camp; and by following us we shall be certain they will tell no one."

"We are gentlemen, monseigneur," said Athos; "put us on our honour, and give yourself no uneasiness. Thank God, we can keep a secret."

The cardinal fixed his keen eyes on the bold speaker.

"You have a quick ear, Monsieur Athos," said the cardinal; "but now listen to this: it is not from mistrust that I ask you to follow me, but for my security. No doubt your companions are MM. Porthos and Aramis."

"Yes, your Eminence," said Athos, while the two musketeers who had remained behind advanced, hat in hand.

"I know you, gentlemen," said the cardinal, "I know you. I know you are not altogether my friends, and I am sorry for it ; but I know you are brave and loyal gentlemen, and that confidence may be reposed in you. Monsieur Athos, do me the honour of accompanying me, you and your two friends, and then I shall have an escort to excite envy in his Majesty, if we should meet him."

The three musketeers bowed to the necks of their horses.

"Well, on my honour," said Athos, "your Eminence is right in taking us with you ; we have seen ill-looking faces on the road, and we have even had a quarrel at the Red Dovecot with four of them."

"A quarrel ! and what for, gentlemen ? " asked the cardinal ; "you know I don't like quarrelsome persons."

"And that is why I have the honour to inform your Eminence of what has happened ; for you might learn it from others, and on a false report believe us to be in fault."

"And what was the result of your quarrel ? " demanded the cardinal, knitting his brow.

"My friend Aramis here received a slight sword-wound in his arm, but it will not prevent him, as your Eminence may see, from mounting to the assault to-morrow, if your Eminence orders an escalade."

"But you are not men to allow sword-wounds to be inflicted on you in this way," said the cardinal. "Come, be frank, gentlemen—you have given some in return ; confess —you know I have the right of giving absolution."

"Monseigneur," said Athos, "I did not even draw my sword, but I took the man who offended me round the body, and flung him out of the window. It seems that in falling," continued Athos, with some hesitation, "he broke his hip."

"Ah, ha ! " said the cardinal.—"And you, Monsieur Porthos ? "

"I, monseigneur, knowing that duelling is prohibited, I seized a bench, and gave one of these brigands a blow which I believe broke his shoulder."

"Very well ! " said the cardinal.—"And you, Monsieur Aramis ? "

"Monseigneur, as I am of a very mild disposition, and as I am likewise about to enter into orders (which monseigneur, perhaps, does not know), I was trying to appease my comrades, when one of these wretches treacherously gave me a sword-thrust through my left arm. Then my patience failed me ; I drew my sword in my turn, and when he came back to the charge, I fancied I felt that in throwing himself on me he let it pass through his body. I only know for a certainty that he fell, and it seemed to me he was carried off with his two companions.'

"The devil, gentlemen!" said the cardinal; "three men disabled in a saloon squabble! You don't do your work by halves. And pray what was your quarrel about?"

"These fellows were drunk," said Athos, "and knowing that a lady had arrived at the tavern this evening, they were on the point of forcing her door."

"Forcing her door!" said the cardinal; "and for what purpose?"

"To do her violence. without doubt," said Athos. "I have had the honour of informing your Eminence that these wretches were drunk."

"And was the lady young and handsome?" asked the cardinal in some anxiety.

"We did not see her, monseigneur," said Athos.

"You did not see her! Ah, very well," replied the cardinal quickly; "you acted quite right in defending a woman's honour; and as I myself am going to the Red Dovecot, I shall know whether you have told me truth or not."

"Monseigneur," said Athos haughtily, "to save our lives, we would not tell a lie."

"Therefore I do not doubt what you say, Monsieur Athos, I do not doubt it for a single instant; but," he added, to change the conversation, "the lady was alone, I suppose?"

"The lady had a cavalier in the room with her," said Athos, "but as this cavalier did not show himself in spite of the noise, it is to be presumed that he is a coward."

"'Judge not rashly,' says the Gospel," replied the cardinal. Athos bowed.

"And now, gentlemen, that's all very well," continued his Eminence. "I know what I wanted to know. Follow me."

The three musketeers fell behind his Eminence, who again enveloped his face in his cloak and started up his horse, keeping at from eight to ten paces in advance of his four companions.

They soon reached the silent, solitary tavern. The landlord doubtless knew what illustrious visitor was coming, and had consequently sent intruders away.

At ten paces from the door the cardinal made a sign to his attendant and the three musketeers to halt. A saddled horse was fastened to the window-shutter. The cardinal knocked three times in a peculiar manner.

A man enveloped in a cloak immediately came out, and exchanged some rapid words with the cardinal; after which he got on horseback and set off in the direction of Surgères, which was likewise that of Paris.

"Advance, gentlemen," said the cardinal.

"You have told me the truth, gentlemen," said he, addressing the three musketeers, "and it will not be my fault if our meeting this evening be not advantageous to you; meanwhile follow me."

The cardinal alighted; the three musketeers followed his example. The cardinal threw the bridle of his horse to his attendant; the three musketeers fastened their horses to the shutters.

The landlord stood at the door; for him, the cardinal was only an officer coming to visit a lady.

"Have you a room on the ground floor where these gentlemen can wait, near a good fire?" the cardinal asked.

The landlord opened the door of a large room, in which a poor stove had just been replaced by a large and excellent fireplace.

"I have this, sir," said he.

"That will do," replied the cardinal.—"Come in, gentlemen, and be kind enough to wait for me; I shall not be more than half an hour."

And while the three musketeers were going into the ground-floor room, the cardinal, without asking further information, mounted the staircase like a man who has no need of his way being pointed out to him.

CHAPTER XLIV.

THE UTILITY OF STOVE-PIPES.

It was evident that without suspecting it, and actuated solely by their chivalric and adventurous characters, our three friends had just rendered a service to some one whom the cardinal honoured with his special protection.

Now who was that some one? This was the question the three musketeers put to each other. Then, seeing that none of the replies their wits could furnish was satisfactory, Porthos called the landlord and asked for dice.

Porthos and Aramis sat down at the table and began to play. Athos walked about in a contemplative mood.

While thinking and walking, Athos kept passing and re-passing before the stove-pipe, broken in half, the other end of which went into the upper chamber; and every time he passed he heard a murmur of words, which at length attracted his attention. Athos went close to it, and distinguished some words which undoubtedly seemed to deserve so deep an interest that he beckoned to his friends to be silent, remaining himself bent, with his ear placed against the opening of the lower orifice.

"Listen, milady," said the cardinal; "the affair is important. Sit down and let us talk."

"Milady!" murmured Athos.

"I am listening to your Eminence with the greatest attention," replied a woman's voice that made the musketeer start.

"A small vessel, with an English crew, whose captain is devoted to me, awaits you at the mouth of the Charente, at Fort de la Pointe. He will set sail to-morrow morning."

"I must go there to-night, then?"

"Instantly! That is to say, as soon as you have received my instructions. Two men, whom you will find at the door on going out, will serve as your escort. You will let me leave first, and, half an hour after, you can go away in your turn."

"Yes, monseigneur. Now let us return to the mission in which you wish to employ me, and, as I desire to continue to merit your Eminence's confidence, deign to explain it to me in clear and precise terms, so that I may not commit any error."

There was a moment of deep silence between the two speakers. It was evident the cardinal was weighing beforehand the terms in which he was about to speak, and that milady was collecting all the powers of her mind to understand the things he was about to say, and to engrave them in her memory when they were spoken.

Athos took advantage of this moment to tell his two companions to fasten the door on the inside, and to beckon them to come and listen with him.

The two musketeers, who loved their ease, each brought a chair for himself and one for Athos. All three then sat down with their heads together and their ears alert.

"You will go to London," pursued the cardinal; "when you reach London you will seek out Buckingham."

"I must beg your Eminence to observe," said milady, "that since the affair of the diamond studs, about which the duke always suspected me, his Grace has been very mistrustful of me."

"Well, this time," said the cardinal, "it is not a question of worming yourself into his confidence, but you will present yourself frankly and loyally as a negotiator."

"Frankly and loyally," repeated milady, in an unspeakable tone of duplicity.

"Yes, frankly and loyally," replied the cardinal, in the same tone. "This whole negotiation is to be carried on openly."

"I will follow your Eminence's instructions to the letter. I only await your giving them."

"You will go to Buckingham in my behalf, and you will tell him I am acquainted with all the preparations he has made; but that they give me no uneasiness, since at the first step he takes I will ruin the queen."

"Will he believe that your Eminence is in a position to accomplish the threat you make him?"

"Yes, for I have the proofs."

"I must be able to present these proofs so as to convince him."

"Unquestionably. And you will tell him I will publish the report of Bois-Robert and of the Marquis de Beautru, regarding the interview with the queen which the duke had at the constable's residence, on the evening Madame la Connétable gave a masked ball. You will tell him, in order that he may not doubt anything, that he came there in the costume of the Great Mogul, which the Chevalier de Guise was to have worn, and which he bought for three thousand pistoles."

"Very well, monseigneur."

"All the details of his entrance and departure on the night when he was introduced into the palace in the character of an Italian fortune-teller you will tell him, in order that he may not doubt the correctness of my information; that he wore under his cloak a large white robe dotted with black tears, skulls, and cross-bones—for, in case of a surprise, he was to pass for the Phantom of the White Lady, who, as every one is aware, appears at the Louvre every time any great event is about to happen."

"Is that all, monseigneur?"

"Tell him also that I am acquainted with all the details of the adventure at Amiens; that I will have a little romance made of it, wittily turned, with a plan of the garden and portraits of the principal actors in that nocturnal romance."

" I will tell him that."

" Tell him, further, Montague is in my power ; that Montague is in the Bastille ; that no letters were found on him, it is true, but that torture may make him tell what he knows, and even what he does not know."

" Exactly."

" Then add that his Grace in his precipitation to quit the Isle of Ré forgot and left behind him in his lodging a letter from Madame de Chevreuse, which singularly compromises the queen, inasmuch as it proves not only that her Majesty can love the king's enemies, but that she can conspire with the enemies of France. You recollect perfectly all I have told you, do you not ? "

" Your Eminence will judge : Madame la Connétable's ball ; the night at the Louvre ; the evening at Amiens ; the arrest of Montague ; the letter of Madame de Chevreuse."

" That's it," said the cardinal—" that's it. You have an excellent memory, milady."

" But," resumed the lady to whom the cardinal had just addressed this flattering compliment, " if, in spite of all these reasons, the duke does not yield, and continues to threaten France ? "

" The duke is madly, or rather insanely, in love," replied Richelieu, with great bitterness. " Like the paladins of old, he has undertaken this war merely to obtain a look from his lady-love. If he becomes certain that this war will cost the honour and perhaps the liberty of the lady of his thoughts, as he calls her, I will answer for it he will look at it twice."

" And yet," said milady, with a persistence that proved she wished to see clearly to the end of the mission with which she was about to be charged—" and yet, if he persists ? "

" If he persists ? " said the cardinal. " That is not probable."

" It is possible," said milady.

" If he persists——" His Eminence made a pause, and resumed : " If he persists—well, then I shall hope for one of those events which change the destinies of states."

" If your Eminence would quote to me some one of these events in history," said milady, " perhaps I should partake of your confidence in the future."

"Well, here, then, for example," said Richelieu. "When in 1610, for a cause almost similar to the one that moves the duke, King Henry IV., of glorious memory, was about to invade Flanders and Italy at the same time, in order to attack Austria on both sides—well, did there not happen an event which saved Austria? Why should not the king of France have the same chance as the emperor?"

"Your Eminence means the knife-stab of the Rue de la Ferronnerie?"

"Exactly so," said the cardinal.

"Does not your Eminence fear that the punishment inflicted on Ravaillac may deter any one who might think of imitating him?"

"There will be, in all times and in all countries, particularly if religious divisions exist in those countries, fanatics who ask nothing better than to become martyrs. And observe, it just occurs to me that the Puritans are furious against the Duke of Buckingham, and their preachers designate him as Antichrist."

"Well?" said milady.

"Well," continued the cardinal, in an indifferent tone, "the only difficulty at this moment is to find some woman, handsome, young, and clever, who wants to get revenge on the duke. Such a woman may be found. The duke has had many love affairs, and if he has succeeded in many of his intrigues by his promises of eternal constancy, he must likewise have sown the seeds of many hatreds by his eternal infidelities."

"No doubt," said milady coolly, "such a woman may be found."

"Well, such a woman, who would put Jacques Clement's knife or Ravaillac's in a fanatic's hands, would save France."

"Yes; but she would be implicated in an assassination."

"Were Ravaillac's accomplices or Jacques Clement's ever known?"

"No, for perhaps they were too high for any one to dare look for them where they were. The Palace of Justice would not be burnt down for every one, monseigneur."

"So you think the fire at the Palace of Justice was not caused by chance?" asked Richelieu, in a tone such as he would have used in putting a question of no importance.

"I, monseigneur?" replied milady. "I think nothing; I quote a fact, that is all. Only I say that if my name were Mademoiselle de Montpensier or the Queen Marie de' Medici,

I should take less precautions than I take, being simply called Lady Clarick."

"That is but just," said Richelieu. "What do you require, then?"

"I require an order which would ratify beforehand all that I should think proper to do for the greatest good of France."

"But, in the first place, we must find the woman I have described, who is anxious to avenge herself on the duke."

"She is found," said milady.

"Then we must find the miserable fanatic who will serve as an instrument of God's justice."

"He will be found."

"Well," said the cardinal, "then it will be time to demand the order which you just now asked for."

"Your Eminence is right," replied milady, "and I have been wrong in seeing in the mission with which you honour me anything but what it really is—that is to say, to announce to his Grace, from your Eminence, that you are acquainted with the different disguises by means of which he succeeded in approaching the queen during the ball given at the constable's; that you have proofs of the interview granted at the Louvre by the queen to a certain Italian astrologer, who was no one else than the Duke of Buckingham; that you have ordered a little romance of a satirical nature to be written on the adventure of Amiens, with a plan of the gardens in which that adventure took place, and portraits of the actors who took part in it; that Montague is in the Bastille, and that torture may make him say things he remembers, and even things he has forgotten; finally, that you have in your possession a letter from Madame de Chevreuse, found in his Grace's headquarters, which singularly compromises not only her who wrote it, but also the lady in whose name it was written. Then if he persists, in spite of all this, inasmuch as what I have just said is the limit of my mission, I shall have nothing more to do but to pray God to work a miracle for the salvation of France. That is it, is it not, monseigneur, and I shall have nothing else to do?"

"That is it," replied the cardinal dryly.

"And now," said milady, without appearing to remark the change of the duke's tone toward her—"now that I have received your Eminence's instructions regarding your enemies, will monseigneur permit me to say a few words to him of mine?"

"Why, have you enemies?" asked Richelieu.

"Yes, monseigneur, enemies against whom you owe me all your support, for I made them by serving your Eminence."

"Who are they?" replied the duke.

"In the first place, there is a little intriguing woman named Bonacieux."

"She is in the prison of Nantes."

"That is to say, she was there," replied milady; "but the queen obtained an order from the king, by means of which she has been conveyed to a convent."

"To a convent?" exclaimed the duke.

"Yes, to a convent."

"And what convent?"

"I don't know; the secret has been well kept."

"But I will know!"

"And will your Eminence tell me in what convent this woman is?"

"I see nothing improper in that," said the cardinal.

"Well, now I have an enemy much more to be dreaded by me than this little Madame Bonacieux."

"Who is that?"

"Her lover."

"What is his name?"

"Oh, your Eminence knows him well," cried milady, carried away by her anger. "He is the evil genius of both of us. In an encounter with your Eminence's guards, he decided the victory in favour of the king's musketeers; he gave three desperate wounds to De Wardes, your emissary, and he caused the affair of the diamond studs to fail; and he, knowing I had Madame Bonacieux abducted, has sworn my death."

"Ah, ha!" said the cardinal; "I know whom you mean."

"I mean that wretch D'Artagnan."

"He is a bold fellow," said the cardinal.

"And because he is a bold fellow he is the more to be feared."

"I must have," said the duke, "a proof of his connection with Buckingham."

"A proof!" cried milady; "I will find you ten."

"Well, then, it is the simplest thing in the world. Get me your proof, and I will send him to the Bastille."

"So far so good, monseigneur; but afterwards?"

"When one is in the Bastille there is no afterwards!"

said the cardinal in a low voice. "Ah, by God!" continued he, "if it were as easy for me to get rid of my enemy as it is easy to get rid of yours, and if it were only against such people you required impunity——"

"Monseigneur," replied milady, "a fair exchange—life for life, man for man; give me one, I will give you the other."

"I don't know what you mean, nor do I even wish to know what you mean," replied the cardinal; "but I wish to please you, and see nothing out of the way in giving you what you ask for with respect to so mean a creature—the more so as you tell me this petty D'Artagnan is a libertine, a duellist, a traitor."

"An infamous scoundrel, monseigneur, an infamous scoundrel!"

"Give me paper, a pen, and some ink, then," said the cardinal.

"Here they are, monseigneur."

There was a moment of silence, which proved that the cardinal was engaged in seeking the terms in which he should write the note, or else in writing it. Athos, who had not lost a word of the conversation, took his two companions by the hand and led them to the other end of the room.

"Well," said Porthos, "what do you want, and why do you not let us listen to the end of the conversation?"

"Hush!" said Athos, speaking in a low voice; "we have heard all it was necessary for us to hear; besides, I don't prevent you from listening, but I must be gone."

"You must be gone!" said Porthos; "and if the cardinal asks for you, what answer can we make?"

"You will not wait till he asks; you will speak first, and tell him that I am gone as a scout, because certain expressions of our landlord have made me think the road is not safe. I will say a word or two about it to the cardinal's attendant likewise. The rest concerns myself; don't be anxious about that."

"Be prudent, Athos," said Aramis.

"Don't be worried," replied Athos.

Porthos and Aramis resumed their places by the stove-pipe.

Athos went out without any mystery, took his horse, which was tied with those of his friends to the fastenings of the shutters, in four words convinced the attendant of the necessity of a vanguard for their return, carefully examined the priming of his pistol, drew his sword, and, like a forlorn hope, took the road to the camp.

CHAPTER XLV.

A CONJUGAL SCENE.

As Athos had foreseen, the cardinal soon came down. He opened the door of the room where the musketeers were, and found Porthos playing an earnest game at dice with Aramis. He cast a rapid glance round the room, and perceived that one of his men was missing.

"What has become of Monsieur Athos?" asked he.

"Monseigneur," replied Porthos, "he has gone on as a scout, owing to some expressions dropped by our landlord making him fear the road was not safe."

"And how have you been amusing yourself, M. Porthos?"

"I have won five pistoles from Aramis, monseigneur."

"Well; now will you return with me?"

"We are at your Eminence's orders."

"To horse, then, gentlemen, for it is getting late."

The attendant was at the door, holding the cardinal's horse by the bridle. A short distance away a group of two men and three horses appeared in the shade; these were the two men who were to conduct milady to Fort de la Pointe, and superintend her embarkation.

The attendant confirmed to the cardinal what the two musketeers had already said regarding Athos. The cardinal made an approving gesture, and started to return with the same precautions he had used in coming.

Let us leave him to follow the road to the camp, protected by his attendant and the two musketeers, and return to Athos.

For a hundred paces he maintained the gait with which he started, but when once out of sight, he turned his horse to the right, made a circuit, and came back to within twenty paces, where, shielded by a coppice, he might watch the passage of the little troop. Having recognized his companions' laced hats and the golden fringe of the cardinal's cloak, he waited till the horsemen had turned the angle of the road, and having lost them from sight, he returned at a gallop to the tavern, which was opened to him without hesitation.

The landlord recognized him.

"My officer," said Athos, "has forgotten to give a piece of very important information to the lady, and has sent me back to repair his forgetfulness."

"Go up," said the host; "she is still in her room."

Athos availed himself of the permission, mounted the stairs with his lightest step, gained the landing, and through the open door saw milady putting on her hat.

He went straight into the chamber and closed the door behind him.

At the noise he made in bolting it milady turned round.

Athos was standing before the door, enveloped in his cloak, with his hat pulled down over his eyes. On seeing that figure, mute and motionless like a statue, milady was startled.

"Who are you, and what do you want ?" cried she.

"There now !" murmured Athos ; "it is certainly she !"

And dropping his cloak and raising his hat, he advanced toward milady.

"Do you know me, madame ?" said he.

Milady took one step forward, and then grew pale, as though she saw a serpent.

"Come," said Athos. "Good ! I see you know me."

"The Comte de la Fère !" murmured milady, drawing back till the wall prevented her going any farther.

"Yes, milady," replied Athos ; "the Comte de la Fère in person, who comes expressly from the other world to have the pleasure of seeing you. Sit down, then, and let us talk, as the cardinal said."

Milady, under the influence of inexpressible terror, sat down without uttering a word.

"You are a demon sent to earth !" said Athos. "Your power is great, I know ; but you also know that with God's aid men have often conquered the most terrible demons. You have once before crossed my path. I thought I had crushed you, madame ; but either I was deceived, or hell has brought you to life again."

Milady at these words, which recalled frightful remembrances, hung her head, with a suppressed groan.

"Yes, hell has brought you to life again," continued Athos, "hell has made you rich, hell has given you another name, hell has almost made you another countenance ; but it has effaced neither the stains from your soul nor the brand from your body ! "

Milady started up as if moved by a spring, and her eyes flashed lightning. Athos remained sitting.

"You believed me to be dead, did you not, as I believed you to be ? And the name of Athos as well concealed the Comte de la Fère as the name of Lady Clarick concealed Anne de Bueil ! Were you not so called when your honoured brother married us? Our position is truly strange," pursued Athos, laughing. "We have lived up to the present time only because we believed each other to be dead, and because a remembrance is less oppressive than a living creature, though sometimes a remembrance is a devouring thing!"

"But," said milady, in a hollow, faint voice, "what brings you back to me? and what do you want with me?"

"I wish to tell you that, though I have remained invisible to your eyes, I have not lost sight of you. I can tell you of your actions day by day from the time you entered the cardinal's service until this evening."

A smile of incredulity passed over milady's pale lips.

"Listen! You cut off the two diamond studs from the Duke of Buckingham's shoulder; you had Madame Bonacieux abducted; you were in love with De Wardes, and, thinking to pass the night with him, opened the door to M. d'Artagnan; you believed that De Wardes had deceived you, and tried to have him killed by his rival; when his rival had discovered your infamous secret, you tried to have him killed in his turn by two assassins, whom you sent in pursuit of him; finding the balls had missed their mark, you sent poisoned wine with a forged letter, to make your victim believe that the wine came from his friends; and lastly, you have just now been sitting in this chamber, in this very chair where I am now, and have entered into an engagement with Cardinal Richelieu to have the Duke of Buckingham assassinated, in exchange for the promise he made you to have D'Artagnan assassinated for your sake."

Milady was livid.

"You must be Satan!" cried she.

"Perhaps," said Athos. "But, at least, listen to what I say. Assassinate the Duke of Buckingham, or have him assassinated; it makes no difference to me. I don't know him; besides, he is an Englishman. But do not touch with the tip of your finger a single hair of D'Artagnan, who is a faithful friend, whom I love and defend, or I swear to you by my father's life the crime which you shall have committed shall be your last."

"M. d'Artagnan has cruelly insulted me," said milady, in a hollow voice; "M. d'Artagnan shall die!"

"Indeed! Is it possible to insult you, madame?" said Athos, laughing. "He has insulted you, and he shall die!"

"He shall die!" replied milady; "she first, then he."

Athos was seized with a kind of vertigo. The sight of

this creature, who had nothing womanly about her, recalled devouring remembrances. He recalled how one day, in a less dangerous situation than the one in which he was now placed, he had already tried to sacrifice her to his honour. His desire for her death returned, burning, and pervaded him like a raging fever. He arose, put his hand to his belt, drew out a pistol, and cocked it.

Milady, pale as a corpse, struggled to cry out; but her frozen tongue could utter only a hoarse sound, which had nothing human in it, and seemed a wild beast's rattle. Clinging to the dark tapestry, she appeared, with her hair in disorder, like the frightful image of terror.

Athos slowly raised his pistol, stretched out his arm, so that the weapon almost touched milady's forehead; and then, in a voice the more terrible from having the supreme calmness of an inflexible resolution,—

"Madame," said he, "you will this instant deliver to me the paper the cardinal signed; or, on my soul, I will blow your brains out."

With another man, milady might have preserved some doubt; but she knew Athos, yet she remained motionless.

"You have one second to decide," said he.

Milady saw by the contraction of his countenance that he was about to pull the trigger; she put her hand quickly into her bosom, pulled out a paper, and held it toward Athos.

"Take it," said she, "and be damned!"

Athos took the paper, returned the pistol to his belt, approached the lamp to be assured that it was the right paper, unfolded it, and read,—

"August 5, 1628.

"By my order, and for the good of the State, the bearer hereof has done what he has done.   RICHELIEU."

"And now," said Athos, taking up his cloak again and putting on his hat—"now that I have drawn your teeth, viper, bite if you can."

And he left the chamber without once looking behind him.

At the door he found the two men, and the horse which they held.

"Gentlemen," said he, "you know monseigneur's order is for you to conduct that woman, without losing time, to Fort de la Pointe, and not to leave her till she is on board."

As his words agreed exactly with the order they had received, they bowed in sign of assent.

Athos leaped lightly into his saddle, and set out at full

gallop ; only, instead of following the road, he took across the fields, urging his horse to the utmost, and stopping occasionally to listen.

In one of his halts he heard the trampling of several horses on the road. He had no doubt it was the cardinal and his escort. He immediately galloped on ahead, rubbed his horse down with some heather and leaves of trees, and then placed himself in the middle of the road, about two hundred paces from the camp.

" Who goes there ? " cried he, as soon as he saw the horsemen coming.

" That is our brave musketeer, I think," said the cardinal.

" Yes, monseigneur," said Porthos, " it is he."

" Monsieur Athos," said Richelieu, " receive my thanks for the good guard you have kept. Gentlemen, we are here ; take the gate on the left. The watchword is ' King and Ré.' "

On saying these words the cardinal bent his head in salutation of the three friends, and took the right hand, followed by his attendant, for that night he himself was to sleep in camp.

" Well," said Porthos and Aramis together, as soon as the cardinal was out of hearing—" well, he signed the paper she asked for ! "

" I know he did," said Athos, " and here it is."

And the three friends did not exchange another word till they got to their quarters, except to give the watchword to the sentinels.

But they sent Mousqueton to tell Planchet that his master was requested to come to the quarters of the musketeers the instant he left the trenches.

Milady, as Athos had foreseen, on finding the two men awaiting her, made no objection to going with them. She had indeed for an instant felt an inclination to be taken back to the cardinal and relate everything to him ; but a revelation on her own account would bring about a revelation from Athos. She might say that Athos had hanged her ; but then Athos would tell that she was branded. She thought it was therefore best to preserve silence, to set off discreetly, to accomplish her difficult mission with her usual skill ; and then, all things being performed to the cardinal's satisfaction, to come back and claim her vengeance.

Consequently, after travelling all night, she was at seven o'clock at Fort de la Pointe ; at eight o'clock she had embarked ; and at nine the vessel, which, with letters of marque from the cardinal, was supposed to be going to Bayonne, raised anchor and set sail toward England.

CHAPTER XLVI.

THE BASTION ST. GERVAIS.

ON rejoining his three friends, D'Artagnan found them assembled in the same room. Athos was meditating, Porthos was twirling his moustache, Aramis was reading prayers in a charming little Book of Hours, bound in blue velvet.

"By Jove," said he, "gentlemen, I hope what you have to tell me is worth the trouble ; or else, I warn you, I will not pardon you for making me come here instead of getting a little rest, after a night spent in taking and dismantling a bastion. Ah ! why were you not there, gentlemen ? It was warm work."

"We were in a place where it was not very cold !" replied Porthos, giving his moustache a twirl that was peculiar to him.

"Hush !" said Athos.

"Oh, ho !" said D'Artagnan, comprehending the musketeer's slight frown ; "it appears there is something new on hand."

"Aramis," said Athos, "you went to breakfast the day before yesterday at the tavern of the Infidel,* I believe ?"

"Yes."

"How did you fare ?"

"For my part, I ate but little. The day before yesterday was a fast-day, and they had nothing but meat."

"What !" said Athos ; "no fish at a seaport ?"

"They say," said Aramis, resuming his pious reading, "that the dike which the cardinal is making drives them all out into the open sea."

"But that is not quite what I asked you," replied Athos. "I want to know if you were left alone, and nobody interrupted you."

* "Le Parpaillot." Parpaillot was an opprobrious term applied to Calvinists. It is derived either from *papillon*, a butterfly ; or from *parpillote*, a small piece of money used by the religious partisans of the 16th century ; or from the Sieur Parpaille, a native of Orange, who, after propagating Protestantism in the Comptat, was put to death in 1562. The word came to mean, in familiar language, a man who had no religion.

"Why, I think there were not many intruders. Yes, Athos, I know what you mean ; we shall do very well at the Infidel."

"Let us go to the Infidel, then ; for here the walls are like sheets of paper."

D'Artagnan, who was accustomed to his friend's manner of acting, and perceived immediately by a word, a gesture, or a sign from him that the circumstances were serious, took Athos's arm, and went out with him without saying anything. Porthos followed, chatting with Aramis.

On their way they fell in with Grimaud. Athos beckoned him to come with them. Grimaud, as usual, silently obeyed ; the poor lad had nearly come to the pass of forgetting how to speak.

They arrived at the taproom of the Infidel ; it was seven o'clock in the morning, and daylight began to appear. The three friends ordered breakfast, and went into a room in which, the host said, they were not likely to be disturbed.

Unfortunately, the hour was badly chosen for a private conference. Reveille had just been beaten ; every one was shaking off the drowsiness of night, and, to dispel the humid morning air, came to take a drop at the bar. Dragoons, Swiss, guardsmen, musketeers, light-horsemen succeeded one another with a rapidity which might answer the land-lord's purposes very well, but agreed badly with the views of the four friends. Thus they replied very curtly to the salutations, healths, and jokes of their companions.

"Come," said Athos ; "we shall get into some pretty quarrel or other, and we don't need one just now. D'Artagnan, tell us what sort of a night you had, and we will describe ours afterwards."

"Ah, yes !" said a light-horseman, lolling about with a glass of brandy in his hand, which he was leisurely sipping —"ah, yes ! You gentlemen of the guards were in the trenches last night, and you had a bone to pick with the Rochellais."

D'Artagnan looked at Athos to know if he ought to reply to this intruder, who mixed unasked in their conversation.

"Well," said Athos, "don't you hear M. de Busigny, who does you the honour of asking you a question ? Relate what has passed during the night, since these gentlemen wish to know."

"Did you not take a bastion ?" asked a Swiss, who was drinking rum out of a beer-glass.

"Yes, sir," said D'Artagnan, bowing ; "we had that

honour. As you may have heard, we even put a barrel
of powder under one of the angles, which, when it blew up,
made a very pretty breach — without reckoning that, as
the bastion was not built yesterday, all the rest of the
building was much shaken."

"And which bastion was it?" asked a dragoon, with his
sabre run through a goose, which he was taking to have
cooked."

"The bastion St. Gervais," replied D'Artagnan, "from
behind which the Rochellais have been annoying our workmen."

"Was the affair hot?"

"Yes, moderately so. We lost five men, and the Rochellais
eight or ten."

"Balzempleu!" said the Swiss, who, notwithstanding
the admirable stock of oaths possessed by the German language, had acquired the habit of swearing in French.

"But," said the light-horseman, "probably they will send
pioneers this morning to repair the bastion."

"Yes, probably," said D'Artagnan.

"Gentlemen," said Athos, "I have a wager to propose."

"Ah, ha! a vager!" cried the Swiss.

"What is it?" said the light-horseman.

"Stop a bit," said the dragoon, placing his sabre like a
spit upon the two large iron dogs which held the firebrands
on the hearth—"stop a bit; I am in it.—You dog of a landlord! a dripping-pan instantly, that I may not lose a drop
of the fat of this estimable bird."

"You are qvite right," said the Swiss; "koose-krease is
koot vith bastry."

"There!" said the dragoon. "Now for the wager. We
are all attention, M. Athos."

"Ah, now for the wager!" said the light-horseman.

"Well, Monsieur de Busigny, I will bet you," said
Athos, "that my three companions, MM. Porthos, Aramis,
and D'Artagnan, and myself, will go and breakfast in the
bastion St. Gervais, and will remain there an hour, by
the watch, whatever the enemy may do to dislodge us."

Porthos and Aramis looked at each other; they began to
understand.

"Well, but," said D'Artagnan, in Athos's ear, "you are
going to get us all killed without mercy."

"We are much more likely to be killed," said Athos, "if
we do not go."

"'Pon my word, gentlemen!" said Porthos, turning

round upon his chair and twirling his moustache, "that's a fine bet, I hope."

"I take it," said M. de Busigny. "Now let us fix the stake."

"Why, you are four, gentlemen," said Athos, "and we are four: a dinner for eight. Will that do?"

"Capitally," replied M. de Busigny.

"Perfectly well," said the dragoon.

"Dat suits me," said the Swiss.

The fourth auditor, who during all this conversation had played a mute part, nodded to show that he acquiesced in the proposition.

"The breakfast for these gentlemen is ready," said the landlord.

"Well, bring it in," said Athos.

The landlord obeyed. Athos called Grimaud, pointed to a large basket standing in a corner, and made a sign to him to wrap the food up in the napkins.

Grimaud perceived that it was to be a breakfast on the grass, packed the viands into the basket, added the bottles, and then took the basket on his arm.

"But where are you going to eat my breakfast?" said the landlord.

"Of what consequence is that to you, if you are paid for it?" said Athos, and he threw two pistoles majestically on the table.

"Shall I give you the change, officer?" said the host.

"No; only add two bottles of champagne, and the difference will be for the napkins."

The landlord had not quite so good a bargain as he at first hoped for, but he made up for it by slipping in two bottles of Anjou wine instead of two bottles of champagne.

"Monsieur de Busigny," said Athos, "will you be so kind as to set your watch with mine, or permit me to regulate mine by yours?"

"Certainly, sir," said the light-horseman, drawing from his fob a very handsome watch set in diamonds. "Half-past seven," said he.

"Thirty-five minutes after seven," said Athos; "we shall know that I am five minutes faster than you, sir."

And bowing to all the astonished spectators, the young men started off for the bastion St. Gervais, followed by Grimaud carrying the basket, ignorant of where he was going, but, in the passive obedience which Athos had taught him, not even thinking of asking.

As long as they were within the camp the four friends did not exchange a word; besides, they were followed by inquisitive loungers, who, hearing of the wager, were anxious to know how they would succeed. But when once they had passed the line of circumvallation, and found themselves in the open field, D'Artagnan, who was completely ignorant of what was going on, thought it was time to demand an explanation.

"And now, my dear Athos," said he, "do me the kindness to tell me where we are going."

"Why, you see plainly enough we are going to the bastion."

"But what are we going to do there?"

"Why, you know well enough we are going to breakfast there."

"But why did we not breakfast at the Infidel?"

"Because we have some very important things to talk over, and it was impossible to talk five minutes in that tavern without being annoyed by all those importunate fellows, who keep coming in, saluting you, and addressing you. Yonder, at least," said Athos, pointing to the bastion, "they will not come and disturb us."

"It seems to me," said D'Artagnan, with that prudence which was so naturally allied with his extreme bravery— "it seems to me that we could have found some retired place on the downs or by the seashore."

"Where we should have been seen all four conferring together, so that at the end of a quarter of an hour the cardinal would have been informed by his spies that we were holding a council."

"Yes," said Aramis, "Athos is right: *Animadvertuntur in desertis.*"

"A desert would not have been amiss," said Porthos; "but the question was where to find it."

"There is no desert where a bird cannot fly over one's head, where a fish cannot leap out of the water, where a rabbit cannot come out of its burrow; and I believe that bird, fish, and rabbit would all be the cardinal's spies. Better, then, carry out our undertaking, from which, besides, we cannot retreat without shame. We have made a wager, a wager which could not be foreseen, and of which I defy any one to guess the true cause. In order to win it, we are going to stay an hour in the bastion. We shall either be attacked, or we shall not be. If we are not, we shall have all the time to talk, and nobody will hear us.

for I will answer for it the walls of the bastion have no ears. If we are attacked, we will talk of our affairs just the same, and while defending ourselves we shall cover ourselves with glory. You see that everything is to our advantage."

"Yes," said D'Artagnan; "but undoubtedly we shall receive a bullet."

"Well, my dear," replied Athos, "you know well that the bullets most to be dreaded are not from open enemies."

"But for such an expedition we surely ought to have brought our muskets."

"You are stupid, friend Porthos. Why load ourselves with a useless burden?"

"I think a good musket, a dozen cartridges, and a powder-flask are not very useless things in face of an enemy."

"Well," replied Athos, "didn't you hear what D'Artagnan said?"

"What did D'Artagnan say?"

"D'Artagnan said that in the attack last night eight or ten Frenchmen were killed and as many Rochellais."

"What then?"

"They did not have time to plunder the bodies, did they, seeing that for the moment they had something more urgent to do?"

"Well?"

"Well, we shall find their muskets, their cartridges, and their powder-flasks; and instead of four musketoons and a dozen balls, we shall have fifteen guns and a hundred charges to fire."

"O Athos!" said Aramis, "truly thou art a great man."

Porthos bowed in sign of acquiescence. D'Artagnan alone did not appear to be quite satisfied.

Grimaud, no doubt, shared the young man's misgivings, for seeing that they continued to advance toward the bastion, a thing which he had not at first suspected, he pulled his master by the skirt of his coat.

"Where are we going?" asked he by a gesture.

Athos pointed to the bastion.

"But," said the silent Grimaud, still in the same dialect, "we shall leave our hides there."

Athos raised his eyes and his finger toward heaven.

Grimaud put his basket on the ground and sat down, shaking his head.

Athos took a pistol from his belt, looked to see if it

was properly primed, cocked it, and placed the muzzle close to Grimaud's ear.

Grimaud was on his legs again, as if moved by a spring. Athos then made him a sign to take up his basket, and to walk on first. Grimaud obeyed. All that Grimaud gained by this moment's pantomime was that he was promoted from the rear-guard to the vanguard.

When they reached the bastion the four friends turned round.

More than three hundred soldiers of all kinds were assembled at the gate of the camp ; and in a separate group they could distinguish M. de Busigny, the dragoon, the Swiss, and the fourth wagerer.

Athos took off his hat, put it on the end of his sword, and waved it in the air. All the spectators returned him his salute, accompanying this politeness with a loud hurrah, which they plainly heard. After which they all four disappeared in the bastion, where Grimaud had already preceded them.

CHAPTER XLVII.

THE COUNCIL OF THE MUSKETEERS.

As Athos had foreseen, the bastion was occupied only by a dozen dead bodies, French and Rochellais.

"Gentlemen," said Athos, who had assumed the command of the expedition, "while Grimaud is laying out the breakfast, let us begin by getting together the guns and cartridges ; we can talk while performing that task. These gentlemen," added he, pointing to the bodies, "will not hear us."

"But still we might throw them into the ditch," said Porthos, "after assuring ourselves they have nothing in their pockets."

"Yes," said Athos ; "that's Grimaud's business."

"Well, then," cried D'Artagnan, "let Grimaud search them, and throw them over the walls."

"By no means," said Athos ; "they may be useful to us."

"These dead bodies useful to us ?" exclaimed Porthos. "Why, you are crazy, my dear friend."

"'Judge not rashly,' say the Gospels and the cardinal," replied Athos. "How many guns, gentlemen ?"

"Twelve," replied Aramis.

"How many cartridges ?"

" A hundred."

" That's quite as many as we shall want. Let us load the guns."

The four musketeers went to work. As they were loading the last musket Grimaud signified that breakfast was ready.

Athos replied, still by gestures, that it was all right, and showed Grimaud a kind of pepper-box, making him understand that he was to stand as sentinel. Only, to alleviate the tedium of the duty, Athos allowed him to take a loaf, two cutlets, and a bottle of wine.

" And now, to table," said Athos.

The four friends sat down on the ground, with their legs crossed, like Turks or tailors.

" There now," said D'Artagnan ; " as there is no longer any fear of being overheard, I hope you are going to let us into your secret."

" I hope at the same time to provide you with amusement and glory, gentlemen," said Athos. " I have taken you on a very pleasant walk ; here is a most delicious breakfast ; and five hundred people yonder, as you may see through the loopholes, are taking us for heroes or madmen—two classes of imbeciles sufficiently alike."

" But the secret ? " said D'Artagnan.

" The secret is," said Athos, " that I saw milady last night."

D'Artagnan was lifting a glass to his lips, but at the mention of milady his hand shook so that he put the glass on the ground again, for fear of spilling the contents.

" You saw your wi——"

" Hush ! " interrupted Athos ; " you forget, my dear, that these gentlemen have not been initiated, as you have, into the secrets of my family affairs. I saw milady."

" And where ? " demanded D'Artagnan.

" About two leagues from here, at the tavern of the Red Dovecot."

" In that case I am lost," said D'Artagnan.

" No, not quite so yet," replied Athos, " for by this time she must have left the shores of France."

" But, after all," asked Porthos, " who is milady ? "

" A very charming woman ! " said Athos, sipping a glass of sparkling wine. " That rascally landlord ! " cried he ; " he has given us Anjou wine instead of champagne, and fancies we know no better ! Yes," continued he, " a very charming woman, who bestowed her favours on our friend D'Artagnan, while he, on his part, has given her some

offence for which she tried to pay him off, a month ago, by
having him killed by two musket-shots; a week ago by
attempting to poison him; and yesterday by demanding
his head of the cardinal."

"What! by demanding my head of the cardinal?"
cried D'Artagnan.

"Yes, that is as true as the gospel," said Porthos; "I
heard her with my own ears."

"So did I," said Aramis.

"But I can never escape," said D'Artagnan, "with such
enemies. First, there is my unknown man of Meung; then
De Wardes, on whom I have inflicted three wounds; next,
milady, whose secret I have discovered; and last, the
cardinal, whose vengeance I have balked."

"Well," said Athos, "that only makes four; and we are
four—one for one. By Jove! if we may believe the signs
Grimaud is making, we are about to have to do with a much
greater number of people."

"What's the matter, Grimaud?" said Athos. "Considering the seriousness of the case, I permit you to speak,
my friend; but be brief, I beg of you. What do you see?"

"A troop."

"How many persons?"

"Twenty men."

"What sort of men?"

"Sixteen pioneers, four soldiers."

"How far distant?"

"Five hundred paces."

"Good! We have just time to finish this fowl, and to
drink one glass of wine to your health, D'Artagnan!"

"To your health," repeated Porthos and Aramis.

"Well, then, to my health, though I do not believe that
your good wishes will be of much service to me."

"Bah!" said Athos; "'God is great,' as the followers
of Mahomet say, and the future is in His hands."

Then swallowing the contents of his glass, which he
put down close to him, Athos arose carelessly, took the
nearest musket, and went to one of the loopholes.

Porthos, Aramis, and D'Artagnan did the same. Grimaud
was ordered to place himself behind the four friends, in
order to reload their guns.

In a moment the troop appeared; they were advancing
along a sort of branch trench, which gave communication
between the bastion and the city.

"By Jove!" said Athos, "it was hardly worth while

to disturb ourselves for twenty fellows armed with pick-axes, mattocks, and shovels! Grimaud needed only make them a sign to go away, and I am sure they would have left us alone."

"I doubt that," replied D'Artagnan, "for they are advancing very resolutely. Besides, in addition to the pioneers, there are four soldiers and a corporal armed with muskets."

"That's because they didn't see us," said Athos.

"Faith!" said Aramis, "I vow it goes against my grain to fire on these poor devils of bourgeois."

"He is a bad priest," said Porthos, "who pities heretics."

"In truth," said Athos, "Aramis is right. I will warn them."

"What the devil are you going about?" cried D'Artagnan; "you will be shot, my dear!"

But Athos took no heed of his advice; and mounting on the breach, with his musket in one hand and his hat in the other,—

"Gentlemen," said he, bowing courteously, and address-ing the soldiers and the pioneers, who, astonished to see him, stopped at fifty paces from the bastion—"gentlemen, a few friends and myself are engaged at breakfast in this bastion. Now, you know nothing is more disagreeable than being disturbed when one is at breakfast. We request you, then, if you really have business here, to wait till we have finished our repast, or to come later on—unless you are wisely desirous of deserting the rebels, and will come and drink with us to the health of the king of France."

"Take care, Athos!" cried D'Artagnan; "don't you see they are aiming at you?"

"Yes, yes," said Athos; "but they are only bourgeois—very bad marksmen; they will be sure to miss me."

In fact, at the same instant four shots were fired, and the bullets flattened against the wall round Athos, but not one hit him. Four shots replied to them, almost in-stantaneously, but much better aimed than those of the aggressors. Three soldiers fell dead, and one of the pioneers was wounded.

"Grimaud," said Athos, still on the breach, "another musket."

Grimaud instantly obeyed. The three friends had re-loaded their arms; another discharge followed the second. The corporal and two pioneers fell dead; the rest of the troop took to flight.

"Now, gentlemen, for a sortie!" cried Athos.

And the four friends rushed out of the fort, gained the field of battle, picked up the muskets of the four soldiers, and the corporal's half-pike; and, convinced that the fugitives would not stop till they got to the city, turned again toward the bastion, bearing with them the trophies of their victory.

"Reload the muskets, Grimaud," said Athos; "and we, gentlemen, will go on with our breakfast and resume our conversation. Where were we?"

"I remember," said D'Artagnan; "you were saying that after demanding my head of the cardinal, milady left the shores of France. Where is she going?" added he, considerably interested in the itinerary which milady was following.

"She is going to England," said Athos.

"What for?"

"To assassinate the Duke of Buckingham, or cause him to be assassinated."

D'Artagnan uttered an exclamation of surprise and indignation.

"But this is infamous!" cried he.

"I beg you to believe," said Athos, "that I care very little about that.—Now you have done, Grimaud, take our corporal's half-pike, tie a napkin to it, and plant it at the top of our bastion, that these rebels of Rochellais may see that they have to deal with brave and loyal soldiers of the king."

Grimaud obeyed without replying.

An instant afterwards the white flag was floating over the heads of the four friends. A thunder of applause saluted its appearance; half the camp was at the barrier.

"But why do you care so little whether she kills Buckingham or not? The duke is our friend."

"The duke is an Englishman, the duke is fighting against us. Let her do what she likes with the duke; I care no more for him than for an empty bottle."

"One moment!" said D'Artagnan. "I will not give up Buckingham in this way; he gave us some very fine horses."

"And, above all, some very handsome saddles," said Porthos, who at that very moment was wearing the lace of his on his cloak.

"Besides," said Aramis, "God desires the conversion and not the death of a sinner."

"Amen!" said Athos; "and we will return to that

subject later, if such be your pleasure. But what I was most anxious about at the moment—and I am sure you will understand me, D'Artagnan—was to secure from this woman a kind of carte-blanche, which she had extorted from the cardinal, and by means of which she could with impunity get rid of you and perhaps of us."

"But this creature must be a demon!" said Porthos, holding out his plate to Aramis, who was carving a fowl.

"And this carte-blanche," asked D'Artagnan—"this carte-blanche, has she it still?"

"No, I got it; I will not say without trouble, for if I did I should tell a lie."

"My dear Athos, I shall give up counting the number of times you have saved my life."

"So you left us to go to her!" exclaimed Aramis.

"Exactly so."

"And you have that letter of the cardinal's?"

"Here it is," said Athos.

And he took the precious paper from his coat pocket.

D'Artagnan unfolded it with a hand the trembling of which he did not even attempt to conceal, and read,—

"August 5, 1628.

"By my order, and for the good of the State, the bearer hereof has done what he has done. RICHELIEU."

"In fact," said Aramis, "it is an absolution in all its forms."

"That paper must be torn in pieces," said D'Artagnan, who fancied he read in it his death sentence.

"On the contrary," said Athos, "it must be preserved carefully. I would not give this paper for as many gold pieces as would cover it."

"And what is she going to do now?" asked the young man.

"Well," replied Athos carelessly, "she is probably going to write to the cardinal that a damned musketeer, named Athos, has taken her safe-conduct from her by force. She will advise him, in the same letter, to get rid of his two friends, Aramis and Porthos, at the same time he disposes of him. The cardinal will remember that these are the same men who are always crossing his path. Then, some fine morning, he will have D'Artagnan arrested, and for fear he should feel bored in his loneliness, he will have us sent to keep him company in the Bastille."

"There, now! It seems to me you are making but very dull jokes, my dear," said Porthos.

"I am not joking," said Athos.

"Do you know," said Porthos, "that to twist that damned milady's neck would be less of a sin than to twist the necks of these poor Huguenot devils, who have committed no other crimes than singing in French the Psalms that we sing in Latin?"

"What says the abbé?" asked Athos quietly.

"I say I am entirely of Porthos's opinion," replied Aramis.

"And I too," said D'Artagnan.

"Fortunately, she is a good way off," said Porthos, "for I confess she would make me very uncomfortable if she were here."

"She makes me uncomfortable in England as well as in France," said Athos.

"She makes me uncomfortable wherever she is," said D'Artagnan.

"But when you had her in your power, why did you not drown her, or strangle her, or hang her?" said Porthos. "It is only the dead who don't come back again."

"You think so, do you, Porthos?" replied the musketeer, with a sad smile, which D'Artagnan alone understood.

"I have an idea," said D'Artagnan.

"What is it?" cried the musketeers.

"To arms!" shouted Grimaud.

The young men sprang up and seized their muskets.

This time a small troop advanced, consisting of from twenty to twenty-five men; but this time they were not pioneers, but soldiers of the garrison.

"Shall we return to the camp?" suggested Porthos. "I don't think the sides are equal."

"Impossible, for three reasons," replied Athos. "The first is, that we have not finished breakfast; the second is, that we have still some very important things to talk about; and the third is, that it yet lacks ten minutes before the hour will be over."

"Well, then," said Aramis, "we must form a plan of battle."

"It's very simple," replied Athos. "As soon as the enemy are within range, we must fire on them. If they continue to advance, we must fire again. We must fire as long as we have loaded guns. Then, if the rest of the troop persist in mounting to the assault, we will allow the besiegers to reach the ditch, and then we will push down on their heads that strip of wall which seems to stand only by a miracle of equilibrium."

" Bravo ! " cried Porthos. " Decidedly, Athos, you were born to be a general, and the cardinal, who fancies himself a great captain, is nothing to you."

"Gentlemen," said Athos, " no divided attention, I beg. Let each one pick out his man."

" I cover mine," said D'Artagnan.

"And I mine," said Porthos.

" And I *idem*," said Aramis.

" Fire, then ! " said Athos.

The four muskets made but one report, but four men fell.

The drum immediately beat, and the little troop advanced double-quick.

Then the musket-shots were repeated without regularity, but always aimed with the same correctness. Nevertheless, as if they had been aware of the numerical weakness of the friends, the Rochellais continued to advance on the run.

At every three shots at least two men fell ; but the approach of those who remained was not slackened.

On reaching the foot of the bastion, there were still more than a dozen or fifteen of the enemy. A last discharge welcomed them, but did not stop them. They leaped into the ditch, and prepared to scale the breach.

" Now, my friends," said Athos, " finish them at a blow. To the wall ! to the wall ! "

And the four friends, aided by Grimaud, pushed with the barrels of their muskets an enormous side of the wall, which bent over as if swayed by the wind, and giving way from its base, fell with a horrible crash into the ditch. Then a fearful cry was heard, a cloud of dust mounted toward the sky, and all was over !

" Can we have destroyed them all, from the first to the last ? " said Athos.

" Faith, it seems so," said D'Artagnan.

" No," cried Porthos ; " there go three or four, limping away."

In fact, three or four of these unfortunate men, covered with dirt and blood, were escaping along the hollow way, and were making for the city. These were all that were left of the little troop.

Athos looked at his watch.

" Gentlemen," said he, " we have been here an hour, and

our wager is won; but we will be fair players. Besides, D'Artagnan has not told us his idea yet.''

And the musketeer, with his usual coolness, went and sat down again before the remains of the breakfast.

"My idea ? " said D'Artagnan.

"Yes; you said you had an idea," said Athos.

"Oh, I remember now," said D'Artagnan. "Well, I will go to England again ; I will go and find Buckingham."

"You shall not do that, D'Artagnan," said Athos coolly.

"And why not ?   Have I not been there once ? "

"Yes ; but at that period we were not at war.   At that period Buckingham was an ally, and not an enemy.   What you now contemplate doing would amount to treason."

D'Artagnan perceived the force of this reasoning, and was silent.

"But," said Porthos, "I think I have an idea in my turn."

"Silence for M. Porthos's idea ! " said Aramis.

"I will ask leave of absence of M. de Tréville, on some pretext or other, which you must find out, as I am not very clever at pretexts.   Milady does not know me.   I will get access to her without her suspecting who I am; and when I catch my beauty, I will strangle her."

"Well," replied Athos, "I am not far from approving M. Porthos's idea."

"For shame ! " said Aramis—"kill a woman ! No. Listen to me ; I have a genuine idea."

"Let us have your idea, Aramis," said Athos, who entertained great deference for the young musketeer.

"We must inform the queen."

"Ah, 'pon my word, yes," said Porthos and D'Artagnan at the same time.   "I think we are getting at the proper means."

"Inform the queen ! " said Athos.   "And how ?   Have we any friends at court ?   Can we send any one to Paris without its being known in the camp ?   It is a hundred and forty leagues from here to Paris ; before our letter reached Angers we should be in a dungeon."

"As to sending a letter safely to her Majesty," said Aramis, "I will take that on myself.   I know a clever person at Tours——"

Aramis stopped on seeing Athos smile.

"Well, do you not adopt this means, Athos ? " asked D'Artagnan.

"I do not reject it altogether," said Athos, "but I wish to remind Aramis that he cannot quit the camp, and that no one but one of us can be trusted ; that two hours after the messenger has set out, all the capuchins, all the alguazils, all the black caps of the cardinal, will know your letter by heart, and you and your clever person will be arrested."

" Without reckoning that the queen would save Buckingham, but would take no heed of us at all."

" Gentlemen," said D'Artagnan, " what Porthos says is full of sense."

" Ah, ha ! but what's going on in the city ? " exclaimed Athos.

" They are beating the alarm."

The four friends listened, and all heard distinctly the sound of the drum.

" You will see they are going to send a whole regiment against us," said Athos.

" You don't think of holding out against a whole regiment, do you ? " inquired Porthos.

" Why not ? " said the musketeer. " I feel myself quite in a humour for it ; and I would hold out before an army if we had only taken the precaution to bring a dozen more bottles of wine."

" 'Pon my word, the drum is approaching," said D'Artagnan.

" Let it come," said Athos. " It is a quarter of an hour's journey from here to the city, consequently a quarter of an hour's journey from the city here. That is more time than we need to devise a plan. If we go from this place, we shall never find another so suitable. Ah, stop ! I have it, gentlemen ; the right idea has just occurred to me."

" Tell us, then."

" Allow me to give Grimaud some indispensable orders."

Athos made a sign for his lackey to draw near.

" Grimaud," said Athos, pointing to the bodies which lay in the bastion, " take those gentlemen, set them up against the wall, put their hats on their heads, and their guns in their hands."

" Oh, great man ! " cried D'Artagnan, " I understand now."

" You understand ? " said Porthos.

" And do you understand, Grimaud ? " said Aramis.

Grimaud made a sign in the affirmative.

" That's all that's necessary," said Athos ; " now for my idea."

" I should like, however, to understand," said Porthos.

" It is not necessary."

"Yes, yes! Athos's idea!" cried Aramis and D'Artagnan at the same time.

"This milady — this woman — this creature — this demon has a brother-in-law, as I think you have told me, D'Artagnan?"

"Yes, I know him very well; and I also believe that he has not a very warm affection for his sister-in-law."

"There is no harm in that; if he detested her, it would be all the better," replied Athos.

"In that case, we are as well off as we could wish."

"And now," said Porthos, "I should like to understand what Grimaud is up to."

"Silence, Porthos!" said Aramis.

"What is her brother-in-law's name?"

"Lord Winter."

"Where is he now?"

"He returned to London at the first rumour of war."

"Well, he's just the man we want," said Athos; "we must warn him. We will send him word that his sister-in-law is on the point of assassinating some one, and we will beg of him not to lose sight of her. There is in London, I hope, some establishment like that of the Magdalens, or of the Repentant Women. He will place his sister in one of these, and we are in peace."

"Yes," said D'Artagnan, "until she gets out again."

"Ah, 'pon my word!" said Athos, "you require too much, D'Artagnan; I have given you all I had, and I beg leave to tell you that this is the end of my rope."

"But I think it would be still better," said Aramis, "to inform the queen and Lord Winter at the same time."

"Yes; but who is to carry the letter to Tours, and who the letter to London?"

"I answer for Bazin," said Aramis.

"And I for Planchet," said D'Artagnan.

"That is so," said Porthos; "if we cannot leave the camp, our lackeys may."

"To be sure they may," said Aramis; "and this very day we write the letters, we give them money, and they set out."

"We will give them money?" replied Athos. "Have you any money, then?"

The four friends looked at one another, and a cloud came over the brows which had been for an instant so cheerful.

"Quick!" cried D'Artagnan; "I see black points and

red points moving yonder. What did you say about a regiment, Athos ? It is a whole army ! ''

" 'Pon my word,'' said Athos ; " yes, there they are. Do you see the sneaks coming without drums or trumpets ? —Ah ! have you finished, Grimaud ? ''

Grimaud made a sign in the affirmative, and pointed to a dozen bodies which he had set up in the most picturesque attitudes—some carrying arms, others seeming to aim, and the rest sword in hand.

" Bravo ! '' said Athos ; " that does honour to your imagination.''

" Very good,'' said Porthos. " I should like, however, to understand.''

" Let us get away first,'' said D'Artagnan ; " and you can understand afterwards.''

" One moment, gentlemen, one moment ; give Grimaud time to clear away the things.''

" Ah, ha ! '' said Aramis ; " the black points and the red points are visibly growing larger. I agree with D'Artagnan : I believe we have no time to lose to regain our camp.''

" Faith ! '' said Athos, " I have nothing more to say against a retreat. Our wager called for an hour : we have stayed an hour and a half. Nothing can be said ; let us be off, gentlemen, let us be off ! ''

Grimaud had already gone on with the basket and the dessert. The four friends followed, and had gone about ten paces.

" Ah ! '' cried Athos. " What the devil shall we do now, gentlemen ? ''

" Have you forgotten something ? '' said Aramis.

" The flag, 'sdeath ! We must not leave a flag in the enemy's hands, even though that flag be but a napkin.''

And Athos ran back to the bastion, mounted the platform, and brought off the flag ; but as the Rochellais had come within musket range, they opened a terrible fire on this man, who appeared to be exposing himself for the pleasure of it.

But Athos might be said to bear a charmed life : the balls whistled all around him ; not one hit him. He waved his flag, turning his back to the guards of the city and saluting those of the camp. On both sides loud shouts arose—on the one side cries of anger, on the other shouts of enthusiasm.

A second discharge followed the first, and three balls, by passing through it, made the napkin really a flag. Shouts were heard from the camp—" Come down ! come down ! ''

Athos came down; his friends were anxiously waiting for him.

"Come on, Athos, come on!" cried D'Artagnan; "now we have found everything except money, it would be stupid to be killed."

But Athos continued to march majestically, in spite of all the remarks his companions made to him; and they, finding their remarks idle, regulated their pace by his.

Grimaud and his basket had got far in advance, and both were out of reach of the balls.

An instant later a furious firing was heard.

"What's that?" asked Porthos; "what are they firing at now? I hear no balls, and I see no one!"

"They are firing on our dead men," replied Athos.

"But our dead men will not return their fire."

"You are right. Then they will fancy it is an ambuscade, they will deliberate; and by the time they find out the joke we shall be out of range. That's why it is useless to get a pleurisy by going too fast."

"Oh, I understand now," said the astonished Porthos.

"That's very lucky," said Athos, shrugging his shoulders.

The French, seeing the four friends returning leisurely, uttered shouts of enthusiasm.

At length a fresh discharge was heard, and this time the balls came rattling among the stones around the four friends, and whistling sharply in their ears. The Rochellais had just taken possession of the bastion.

"What bunglers!" said Athos. "How many have we killed of them—a dozen?"

"Or fifteen."

"How many did we crush under the wall?"

"Eight or ten."

"And in exchange for all that, not a scratch! Ah! but what is the matter with your hand, D'Artagnan? It seems to me it is bleeding."

"Oh, it's nothing," said D'Artagnan.

"A spent ball?"

"Not even that."

"What is it, then?"

We have said that Athos loved D'Artagnan as though he was his son, and this sombre and inflexible character sometimes felt a parent's anxiety for the young man.

"Only grazed a little," replied D'Artagnan. "My fingers were caught between the stone of the wall and the stone of my ring, and the skin was broken."

"That comes of wearing diamonds, my master," said Athos disdainfully.

"Ah, to be sure," cried Porthos; "there is really a diamond. Why the devil, then, do we plague ourselves about money when there is a diamond?"

"Come, that's a fact!" said Aramis.

"Well thought of, Porthos; this time you have an idea."

"Certainly I have," said Porthos, drawing himself up proudly at Athos's compliment. "Since there is a diamond, let us sell it."

"But," said D'Artagnan, "it is the queen's diamond."

"All the more reason why it should be sold," replied Athos. "As the queen is saving Buckingham, her lover, nothing could be more just; the queen is saving us, her friends—nothing more moral. Let us sell the diamond. What says Monsieur l'Abbé? I don't ask Porthos; his opinion has been given."

"Why, I think," said Aramis, "that since his ring does not come from a mistress, and consequently is not a love-token, D'Artagnan may sell it."

"My dear Aramis, you speak like theology personified. Your opinion, then, is——"

"Sell the diamond."

"Well, then," said D'Artagnan gaily, "let us sell the diamond, and say no more about it."

The fusillade was still going on; but the friends were out of range, and the Rochellais only fired to soothe their consciences.

"Faith! it was time that idea came into Porthos's head. Here we are in camp; therefore, gentlemen, not a word more of this affair. We are observed; they are coming to meet us; we shall be borne in in triumph."

In fact, as we have said, the whole camp was in commotion. More than two thousand persons had been present, as at a play, at this fortunate escapade of the four friends —an escapade of the real motive of which no one had a suspicion. Nothing was heard but cries of "Hurrah for the musketeers! Hurrah for the guards!" M. de Busigny was the first to come and shake Athos by the hand, and acknowledge that the wager was lost. The dragoon and the Swiss followed him, and all their comrades followed the dragoon and the Swiss. There was no end to the congratulations, pressures of the hand, and embraces; there was inextinguishable laughter at the Rochellais. The tumult at

length became so great that the cardinal fancied there was
a riot, and sent La Houdinière, his captain of the guards, to
find out what was going on.

The affair was described to the messenger with all the
effervescence of enthusiasm.

" Well ? " asked the cardinal, on seeing La Houdinière
return.

" Well, monseigneur," replied the latter, " three musketeers and a guardsman laid a wager with M. de Busigny
that they would go and breakfast in the Bastion St.
Gervais, and while breakfasting they held it for two hours
against the enemy, and have killed I don't know how many
Rochellais."

" Did you inquire the names of the three musketeers ? "

" Yes, monseigneur."

" What are their names ? "

" MM. Athos, Porthos, and Aramis."

" Always my three brave fellows ! " murmured the cardinal.   " And the guard ? "

" M. d'Artagnan."

" Still my young scapegrace. Positively, these four men
must be mine."

That same evening the cardinal spoke to M. de Tréville
of the morning's exploit, which was the talk of the whole
camp. M. de Tréville, who had received the account of
the adventure from the very mouths of the heroes of it,
related it in all its details to his Eminence, not forgetting
the episode of the napkin.

" Very well, Monsieur de Tréville," said the cardinal ;
" pray let me have that napkin. I will have three fleurs-
de-lis embroidered on it in gold, and will give it to your
company as a standard."

" Monseigneur," said M. de Tréville, " that will hardly be
doing justice to the guards. M. d'Artagnan is not mine ; he
serves under M. des Essarts."

" Well, then, take him," said the cardinal ; " when four
men are so much attached to one another, it is only fair that
they should serve in the same company."

That same evening M. de Tréville announced this good
news to the three musketeers and D'Artagnan, inviting all
four to breakfast with him next morning.

D'Artagnan was beside himself with joy. We know that
the dream of his life had been to become a musketeer.

The three friends were likewise greatly delighted.

" Faith ! " said D'Artagnan to Athos, " that was a

triumphant idea of yours ! As you said, we have acquired glory, and were enabled to carry on a conversation of the greatest importance."

" Which we can resume now without anybody suspecting us, for, with God's aid, we shall henceforth pass for cardinalists."

That evening D'Artagnan went to present his compliments to M. des Essarts, and to inform him of his promotion.

M. des Essarts, who esteemed D'Artagnan, offered to aid him in any way, as this change of corps would entail expenses for outfit.

D'Artagnan respectfully declined, but thinking the opportunity a good one, he begged him to have the diamond he put into his hand valued, as he wished to turn it into money.

By eight o'clock next morning M. des Essarts's valet came to D'Artagnan's lodging, and gave him a purse containing seven thousand livres.

This was the price of the queen's diamond.

CHAPTER XLVIII.

A FAMILY AFFAIR.

ATHOS had invented the phrase, *family affair*. A family affair was not subject to the cardinal's investigation ; a family affair concerned no one ; people might employ themselves in a family affair before all the world.

Thus Athos had discovered the words, *family affair*.

Aramis had discovered the idea, the lackeys.

Porthos had discovered the means, the diamond.

D'Artagnan alone had discovered nothing—he, ordinarily, the most inventive of the four ; but it must also be said that the mere mention of milady paralyzed him.

Oh no ! we were mistaken ; he had discovered a purchaser for his diamond.

The breakfast at M. de Tréville's was delightfully gay. D'Artagnan was already in his uniform, for as he was nearly of the same size as Aramis, and as Aramis had been so liberally paid by the bookseller who purchased his poem, as we remember, he had bought two of everything, and so he furnished his friend with a complete outfit.

D'Artagnan would have been at the height of his wishes

if he had not constantly seen milady, like a dark cloud, on the horizon.

After breakfast it was agreed that they should meet again in the evening at Athos's lodging, and would there end the affair.

D'Artagnan passed the day in exhibiting his musketeer's uniform in every street of the camp.

In the evening, at the appointed hour, the four friends met. There remained only three things to be decided on— what they should write to milady's brother; what they should write to the clever person at Tours; and which should be the lackeys to carry the letters.

Each one offered his own. Athos talked of the discretion of Grimaud, who never spoke a word but when his master unlocked his mouth. Porthos boasted of the strength of Mousqueton, who was big enough to thrash four men of ordinary size. Aramis, confiding in Bazin's skill, delivered a pompous eulogy of his candidate; and finally, D'Artagnan had entire faith in Planchet's bravery, and reminded them of the manner in which he had conducted himself in the ticklish affair at Boulogne.

These four virtues disputed the prize for a long time, and gave opportunity for magnificent speeches, which we will not repeat here, lest they should be deemed wearisome.

"Unfortunately," said Athos, "the one we send must possess in himself alone the four qualities united."

"But where is such a lackey to be found?"

"Not to be found!" cried Athos. "I know that; so take Grimaud."

"Take Mousqueton!"

"Take Bazin!"

"Take Planchet. Planchet is brave and shrewd; that's two qualities out of the four."

"Gentlemen," said Aramis, "the chief point is not to know which of our four lackeys is the discreetest, the strongest, the cleverest, or the bravest; the thing is to know which loves money the best."

"What Aramis says is very sensible," replied Athos: "we must speculate on people's faults, and not on their virtues. Abbé, you are a great moralist."

"Doubtless," said Aramis; "for we not only require to be well served in order to succeed, but, still more, in order not to fail; for in case of failure, heads are at stake, not for our lackeys——"

"Speak lower, Aramis," said Athos.

"**You are** right. Not the lackey's," resumed Aramis, "but the master's. And even the masters'! Are our lackeys sufficiently devoted to us to risk their lives for us? No."

"Faith!" said D'Artagnan, "I would almost answer for Planchet."

"Well, my dear friend, add to his natural devotion a good sum of money which may give him some comfort, and then, instead of answering for him once, answer for him twice."

"Why, good Heavens! you will be deceived just the same," said Athos, who was an optimist when things were concerned, and a pessimist when men were in question. "They will promise everything for the sake of the money, and on the road fear will prevent them from acting. Once taken, they will be put to the torture; when put to the torture they will confess everything. What the devil! we are not children. To go to England" (Athos lowered his voice) "they must cross all France covered with the cardinal's spies and creatures; a pass must be obtained to set sail; and one ought to know English in order to inquire the way to London. Really, I consider the thing very difficult!"

"Not at all," cried D'Artagnan, who was very anxious the thing should be done. "On the contrary, I think it is very easy. It would be, no doubt. Of course, by Jove! if we write to Lord Winter about affairs of vast importance, of the cardinal's horrors——"

"Speak lower!" said Athos.

"Of state intrigues and secrets," continued D'Artagnan, complying with the recommendation, "no doubt we shall be all broken on the wheel; but, for God's sake, do not forget, as you yourself said, Athos, that we only write to him concerning a family affair—that we only write to him to entreat that as soon as milady arrives in London, he will put it out of her power to injure us. I will write to him, then, nearly in the following terms."

"Let us see," said Athos, assuming a critical look.

"'Sir, and dear friend——'"

"Ah, yes! 'dear friend' to an Englishman," interrupted Athos—"a fine beginning! Bravo, D'Artagnan! With that one word you would be quartered instead of broken on the wheel."

"Well, so be it. I will say, then, 'Sir,' quite short."

"You may even say 'Milord,'" replied Athos, who stickled for propriety.

" ' Milord, do you remember the little goat pasture of the Luxembourg ? ' "

" Good ! the Luxembourg, now ! They will suppose it is an allusion to the queen-mother ! That's ingenious," said Athos.

" Well, then, we will put simply, ' Milord, do you remember a certain little inclosure where your life was spared ? ' "

" My dear D'Artagnan, you will never make anything but a very bad secretary. ' Where your life was spared ! ' For shame ! that's unworthy. A man of spirit is not to be reminded of such services. To reproach a person with a benefit conferred is an insult."

" Oh, my dear ! " said D'Artagnan, " you are insupportable ! If the letter must be written under your censure, 'pon my word, I renounce the task."

" And you do right. Handle the musket and the sword, my dear fellow ; you come off splendidly at these two exercises. But hand the pen over to the abbé ; that's his province."

" Ay, ay," said Porthos ; " hand the pen over to Aramis ; he writes theses in Latin."

" Well, so be it," said D'Artagnan. " Draw up this note for us, Aramis ; but, by our holy father the Pope, be concise, for I shall pluck you in my turn, I warn you."

" I ask nothing better," said Aramis, with that ingenuous self-confidence which every poet has ; " but let me know what I am about. I have heard, in one way and another, that Lord Winter's sister-in-law was vile. It was even proved to me when I overheard her conversation with the cardinal."

" Worse than vile, ye gods ! " said Athos.

" But," continued Aramis, " the details escape me."

" And me also," said Porthos.

D'Artagnan and Athos looked at each other for some time in silence. At length Athos, after reflection, and growing paler than usual, gave an affirmative nod. D'Artagnan understood by it he was at liberty to speak.

" Well, this is what you have to say," said D'Artagnan: " Milord, your sister-in-law is an infamous woman, who has wished to have you killed, that she might inherit your wealth. But she could not be your brother's wife, as she had already been married in France, and had been——"

D'Artagnan stopped, as if seeking for the word, and looked at Athos.

" Repudiated by her husband."

" Because she had been branded," continued D'Artagnan.

" Bah ! " cried Porthos, " impossible ! She wanted to have her brother-in-law killed ? "

" Yes."

" And she had been married ? " asked Aramis.

" Yes."

" And her husband found out that she had a fleur-de-lis on her shoulder ? " cried Porthos.

" Yes."

Three times Athos had said " yes," and each time with a deeper intonation.

" And who has seen this fleur-de-lis ? " asked Aramis.

" D'Artagnan and I ; or rather, to observe the chronological order, I and D'Artagnan," replied Athos.

" And does this frightful creature's husband still live ? " asked Aramis.

" He still lives."

" Are you quite sure of it ? "

" I am."

There was a moment of chilling silence, during which every one was affected, according to his nature.

" This time," said Athos, first breaking the silence, " D'Artagnan has given us an excellent programme, and this must be written at once."

" The devil ! you are right, Athos," said Aramis ; " and the wording of it is difficult. The chancellor himself would be puzzled how to write such a letter, and yet the chancellor draws up a report very agreeably. Never mind ! Be silent ; I will write it."

Aramis accordingly took the pen, reflected for a few moments, wrote eight or ten lines in a charming little feminine hand, and then, in a soft, slow voice, as if each word had been scrupulously weighed, he read the following :—

" MILORD,—The person who writes these lines had the honour of crossing swords with you in a little yard near the Rue d'Enfer. As you have several times since been kind enough to call yourself that person's friend, he thinks it his duty to respond to your friendship by sending you important information. Twice you have almost been the victim of a near relative whom you believe to be your heir, because you do not know that before she contracted a marriage in England she was already married in France. But the third time, which is this, you may succumb. Your

relative left Rochelle for England during the night. Be
on the watch for her arrival, for she has great and terrible
projects. If you absolutely insist on knowing what she is
capable of, read her past history upon her left shoulder."

"Well, now, that's wonderfully well done," said Athos;
"really, my dear Aramis, you have the pen of a secretary
of state. Lord Winter will now be upon his guard, if the
letter should reach him; and even if it should fall into the
cardinal's hands, we shall not be compromised. But as the
lackey who goes may make us believe he has been to London
and may stop at Châtellerault, let us give him only half the
sum with the letter, promising that he shall have the other
half in exchange for the reply. Have you the diamond?"
continued Athos.

"I have what is still better: I have the value of it."

And D'Artagnan threw the purse on the table. At the
sound of the gold Aramis raised his eyes and Porthos
started; Athos remained unmoved.

"How much is there in that purse?"

"Seven thousand livres, in louis of twelve francs."

"Seven thousand livres!" cried Porthos—"that wretched
little diamond was worth seven thousand livres?"

"It seems so," said Athos, "since here they are. I don't
suppose that our friend D'Artagnan has added any of his
own."

"But, gentlemen, in all this," said D'Artagnan, "we
have no thought of the queen. Let us look a little after her
dear Buckingham's health. That is the least we owe her."

"You are right," said Athos; "but that falls to Aramis."

"Well," replied the latter, "what must I do?"

"Oh, it's simple enough," replied Athos. "Write a
second letter for that clever personage who lives at Tours."

Aramis resumed his pen, reflected a little more, and wrote
the following lines, which he immediately submitted to his
friends' approbation,—

"My dear cousin."

"Ah, ha!" said Athos; "this clever lady is your relative,
then?"

"She's my cousin-german."

"Good—for your cousin, then!"

Aramis continued:—

"MY DEAR COUSIN,—His Eminence the cardinal, whom
God preserve for the happiness of France and the confusion

of the enemies of the kingdom, is on the point of finishing up with the heretic rebels of Rochelle ; it is probable that the aid of the English fleet will never even arrive in sight of the place. I will even venture to say that I am certain the Duke of Buckingham will be prevented from starting for there by some great event. His Eminence is the most illustrious politician of times past, of times present, and probably of times to come. He would extinguish the sun, if the sun incommoded him. Give these happy tidings to your sister, my dear cousin. I have dreamed that that cursed Englishman was dead. I cannot recollect whether it was by steel or by poison ; only I am sure of this : I have dreamed he was dead, and you know my dreams never deceive me. Be assured, then, of seeing me soon return."

"Capital," cried Athos ; "you are the king of poets, my dear Aramis. You speak like the Apocalypse, and you are as true as the gospel. There is nothing now for you to do but to put the address on your letter."

"That's easily done," said Aramis.

He folded the letter coquettishly, took it, and wrote,—

"To Mademoiselle Michon, seamstress, Tours."

The three friends looked at each other and laughed ; they were caught.

"Now," said Aramis, "you understand, gentlemen, that Bazin is the only person who can carry this letter to Tours. My cousin knows no one but Bazin, and places confidence in no one else ; any other person would fail. Besides, Bazin is ambitious and learned ; Bazin has read history, gentlemen. He knows that Sixtus V. became pope after having tended pigs. Then, as he means to enter holy orders at the same time as myself, he does not despair of becoming a pope in his turn, or at least a cardinal. You understand that a man who has such views will never allow himself to be taken, or if taken, will undergo martyrdom rather than speak."

"Well, well," said D'Artagnan, "I grant you Bazin with all my heart, but let me have Planchet. Milady one day had him turned out of doors, with a sound caning. Now Planchet has an excellent memory, and I will be bound that if he can see possible means of vengeance, he will let himself be beaten to death rather than fail. If your affairs of Tours are your affairs, Aramis, those of London are mine. I beg, then, that Planchet may be chosen, especially as he has already been to London with me, and knows how to say very correctly, *London, sir, if you please,* and, *My master, Lord d'Artagnan.* With that, you may be satisfied, he can make his way, both going and returning."

"In that case," said Athos, "Planchet must receive seven hundred livres for going, and seven hundred livres for coming back; and Bazin, three hundred livres for going, and three hundred livres for coming back. That will reduce the sum to five thousand livres. We will each take a thousand livres, to be employed as seems good to each, and we will leave a fund of a thousand livres, in the guardianship of the abbé here, for extraordinary occasions or common necessities. Does that suit you?"

"My dear Athos," said Aramis, "you speak like Nestor."

Planchet was sent for, and instructions were given him. He had already been notified by D'Artagnan, who had shown him first the glory, next the money, and then the danger.

"I will carry the letter in the lining of my coat," said Planchet, "and if I am taken I will swallow it."

"Well, but then you will not be able to fulfil your commission," said D'Artagnan.

"You will give me a copy of it this evening, and I will know it by heart before morning."

D'Artagnan looked at his friends, as if to say, "Well, what did I promise you?"

"Now," continued he, addressing Planchet, "you have eight days to get to Lord Winter, you have eight days to return in—in all sixteen days; if on the sixteenth day after your departure, at eight o'clock in the evening, you are not here, no money, even if it be but five minutes past eight."

"Then, sir," said Planchet, "buy me a watch."

"Take this," said Athos, with his usual careless generosity, giving him his own, "and be a good lad. Remember, if you talk, if you babble, if you get drunk, you risk your master's head—your master, who has so much confidence in your fidelity that he is responsible to us for you. But remember, also, that if, by your fault, any evil happens to D'Artagnan, I will find you, wherever you are, and for the express purpose of disembowelling you."

"O sir!" said Planchet, humiliated by the suspicion, and, above all, terrified at the musketeer's calm air.

"And I," said Porthos, rolling his big eyes—"remember, I will skin you alive."

"Ah, sir!"

"And I," said Aramis, in his soft, melodious voice—"remember that I will roast you at a slow fire, like a savage."

"Ah, sir!"

And Planchet began to weep. We will not venture to say whether it was from terror caused by the threats, or from tenderness at seeing four friends so closely united.

D'Artagnan took his hand and kissed him.

"See, Planchet," said he, "these gentlemen only say all this out of affection for me, but at heart they all respect you."

"Ah, sir!" said Planchet, "I will succeed, or I will consent to be quartered; and if they quarter me, be assured that not a morsel of me will speak."

It was decided that Planchet should set out at eight o'clock the next morning, in order, as he had said, that he might learn the letter by heart during the night. He gained just twelve hours by this arrangement; he was to be back on the sixteenth day, by eight o'clock in the evening.

In the morning, as he was mounting his horse, D'Artagnan, who felt at the bottom of his heart a partiality for the duke, took Planchet aside.

"Listen," said he to him. "When you have given the letter to Lord Winter, and he has read it, you will further say to him, 'Watch over his Grace, Lord Buckingham, for there is a plot to assassinate him.' But, Planchet, you see this is so serious and important that I have not informed my friends that I would entrust this secret to you; and for a captain's commission I would not write it."

"Be at rest, sir," said Planchet; "you shall see whether confidence can be placed in me or not."

And mounted on an excellent horse, which he was to leave at the end of twenty leagues to take the post, Planchet set off at a gallop, a little anxious by the threefold threat made him by the musketeers, but otherwise as light-hearted as possible.

Bazin set out the next day for Tours, and was allowed a week in which to perform his commission.

The four friends, all the while these two were away, had, as may well be supposed, their eyes more than ever on the watch, their ears pricked up, and every sense alert. Their days were spent in trying to catch whatever was said, in observing the cardinal's proceedings, and in looking out for all the couriers who arrived. More than once an insurmountable trembling seized them when called upon for any unexpected service. They had, besides, to look constantly to their own safety ; milady was a phantom which, when it had once appeared to people, did not allow them to sleep very quietly.

On the morning of the eighth day Bazin, fresh as ever and smiling as usual, entered the tavern of the Infidel as the four friends were sitting down to breakfast, saying, as had been agreed upon,—

"Monsieur Aramis, here is your cousin's answer."

The four friends exchanged a joyful glance. Half of the work was done. It is true, however, that it was the shortest and the easiest half.

Aramis took the letter, which was in a large, coarse hand, and ill-spelt.

"Good gracious!" cried he, laughing, "I really despair of my poor Michon ; she will never write like M. de Voiture."

"Vot do you mean by your boor Migeon ?" asked the Swiss, who was chatting with the four friends when the letter arrived.

"Oh, by Jove! less than nothing," said Aramis ; "a little charming seamstress, whom I love dearly, and from whom I requested a few autograph lines as a sort of keepsake."

"Ze teffil !" said the Swiss ; "if ze lady is as kreat as her writing is large, you are lucky fellow, gomrat !"

Aramis read the letter, and passed it to Athos.

"See what she writes to me, Athos," said he.

Athos cast a glance over the epistle, and, to dissipate all the suspicions that might have been created, read aloud,—

"MY COUSIN,—My sister and I are very skilful in interpreting dreams, and even entertain great fear of them ; but of yours it may be said, I hope, every dream is an illusion. Farewell ! Take care of yourself, and act so that we may, from time to time, hear you spoken of.

"MARIE MICHON."

"And what dream does she mean ?" asked the dragoon, who had approached during the reading.

"Yes ; what's the tream ?" said the Swiss.

"Well, by Jove!" said Aramis, "it was only this : I had a dream, and I related it to her."

"Oh yes, py Kot, yes ; it's simple enough to dell a tream ven you haff vun ; but I neffer tream."

"You are very fortunate," said Athos, rising; "I wish I could say as much!"

"Neffer!" replied the Swiss, enchanted that a man like Athos could envy him anything. "Neffer! neffer!"

D'Artagnan, seeing Athos rise, did the same, took his arm, and went out.

Porthos and Aramis remained behind to encounter the jokes of the dragoon and the Swiss.

Bazin went and lay down on a truss of straw; and as he had more imagination than the Swiss, he dreamed that Aramis had become a pope, and was adorning his head with a cardinal's hat.

But as we have said, Bazin, by his fortunate return, had removed only a part of the uneasiness which weighed on the four friends. Days of expectation are long, and D'Artagnan in particular would have wagered that these days contained forty-eight hours. He forgot the necessary slowness of navigation; he mentally exaggerated milady's power. He came to believe that this woman, who seemed to him like a demon, had auxiliaries as supernatural as herself. At the least noise he imagined that he was about to be arrested, and that Planchet was being brought back to be confronted with himself and his friends. Moreover, his confidence in the worthy Picard, at one time so great, grew less each day. His anxiety became so great that it even extended to Aramis and Porthos. Athos alone remained calm, as though no danger hovered over him, and as though he were breathing his usual atmosphere.

On the sixteenth day in particular these signs of anxiety were so manifest in D'Artagnan and his two friends that they could not remain quiet in one place, and they wandered about like ghosts on the road by which Planchet was expected.

"Really," said Athos, "you are not men, but children, to let a woman terrify you so! And what is it all about after all? Being imprisoned? Well, but we should be got out of prison; Madame Bonacieux got out. Being beheaded? Why, every day in the trenches we go cheerfully to expose ourselves to worse than that, for a bullet may break a leg, and I am convinced a surgeon would give us more pain in cutting our thighs than an executioner would in cutting off our heads. Wait quietly, then; in two hours, in four, in six hours at the latest, Planchet will be here. He promised to be here, and I have very great faith in Planchet's promises; I think him a very good lad."

"But if he does not come?" said D'Artagnan.

"Well, if he does not come, it will be because he has been delayed, that's all. He may have fallen from his horse; he may have slipped down on the deck; he may have travelled so fast as to get inflammation of the lungs. Eh, gentlemen, let us reckon upon accidents! Life is a chaplet of little miseries, which the philosopher, with a smile, tells off one at a time. Be philosophers, as I am, gentlemen; sit down at the table and let us drink. Nothing makes the future look so bright as surveying it through a glass of chambertin."

"That's very well," replied D'Artagnan, "but I am tired of fearing, when I open a fresh bottle, that the wine may come from milady's cellar."

"You are hard to suit," said Athos; "such a beautiful woman!"

"A woman of mark!" said Porthos, with his loud laugh.

Athos started, passed his hand over his brow to wipe off the drops of perspiration, and rose in his turn with a nervous movement he could not repress.

The day, however, passed away, and the evening came on slower than ever, but it came. The taprooms were filled with drinkers. Athos, who had pocketed his share of the diamond, seldom quitted the Infidel. He had found in M. de Busigny—who, by the way, had given them a magnificent dinner—a partner worthy of his company. They were playing together as usual when seven o'clock struck; the patrols were heard passing to double the posts. At half-past seven tattoo was sounded.

"We are lost," said D'Artagnan in Athos's ear.

"You mean we have lost," said Athos quietly, drawing four pistoles from his pocket and flinging them on the table. "Come, gentlemen," said he, "they are beating the tattoo; to bed, to bed!"

And Athos went out of the Infidel, followed by D'Artagnan. Aramis came behind, giving his arm to Porthos. Aramis mumbled verses, and Porthos from time to time pulled a hair or two from his moustache, as a sign of despair.

But behold! suddenly a shadow appears in the darkness, the outline of which is familiar to D'Artagnan, and a well-known voice says,—

"Sir, I have brought your cloak, for it is chilly this evening."

"Planchet!" cried D'Artagnan, intoxicated with joy.

"Planchet!" repeated Aramis and Porthos.

"Well, certainly Planchet," said Athos; "what is there astonishing in that? He promised to be back by eight o'clock, and eight is just now striking. Bravo, Planchet! you are a lad of your word, and if ever you leave your master I promise you a place in my service."

"Oh no, never!" said Planchet. "I will never leave M. d'Artagnan."

At the same time D'Artagnan felt Planchet slipping a note into his hand.

D'Artagnan was strongly inclined to kiss Planchet on his return as he had kissed him on his departure; but he feared lest such effusiveness lavished on his lackey in the open street might appear extraordinary to some spectator, and he restrained himself.

"I have a note," said he to Athos and his friends.

"Very well," said Athos; "let us go home and we will read it."

The note burned in D'Artagnan's hand. He wished to hasten; but Athos took his arm and passed it under his own, and the young man was obliged to regulate his pace by his friend's.

At length they reached the tent, lit a lamp, and whilst Planchet stood at the entrance, so that the four friends might not be surprised, D'Artagnan with a trembling hand broke the seal and opened the letter so anxiously expected.

It contained half a line in a thoroughly British hand, and of thoroughly Spartan brevity:—

"*Thank you. Be easy.*"

Athos took the letter from D'Artagnan's hands, drew near to the lamp, set fire to it, and did not let it go till it was reduced to ashes.

Then calling Planchet,—

"Now, my lad," said he, "you may claim your seven hundred livres; but you did not run much risk with such a note as that."

"'Twas not from lack of trying every means to compass it," said Planchet.

"Well," cried D'Artagnan, "tell us about it."

"Ah, sir, it's a very long story."

"You are right, Planchet," said Athos; "besides, tattoo has been sounded, and we should be observed if we kept a light burning longer than the others."

"So be it," said D'Artagnan. "Let us go to bed. Planchet, sleep soundly."

"Faith, sir, it will be the first time I have done so these sixteen days!"

"Or I either!" said D'Artagnan.

"Or I either!" said Porthos.

"Or I either!" said Aramis.

"Well, if I must tell you the truth—or I either!" said Athos.

CHAPTER XLIX.

FATALITY.

MEANTIME milady, drunk with rage, roaring on the deck of the vessel like a lioness embarked, had been tempted to leap into the sea in order to regain the coast, for she could not get rid of the idea that she had been insulted by D'Artagnan and threatened by Athos, and after all was leaving France without being revenged on either.

This idea soon became so insupportable to her that, at the risk of whatever terrible consequences might result to herself from it, she implored the captain to put her on shore; but the captain, anxious to escape from his false position—placed between French and English cruisers like the bat between the rats and the birds—was in great haste to reach the English coast, and positively refused to obey what he considered a woman's whim, though he promised his passenger, since she had been particularly recommended to him by the cardinal, to land her at one of the ports of Brittany, either at Lorient or Brest, if the sea and the French permitted. But the wind was contrary, the sea rough; they kept beating to windward and tacking about. Nine days after leaving the Charente, milady, pale with anger and annoyance, saw only the blue coasts of Finisterre appear.

She calculated that to cross this corner of France and return to the cardinal would take her at least three days; add another day for landing, and that made four; add these four days to the others, that would be thirteen days lost—thirteen days, during which so many important events might happen in London. She reflected, likewise, that the cardinal would be angry at her return, and, consequently, would be more disposed to listen to the complaints made against her than to the accusations she brought against others.

She therefore allowed the vessel to pass Lorient and Brest without repeating her request to the captain, and he took care not to remind her of it. So milady continued her voyage, and on the very day that Planchet embarked at Portsmouth for France, his Eminence's messenger entered the port in triumph.

All the city was stirred by an extraordinary commotion: four large ships, recently built, had just been launched. Standing on the jetty, his clothes bedizened with gold, glittering as usual with diamonds and precious stones, his hat ornamented with a white feather which drooped on his shoulder, Buckingham was seen, surrounded by a staff almost as brilliant as himself.

It was one of those rare and beautiful winter days when England remembers that there is a sun. The orb, pale, but nevertheless splendid still, was declining toward the horizon, tingeing at once the heavens and the sea with bands of purple fire, and casting on the towers and the old houses of the city a last golden ray, making the windows sparkle like the reflection of a fire. Milady, on breathing that sea air, which grows more and more invigorating and balsamic according as one nears the land, on contemplating all the power of that army which she was to combat alone—she, a woman, with a few bags of gold—compared herself mentally to Judith, the terrible Jewess, when she penetrated into the camp of the Assyrians, and beheld the enormous mass of chariots, horses, men, and arms, which a gesture of her hand was to dissipate like a cloud of smoke.

They entered the roadstead; but as they were making ready to cast anchor, a little cutter, formidably armed and purporting to be a coastguard, approached the merchant vessel, and dropped into the sea its gig, which directed its course to the ladder. The gig contained an officer, a boatswain, and eight oarsmen. The officer alone got on board, where he was received with all the deference inspired by a uniform.

The officer conversed a few moments with the captain, had him read several papers of which he was the bearer; and on the merchant-captain's order, all on board, both passengers and crew, were called on deck.

After this kind of summons had been given, the officer inquired aloud about the place of the brig's departure, of her route, of her landings; and all these questions the captain answered without hesitation and without difficulty.

Then the officer began to pass in review all the individuals, one after the other; and stopping in front of milady, surveyed her very closely, but without addressing a single word to her. He then went up to the captain, again said a few words to him, and, as if from that moment the vessel was under his command, he ordered a manœuvre which the crew immediately executed.

Then the vessel resumed her course, still escorted by the little cutter, which sailed side by side with it, threatening her side with the mouths of its six cannon, while the boat followed in the wake of the ship.

While the officer made his scrutiny of milady, milady, as may well be imagined, had been sharply eyeing him. But great as was the power of this woman, with eyes of flame, in reading the hearts of those whose secrets she wished to divine, she met this time with a face so impenetrable that no discovery followed her investigation. The officer who had stopped before her and silently studied her with so much care might have been twenty-five or twenty-six years old. He had a pale complexion, with clear blue eyes, rather deeply set; his mouth, fine and well cut, remained motionless in its correct lines; his chin, strongly set, denoted that strength of will which, in the ordinary Britannic type, usually stands only for obstinacy; a brow a little receding, as is proper for poets, enthusiasts, and soldiers, was scarcely shaded by short thin hair, which, like the beard covering the lower part of his face, was of a beautiful deep-chestnut colour.

When they entered the port it was already nightfall. The fog made the darkness still denser, and formed round the beacons and the lantern of the jetty a circle like that which surrounds the moon when the weather threatens to become rainy. The air they breathed was gloomy, damp, and cold.

Milady, courageous as she was, shivered in spite of herself.

The officer desired to have milady's luggage pointed out to him, ordered it to be placed in the boat; and when this operation was completed, he offered her his hand and invited her to descend.

Milady looked at the man and hesitated.

"Who are you, sir," she asked, "that you are so kind as to busy yourself so particularly on my account?"

"You must see, madame, by my uniform, that I am an officer in the English navy," replied the young man.

"But is it the custom for officers in the English navy to give their services to their female compatriots who land at a port of Great Britain, and to carry their gallantry so far as to bring them ashore?"

"Yes, madame, it is our custom, not from gallantry, but prudence, in time of war, to bring foreigners to certain hotels, in order that they may be under the eye of the government until full information can be obtained about them."

These words were spoken with the most exact politeness and the most perfect calmness. Nevertheless, they had not the power of convincing milady.

"But I am not a foreigner, sir," said she, with an accent as pure as ever was heard between Portsmouth and Manchester; "my name is Lady Clarick, and this measure——"

"This measure is general, madame, and you would not succeed in escaping from it."

"I will follow you, then, sir."

And accepting the officer's hand, she began to climb down the ladder, at the foot of which the gig was awaiting her. The officer followed her. A large cloak was spread in the stern. The officer had her sit down on the cloak, and placed himself beside her.

"Give way!" said he to the sailors.

The eight oars fell at once into the sea, making but a single sound, giving a single stroke, and the gig seemed to fly over the surface of the water.

At the end of five minutes they reached shore.

The officer sprang on the quay and offered milady his hand.

A carriage was in waiting.

"Is this carriage for us?" asked milady.

"Yes, madame," replied the officer.

"So the hotel is at some distance?"

"At the other end of the town."

"Very well," said milady; and she got resolutely into the carriage.

The officer saw that the baggage was fastened carefully behind the carriage; and when this operation was over, he took his place beside milady, and shut the door.

Instantly, without any order being given, or place of destination indicated, the coachman set off at a gallop, and plunged into the streets of the town.

Such a strange reception naturally gave milady ample matter for reflection ; so, seeing that the young officer did not seem at all disposed to talk, she reclined in her corner of the carriage, and passed in review all the suppositions which presented themselves, one after the other, to her mind.

At the end of a quarter of an hour, however, surprised at the length of the road, she leaned forward toward the window to see where she was going. No houses were to be seen ; trees appeared in the darkness like great black phantoms running after one another.

Milady shuddered.

"But we are no longer in the town, sir," said she.

The young officer was silent.

"I will go no farther unless you tell me where you are taking me. I warn you, sir."

This threat brought no reply.

"Oh, but this is too much," cried milady. "Help ! help ! "

No voice replied to hers. The carriage continued to roll rapidly on. The officer seemed like a statue.

Milady looked at the officer with one of those terrible expressions characteristic of her face, and which so rarely failed of their effect. Anger made her eyes flash in the darkness.

The young man remained unmoved.

Milady tried to open the door and throw herself out.

"Take care, madame," said the young man coldly ; "you will kill yourself if you attempt to jump out."

Milady sat down again, foaming with rage. The officer leaned forward, looked at her, and seemed surprised to see that face, but just before so beautiful, distorted with passion and become almost hideous.

The artful creature realized that she was injuring herself by allowing him thus to read her soul. She composed her features, and in a complaining voice said,—

"In the name of Heaven, sir, tell me if I am to attribute the violence that is done me to you, or to your government, or to an enemy."

"No violence is done you, madame ; and what happens to you is the result of a very simple measure which we are compelled to take with all who land in England."

"Then you don't know me, sir ? "

"It is the first time I ever had the honour of seeing you."

" And, on your honour, you have no cause of hatred against me ? "

" None, I swear to you."

There was so much serenity, coolness, mildness even, in the young man's voice that milady felt reassured.

At length, after nearly an hour's ride, the carriage stopped before an iron gate, which shut in a sunken avenue leading to a castle severe in form, massive, and isolated. Then, as the wheels rolled over a fine gravel, milady could hear a dull roar, which she recognized as the noise of the sea dashing against a rock-bound coast.

The carriage passed under two arched gateways, and at length stopped in a dark, square court. Almost immediately the carriage door was opened, the young man sprang lightly to the ground, and gave milady his hand. She leaned on it, and in her turn alighted quite calmly.

" Still, the fact is I am a prisoner," said milady, looking around her, and then fixing her eyes on the young officer with a most gracious smile ; " but I feel assured it will not be for long," added she. " My own conscience and your politeness, sir, are the guarantees of that."

Flattering as this compliment was, the officer made no reply, but drawing from his belt a little silver whistle, such as boatswains use in ships of war, he whistled three times, with three different modulations. Several men then appeared, unharnessed the smoking horses, and put the carriage into a coach-house.

The officer, always with the same calm politeness, invited his prisoner to enter the house. She, always with the same smiling countenance, took his arm, and passed with him under a low arched door, which, by a vaulted passage, lighted only at the farther end, led to a stone staircase turning round a stone column. Then they paused before a massive door, which, after the young officer had inserted a key into the lock, turned heavily on its hinges, and disclosed the chamber destined for milady.

With a single glance the prisoner took in the apartment in its minutest details.

It was a chamber the furniture of which was at once suited to a prison or the dwelling of a free man ; yet the bars at the windows and the outside bolts on the door decided the question in favour of the prison. For an instant all this creature's strength of mind abandoned her. She sank into an armchair, with her arms folded, her head hanging down, and expecting every instant to see a judge enter to question her.

But no one entered except two marines, who brought in her trunks and packages, deposited them in a corner of the room, and retired without speaking.

The officer presided over all these details with the same calmness milady had always observed in him, never uttering a word, and making himself obeyed by a gesture of his hand or a sound of his whistle.

One might have said that between this man and his inferiors spoken language did not exist, or had become useless.

At length milady could hold out no longer. She broke the silence.

"In the name of Heaven, sir," cried she, "what is the meaning of all this? Put an end to my doubts. I have courage enough for any danger I can foresee, for any misfortune I can comprehend. Where am I, and why am I here? If I am free, why these bars and these doors? If I am a prisoner, what crime have I committed?"

"You are here in the apartment destined for you, madame. I received orders to go and take charge of you at sea, and to conduct you to this castle. This order, I believe, I have accomplished with all a soldier's strictness, but also with all the courtesy of a gentleman. Here ends, at least for the present, the duty I had to fulfil toward you; the rest concerns another person."

"And who is this other person?" asked milady. "Can you not tell me his name?"

At that moment a great jingling of spurs was heard on the stairs. People talking together went by, the sounds of voices died away, and the noise made by a single footstep approached the door.

"Here he is, madame," said the officer, leaving the entrance clear, and drawing himself up in an attitude of respect and submission.

At the same time the door opened; a man appeared on the threshold.

He had no hat on, wore a sword at his side, and was crushing a handkerchief in his hand.

Milady thought she recognized this shadow in the gloom; she leaned with one hand on the arm of the chair, and protruded her head as if to meet a certainty.

Then the stranger advanced slowly, and as he advanced into the circle of light projected by the lamp, milady involuntarily drew back.

Then, when she had no longer any doubt,—

"What! my brother!" cried she, at the culmination of her amazement; "is it you?"

"Yes, fair lady," replied Lord Winter, making a bow, half courteous, half ironical; "it is I, myself."

"Then this castle?"

"Is mine."

"This room?"

"Is yours."

"I am your prisoner, then?"

"Nearly so."

"But this is a frightful abuse of power!"

"No high-sounding words. Let us sit down and talk calmly, as brother and sister ought to do."

Then turning toward the door, and seeing that the young officer was waiting for his last orders,—

"It is all right," said he; "I thank you. Now leave us alone, Mr. Felton."

CHAPTER L.

BROTHER AND SISTER.

WHILE Lord Winter was shutting the door, closing a shutter, and drawing a chair near to his sister-in-law's armchair, milady was thoughtfully plunging her glance into the depths of possibility, and discovered the whole plot, not even a glimpse of which she could get so long as she was ignorant into whose hands she had fallen. She knew her brother-in-law was a worthy gentleman, a bold huntsman, an intrepid player, enterprising with women, but with less than average skill in intrigues. How could he have discovered her arrival and caused her to be seized? Why did he detain her?

Athos had indeed said some words which proved that the conversation she had had with the cardinal had fallen into others' ears; but she could not suppose that he had dug a counter-mine so promptly and so boldly. She feared, rather, that her preceding operations in England had been discovered. Buckingham might have guessed that it was she who had cut off the two studs, and avenged himself for that little treachery. But Buckingham was incapable of going to any excess against a woman, particularly if that woman was supposed to have acted from a feeling of jealousy.

This supposition appeared to her the most reasonable:

it seemed to her that they wanted to revenge the past, and not to anticipate the future. At all events, she congratulated herself on having fallen into the hands of her brother-in-law, with whom she reckoned she could come off easily, rather than into the hands of an avowed and intelligent enemy.

"Yes, let us talk, brother," said she, with a kind of sprightliness, now that she had decided to get from the conversation, in spite of all dissimulation Lord Winter could bring to it, the information of which she stood in need for regulating her future conduct.

"So you decided to come to England again," said Lord Winter, "in spite of the resolutions you so often manifested in Paris never to set your foot again on British soil ?"

Milady replied to this question by another question.

"Before everything," said she, "tell me how you had me watched so closely as to be aware in advance not only of my arrival, but, still more, of the day, the hour, and the port at which I should arrive ?"

Lord Winter adopted the same tactics as milady, thinking that as his sister-in-law employed them they must be good.

"But tell me, my dear sister," replied he—"what have you come to do in England ?"

"Why, to see you," replied milady, without knowing how much she aggravated by this reply the suspicions which D'Artagnan's letter had given birth to in her brother-in-law's mind, and only desiring to gain her auditor's good-will by a falsehood.

"Ah, to see me ?" said Lord Winter craftily.

"Certainly, to see you. What is there astonishing in that ?"

"And you had no other object in coming to England but to see me ?"

"No."

"So it was for my sake alone you took the trouble to cross the Channel ?"

"For your sake only."

"The deuce ! What affection, my sister !"

"Why, am I not your nearest relative ?" demanded milady, in a tone of the most touching ingenuousness.

"And my only heir, are you not ?" said Lord Winter in his turn, fixing his eyes on milady's.

In spite of herself milady could not help starting; and as in pronouncing the last words Lord Winter laid his hand on his sister's arm, this start did not escape him.

In fact, the blow was direct and deep. The first idea that occurred to milady's mind was that she had been betrayed by Kitty, and that she had told the baron about her interested aversion toward him, of which she had imprudently allowed some marks to escape her before her servant; she also recollected the furious and imprudent attack she had made upon D'Artagnan when he spared her brother's life.

"I do not comprehend, my lord," said she, to gain time and make her adversary speak out. "What do you mean? Is there any secret meaning concealed beneath your words?"

"Oh, dear me, no!" said Lord Winter, with apparent good-nature. "You wish to see me, and you come to England. I learn of this desire, or rather I suspect that you feel it, and in order to spare you all the annoyances of an arrival at night in a port, and all the fatigues of landing, I send one of my officers to meet you, I place a carriage at his orders, and he brings you here to this castle, of which I am governor, where I come every day, and where, in order to satisfy our mutual desire of seeing each other, I have prepared a chamber for you. What is there in all that I have said to you more astonishing than in what you have told me?"

"No; but what I find astonishing is that you should be informed of my coming."

"And yet that is the most simple thing in the world, my dear sister. Did you not observe that the captain of your little vessel, on entering the road, sent forward, to obtain permission to enter the port, a small gig bearing his logbook and the register of his crew? I am commandant of the port; they brought me that book. I recognized your name in it. My heart told me what your mouth has just confirmed—that is to say, with what view you have exposed yourself to the dangers of such a perilous sea, or at least a sea so wearisome just at this time—and I sent my cutter to meet you. You know the rest."

Milady comprehended that Lord Winter lied, and was only the more alarmed.

"Brother," continued she, "was not that my Lord Buckingham whom I saw on the jetty this evening as we entered the port?"

"It was indeed. Ah, I can understand how the sight of him struck you," replied Lord Winter. "You come from a country where he must be very much talked about, and I know that his armaments against France greatly engage your friend the cardinal's attention."

"My friend the cardinal!" cried milady, seeing that on this point as well as on the other Lord Winter seemed perfectly well informed.

"Is he not your friend?" replied the baron negligently. "Ah! I beg your pardon; I thought he was. But we will return to my lord duke presently. Let us not depart from the quite sentimental turn our conversation had taken. You said you came to see me?"

"Yes."

"Well, I reply that your every wish should be fulfilled, and that we should see each other every day."

"Am I, then, to remain here eternally?" demanded milady in some terror.

"Do you find yourself poorly lodged, sister? Ask for anything you lack, and I will hasten to have you furnished with it."

"But I have neither my women nor my people."

"You shall have all that, madame. Tell me on what footing your household was established by your first husband, and though I am only your brother-in-law, I will arrange it on a similar one."

"My first husband!" cried milady, looking at Lord Winter with startled eyes.

"Yes, your French husband; I don't speak of my brother. However, if you have forgotten, as he is still living, I could write to him, and he would send me information on the subject."

A cold sweat started from milady's brow.

"You are joking!" said she, in a hollow voice.

"Do I look as if I were?" asked the baron, rising and taking a step backward.

"Or, rather, you insult me," continued she, pressing with her contracted hands the two arms of her chair, and raising herself up on her wrists.

"I insult you!" said Lord Winter contemptuously. "In truth, madame, do you think that is possible?"

"In truth, sir," said milady, "you are either drunk or mad. Leave the room, sir, and send me a woman."

"Women are very indiscreet, sister. Couldn't I serve you as a waiting-maid? By that means, all our secrets would be kept in the family."

"Insolent wretch!" cried milady. And as if moved by a spring, she sprang toward the baron, who was waiting her attack with his arms folded, but with one hand on the hilt of his sword.

"Come, come!" said he; "I know you have the habit of assassinating people; but I shall defend myself, I warn you, even against you."

"No doubt you would," said she; "you have every appearance of being coward enough to lift your hand against a woman."

"Perhaps I am. Besides, I have an excuse, for mine would not be the first man's hand that has been placed upon you, I imagine."

And the baron pointed with a slow and accusing gesture to milady's left shoulder, which he almost touched with his finger.

Milady uttered a muffled roar, and retreated to a corner of the room, like a panther when she draws back to leap.

"Oh, roar as much as you please," cried Lord Winter, "but don't try to bite, for I warn you the thing would be to your prejudice. Here there are no solicitors who regulate successions beforehand; there is no knight-errant to come and seek a quarrel with me on account of the fair lady I detain a prisoner; but I have judges all ready who will quickly dispose of a woman so shameless as to come and steal, a bigamist, into the bed of my oldest brother, Lord Winter; and these judges, I warn you, will give you over to a hangman, who will make both your shoulders alike."

He continued, but with increasing warmth,—

"Yes, I understand how, after inheriting my brother's fortune, it would have been very agreeable to you to be my heir likewise; but know beforehand, if you kill me, or cause me to be killed, my precautions are taken: not a penny of what I possess will pass into your hands. Are you not already rich enough, possessing now nearly a million? And could you not stop your fatal career, if you did not do evil only for the infinite and supreme delight of doing it? Oh, be assured, if my brother's memory were not sacred to me, you should rot in a state dungeon, or satisfy the curiosity of sailors at Tyburn. I will be silent, but you must endure your captivity quietly. In fifteen or twenty days I shall set out for Rochelle with the army; but before my departure, a vessel which I shall see set sail will take you away and convey you to our southern colonies. And be assured I will give you a companion who will blow your brains out at the first attempt you may make to return to England or the Continent."

Milady listened with an attention that dilated her inflamed eyes.

"Yes, at present," continued Lord Winter, "you will remain in this castle. The walls of it are thick, the doors strong, and the bars solid. Moreover, your window opens immediately over the sea. The men of my crew, who are devoted to me for life and death, mount guard around this apartment, and watch all the passages leading to the castle yard. Even if you gained the yard, there would still be three iron gates for you to pass through. The order given is positive: a step, a gesture, a word, on your part, implying an effort to escape, and you will be fired upon. If they kill you, English justice will be under obligations to me for saving it trouble. Ah! your features are resuming their calmness, your countenance is recovering its assurance. 'Fifteen days, twenty days!' say you. 'Bah! I have an inventive mind; before that has expired some idea will occur to me. I have an infernal spirit; I shall find some victim. Before a fortnight has gone by,' you say to yourself, 'I shall be away from here!' Well, try! The officer who commands alone here in my absence you have seen, and therefore already know him. As you must have observed, he knows how to obey orders, for I am sure you did not come from Portsmouth here without trying to make him speak. What do you say to that? Could a statue of marble have been more impassive and more mute? You have already tried the power of your seductions on many men, and, unfortunately, you have always succeeded. Try them on him. By God! if you succeed with him, I pronounce you the demon himself."

He went to the door and opened it hastily.

"Call Mr. Felton," said he.—"Wait a minute longer, and I will commend you to him."

Between these two people a strange silence ensued, during which the sound of a slow and regular step was heard approaching. Soon a human form appeared in the shade of the corridor, and the young lieutenant, whose acquaintance we have already made, stopped at the door to receive the baron's orders.

"Come in, my dear John," said Lord Winter—"come in and shut the door."

The young officer entered.

"Now," said the baron, "look at this woman. She is

young, she is beautiful, she has all earthly seductions. Well, she is a monster, who, at twenty-five, has been guilty of as many crimes as you could read of in a year in the archives of our tribunals. Her voice prejudices in her favour; her beauty serves as a bait to her victims; her body even pays what she promises—I must do her that justice. She will try to seduce you, perhaps she will even try to kill you. I have extricated you from poverty, Felton; I have had you made lieutenant; I once saved your life—you know on what occasion. I am not only your protector, but your friend; not only a benefactor, but a father to you. This woman came back again into England for the purpose of conspiring against my life. I hold this serpent in my hands. Well, I call on you and say to you: Friend Felton, John, my son, guard me, and more particularly guard thyself, against this woman. Swear by thy hopes of salvation to keep her safely for the punishment she has deserved. John Felton, I trust in thy word! John Felton, I believe in thy loyalty!"

"My lord," said the young officer, summoning to his mild countenance all the hatred he could find in his heart —"my lord, I swear to you all shall be done as you desire."

Milady received this look like a resigned victim. It was impossible to imagine a more submissive or a milder expression than that which prevailed on her beautiful countenance. Lord Winter himself could scarcely recognize the tigress whom, a minute before, he was preparing to fight.

"She is never to leave this room, understand, John; she is not to correspond with any one; she is to speak to no one but you—if, indeed, you wish to do her the honour of addressing a word to her."

"That is quite sufficient, my lord! I have sworn."

"And now, madame, try to make your peace with God, for you are judged by men!"

Milady let her head sink, as if she felt herself crushed by this sentence. Lord Winter went out, making a sign to Felton, who followed him and shut the door.

An instant after, the heavy step of a marine was heard in the corridor, serving on sentinel's duty, with his axe in his girdle and his musket on his shoulder.

Milady remained for some minutes in the same position, for she thought they might perhaps be watching her through the keyhole. Then she slowly raised her head, and assuming a formidable expression of menace and defiance, ran to the door to listen, looked out of her window, and returning to bury herself again in her large armchair, she reflected.

CHAPTER LI.

OFFICER.

MEANWHILE the cardinal was anxiously looking for news from England ; but no news arrived, except what was annoying and threatening.

Well as Rochelle was invested, certain as success might appear, owing to the precautions taken, and above all, to the dike preventing the entrance of any vessel into the besieged city, yet still the blockade might last for a long time ; and this was a great affront to the king's arms, and a great inconvenience to the cardinal, who had no longer, it is true, to embroil Louis XIII. with Anne of Austria, for that affair was done, but he had to reconcile M. de Bassompierre and the Duc d'Angoulême, who were engaged in a quarrel.

Monsieur, who had begun the siege, now left to the cardinal the task of finishing it.

The city, notwithstanding its mayor's incredible perseverance, had attempted a sort of mutiny in favour of surrendering ; the mayor had hanged the ringleaders. This execution subdued the worst of the mutineers, who then resolved to allow themselves to die of hunger. This death always seemed to them slower and not so sure as death by strangulation.

The besiegers from time to time took the messengers which the Rochellais sent to Buckingham, or the spies which Buckingham sent to the Rochellais. In either case the trial was soon over. The cardinal pronounced the single word " Hanged ! " The king was invited to come and see the hanging. The king came languidly, placing himself in a good situation to see all the details. This always amused him a little, and made him endure the siege patiently ; but it did not prevent his getting very much bored, or from talking at every moment of returning to Paris ; so that if the messengers and the spies had failed, his Eminence, in spite of all his imagination, would have found himself very much embarrassed.

Nevertheless, time went on, and the Rochellais did not surrender. The last spy taken was the bearer of a letter.

The letter, to be sure, informed Buckingham that the city was reduced to the last extremity; but instead of adding, "If your aid does not arrive within a fortnight, we shall surrender," it merely added, "If your aid does not arrive within a fortnight, we shall all be dead of starvation when it does arrive."

The Rochellais, then, had no hope except in Buckingham; Buckingham was their Messiah. It was evident that if they one day learned to a certainty that they could no longer count on Buckingham, their courage would fail with their hope.

So the cardinal was most impatiently awaiting news from England that would announce to him that Buckingham would not come.

The question of carrying the city by assault, though often debated in the king's council, had always been rejected. In the first place, Rochelle appeared impregnable; then the cardinal, whatever he said, knew very well that the horrible bloodshed in this encounter, when Frenchmen would be fighting against Frenchmen, meant a retrograde movement of sixty years impressed on politics, and the cardinal was for those days what we now call a man of progress. In fact, the sacking of Rochelle, and the massacre of three or four thousand Huguenots who would allow themselves to be butchered, would resemble too closely, in 1628, the massacre of St. Bartholomew in 1572. And then, above all, this extreme measure, to which the king, being a good Catholic, felt no repugnance at all, always fell to the ground before the one argument of the besieging generals—Rochelle is impregnable except by famine.

The cardinal could not drive from his mind the fear he entertained concerning his terrible emissary, for he well understood this woman's strange qualities, now serpent-like, now lion-like. Had she betrayed him? Was she dead? He knew her well enough in all cases to know that while acting for him or against him, as a friend or an enemy, she would not remain motionless unless blocked by great obstacles. But whence did such obstacles arise? That was what he could not know.

However, he reckoned, and rightly, on milady. He had divined in this woman's past terrible things which his red cloak alone could cover; and he felt that, from one cause or another, this woman was his own, as she could find in no one but in him a support superior to the danger which threatened her.

He resolved, therefore, to carry on the war alone, and to look for any success foreign to himself only as we look for a fortunate chance. He continued to push the building of the famous dike which was to starve Rochelle. Meanwhile he cast his eyes over that unfortunate city, which contained so much deep misery and so many heroic virtues, and recalling the saying of Louis XI., his political predecessor as he himself was Robespierre's predecessor, he repeated this maxim of Tristan's royal gossip : "Divide in order to reign."

Henry IV., when besieging Paris, had loaves and provisions thrown over the walls. The cardinal had little notes thrown over, in which he represented to the Rochellais how unjust, selfish, and barbarous was the conduct of their leaders. These leaders had corn in abundance, and would not let them partake of it. They adopted this maxim—for they, too, had maxims—that it was of very little consequence whether the women, the children, and the old men died, so long as the men who were to defend the walls remained strong and healthy. Up to that time, whether from devotion or from want of power to resist it, this maxim, without being generally adopted, had, nevertheless, passed from theory to practice. But the notes did it injury. The notes reminded the men that the children, women, and old men who were allowed to die were their sons, their wives, and their fathers, and that it would be more just if every one were reduced to the common level of poverty, in order that one and the same position might give birth to unanimous resolutions.

These notes had all the effect that he who wrote them could expect, for they induced a great number of the inhabitants to open private negotiations with the royal army.

But just as the cardinal saw his scheme already bearing fruit, and was applauding himself for having put it in action, an inhabitant of Rochelle, who had succeeded somehow in passing the royal lines, in spite of the watchfulness of Bassompierre, Schomberg, and the Duc d'Angoulême, themselves watched by the cardinal—an inhabitant of Rochelle, we say, entered the city, coming from Portsmouth, and said that he had seen a magnificent fleet ready to sail within a week. Moreover, Buckingham announced to the mayor that at length the great league against France was about to be proclaimed, and that the kingdom would be at once invaded by the English, Imperial, and Spanish armies. This letter was read publicly in all the squares, copies were posted at the corners of the streets, and even those who had begun to open negotiations interrupted them, determined to await the aid so pompously announced.

This unexpected circumstance brought back Richelieu's former anxieties, and forced him, in spite of himself, to turn his eyes once more to the other side of the sea.

During this time, exempt from these anxieties of its only real leader, the royal army led a jolly life, there being no lack of provisions, or money either, in the camp. All the corps rivalled one another in audacity and gaiety. To take spies and hang them, to make hazardous expeditions upon the dike or the sea, to conjure up foolish plans and execute them coolly—such were the pastimes which made the army find these days short, which were so long not only to the Rochellais, a prey to famine and distress, but also to the cardinal, who was blockading them so closely.

Sometimes when the cardinal, who was always on horse-back, like the lowest gendarme of the army, was casting a pensive glance over those works, which the engineers, brought from all the corners of France, were executing under his orders, though at a pace hardly commensurate with his desires, and met a musketeer of Tréville's company, he would draw near and look at him in a peculiar manner; but if he did not recognize in him one of our four companions, he would turn his keen eyes and mighty thoughts in some other direction.

One day when the cardinal, oppressed by mortal weariness of mind, hopeless of the negotiations with the city, without news from England, had gone out with no other aim than to ride, accompanied only by Cahusac and La Houdinière, skirting the beach and mingling the immensity of his dreams with the immensity of the ocean, he came ambling along to a hill, from the top of which he perceived, behind a hedge, reclining on the sand, in the sun so rare at this period of the year, seven men surrounded by empty bottles. Four of these men were our musketeers, preparing to listen to a letter one of them had just received. This letter was so important that it caused them to abandon their cards and their dice on a drum-head.

The other three were occupied in uncorking an enormous demijohn of Collioure wine; they were the gentlemen's lackeys.

The cardinal was, as we have said, in very low spirits; and when he was in that state of mind, nothing increased his depression so much as gaiety in others. Besides, he had another strange fancy, which was always to believe that the causes of his sadness created the gaiety of others. Making a sign to La Houdinière and Cahusac to stop, he alighted from his horse, and went toward these suspected merry-makers, hoping, by means of the sand which deadened the sound of his steps, and of the hedge which concealed his approach, to catch some words of a conversation which seemed so interesting. Ten paces from the hedge he recognized the Gascon prattle, and as he had already perceived that these men were musketeers, he had no doubt that the three others were those called "the inseparables"—that is to say, Athos, Porthos, and Aramis.

As may well be supposed, his desire to hear the conversation was increased by his discovery. His eyes took on a strange expression, and with the step of a cat he advanced toward the hedge. But he had not been able as yet to make out anything more than vague syllables without any positive sense, when a short, sonorous cry made him start, and attracted the attention of the musketeers.

"Officer!" cried Grimaud.

"I believe you are speaking, you rascal!" said Athos, rising on his elbow, and fascinating Grimaud with his flashing eyes.

Grimaud therefore said not a word more, but contented himself with pointing his index finger at the hedge, signifying by this gesture the presence of the cardinal and his escort.

With a single bound the musketeers were on their feet, and saluted respectfully.

The cardinal seemed furious.

"It seems that the musketeers set sentinels for themselves," said he. "Are the English expected by land, or do the musketeers consider themselves officers of rank?"

"Monseigneur," replied Athos, for amidst the general alarm he alone had preserved that calmness and *sang froid* which never forsook him—"monseigneur, the musketeers, when they are not on duty, or when their duty is over, drink and play at dice, and they are officers of very high rank to their lackeys."

"Lackeys!" grumbled the cardinal. "Lackeys who are ordered to warn their masters when any one passes are not lackeys; they are sentinels."

"Your Eminence may perceive that if we had not taken this precaution, we should have been in danger of letting

you pass without presenting you our respects, or offering you our thanks for the favour you have done us in uniting us.—D'Artagnan," continued Athos, "you were only just now so anxious for such an opportunity for expressing your thanks to monseigneur.   Here it is ; avail yourself of it."

These words were pronounced with that perfect imperturbability which distinguished Athos in the hour of danger, and with that excessive politeness which made of him at certain moments a king more majestic than kings by birth.

D'Artagnan came forward and stammered out a few words of thanks, which soon expired under the cardinal's gloomy looks.

"No matter, gentlemen," continued the cardinal, without appearing to be in the least diverted from his first intention by the incident which Athos had raised—"no matter, gentlemen.   I do not like simple soldiers, because they have the advantage of serving in a privileged corps, thus to play the great lords ; and discipline is the same for them as for everybody else."

Athos allowed the cardinal to finish his sentence completely, and bowing in sign of assent, he replied in his turn,—

"Discipline, monseigneur, has in no way, I hope, been forgotten by us.   We are not on duty, and we believe that, as we are not on duty, we are at liberty to dispose of our time as we please.   If we are so fortunate as to have some particular command from your Eminence, we are ready to obey you.   Your Eminence may perceive," continued Athos, frowning, for such an investigation began to annoy him, "that we have come out with our arms, so as to be ready for the least alarm."

And he showed the cardinal the four muskets stacked near the drum, on which were the cards and dice.

"We beg your Eminence to believe," added D'Artagnan, "that we should have come to meet you, if we could have supposed it was you coming toward us with so few attendants."

"Do you know what you look like, always together, as you are, armed, and sentinelled by your lackeys ? " said the cardinal.   "You look like four conspirators."

"Oh, so far, monseigneur, it's true," said Athos ; "we do conspire, as your Eminence might have seen the other day, only we conspire against the Rochellais."

"Eh, politicians ! " replied the cardinal, frowning in his turn ; "the secret of many things unknown might perhaps be found in your brains, if we could read in them as you were reading that letter which you concealed when you saw me coming."

The colour mounted to Athos's face, and he made a step toward his Eminence.

"One would think that you really suspected us, monseigneur, and that we are undergoing a cross-examination. If it be so, we trust your Eminence will deign to explain yourself, and we shall then at least be acquainted with our real position."

"And if it were an examination," replied the cardinal, "others beside you have undergone such, Monsieur Athos, and have replied to them."

"So, monseigneur, I have told your Eminence that you had but to question us, and we are ready to reply."

"What was that letter you were about to read, Monsieur Aramis, and which you concealed?"

"A woman's letter, monseigneur."

"Oh, I understand. We must be discreet with such letters. But nevertheless we may show them to a confessor, and you know I have taken orders."

"Monseigneur," said Athos, with a calmness all the more terrible that he risked his life when he made this reply, "the letter is a woman's, but it is neither signed Marion de Lorme nor Madame d'Arguillon."

The cardinal became as pale as death. A flash of fire darted from his eyes. He turned round as if to give an order to Cahusac and Houdinière. Athos saw the movement; he took a step toward the muskets, on which the other three friends had fixed their eyes like men ill-disposed to allow themselves to be arrested. The cardinal's party consisted of only three; the musketeers, lackeys included, numbered seven. He judged that the match would be so much the less equal if Athos and his companions were really plotting; and by one of those quick changes which he always had at command, all his anger faded away into a smile.

"Come, come!" said he, "you are brave young men, proud in daylight, faithful in darkness; no fault can be found with you for watching over yourselves when you watch so carefully over others. Gentlemen, I have not forgotten the night in which you served me as an escort to the Red Dovecot. If there were any danger to be apprehended on the road I am going, I should request you to accompany me; but as there is none, remain where you are, finish your bottles, your game, and your letter. Farewell, gentlemen ! "

And remounting his horse, which Cahusac had led to him, he saluted them with his hand and rode away.

The four young men, standing motionless, followed him with their eyes without speaking a single word until he had disappeared.

Then they looked at one another.

All showed their consternation and terror in their faces ; for notwithstanding his Eminence's friendly farewell, they plainly perceived that the cardinal went away with rage in his heart.

Athos alone smiled with a self-possessed, disdainful smile.

When the cardinal was out of hearing and sight,—

" That Grimaud kept but tardy watch ! " cried Porthos, anxious to visit his ill-humour on some one.

Grimaud was about to excuse himself. Athos lifted his finger, and Grimaud was silent.

" Would you have given up the letter, Aramis ? " said D'Artagnan.

" I," said Aramis, in his most flute-like tone—" I had made up my mind. If he had insisted on the letter being given up to him, I would have presented the letter to him with one hand, and with the other I would have run my sword through his body."

" I expected as much," said Athos ; " and that was why I interfered between you and him. Truly, this man is very unwise to talk in this way to other men ; one would say he had never had to do with any but women and children."

" My dear Athos," said D'Artagnan, " I admire you very much, but, nevertheless, we were in the wrong, after all."

" How in the wrong ? " exclaimed Athos. " Whose, then, is the air we breathe ? Whose is the ocean on which we look ? Whose is the sand on which we were reclining ? Whose is that letter of your mistress's ? The cardinal's ? 'Pon my honour, this man fancies the world belongs to him. There you stood, stammering, stupefied, confounded. One might have supposed that the Bastille appeared before you, and that the gigantic Medusa was converting you into stone. Come, now, is to be in love conspiring ? You are in love with a woman whom the cardinal has caused to be shut up, and you wish to get her out of the cardinal's hands. That's a game you are playing with his Eminence ;

this letter is your hand. Why should you show your hand to your adversary? That is never done. If he finds it out, well and good. We are finding out his, aren't we?"

"In truth, what you say has sense in it, Athos," said D'Artagnan.

"In that case let there be no more question of what has just occurred, and let Aramis resume the letter from his cousin where the cardinal interrupted him."

Aramis took the letter from his pocket, the three friends surrounded him, and the three lackeys grouped themselves again near the demijohn.

"You had only read a line or two," said D'Artagnan, "so begin the letter over again."

"Willingly," said Aramis.

"MY DEAR COUSIN,—I think I shall decide to set out for Béthune, where my sister has placed our little servant in the convent of the Carmelites. This poor child is resigned; she knows she cannot live elsewhere without risking the salvation of her soul. However, if the affairs of our family are settled, as we hope they will be, I believe she will run the risk of being damned, and will return to those whom she misses, particularly as she knows they are always thinking of her. In the meanwhile, she is not altogether wretched; what she most desires is a letter from her intended. I know that such commodities pass with difficulty through the gratings; but after all, as I have proved to you, my dear cousin, I am not unskilled, and I will take charge of the commission. My sister thanks you for your good and eternal remembrance. She underwent for a moment considerable anxiety; but she is now at length a little reassured, having sent her secretary yonder, in order that nothing may happen unexpectedly.

"Farewell, my dear cousin. Let us hear from you as often as possible—that is to say, whenever you can send with safety. I embrace you.   MARIE MICHON."

"Oh, what do I not owe you, Aramis?" cried D'Artagnan. "Dear Constance! I have at length, then, news of her. She lives; she is in safety in a convent; she is at Béthune! Where do you suppose Béthune is, Athos?"

"Why, upon the frontiers of Artois and of Flanders. When the siege is once over we shall be able to make a tour in that direction."

"And that will not be long, it is to be hoped," said

Porthos; "for this morning they hung a spy who confessed that the Rochellais had come to the leather of their shoes. Supposing that after having eaten the leather they eat the soles, I cannot see what they have left, unless they eat one another."

"Poor fools!" said Athos, emptying a glass of excellent Bordeaux wine, which, without having at that period the reputation it now enjoys, no less merited it—"poor fools! As if the Catholic religion was not the most agreeable of all religions! All the same," resumed he, after having smacked his tongue against his palate, "they are brave fellows. But what the devil are you about, Aramis?" continued Athos. "Why, you are squeezing that letter into your pocket!"

"Yes," said D'Artagnan, "Athos is right; it must be burnt. Who knows whether the cardinal has not a secret for examining ashes?"

"He must have one," said Athos.

"What are you going to do with the letter, then?" asked Porthos.

"Come here, Grimaud," said Athos.

Grimaud got up and obeyed.

"As a punishment for having spoken without permission, my friend, you will please eat this piece of paper. Then, to recompense you for the service you will have rendered us, you shall afterwards drink this glass of wine. Here is the letter. First, chew vigorously."

Grimaud smiled; and with his eyes fixed on the glass which Athos had just filled to the brim, he crushed the paper and swallowed it.

"Bravo, Master Grimaud!" said Athos. "And now take this. Good! I excuse you from saying 'Thank you.'"

Grimaud silently swallowed the glass of Bordeaux wine; but his eyes, raised toward heaven during the whole time this delicious occupation lasted, spoke a language which, though mute, was none the less expressive.

"And now," said Athos, "unless the cardinal should form the ingenious idea of ripping up Grimaud, I think we may be almost free from anxiety."

Meantime his Eminence was continuing his melancholy ride, murmuring between his moustaches what he so often said before,—

"These four men must positively be mine."

CHAPTER LII.

THE FIRST DAY OF CAPTIVITY.

LET us return to milady, whom our eyes, turned toward the coast of France, have lost from sight for an instant.

We shall find her in the despairing attitude in which we left her, plunged in an abyss of dismal reflections, a dismal hell, at the gate of which she has almost left hope behind; for now for the first time she doubts, for the first time she fears.

On two occasions her fortune has failed her, on two occasions she has found herself discovered and betrayed; and on both these occasions she failed before the fatal genius sent doubtlessly by Heaven to combat her: D'Artagnan has conquered her—her, the invincible power of evil.

He has deceived her love, humbled her pride, thwarted her ambition; and now he is ruining her fortune, depriving her of liberty, and even threatening her life. Moreover, he has lifted the corner of her mask—that ægis with which she covered herself, and which rendered her so strong.

From Buckingham, whom she hates as she hates all she has loved, D'Artagnan averted the tempest with which Richelieu threatened him in the person of the queen. D'Artagnan had passed himself off on her as De Wardes, for whom she had conceived one of those invincible tigress-like fancies common to women of her character. D'Artagnan knows the terrible secret which she has sworn no one should know without dying. Finally, just as she has obtained from Richelieu a signed permit by means of which she is going to take vengeance on her enemy, this paper is torn from her hands, and D'Artagnan holds her prisoner, and is about to send her to some filthy Botany Bay, some infamous Tyburn of the Indian Ocean.

For all this, doubtless, D'Artagnan is responsible. From whom can come so many disgraces heaped on her head, if not from him? He alone could have transmitted to Lord Winter all these frightful secrets, which he has discovered, one after another, in consequence of Fate. He knows her brother-in-law; he must have written to him.

What hatred she distils! There, motionless, with her burning, fixed eyes, in her lonely room, how well the paroxysms of her muffled roaring, which at times escape with her breathing from the depths of her chest, accompany the sound of the surge which rises, growls, roars, and breaks against the rocks on which is built this dark and haughty castle! By the light of the flashes with which her tempestuous passion illumines her mind, how many magnificent projects of vengeance she conceives against Madame Bonacieux, against Buckingham, but above all, against D'Artagnan—projects lost in the distances of the future!

Yes, but in order to avenge herself she must be free; and to be free, a prisoner has to pierce a wall, unfasten bars, cut through a floor—all undertakings which a strong, patient man may accomplish, but in which a woman's feverish nervousness must fail. Besides, to do all this, time is necessary—months, years; and she has ten or twelve days, as Lord Winter, her fraternal and terrible jailer, told her.

And yet if she were a man she would attempt all this, and perhaps would succeed. Why, then, did Heaven make the mistake of placing a masculine soul in her frail, delicate body?

The first moments of her captivity, therefore, were terrible; but a few convulsions of rage which she could not overcome paid to nature her debt of feminine weakness. But by degrees she subdued the outbursts of her mad passion; the nervous tremblings which agitated her frame disappeared, and now she remained folded back on herself, like a fatigued serpent reposing.

"Come, come! I must have been mad to be carried away so," says she, plunging into the glass, which reflects back the burning glance by which she seems to question herself. "No violence; violence is a proof of weakness. In the first place, I have never succeeded by that means. Perhaps if I employed my strength against women, I should have a chance to find them weaker than myself, and consequently to conquer them. But I battle with men, and for them I am only a woman. Let me battle like a woman, then. My strength is in my weakness."

Then, as if to render an account to herself of the changes she could impose upon her countenance, so mobile and so expressive, she made it assume successively all expressions, from passionate anger, which convulsed her features, to the sweetest, most affectionate, and most seducing smile. Then her hair in turn, under her skilful hands, took on all the undulations she thought might assist the charms of her face. At length she murmured, satisfied with herself,—

"Come, nothing is lost. I am still beautiful."

It was then almost eight o'clock in the evening. Milady perceived a bed; she felt that a few hours' repose would refresh not only her brain and her ideas, but, still further, her complexion. A better idea, however, came into her mind before going to bed. She had heard something said about supper. She had already been an hour in this apartment. It could not be long before her repast would be brought. The prisoner was anxious not to lose any time. She resolved to make that very evening some attempts to ascertain the lie of the land by studying the characters of the people to whose guardianship she was committed.

A light appeared under the door. This light announced the reappearance of her jailers. Milady, who had arisen, quickly sat down again in her armchair, her head thrown back, her beautiful hair unbound and dishevelled, her bosom half bare beneath her crumpled laces, one hand on her heart and the other hanging down.

The bolts were drawn, the door creaked on its hinges, steps sounded in the chamber and drew near.

"Stand that table there," said a voice which the prisoner recognized as Felton's.

The order was obeyed.

"You will bring lights and relieve the sentinel," continued Felton.

This double order, which the young lieutenant gave to the same individuals, proved to milady that her servants were the same men as her guards—that is to say, soldiers.

Felton's orders were, moreover, executed with a silent rapidity that proved the excellent state in which he maintained discipline.

At length Felton, who had not yet looked at milady, turned toward her.

"Ah, ha!" said he, "she is asleep; 'tis well. When she wakes she can sup."

And he took some steps toward the door.

"But, lieutenant," said a soldier a little less stoical than his officer, and who had approached milady, "this woman is not asleep."

"What! not asleep!" said Felton.

"She has fainted away. Her face is very pale, and I have listened in vain; I can't hear her breathe."

"You are right," said Felton, after looking at milady from the spot on which he stood, without moving a step toward her. "Go and tell Lord Winter that his prisoner has fainted. The case not having been foreseen, I don't know what to do."

The soldier went out to obey his officer's orders. Felton sat down on an armchair which happened to be near the door, and waited without speaking a word, without making a gesture. Milady possessed that great art, so much studied by women, of looking through her long eyelashes without appearing to open the lids. She perceived Felton, as he sat with his back to her. She continued to look at him during nearly ten minutes, and in these ten minutes the impassive guardian never once turned round.

She then thought that Lord Winter would come, and by his presence give fresh strength to her jailer. Her first trial was lost; she decided like a woman who reckons on her resources. Consequently she raised her head, opened her eyes, and sighed feebly.

At this sigh Felton at last turned round.

"Ah, you are awake again, madame," he said; "then I have nothing more to do here. If you want anything, you can ring."

"Oh, my God, my God! how I have suffered," murmured milady in her musical voice, which, like those of the ancient enchantresses, charmed all whom she wished to destroy.

And as she sat up in the armchair, she assumed a still more graceful and voluptuous position than that she had exhibited when reclining.

Felton rose.

"You will be served thus, madame, three times a day," said he. "In the morning at nine o'clock, in the day at one o'clock, and in the evening at eight. If that does not suit you, you can point out what other hours you prefer, and in this respect your wishes will be complied with."

"But am I to remain always alone in this vast and dismal chamber?" asked milady.

"A woman of the neighbourhood has been sent for, who will be at the castle to-morrow. She will come to you as often as you desire her presence."

"I thank you, sir," replied the prisoner humbly.

Felton made a slight bow and started toward the door. Just as he was about to cross the threshold Lord Winter appeared in the corridor, followed by the soldier who had been sent to inform him of milady's fainting. He held a vial of salts in his hand.

"Well, what's going on here?" said he, in a jeering voice,

on seeing the prisoner sitting up and Felton about to go out. "Has this dead woman come to life again already? By Jove! Felton, my lad, did you not see that she took you for a novice, and that we have been seeing the first act of a comedy of which we shall doubtless have the pleasure of following out all the developments?"

"I imagined that might be the case, my lord," said Felton. "But as the prisoner is a woman, after all, I wished to pay her the attention that every man of gentle birth owes to a woman, if not on her account, at least on his own."

Milady shuddered through her whole frame. These words of Felton's passed like ice through her veins.

"So," replied Lord Winter, laughing, "that beautiful hair, so skilfully dishevelled, that white skin and that languishing look, have not yet seduced you, you heart of stone?"

"No, my lord," replied the unfeeling young man; "and, believe me, it requires more than the tricks and coquetries of a woman to corrupt me."

"In that case, my brave lieutenant, let us leave milady to invent something else, and let us go to supper. But don't you worry. She has a fruitful imagination, and the second act of the comedy will follow not long after the first."

And at these words Lord Winter passed his arm through Felton's, and led him out, laughing.

"Oh, I will be a match for you!" muttered milady between her teeth. "Be assured of that, you miserable would-be monk, you miserable converted soldier, who have cut your uniform out of a friar's frock!"

"By the way, milady," resumed Lord Winter, stopping at the door, "you must not let this check take away your appetite. Taste that fowl and those fish. 'Pon honour, they are not poisoned. I agree very well with my cook, and he is not to be my heir. I have full and perfect confidence in him. Do as I do. Farewell, dear sister, till your next fainting fit."

This was all milady could endure, and when she was alone a fresh fit of despair seized her. She cast her eyes on the table, saw a knife glittering, rushed toward it and clutched it. But her disappointment was cruel: the blade was blunt, and of flexible silver.

A burst of laughter resounded from the other side of the half-closed door, and the door was reopened.

"Ha, ha, ha!" cried Lord Winter; "ha, ha, ha! Don't you see, my brave Felton, don't you see what I told you? That knife was for you, my lad; she would have killed you. Observe, this is one of her eccentricities, to get rid thus, in one way or another, of all the people who inconvenience her. If I had listened to you, the knife would have been pointed and of steel. Then it would have been all over with Felton. She would have cut your throat, and afterwards that of every one else. See, John, how well she knows how to handle a knife."

In fact, milady still held the weapon of offence in her clenched hand; but these last words, this supreme insult, relaxed her hands, her strength, and even her will.

The knife fell to the ground.

"You are right, my lord," said Felton, in a tone of profound disgust, which sounded to the very bottom of milady's heart—"you are right, my lord; I was in the wrong."

And both left the room again.

But this time milady lent a more attentive ear than she did the first time, and she heard their steps die away at the remotest end of the corridor.

"I am lost," murmured she; "I am in the power of men on whom I can have no more influence than if they were bronze statues or granite. They know me by heart, and are hardened against all my weapons. Nevertheless it is impossible that this should end as they have decreed."

In fact, as was shown by this last reflection—this instinctive return to hope—sentiments of weakness or fear did not dwell long in that deep soul. Milady sat down to table, ate of several dishes, drank a little Spanish wine, and felt all her resolution return.

Before she went to bed she had commented on, analyzed, turned on all sides, examined on all points, the words, the gestures, the signs, and even the silence of the two men; and the result of her commentary, her analysis, her study, was that Felton, everything considered, was decided to be the more vulnerable of her two persecutors.

One expression above all kept recurring to the prisoner's mind.

"If I had listened to you," Lord Winter had said to Felton.

Felton, then, had spoken in her favour, since Lord Winter had not been willing to listen to Felton.

"Weak or strong," repeated milady, "that man has a spark of pity in his soul. Of that spark I will make a flame that shall devour him. As to the other, he knows me, he fears me, and knows what he has to expect of me if ever I escape from his hands. So it is useless to attempt anything with him. But Felton—that's another thing. He is an ingenuous, pure, and apparently virtuous young man; there is a way of getting him."

And milady went to bed, and fell asleep with a smile on her lips. Any one who had seen her sleeping might have said she was a young girl dreaming of the crown of flowers she was to wear on her brow at the next fête.

CHAPTER LIII.

THE SECOND DAY OF CAPTIVITY.

MILADY dreamed that she at length had D'Artagnan in her power, that she was present at his execution; the sight of his odious blood, flowing beneath the executioner's axe, spread that charming smile upon her lips.

She slept as a prisoner sleeps who is rocked by his first hope.

In the morning when they entered her chamber she was still in bed. Felton remained in the corridor. He brought with him the woman of whom he had spoken the evening before, and who had just arrived; this woman entered, and approaching milady's bed, offered her services.

Milady was habitually pale. Her complexion might therefore deceive a person who saw her for the first time.

"I am in a fever," said she; "I have not slept a single instant during all this long night; I am in frightful pain. Will you be more humane to me than others were to me yesterday? Besides, all I ask is permission to stay in bed."

"Would you like a physician sent for?" asked the woman.

Felton listened to this dialogue without speaking a word.

Milady reflected that the more people she had around her, the more she should have to work upon, and the stricter would be the watch Lord Winter kept over her. Besides, the physician might declare the malady was feigned; and milady, having lost the first game, was not willing to lose the second.

"Send for a physician!" said she. "What would be the good of that? These gentlemen declared yesterday that my illness was a comedy; it would be just the same to-day, no doubt, for since yesterday evening they have had plenty of time to send for a doctor."

"Then," said Felton, becoming impatient, "say yourself, madame, what treatment you wish followed."

"Eh! how can I tell? My God! I know that I am in pain, that's all. Give me anything you like; it is of very little consequence to me."

"Go, get Lord Winter," said Felton, tired of these eternal complaints.

"Oh no, no!" cried milady; "no, sir, do not call him, I conjure you. I am well, I want nothing; do not call him."

She put such prodigious vehemence, such irresistible eloquence, into this exclamation that Felton, in spite of himself, advanced some steps into the room.

"He has come!" thought milady.

"Now, if you are *really* in pain," said Felton, "a physician shall be sent for; and if you deceive us—well, why, it will be so much the worse for you. But at least we shall not have to reproach ourselves with anything."

Milady made no reply, but turning her beautiful head over on her pillow, she burst into tears, and sobbed as though her heart would break.

Felton surveyed her for an instant with his usual coolness; then, seeing that the crisis threatened to be prolonged, he left the room. The woman followed him, and Lord Winter did not appear.

"I fancy I begin to see my way," murmured milady, with a savage joy, burying herself under the clothes to conceal from anybody who might be watching her this burst of inward satisfaction.

Two hours passed away.

"Now it is time that the malady should be over," said she; "let me get up and obtain some success this very day. I have but ten days, and this evening two will be gone."

On entering milady's room in the morning they had brought her breakfast; now she thought it could not be long before they would come to clear the table, and that she should see Felton.

Milady was not mistaken. Felton reappeared again, and without observing whether she had or had not touched her repast, he made a sign for the table to be carried out of the room, as it was brought in all set.

Felton remained behind; he held a book in his hand.

Milady, reclining in an armchair near the fireplace, beautiful, pale, and resigned, looked like a holy virgin awaiting martyrdom.

Felton approached her, and said,—

"Lord Winter, who is a Catholic, as well as yourself, madame, thinking that the privation of the rites and ceremonies of your church might be painful to you, has consented that you should read every day the ordinary of *your mass*, and here is a book which contains the ritual of it."

At the manner in which Felton laid the book on the little table near which milady was sitting, at the tone in which he pronounced the two words "your mass," at the disdainful smile with which he accompanied them, milady raised her head and looked more attentively at the officer.

Then, by the plain arrangement of his hair, by his costume of exaggerated simplicity, by his brow polished like marble, but hard and impenetrable like it, she recognized one of those gloomy Puritans she had so often met with, both at the court of King James and at the court of the king of France, where, in spite of the remembrance of St. Bartholomew's, they sometimes came to seek refuge.

She then had one of those sudden inspirations which only people of genius have in great crises, in the supreme moments which are to decide their fortunes or their lives.

Those two words, "your mass," and a simple glance cast on Felton, revealed to her all the importance of the reply she was about to make.

But with that rapidity of intelligence which was peculiar to her, this reply, ready arranged, presented itself to her lips,—

"I," said she, with an accent of disdain struck in unison with that which she had remarked in the young officer's voice—"I, sir? *My mass?* Lord Winter, the corrupted Catholic, knows very well that I am not of his religion, and this is a snare he wishes to set for me!"

"And of what religion are you, then, madame?" asked Felton.

"I will tell," cried milady, with a feigned enthusiasm, "on the day when I shall have suffered sufficiently for my faith."

Felton's look revealed to milady the full extent of the space she had just opened for herself by this single word.

The young officer, however, remained mute and motionless. His look alone had spoken.

"I am in the hands of mine enemies," continued she, with that tone of enthusiasm which she knew was familiar to the Puritans. "Well, let my God save me, or let me perish for my God! That is the reply I beg you to make to Lord Winter. And as to this book," added she, pointing to the ritual with her finger, but without touching it, as though she would be contaminated by the touch, "you may carry it back and make use of it yourself; for doubtless you are doubly Lord Winter's accomplice—the accomplice in his persecutions, the accomplice in his heresies."

Felton made no reply, took the book with the same appearance of repugnance which he had before manifested, and retired thoughtfully.

Lord Winter came toward five o'clock in the evening. Milady had had time, during all that day, to lay out her plan of conduct. She received him like a woman who has already recovered all her advantages.

"It seems," said the baron, seating himself in the arm-chair opposite the one occupied by milady, and stretching out his legs carelessly on the hearth—"it seems we have made a little apostasy!"

"What do you mean, sir?"

"I mean that, since we last met, we have changed our religion. Can you by chance have married a Protestant for a third husband?"

"Explain yourself, my lord," replied the prisoner majestically; "for though I hear your words, I declare I do not understand them."

"Then you have no religion at all. I like that best," replied Lord Winter, sneering.

"Certainly, that is more accordant with your own principles," replied milady coldly.

"Well, I confess it makes no difference at all to me."

"Oh, you need not avow your religious indifference, my lord; your debaucheries and crimes would make it perfectly credible."

"What! you talk of debaucheries, Madame Messalina, Lady Macbeth! Either I misunderstand you, or, by God, you are mighty impudent!"

"You only speak so because you know you are listened to, sir," replied milady coldly; "and you wish to interest your jailers and your hangmen against me."

"My jailers and my hangmen! Heyday, madame! You are assuming quite a poetical tone, and yesterday's comedy is turning this evening into a tragedy. As to the rest, in a week you will be where you ought to be, and my task will be completed."

"Infamous task! impious task!" cried milady, with the exultation of a victim provoking the judge.

"On my word of honour," said Lord Winter, rising, "I think the hussy is going mad! Come, come, calm yourself, Madame Puritan, or I'll have you put in the dungeon. By Jove! my Spanish wine has gone to your head, has it not? But never mind; that sort of intoxication is not dangerous and will have no consequences."

And Lord Winter retired swearing, a habit at that period very cavalier-like.

Felton was, in fact, behind the door, and had not lost one word of the scene.

Milady had guessed correctly.

"Yes, go! go!" said she to her brother; "on the contrary, the consequences are drawing near. But you, weak fool, will not see them until it will be too late to avoid them."

Silence was re-established. Two hours passed away. Milady's supper was brought in, and she was found deeply engaged in saying her prayers aloud—prayers which she had learned of an old servant of her second husband's, a most austere Puritan. She appeared to be in an ecstasy, and paid not the slightest attention to what was going on around her. Felton made a sign that she should not be disturbed, and when all was arranged he went out quietly with the soldiers.

Milady knew she might be watched, so she continued her prayers to the end; and it seemed to her that the soldier on duty at her door no longer marched with the same step, but seemed to be listening.

For the moment she required nothing further. She rose, placed herself at table, ate but little, and drank only water.

An hour after, her table was cleared; but milady remarked that this time Felton did not accompany the soldiers.

He feared, then, to see her too often.

She turned toward the wall to smile, for there was in her smile such an expression of triumph that this single smile would have betrayed her. She allowed, therefore, half an hour to pass away; and as at that moment all was silent in the old castle, as nothing was heard but the eternal murmur of the waves—that immense respiration of the ocean—with her pure, harmonious, and powerful voice she began the first stanza of the psalm then in greatest favour with the Puritans,—

> "Thou leavest still Thy servants, Lord,
> To see if they be strong;
> But soon again Thou dost afford
> Thy hand to lead them on."

These verses were not excellent—very far from it, even ; but as it is well known, the Puritans did not pique themselves on their poetry.

As she was singing milady listened. The soldier on guard at her door stopped, as if he had been changed into stone. Milady could therefore judge of the effect she had produced.

Then she continued her singing with inexpressible fervour and feeling. It seemed to her that the sounds spread afar beneath the vaults, and carried with them a magic charm to soften her jailers' hearts. It, however, seemed that the soldier on duty, a zealous Catholic no doubt, shook off the charm, for through the door,—

"Be quiet, madame !" said he ; "your song is as dismal as a *De profundis ;* and if, besides the pleasure of being in garrison here, we must hear such things as these, no mortal can stand it."

"Silence !" then said a stern voice, which milady recognized as Felton's. "What business is it of yours, you rascal ? Have you been ordered to prevent this woman from singing ? No ; you were told to guard her—to fire at her if she attempted to fly. Guard her. If she flies, kill her. But don't exceed your orders."

An expression of unspeakable joy lightened milady's countenance ; but this expression was fleeting as the reflection of lightning, and without appearing to have heard the dialogue, of which she had not lost a word, she began again, giving her voice all the charm, all the power, all the seduction the demon had bestowed upon it,—

> "For all my tears and all my cares,
>   My exile and my chains,
> I have my youth, I have my prayers,
>   And God, who counts my pains."

Her voice, of unusual range and of sublime expression, gave to the rude, unpolished poetry of these psalms a magic and an effect which the most exalted Puritans rarely found in the songs of their brethren. They were obliged, indeed, to ornament them with all the resources of their imagination. Felton believed he heard the singing of the angel who consoled the three Hebrews in the furnace.

Milady continued,—

> "But soon the day of our release,
>   Almighty God, will come ;
> And if our earthly hope must cease,
>   We'll go to martyrdom !"

This stanza, into which the terrible enchantress tried to throw her whole soul, completed the trouble which had entered the young officer's heart. He quickly opened the door, and milady saw him appear, pale as usual, but with his eyes inflamed and almost wild.

"Why do you sing thus, and with such a voice?" said he.

"I crave your pardon, sir," said milady softly; "I forgot that my songs are out of place in this house. I have perhaps offended you in your religious beliefs; but it was without meaning to do so, I assure you. Pardon me, then, a fault which is perhaps great, but which certainly was involuntary."

Milady was so beautiful at this moment, the religious ecstasy in which she appeared to be plunged gave such an expression to her countenance, that Felton was dazzled, and fancied he beheld the angel whom just before he thought he heard.

"Yes, yes," said he, "you disturb, you agitate the people who inhabit the castle."

And the poor fanatic was not himself aware of the incoherence of his words, while milady was reading with her lynx's eyes the very depths of his heart.

"I will be silent," said milady, casting down her eyes, with all the sweetness she could give to her voice, with all the resignation she could express in her manner.

"No, no, madame," said Felton; "only do not sing so loud, particularly at night."

And at these words Felton, feeling that he could not long maintain his severity toward his prisoner, rushed out of the room.

"You have done right, lieutenant," said the soldier. "Her songs disturb the mind; and yet we get accustomed to them, her voice is so beautiful."

CHAPTER LIV.

THE THIRD DAY OF CAPTIVITY.

FELTON had come, but there was still another step to be taken. He must be retained, or, rather, he must be left quite alone; and milady as yet perceived but dimly the means which could bring her to this result.

Still more must be done. He must be made to speak, in order that she might speak to him; for milady very well knew that her greatest charm was in her voice, which so skilfully ran over the whole gamut of tones, from human speech to celestial language.

And yet, in spite of all this charm, milady might fail; for Felton was forewarned, even against the least chance. From that moment she watched all his actions, all his words, to the simplest glance of his eyes, to his gestures, even to a respiration that might be interpreted as a sigh; in short, she studied everything like a clever actor to whom a new part has just been assigned in a line he has not been accustomed to follow.

Toward Lord Winter her plan of conduct was more easy; therefore she had determined on that the evening before. To remain silent and dignified in his presence; from time to time to irritate him by an affected disdain, by a contemptuous word; to provoke him to threats and violence, which would contrast with her own resignation—such was her plan. Felton would see; perhaps he would say nothing, but he would see.

In the morning Felton came as usual; but milady allowed him to preside over all the preparations for the breakfast without addressing a word to him. Just as he was on the point of retiring she was cheered by a ray of hope, for she thought he was about to speak; but his lips moved without any sound coming from his mouth, and making a powerful effort over himself, he sent back to his heart the words that were about to escape from his lips, and went out.

Toward noon Lord Winter came in.

It was quite a fine winter's day, and a ray of that pale English sun, which lightens but does not warm, passed through the bars of her prison.

Milady was looking out of the window, and pretended not to hear the door as it opened.

"Ah, ha!" said Lord Winter, "after having played comedy, after having played tragedy, we are now playing melancholy, eh?"

The prisoner made no reply.

"Yes, yes," continued Lord Winter; "I understand. You would like very well to be at liberty on that shore! You would like very well to be in a good ship, ploughing the waves of that emerald-green sea! You would like very well, either on land or on the ocean, to lay for me one of those nice little ambuscades you are so skilful in planning! Patience, patience! In a few days the shore will be at your command, the sea will be open to you—more open than will, perhaps, be agreeable to you ; for in a few days England will be relieved of your presence."

Milady clasped her hands, and raising her fine eyes toward heaven,—

"Lord, Lord," said she, with an angelic meekness of gesture and tone, "pardon this man, as I myself pardon him."

"Yes, pray, accursed woman !" cried the baron ; "your prayer is so much the more generous from your being, I swear to you, in the power of a man who will never pardon you !"

And he left the room.

At the moment he went out her piercing glance darted through the half-closed door, and she perceived Felton quickly stepping to one side lest he should be seen by her.

Then she threw herself upon her knees and began to pray.

"My God, my God !" said she, "Thou knowest in what holy cause I suffer ; give me, then, the strength to suffer."

The door opened gently ; the beautiful suppliant pretended not to hear the noise, and in a voice broken by tears she continued,—

"God of vengeance ! God of goodness ! wilt Thou allow this man's frightful projects to be accomplished ?"

Then only did she feign to hear the sound of Felton's steps ; and rising quick as thought, she blushed, as if ashamed of being surprised on her knees.

"I do not like to disturb those who pray, madame," said Felton seriously ; "do not disturb yourself on my account, I beseech you."

"How do you know I was praying, sir ?" said milady, in a voice choked by sobs. "You were mistaken, sir ; I was not praying."

"Do you think, then, madame," replied Felton, in the same serious voice, but in a milder tone—"do you think I assume the right of preventing a creature from prostrating herself before her Creator ? God forbid ! Besides, repentance is becoming to the guilty. Whatever crimes they may have committed, for me the guilty are sacred at the feet of God."

"Guilty !—I ?" said milady, with a smile which might have disarmed the angel of the last judgment. "Guilty ! Oh, my God, Thou knowest whether I am guilty ! Say I am condemned, sir, if you please ; but you know that God, who loves martyrs, sometimes permits the innocent to be condemned."

"Were you condemned, were you innocent, were you a martyr," replied Felton, "the greater would be the need of prayer ; and I myself will aid you with my prayers."

"Oh, you are a just man ! " cried milady, throwing herself on her knees at his feet. "I can stand it no longer, for I fear I shall be wanting in strength in the moment at which I shall be forced to undergo the struggle and confess my faith. Listen, then, to the supplication of a despairing woman. You are made a tool of, sir ; but that is not the question. I ask you only one favour, and if you grant it me, I will bless you in this world and in the world to come."

"Speak to the master, madame," said Felton ; "happily I am not charged with the power either of pardoning or punishing. God has laid this responsibility on one higher placed than I am."

"To you—no, to you alone ! Listen to me rather than contribute to my destruction, rather than contribute to my ignominy."

"If you have deserved this shame, madame, if you have incurred this ignominy, you must submit to it as an offering to God."

"What do you say ? Oh, you do not understand me! When I speak of ignominy, you think I speak of some punishment or other, of imprisonment or death ! Would to Heaven it were no worse ! Of what consequence to me is imprisonment or death ? "

"I no longer understand you, madame," said Felton.

"Or, rather, you pretend not to understand me, sir ! " replied the prisoner, with a doubting smile.

"No, madame, on the honour of a soldier, on the faith of a Christian."

"What ! You are ignorant of Lord Winter's designs on me ? "

"I am."

"Impossible ! You are his confidant ! "

"I never lie, madame."

"Oh, he makes too little concealment of them for you not to guess them."

"I seek to guess nothing, madame ; I wait till I am confided in ; and apart from what Lord Winter has said to me before you, he has confided nothing to me."

"Why, then," cried milady, with an incredible accent of truthfulness—"why, then, you are not his accomplice ; you do not know that he destines me to a disgrace which all the punishments of the world cannot equal in horror ? "

"You are mistaken, madame," said Felton, reddening; "Lord Winter is not capable of such a crime."

"Good!" said milady to herself; "without knowing what it is, he calls it a crime!"

Then aloud,—

"The friend of the infamous is capable of everything."

"Whom do you call the infamous?" asked Felton.

"Are there, then, in England two men to whom such an epithet can be applied?"

"You mean George Villiers?" said Felton, and his eyes flashed fire.

"Whom pagans and infidel gentiles call the Duke of Buckingham," replied milady. "I could not have thought that there was an Englishman in all England who would have required so long an explanation to understand of whom I was speaking."

"The hand of the Lord is stretched over him," said Felton; "he will not escape the chastisement he deserves."

Felton only expressed regarding the duke the execration which all the English felt for a man whom the Catholics themselves called the extortioner, the pillager, the profligate, and whom the Puritans styled simply Satan.

"Oh, my God, my God!" cried milady; "when I supplicate Thee to pour on this man the chastisement which is his due, Thou knowest that I pursue not my own vengeance, but that I pray for the deliverance of a whole nation!"

"Do you know him, then?" asked Felton.

"At length he questions me!" said milady to herself, at the height of joy at having obtained so quickly such a great result. "Oh, do I know him? Yes; to my misfortune, to my eternal misfortune!"

And milady wrung her hands, as if she had reached the very paroxysm of grief.

Felton no doubt felt within himself that his strength was deserting him, and he took several steps toward the door; but the prisoner, whose eye was never off him, sprang after him and stopped him.

"Sir," cried she, "be kind, be clement, listen to my prayer. That knife, which the baron's fatal prudence deprived me of, because he knows the use I would make of it— Oh, hear me to the end! That knife—give it to me for a minute only, for mercy's, for pity's sake! I will embrace your knees! You shall shut the door, that you may be certain I am not angry with you! My God! the idea of being angry with you, the only just, good, and compassionate being I have met with!—you, my saviour perhaps! One minute, that knife, one minute, a single minute, and I will restore it to you through the grating of the door; only one minute, Mr. Felton, and you will have saved my honour."

"To kill yourself?" cried Felton, in terror, forgetting to withdraw his hands from the hands of the prisoner—"to kill yourself?"

"I have said, sir," murmured milady, lowering her voice, and allowing herself to sink overpowered to the ground—"I have told my secret! He knows all!—My God, I am lost!"

Felton remained standing, motionless and undecided.

"He still doubts," thought milady; "I have not been sufficiently genuine."

Some one was heard walking in the corridor. Milady recognized Lord Winter's step.

Felton recognized it also, and took a step toward the door.

Milady sprang forward.

"Oh, not a word," said she, in a concentrated voice—"not a word to this man of all I have said to you, or I am lost, and it would be you—you——"

Then as the steps drew near she became silent for fear of being heard, applying, with a gesture of infinite terror, her beautiful hand to Felton's mouth.

Felton gently pushed milady from him, and she sank into an easy-chair.

Lord Winter passed before the door without stopping, and they heard the sound of his footsteps in the distance.

Felton, as pale as death, remained some instants with his ear alert and listening; then, when the sound had entirely died away, he breathed like a man awaking from a dream, and rushed out of the apartment.

"Ah," said milady, listening in her turn to the noise of Felton's steps, which faded away in a direction opposite to Lord Winter's—"ah, at length thou art mine!"

Then her brow darkened.

"If he tells the baron," said she, "I am lost; for the baron, who knows very well that I shall not kill myself, will place me before him with a knife in my hand, and he will discover that all this great despair was only a trick."

She went and stood before the glass and looked at herself closely. Never had she appeared more beautiful.

"Yes, yes!" said she smiling; "but he won't tell him!"

In the evening Lord Winter came when the supper was brought.

"Sir," said milady, "is your presence an indispensable accessory of my captivity? Could you not spare me the additional tortures which your visits inflict on me?"

"How now, my dear sister!" said Lord Winter. "Did you not sentimentally inform me, with that pretty mouth of yours, so cruel to me to-day, that you came to England solely for the pleasure of seeing me at your ease, an enjoyment of which you told me you so sensibly felt the privation that you had risked everything for it—seasickness, tempests, captivity? Well, here I am; be satisfied. Besides, this time my visit has a motive."

Milady trembled; she thought Felton had told all. Perhaps never in her life had this woman, who had experienced so many opposite and powerful emotions, felt her heart beat so violently.

She was seated. Lord Winter took an armchair, drew it toward her, and sat down near her; then pulling a paper out of his pocket, he unfolded it slowly.

"Here," said he, "I wanted to show you the kind of passport which I myself have drawn up, and which will serve you henceforward as an order-book in the life I am willing to grant you."

Then turning his eyes from milady to the paper, he read,—

"'Order to conduct to ——' The name is blank," interrupted Lord Winter. "If you have any preference you may indicate it to me, and if it be not within a thousand leagues of London, attention will be paid to your wishes. I will begin again, then. 'Order to conduct to —— the person named Charlotte Backson, branded by the justice of the kingdom of France, but liberated after chastisement. She is to dwell in this place, without ever going more than three leagues from it. In case of any attempt to escape, the penalty of death is to be applied. She will receive five shillings per day for lodging and food.'"

"This order does not concern me," replied milady coldly, "since it bears another name than mine."

"A name! Have you a name?"

"I bear your brother's."

"You are mistaken; my brother is only your second husband, and your first is still living. Tell me his name, and I will put it in the place of the name of Charlotte Backson. No?—you will not?—you are silent? Well, then, you must be registered as Charlotte Backson."

Milady remained silent ; only this time it was no longer from affectation, but from terror. She believed the order was on the point of being put into execution. She thought that Lord Winter had hastened her departure. She believed she was condemned to start that very evening. Everything in her mind was lost for an instant, when suddenly she perceived that no signature was attached to the order.

The joy she felt at this discovery was so great she could not conceal it.

"Yes, yes," said Lord Winter, who perceived what was passing in her mind—"yes, you look for the signature, and you say to yourself, 'All is not lost, for that order is not signed. It is only shown to me to terrify me ; that's all.' You are mistaken. To-morrow this order will be sent to the Duke of Buckingham ; the day after to-morrow it will return signed by his hand and marked with his seal ; and twenty-four hours later I will answer for its being put into execution. Farewell, madame ; this is all I had to say to you."

"And I reply to you, sir, that this abuse of power, this exile under a false name, is infamous ! "

"You would prefer to be hanged in your true name, milady ? You know the English laws are inexorable on the abuse of marriage vows ! Speak freely. Though my name, or rather my brother's, would be mixed up in the affair, I will risk the scandal of a public trial to make myself certain of getting rid of you."

Milady made no reply.

"Oh, I see you prefer peregrination. That's well, milady ; and there is an old proverb that says, 'Travelling forms youth.' Faith, you are not wrong after all, and life is sweet. That's the reason why I take such care you shall not deprive me of mine. There only remains, then, the question of the five shillings to be settled. I seem rather parsimonious—do I not ? That's because I don't care to leave you the means of bribing your jailers. Besides, you will always have your charms left to seduce them with. Employ them, if your check with Felton has not disgusted you with temptations of that kind."

"Felton has not told him," said milady to herself ; "nothing is lost, then."

"And now, madame, till I see you again. To-morrow I will come and announce to you the departure of my messenger."

Lord Winter rose, saluted milady ironically, and left the room.

Milady breathed again; she had still four days before her. Four days would be sufficient for her to complete the conquest of Felton.

A terrible idea, however, occurred to her. She thought that Lord Winter would perhaps send Felton himself to get the order signed by Buckingham. In that case Felton would escape her; for in order to ensure success, the magic of an uninterrupted seduction was necessary.

Nevertheless, as we have said, one circumstance reassured her—Felton had not spoken.

As she did not wish to seem at all agitated by Lord Winter's threats, she took her place at table and ate.

Then, as she had done the evening before, she fell on her knees and repeated her prayers aloud. As on the evening before, the soldier stopped his march to listen to her.

Soon after she heard lighter steps than the sentinel's coming from the end of the corridor and stopping before her door.

" That is he," said she.

And she began the same religious chant which had so strongly stirred Felton the evening before.

But though her sweet, full, and sonorous voice vibrated more harmoniously and affectingly than ever, the door remained shut. It seemed, however, to milady that in one of the furtive glances she darted from time to time at the small grating she saw the young man's ardent eyes through the narrow opening. But whether this was a reality or not, this time he had sufficient self-control not to enter.

Only, a few instants after she had finished her religious song, milady thought she heard a deep sigh; then the same steps she had heard approach departed slowly, and as though regretfully.

CHAPTER LV.

THE FOURTH DAY OF CAPTIVITY.

THE next day, when Felton entered milady's apartment he found her standing upon a chair, holding in her hands a cord made of several cambric handkerchiefs torn into strips, twisted together into a kind of rope, and tied at the ends. At the noise Felton made in opening the door milady leaped lightly to the ground and tried to hide behind her the improvised cord she held in her hand.

The young man was even paler than usual, and his eyes, inflamed by lack of sleep, showed that he had passed a feverish night.

Nevertheless, his brow was armed with a sternness more severe than ever.

He advanced slowly toward milady, who had sat down, and taking one end of the murderous rope, which, by mistake or perhaps by design, she allowed to appear,—

"What is this, madame?" he asked coldly.

"This? Nothing," said milady, smiling with that melancholy expression which she knew so well how to give to her smile. "*Ennui* is the mortal enemy of prisoners; I was blue, and I amused myself with twisting a rope."

Felton turned his eyes toward that part of the wall of the apartment before which he had found milady standing in the chair in which she was now seated, and over her head he perceived a gilt-headed screw, fixed in the wall for the purpose of hanging up clothes or arms.

He started, and the prisoner saw that start; for though her eyes were cast down, nothing escaped her.

"And what were you doing standing on that chair?" asked he.

"What difference does that make to you?" replied milady.

"But," replied Felton, "I wish to know."

"Do not question me," said the prisoner; "you know that we true Christians are forbidden to tell falsehoods."

"Well, then," said Felton, "I will tell you what you were doing, or rather what you were going to do: you were going to finish the fatal work you cherish in your mind. Remember, madame, if our God forbids us to tell falsehoods, He much more severely forbids suicide."

"When God sees one of His creatures unjustly persecuted, placed between suicide and dishonour, believe me, sir," replied milady, in a tone of deep conviction, "God pardons suicide, for then suicide is martyrdom."

"You say either too much or too little. Speak, madame; in Heaven's name, explain yourself."

"Relate my misfortunes to you, for you to treat them as fables; tell you my plans, for you to go and denounce them to my persecutor! No, sir. Besides, what difference to you is the life or death of a condemned wretch? You are only responsible for my body, aren't you? And provided you produce a corpse recognized as mine, they will require no more of you; and perhaps, even, you will have a double reward."

"I, madame, I!" cried Felton—"to suppose that I would ever accept the price of your life! Oh, you cannot think what you say!"

"Let me act as I please, Felton, let me act as I please," said milady, becoming excited. "Every soldier must be ambitious, must he not? You are a lieutenant: well, you will follow my bier with the rank of captain."

"Now, what have I done to you," said Felton, disturbed, "that you should load me with such a responsibility before God and before men? In a few days you will be away from this place; your life, madame, will then no longer be under my care, and," added he, with a sigh, "then you can do what you will with it."

"So," cried milady, as if she could not resist a pious indignation, "you, a religious man, you, who are called a just man, ask but one thing, and that is that you may not be inculpated, annoyed, by my death."

"It is my duty to watch over your life, madame, and I shall watch over it."

"But do you understand the mission you are fulfilling? A sufficiently cruel one, if I am guilty; but what name can you give it, what name will the Lord give it, if I am innocent?"

"I am a soldier, madame, and fulfil the orders I have received."

"Do you believe, then, that at the day of judgment God will separate blind executioners from iniquitous judges? You are not willing that I should kill my body, and you make yourself the agent of him who would kill my soul!"

"But I repeat it again to you," replied Felton, in great emotion—"no danger threatens you. I will answer for Lord Winter as for myself."

"Foolish man!" cried milady—"poor, foolish man! venturing to answer for another, when the wisest, when those most after God's own heart, hesitate to answer for themselves; and ranging yourself on the side of the strongest and the most fortunate, to crush the weakest and the most unfortunate."

"Impossible, madame, impossible," murmured Felton, who felt to the bottom of his heart the force of her argument. "A prisoner, you shall not through me recover your liberty; living, you shall not through me lose your life!"

"Yes," cried milady, "but I shall lose what is much

dearer to me than life—I shall lose my honour, Felton; and you—you I make responsible, before God and before men, for my shame and my infamy."

This time Felton, unmoved as he was or appeared to be, could not resist the secret influence which had already taken possession of him. To see such a beautiful woman, fair as the brightest vision, to see her now overcome by grief and now threatening, to undergo at the same time the ascendency of grief and beauty, was too much for a visionary, too much for a brain weakened by the ardent dreams of an ecstatic faith, too much for a heart corroded both by the burning love of Heaven and by the devouring hatred of men.

Milady saw his trouble, she felt by intuition the flame of opposing passions which burned the blood in the young fanatic's veins; and as a skilful general, who, seeing the enemy ready to surrender, marches toward him with a cry of victory, she rose, beautiful as a priestess of old, inspired like a Christian virgin, her arms extended, her throat uncovered, her hair dishevelled, holding with one hand her dress modestly drawn over her bosom, her look illumined by that fire which had already created such disorder in the young Puritan's senses, she stepped toward him, crying out in a vehement melody, and in her sweet voice, to which on occasion she could give a terrible accent,—

> " Let his victim to Baal be sent,
>   To the lions the martyr be thrown;
> Thy God He shall make thee repent;
>   From th' abyss He'll give ear to my moan."

Felton stood before this strange apparition like one petrified.

"Who art thou? who art thou?" cried he, clasping his hands. "Art thou a messenger from God, art thou a minister from hell, art thou an angel or a demon, callest thou thyself Eloa or Astarte?"

"Do you not know me, Felton? I am neither an angel nor a demon; I am a daughter of earth, I am a sister of thy faith, that is all."

"Yes, yes!" said Felton; "I doubted, but now I believe."

"You believe, and still you are an accomplice of that child of Belial who is called Lord Winter! You believe, and yet you abandon me in the hands of my enemies, of the enemy of England, of the enemy of God! You believe, and yet you deliver me up to him who fills and defiles the world with his heresies and debaucheries, to that infamous Sardanapalus, whom the blind call the Duke of Buckingham, and whom true believers name Antichrist!"

"I deliver you up to Buckingham! I! What mean you by that?"

"They have eyes," cried milady, "but they see not; ears have they, but they hear not."

"Yes, yes!" said Felton, passing his hands over his brow, covered with sweat, as if to remove his last doubt. "Yes, I recognize the voice which speaks to me in my dreams; yes, I recognize the features of the angel that appears to me every night, crying to my soul, which cannot sleep: 'Strike, save England, save thyself, for thou wilt die without having appeased God!' Speak, speak!" cried Felton; "I can understand you now."

A flash of terrible joy, but rapid as thought, gleamed from milady's eyes.

Fugitive as this homicidal flash was, Felton saw it, and started as if its light had revealed the abysses of this woman's heart.

He suddenly recalled Lord Winter's warnings, milady's seductions, her first attempts after her arrival. He drew back a step and hung his head, without ceasing, however, to look at her. As if fascinated by this strange creature, he could not remove his eyes from hers.

Milady was not a woman to misunderstand the meaning of this hesitation. Under her apparent emotions, her icy coolness never abandoned her. Before Felton replied, and before she should be forced to resume a conversation so difficult to be sustained in the same exalted key, she let her hands fall, and as if the weakness of the woman overpowered the enthusiasm of the inspired fanatic, she said,—

"But no; it is not for me to be the Judith to deliver Bethulia from this Holofernes. The sword of the Eternal is too heavy for my arm. Allow me, then, to avoid dishonour by death; let me take refuge in martyrdom. I do not ask you for liberty, as one who was guilty would, nor for vengeance, as a pagan would. Let me die—that is all. I beg you, I implore you on my knees; let me die, and my last sigh shall be a blessing for my saviour."

At her voice, so sweet and beseeching, at her look, so timid and downcast, Felton drew near. Little by little the enchantress had clothed herself with that magic which she assumed and threw aside at will—that is to say, beauty, meekness, and tears, and above all, the irresistible attraction of mystical voluptuousness, the most consuming of all voluptuousness.

" Alas ! " said Felton, " I can do but one thing, and that is to pity you, if you prove to me you are a victim. Lord Winter alleges cruel accusations against you. You are a Christian, you are my sister in religion. I feel myself drawn toward you—I, who have never loved any one but my benefactor—I, who have met with nothing in life but traitors and impious men. But you, madame, so beautiful in reality, you, so pure in appearance, must have committed great iniquities for Lord Winter to pursue you thus."

" They have eyes," repeated milady, with an accent of indescribable grief, " but they see not ; ears have they, but they hear not."

" But," cried the young officer, " speak, speak, then ! "

' Confide my shame to you ! " cried milady, with the blush of modesty on her face—" for often the crime of one becomes the shame of another—confide my shame to you, a man, and I a woman ! Oh," continued she, placing her hand modestly over her beautiful eyes, " never ! never ! —I could not."

" But to me, to a brother ? " said Felton.

Milady looked at him for some time with an expression which the young man took for doubt, but which, however, was nothing but observation—above all, the desire to fascinate.

Felton, a suppliant in his turn, clasped his hands.

" Well, then," said milady, " I confide in my brother. I will dare——"

At this moment Lord Winter's steps were heard ; but this time milady's terrible brother-in-law did not content himself, as on the preceding day, with passing before the door and going away again. He stopped, exchanged some words with the sentinel ; then the door opened, and he appeared.

During these few words Felton had quickly drawn back, and when Lord Winter entered he was several paces from the prisoner.

The baron entered slowly, casting a scrutinizing glance from milady to the young officer.

" You have been a long time here, John," said he. " Has this woman been relating her crimes to you ? In that case, I can comprehend the length of the conversation."

Felton started, and milady felt she was lost if she did not come to the assistance of the disconcerted Puritan.

" Ah ! you fear your prisoner may escape," said she.

"Well, ask your worthy jailer what favour I was but this instant asking him."

"You were asking a favour?" said the baron suspiciously.

"Yes, my lord," replied the young man, in some confusion.

"And what favour, pray?" asked Lord Winter.

"A knife, which she would return to me through the grating of the door a minute after she had received it," replied Felton.

"So there is some one concealed here whose throat this amiable lady is desirous of cutting," said Lord Winter in his ironical, contemptuous tone.

"There is myself," replied milady.

"I have given you the choice between America and Tyburn," replied Lord Winter. "Choose Tyburn, milady. Believe me, the cord is more certain than the knife."

Felton grew pale and made a step forward, remembering that at the moment he entered milady had a rope in her hand.

"You are right," said she; "I had already thought of it." Then she added in a low voice, "I will think of it again."

Felton felt a shudder run to the marrow of his bones; probably Lord Winter perceived his emotion.

"Mistrust yourself, John," said he; "I have placed reliance on you, my friend. Beware! I have warned you! But be of good courage, my lad; in three days we shall be delivered from this creature, and where I shall send her to she can no longer hurt anybody."

"You hear him!" cried milady vehemently, so that the baron might believe she was addressing Heaven, and that Felton might understand she was addressing him.

Felton hung his head and seemed buried in thought.

The baron took the young officer by the arm, and kept looking over his own shoulder so as not to lose sight of milady till he had gone out.

"Alas!" said the prisoner, when the door was shut, "I fear I am not so far advanced as I expected. Lord Winter has changed his usual stupidity into a prudence hitherto foreign to him. That's what the desire of vengeance is; and how that desire forms a man! Felton hesitates. Ah, he is not a man like that cursed D'Artagnan. A Puritan only adores virgins, and he adores them by clasping his hands. A musketeer loves women, and he loves them by clasping his arms round them."

Meantime milady waited with great impatience, for she feared the day would pass without her seeing Felton again. At last, an hour after the scene we have just related, she heard some one speaking in a low voice at the door. Soon after the door opened, and she perceived Felton.

The young man advanced into the room with a quick step, leaving the door open behind him, and making a sign to milady to be silent. His face was much agitated.

"What do you want with me?" she asked.

"Listen," replied Felton in a low voice. "I have just sent away the sentinel, that I might remain here without any one knowing I had come to speak to you, without having what I say to you overheard by others. The baron has just related a frightful story to me."

Milady assumed her smile of a victim resigned, and shook her head.

"Either you are a demon," continued Felton, "or the baron, my benefactor, my father, is a monster. I have known you four days, I have loved him two years. I therefore may hesitate between you. But be not alarmed at what I say; I need to be convinced. To-night, after twelve, I will come to see, and you will convince me."

"No, Felton, no, my brother; the sacrifice is too great, and I feel what it must cost you. No; I am lost. Do not be lost with me. My death will be much more eloquent than my life, and the silence of the corpse will convince you much better than the prisoner's words."

"Be silent, madame," cried Felton, "and do not speak to me in this way. I came to entreat you to promise me on your honour, to swear to me by what you hold most sacred, that you will make no attempt on your life."

"I will not promise," said milady, "for no one has more respect for a promise or an oath than I have, and if I made a promise I should have to keep it."

"Well," said Felton, "only promise till after you have seen me again. If, when you have seen me again, you still persist—well, then you shall be free, and I myself will give you the weapon you asked me for."

"Well," said milady, "for your sake I will wait."

"Swear it."

"I swear I will, by our God. Are you satisfied?"

"I am," said Felton. "Till night, then."

And he darted out of the room, shut the door, and waited in the corridor, the soldier's half-pike in his hand, and as if he had mounted guard in his place.

When the soldier returned Felton gave him back his weapon.

Then, through the grating to which she had come, milady saw the young man cross himself with a delirious fervour, and go down the corridor in an apparent transport of joy.

She herself returned to her place with a smile of savage contempt on her lips, and repeated, blaspheming, that terrible name of God, by whom she had just sworn without ever having learned to know Him.

"My God," said she, "what an insane fanatic! My God, I shall avenge myself, and he will help me!"

CHAPTER LVI.

THE FIFTH DAY OF CAPTIVITY.

MILADY had achieved a half-triumph, and the success obtained doubled her strength.

It was not a difficult thing to conquer, as she had hitherto done, men who were quick to let themselves be seduced, and whom the gallant education of a court led readily into her snares. Milady was handsome enough not to find resistance on the part of the flesh, and she was clever enough to prevail over all the obstacles of the mind.

But this time she had to contend with an uncultivated nature, concentrated and insensible by dint of austerity. Religion and penance had made Felton a man inaccessible to ordinary seductions. In his heated brain fermented plans so vast, projects so tumultuous, that no room remained for any capricious or material love—that sentiment which feeds on leisure and grows by corruption. Milady therefore had made a breach with her false virtue in the opinion of a man horribly prejudiced against her, and with her beauty in the heart of a man hitherto chaste and pure. In short, by this experiment, made upon the most rebellious subject that nature and religion could submit to her study, she had acquired a knowledge of her own resources hitherto unknown to herself.

Many times, nevertheless, during the evening she despaired of fate and of herself. She did not invoke God, we know, but she had faith in the genius of evil—that immense sovereignty which reigns in all the details of human life, and by which, as in the Arabian fable, a single pomegranate seed is sufficient to reconstruct a ruined world.

Milady, being well prepared for Felton's reception, was able to erect her batteries for the next day. She knew she had only two days left ; that when once the order was signed by Buckingham—and Buckingham would sign it the more readily from its bearing a false name, and because he could not therefore recognize the woman in question—when once this order was signed, we say, the baron would make her embark immediately ; and she knew also that women condemned to transportation employ arms much less powerful in their seductions than pretendedly virtuous women whose beauty is illuminated by the sun of society, whose kind the voice of fashion lauds, and whom a halo of aristocracy gilds with its magic splendours. To be a woman condemned to a painful and infamous punishment does not prevent her from being beautiful, but it is an obstacle to the regaining of power. Like all persons of real genius, milady knew what suited her nature and her means. Poverty was destruction to her ; degradation took away two-thirds of her greatness. Milady was a queen only among queens. The pleasure of satisfied pride was necessary for her domination. To command inferior beings was rather a humiliation than a pleasure for her.

She should certainly return from her exile—she did not doubt that a single instant. But how long might this exile last ? For an active, ambitious nature like milady's, days not spent in climbing are days of ill-omen. What word, then, can be found to describe those days when they are descending ? To lose a year, two years, three years—that is to say, an eternity ; to return when D'Artagnan and his friends, happy and triumphant, should have received from the queen the reward they had deserved by the services they had rendered her—these were devouring ideas which a woman like milady could not endure. Besides, the storm raging within her doubled her strength, and she would have burst the walls of her prison if her body could for a single instant have assumed the proportions of her mind.

Then what spurred her on still more in the midst of all this was the remembrance of the cardinal. What must the mistrustful, restless, suspicious cardinal think of her silence—the cardinal, not merely her only support, her only prop, her only protector in the present, but still further, the principal instrument of her future fortune and vengeance ? She knew him—she knew that on her return after a fruitless journey it would be idle to allege her imprisonment as an excuse, idle to enlarge on the sufferings she had undergone. The cardinal would reply, with the sarcastic calmness of the sceptic, strong at once by power and genius,—

" You should not have allowed yourself to be taken."

Then milady collected all her energies, murmuring in the depths of her soul the name of Felton, the only beam of light penetrating to her in the depths of the hell into which she was fallen ; and like a serpent which folds and unfolds its rings to ascertain its strength, she enveloped Felton beforehand in the thousand meshes of her inventive imagination.

Meanwhile the time was passing. The hours, one after another, seemed to awaken the bell as they passed, and every blow of the brazen hammer resounded on the prisoner's heart. At nine o'clock Lord Winter made his usual visit, examined the window and the bars, sounded the floor and the walls, looked to the chimney and the doors ; but during this long and minute examination neither he nor milady uttered a single word.

Doubtless both of them understood that the situation had become too serious to waste time in idle words and ineffectual anger.

" Well," said the baron on leaving her, " you will not escape for one more night ! "

At ten o'clock Felton came and placed the sentinel. Milady recognized his step. She was as well acquainted with it now as a mistress is with the footfall of the lover of her heart, and yet milady at the same time detested and despised this weak fanatic.

It was not the appointed hour ; Felton did not come in.

Two hours after, as the clock struck twelve, the sentinel was relieved.

This time it was the hour, and from this moment milady waited impatiently.

The new sentinel began his walk in the corridor.

At the end of ten minutes Felton came. Milady was all attention.

" Listen," said the young man to the sentinel. " On no pretence leave the door, for you know that last night my lord punished a soldier for quitting his post for an instant, though I watched in his place during his absence."

" Yes, I know he did," said the soldier.

" I recommend you, therefore, to keep the strictest watch. I am going to pay a second visit to this woman, who, I fear, entertains sinister intentions on her own life, and I have received orders to watch her."

"Good!" murmured milady; "here's the austere Puritan telling a lie!"

The soldier only smiled.

"Plague take it, lieutenant!" said he; "you are not very unlucky in being charged with such commissions, particularly if my lord has authorized you to look in her bed!"

Felton reddened. In any other circumstances he would have reprimanded the soldier for indulging in such a joke, but his conscience murmured too loud for his mouth to dare to speak.

"If I call, come in," said he; "if any one comes, call me."

"I will, lieutenant," said the soldier.

Felton entered milady's apartment. Milady arose.

"So here you are!" said she.

"I promised you I would come," said Felton, "and I have come."

"You promised me something else."

"What? My God!" said the young man, who, in spite of his self-command, felt his knees tremble and the sweat start from his brow.

"You promised to bring a knife, and to leave it with me after our conversation."

"Say no more of that, madame," said Felton. "There is no situation, however terrible, that can authorize one of God's creatures to inflict death upon itself. I have reflected that I could never become guilty of such a sin."

"Ah, you have reflected!" said the prisoner, sitting down in her armchair with a smile of disdain; "and I also have reflected."

"About what?"

"That I can have nothing to say to a man who does not keep his word."

"Oh, my God!" murmured Felton.

"You may retire," said milady. "I shall not speak."

"Here is the knife," said Felton, drawing from his pocket the weapon which, according to his promise, he had brought, but which he hesitated to give to his prisoner.

"Let me see it," said milady.

"For what purpose?"

"On my honour I will instantly return it to you. You shall place it on that table, and you may remain between it and me."

Felton handed the weapon to milady, who examined the temper of it attentively, and tried the point on the tip of her finger.

"Well," said she, returning the knife to the young officer, "this is fine and good steel. You are a faithful friend, Felton."

Felton took back the weapon and laid it on the table, in accordance with his agreement with his prisoner.

Milady followed him with her eyes, and made a gesture of satisfaction.

"Now," said she, "listen to me."

The recommendation was useless. The young officer was standing before her, awaiting her words as if to devour them.

"Felton," said milady, with a solemnity full of melancholy, "if your sister, your father's daughter, said to you,—

"While still young, unfortunately beautiful, I was dragged into a snare. I resisted. Ambushes, acts of violence, were multiplied around me. I resisted. The religion I serve, the God I adore, were blasphemed because I called to my aid my religion and my God. I resisted. Then outrages were heaped upon me, and when they could not ruin my soul they determined to defile my body for ever. Finally——"

Milady stopped, and a bitter smile passed over her lips.

"Finally," said Felton—"finally, what did they do?"

"Finally, one evening, they resolved to paralyze my unconquerable resistance. One evening a powerful narcotic was mixed with my water. Scarcely had I finished my repast when I felt myself sink by degrees into a strange torpor. Though I was without suspicion, a vague fear seized me, and I tried to struggle against sleep. I arose. I endeavoured to run to the window and call for help, but my legs refused to carry me. It seemed as if the ceiling were sinking down on my head and crushing me under its weight. I stretched out my arms; I tried to speak; I could only utter inarticulate sounds. An irresistible faintness came over me. I supported myself by an armchair, feeling that I was about to fall, but this support was soon insufficient for my weak arms. I fell on one knee, then on both. I tried to pray, but my tongue was frozen. God, doubtless, neither heard nor saw me, and I sank down on the floor, a prey to a sleep which was like death.

"Of all that passed during my sleep, or the time that glided away while it lasted, I have no recollection. The only thing I recollect is, that I woke in bed, in a round chamber, the furniture of which was sumptuous, and into which light penetrated only by an opening in the ceiling.

Moreover, no door seemed to give entrance to the room. It might have been called a magnificent prison.

"It was long before I could make out where I was, or could take account of the details I describe. My mind seemed to strive in vain to shake off the heavy darkness of the sleep from which I could not rouse myself. I had vague perceptions of a space travelled over, of the rolling of a carriage, of a horrible dream in which my strength was exhausted; but all this was so dark and so indistinct in my mind that these events seemed to belong to another life than mine, and yet mixed with mine by a fantastic duality.

"For some time the state into which I had fallen appeared so strange that I thought I was dreaming. I arose tremblingly. My clothes were near me on a chair. I neither remembered having undressed myself, nor going to bed. Then little by little the reality broke upon me, full of chaste terrors. I was no longer in the house where I had been dwelling. As well as I could judge by the light of the sun, the day was already two-thirds gone. It was the evening before that I had fallen asleep; my sleep, then, must have already lasted nearly twenty-four hours! What had happened during this long sleep?

"I dressed myself as quickly as possible. My slow and stiff motions all attested that the effects of the narcotic were still not entirely dissipated. The chamber was evidently furnished for a woman's reception; and the most finished coquette could not have formed a wish which, on looking round the apartment, she would not have found gratified.

"Certainly I was not the first captive who had been shut up in this splendid prison. But you understand, Felton, the more superb the prison, the greater was my terror.

"Yes, it was a prison, for I vainly tried to get out of it. I sounded all the walls in the hopes of discovering a door, but everywhere the walls returned a full, dull sound.

"I made the circuit of the room perhaps twenty times, in search of an outlet of some kind; there was none. I sank exhausted with fatigue and terror into an armchair.

"In the meantime night was rapidly coming on, and with night my terrors increased. I did not know but I had best remain where I was seated. I seemed to be surrounded by unknown dangers, into which I was likely to fall at every step. Although I had eaten nothing since the evening before, my fears prevented me from feeling hungry.

"No noise from without by which I could measure the

time reached me. I only supposed it might be seven or eight o'clock in the evening, for it was October and quite dark.

"All at once a door, creaking on its hinges, made me start. A globe of fire appeared above the glazed opening of the ceiling, casting a strong light into my chamber, and I perceived with terror that a man was standing within a few paces of me.

"A table, with two covers, bearing a supper ready prepared, stood, as if by magic, in the middle of the apartment.

"That man was he who had pursued me during a whole year, who had vowed my dishonour, and who, by the first words that issued from his mouth, gave me to understand he had accomplished it the preceding night."

"The scoundrel!" murmured Felton.

"Oh yes, the scoundrel!" cried milady, seeing the interest which the young officer, whose soul seemed to hang on her lips, took in her strange story—"oh yes, the scoundrel! He believed that, by having triumphed over me in my sleep, all was completed. He came, hoping that I should accept my shame, since my shame was consummated. He came to offer his fortune in exchange for my love.

"All the haughty contempt and disdainful words that the heart of a woman can contain I poured out upon this man. Doubtless he was accustomed to such reproaches, for he listened to me calm and smiling, with his arms folded over his breast. Then, when he thought I had said all, he advanced toward me. I sprang to the table, I seized a knife, I placed it to my breast.

"'Take one step more,' said I, 'and in addition to my dishonour, you shall have my death to reproach yourself with!'

"Unquestionably there was in my look, my voice, my whole person, such sincerity of gesture, of attitude and action, as carries conviction to the most perverse minds, for he stopped.

"'Your death!' said he. 'Oh no; you are too charming a mistress to allow me to consent to lose you thus, after having had the good fortune to have you once in my possession. Good-bye, my charmer; I will defer paying you my next visit till you are in a better humour.'

"At these words he blew a whistle. The globe of fire which lighted the room reascended and disappeared. I found myself again in complete darkness. The same noise of the door opening and shutting was repeated the instant after, the flaming globe descended again, and I was alone.

"That moment was frightful If I had still any doubts of my misfortune, these doubts had vanished in an overwhelming reality. I was in the hands of a man whom I not only detested, but despised ; of a man capable of anything, and who had already given me a fatal proof of what it was in his power to do."

"But, pray, who was this man ? " asked Felton.

"I spent the night in a chair, starting at the least noise ; for about midnight the lamp went out, and I again was in darkness. But the night passed without any fresh attempt on the part of my persecutor. Day came ; the table had disappeared, only I had still the knife in my hand.

"That knife was my only hope.

"I was worn out with fatigue. Lack of sleep inflamed my eyes ; I had not dared to sleep a single instant. The light of day reassured me. I went and threw myself on the bed, without parting with the emancipating knife, which I concealed under my pillow.

"When I awoke another meal was served.

"This time, in spite of my terrors, in spite of my agony, I began to feel a devouring hunger. It was forty eight hours since I had taken any nourishment. I ate some bread and some fruit ; then remembering the narcotic mixed with the water I had drunk, I did not touch that which was placed on the table, but filled my glass at a marble fountain fixed in the wall over my dressing-table.

"And yet, in spite of this precaution, I remained for some time still in a terrible agitation of mind. But this time my fears were unfounded ; I spent the day without experiencing anything like what I dreaded.

"I took the precaution to half empty the carafe, so that my suspicions might not be noticed.

"The evening came on, and with it darkness ; but deep as this darkness was, my eyes began to be accustomed to it. I saw the table sink through the floor. A quarter of an hour after it appeared again, bearing my supper. And in an instant, thanks to the same lamp, my chamber was once more lighted.

"I was determined to eat only such things as could not possibly have anything soporific introduced into them. Two eggs and some fruit composed my repast. Then I drew another glass of water from my protecting fountain, and drank it.

"After swallowing a mouthful or two, it seemed to me not to have the same taste as in the morning. A swift suspicion instantly seized me. I stopped, but I had already drunk half a glassful of it.

"I threw the rest away with horror, and waited, with the dew of fear on my brow.

"No doubt some invisible witness had seen me draw the water from that fountain, and had taken advantage of my very confidence in it the better to assure my ruin so coolly resolved upon, so cruelly pursued.

"Half an hour had not passed when the same symptoms began to appear; only, as I had drunk but half a glass of the water, I struggled longer, and instead of falling entirely asleep, I sank into a state of lethargy, which left me a perception of what was happening around me, while it deprived me of the strength either to defend myself or to fly.

"I dragged myself toward the bed, to seek the only defence left me—my saving knife; but I could not reach the bolster. I sank on my knees, my hands clasped round one of the bedposts; then I realized that I was lost."

Felton became frightfully pale, and a convulsive shudder crept through his whole body.

"And what was most terrible," continued milady, with altered voice, as if she still experienced the same agony as at that awful moment, "was that this time I retained a consciousness of the danger threatening me; was that my soul, so to speak, was still awake in my sleeping body; was that I saw; was that I heard! It is true that all was like a dream, but it was only the more frightful.

"I saw the lamp ascending and gradually leaving me in darkness; then I heard the creaking of the door so well known, though I had heard it open but twice.

"I felt instinctively that some one was approaching me. It is said that the doomed wretch in the deserts of America thus feels the approach of the serpent.

"I strove to make an effort, I tried to cry out; by an incredible effort of will I even raised myself up, but only to sink down again immediately, and to fall into my perse-cutor's arms."

"Tell me, pray, who this man was?" cried the young officer.

Milady saw at a single glance all the painful feelings which she inspired in Felton by dwelling on every detail of her recital. But she would not spare him a single pang. The more profoundly she wounded his heart, the more certain he would be to avenge her; so she went on as if she had not heard his exclamation, or as if she thought the moment was not yet come to reply to it.

"Only this time it was no longer a kind of inert corpse, without feeling, that the villain had to deal with. I told you that without being able to regain the complete exercise of my faculties I retained the sense of my danger. I struggled, then, with all my strength, and weak as I was, doubtless opposed a long resistance, for I heard him cry out,—

"'These miserable Puritan girls! I knew very well that they tired out their executioners, but I thought them less strong against their lovers!'

"Alas! my desperate resistance could not last long. I felt my strength fail, and this time it was not my sleep that enabled the scoundrel to prevail, but my swooning."

Felton listened without making any sound but a kind of suppressed roar. Only the sweat streamed down his marble brow, and his hand, under his coat, tore his breast.

"My first impulse on coming to myself was to feel under my pillow for the knife I had not been able to reach. If it had not come into play for defence, it might at least serve in expiation.

"But on taking that knife, Felton, a terrible idea occurred to me. I have sworn to tell you all, and I will tell you all. I promised you the truth: I will tell it, though it destroy me."

"The idea came into your mind to avenge yourself on that man, did it not?" cried Felton.

"It certainly did!" said milady. "The idea was not a Christian one. I know; but undoubtedly that eternal enemy of our souls, that lion roaring constantly around us, breathed it into my mind. In short, what shall I say to you, Felton?" continued milady, in the tone of a woman accusing herself of a crime. "This idea occurred to me, and did not leave me. I am to-day bearing the punishment of that homicidal thought."

"Go on! go on!" said Felton; "I am eager to see you come to your vengeance!"

"Oh, I resolved that it should take place as soon as possible. I had no doubt he would return the following night. During the day I had nothing to fear.

"When the breakfast hour came, therefore, I did not hesitate to eat and drink. I determined to make believe sup, but to take nothing; so by the nourishment of the morning I was to combat the fast of the evening.

"Only I concealed a glass of water, which formed part

of my breakfast, thirst having made me suffer the most when I had remained forty-eight hours without eating or drinking.

"The day passed without having any other influence on me than to strengthen the resolution I had formed, only I took care that my face should not betray the slightest thoughts of my heart, for I had no doubt I was watched. Several times, even, I felt a smile on my lips. Felton, I dare not tell you at what idea I smiled; you would hold me in horror——"

"Go on! go on!" said Felton; "you see plainly that I listen, and that I am anxious to know the end."

"Evening came; the ordinary events took place. During the darkness, as before, my table was covered; then the lamp was lighted, and I sat down to table. I ate some fruit only. I pretended to pour out water from the carafe, but I drank only what I had saved in my glass. Moreover, the substitution was made so carefully that my spies, if I had any, could have no suspicion of it.

"After supper I exhibited the same marks of languor as on the preceding evening. But this time, as if I yielded to fatigue, or as if I had become familiarized with danger, I dragged myself toward my bed, let my dress fall, and got in.

"I found my knife where I had placed it under my pillow, and while feigning to sleep, my hand convulsively grasped the handle of it.

"Two hours passed without anything new occurring. This time—oh, my God! who could have told me that the evening before?—I began to fear he would not come.

"At length I saw the lamp rising softly, and disappearing in the depths of the ceiling. My room was filled with darkness and obscurity, but I made an effort to see through this darkness and obscurity.

"Nearly ten minutes passed; I heard no other noise but the beating of my own heart.

"I implored Heaven that he might come.

"At length I heard the well-known noise of the door opening and shutting. In spite of the thickness of the carpet, I heard a step which made the floor creak. In spite of the darkness, I saw a shadow approaching my bed."

"Make haste! make haste!" said Felton; "do you not see that every one of your words burns me like molten lead?"

"Then," continued milady, "I collected all my strength;

I recalled to my mind that the moment of vengeance, or rather of justice, had struck. I looked upon myself as another Judith. I gathered myself up, knife in hand, and when I saw him near me, stretching out his arms to find his victim, then, with a last cry of agony and despair, I struck him in the middle of his breast.

"The scoundrel! He had foreseen all. His breast was covered with a coat of mail; the edge of the knife was turned.

"'Ah, ha!' cried he, seizing my arm, and wresting from me the weapon that had served me so ill, 'you want to take my life, do you, my pretty Puritan? But this is more than dislike, this is ingratitude! Come, come, calm yourself, my sweet girl! I thought you were become kinder. I am not one of those tyrants who detain women by force. You don't love me. With my usual fatuity, I doubted it; now I am convinced. To-morrow you shall be free.'

"I had but one wish, and that was that he should kill me.

"'Beware!' said I, 'for my liberty is your dishonour.'

"'Explain yourself, my pretty sibyl.'

"'Yes; for no sooner shall I have left this place than I will tell everything. I will proclaim the violence you have used toward me. I will describe my captivity. I will denounce this palace of infamy. You are placed very high, my lord, but tremble! Above you there is the king. Above the king there is God.'

"Perfect master as he seemed over himself, my persecutor allowed a movement of anger to escape him. I could not see the expression of his face, but I felt the arm on which my hand was placed tremble.

"'Then you shall not go from here,' said he.

"'Very well,' cried I; 'then the place of my punishment will be also my tomb. So be it, I will die here; and you will see if an accusing phantom is not more terrible than a living being who threatens!'

"'No weapon shall be left in your hands.'

"'There is a weapon which despair has placed within reach of every creature that has the courage to make use of it. I will allow myself to die of hunger.'

"'Come, come,' said the wretch; 'is not peace much better than such a war? I will restore you to liberty this moment. I will proclaim you a piece of immaculate virtue. I will name you the Lucretia of England.'

"'And I will say that you are the Sextus. I will denounce you before men as I have even now denounced you before God ; and if it be necessary that, like Lucretia, I should sign my accusation with my blood, I will sign it.'

" ' Ah, ha ! ' said my enemy in a jeering tone, ' that's quite another thing. Faith ! everything considered, you are very well off here. You shall want for nothing, and if you choose to die of hunger, why, that will be your own fault.'

" At these words he retired. I heard the door open and shut, and I remained overwhelmed, yet less, I confess, by my grief than by the shame of not having avenged myself.

" He kept his word. All that day, all the next night, passed away without my seeing him. But I also kept my word with him, and I neither ate nor drank. I was, as I had told him, determined to starve myself to death.

" I passed the day and the night in prayer, for I hoped that God would pardon me my suicide.

" The second night the door opened. I was lying on the floor, for my strength was beginning to abandon me.

" At the noise I raised myself up on one hand.

" ' Well,' said a voice, which vibrated in too terrible a manner in my ear not to be recognized—' well, are we softened a little ? Will we not pay for our liberty by the mere promise of silence ? Come, I am a good sort of a prince,' added he, ' and though I do not like Puritans, I do them justice, as well as Puritan women when they are pretty. Come, take a little oath for me on the cross ; I won't ask anything more of you.'

" ' On the cross,' cried I, rising up, for at that abhorred voice I had recovered all my strength—' on the cross, I swear that no promise, no threat, no force, no torture, shall close my mouth ! On the cross, I swear to denounce you everywhere as a murderer, as a despoiler of honour, as a base coward ! On the cross, I swear, if I ever succeed in escaping from this place, to call down vengeance on you from the whole human race !'

" ' Beware ! ' said the voice, in a threatening accent that I had never yet heard. ' I have one supreme means, which I will not employ except in the last extremity, to close your mouth, or at least to prevent any one from believing a single word you may utter.'

" I mustered all my strength to reply to him with a burst of laughter.

" He saw that it was an eternal war, a war to the death, between us from that time forth.

" ' Listen,' said he : ' I give you the rest of this night and all to-morrow.   Reflect : promise to be silent, and riches, consideration, even honour, shall surround you.   Threaten to speak, and I will condemn you to infamy.'

" ' You,' cried I, ' you ! '

" ' To eternal, ineffaceable infamy ! '

" ' You ! ' repeated I.   Oh, I declare to you, Felton, I thought him mad !

" ' Yes, I ! ' replied he.

" ' Oh, leave me,' said I ; ' begone, if you do not wish to see me dash my head against that wall, before your eyes ! '

" ' Very well,' replied he.   ' It is your own doing.   Till to-morrow evening, then ! '

" ' Till to-morrow evening,' I repeated, allowing myself to fall, and biting the carpet with rage.''

Felton leaned for support on a piece of furniture, and milady saw, with a demon's joy, that his strength would fail him, perhaps before the end of her recital.

CHAPTER LVII.

A DEVICE OF CLASSICAL TRAGEDY.

AFTER a moment's silence, employed by milady in observing the young man who was listening to her, milady continued her recital.

" It was nearly three days since I had eaten or drunk any-thing.   I was suffering frightful torments.   At times there passed before me something like clouds compressing my brow, veiling my eyes.   It was delirium.

" When evening came I was so weak that almost every instant I fainted, and every time that I fainted I thanked God, for I thought I was going to die.

" In the midst of one of these fainting fits I heard the door open.   Terror recalled me to myself.

" He entered the apartment, followed by a man in a mask.   He himself was masked, but I knew his step, I knew his voice, I knew him by that imposing carriage which hell bestowed on his person for the curse of hu-manity.

" ' Well,' said he to me, ' have you made up your mind to take the oath I requested of you ? '

" ' You have said Puritans have but one word.   Mine you have heard, and that is to pursue you on earth before the tribunal of men, in heaven before the tribunal of God.'

" ' You persist, then ? '

" ' I swear it before the God who hears me. I will take the whole world as a witness of your crime, and that until I have found an avenger.'

" ' You are a prostitute,' said he, in a voice of thunder, ' and you shall undergo the punishment of prostitutes ! Disgraced in the eyes of the world you will invoke, try to prove to that world that you are neither guilty nor mad ! '

" Then addressing the man who accompanied him,—

" ' Executioner,' said he, ' do your duty.' "

" Oh, his name, his name ! " cried Felton ; " tell it me ! "

" Then in spite of my cries, in spite of my resistance—for I began to realize that for me there was a question of something worse than death—the executioner seized me, threw me on the floor, bruised me with his rough grasp. Suffocated by sobs, almost without consciousness, invoking God, who did not listen to me, I suddenly uttered a frightful cry of pain and shame. A burning fire, a red-hot iron, the iron of the executioner, was imprinted on my shoulder."

Felton uttered a groan.

" Here," said milady, rising with the majesty of a queen— " here, Felton, behold the new martyrdom invented for a young girl, pure, and yet the victim of a scoundrel's brutality. Learn to know the hearts of men, and henceforth make yourself less easily the instrument of their unjust revenges."

Milady, with a swift gesture, opened her dress, tore the cambric that covered her bosom, and, red with feigned anger and simulated modesty, showed the young man the ineffaceable impression which dishonoured her beautiful shoulder.

" But," cried Felton, " it is a fleur-de-lis which I see there."

" And therein consisted the infamy," replied milady. " The brand of England !—it would have been necessary to prove what tribunal had imposed it on me, and I could have made a public appeal to all the tribunals of the kingdom ; but the brand of France ! — oh, by that, by that I was branded indeed ! "

This was too much for Felton.

Pale, motionless, overwhelmed by this frightful revelation, dazzled by the superhuman beauty of this woman, who unveiled herself before him with a shamelessness which appeared to him sublime, he ended by falling on his knees before her, as the early Christians did before those pure and holy martyrs whom the persecution of the emperors gave up in the circus to the bloodthirsty lewdness of the populace. The brand disappeared; the beauty alone remained.

"Pardon! pardon!" cried Felton; "oh, pardon!"

Milady read in his eyes, "Love! love!"

"Pardon for what?" asked she.

"Pardon me for having joined your persecutors."

Milady held out her hand to him.

"So beautiful! so young!" cried Felton, covering that hand with his kisses.

Milady cast on him one of those looks which make a slave into a king.

Felton was a Puritan. He dropped this woman's hand to kiss her feet.

He more than loved her; he adored her.

When this crisis was past; when milady seemed to have recovered her self-control, which she had not lost even for an instant; when Felton had seen her cover again with the veil of chastity those treasures of love which were concealed from him only to make him desire them the more ardently,—

"Ah, now!" said he, "I have only one thing to ask of you—that is, the name of your true executioner. For in my eyes there is but one. The other was the instrument, that was all."

"What, brother!" cried milady; "must I name him? Have you not yet divined who he is?"

"What!" cried Felton; "he!—he again!—he always! What!—the real culprit!"

"The real culprit," said milady, "is the ravager of England, the persecutor of true believers, the cowardly ravisher of the honour of so many women—he who, to satisfy a caprice of his corrupt heart, is about to make England shed so much blood, who protects the Protestants to-day and will betray them to-morrow——"

"Buckingham! Then it is Buckingham!" cried Felton, in exasperation.

Milady hid her face in her hands, as if she could not endure the shame which this name recalled to her.

"Buckingham, the executioner of this angelic creature!" cried Felton. "And Thou hast not hurled Thy thunder at him, my God! And Thou hast left him noble, honoured, powerful, for the ruin of us all!"

"God abandons him who abandons himself," said milady.

"But He will draw down on his head the punishment

reserved for the damned!" said Felton, with increasing excitement. "He wishes that human vengeance should precede heavenly justice."

"Men fear him and spare him."

"I," said Felton—"I do not fear him, nor will I spare him!"

Milady felt her soul bathed in a hellish joy.

"But how can Lord Winter, my protector, my father," asked Felton, "be mixed up with all this?"

"Listen, Felton," resumed milady. "Because by the side of base and contemptible men there are often found great and generous natures. I had an affianced husband, a man whom I loved, and who loved me—a heart like yours, Felton, a man like you. I went to him and told him all; he knew me, that man did, and did not doubt an instant. He was a nobleman, a man equal to Buckingham in every respect. He said nothing; he only girded on his sword, enveloped himself in his cloak, and went straight to Buckingham Palace."

"Yes, yes," said Felton, "I understand; though with such men not the sword, but the dagger, should be used."

"Buckingham had left England the day before, sent as ambassador to Spain, to demand the hand of the Infanta for King Charles I., who was then only Prince of Wales. My affianced husband returned.

"'Hear me,' said he. 'That man has gone, and has therefore for the moment escaped my vengeance; but meanwhile let us be united, as we were to have been. Then leave Lord Winter to maintain his own honour and his wife's.'"

"Lord Winter!" cried Felton.

"Yes," said milady, "Lord Winter. And now you can understand it all, can you not? Buckingham was absent nearly a year. A week before his return Lord Winter died suddenly, leaving me his sole heir. Whence came the blow? God who knows all doubtless knows this, but I accuse no one."

"Oh, what an abyss! what an abyss!" cried Felton.

"Lord Winter died without revealing anything to his brother. The terrible secret was to be concealed from all till it burst like a thunderclap over the head of the guilty one. Your protector had regretfully seen his elder brother's marriage with a portionless girl. I felt that I could look for no support from a man disappointed in his hopes of an inheritance. I went to France, intending to remain there for the rest of my life. But all my fortune is in England. Communication being closed by the war, I was in want of everything. So I was obliged to come back again. Six days ago I landed at Portsmouth."

"Well?" said Felton.

"Well, Buckingham heard by some means, no doubt, of my return. He spoke of me to Lord Winter, already prejudiced against me, and told him that his sister-in-law was a prostitute, a branded woman. My husband's voice, pure and noble, was no longer there to defend me. Lord Winter believed all that was told him, with so much the more facility because it was his interest to believe it. He had me arrested, brought me here, and placed me under your guard. You know the rest. The day after to-morrow he banishes me, he transports me; the day after to-morrow he exiles me among the infamous. Oh, the net is well woven, the plot is clever, and my honour will not survive it! You see, then, Felton, I must die! Felton, give me that knife!"

And at these words, as if all her strength was exhausted, milady sank, weak and languishing, into the arms of the young officer, who, intoxicated with love, anger, and hitherto unknown sensations of delight, held her with transport, pressed her to his heart, all trembling at the breath from her lovely mouth, bewildered by the contact with her palpitating bosom.

"No, no," said he, "no; you shall live honoured and pure, you shall live to triumph over your enemies."

Milady slowly pushed him from her with her hand, while drawing him nearer with her look. But Felton embraced her more closely, imploring her as though she were a divinity.

"Oh, death, death!" said she, lowering her voice and her eyelids; "oh, death rather than shame! Felton, my brother, my friend, I conjure you!"

"No," cried Felton, "no; you shall live, and you shall be avenged."

"Felton, I bring misfortune to all who surround me! Felton, abandon me! Felton, let me die!"

"Well, then, we will die together!" cried he, pressing his lips to the prisoner's.

Several knocks resounded on the door. This time milady really pushed him away from her.

"Hark!" said she; "we have been overheard. Some one is coming! All is over! We are lost!"

"No," said Felton; "it is only the sentinel warning me that they are about to change guard."

"Then run to the door and open it yourself."

Felton obeyed. This woman was already his whole thought, his whole soul.

He found a sergeant in command of a watch patrol.

"Well, what is the matter?" asked the young lieutenant.

"You told me to open the door if I heard any one cry out," said the soldier; "but you forgot to leave me the key. I heard you cry out without understanding what you said. I tried to open the door, but it was locked inside; then I called the sergeant."

"And here I am," said the sergeant.

Felton, bewildered, almost mad, stood speechless.

Milady, perceiving that it was now her turn to come forward, ran to the table, and seizing the knife which Felton had laid down,—

"And what right have you to prevent me from dying?" said she.

"Great God!" exclaimed Felton, on seeing the knife glitter in her hand.

At that moment a burst of ironical laughter resounded through the corridor. Attracted by the noise, the baron, in his dressing-gown, his sword under his arm, was standing in the doorway.

"Ah, ha!" said he; "here we are, at the last act of the tragedy. You see, Felton, the drama has gone through all the phases I named. But be at ease; no blood will flow.'

Milady perceived that all was lost unless she gave Felton an instant and terrible proof of her courage.

"You are mistaken, my lord—blood will flow; and may that blood fall back on those who cause it to flow!"

Felton uttered a cry and rushed toward her. He was too late; milady had stabbed herself.

But the knife had very fortunately, we should say skilfully, come in contact with the steel busk which at that period, like a cuirass, defended women's bosoms; it had glided down it, tearing her dress, and had penetrated slantingly between the flesh and the ribs.

Milady's robe was none the less stained with blood in a second. Milady fell backward and seemed to have fainted.

Felton snatched away the knife.

"See, my lord," said he, in a deep, gloomy tone, "here is a woman who was under my guard, and who has killed herself!"

"Do not worry, Felton," said Lord Winter. "She is not

dead ; demons do not die so easily.   Do not worry, but go wait for me in my chamber."

"But, my lord——"

"Go, sir ; I command you."

At this injunction from his superior, Felton obeyed ; but as he went out he put the knife into his bosom.

Lord Winter contented himself with calling the woman who waited on milady, and when she came he recommended the prisoner, who was still in a swoon, to her care, and left her alone with her.

But as the wound after all might be serious, he immediately sent off a man on horseback to fetch a doctor.

CHAPTER LVIII.

ESCAPE.

As Lord Winter had thought, milady's wound was not dangerous.   So soon as she was left alone with the woman whom the baron had summoned, and who hastened to her, she opened her eyes.

It was necessary, however, to affect weakness and pain, but this was not a very difficult task for an actress like milady.   Thus the poor woman was completely the prisoner's dupe, and notwithstanding her entreaties, she persisted in watching all night.

But this woman's presence did not prevent milady from thinking.

There was no longer any doubt that Felton was convinced ; Felton was hers.   If an angel appeared to that young man to accuse milady, he would certainly, in the disposition of mind he was then in, regard him as a messenger from the demon.

Milady smiled at this thought, for Felton was henceforth her only hope. her only means of safety.

But Lord Winter might have suspected him ! But Felton himself might now be watched !

Toward four o'clock in the morning the doctor came. Since milady had stabbed herself the wound had already closed.   The doctor could therefore measure neither its direction nor depth.   He only recognized by milady's pulse that her case was not serious.

In the morning milady, under the pretence of not having

slept during the night and wanting rest, sent away the woman who attended her.

She had one hope—that Felton would appear at the breakfast hour; but Felton did not come.

Were her fears realized? Was Felton, suspected by the baron, about to fail her at the decisive moment? She had only one day left. Lord Winter had announced her embarkation for the 23rd, and it was now the morning of the 22nd.

Nevertheless she still waited patiently till the dinner hour.

Though she had eaten nothing in the morning, the dinner was brought in at its usual time. Milady then perceived with terror that the uniform of the soldiers who guarded her was changed.

Then she ventured to ask what had become of Felton.

She was told that he had left the castle an hour before on horseback. She inquired whether the baron was still at the castle. The soldier replied that he was, and that he had given orders to be informed if the prisoner wished to speak to him.

Milady replied that she was too weak at present, and that her only desire was to be left alone.

The soldier went out, leaving the dinner served.

Felton was sent away; the marines were changed. Felton, then, was mistrusted!

This was the last blow to the prisoner.

Left alone, she got up. The bed in which she had remained for prudence, and in order that she might be believed to be seriously wounded, burnt her like a blazing fire. She cast a glance at the door. The baron had had a plank nailed over the grating. He feared, no doubt, that through this opening she might still, by some diabolical means, succeed in corrupting her guards.

Milady smiled for joy. She was free now to give way to her transports without being observed. She walked up and down her chamber with the fury of a crazy woman, or a tigress shut up in an iron cage. Assuredly if the knife had been left in her hands she would now have thought, not of killing herself, but of killing the baron.

At six o'clock Lord Winter came in. He was armed to the teeth. This man, in whom milady till that time had only seen a rather silly gentleman, had become an admirable jailer. He appeared to foresee everything, to divine everything, to anticipate everything.

A single look at milady informed him of all that was passing in her mind.

"Ay!" said he, "I see; but you will not kill me to-day either. You have no longer a weapon; and besides, I am on my guard. You began to pervert my poor Felton. He was already yielding to your infernal influence. But I intend to save him. He will never see you again; all is over. Get your clothes together; to-morrow you will go. I had fixed the embarkation for the 24th. But I have reflected that the more promptly the affair takes place, the more certain it will be. To-morrow at noon I shall have the order for your exile, signed 'Buckingham.' If you speak a single word to any one before you are on shipboard, my sergeant will blow your brains out. He has orders to do so. If, when on board, you speak a single word to any one before the captain permits you, the captain will have you thrown into the sea; that is determined. *Au revoir*, then. That is all I have to say to you to-day. To-morrow I will see you again, to take my leave of you."

And at these words the baron went out. Milady had listened to all this tirade of threats with a smile of disdain on her lips, but with rage in her heart.

The supper was served. Milady felt that she needed all her strength. She did not know what might take place during this night, which was approaching portentously, for enormous clouds were rolling over the face of the sky, and distant lightning announced a storm.

The storm broke about ten o'clock. Milady felt a consolation at seeing nature share the disorder of her heart; the thunder growled in the air like the anger in her thoughts. It seemed to her that the blast sweeping along dishevelled her brow, as it bowed the branches and bore away their leaves. She howled as the hurricane howled, and her voice was lost in the great voice of nature, which seemed also to groan with despair.

Suddenly she heard a tap at her window, and by the help of a flash of lightning she saw the face of a man appear behind the bars.

She ran to the window and opened it.

"Felton!" cried she. "I am saved!"

"Yes," said Felton; "but be silent, be silent! I must have time to file through these bars. Only take care that they do not see me through the grating of the door."

"Oh, it is a proof that the Lord is on our side, Felton!" replied milady. "The grating is closed with a board."

"That is well; God has made them mad!" said Felton.

"But what must I do?" asked milady.

"Nothing, nothing—only shut the window. Go to bed, or at least lie down with your clothes on. As soon as I have finished I will knock on the panes. But are you strong enough to follow me?"

"Oh yes!"

"Your wound?"

"Pains me, but will not prevent my walking."

"Be ready, then, at the first signal."

Milady shut the window, extinguished the lamp, and went, as Felton had desired her, to lie down on the bed. Amid the moaning of the storm she heard the grinding of the file on the bars, and by the light of every flash she saw Felton's shadow behind the panes.

She spent an hour scarcely breathing, panting, with a cold sweat on her brow, and her heart oppressed by frightful agony at every movement she heard in the corridor.

There are hours that last a year.

At the end of an hour Felton tapped again.

Milady sprang out of bed and opened the window. Two bars removed made an opening large enough for a man to pass through.

"Are you ready?" asked Felton.

"Yes. Must I take anything with me?"

"Money, if you have any."

"Yes; fortunately they have left me all I had."

"So much the better, for I have expended all mine in hiring a vessel."

"Here!" said milady, placing a bag full of louis in Felton's hands. Felton took the bag and threw it to the foot of the wall.

"Now," said he, "will you come?"

"I am here."

Milady climbed on a chair, and leaned the upper part of her body through the window. She saw the young officer suspended over the abyss by a rope ladder. For the first time a feeling of terror reminded her that she was a woman. The dark space frightened her.

"I expected this," said Felton.

"Oh, it's nothing, it's nothing!" said milady; "I will descend with my eyes shut."

"Have you confidence in me?" said Felton.

"Can you ask me such a question?"

"Put your two hands together. Cross them; that's right!"

Felton fastened her two wrists together with a handkerchief, and then tied a cord over the handkerchief.

"What are you doing?" asked milady in surprise.

"Put your arms round my neck, and fear nothing."

"But I shall make you lose you balance, and we shall both be dashed to pieces."

"Don't be afraid. I am a sailor."

Not a second was to be lost. Milady put her arms round Felton's neck, and let herself slip out of the window.

Felton began to descend the ladder slowly, step by step. In spite of the weight of their bodies, the blast of the hurricane made them swing to and fro in the air.

All at once Felton stopped, anxious and alert, listening.

"What is it?" asked milady.

"Silence!" said Felton; "I hear footsteps."

"We are discovered!"

There was a silence of several seconds.

"No," said Felton; "it is nothing."

"But what noise was that, then?"

"The patrol going their round."

"Where is their round?"

"Just under us."

"They will discover us!"

"No; unless it lightens they will not."

"But they will run against the ladder."

"Fortunately it is too short by six feet."

"Here they are! My God!"

"Silence!"

Both remained in suspense, motionless and breathless, within twenty feet of the ground, while the soldiers were passing beneath them, laughing and talking.

The patrol passed. The noise of their retreating footsteps and the murmur of their voices soon died away.

"Now," said Felton, "we are safe!"

Milady breathed a deep sigh and fainted.

Felton continued to descend. When he reached the bottom of the ladder, and found no more support for his feet, he clung to it with his hands. At length, coming to the last round, he hung by his hands and touched the ground. He stooped down, picked up the bag of money, and took it in his teeth.

Then he seized milady in his arms, and set off briskly in the direction opposite to the one the patrol had taken. He soon left the beat, climbed across the rocks, and when he reached the shore of the sea, whistled.

A similar signal replied to him, and five minutes after a boat appeared, rowed by four men.

The boat approached as near as it could to the shore, but there was not water deep enough for it to touch ; and Felton walked into the sea up to his waist, being unwilling to trust his precious burden to any one.

Fortunately the storm was beginning to die away, but the sea was still rough. The little boat bounded over the waves like a nutshell.

"To the sloop," said Felton, "and give way lively."

The four men bent to their oars, but the sea was too high to let them get much hold of it.

At all events, they were leaving the castle behind them. That was the main thing. The night was extremely dark ; it was already almost impossible to make out the shore from the boat ; it was therefore even more difficult to make out the boat from the shore.

A black speck was rocking on the sea. It was the sloop.

While the boat was advancing with all the speed its four oarsmen could give it, Felton untied the cord, and then the handkerchief that bound milady's hands together. Then when her hands were loosed he took some sea-water and sprinkled it over her face.

Milady drew a deep breath and opened her eyes.

"Where am I ?" she asked.

"Saved," replied the young officer.

"Oh, saved ! saved !" cried she. "Yes, there is the sky, here is the sea ! The air I breathe is the air of liberty ! Ah, thank you, Felton, thank you !"

The young man pressed her to his heart.

"But what is the matter with my hands ?" asked milady ; "it seems as if my wrists had been crushed in a vice."

Milady held out her arms ; her wrists were bruised.

"Alas !" said Felton, looking at her beautiful hands and gently shaking his head.

"Oh, it's nothing, it's nothing !" cried milady ; "now I remember."

Milady looked searchingly around her.

"There it is," said Felton, touching the money-bag with his foot.

They drew near to the sloop. A sailor on watch hailed the boat ; the boat replied.

"What vessel is this ?" asked milady.

"One I hired for you."

"Where is it going to carry me ?"

" Wherever you please, after you have landed me at Portsmouth."

" What are you going to do at Portsmouth ? " asked milady.

" Fulfil Lord Winter's orders," said Felton, with a gloomy smile.

" What orders ? " insisted milady.

" Do you not understand ? " asked Felton.

" No ; explain yourself, I beg of you."

" As he mistrusted me, he determined to guard you himself, and sent me in his place to get Buckingham to sign the order for your transportation."

" But if he mistrusted you, how could he confide such an order to you ? "

" Could I be supposed to know what I was the bearer of ? "

" True ! And you are going to Portsmouth ? "

" I have no time to lose. To-morrow is the 23rd, and Buckingham sets sail to-morrow with his fleet."

" He sets sail to-morrow ! Where for ? "

" For Rochelle."

" He must not sail ! " cried milady, forgetting her usual presence of mind.

" Do not worry ! " replied Felton ; " he will not sail."

Milady started with joy. She had just read to the depths of this young man's heart : Buckingham's death was written there at full length.

" Felton," cried she, " you are as great as Judas Maccabæus ! If you die, I will die with you ; that is all I can say to you."

" Silence ! " cried Felton ; " we are here."

In fact they were grazing the sloop.

Felton climbed up the ladder first, and gave milady his hand, while the sailors supported her, for the sea was still very turbulent.

An instant after they were on the deck.

" Captain," said Felton, " this is the lady of whom I spoke to you, and whom you must convey safe and sound to France."

" For a thousand pistoles," said the captain.

" I have paid you five hundred of them."

" That's correct," said the captain.

" And here are the other five hundred," replied milady, placing her hand upon the bag of gold.

" No," said the captain, " I stick to my bargain, and I

agreed with this young man that the other five hundred shall not be due me till we arrive at Boulogne."

"And shall we arrive there?"

"Safe and sound," said the captain; "as true as my name's Jack Butler."

"Well," said milady, "if you keep your word, instead of five hundred I will give you a thousand pistoles."

"Hurrah for you, then, my pretty lady!" cried the captain; "and may God often send me such passengers as your ladyship."

"In the meanwhile," said Felton, "convey me to the little bay of —— ; you know it was agreed you should put in there."

The captain replied by ordering the necessary manœuvres, and toward seven o'clock in the morning the little vessel was casting anchor in the designated bay.

During this passage Felton related everything to milady—how, instead of going to London, he had hired the little vessel; how he had returned; how he had scaled the wall by fastening cramps in the interstices of the stones as he ascended, to give him foothold; and how, when he had reached the bars, he fastened his ladder. Milady knew the rest.

Milady tried to encourage Felton in his project, but at the first words that issued from her mouth she plainly saw that the young fanatic stood more in need of being moderated than urged on.

It was agreed that milady should wait for Felton till ten o'clock. If he did not return by ten o'clock, she was to sail without him.

Then, in case he was free, he was to rejoin her in France, at the convent of the Carmelites, at Béthune.

CHAPTER LIX.

WHAT TOOK PLACE AT PORTSMOUTH, AUGUST 23, 1628.

FELTON took leave of milady as a brother about to go for a mere walk takes leave of his sister—by kissing her hand.

His whole person appeared in its ordinary state of calmness, only an unusual fire beamed from his eyes, like the glow of a fever; his brow was even paler than usual, his teeth were set, and his speech had a short, dry accent, indicating that something dark was going on within him.

As long as he remained in the boat which conveyed him to land he kept his face toward milady, who, standing on the deck, followed him with her eyes. Both felt sufficiently relieved from the fear of pursuit. No one ever came into milady's apartment before nine o'clock, and it would require three hours to go from the castle to London.

Felton leaped ashore, climbed the little ascent leading to the top of the beach, saluted milady a last time, and took his course toward the city.

At the end of a hundred paces, as the ground kept sloping down, he could, on turning round, only see the mast of the sloop.

He immediately ran in the direction of Portsmouth, which he saw about half a mile before him, standing out in the haze of the morning, with its towers and houses.

Beyond Portsmouth the sea was covered with vessels, the masts of which, like a forest of poplars stripped by the winter, were swaying with each breath of the wind.

Felton in his swift walk reviewed all the accusations, true or false, with which two years of mature meditations and long residence among the Puritans had armed him against the favourite of James I. and Charles I.

When he compared this minister's public crimes—startling crimes, European crimes, if we may say so—with the private and unknown crimes with which milady had charged him, Felton found that the more culpable of the two men who composed Buckingham's character was the one whose life the public did not know. This was because his love, so strange, so new, and so ardent, made him view Lady Winter's infamous and imaginary accusations as, through a magnifying glass, we see frightful monsters which are in reality only atoms imperceptibly small compared to ants.

The swiftness of his walk heated his blood still more. The idea that he was leaving behind him, exposed to a frightful vengeance, the woman whom he loved, or rather adored as a saint, the emotion he had experienced, his present fatigue—all together exalted his mind above human feeling.

He entered Portsmouth about eight o'clock in the morning. The whole population was on foot. Drums were beating in the streets and in the port. The troops about to be embarked were marching toward the sea.

Felton arrived at the palace of the Admiralty covered with dust and streaming with perspiration. His face, usually so pale, was purple with heat and passion. The sentinel was about to keep him away, but Felton called to the officer of the post, and drawing from his pocket the letter of which he was the bearer,—

"A pressing message from Lord Winter," said he.

At the name of Lord Winter, who was known to be one of his Grace's most intimate friends, the officer of the post gave orders to pass Felton, who, indeed, wore a naval officer's uniform.

Felton darted into the palace.

At the moment he entered the vestibule another man was entering likewise, covered with dust and out of breath, leaving at the gate a post-horse, which, as soon as he had alighted from it, sank down exhausted.

Felton and he addressed Patrick, the duke's confidential valet, at the same moment. Felton named Lord Winter. The stranger would give no name, and asserted that he could make himself known to the duke alone. Each insisted on being admitted before the other.

Patrick, who knew Lord Winter had official dealings and friendly relations with the duke, gave the preference to the one who came in his name. The other was forced to wait, and it was easy to see how he cursed the delay.

The valet led Felton through a large hall, in which were waiting the deputies from Rochelle, headed by the Prince de Soubise, and introduced him into a closet, where Buckingham, just out of the bath, was finishing his toilet, on which, as usual, he was bestowing extraordinary attention.

"Lieutenant Felton, from Lord Winter," said Patrick.

"From Lord Winter!" repeated Buckingham. "Let him come in."

Felton entered. Buckingham was in the act of throwing on a couch a rich dressing-gown worked with gold, to put on a blue velvet doublet embroidered with pearls.

"Why did not the baron come himself?" demanded Buckingham. "I expected him this morning."

"He desired me to tell your Grace," replied Felton, "that he very much regretted not having that honour, but that he was prevented by the guard he is obliged to keep at the castle."

"Yes, yes," said Buckingham; "I know he has a prisoner."

"I wish to speak to your Grace of that prisoner," replied Felton.

"Well, then, speak!"

"What I have to say of her can only be heard by yourself, my lord!"

"Leave us, Patrick," said Buckingham, "but remain within sound of the bell. I will call you presently."

Patrick went out.

"We are alone, sir," said Buckingham; "speak!"

"My lord," said Felton, "the Baron Winter wrote to you the other day to request you to sign an order of embarkation relative to a young woman named Charlotte Backson."

"Yes, sir; and I answered him that if he would bring or send me the order I would sign it."

"Here it is, my lord."

"Give it to me," said the duke.

And taking it from Felton, he cast a rapid glance over the paper. Then perceiving that it was the one that had been mentioned to him, he laid it on the table, took a pen, and prepared to sign it.

"Pardon, my lord," said Felton, stopping the duke; "but does your Grace know that Charlotte Backson is not this young woman's real name?"

"Yes, sir, I know it," replied the duke, dipping the pen into the ink.

"Then your Grace knows her real name?" asked Felton, in a sharp tone.

"I know it."

And the duke put the pen to the paper. Felton grew pale.

"And knowing her real name, my lord," replied Felton, "will you sign it all the same?"

"I certainly will," said Buckingham, "and sooner twice than once."

"I cannot believe," continued Felton, in a voice that became sharper and harsher, "that your Grace knows that this concerns Lady Winter."

"I know it perfectly well, though I am astonished that you know it."

"And will your Grace sign that order without remorse?"

Buckingham looked at the young man haughtily.

"Indeed, sir, do you know you are asking me strange questions, and that I am very silly to reply to them?"

"Reply to them, my lord," said Felton; "the circumstances are more serious than perhaps you imagine."

Buckingham reflected that the young man, coming from Lord Winter, very likely spoke in his name, and softened his manner a little.

"Without remorse," said he. "And the baron knows as well as myself that Lady Winter is a very guilty woman, and it is almost equivalent to pardoning her to reduce her punishment to transportation."

The duke put his pen to the paper.

"You will not sign that order, my lord!" said Felton, taking a step toward the duke.

"Not sign this order!" said Buckingham. "And why not?"

"Because you will look into your own heart, and you will do justice to Lady Winter."

"I should do justice to Lady Winter by sending her to Tyburn," said Buckingham; "Lady Winter is an infamous woman."

"My lord, Lady Winter is an angel. You know that she is, and I demand her liberty of you."

"Come, come!" exclaimed Buckingham; "are you mad, to speak to me in this manner?"

"My lord, excuse me! I speak as I can; I am restraining myself. But, my lord, think of what you are on the point of doing, and beware lest you go too far!"

"What do you say? God pardon me!" cried Buckingham; "I think he threatens me!"

"No, my lord, I still pray; and I say to you, One drop of water suffices to make the full vase overflow; one slight fault may draw down punishment on the life spared in spite of so many crimes."

"Mr. Felton," said Buckingham, "you will please to withdraw, and place yourself under arrest immediately."

"You shall hear me to the end, my lord! You seduced this young girl, you outraged, defiled her! Repair your crimes toward her, let her go free, and I will not require anything else from you."

"You will not require!" said Buckingham, looking at Felton with astonishment, and dwelling upon each syllable of the four words which he had just pronounced.

"My lord," continued Felton, becoming more excited as he spoke—"my lord, beware! All England is weary of your iniquities. My lord, you have abused the royal power, which you have almost usurped. My lord, you are held in horror by God and men. God will punish you hereafter, but I will punish you here!"

"Ah, this is too much!" cried Buckingham, taking a step toward the door.

Felton barred his passage.

"I ask it humbly of you, my lord," said he; "sign the order for Lady Winter's liberation. Reflect—she is a woman you have dishonoured."

"Withdraw, sir," said Buckingham, "or I will call my attendant and have you placed in irons."

"You shall not call," said Felton, throwing himself between the duke and the bell, placed on a silver-mounted stand. "Beware, my lord; you are in God's hands!"

"In the devil's hands, you mean!" cried Buckingham, raising his voice so as to attract the notice of his people without absolutely calling.

"Sign, my lord—sign Lady Winter's liberation," said Felton, holding a paper to the duke.

"What! by force? You are joking!—Hello, Patrick!"

"Sign, my lord!"

"Never."

"Never?"

"Help!" cried the duke, and at the same time sprang toward his sword.

But Felton gave him no time to draw it. He held the knife with which milady had stabbed herself open in his bosom. With one bound he was on the duke.

At that moment Patrick entered the room, crying,—

"A letter from France, my lord!"

"From France!" cried Buckingham, forgetting everything on thinking from whom that letter came.

Felton took advantage of this moment, and plunged the knife into his side up to the handle.

"Ah, traitor!" cried Buckingham, "thou hast killed me!"

"Murder!" screamed Patrick.

Felton cast his eyes round for means of escape, and seeing the door free, he rushed into the next chamber, in which, as we said, the deputies from Rochelle were waiting, crossed it as quickly as possible, and sprang toward the staircase. But on the first step he met Lord Winter, who, seeing him pale, wild, livid, and stained with blood, both on his hands and face, seized him by the throat, crying,—

"I knew it! I guessed it! A minute too late! Oh, unfortunate, unfortunate that I am!"

Felton made no resistance. Lord Winter placed him in the hands of the guards, who led him, until they should receive fresh orders, to a little terrace looking out over the sea; and then he rushed into Buckingham's room.

At the cry uttered by the duke and Patrick's scream the

man whom Felton had met in the antechamber darted into the closet.

He found the duke lying on a sofa, with his hand pressed convulsively over the wound.

"La Porte," said the duke in a faint voice—"La Porte, do you come from her ? "

"Yes, monseigneur," replied Anne of Austria's faithful cloakbearer, " but too late, perhaps."

"Silence, La Porte ; you may be overheard.—Patrick, let no one enter.—Oh, I shall not know what she says to me ! —My God ! I am dying ! "

And the duke fainted.

In the meanwhile Lord Winter, the deputies, the leaders of the expedition, the officers of Buckingham's household, had all made their way into the chamber. Cries of despair resounded on all sides. The news which filled the palace with tears and groans soon became known, and spread throughout the city.

The report of a cannon announced that something new and unexpected had taken place.

Lord Winter was tearing his hair.

"Too late by a minute ! " cried he, " too late by a minute ! Oh, my God, my God ! what a misfortune ! "

In fact, he had been informed at seven o'clock in the morning that a rope ladder was swaying from one of the castle windows. He had hastened to milady's chamber, found it empty, the window open and the bars filed, had remembered the verbal caution D'Artagnan had transmitted to him by his messenger, had trembled for the duke, and running to the stable, without taking time to have a horse saddled, had jumped upon the first he came to, had galloped off at full speed, had alighted in the courtyard, had ascended the stairs precipitately, and on the top step, as we have said, had met Felton.

The duke, however, was not dead. He recovered a little, opened his eyes, and hope revived in all hearts.

"Gentlemen," said he, " leave me alone with Patrick and La Porte.—Ah, is that you, De Winter ? You sent me a strange madman this morning. See what a condition he has brought me to ! "

"Oh, my lord ! " cried the baron, " I shall never console myself for it."

"And you would be quite wrong, my dear De Winter," said Buckingham, holding out his hand to him ; " I do not know the man who deserves being regretted during the whole of another man's life. But leave us, I pray you."

The baron went out sobbing.

Only the wounded duke, La Porte, and Patrick remained in the closet. A surgeon had been sent for, but none could be found.

"You will live, my lord, you will live!" repeated Anne of Austria's faithful servant, on his knees before the duke's sofa.

"What did she write me?" said Buckingham feebly, streaming with blood and suppressing his frightful agony to speak of her he loved; "what did she write me? Read me her letter."

"Oh, my lord!" said La Porte.

"Obey, La Porte. Do you not see I have no time to lose?"

La Porte broke the seal and placed the paper before the duke's eyes; but Buckingham tried in vain to make out the writing.

"Read it!" said he—"read it! I cannot see. Read, then! for soon, perhaps, I shall not hear, and I shall die without knowing what she has written me."

La Porte made no further objection, and read,—

"MILORD,—By what I have suffered by you and for you since I have known you, I conjure you, if you have any care for my repose, to interrupt those great armaments which you are preparing against France, to put an end to a war the ostensible cause of which is publicly said to be religion, and the hidden and real cause of which is privately whispered to be your love for me. This war may bring not only great catastrophes on England and France, but misfortunes on you, milord, for which I should never console myself.

"Be careful of your life, which is threatened, and which will be dear to me from the moment I am not obliged to see an enemy in you.—Your affectionate   ANNE."

Buckingham collected all his remaining strength to listen to the reading of the letter. Then when it was ended, as if he had met with a bitter disappointment in it,—

"Have you nothing else to say to me verbally, La Porte?" asked he.

"Yes, monseigneur. The queen charged me to bid you be on your guard, for she has been informed that your assassination would be attempted."

"And is that all, is that all?" replied Buckingham impatiently.

"She likewise charged me to tell you that she still loved you."

"Ah," said Buckingham, "God be praised! My death, then, will not be to her as the death of a stranger."

La Porte burst into tears.

"Patrick," said the duke, "bring me the casket in which the diamond studs were kept."

Patrick brought the object desired, which La Porte recognized as having belonged to the queen.

"Now the white satin sachet on which her monogram is embroidered in pearls."

Patrick again obeyed.

"Here, La Porte," said Buckingham, "these are the only remembrances I ever received from her—this silver casket and these two letters. You will restore them to her Majesty; and as a last memorial"—he looked round for some valuable object—"you will add to them——"

He still looked; but his eyes, darkened by death, saw only the knife which had fallen from Felton's hand, still steaming with the red blood spread over its blade.

"And you will add to them this knife," said the duke, pressing the hand of La Porte.

He had just strength enough to place the sachet at the bottom of the silver casket, and to let the knife fall into it, making a sign to La Porte that he was no longer able to speak. Then, in a last convulsion, which he had no longer the power to resist, he slipped from the sofa to the floor.

Patrick uttered a loud cry.

Buckingham tried to smile a last time, but death checked his wish, which remained graven on his brow like a last kiss of love.

At this moment the duke's surgeon arrived, quite terrified. He was already on board the admiral's ship, where they had been obliged to go for him.

He approached the duke, took his hand, held it for an instant in his own, and letting it fall,—

"All is useless," said he; "he is dead."

"Dead! dead!" cried Patrick.

At this cry all the crowd came again into the apartment, and everywhere nothing but consternation and tumult prevailed.

As soon as Lord Winter saw Buckingham was dead he ran to Felton, whom the soldiers were still guarding on the terrace of the palace.

"Miserable wretch!" said he to the young man, who since Buckingham's death had regained the coolness and self-possession which was never again to abandon him—"miserable wretch! What hast thou done?"

"I have avenged myself!" said he.

"Avenged yourself!" said the baron. "Rather say that you have served as an instrument for that cursed woman. But I swear to you that this crime shall be her last."

"I don't know what you mean," replied Felton quietly, "and I am ignorant of whom you are speaking, my lord. I killed the Duke of Buckingham because he twice refused your request to have me appointed captain. I punished him for his injustice, that is all."

De Winter, stupefied, looked on while the soldiers bound Felton, and did not know what to think of such insensibility.

One thing alone, however, cast a shade over Felton's pallid brow. At every noise he heard the simple Puritan fancied he recognized milady's step and voice coming to throw herself into his arms, to accuse herself and meet death with him.

Suddenly he started. His eyes became fixed upon a point of the sea which the terrace where he was overlooked. With a sailor's eagle eye, he had recognized there, where another would have seen only a gull hovering over the waves, the sail of the sloop, sailing toward the coast of France.

He grew deadly pale, placed his hand on his breaking heart, and perceived how he had been betrayed.

"One last favour, my lord!" said he to the baron.

"What is that?" replied his lordship.

"What time is it?"

The baron drew out his watch.

"It wants ten minutes to nine," said he.

Milady had hastened her departure by an hour and a half. As soon as she heard the cannon announcing the fatal event, she had ordered the anchor to be weighed.

The vessel was sailing away under a blue sky at a great distance from the coast.

"God has so willed it!" said he, with a fanatic's resignation, but without, however, being able to take his eyes from that ship, on board of which he doubtless fancied he could distinguish the white phantom of her to whom his life was to be sacrificed.

Lord Winter followed his look, observed his suffering, and guessed all.

"Be punished *alone*, in the first place, miserable man!" said Lord Winter to Felton, who allowed himself to be dragged away with his eyes turned toward the sea ; "but I swear to you, by the memory of my brother whom I loved so much, that your accomplice is not saved."

Felton hung down his head without pronouncing a syllable.

Lord Winter descended the stairs rapidly, and went to the port.

CHAPTER LX.

IN FRANCE.

THE first fear of the king of England, Charles I., on learning of the duke's death, was that such terrible news might discourage the Rochellais. He tried, says Richelieu in his memoirs, to conceal it from them as long as possible, closing all the ports of his kingdom, and carefully keeping watch that no vessel should go out until the army which Buckingham was getting together had set sail, taking upon himself, in default of Buckingham, to superintend its departure.

He carried the strictness of this order so far as to detain in England the ambassadors of Denmark, who had taken leave, and the ordinary ambassador of Holland, who was to take back to the port of Flushing the Indian merchant-men which Charles I. had caused to be restored to the United Provinces.

But as it did not occur to him to give this order till five hours after the event—that is to say, till two o'clock in the afternoon—two vessels had already left the port, one bearing, as we know, milady, who, already anticipating the event, was further confirmed in that belief by seeing the black flag flying at the mast-head of the admiral's ship.

As to the second vessel, we will relate hereafter whom it carried and how it set sail.

During all this time nothing new happened in the camp at Rochelle. Only the king, who was much bored as usual, but perhaps a little more so in the camp than elsewhere, resolved to go incognito and spend the festival of St. Louis at St. Germain, and asked the cardinal to order him an escort of twenty musketeers only. The cardinal, who was sometimes affected by the king's unrest, granted this leave of absence with great pleasure to his royal lieutenant, who promised to return about the 15th of September.

M. de Tréville, on being informed by his Eminence, packed his portmanteau, and as, without knowing the cause, he knew the great desire and even imperative need that his friends had of returning to Paris, he fixed on them, of course, to form part of the escort.

The four young men heard the news a quarter of an hour after M. de Tréville, for they were the first to whom he communicated it. Then D'Artagnan appreciated the favour the cardinal had conferred on him by transferring him at last to the musketeers, for had it not been for that circumstance, he would have been forced to remain in the camp while his companions left it.

His impatience to return toward Paris, of course, had for its cause the danger which Madame Bonacieux would run of meeting at the convent of Béthune with milady, her mortal enemy. Aramis, therefore, as we have said, had written immediately to Marie Michon, the seamstress at Tours, who had such fine acquaintances, to obtain from the queen permission for Madame Bonacieux to leave the convent, and to retire either into Lorraine or Belgium. They had not long to wait for an answer, and eight or ten days later Aramis received the following letter :—

" MY DEAR COUSIN,—Here is my sister's permission to withdraw our little servant from the convent of Béthune, the air of which you think does not agree with her. My sister sends you her permission with great pleasure, for she is very fond of the little girl, to whom she intends to be more serviceable hereafter.—I salute you,
" MARIE MICHON."

In this letter was enclosed an order conceived in these terms :—

" The superior of the convent of Béthune will place in the hands of the person who shall present this note to her the novice who entered the convent on my recommendation and under my patronage.
" At the Louvre, August 10, 1628. ANNE."

It may be easily imagined how the relationship between Aramis and a seamstress who called the queen her sister amused the young men ; but Aramis begged his friends not to revert to the subject again, declaring that if another single word were said to him about it, he would never again employ his cousin to interfere in such affairs.

There was no more talk, therefore, of Marie Michon among the four musketeers, who, besides, had what they wanted—that is to say, the order for withdrawing Madame Bonacieux from the convent of the Carmelites at Béthune. To be sure this order would not be of great use to them while they were in camp at Rochelle—that is to say, at the other end of France. So D'Artagnan was on the point of asking leave of absence of M. de Tréville, at the same time candidly confiding to him the importance of his departure, when the news was transmitted to him, as well as to his three friends, that the king was about to set out for Paris with an escort of twenty musketeers, and that they formed part of the escort.

Their joy was great. They sent their lackeys on in advance with the baggage, and set out on the morning of the 16th.

The cardinal accompanied his Majesty from Surgères to Mauzé, and there the king and his minister took leave of each other with great demonstrations of friendship.

The king, however, who was after amusement, while travelling as fast as possible—for he was anxious to be in Paris by the 23rd—stopped from time to time to fly the magpie, a pastime the taste for which had been formerly inspired in him by De Luynes, and for which he had always preserved a great liking. Sixteen of the twenty musketeers, when the thing happened, rejoiced greatly at this relaxation, but four cursed it heartily. D'Artagnan in particular had a perpetual buzzing in his ears, which Porthos explained in this way,—

" A very great lady has told me that that means somebody is talking of you somewhere."

At length the escort passed through Paris on the 23rd, in the night. The king thanked M. de Tréville, and permitted him to give out furloughs of four days, on condition that not one of those so favoured should appear in any public place, under penalty of the Bastille.

The first four furloughs granted, as may be imagined, were to our four friends. Moreover, Athos obtained of M. de Tréville six days instead of four, and got these six days lengthened by two nights more, for they set out on the 24th at five o'clock in the evening, and as a further kindness, M. de Tréville post-dated the furlough to the morning of the 25th.

"Good Lord!" said D'Artagnan, who, as we know, never scrupled at anything; "it seems to me we are making a great trouble for a very simple thing. In two days, by using up two or three horses (which I care little about, as I have money), I am at Béthune, I present my letter from the queen to the superior, and I bring back the dear treasure I go to seek, not into Lorraine, not into Belgium, but to Paris, where she will be much better concealed, particularly while the cardinal is at Rochelle. Then once back from the campaign, half by the protection of her cousin, half as a favour for what we have personally done for her, we shall obtain from the queen what we desire. Stay here, then, and do not exhaust yourselves with useless fatigue. Myself and Planchet are all that such a simple expedition requires."

To this Athos replied calmly,—

"We also have money left, for I have not yet drunk up all my share of the diamond, and Porthos and Aramis have not entirely eaten theirs. So we will use up four horses as well as one. But consider, D'Artagnan," added he, in a tone so solemn that it made the young man shudder—"consider that Béthune is a city where the cardinal agreed to meet a woman, who, wherever she goes, brings misery with her. If you had only to deal with four men, D'Artagnan, I would let you go alone. You have to do with that woman. All four of us will go; and I hope to God that, with our four lackeys, there may be enough of us."

"You terrify me, Athos!" cried D'Artagnan. "But what do you fear?"

"Everything!" replied Athos.

D'Artagnan studied his companions' faces, which, like Athos's, wore an expression of deep anxiety, and they continued their route as fast as their horses could carry them, but without adding another word.

On the evening of the 25th, as they were entering Arras, and as D'Artagnan was dismounting at the tavern of the Golden Harrow to drink a glass of wine, a horseman came out of the post-yard, where he had just had a relay, starting off at a gallop, with a fresh horse, on the road to Paris. At the moment he was passing through the gateway into the street the wind blew open the cloak in which he was wrapped, though it was August, and lifted his hat, which the traveller seized with his hand just as it left his head, and pulled it down quickly over his eyes.

D'Artagnan, who had his eyes fixed on this man, became very pale, and let his glass fall.

"What is the matter, sir?" asked Planchet.—"Oh, come, gentlemen, gentlemen! My master is ill!"

The three friends hastened to D'Artagnan, but instead of finding him ill, met him running for his horse. They stopped him at the door.

"Now, where the devil are you going in this way?" cried Athos.

"It is he!" cried D'Artagnan, pale with passion, and with the sweat on his brow; "it is he! Let me overtake him!"

"He—who?" asked Athos.

"He—my man!"

"What man?"

"That cursed man, my evil genius, whom I have always seen when threatened by some misfortune; he who accompanied the horrible woman when I met her for the first time; he whom I was seeking when I offended our friend Athos; he whom I saw on the very morning of the day Madame Bonacieux was carried off! I just saw him! It is he! I recognized him when his cloak blew open!"

"The devil!" said Athos musingly.

"To horse, gentlemen, to horse! Let us pursue him! We shall overtake him!"

"My dear friend," said Aramis, "remember that he's gone in an opposite direction to that in which we are going; that he has a fresh horse, and ours are fatigued; that consequently we shall disable our own horses without even the chance of overtaking him. Let the man go, D'Artagnan; let us save the woman."

"Hello, sir!" cried an hostler, running out and looking after the unknown—"hello, sir! here is a paper which dropped out of your hat. Hello, sir! Hello!"

"Friend," said D'Artagnan, "a half-pistole for that paper!"

"Faith, sir, with great pleasure! Here it is!"

The hostler, delighted with the good day's work he had done, went into the yard again. D'Artagnan unfolded the paper.

"Well?" eagerly demanded all his three friends, surrounding him.

"Only one word!" said D'Artagnan.

"Yes," said Aramis; "but that one word is the name of some town or village."

"*Armentières!*" read Porthos—"Armentières! I don't know it."

"And that name of a town or village is written in her hand!" cried Athos.

"Come on! come on!" said D'Artagnan; "let us keep that paper carefully; perhaps I have not lost my last pistole. To horse, my friends, to horse!"

And the four friends galloped off on the road to Béthune.

CHAPTER LXI.

THE CARMELITE CONVENT AT BÉTHUNE.

GREAT criminals carry with them a kind of predestination, causing them to surmount all obstacles, causing them to escape all dangers up to the moment which Providence, exhausted, has designated as the reef of their impious fortunes.

Thus it was with milady. She passed through the cruisers of both nations, and reached Boulogne without accident.

On landing at Portsmouth milady was an Englishwoman, driven from Rochelle by the persecutions of the French. On landing at Boulogne, after a two days' passage, she claimed to be a Frenchwoman, whom the English persecuted at Portsmouth, out of their hatred for France.

Milady had likewise the most efficacious of passports—her beauty, her noble appearance, and the generosity with which she scattered pistoles. Freed from the usual formalities by the affable smile and gallant manners of an old governor of the port, who kissed her hand, she only stayed long enough at Boulogne to post a letter, conceived in the following terms :—

"To his Eminence Monseigneur Cardinal Richelieu, in his camp before Rochelle :—

"Monseigneur, let your Eminence be reassured: his Grace the Duke of Buckingham *will not set out* for France.

"Boulogne, evening of the 25th.

"LADY DE ——.

"P.S.—According to your Eminence's desire, I am going to the convent of the Carmelites at Béthune, where I will await your orders."

In fact, that same evening milady began her journey. Night overtook her. She stopped and slept at an inn.

At five o'clock the next morning she was on her way again, and three hours later entered Béthune.

She inquired for the Carmelite convent, and went to it immediately.

The superior came to meet her. Milady showed her the cardinal's order. The abbess assigned her a chamber, and had breakfast served.

All the past was already effaced from this woman's eyes, and her looks, fixed on the future, beheld only the high fortunes reserved for her by the cardinal, whom she had so successfully served without his name being in any way mixed up with the sanguinary affair. The ever-new passions consuming her gave to her life the appearance of those clouds which float in the sky, reflecting sometimes its azure, sometimes the fire, sometimes the opaque blackness of the tempest, and which leave behind them no traces on the earth but devastation and death.

After breakfast the abbess came to pay her a visit. There are very few distractions in the cloister, and the good mother-superior was eager to make acquaintance with her new inmate.

Milady wished to please the abbess. Now this was an easy matter for a woman so really superior as she was. She tried to be agreeable. She was charming, and won the good nun by her varied conversation, and by the graces of her whole person.

The abbess, who was the daughter of a noble house, took particular delight in those stories of the court which so seldom travel to the extremities of the kingdom, and which, above all, have so much difficulty in penetrating the walls of convents, on whose thresholds the noise of the world dies away.

Milady, on the contrary, was quite conversant with all aristocratic intrigues, in the midst of which she had constantly lived for five or six years. So she made it her business to entertain the good abbess with the mundane practices of the court of France, mixed with the king's extravagant devotions. She related to her the entire budget of gossip and scandal concerning the lords and ladies of the court, whom the abbess knew perfectly by name ; touched lightly on the amours of the queen and the Duke of Buckingham, talking a great deal to induce her auditor to talk a little.

But the abbess was content to listen and smile, without replying at all. Milady, however, saw that this style of conversation amused her very much, and continued. But now she let the conversation fall on the cardinal.

But here she was greatly embarrassed. She did not know whether the abbess was a royalist or a cardinalist; she therefore confined herself to a prudent middle course. But the abbess on her part maintained a still more prudent reserve, contenting herself with making a profound inclination of the head every time that the fair traveller pronounced his Eminence's name.

Milady began to think she should be very greatly bored in the convent; so she resolved to risk something, in order immediately to know how to act afterwards. Desirous of seeing how far the good abbess's discretion would go, she began to tell a scandal, carefully veiled at first, but very circumstantial afterwards, about the cardinal, relating the minister's amours with Madame d'Aiguillon, Marion de Lorme, and several other women of easy virtue.

The abbess listened more attentively, grew animated by degrees, and smiled.

"Good!" thought milady; "she likes my conversation. If she is a cardinalist, she has no fanaticism, at least, in it."

She then went on to describe the persecutions wreaked by the cardinal on his enemies. The abbess only crossed herself without approving or disapproving. This confirmed milady in her opinion that the nun was rather a royalist than a cardinalist. Milady, therefore, continued colouring her narrations more and more.

"I am very ignorant about all these matters," said the abbess at length; "but though we are distant from the court and remote from the interests of the world, we have very sad examples of what you have related; and one of our inmates has suffered much from the cardinal's vengeance and persecution."

"One of your inmates!" said milady. "O Heavens! Poor woman, I pity her, then!"

"And you are right, for she is much to be pitied. Imprisonment, threats, ill-treatment—she has suffered everything. But after all," resumed the abbess, "the cardinal has perhaps plausible motives for acting thus; and though she has the look of an angel, we must not always judge people by appearances."

"Good!" said milady to herself; "who knows! Perhaps I am about to discover something here. I am in luck!"

And she tried to give her countenance an appearance of perfect candour.

"Alas!" said milady, "I know it is so. It is said that we must not believe in faces. But in what, then, shall we place confidence, if not in the most beautiful work of the Lord? I shall be deceived all my life, perhaps, but I shall always have faith in a person whose face inspires me with sympathy."

"You would, then, be tempted to believe," said the abbess, "that this young woman is innocent?"

"The cardinal does not only pursue crimes," said she; "there are certain virtues which he pursues more severely than certain offences."

"Permit me, madame, to express my surprise," said the abbess.

"At what?" asked milady naïvely.

"At the language you use."

"What do you find so astonishing in my language?" asked milady, smiling.

"You are the cardinal's friend, for he sends you here, and yet——"

"And yet I speak ill of him," replied milady, finishing the mother-superior's thought.

"At least, you don't speak well of him."

"That is because I am not his friend," said she, sighing, "but his victim!"

"But yet the letter in which he recommends you to me?"

"Is an order for me to keep myself in a kind of prison from which he will release me through some of his satellites."

"But why did you not escape?"

"Where should I go? Do you believe there is a spot on earth which the cardinal cannot reach, if he takes the trouble to stretch forth his hand? If I were a man, that might really be possible; but what can a woman do? This young inmate of yours—has she tried to escape?"

"No, she has not; but she—that is another thing; I believe she is detained in France by some love affair."

"Then," said milady, with a sigh "if she is in love, she is not altogether wretched."

"And so," said the abbess, looking at her with increasing interest, "I behold another poor persecuted woman?"

"Alas, yes!" said milady.

The abbess looked at her for an instant anxiously, as if a fresh thought were rising in her mind.

"You are not an enemy of our holy faith?" said she hesitatingly.

"I?" cried milady; "I a Protestant? Oh no! I call to witness the God who hears us that, on the contrary, I am a fervent Catholic!"

"Then, madame," said the abbess, smiling, "be re-assured. The house in which you are will not be a very hard prison, and we will do all in our power to make you love your captivity. You will find here, moreover, that young woman who is persecuted, no doubt, in consequence of some court intrigue. She is amiable and courteous."

"What is her name?"

"She was sent to me by some one of very high rank, under the name of Kitty. I have made no effort to learn her other name."

"Kitty!" cried milady; "what! Are you sure?"

"That she is called so? Yes, madame. Do you know her?"

Milady smiled to herself at the idea which had occurred to her, that this might be her former waiting-maid. There was connected with the recollection of this girl a recollection of anger; and a desire of vengeance disordered milady's features, which, however, immediately recovered the calm and benevolent expression which this woman of a hundred faces had for a moment allowed them to lose.

"And when can I see this young lady, for whom I already feel so great a sympathy?" asked milady.

"Why, this evening," said the abbess; "even during the day. But you told me you had been travelling these four days. This morning you rose at five o'clock; you must need rest. Go to bed and sleep; at dinner-time we will wake you."

Though milady would very willingly have gone without sleep, sustained as she was by all the excitements that a fresh adventure was awakening in her heart, ever thirsting for intrigues, she nevertheless accepted the mother-superior's advice. During the preceding twelve or fifteen days she had experienced so many different emotions that if her iron frame was still capable of supporting fatigue, her mind required repose.

She therefore took leave of the abbess and went to bed, gently rocked by the ideas of vengeance which the name of Kitty had naturally evoked. She remembered that almost unlimited promise which the cardinal had given her if she succeeded in her enterprise. She had succeeded. D'Artagnan was therefore in her power!

One thing alone frightened her : that was the remembrance of her husband, the Comte de la Fère, whom she had thought dead, or at least expatriated, and whom she found again in Athos, D'Artagnan's best friend.

But also if he was D'Artagnan's friend he must have lent him his assistance in all the measures by which the queen had defeated his Eminence's projects. If he was D'Artagnan's friend he was the cardinal's enemy ; and she, doubtless, would succeed in enveloping him in that vengeance by the coils of which she hoped to suffocate the young musketeer.

All these hopes were sweet thoughts to milady ; so, rocked by them, she soon fell asleep.

She was awakened by a gentle voice sounding at the foot of her bed. She opened her eyes, and saw the abbess, accompanied by a young woman with light hair and a delicate complexion, who was giving her a look full of benevolent curiosity.

The young woman's face was quite unknown to her. Each examined the other with great attention while exchanging the customary compliments. Both were very handsome, but of quite different styles of beauty. Milady, however, smiled on observing that she excelled the young woman by far in her noble air and aristocratic bearing. To be sure, the novice's habit which the young woman wore was not very advantageous in sustaining a contest of this kind.

The abbess introduced them to each other. Then when this formality was accomplished, as her duties called her to the church, she left the two young women alone.

The novice, seeing milady remained in bed, was about to follow the mother-superior, but milady stopped her.

" How, madame," said she ; " I have scarcely seen you, and you already wish to deprive me of your company, on which I had nevertheless counted a little, I must confess, for the time I have to pass here ? "

" No, madame," replied the novice ; " only I thought I had chosen my time badly. You were asleep ; you are fatigued."

" Well," said milady, " what can sleeping people wish for ? A happy awakening.! This awakening you have given me. So let me enjoy it at my ease." And taking her hand, she drew her to an armchair which was near her bed.

The novice sat down.

" Heavens ! how unfortunate I am ! " said she ; " I have

been here six months without the shadow of an amusement. You arrive, and your presence was likely to afford me delightful company; and now here I am, according to all probability, likely to leave the convent at any moment!"

"What! are you going soon?" asked milady.

"At least I hope so," said the novice, with an expression of joy which she made no effort to disguise.

"I think I heard you had suffered through the cardinal," continued milady. "That would have been another motive for sympathy between us."

"So what I have heard from our good mother is true! You likewise been a victim of that wicked priest?"

"Hush!" said milady; "let us not, even here, speak thus of him. All my misfortunes arise from my having said almost the same as you have just said before a woman who I thought was my friend, and who betrayed me. And are you also the victim of treachery?"

"No," said the novice, "but of my devotion—of a devotion to a woman I loved, for whom I would have laid down my life, for whom I would still do so."

"And who has abandoned you. Is that it?"

"I have been unjust enough to believe so. But during the last two or three days I have had proof to the contrary, and I thank God for it! I should have been sorry to think she had forgotten me. But you, madame," continued the novice—"you appear to be free; and if you were inclined to escape, it would only rest with yourself to do so."

"Where would you have me go, without friends, without money, in a part of France with which I am unacquainted, and where I have never been before?"

"Oh," cried the novice, "as to friends, you would have them wherever you went, you appear so good and are so beautiful!"

"That does not prevent," replied milady, softening her smile so as to give it an angelic expression, "my being alone or being persecuted."

"Hear me," said the novice; "we must trust in Heaven. There always comes a moment when the good you have done pleads your cause before God. And see! Perhaps it is your good fortune that you have met with me, humble and powerless as I am; for if I leave this place—well, I shall have powerful friends, who, after exerting themselves on my account, may also exert themselves for you."

"Oh, when I said I was alone," said milady, hoping to make the novice speak by speaking of herself, "it is not for want of some friends high in station. But these friends themselves tremble before the cardinal. The queen herself does not dare to oppose the terrible minister. I have proof that her Majesty, notwithstanding her excellent heart, has more than once been obliged to abandon to the anger of his Eminence persons who had served her."

"Trust me, madame; the queen may seem to have abandoned those persons, but we must not put faith in appearances. The more they are persecuted the more she thinks of them, and often when they the least expect it they receive proofs of kind remembrance."

"Alas!" said milady, "I believe so. The queen is so good!"

"Oh, you know her, then, that lovely and noble queen, by your speaking of her in this way!" cried the novice enthusiastically.

"That is to say," replied milady, driven into her intrenchments, "I have not the honour of knowing her personally. But I know a great number of her most intimate friends. I am acquainted with M. de Putange; I met M. Dujart in England; I know M. de Tréville."

"M. de Tréville!" exclaimed the novice. "Do you know M. de Tréville?"

"Yes, perfectly well—intimately, even."

"What! the captain of the king's musketeers?"

"Yes, the captain of the king's musketeers."

"Oh, why, then, only see!" cried the novice; "we shall soon be well acquainted, almost friends. If you know M. de Tréville, you must have been at his house?"

"Often!" said milady, who having entered on this track, and perceiving that her falsehood was succeeding, was determined to carry it through.

"If you have visited him, you must have met some of his musketeers?"

"All those he is in the habit of receiving!" replied milady, for whom this conversation began to have a real interest.

"Name a few of those you know, and you will find they are my friends."

"Well," said milady, a little embarrassed, "I know M. de Souvigny, M. de Courtivron, M. de Férusac."

The novice let her speak, but observing she stopped,—

"Don't you know," said she, "a gentleman named Athos?"

Milady became as pale as the sheets in which she was

lying, and mistress as she was of herself, could not help uttering a cry, seizing the novice's hand, and devouring her with her looks.

"What is the matter? O Heavens!" asked the poor woman; "have I said anything that hurt your feelings?"

"No, no; but the name struck me, because I also used to know that gentleman, and it appeared strange to me to meet with a person who appears to know him well."

"Oh yes, well, very well! Not only him, but also his friends Porthos and Aramis!"

"Indeed! you know them likewise? I know them!" cried milady, who felt a chill penetrating to her heart.

"Well, if you know them, you know that they are good and worthy gentlemen. Why do you not apply to them if you need support?"

"That is to say," stammered milady, "I am not really very intimate with any of them. I know them from having heard one of their friends, Monsieur d'Artagnan, say a great deal about them."

"You know M. d'Artagnan!" cried the novice, in her turn seizing milady's hand and devouring her with her eyes.

Then remarking the strange expression of milady's face,—

"Pardon me, madame," said she; "you know him—how?"

"Why," replied milady, considerably embarrassed—"why, as a friend."

"You are deceiving me, madame," said the novice. "You have been his mistress!"

"It is you who have been his mistress, madame," cried milady in her turn.

"I!" exclaimed the novice.

"Yes, you. I know you now. You are Madame Bona-cieux."

The young woman drew back in surprise and terror.

"Oh, do not deny it! Answer!" continued milady.

"Well, yes, madame!" said the novice. "Are we rivals?"

Milady's face was illumined by such a savage joy that in any other circumstances Madame Bonacieux would have fled in terror. But she was absorbed by her jealousy.

"Speak, madame!" resumed Madame Bonacieux, with an energy of which one would not have thought her capable. "Have you been, or are you, his mistress?"

"Oh no!" cried milady, with a tone that admitted no doubt of her truth; "never! never!"

"I believe you," said Madame Bonacieux. "But why, then, did you cry out so?"

"Do you not understand?" said milady, who had already overcome her agitation and recovered all her presence of mind.

"How can I understand? I know nothing."

"Can you not understand that M. d'Artagnan, being my friend, might take me into his confidence?"

"Indeed!"

"Do you not perceive that I know all — your being carried off from the little house at St. Germain, his despair, that of his friends, and their useless inquiries from that moment? How could I help being astonished when, without having the least expectation of such a thing, I meet you face to face—you of whom we have so often spoken together, you whom he loves with all his soul, you whom he had taught me to love before I had seen you! Ah, dear Constance, I have found you, then; I see you at last!"

And milady stretched out her arms to Madame Bonacieux, who, convinced by what she had just said, saw nothing in this woman, whom an instant before she had believed to be her rival, but a sincere and devoted friend.

"Oh, pardon me!" cried she, sinking upon milady's shoulders; "I love him so dearly!"

The two women held each other for an instant in a close embrace. Assuredly, if milady's strength had been equal to her hatred, Madame Bonacieux would never have escaped alive from that embrace.

But as she could not stifle her, she smiled on her.

"Oh, dear, pretty, good little creature!" said milady; "how delighted I am to see you! Let me look at you!" And while saying these words, she absolutely devoured her with her eyes. "Oh yes, it is you indeed! From what he has told me, I know you now. I recognize you perfectly."

The poor young woman could not possibly suspect the frightfully cruel thought behind the rampart of that pure brow, behind those brilliant eyes, in which she read nothing but interest and compassion.

"Then you know what I have suffered," said Madame Bonacieux, "since he has told you what he has suffered; but to suffer for him is happiness."

Milady replied mechanically, "Yes, that is happiness."

She was thinking of something else.

"And then," continued Madame Bonacieux, "my punishment is drawing to a close. To-morrow, perhaps this evening, I shall see him again ; and then the past will no longer exist."

"This evening?" asked milady, roused from her reverie by these words. "What do you mean? Are you expecting some news from him?"

"I expect D'Artagnan himself."

"Himself! D'Artagnan here!"

"Yes, D'Artagnan himself!"

"But that's impossible! He is at the siege of Rochelle with the cardinal. He will not return till after the taking of the city."

"Ah! you fancy so. But is there anything impossible for my D'Artagnan, the noble and loyal gentleman?"

"Oh, I cannot believe you!"

"Well, read, then!" said the unhappy young woman, in the excess of her pride and joy presenting a letter to milady.

"Humph! Madame de Chevreuse's writing!" said milady to herself. "Ah! I was very sure messages came from that quarter."

And she greedily read the following few lines :—

"MY DEAR CHILD,—Hold yourself in readiness. *Our friend* will see you soon, and he will see you only to release you from the imprisonment in which your safety required you should be concealed. Prepare, then, for your departure, and never despair of us.

"Our charming Gascon has just proved himself as brave and faithful as ever. Tell him that certain parties are grateful to him for the warning he has given."

"Yes, yes," said milady; "the letter is precise. Do you know what that warning was?"

"No; I only suspect he has warned the queen against some fresh machinations of the cardinal."

"Yes, that's it, no doubt!" said milady, returning the letter to Madame Bonacieux, and allowing her head to sink thoughtfully on her bosom.

At that moment the galloping of a horse was heard.

"Oh!" cried Madame Bonacieux, darting to the window, "can it be he already?"

Milady stayed in bed, petrified by surprise. So many unexpected things were happening to her all at once that for the first time she was at a loss.

"D'Artagnan!" murmured she; "can it be he?" And she remained in bed with her eyes staring.

"Alas, no!" said Madame Bonacieux. "It is a man I don't know. And yet he seems to be coming here. Yes, he has reined in his horse—he stops at the gate—he rings."

Milady sprang out of bed.

"Are you very sure it is not he?" said she.

"Oh yes—very sure!"

"Perhaps you did not see him plainly."

"Oh, if I were to see the plume of his hat, the end of his cloak, I should know him!"

Milady continued to dress herself.

"Never mind! The man is coming here, do you say?"

"Yes, he has come in."

"He must come either for you or for me."

"My God! how agitated you seem."

"Yes, I admit I am. I have not your confidence; I am in dread of the cardinal."

"Hush!" said Madame Bonacieux; "some one is coming."

In fact, the door opened, and the mother-superior entered.

"Did you come from Boulogne?" demanded she of milady.

"Yes, I did," replied she, trying to recover her self-possession. "Who wants me?"

"A man who will not tell his name, but who comes from the cardinal."

"And wishes to speak with me?" asked milady.

"He wishes to speak to a lady just come from Boulogne."

"Then let him come in, if you please."

"Oh, my God, my God!" cried Madame Bonacieux; "can it be any bad news?"

"I am afraid so."

"I will leave you with this stranger; but as soon as he is gone, if you will permit me, I will return."

"Certainly! I beg you will."

The mother-superior and Madame Bonacieux retired.

Milady was left alone, with her eyes fixed on the door. An instant after the jingling of spurs was heard on the stairs, then steps approached, the door opened, and a man appeared.

Milady uttered a cry of joy. This man was the Comte de Rochefort, the cardinal's personal agent.

CHAPTER LXII.

TWO KINDS OF DEMONS.

"AH!" cried milady and Rochefort together, "so it is you?"

"Yes, it is."

"And you come?" asked milady.

"From Rochelle.   And you?"

"From England."

"Buckingham?"

"Dead or desperately wounded, as I was leaving without having succeeded in obtaining anything from him.   A fanatic assassinated him."

"Ah!" said Rochefort, with a smile, "this is a piece of good luck—one that will delight his Eminence!   Have you informed him of it?"

"I wrote to him from Boulogne.   But what brings you here?"

"His Eminence was uneasy, and sent me to inquire after you."

"I only arrived yesterday."

"And what have you been doing since yesterday?"

"I have not wasted my time."

"Oh, I have no fear of that."

"Do you know whom I have found here?"

"No."

"Guess."

"How can I?"

"That young woman whom the queen took out of prison."

"The mistress of that fellow D'Artagnan?"

"Yes; Madame Bonacieux, with whose hiding-place the cardinal was unacquainted."

"Upon my word," said De Rochefort, "here is a chance that may be coupled with the other!   Truly, the cardinal is a privileged man!"

"Can you imagine my astonishment," continued milady, "when I found myself face to face with this woman?"

"Does she know you?"

"No."

"Then she looks on you as a stranger?"

Milady smiled.

"I am her best friend."

"Upon my honour, only you, my dear countess, can perform such miracles!"

"And it is well I can, chevalier," said milady; "for do you know what is going on?"

"No."

"They are going to take her away to-morrow or the day after, on an order from the queen."

"Indeed! And who is going to do that?"

"D'Artagnan and his friends."

"They are certainly going to such lengths that we shall have to send them to the Bastille."

"Why has it not been done already?"

"Well, because the cardinal has a weakness for these men which I do not understand."

"Indeed!"

"Yes."

"Well, then, tell him this, Rochefort. Tell him that our conversation at the inn of the Red Dovecot was overheard by these four men. Tell him that after his departure one of them came to me, and took from me, by violence, the safe-conduct which he had given me. Tell him they warned Lord Winter of my journey to England; that this time again they nearly made me fail in my mission, as they did in the affair of the studs. Tell him that among these four men two only are to be feared—D'Artagnan and Athos. Tell him that the third, Aramis, is Madame de Chevreuse's lover. He must be left alone; we know his secret, and he may be useful. As to the fourth, Porthos, he is a fool, a simpleton, a booby, not worth troubling himself about."

"But these four men must be now at the siege of Rochelle?"

"I thought so too; but a letter which Madame Bonacieux has received from Madame la Connétable, and which she had the imprudence to show me, leads me to believe that these four men, on the contrary, are on the road here to take her away."

"The devil! What's to be done?"

"What did the cardinal say with respect to me?"

"I was to take your dispatches, written or verbal, to return post-haste; and when he shall know what you have done, he will think of what you have to do."

"So I must remain here?"

"Here, or in the neighbourhood."

"You cannot take me with you?"

"No; the order is imperative. Near the camp you might be recognized; and your presence, you must be aware, would compromise his Eminence."

"Then I must wait here or in this vicinity?"

"Only tell me beforehand where you will wait for commands from the cardinal. Let me know always where to find you."

"Listen: it is probable I may not be able to remain here."

"Why not?"

"You forget that my enemies may arrive at any minute."

"True; but, then, is this little woman to escape his Eminence?"

"Bah!" said milady, with a smile that only belonged to herself, "didn't I tell you I am her best friend?"

"Ah, true! I may then tell the cardinal, respecting this woman——"

"That he need not be anxious."

"Is that all?"

"He will know what that means."

"He will guess, at least. Now, then, what had I better do?"

"Go back again directly. It seems to me the news you bear is worth the trouble of a little diligence."

"My chaise broke down coming into Lilliers."

"Capital!"

"Why capital?"

"Yes; I want your chaise."

"And how shall I travel, then?"

"At a gallop."

"That's very easy for you to say—a hundred and eighty leagues!"

"What's that?"

"Well, it shall be done. And then?"

"Then, why, as you pass through Lilliers you will send me your chaise, with an order to your servant to place himself at my disposal."

"Well."

"You have, no doubt, about you some order from the cardinal?"

"I have 'full powers.'"

"Show it to the abbess, and tell her that some one will come and fetch me either to-day or to-morrow, and that I am to follow the person who presents himself in your name."

"Very well."

"Don't forget to speak harshly of me when you talk of me to the abbess."

"Why so?"

"I am one of the cardinal's victims. I must inspire confidence in poor little Madame Bonacieux."

"You are right. Now, will you make me a report of all that has happened?"

"Why, I have related the events to you. You have a good memory; repeat what I have told you. A paper may get lost."

"You are right; only let me know where to find you, so that I may not lose my time in hunting for you about the neighbourhood."

"You are right; wait."

"Do you want a map?"

"Oh, I know this country well."

"You? When were you here before?"

"I was brought up here."

"Indeed!"

"It is worth something, you see, to have been brought up somewhere."

"You will wait for me, then, at——"

"Let me reflect a moment. Oh yes, at Armentières."

"What is Armentières?"

"A little town upon the Lys. I shall only have to cross the river, and I shall be in a foreign country."

"Capital! But it is understood you will cross the river only in case of danger."

"Certainly."

"And in that case, how shall I know where you are?"

"You do not want your lackey?"

"No."

"Is he to be depended on?"

"Perfectly."

"Let me have him, then; no one knows him. I will leave him at the place I quit, and he will bring you to me."

"And you say you will wait for me at Armentières?"

"At Armentières."

"Write that name on a piece of paper, lest I forget it. That is not compromising; a name of a town, is it?"

"Eh! who knows? No matter," said milady, writing the name on a half sheet of paper; "I will run the risk."

"Good!" said Rochefort, taking the paper from milady, folding it, and placing it in the lining of his hat. "Besides, do not worry. I will do as children do, and in case I lose the paper, I will repeat the name as I go along. Now, is that all?"

"I believe so."

"Let us see: Buckingham dead or grievously wounded; your conversation with the cardinal overheard by the four musketeers; Lord Winter warned of your arrival at Portsmouth; D'Artagnan and Athos to the Bastille; Aramis Madame de Chevreuse's lover; Porthos a fool; Madame Bonacieux found again; to send you the chaise as soon as possible; to place my lackey at your disposal; to make you out to be a victim of the cardinal, in order that the abbess may entertain no suspicion; Armentières, on the banks of the Lys. Is that all correct?"

"In good truth, my dear chevalier, you are a miracle of memory. By the way, one thing more——"

"What is that?"

"I saw some very pretty woods which must be next the convent garden. Say that I am to be permitted to walk in those woods. Who knows? Perhaps I may need to go out of a back door."

"You think of everything."

"And you forget one thing."

"What's that?"

"To ask me whether I need money."

"True; how much do you want?"

"All you have in gold."

"I have five hundred pistoles, or thereabouts."

"I have as much. With a thousand pistoles one can face everything. Empty your pockets."

"Here it is."

"Good! When do you start?"

"In an hour—time to eat a morsel while I am sending for a post-horse."

"Capital Farewell, chevalier!"

"Farewell, countess!"

"Recommend me warmly to his Eminence!"

"Recommend me to Satan!"

Milady and Rochefort exchanged a smile and separated.

An hour afterwards Rochefort set out at his horse's best speed; five hours after that he was passing through Arras.

Our readers already know how he was recognized by D'Artagnan, and how that fact, by suggesting fears to the four musketeers, gave fresh activity to their journey.

CHAPTER LXIII.

THE DROP OF WATER.

ROCHEFORT had scarcely departed when Madame Bonacieux came back. She found milady with a smiling countenance.

"Well," said the young woman, "what you dreaded has happened: this evening or to-morrow the cardinal will send some one to take you away."

"Who told you that, my dear?" asked milady.

"I heard it from the mouth of the messenger himself."

"Come and sit down close to me," said milady

"Here I am."

"Wait till I am sure no one can hear us."

"Why all these precautions?"

"You shall know."

Milady arose and went to the door, opened it, looked down the corridor, and then returned and seated herself near Madame Bonacieux.

"Then," said she, "he has well played his part."

"Who has?"

"He who just now presented himself to the abbess as the cardinal's messenger?"

"So he was playing a part?"

"Yes, my dear."

"That man, then, is not——"

"That man," said milady, lowering her voice, "is my brother!"

"Your brother!" cried Madame Bonacieux.

"Well, no one must know this secret, my dear, but yourself. If you reveal it to any one at all I shall be lost, and you also, perhaps."

"O Heavens!"

"Listen to me. This is what has happened: My brother, who was coming to my assistance, to take me away by force if it were necessary, fell in with the cardinal's emissary coming in search of me. He followed him. Reaching a solitary and retired part of the road, he drew his sword and required the messenger to deliver up to him the papers of which he was the bearer. The messenger resisted; my brother killed him."

"Oh!" said Madame Bonacieux, with a shudder.

"Remember that was the only way. Then my brother determined to substitute cunning for force. He took the papers, and presented himself here as the cardinal's emissary, and in an hour or two a carriage will come to take me away by order of his Eminence."

"I understand. Your brother sends the carriage."

"Exactly so; but that is not all. That letter you have received, and which you believe to be from Madame de Chevreuse——"

"Well?"

"It is a forgery."

"How can that be?"

"Yes, a forgery; it is a snare to prevent your making any resistance when the persons come to fetch you."

"But D'Artagnan is coming!"

"Do not be deceived. D'Artagnan and his friends are detained at the siege of Rochelle."

"How do you know that?"

"My brother met some of the cardinal's emissaries in the uniform of musketeers. You would have been summoned to the gate; you would have thought you went to meet friends; you would have been carried off and taken back again to Paris."

"Oh, my God! my senses fail me amid such a chaos of iniquities. I feel, if this continues," said Madame Bonacieux, raising her hands to her forehead, "I shall go mad!"

"Stop——"

"What?"

"I hear a horse's steps; it is my brother setting off again. I want to give him a last farewell. Come."

Milady opened the window and beckoned to Madame Bonacieux to join her. The young woman complied.

Rochefort passed at a gallop.

"Farewell, brother!" cried milady.

The chevalier raised his head, saw the two young women, and without stopping waved his hand in a friendly way to milady.

"Dear, good George," said she, closing the window with an expression of face full of affection and melancholy.

And she resumed her seat as if plunged in entirely personal reflections.

"Dear lady," said Madame Bonacieux, "pardon me for interrupting you, but what do you advise me to do? Good Heavens! You have more experience than I have. Speak! I will listen."

"In the first place," said milady, "it is possible that I may be mistaken, and D'Artagnan and his three friends may really come to your assistance."

"Oh, that would be too beautiful!" cried Madame Bonacieux. "So much happiness is not destined for me!"

"Then you perceive it would be only a question of time, a kind of race, which should arrive first. If your friends are the speedier, you are saved; if the cardinal's satellites are, you are lost!"

"Oh yes, yes — lost beyond redemption! What am I to do, then? What am I to do?"

"There would be a very simple way, very natural——"

"What? Say!"

"To wait, concealed in the neighbourhood, until you satisfied yourself who the men were who came to ask for you."

"But where can I wait?"

"Oh, there is no difficulty in that. I shall stop and conceal myself at a few leagues from here, till my brother can rejoin me. Well, I will take you with me. We can conceal ourselves and wait together."

"But I shall not be allowed to go; I am almost a prisoner here."

"As I am supposed to go by an order from the cardinal, no one will believe you are anxious to follow me."

"Well?"

"Well, the carriage is at the door; you bid me farewell; you get on the step to embrace me a last time. My brother's servant, who comes to fetch me, is forewarned; he makes a sign to the postillion, and we set off at a gallop."

"But D'Artagnan, D'Artagnan! if he should come!"

"Well, shall we not know it?"

"How?"

"Nothing more easy. We will send my brother's servant back to Béthune, and as I told you we can trust him. He shall assume a disguise, and place himself in front of the convent. If the cardinal's emissaries arrive, he will not stir; if M. d'Artagnan and his friends come, he will bring them to us."

"He knows them, then?"

"Certainly he does. Has he not seen M. d'Artagnan at my house?"

"Oh yes, yes; you are right. In this way all will go well—all will be for the best; but do not go far from here."

"Seven or eight leagues at most. We will stay on the frontier, for instance; and at the first alarm we can leave France."

" And what shall we do meantime ? "

" Wait."

" But if they come ? "

" My brother's carriage will be here before them."

" Supposing I am at a distance from you when the carriage comes for you—at dinner or supper, for instance ? "

" Do one thing."

" What ? "

" Tell your good mother-superior that, in order that we may be as much together as possible, you beg her to let you take your meals with me."

" Will she let me ? "

" What harm is there in it ? "

" Oh, very good ! In this way we shall not be separated for an instant."

" Well, go down to her, then, and make your request. My head feels a little heavy. I will take a turn in the garden."

" Go ; and where shall I find you ? "

" Here, in an hour."

" Here, in an hour. Oh, how good you are ! and I thank you ! "

" How could I help being interested in you ? If you were not so beautiful and so amiable, are you not the beloved of one of my best friends ? "

" Dear D'Artagnan ! Oh, how he will thank you ! "

" I hope so. Now, then, all is agreed ; let us go down."

" You are going into the garden ? "

" Yes."

" Go along this corridor, and a little staircase will bring you to it."

" Excellent ; thank you ! "

And the two women parted, exchanging affectionate smiles.

Milady had told the truth : her head was heavy, for her ill-arranged plans clashed against one another like a chaos. She needed to be alone in order to collect her thoughts a little. She saw vaguely into the future, but she needed silence and quiet in order to give all her ideas, still in confusion, a distinct form and a regular plan.

The most pressing thing was to get Madame Bonacieux away, and convey her to a place of safety, and there, in case of necessity, use her as a hostage. Milady began to question the issue of this terrible duel, in which her enemies showed as much perseverance as she did animosity.

Besides, she felt as we feel when a storm is approaching —that this issue was near and could not fail to be terrible.

The principal thing for her then was, as we have said, to keep Madame Bonacieux in her power. Madame Bonacieux was D'Artagnan's very life; the life of the woman he loved was more than his life: in case of ill-fortune, this was a way of negotiating and of certainly obtaining favourable conditions.

Now this point was settled; Madame Bonacieux, without any suspicion, accompanied her. Once concealed with her at Armentières, it would be easy to make her believe that D'Artagnan had not come to Béthune. In a fortnight, at the most, Rochefort would be back again. During that fortnight, moreover, she would have time to think how she could best be revenged on the four friends. She entertained no fear of being bored, thank God! for she should enjoy the sweetest pastime events could offer to a woman of her character—the perfecting of a cruel vengeance.

While revolving all this in her mind, she was casting her eyes around her, and arranging in her head the topography of the garden. Milady was like a good general, who looks out alike for victory and defeat, and is quite prepared, according to the chances of the battle, to march forward or to beat a retreat.

At the end of an hour she heard a sweet voice calling her. It was Madame Bonacieux's. The good abbess had naturally consented to everything, and as a beginning they were to sup together.

On reaching the courtyard they heard the noise of a carriage stopping at the gate.

Milady listened.

" Do you hear ? " said she.

" Yes, the rolling of a carriage."

" It is the one my brother sends for us."

" Oh, my God ! "

" Come, come ! Courage ! "

The bell of the convent gate rang; milady was not mistaken.

" Go up to your chamber," said she to Madame Bonacieux; " of course you have some jewels you would like to take with you."

" I have his letters," said she.

" Well, go get them, and come to my room ; we will have a bite of supper. We shall travel part of the night perhaps, and must keep our strength up."

"Great Heavens!" said Madame Bonacieux, placing her hand on her bosom; "my heart beats so I cannot walk."

"Courage, my dear, courage! Remember that in a quarter of an hour you will be safe; and think that what you are about to do is for his sake."

"Yes, yes—everything for his sake. You have restored my courage by a single word. Go; I will be with you directly."

Milady hastily ran up to her room. There she found Rochefort's lackey, and gave him his instructions.

He was to wait at the gate. If by chance the musketeers should appear, the carriage was to drive off as fast as possible, pass round the convent, and go and wait for milady at a little village situated at the other side of the wood. In this case milady was to cross the garden and gain the village on foot. We have already said milady was perfectly acquainted with this part of France.

If the musketeers did not appear, things were to go on as had been agreed. Madame Bonacieux was to get into the carriage as if to bid her farewell, and she was to take away Madame Bonacieux.

Madame Bonacieux came in, and to remove all suspicion, if she had any, milady repeated to the lackey, before her, all the last part of her instructions.

Milady asked some questions about the carriage. It was a three-horse chaise driven by a postillion. Rochefort's lackey was to precede it as a courier.

Milady was wrong in fearing that Madame Bonacieux would have any suspicions. The poor young woman was too innocent to suppose that any woman could be guilty of such perfidy. Besides, the name of the Countess Winter, which she had heard the abbess pronounce, was perfectly unknown to her, and she was even ignorant that she had so great and so fatal a share in the misfortunes of her life.

"You see," said she, when the lackey had gone out, "everything is ready. The abbess suspects nothing, and believes that they have come after me by the cardinal's command. The man has gone to give his last orders; take a mouthful to eat, drink a swallow of wine, and let us go."

"Yes," said Madame Bonacieux mechanically; "let us go."

Milady made her a sign to sit down before her, poured out a small glass of Spanish wine for her, and helped her to some of the breast of a chicken.

"See," said she, "how propitious everything is! Here is night coming on; by daybreak we shall have gained our retreat, and no one can have any suspicion where we are. Come, courage! take something."

Madame Bonacieux ate a few mouthfuls mechanically, and just touched the glass to her lips.

"Come, come!" said milady, lifting hers to her mouth, "do as I do."

But just as she was putting hers to her mouth her hand remained suspended. She had heard something on the road which sounded like the far-off beat of hoofs approaching; then, almost at the same time, it seemed to her that she heard the neighing of horses.

This noise roused her from her joy as a storm awakens the sleeper in the midst of a beautiful dream. She grew pale and ran to the window, while Madame Bonacieux, rising all of a tremble, supported herself on her chair to avoid falling.

Nothing was yet to be seen, only they heard the galloping constantly draw nearer.

"O Heavens!" cried Madame Bonacieux, "what is that noise?"

"It is either our friends or our enemies," said milady, with her terrible coolness. "Stay where you are. I will tell you."

Madame Bonacieux remained standing, mute, pale, and motionless.

The noise became louder; the horses could not be more than a hundred paces distant. If they were not yet to be seen, it was because the road made a bend. Yet the noise became so distinct that the horses might be counted by the sharply defined sound of their hoofs.

Milady gazed with all her eyes; it was just light enough for her to recognize those who were coming.

Suddenly, at a turn of the road, she saw the glitter of laced hats and the waving of plumes; she counted two, then five, then eight horsemen. One of them was two lengths of his horse in advance of the others.

Milady uttered a stifled groan. In the first horseman she recognized D'Artagnan.

"O Heavens, Heavens!" cried Madame Bonacieux, "what is it? what is it?"

"It is the cardinal's guards—not an instant to be lost!" cried milady. "Let us fly! let us fly!"

"Yes, yes, let us fly!" repeated Madame Bonacieux,

but without being able to take a step, fixed to the spot as she was by terror.

They heard the horsemen riding under the windows.

" Come on, then ! do come on ! " cried milady, striving to drag the young woman along by the arm.   " Thanks to the garden, we yet can escape.   I have the key.   But let us make haste.   In five minutes it will be too late ! "

Madame Bonacieux tried to walk, took two steps, and sank on her knees.

Milady strove to lift her up and carry her, but could not succeed.

At this moment they heard the rolling of the carriage, which as soon as the musketeers were seen set off at a gallop.   Then three or four shots were fired.

" For the last time, will you come ? " cried milady.

" Oh, my God, my God !   You see my strength fails me. You see plainly I cannot walk.   Escape yourself ! "

" Escape myself, and leave you here !   No, no, never ! " cried milady.

All at once she stopped ; a livid flash darted from her eyes.   She ran to the table, poured into Madame Bonacieux's glass the contents of a ring which she opened with singular quickness.

It was a grain of a reddish colour, which instantly melted.

Then taking the glass with a firm hand,—

" Drink," said she ;   " this wine will give you strength— drink ! "

And she put the glass to the lips of the young woman, who drank mechanically.

" This is not the way I wanted to avenge myself," said milady, setting the glass on the table with an infernal smile, " but, faith ! one does what one can."

And she rushed out of the room.

Madame Bonacieux saw her go without being able to follow her.   She was like those people who dream they are pursued, and who vainly struggle to walk.

A few moments passed.   A frightful noise was heard at the gate.   Every instant Madame Bonacieux expected to see milady, but she did not return.

At length she heard the grating of the hinges of the opening gates ; the noise of boots and spurs resounded on the stairs.   There was a great murmur of voices coming nearer and nearer ; it seemed to her she heard her own name pronounced.

All at once she uttered a loud cry of joy, and darted

toward the door. She had recognized D'Artagnan's voice.

"D'Artagnan! D'Artagnan!" cried she, "is it you? This way! this way!"

"Constance! Constance!" replied the young man, "where are you? My God!"

At the same moment the door of the cell yielded to a shock, rather than opened. Several men rushed into the room. Madame Bonacieux had sunk into an armchair, without the power of moving.

D'Artagnan threw down a pistol, still smoking, which he held in his hand, and fell on his knees before his mistress. Athos replaced his in his belt. Porthos and Aramis, who held their drawn swords in their hands, returned them to their scabbards.

"O D'Artagnan! my beloved D'Artagnan! You have come, then, at last. You have not deceived me! It is indeed you!"

"Yes, yes, Constance!—reunited!"

"Oh, how foolish *she* was to tell me you would not come! I hoped silently. I was not willing to flee. Oh, how rightly I have acted! How happy I am!"

At the word *she*, Athos, who had quietly seated himself, suddenly got up.

"*She!* Who?" asked D'Artagnan.

"Why, my companion. She who, out of friendship for me, wished to save me from my persecutors. She who, mistaking you for the cardinal's guards, has just made her escape."

"Your companion!" cried D'Artagnan, becoming paler than his mistress's white veil. "What companion do you mean?"

"She whose carriage was at the gate; a woman who calls herself your friend, D'Artagnan; a woman to whom you have told everything."

"But her name, her name!" cried D'Artagnan; "my God! don't you know her name?"

"Yes, it was pronounced before me. Stop—but—it is strange—oh, my God! my head swims—I cannot see!"

"Help, friends, help! Her hands are like ice!" cried D'Artagnan; "she is ill! Great God, she is growing unconscious!"

While Porthos was calling for help at the top of his voice, Aramis ran to the table to get a glass of water. But he stopped at seeing the horrible alteration that had taken place in the face of Athos, who, standing before the table, his hair rising from his head, his eyes fixed in stupor, was looking at one of the glasses, and seemed a prey to the most horrible doubt.

"Oh," said Athos, "oh no! It is impossible! God would not permit such a crime!"

"Water! water!" cried D'Artagnan—"water!"

"Oh, poor woman! poor woman!" murmured Athos, in a broken voice.

Madame Bonacieux opened her eyes under D'Artagnan's kisses.

"She revives!" cried the young man.

"Madame," said Athos—"madame, in Heaven's name, whose empty glass is this?"

"Mine, sir," said the young woman, in a dying voice.

"But who poured out for you the wine that was in this glass?"

"_She._"

"But who is _she_?"

"Oh, I remember," said Madame Bonacieux; "the Countess Winter."

The four friends uttered one and the same cry, but the cry of Athos dominated over all the rest.

At that moment Madame Bonacieux's face grew livid, a stifled agony overcame her, and she sank panting into the arms of Porthos and Aramis.

D'Artagnan seized Athos's hand with an anguish difficult to describe.

"What! do you believe——"

His voice was stifled by sobs.

"I believe everything," said Athos.

"D'Artagnan! D'Artagnan!" cried Madame Bonacieux, "where art thou? Do not leave me! Thou seest that I am dying!"

D'Artagnan let fall Athos's hand, which he still held convulsively clasped in his, and hastened to her.

Her beautiful face was distorted, her glassy eyes were fixed, a convulsive shuddering shook her body, the sweat stood on her brow.

"In Heaven's name, run, call! Aramis! Porthos! call for help!"

"Useless!" said Athos, "useless! For the poison which she pours out there is no antidote."

"Yes, yes! help, help!" murmured Madame Bonacieux —"help!"

Then collecting all her strength, she took the young man's head between her hands, looked at him for an instant as if her whole soul had passed into her look, and pressed her lips to his.

"Constance! Constance!" cried D'Artagnan wildly.

A sigh escaped from Madame Bonacieux's mouth and dwelt for an instant on D'Artagnan's lips. That sigh was her soul, so chaste and so loving, reascending to heaven.

D'Artagnan held only a corpse pressed to his heart.

The young man uttered a cry, and fell by his mistress's side as pale and as cold as she was.

Porthos wept, Aramis lifted his hand toward heaven, Athos made the sign of the cross.

At that moment a man appeared in the doorway, almost as pale as those in the room, looked round him, saw Madame Bonacieux dead and D'Artagnan fainting.

He appeared just at that moment of stupor which follows great catastrophes.

"I was not mistaken," said he. "Here is M. d'Artagnan, and you are his three friends, MM. Athos, Porthos, and Aramis."

The persons whose names had just been pronounced looked at the stranger in astonishment. All three thought they knew him.

"Gentlemen," resumed the newcomer, "you are, as I am, in search of a woman, who," added he, with a terrible smile, "must have passed this way, for I see a corpse here!"

The three friends remained mute. But the voice, as well as the face, reminded them of a man they had seen, and yet they could not remember in what circumstances.

"Gentlemen," continued the stranger, "since you will not recognize a man who probably owes his life to you twice, I must name myself. I am the Lord Winter—that woman's brother-in-law."

The three friends uttered a cry of surprise.

Athos rose and offered him his hand.

"You are welcome, milord," said he; "you are one of our friends."

"I left Portsmouth five hours after her," said Lord Winter. "I arrived three hours after her at Boulogne. I missed her by twenty minutes at St. Omer. At last at Lilliers I lost trace of her. I was going about at haphazard, inquiring of every one, when I saw you gallop by. I recognized M. d'Artagnan. I called to you; you did not answer. I tried to follow you, but my horse was too tired to go at the same rate as yours. And yet it seems that, in spite of all your diligence, you still arrived too late."

" You see ! " said Athos, pointing to Madame Bonacieux dead, and to D'Artagnan, whom Porthos and Aramis were trying to recall to life.

" Are they both dead ? " asked Lord Winter coldly.

" No," replied Athos ; " fortunately, M. d'Artagnan has only fainted."

" Ah ! so much the better ! " said Lord Winter.

At that moment D'Artagnan opened his eyes.

He tore himself from the arms of Porthos and Aramis, and threw himself like a madman on his mistress's dead body.

Athos rose, walked up to his friend with a slow and solemn step, kissed him tenderly, and as he burst into violent sobs, said to him, with his noble and persuasive voice,—

" Friend, be a man ! Women weep for the dead ; men avenge them ! "

" Oh yes," cried D'Artagnan, " yes ! If it is to avenge her, I am ready to follow you."

Athos took advantage of this moment of strength, which the hope of vengeance restored to his unfortunate friend, to make a sign to Porthos and Aramis to go and fetch the mother-superior.

The two friends met her in the corridor, still in great anxiety and agitation at such events. She summoned some of the nuns, who, contrary to all convent customs, found themselves in the presence of five men.

" Madame," said Athos, passing his arm under D'Artagnan's, " we abandon to your pious care the body of this unfortunate woman. Treat her as one of your sisterhood. We will return some day to pray over her grave ! "

D'Artagnan hid his face in Athos's bosom and burst into sobs.

" Weep," said Athos — " weep, heart full of love, youth, and life ! Alas ! would that I could weep as thou dost ! "

And affectionate as a father, consoling as a priest, great as a man who has suffered much, he drew away his friend.

All five, followed by their lackeys leading their horses, took their way to the town of Béthune, the outlying houses of which they saw, and stopped at the first inn to which they came.

" But," said D'Artagnan, " are we not to pursue that woman ? "

"Presently," said Athos; "I have certain measures to take."

"She will escape us," replied the young man—"she will escape us, Athos, and it will be your fault."

"I will answer for her," said Athos.

D'Artagnan had such trust in his friend's word that he bowed his head, and entered the inn without making a reply.

Porthos and Aramis looked at each other, not at all understanding Athos's confidence.

Lord Winter thought he spoke in this way to assuage D'Artagnan's sorrow.

"Now, gentlemen," said Athos, when he had ascertained there were five vacant rooms in the hotel, "let us each retire to his own chamber. D'Artagnan needs to be alone, to weep and to sleep. I take charge of everything. Do not worry."

"It seems to me, however," said Lord Winter, "that if there are any measures to be taken against the countess, it concerns me; she is my sister-in-law."

"Me also!" said Athos; "she is my wife."

D'Artagnan smiled, for he realized that Athos was sure of his vengeance since he revealed such a secret. Porthos and Aramis looked at each other. Lord Winter thought Athos was mad.

"Now, all go to your rooms," said Athos, "and leave me to act. You must perceive that in my quality of a husband this concerns me. Only, D'Artagnan, if you have not lost it, give me the piece of paper which fell from that man's hat. The name of the village of —— is written on it."

"Ah!" said D'Artagnan, "I understand now. That name written in her hand——"

"You see," said Athos, "there is a God in heaven!"

CHAPTER LXIV.

THE MAN IN THE RED CLOAK.

ATHOS's despair had given place to a concentrated grief, which made this man's brilliant mental faculties keener than ever.

Possessed by a single thought—that of the promise he had made, and of the responsibility he had assumed—he was the last to retire to his room. He begged the host to get him a map of the province, bent over it, examined the lines traced on it, perceived that there were four different roads from Béthune to Armentières, and called the valets.

Planchet, Grimaud, Bazin, and Mousqueton presented themselves, and received Athos's clear, positive, and serious orders. They were to set out the next morning at daybreak, and to go to Armentières—each by a different route. Planchet, the most intelligent of the four, was to follow the road by which had passed the carriage on which the four friends had fired, and which was accompanied, as will be remembered, by Rochefort's servant.

Athos set the lackeys to work first, because, since these men had been in the service of himself and his friends, he had discovered in each of them different and essential qualities.

Besides, lackeys asking questions inspire less mistrust in strangers than their masters, and meet with more sympathy among those to whom they apply.

Finally, milady was acquainted with the masters, but did not know the lackeys; while, on the contrary, the lackeys knew milady perfectly well.

All four were to meet the next day at eleven o'clock. If they had discovered milady's retreat, three were to remain on guard; the fourth was to return to Béthune, to inform Athos and serve as a guide to the four friends.

When these arrangements were made the lackeys retired.

Athos then arose from his chair, girded on his sword, enveloped himself in his cloak, and left the hotel. It was nearly ten o'clock. At ten o'clock in the evening, we know, the streets in provincial towns are very little frequented. Athos, however, was visibly anxious to find some one of whom he could ask a question. At length he met a belated passer-by, went up to him, and spoke a few words to him. The man he addressed drew back in terror, yet he answered the musketeer by a gesture. Athos offered the man half a pistole to go with him, but the man refused.

Athos then plunged into the street the man had indicated with his finger. But on arriving at a cross-way, he stopped again, evidently embarrassed. However, as he had a better chance of meeting some one at the cross-way than anywhere else, he stood still. In fact, after a few minutes a night-watch passed. Athos repeated to him the same question he had asked the first person he had met. The night-watch evinced the same terror, refused also to go with Athos, and only showed him with his hand the road he should take.

Athos walked in the direction indicated, and reached the suburb, situated at the end of the city, opposite where he and his friends had entered it. Here he again appeared uneasy and embarrassed, and stopped for the third time.

Fortunately, a beggar passed and came up to Athos to ask charity. Athos offered him a crown to accompany him where he was going. The beggar hesitated at first, but at the sight of the piece of silver glittering in the darkness, he consented, and walked on before Athos.

Reaching the corner of a street, he showed in the distance a small house, isolated, solitary, dismal. Athos went to the house, while the beggar, having received his reward, hurried away as fast as he could walk.

Athos went round the house before he could distinguish the door from the reddish colour in which the house was painted. No light shone through the chinks of the shutters; no sound gave reason to believe that it was inhabited. It was dark and silent as a tomb.

Three times Athos knocked and no one responded. At the third knock, however, the door was half opened, and a man of lofty stature, pale complexion, and black hair and beard appeared.

Athos and he exchanged some words in a low voice. Then the tall man made a sign to the musketeer that he might come in. Athos immediately took advantage of the permission, and the door closed after him.

The man whom Athos had come so far to seek, and whom he had found with so much trouble, introduced him into his laboratory, where he was engaged in fastening together with iron wire the rattling bones of a skeleton. All the frame was already adjusted. The skull only lay on the table.

All the rest of the furniture indicated that the occupant of this house was engaged in the study of the natural sciences. There were jars filled with snakes labelled according to their species. Dried lizards shone like emeralds set in great squares of black wood; bunches of wild, odoriferous herbs, doubtless having qualities unknown to ordinary men, were fastened to the ceiling and hung down in the corners of the apartment.

But there was no family, no servant. The tall man dwelt alone in this house.

Athos cast a cold and indifferent glance on all the objects

we have described, and at the invitation of the man he came to seek sat down near him.

Then he explained to him the cause of his visit, and the service he required of him. But scarcely had he expressed his request when the unknown, who had remained standing before the musketeer, drew back in terror, and refused. Then Athos took from his pocket a small paper, on which were written two lines, accompanied by a signature and a seal, and presented them to him who had been too premature in showing these signs of repugnance. The tall man had scarcely read the two lines, seen the signature, and recognized the seal, when he bowed to denote that he had no longer any objection to make, and that he was ready to obey.

Athos required no more. He arose, bowed, went out, returned by the same way he had come, re-entered the hotel, and shut himself up in his room.

At daybreak D'Artagnan came to him, and asked him what was to be done.

" Wait ! " replied Athos.

Some minutes later the mother-superior of the convent sent to inform the musketeers that the funeral would take place at noon. There was no news of the poisoner, only she must have escaped through the garden, on the sand of which her footsteps could be traced, and the gate of which had been found locked. The key had disappeared.

At the hour appointed Lord Winter and the four friends repaired to the convent. The bells were tolling solemnly, the chapel was open, the grating of the choir was closed. In the centre of the choir the body of the victim, clothed in her novitiate dress, was exposed. On each side of the choir, and behind the gratings opening from the convent, were assembled the whole community of the Carmelites, who were listening to the divine service, and mingling their chants with the chants of the priests without seeing the lay auditors or being seen by them.

At the chapel door D'Artagnan felt his courage failing him again, and turned to look for Athos, but Athos had disappeared.

Faithful to his mission of vengeance, Athos had asked to be taken to the garden ; and there, on the sand, following the light steps of this woman who had left a bloody track wherever she had gone, he proceeded as far as the gate leading into the wood, had it opened, and plunged into the forest.

Then all his suspicions were confirmed. The road by which the carriage had disappeared skirted the forest. Athos pursued the road for some time with his eyes fixed on the ground. Slight bloodstains, coming from the wound inflicted either on the man who accompanied the carriage as a courier or from one of the horses, spotted the road. At the end of three-quarters of a league, about fifty paces from Festubert, a larger bloodstain showed. The ground was beaten down by horses. Between the forest and this tell-tale place, a little behind the trampled ground, was the same track of small feet as in the garden. Here the carriage had stopped.

At this place milady had come out of the wood and got into the carriage.

Satisfied with this discovery, which confirmed all his suspicions, Athos returned to the hotel and found Planchet impatiently waiting for him.

Everything was as Athos had foreseen.

Planchet had followed the road; like Athos, had noticed the bloodstains; like Athos, had remarked the place where the horses had stopped. But he had gone farther than Athos, so that at the village of Festubert, while drinking at an inn, he had learned, without requiring to ask a question, that about half-past eight the evening before a wounded man, who accompanied a lady travelling in a post-chaise, had been obliged to stop, being unable to proceed. The accident was attributed to robbers, who had stopped the chaise in the wood. The man had remained in the village; the woman had taken a relay of horses and continued her journey.

Planchet went in search of the postillion who had driven the chaise, and found him. He had taken the lady as far as Fromelles, and from Fromelles she had set out for Armentières. Planchet took the short cut, and by seven o'clock in the morning was at Armentières.

There was but one hotel, the Post. Planchet went and presented himself as a lackey out of a place, who was in search of a job. He had not chatted ten minutes with the people of the tavern before he knew that a lady had come there about eleven o'clock the night before alone, had taken a room, had sent for the steward, and told him that she wanted to stay some time in that neighbourhood.

Planchet did not need to know any more. He hastened to the rendezvous, found the three lackeys at their posts, placed them as sentinels at all the doors of the hotel, and came to find Athos, who was just hearing the last of the report when his friends returned.

All their faces were melancholy and anxious, even Aramis's mild face.

" What is to be done ? " asked D'Artagnan.

" Wait," replied Athos.

Each one went to his own room.

At eight o'clock in the evening Athos ordered the horses to be saddled, and had Lord Winter and his friends notified to be prepared for the expedition.

In an instant all five were ready. Each examined his arms, and put them in order. Athos was last to come down, and found D'Artagnan already on horseback and impatient.

" Patience ! " cried Athos ; " one of us is still lacking."

The four gentlemen looked round them in astonishment, for they vainly wondered who this some one lacking could be.

At this moment Planchet brought Athos's horse. The musketeer leaped lightly into the saddle.

" Wait for me," cried he ; " I will be back."

And he set off at a gallop.

In a quarter of an hour he returned, accompanied by a tall man, masked, and enveloped in a large red cloak.

Lord Winter and the three musketeers looked at one another inquiringly. None of them could give the others any information, for all were ignorant who this man was. Nevertheless, they felt that this was as it should be, since the thing was done by Athos's order.

At nine o'clock, guided by Planchet, the little cavalcade set out, following the route the carriage had taken.

It was a melancholy sight, that of these six men, riding silently, each plunged in his own thoughts, sad as despair, sombre as punishment.

CHAPTER LXV.

JUDGMENT.

IT was a dark and stormy night. Monstrous clouds were flying across the sky, concealing the light of the stars. The moon would not rise before midnight.

Occasionally, by the light of a lightning flash gleaming along the horizon, the road could be seen stretching before them, white and solitary. Then when the flash became extinct, all relapsed into darkness.

Every instant Athos was calling D'Artagnan back, who constantly rode in advance of the little troop, and compelling him to fall into rank, though in a moment he was ahead again. He had but one thought, which was to go forward; and he went.

They silently rode through the little village of Festubert, where the wounded servant was; then they skirted the wood of Richebourg. When they had reached Herlier, Planchet, who was still acting as guide, turned to the left.

Several times Lord Winter, or Porthos, or Aramis tried to have a word with the man in the red cloak. But at each question put to him he bowed, without making any reply. The travellers then understood that there must be some reason why the unknown kept silence, and ceased speaking to him.

Moreover, the storm was increasing, the flashes succeeded each other rapidly, the thunder began to growl, and the wind, precursor of a hurricane, whistled in the plumes and the hair of the horsemen.

The cavalcade rode at their utmost speed.

A little beyond Fromelles the storm burst upon them. They put on their cloaks. They had still three leagues before them, and they rode amid torrents of rain.

D'Artagnan had taken off his hat, and did not put on his cloak. He found it pleasant to let the water trickle over his burning brow, and down his body shaken with feverish chills.

Just as the little troop had passed Goskal, and were approaching the Post, a man sheltered under a tree stepped out from its trunk, with which he had been confounded in the darkness, and advanced into the middle of the road, with his finger on his lips.

Athos recognized Grimaud.

"What's the matter?" cried Athos; "has she left Armentières?"

Grimaud nodded. At a movement made by D'Artagnan,—

"Silence, D'Artagnan!" said Athos. "I have taken this whole affair myself, so it is my right to question Grimaud."

"Where is she?" asked Athos.

Grimaud stretched out his hands in the direction of the Lys.

"Far from here?" asked Athos.

Grimaud showed his master his forefinger bent.

"Alone?" asked Athos.

Grimaud made a sign that she was.

" Gentlemen," said Athos, " she is alone, within half a league of here, in the direction of the river. 'Tis good! —Lead us forward, Grimaud."

Grimaud started off across country, and served as a guide to the cavalcade.

At the end of nearly five hundred paces they came to a brook, which they forded.

By a flash of lightning they saw the village of Enguinghem.

" Is she there, Grimaud ? " asked Athos.

Grimaud shook his head.

And the troop continued their route.

Another flash gleamed. Grimaud stretched out his arm, and by the livid light of the fire-serpent they distinguished a little isolated house on the banks of the river, within a hundred paces of a ferry.

One window was lighted.

" Here we are ! " said Athos.

At this moment a man who had been crouching in a ditch jumped up. It was Mousqueton. He pointed his finger to the lighted window.

" She's there," said he.

" And Bazin ? " asked Athos.

" While I was watching the window, he was watching the door."

" Good ! " said Athos ; " you are all faithful servants."

Athos leaped down from his horse, gave the bridle to Grimaud, and advanced toward the window, after having made a sign to the rest of the troop to go toward the door.

The little house was surrounded by a quickset hedge two or three feet high. Athos sprang over the hedge and went up to the window, which was without shutters, but had the half-curtains closely drawn.

He got upon the stone coping, in order to see over the top of the curtain.

By the light of the lamp he saw a woman wrapped in a dark mantle sitting on a stool near a dying fire. Her elbows rested on a mean table, and she leaned her head on her two hands, which were white as ivory.

Her face was not distinguishable, but an ominous smile passed over Athos's lips. There was no mistaking. It was indeed she whom he sought.

At this moment a horse neighed. Milady raised her head, saw Athos's pale face close to the window, and screamed.

Athos saw he was recognized, pushed the window with his knee and hand. It yielded; the panes broke.

And Athos, like the spectre of vengeance, sprang into the room.

Milady ran to the door and opened it; but paler and more threatening still than Athos, D'Artagnan stood on the threshold.

Milady drew back, uttering a cry. D'Artagnan, believing she might have means of flight, and fearing lest she should escape them, drew a pistol from his belt. But Athos raised his hand.

"Put back your weapon, D'Artagnan," said he; "this woman must be judged and not assassinated. Wait but a moment longer, my friend, and you shall be satisfied. Come in, gentlemen."

D'Artagnan obeyed, for Athos had the solemn voice and the mighty gesture of a judge sent by the Lord Himself. So behind D'Artagnan entered Porthos, Aramis, Lord Winter, and the man in the red cloak.

The four lackeys guarded the door and the window.

Milady had sunk into a chair, with her hands extended, as if to conjure away this terrible apparition. On perceiving her brother-in-law she uttered a terrible cry.

"What do you want?" screamed milady.

"We want," said Athos, "Charlotte Backson, who first was called Comtesse de la Fère, and afterwards Lady Winter, Baroness of Sheffield."

"I am she! I am she!" murmured she, at the height of terror. "What do you want of me?"

"We intend to judge you according to your crimes," said Athos. "You shall be free to defend yourself. Justify yourself if you can.—Monsieur d'Artagnan, it is for you to accuse her first."

D'Artagnan stepped forward.

"Before God and before men," said he, "I accuse this woman of poisoning Constance Bonacieux, who died yesterday evening."

He turned to Porthos and Aramis.

"We bear witness to this," said the two musketeers, with one impulse.

D'Artagnan continued,—

"Before God and before men, I accuse this woman of having tried to poison me by wine which she sent me from Villeroi, with a forged letter, purporting that the wine came from my friends. God preserved me, but a man named Brisemont died in my place."

"We bear witness to this," said Porthos and Aramis, in the same voice.

"Before God and before men, I accuse this woman of having urged me to murder the Baron de Wardes. But as no one is present to bear witness to the truth of this accusation. I attest it myself. I have done."

And M. d'Artagnan passed to the other side of the room with Porthos and Aramis.

"It is your turn, milord," said Athos.

The baron came forward.

"Before God and before men," said he "I accuse this woman of having caused the assassination of the Duke of Buckingham."

"The Duke of Buckingham assassinated!" cried all present with one voice.

"Yes," said the baron, "assassinated. On receiving the warning letter you wrote to me, I had this woman arrested, and put her in the charge of a loyal servant. She corrupted this man, she placed the dagger in his hand, she made him kill the duke. And at this moment, perhaps, Felton is paying with his life for this fury's crime!"

A shudder crept through the judges at the revelation of these crimes of which they had not yet heard.

"This is not all," proceeded Lord Winter. "My brother, who made you his heir, died in three hours, of a strange disorder, which left livid traces over all his body. Sister, how did your husband die?"

"Horror!" cried Porthos and Aramis.

"Buckingham's assassin, Felton's assassin, my brother's assassin, I demand justice upon you, and I swear that if it be not granted to me, I will execute it myself."

And Lord Winter ranged himself by D'Artagnan's side, leaving his place free for another accuser.

Milady buried her face in her two hands, and tried to recall her ideas, confused in a mortal vertigo.

"It is my turn," said Athos, himself trembling as the lion trembles at the sight of the serpent—"it is my turn. I married this woman when she was a young girl. I married her in spite of all my family. I gave her my wealth, I gave her my name; and one day I discovered that this woman was branded—this woman was marked with a fleur-de-lis on her left shoulder."

"Oh," said milady, "I defy you to find the tribunal which pronounced that infamous sentence upon me. I defy you to find him who executed it."

"Silence!" said a voice. "It is for me to reply to that!"

And the man in the red cloak came forward in his turn.

"Who is this man? who is this man?" cried milady. She was suffocated by terror; her hair, which had become undone, seemed to stand up over her livid countenance as if it were alive.

All eyes were fixed on this man, for to all except Athos he was unknown.

Even Athos looked at him with as much stupefaction as the others, for he knew not how he could in any way be mixed up with the horrible drama which was at that moment coming to its climax.

After approaching milady with a slow and solemn step, so that the table alone separated them, the unknown took off his mask.

Milady for some time examined with increasing terror his pale face, framed in its black hair and beard, and the only expression of which was icy sternness. Then all at once,—

"Oh no, no!" cried she, rising and retreating to the very wall; "no, no! it is an infernal apparition! It is not he! Help, help!" she screamed in a hoarse voice, turning to the wall as if she could tear an opening in it with her hands.

"But who are you, then?" cried all the witnesses of this scene.

"Ask this woman," said the man in the red cloak, "for you see well enough she knows me!"

"The executioner of Lille! the executioner of Lille!" cried milady, a prey to wild terror, and clinging with her hands to the wall to avoid falling.

Every one drew back, and the man in the red cloak remained standing alone in the middle of the room.

"Oh, forgive me! pardon, pardon!" cried the wretched woman, falling on her knees.

The unknown waited for silence.

"I told you so—that she knew me," he went on to say. "Yes, I am the executioner of the city of Lille, and here is my story."

All eyes were fixed upon this man; his words were awaited with anxious eagerness.

"This young woman when she was a young maiden was as beautiful as she is now. She was a nun in the convent of the Benedictines of Templemar. A young priest, of a simple and believing heart, was the chaplain of that convent. She undertook to seduce him, and succeeded; she would have seduced a saint.

"The vows of both were sacred—irrevocable. Their intrigue could not last long without ruining both. She prevailed on him to leave the country; but for them to leave the country, to escape together, to reach another part of France, where they might live at ease because there they would be unknown, money was necessary. Neither of them had any. The priest stole the sacred utensils and sold them. But as they were preparing to escape together, they were both arrested.

"Within a week she seduced the jailer's son and escaped. The young priest was condemned to ten years in chains, and to be branded. I was executioner of the city of Lille, as this woman has said. I was obliged to brand the guilty man; and the guilty man, gentlemen, was my brother!

"I then swore that this woman who had ruined him, who was more than his accomplice, since she had spurred him on to commit the crime, should share at least his punishment. I suspected the place where she was concealed. I followed her, I caught her, I bound her, and I imprinted the same disgraceful mark on her that I had imprinted on my poor brother.

"The day after my return to Lille, my brother in his turn succeeded in making his escape. I was accused of complicity, and was condemned to stay in prison in his place till he should be again a prisoner. My poor brother was ignorant of my condemnation. He had rejoined this woman. They fled together into Berry, and there he obtained a little curacy. This woman passed for his sister.

"The lord of the estate on which the curate's church was situated saw this pretended sister, and fell in love with her so sincerely that he offered to marry her. Then she left the man whom she had ruined for the man whom she was destined to ruin, and became the Comtesse de la Fère——"

All eyes were turned toward Athos, whose real name this was. He bowed his head in token that all that the executioner had said was true.

"Then," resumed the other, "mad, desperate, determined to get rid of an existence from which she had taken away everything, both honour and happiness, my poor brother returned to Lille, and learning the sentence that had condemned me in his place, gave himself up, and hanged himself that same night from the air-hole of his dungeon cell.

20

"I must say in justice that they who had condemned me kept their word. As soon as the identity of the body was proved, I was set at liberty.

"That is the crime of which I accuse her. That is the cause of her being branded."

"Monsieur d'Artagnan," said Athos, "what penalty do you demand against this woman?"

"The penalty of death," replied D'Artagnan.

"Milord de Winter," continued Athos, "what penalty do you demand against this woman?"

"The penalty of death," replied Lord Winter.

"MM. Porthos and Aramis," repeated Athos, "you who are her judges, what penalty do you pronounce on this woman?"

"The penalty of death," replied the musketeers in a hollow voice.

Milady uttered a frightful shriek, and dragged herself along on her knees several paces toward her judges.

Athos stretched out his hand toward her.

"Charlotte Backson, Comtesse de la Fère, Milady de Winter," said he, "your crimes have wearied men on earth and God in heaven. If you know any prayer, say it; for you are condemned, and you shall die."

At these words, which left her no hope, milady rose to her full height and tried to speak, but her strength failed her. She felt that a powerful and implacable hand was seizing her by the hair, and was dragging her away as irrevocably as fate drags man. She did not, therefore, even attempt to make any resistance, and went out of the cottage.

Lord Winter, D'Artagnan, Athos, Porthos, and Aramis followed her. The lackeys followed their masters, and the room was left desolate, with its broken window, its open door, and its smoky lamp burning forlornly on the table.

CHAPTER LXVI.

EXECUTION.

It was almost midnight. The moon, hollowed by its waning, and red as blood under the last traces of the storm, was rising behind the little town of Armentières, which outlined against its pallid light the dark silhouette of its houses and the skeleton of its high carved belfry. In front of them the Lys was rolling its waters like a river of molten lead; while on the other bank could be seen a black mass of trees, outlined against a stormy sky, which was invaded by huge coppery clouds, creating a kind of twilight amid the night. On the left was an old abandoned windmill, with motionless vans, from the ruins of which an owl was emitting its shrill, periodical, and monotonous cry. Here and there in the plain, on the right and on the left of the road, which the dismal procession followed, appeared a few low, stunted trees looking like deformed dwarfs crouching down as if to watch men at this ominous hour.

From time to time a broad sheet of lightning opened the horizon in its whole width, zigzagged over the black mass of trees, and came like a terrible scimitar, cutting the sky and the water into two parts. Not a breath of wind disturbed the heavy atmosphere. A deathlike silence oppressed all nature. The soil was humid and glistening with the rain which had just fallen, and the refreshed herbs distilled their perfume with increased energy.

Two of the lackeys dragged milady along, each taking one of her arms. The executioner walked behind them, and Lord Winter, D'Artagnan, Porthos, and Aramis walked behind the executioner.

Planchet and Bazin came last.

The two lackeys led milady toward the river. Her mouth was mute, but her eyes spoke with their inexpressible eloquence, supplicating by turns each of those on whom she looked.

When she found herself a few paces in advance, she whispered to the lackeys,—

"A thousand pistoles to each of you if you will protect my flight. But if you deliver me up to your masters, I have at hand avengers who will make you pay dearly for my death."

Grimaud hesitated; Mousqueton trembled in all his limbs.

Athos, hearing milady's voice, came up quickly. Lord Winter did the same.

"Send off these lackeys," said he. "She has spoken to them; they are no longer safe."

Planchet and Bazin were summoned, and took the places of Grimaud and Mousqueton.

When they reached the banks of the river the executioner approached milady and bound her hands and her feet.

Then she broke silence to cry out,—

"You are cowards, you are miserable assassins! It takes ten men of you to murder one woman! Beware! If I am not rescued I shall be avenged."

"You are not a woman," said Athos coldly. "You do not belong to the human species. You are a demon escaped from hell, and we are going to send you back again."

"Ah, you virtuous men!" exclaimed milady; "but remember that he who touches a hair of my head is himself an assassin."

"The executioner can kill, madame, without being on that account an assassin," said the man in the red cloak, striking on his immense sword. "He is the last judge; that is all."

And as he was binding her while saying these words, milady uttered two or three wild cries, which produced a strange effect, flying away into the night and losing themselves in the depth of the woods.

"But if I am guilty, if I have committed the crimes you charge me with," shrieked milady, "take me before a tribunal. You are not judges, you, to condemn me!"

"I offered you Tyburn," said Lord Winter. "Why did you not accept it?"

"Because I do not want to die!" cried milady, writhing; "because I am too young to die!"

"The woman you poisoned at Béthune was even younger than you, madame, and yet she is dead," said D'Artagnan.

"I will enter a cloister; I will become a nun," said milady.

"You were in a cloister," said the executioner, "and you left it to destroy my brother."

Milady uttered a cry of terror and sank on her knees.

The executioner lifted her up by her arms and was carrying her toward the boat.

"Oh, my God!" cried she, "my God! Are you going to drown me?"

These cries had something so heartrending in them that D'Artagnan, who had been at first the most implacable against milady, sank down on a stump and bent his head, covering his ears with the palms of his hands; and yet, notwithstanding this, he still heard her threaten and cry.

D'Artagnan was the youngest of all these men; his heart failed him.

"Oh, I cannot behold this frightful spectacle! I cannot consent that this woman should die thus!"

Milady heard these few words, and caught at a gleam of hope.

"D'Artagnan, D'Artagnan!" cried she, "remember I loved you!"

The young man rose and took a step toward her.

But Athos arose, drew his sword, and placed himself in front of him.

"If you take one step farther, D'Artagnan," said he, "we cross swords."

M. d'Artagnan fell on his knees and prayed.

"Come!" continued Athos; "executioner, do your duty."

"Willingly, monseigneur," said the executioner; "for as true as I am a good Catholic, I firmly believe I am right in performing my functions on this woman."

"'Tis well."

Athos took a step toward milady.

"I pardon you," said he, "the ill you have done me; I pardon you for my blasted future, my lost honour, my defiled love, and my salvation for ever compromised by the despair into which you have cast me. Die in peace!"

Lord Winter advanced next.

"I pardon you," said he, "the poisoning of my brother, the assassination of his Grace the Duke of Buckingham; I pardon you poor Felton's death; I pardon you the attempts on me personally. Die in peace!"

"And I," said D'Artagnan—"pardon me, madame, for having by deceit, unworthy of a gentleman, provoked your anger; and in exchange I pardon you the murder of my poor sweetheart and your cruel vengeance against me. I pardon you, and I weep for you. Die in peace!"

"I am lost!" murmured milady in English; "I must die!"

Then she rose of her own accord, and cast around her one of those keen looks which seemed to dart from a flaming eye.

She saw nothing.

She listened; she heard nothing.

She had only enemies around her.

"Where am I to die?" she asked.

"On the other bank," replied the executioner.

Then he made her enter the boat, and just as he was going to set foot in it himself, Athos handed him a sum of money.

"Here," said he, "is the price of the execution, that it may be plain we are acting as judges."

"Very well," said the executioner. "And now, in her turn, let this woman see that I am not fulfilling my trade, but my duty."

And he threw the money into the river.

The boat moved off toward the left bank of the Lys, bearing the guilty woman and the executioner. All the others remained on the right bank, where they had fallen on their knees.

The boat glided along the ferry-rope under the gleam of a pale cloud which hung over the water at the moment.

It was seen reaching the opposite bank ; the figures were outlined in black against the red-tinted horizon.

Milady during the passage had contrived to untie the cord which fastened her feet ; on reaching the bank, she jumped lightly on shore and took to flight.

But the soil was moist. When she reached the top of the bank she slipped and fell on her knees.

A superstitious idea struck her : she realized that Heaven denied her its aid, and she remained in the attitude in which she had fallen, with her head drooping and her hands clasped.

Then from the other bank the executioner was seen to raise both his arms slowly. A moonbeam fell on the blade of his broadsword. His two arms fell ; they heard the hissing of the scimitar and the victim's cry ; then a truncated mass sank under the blow.

The executioner then took off his red cloak, spread it on the ground, laid the body in it, threw in the head, tied it by the four corners, lifted it on his shoulder, and got into the boat again.

In the middle of the stream he stopped the boat, and holding his burden over the water,—

"Let the justice of God be done!" cried he, in a loud voice.

And he let the body drop into the depths of the waters, which closed over it.

Three days later the four musketeers were in Paris again. They had not exceeded their leave of absence, and that same evening went to pay their customary visit to M. de Tréville.

"Well, gentlemen," asked the excellent captain, "have you enjoyed your excursion ? "

"Prodigiously ! " replied Athos for himself and his companions.

CONCLUSION.

On the sixth of the following month the king, in compliance with the promise he had made the cardinal to leave Paris and to return to Rochelle, departed from his capital, unable to recover from his amazement at the news which was just beginning to spread abroad that Buckingham had been assassinated.

Though warned that the man she had loved so fondly was in danger, the queen, when his death was announced to her, would not lend credence to it ; she was even imprudent enough to exclaim,—

"It is false ; he has just written to me !"

But the next day she was obliged to believe this fatal intelligence. La Porte, detained in England, as every one else had been, by the orders of King Charles I., arrived, bringing the last, the funereal present which Buckingham sent to the queen.

The king's joy had been very lively. He did not trouble to dissemble it, but even displayed it with affectation before the queen. Louis XIII., like all weak minds, was wanting in generosity.

But the king soon became dull and indisposed again ; his brow was not one of the kind that are serene for any length of time. He felt that by returning to his camp he was about to become a slave again, and yet nevertheless he returned.

The cardinal was for him the fascinating serpent, and he was the bird flying from branch to branch without being able to escape.

So the return to Rochelle was profoundly dull. Our four friends in particular astonished their comrades. They travelled together, side by side, with melancholy eyes and hanging heads. Athos alone from time to time raised his broad brow. A flash kindled in his eyes, a bitter smile passed over his lips. Then, like his comrades, he again resumed his reveries.

When the escort arrived in a city, as soon as they had escorted the king to his lodgings the four friends either retired to their own quarters or to some secluded tavern, where they neither drank nor played. They only conversed in a low voice, looking around attentively that no one overheard them.

One day, when the king had halted on the way to fly the magpie, and the four friends, according to their custom, instead of following the sport, had stopped at a tavern on the turnpike, a man, riding full speed from Rochelle, pulled up at the door to drink a glass of wine, and glanced into the room where the four musketeers were sitting at table.

"Hello, Monsieur d'Artagnan !" said he, "isn't it you I see in there ?"

D'Artagnan raised his head and uttered a cry of joy. It was the man he called his phantom; it was the stranger of Meung, of the Rue des Fossoyeurs, and of Arras.

D'Artagnan drew his sword and sprang toward the door.

But this time, instead of eluding him, the stranger leaped from his horse and advanced to meet D'Artagnan.

"Ah, sir!" said the young man, "I meet you, then, at last! This time you shall not escape me!"

"Neither is it my intention, sir, for this time I was seeking you. I arrest you in the name of the king. I tell you that you must surrender your sword to me, sir, and that without resistance. Your life depends upon it. I warn you."

"But who are you?" demanded D'Artagnan, lowering the point of his sword, but without yet surrendering it.

"I am the Chevalier de Rochefort," answered the stranger, "Cardinal Richelieu's equerry, and I have orders to conduct you to his Eminence."

"We are returning to his Eminence, chevalier," said Athos, advancing; "and you will be good enough to accept M. d'Artagnan's word that he will go straight to Rochelle."

"I must place him in the hands of guards who will take him to camp."

"We will serve as his guards, sir, on our word as gentlemen; but, on our word as gentlemen, likewise," added Athos, "M. d'Artagnan shall not leave us."

The Chevalier de Rochefort cast a glance backward, and saw that Porthos and Aramis had taken their places between him and the door. He perceived that he was completely at the mercy of these four men.

"Gentlemen," said he, "if M. d'Artagnan will surrender his sword to me and join his word to yours, I shall be satisfied with your promise to convey M. d'Artagnan to the cardinal's quarters."

"You have my word, sir, and here is my sword."

"This suits me all the better," said Rochefort, "as I must continue my journey."

"If it is to rejoin milady," said Athos coolly, "it is useless. You will not find her."

"What has become of her?" asked Rochefort eagerly.

"Come back with us to the camp and you shall know."

Rochefort remained thoughtful for a moment; then, as they were only a day's journey from Surgères, where the cardinal was coming to meet the king, he resolved to follow Athos's advice and go back with them.

Besides, this return gave him the advantage of watching over his prisoner.

They resumed their route.

At three o'clock the next afternoon they reached Surgères. The cardinal was there awaiting Louis XIII. The minister and the king exchanged numerous caresses, congratulating each other on the fortunate chance which had freed France from the implacable enemy who had been rousing all Europe against her. After this the cardinal, who had been informed by Rochefort that D'Artagnan was arrested, and who was anxious to see him, took leave of the king, inviting him to come the next day to view the works on the dike, which were completed.

The cardinal, on returning in the evening to his headquarters at the bridge of La Pierre, found D'Artagnan, without his sword, and the three musketeers armed, standing before the door of the house which he was occupying.

This time, as he was well attended, he looked at them sternly, and made a sign with his eye and hand for D'Artagnan to follow him.

D'Artagnan obeyed.

"We shall wait for you, D'Artagnan," said Athos, loud enough for the cardinal to hear him.

His Eminence kept on his way without uttering a single word.

D'Artagnan entered after the cardinal, and behind D'Artagnan the door was guarded.

His Eminence went to the room which served him as a study, and made a sign to Rochefort to bring in the young musketeer.

Rochefort obeyed and retired.

D'Artagnan remained alone before the cardinal. This was his second interview with Richelieu, and he afterwards confessed that he felt sure it would be his last.

Richelieu remained standing, leaning against the mantelpiece. A table was between him and D'Artagnan.

"Sir," said the cardinal, "you have been arrested by my orders."

"So I have been told, monseigneur."

"Do you know why?"

"No, monseigneur, for the only thing for which I could be arrested is still unknown to your Eminence."

Richelieu looked steadfastly at the young man.

"Indeed!" said he; "what does that mean?"

"If monseigneur will first tell me what crimes I am

charged with, I will then tell the deeds that I have done."

"You are charged with crimes that have brought down far loftier heads than yours, sir," said the cardinal.

"What are they, monseigneur?" demanded D'Artagnan, with a calmness that astonished the cardinal himself.

"You are charged with having corresponded with the enemies of the kingdom. You are charged with having surprised state secrets. You are charged with having tried to thwart your general's plans."

"And who charges me with this, monseigneur?" said D'Artagnan, who suspected the accusation came from milady—"a woman branded by the law of the country; a woman who was married to one man in France and to another in England; a woman who poisoned her second husband, and who attempted to poison me!"

"What is all this, sir?" cried the cardinal, astonished; "and what woman are you speaking of thus?"

"Of Milady de Winter," replied D'Artagnan—"yes, of Milady de Winter, of whose many crimes your Eminence was doubtless ignorant when you honoured her with your confidence."

"Sir," said the cardinal, "if Milady de Winter has committed the crimes which you say, she shall be punished."

"She is punished, monseigneur."

"And who has punished her?"

"We."

"Is she in prison?"

"She is dead."

"Dead!" repeated the cardinal, who could not believe what he heard. "Dead! Did you say she was dead?"

"Three times she tried to kill me, and I pardoned her. But she killed the woman I loved. Then my friends and I took her, tried her, and condemned her."

D'Artagnan then related the poisoning of Madame Bonacieux in the Carmelite convent of Béthune, the trial in the lonely house, and the execution on the banks of the Lys.

A shudder ran through the cardinal's body, and yet he did not shudder readily.

But suddenly, as if under the influence of a secret thought, the cardinal's face, till that moment gloomy, began gradually to grow serene, and at last recovered the most perfect serenity.

"So," said the cardinal, in a tone the mildness of which contrasted with the severity of his words, "you have constituted yourselves judges, forgetting that they who punish without licence to punish are assassins?"

"Monseigneur, I swear to you that I have never for an instant had the intention of defending my head against you. I will submit to the punishment your Eminence may please to inflict upon me. I do not hold life dear enough to be afraid of death."

"Yes, I know you are a man of courage, sir," said the cardinal, in a tone almost affectionate; "I can therefore tell you beforehand you shall be tried, even condemned."

"Another might reply to your Eminence that he had his pardon in his pocket. I shall content myself with saying, Command, monseigneur; I am ready."

"Your pardon?" said Richelieu, surprised.

"Yes, monseigneur," said D'Artagnan.

"And signed by whom? By the king?"

And the cardinal pronounced these words with a singular expression of contempt.

"No; by your Eminence."

"By me? You are mad, sir!"

"Monseigneur will doubtless recognize his own writing."

And D'Artagnan presented to the cardinal the precious paper which Athos had forced from milady, and which he had given to D'Artagnan to serve him as a safeguard.

His Eminence took the paper and read in a slow voice, dwelling on every syllable:—

"*August 5, 1628.*

"By my order, and for the good of the State, the bearer hereof has done what he has done. RICHELIEU."

The cardinal, after reading these two lines, fell into deep thought, but he did not return the paper to D'Artagnan.

"He is meditating by what sort of punishment he shall put me to death," said D'Artagnan to himself. "Very well! On my faith, he shall see how a gentleman can die!"

The young musketeer was in an excellent disposition to die like a hero.

Richelieu still continued thinking, twisting and untwisting the paper in his hands. At last he raised his head, fixed his eagle look upon D'Artagnan's frank, loyal, intelligent face, read on his face, furrowed with tears, all the sufferings he had endured for a month, and reflected for the third or fourth time what a future this young man had before him, and what resources his activity, his courage, and his understanding could devote to a good master.

On the other hand, milady's crimes, her strength of mind, and her infernal genius had more than once terrified him. He felt something like a secret joy at being for ever rid of such a dangerous accomplice.

He slowly tore the paper which D'Artagnan had generously placed in his hand.

"I am lost!" said D'Artagnan to himself.

And he bowed low before the cardinal, like a man who says, "Lord, Thy will be done!"

The cardinal went to the table, and without sitting down, wrote a few lines on a parchment, two-thirds of which was already filled up, and affixed his seal to it.

"That is my condemnation," thought D'Artagnan. "He will spare me the tedium of the Bastille or the slow processes of a trial. It's another proof of his kindness."

"Here, sir," said the cardinal to the young man; "I have taken from you one signed blank, and I give you another. The name is wanting in this commission, and you yourself will write it in."

D'Artagnan took the paper hesitatingly, and cast his eyes over it.

It was a lieutenant's commission in the musketeers.

D'Artagnan fell at the cardinal's feet.

"Monseigneur," said he, "my life is yours! Henceforward dispose of it. But I do not deserve this favour which you bestow on me. I have three friends who are more meritorious and more worthy——"

"You are an honest fellow, D'Artagnan," interrupted the cardinal, tapping him familiarly on the shoulder, charmed at having subdued this rebellious nature. "Do with this commission what you will. Only remember that though the name is left blank I give it to you."

"I shall never forget it," replied D'Artagnan. "Your Eminence may be certain of that."

The cardinal turned round and said in a loud voice,—

"Rochefort!"

The chevalier, who doubtless was behind the door, entered immediately.

"Rochefort," said the cardinal, "you see M. d'Artagnan. I receive him among the number of my friends. Shake hands, then, and be prudent, if you wish to preserve your heads."

Rochefort and D'Artagnan saluted each other distantly, but the cardinal was there observing them with his vigilant eye.

They left the chamber at the same time.

" We shall meet again, shall we not, sir ? "

" When you please," said D'Artagnan.

" An opportunity will offer," replied Rochefort.

" What's that ? " said the cardinal, opening the door.

The two men smiled at each other, shook hands, and bowed to his Eminence.

" We were beginning to grow impatient," said Athos.

" Here I am, friends," replied D'Artagnan—" not only free, but in favour."

" Will you tell us about it ? "

" This evening."

Accordingly, that same evening D'Artagnan repaired to the quarters of Athos, whom he found in a fair way of emptying his bottle of Spanish wine, an occupation which he religiously fulfilled every night.

He related what had taken place between the cardinal and himself, and drawing the commission from his pocket,—

" Here, my dear Athos," said he ; " this naturally belongs to you."

Athos smiled his sweet, fascinating smile.

" My friend," said he, " for Athos this is too much, for the Comte de la Fère it is too little. Keep the commission ; it is yours. Alas ! my God ! it has cost you enough."

D'Artagnan left Athos's room and went to Porthos's.

He found him dressed in a magnificent coat covered with splendid embroidery, looking at himself in a glass.

" Ah, ha ! " exclaimed Porthos ; " it is you, dear friend. How do you think these garments fit me ? "

" Wonderfully well," said D'Artagnan. " But I have come to offer you a dress which will suit you still better."

" What's that ? " asked Porthos.

" That of a lieutenant in the musketeers."

D'Artagnan related to Porthos his interview with the cardinal, and taking the commission from his pocket,—

" Here, my dear," said he ; " write your name in it, and become my officer."

Porthos cast his eyes over the commission, and returned it to D'Artagnan, to the young man's great astonishment.

" Yes," said he—" yes, that would flatter me very much, but I should not have time enough to enjoy the distinction. During our expedition to Béthune my duchess's husband died ; so that, my dear, since the coffer of the defunct is holding out its arms to me, I am going to marry the widow.

Look here! I was trying on my wedding suit. Keep your lieutenant, my dear, keep it."

The young man entered Aramis's apartment.

He found him kneeling before a praying-desk, with his head leaning on an open prayer-book.

He described to him his interview with the cardinal, and for the third time drawing his commission from his pocket,—

"You, our friend, our intelligence, our invisible protector," said he, "accept this commission. You have deserved it more than any one by your wisdom and your counsels, which were always followed by such happy results."

"Alas! dear friend," said Aramis, "our recent adventures have entirely disgusted me with life and with the sword. This time my determination is irrevocably taken. After the siege I shall enter the house of the Lazarists. Keep the commission, D'Artagnan. The profession of arms suits you. You will be a brave and gallant captain."

D'Artagnan, his eye moist with gratitude and beaming with joy, went back to Athos, whom he found still at table, contemplating the charms of his last glass of Malaga by the light of his lamp.

"Well," said he, "they also have refused this commission!"

"Because, dear friend, no one is more worthy of it than yourself."

And he took a pen, wrote D'Artagnan's name on the commission, and returned it to him.

"I shall then no longer have any friends," said the young man. "Alas! nothing more, only bitter recollections."

And he let his head sink into his hands, while two tears rolled down his cheeks.

"You are young," replied Athos, "and your bitter recollections have time to be changed into sweet memories."

EPILOGUE.

ROCHELLE, deprived of the aid of the English fleet and the reinforcements promised by Buckingham, surrendered after a siege of a year. On the 28th of October, 1628, the capitulation was signed.

The king made his entrance into Paris on December 23, the same year. He was received in triumph, as if he came from conquering an enemy and not Frenchmen. He entered by the Faubourg St. Jacques with magnificent display.

The procession, led by symbolical cars, passed under a dozen triumphal arches, on which all the gods of Olympus were celebrating the unnumbered virtues of Louis the Victorious. An immense throng, stationed along the whole route of the procession, rent the air with their enthusiastic acclamations, greeting the conquerer's return.

D'Artagnan took possession of his rank. Porthos left the service, and during the following year married Madame Coquenard. The coffer so eagerly coveted contained 800,000 livres.

Mousqueton had a magnificent livery, and enjoyed the satisfaction for which he had yearned all his life—that of standing behind a gilded carriage.

Aramis, after a long absence in Lorraine, suddenly disappeared, and ceased to write his friends. They learned long afterwards, through Madame de Chevreuse, who told it to two or three of her lovers, that he had decided to assume the habit in a religious house at Nancy.

Bazin became a lay brother.

Athos remained a musketeer under D'Artagnan's command till the year 1631, when, after a journey which he made to Touraine, he also quitted the service, under the pretext of having just inherited a small property in Roussillon.

Grimaud followed Athos.

D'Artagnan fought three times with Rochefort, and wounded him three times.

"I shall probably kill you the fourth," said he to him, holding out his hand to assist him to rise.

"Then it is better for you and for me that we stop here," answered the wounded man. "Zounds! I am much more your friend than you think; for after our very first encounter, I could, by saying a word to the cardinal, have had your head cut off!"

This time they heartily shook hands, and without retaining any malice.

Planchet obtained from Rochefort the rank of sergeant in the guards.

M. Bonacieux lived on very quietly, perfectly ignorant of what had become of his wife, and caring very little about the matter. One day he had the imprudence to recall himself to the cardinal's memory. The cardinal sent him word that he would see to it that he should never want for anything in future.

In fact, the next day M. Bonacieux left his house at seven o'clock in the evening to go to the Louvre, and he was never seen again in the Rue des Fossoyeurs. The opinion of those who seemed to be best informed was that he was fed and lodged in some royal castle, at the expense of his generous Eminence.

THE END.

Printed in Great Britain by
Thomas Nelson and Sons Ltd, Edinburgh